The Adventures of Elizabeth Stanton
Series Volume 6

Age of Exploration

Vic Broquard

The Adventures of Elizabeth Stanton Series
Volume 6: Age of Exploration

Vic Broquard

Published by:
Broquard eBooks
http://Broquard-eBooks.com
author@Broquard-eBooks.com
103 Timberlane
East Peoria, IL 61611

Artwork by Crooked Willow Studios

For Morgan and L. Ron Hubbard

Table of Contents

Chapter 1 Onto the High Seas We Go

On August 1, 648, the Sleepy Hollow slowly tacked out of Velona's huge harbor. My Explorers Circle is now beginning its maiden voyage of discovery of new lands and of new trading partners. I had always wanted to be at sea. Although I had dreamed of being the captain, I am settling for being the Wid, the leader of this very large Circle of explorers.

My name is-was Elizabeth Stanton, originally anyway, my dearest friends still call me Bethany. When that body died, my next lifetime I was called Bethany Madelyn Adid, until I married and became the wife of Jes Amir, who was the Great Messiah. I was then known as Bethany Madelyn Amir, and I discovered much later, I was called the Blessed Holy Mother. Next, I had a male body known as Ket Bethany. Yes, I have a fetish for the name Bethany and another for long hair, but those are just fleshly body things. Now I am Elizabeth Ann Rose Weston and am just shy of becoming of age, fourteen, well okay, I am thirteen and three-quarters.

You see, I, like you, am a being — an immortal spirit. I've lived in many bodies and will have as many more as I desire, assuming the world, Tarra, our playground, is not destroyed. It began many years ago; I was part of a group of like-minded people, the druwids. In my group, I was revered as the Wid Bethany — the title that I took nearly nine hundred years ago now as I sit here and look back upon my past. I am Truth and Knowledge. Yes, you may call me a witch, a demon or a heretic, but, in doing so, you mark yourself as just another Blind One. I chose this road — this path I follow — knowingly and willingly. I do it for all mankind, even you.

Rats, this is sounding very confusing. Let me begin again. Tarra is our world. Geography plays a major role in this story; so allow me to describe the "known" world here in 648, which is about to be changed considerably with our voyages. The known world consists of one large landmass shaped much like a dog's bone. The narrow section connecting the two large lobes is an impassable desert. On either side, rise tall mountain ranges that make overland travel into the Desert of Desolation impossible as well. All life resides in the western lobe, at least as we knew it in 648.

A great sea, the Med Sea splits the lobe into two portions. The sparsely populated Southlands occupy the southern two-thirds of the lobe, while the upper third is divided into several pieces. The Med Sea, about seventy-five miles wide, spans nearly the entire western lobe, ending in a semi-arid land called Juda Arad. Some hundred miles north of the Med Sea is the eight thousand foot tall Appian Way mountain range, dividing this bottom northern third from the upper two equal sized long portions. Above Juda Arad lies the Northern Steppes, a hilly, grassland. Paralleling the Med Sea coast on the northern side and abutting the steppes are the Sea Princes, actually at one time called the Lands of the Seven Sea Princes.

The Zargarb sector abuts Juda Arad. Going on down the line are Solamina, Pieta, Bonilla, Vito, Barcella, and Velona. Fortress d'Grange, the eighth sector, lies in the mountainous lands just above Velona. On the other side of the Appian Way lies the Greenway and Langdoc region. The Greenway has been broken into numerous small kingdoms, of which Mont Blanc, Langdoc, Calgary, and Southway are the strongest and controlled by us. The easternmost of these Greenway kingdoms abuts with the Northern Steppes. Further north beyond yet another mountain range lies Volksholm where the Axemen live, their home country, I should say, since many have now immigrated south. Recently, we have discovered an isolated island chain in the far northern waters many miles west of West Reach.

Lying just offshore from Calgary, the largest city in the Greenway, is the island called West Reach, or Cymry by the locals.

On the southern shores of the Med Sea lay the Red Desert, largely uninhabited. Further south lies the Southlands, a huge land largely unexplored by us. Big game, diamond mines, gold mines, and heavy jungle regions abound down here. Much heavy, exotic timber comes from this area, which is used in the construction of our many ships.

Just off the western edge of the Southlands lies a series of hundreds of small islands, known collectively as the Spice Islands, from where we get our cocoa and teas, which I dearly love. Finally, on the eastern side of the Southlands, sitting just below the long stem of the dog bone shape continent lies the huge island called Megalos. Its western side nearly touches the Southlands; a Narrow Firth separates the two, where the water level is only a few feet deep at low tide. A huge city lies here called Sud.

On the spiritual side countering the chaos of the world are the Guardians, the Santi del Dio, and the Guardian of the Anuir in the Red Desert, which is Jes Amir's current identity. Jes has no physical body now, but is working his miracles with his devout followers, a rag-tag group of Arad immigrants who fled Juda Arad into this inhospitable desert region. Jes had begun using a different approach, assisting one being at a time to recover much of his latent spiritual abilities. As far as I know, he has now gotten three of his followers trained up to a very powerful state of abilities. He and I made a bargain. He needed time and relative quiet in the world in which to work his miracles on individuals. My task was to handle the fleshly world around Tarra, trying to establish a calm environment in which he could continue to free spiritual beings.

We Guardians were specialized originally into seven areas. The Protector is highly skilled in the fighting arts. The Communicator uses telepathy to provide instant communications. The Healer is highly skilled in the healing arts, though all the Guardians are trained in the basics of healing. The Planner is skilled in design and construction of buildings and other works. The Loremaster is highly skilled in Nature, plants and animals are their specialty. The Judgers are highly skilled in recognizing the truth in disputes and settling them, along with the ability to create illusions that others believe to be real, such as causing guards to fall asleep while on duty. Finally, the Wid has a passion to know all about everything and is the hardest to develop, having a constant need to learn new things. I have always been a Wid.

In the old days, one of each of these seven specialties was joined into a Circle. With the horrible dwindling of our numbers, this optimum arrangement has largely been lost. However, recently, the leader that I had chosen to replace me, when my Ket Bethany body died, was Jenna Rose Weston. She grew up in Zargarb and had been running her own inn prior to the Holy Paladins taking control of her sector. She refused to close down her business, and they abducted her, cut off her hands, and threw her into their Nunnery. After her wounds healed, she and two others managed a nighttime escape and fled to the Santi Fortress next door to the city. From there, she was brought to Velona and into my presence.

Jenna and her two companions were very able spiritual beings, I noted, residing outside their heads. Hence, I proceeded to give all three as much Guardian training as they could master and desired. Jenna excelled above the other two. Only when she reached her tenth year of study and had to pick one of the seven specialties did she run into trouble. Without hands or desire, none of the specialties fit her. She, on the other hand, had her own ideas. She traveled into the Red Desert and was trained by Jes, the Guardian of the Anuir. She regained some spiritual abilities that she had had many lifetimes ago, the ability to move objects without using a fleshly body. Within the Guardians and the Santi, she became very famous for her special ability.

She also developed a special method by which the mental trauma one suffered could be erased! Often, she discovered, the actual genus lay in trauma suffered in previous lifetimes. When these incidents had been totally viewed and re-experienced in their entirety, which often took considerable time, being so mired in pain and unconsciousness, the trauma totally erased. She became the most famous healer on Tarra. I learned her technique and became nearly as good at it as she is. All the traumatized women of the Occupied Sectors were brought to her estate, and she and I erased these women's trauma. The result, these women who had suffered horribly gained a new lease on life, one now worth living.

We discovered that these many women who were so brutalized, losing arms and hands, had been the artists or performing artists in their sectors. Thus, their salvaging became even more important in our eyes, since artists help create civilizations! During this time, I also learned how to move objects from mom.

Over on West Reach up in the Highlands, King Lachlan Laird of Brea, had visions of the destruction of her kingdom. Also, she had visions of these many women artists that we were helping. She donated the entire wealth of her kingdom, nearly a half million gold coins worth, to Jenna to help all these women survive. Shortly after that, the Holy Paladins invaded West Reach and slaughtered her and many in her kingdom, burning her fortress and town to the ground.

The many armless women decided to form the Laird Foundation for the Arts with this money. They build a magnificent twin palace for the arts on Jenna's new estate, where they could work, and the artists from Velona could come as well. There is no structure on Tarra as magnificent as this twin palace. Further, they built other buildings in all the other sectors and several other lands as well, all geared to the full, compete support of artists and performing artists.

One of these, Bard Tal, my son in my last lifetime and an Amir descendent hunted by the assassins of the Church of Jehosanity and the Mano del Dio, has become the foremost musician on Tarra. He has put together a fabulous group combining music and dance into an incredible unit. He is using a number of armless dancers in his show, and he and his fellow musician from the Highlands have even married two of them. They are now residing at Jenna's estate and perform each week at the twin palaces.

The women of the Foundation have established various directors, who are knowledgeable in their specialties. Under their guidance, the arts and the performing arts in Velona have risen to heights never seen on Tarra before.

Over the past number of years and by a number of unusual methods, the Santi have helped Zargarb, Solamina, Barcella, and Pieta become free from the occupation of the Holy Paladins. These four are now free sectors, aided and protected by the Santi. Only Bonilla and Vito remain occupied sectors. However, now the Santi have finally stopped the Holy Paladin's from using the metal encasements. As of 648, no more women are being so brutalized, for which we are now quite grateful indeed.

Finally, peace and quiet have more or less returned to the known world. Hence, I decided now would be the ideal time for us to go exploring the oceans of Tarra, looking for new lands and new trading partners. Only by growth can we prosper. Jenna gave her approval with the restrictions that she pick my traveling companions and could call upon us to return at once should more trouble develop. These conditions I readily agreed to follow. I finally got my wish to sail the seas in a caravel.

The caravel has two main masts with smaller stern mast sporting a spanker sail and with several jibs aft. The Sleepy Hollow has a poop deck, and the captain's station is high atop this stern deck, along with the helm. The best cabins are those in the poop deck, one of which is for Captain Henry Freeze, who's twenty-six with long brown hair and matching eyes. He is a master of sailing. His bosun, Thad Thrush, is likewise from the Greenway with short brown hair and is twenty-five. Part of the crew members are three Santi Guardians, whose job is the protection of the ship and its crew. The Protector is Jason Farthington; his wife, Cathy is the Healer. Their good friend is Sammy Welts, who is their Communicator. All three come from Mont Blanc and are twenty-one.

The Santi lieutenant in charge of the fighters onboard is Bill Weatherspoon, from Calgary. He is the oldest onboard at thirty. His two sergeants are Angel Hattfield and Mary Beth Blackstone; both are twenty-three, with short brown hair, blue eyes, and are fighters from Calgary, who love the longbow. Both are superb archers. Additionally, there are six regular sailors and eight other Santi fighters. In case of trouble, the fighters man the monster ballista in the bow, which shoots a quarrel that is nearly a spear. Three more are located below deck and can be brought up on deck if a fight occurs. Additionally, an enormous catapult lobs flaming oil balls. This device is located near the stern on the main deck. Three more catapults are stowed in the cargo hold. This caravel is serious, if it's attacked.

The plush poop deck cabins hold the three Guardians and the three Santi leaders. When guests are aboard, normally these would make their cabins available, moving below deck into the cargo hold. However, since my party was too large to fit, I requested that they keep their plush cabins. Instead, the stern cargo hold has been modified for our use. Six more cabins were built, each sleeping two and with a small porthole for air located near the ceiling, as high up on the sides of the ship as possible.

My group consists of eleven of us; the Explorers Circle is our title. I, Bethany Rose Weston, am the leader and Wid. As I said, I'm nearly fourteen with long blonde hair and sky blue eyes. Everyone says I look like mom, who is a stunning blonde. Linda Sarah Amir is our Judger, and she is the same age as me. We have been best friends since we could walk and are inseparable. She is also blonde, though her hair is a shade darker than I mine, and has deep blue eyes. Linda is in the peculiar position of having been my daughter when I was Bethany Madelyn Amir and now is my daughter from my previous life as Ket Bethany. Lilly Ann is her mother and my second wife of last lifetime. Lilly Ann is also the Judger for Jenna's Circle. Sometimes, Linda and I get a bit confused with each other, because we are so close and remember well our recent lifetimes.

Next, Benet Donegal, son of Beth Ann, Lilly Ann's twin sister, is our Loremaster. He is eighteen with brown hair and hazel eyes. Emil Amir is our Protector and is the oldest of our Circle's Guardians at nineteen. He has brown hair and blue eyes and is rather handsome and dashing, always looking out for us, as if we were his kid sisters. Our Healer is Tonia Po Woodgrove, daughter of Elona Po, High Priestess and sole monarch of Velona. She is fourteen with long black hair and the greenish eyes of her mother. Cedric Dietz is our Planner and is fifteen. Cedric is cute with dark brown hair and black eyes. He is trying to grow a moustache now.

Finally, we have the fifteen-year-old twins of Andre and Lenkova Pazzio le'Goeur of Zargarb. Rosina has short blonde hair with blue eyes and looks like her mother, the most famous Sisterhood fighter in Zargarb. Her skin has a slight yellowish hue to it, coming from her Northern Steppes heritage. She is our Communicator. Renzo is a Protector and is tall with dark brown hair and the brown eyes of his father. Likewise, his skin has a hint of his steppes ancestry in it. I think Renzo is awfully cute and handsome. Both were originally sent to Jenna to have their horizons broadened. We are certainly accomplishing that goal.

Three others were added to our Circle. Mom insisted that we bring along the very best language translator in Velona. It turned out to be Natale Angela, a young woman who had lost her arms some years back. I had performed her therapy sessions. She is still single and is twenty-four now, with beautiful, long, curly blonde tresses that extended down to her rear, and she has enchantingly, pale blue eyes. Natale proved her worth on our last voyage. For her, this is a linguist's dream come true, voyages to other lands with other languages to learn firsthand.

I thought that Natale was extremely brave for insisting on doing things that she might otherwise not ever attempt again. I still remember what she said to me, "Lizzy Ann, if I give in to it, I am lost. I just have to keep trying to do things for myself somehow, someway. The alternative is just too awful to contemplate. I am alive, and I want to live life and enjoy it. I can't do that if I sit around in a chair all day and let others do everything for me. I can't live like that."

When I had asked Natale why she had not yet gotten married, she replied, "I haven't gotten married, though I've been asked twice by two men. I want to marry just the right man. So many of the other women are artists, and many of their husbands are also artists, so they then have much in common. Also, there is the small matter of love. I'm only going to marry someone I truly love, period. Yet, it's worse than that for me," she sighed.

"Oh, not because of no arms — it's not that. I mean I have a sharp mind. I'm a linguist. I love to learn new languages and speak with those who speak it. I've always wanted to travel and meet new people. Either the men I've met at the dances don't have a keen mind or they don't like anything that I like. I am probably doomed never to find love, but that's okay if I can travel and learn new languages and speak with those people — well, if I can do so every now and then. That's why this trip means so very much to me."

On our previous voyage, Natale so proved her worth that Captain Henry absolutely demanded that she come along on this new voyage. He would not sail without her! I think he was rather smitten with her.

We also had two last minute additions to our Circle, Mireio and Roberto Milienne. She was twenty-four and a victim of those damnable metal encasements and had lost her arms. Both were highly competent musicians. Their goal was to learn the music and songs of the new people that we encountered. She had a fabulous voice with perfect pitch. In addition, she had a nearly photographic memory for a tune. If she heard it once, she could remember every note! Roberto, twenty-six, was a guitarist and music transcriber, having just invented a way to annotate music onto paper. Mireio had lovely, long blonde hair down to her waist and pale blue eyes. Her husband had light brown hair with deep blue eyes. He was madly in love with her and her unique skills with music.

Mireio and Roberto shared a cabin; Natale and I bunked together; Benet and Emil took another cabin; Cedric and Renzo, another; Rosina and Linda shared one cabin, while Tonia currently had a private cabin. The crew had their quarters in the cargo hold bow section of the caravel. Our cargo consisted of a large quantity of provisions along with a good deal of trading goods, just in case such an opportunity arose. Still, the caravel rode high in the water, for it could carry twice the cargo we had with us on this lengthy voyage.

High atop the main mast, the black flag with the red fleur-de-lis cross, the symbol of the Santi del Dio, fluttered in the wind. The huge white sails, which also had red fleur-de-lis crosses on them, puffed out catching the wind. Even the spanker sail was up, along with the several jibs. We were off and running westward out into the open sea.

All of us were up on deck watching the very large city of Velona slowly shrink in size. Always, I found it spectacular to watch the caravels leave the port behind. Such has always fascinated me. I had my arm around Natale's waist, steading us both against the rail so we could watch, the wind blowing our long hair behind us. "I cannot believe this is really happening!" she said. "I'm so excited about this trip!"

"I know. It has long been a dream of mine to sail the high seas, like a free bird," I replied. "I'm just as excited too."

Mireio and Roberto were standing next to us. Like us, her hair was blowing madly behind her. We three had the longest hair on the ship. Yes, as I said, I have a fetish for long hair and the name Bethany. She said, "I'm just as excited as you two! Think of all the fabulous music and instruments we may encounter! Never in a million years would I have dreamed I would be off on such a trip! Only a few years ago, I was convinced my life was over when they busted that metal device off me. Now here I am a few years later embarking on a dream trip that any musician would give anything to take!"

"Well, not just any musician, my love," Roberto put in, "only those who have an overwhelming desire to learn new music of other lands. Many are content just to play the same tunes of the land, but not us!" She gave him a loving kiss.

A little later, Mireio said, "Bethany, Roberto and I can play for everyone whenever you all want some entertainment. Say, Bard Tal said that you used to be a good musician yourself, Bethany. Is that true?"

Memories of my last lifetime flashed before me, when I led the Cymry Minstrels across the Sea Princes, playing music for the local villagers as we went. Bard Tal, who in his previous lifetime had been Caitlyn Amir, my wife, was with me. She played the hammered dulcimer then. Caitlyn was assassinated the very night she gave birth to our twins, Tegid and Tal. She had immediately taken over the baby body now called Bard Tal. I sighed, "Yes, Tal is right. Last lifetime, I was a troubadour. My favorite instrument still is the bass flute. I brought Tal's old one along with me, but I have not had any time to learn to play it this lifetime. It seems like every time I think I have some time, in comes another load of brutalized women who need immediate therapy. I brought it along with me because maybe now I will have the time to practice and re-learn how to play."

"Well, we can help you," Mireio volunteered. "I used to play the harp and sing, though now I can only sing. I have a keen sense of pitch, so I can make sure that you are spot on. You really ought to work on it; life is so utterly dull without music in it!"

"Well, we certainly will have lots of free time on this trip. There are only so many times that the deck needs swabbing," I replied. Natalie chuckled. This was her favorite chore, one that she could do, given sufficient time, of course.

Just then, Captain Henry came down from the poop deck, "Okay, Bethany, it's time to go to the map room and work out where we are heading first. Ladies, care to join me?" He was smiling at Natale, I noticed. Natale and I, along with Linda and Emil, followed him into the poop deck hallway to his rear cabin. His was twice as large as any other cabin, stretching across the entire rear of the stern of the caravel. He had a large table in the center of the room on which he had laid out his maps. Natale, Emil, and I crowded around the table and looked at the map.

"So where to first, Bethany?" Henry asked. "We could try to find this Vihreä that we were told lies further west from Eyrarbakki, the island we visited a few months ago." Vihreä is Old Volksholm meaning green land. "Or we could explore the rumors of an island group somewhere off the coast of the Red Desert. Or we could look for more Spice Islands way down south. Or we could sail in any direction. What will it be, Bethany?"

"Let's be systematical, shall we? We should try to find this Vihreä land first, because it is so far north and winter is coming within a few months. We probably have still maybe three months left to us. Then, we can swing back further south where it is warmer. Personally, I don't like the bitter cold that I experienced in Eyrarbakki."

"That makes perfect sense, Bethany. Part of our job is to create detailed sailing maps. There is no better place to start than way up north and work our way down. I'll issue the orders then. It will be about ten days until we reach Eyrarbakki, because we're more heavily loaded this trip."

That settled, Natale said, "Now remember, Henry, when the next blow comes, I want to be on deck with you throughout it. I'm dying to experience a blow firsthand. You promised me last trip that I could, you know!" She refrained from outright begging, however.

He grinned broadly, "I have not forgotten, Miss Natale. Just remember, it can be a bit dangerous up there in a blow, and once it hits, you can't suddenly change your mind. You are committed until the storm passes."

Undaunted, she replied, "Well you just make sure that I'm securely tied to the ship or whatever. I don't want to be blown into the sea. I've been dreaming about what it must be like, you know, the wind and rain blowing on your face and all that. I've just got to experience it, at least once."

"Believe me, Miss Natale, I won't let that happen. You are the most important person on this ship this trip! Where would we be without our translator? Oh, that reminds me, Miss Natale," his face had a twinge of red in it I noticed. He retrieved a small box from his desk. "When I was ashore in Velona, I picked up a little something for my prized crew member. Here, this is for you Miss Natale." He opened the box. Inside, she saw a golden necklace with a golden Santi fleur-de-lis cross hanging from it.

"Oh my, it's beautiful!" Natale exclaimed, taken by complete surprise.

"Here allow me," and he carefully put it around her neck. It was just the right length to adorn her upper chest. "Now no one can doubt that you are indeed Santi," he beamed.

"It's gorgeous. Henry, but you shouldn't have spent your money on it. I mean this has got to be expensive," she replied, still looking down at it. I noticed that it was of the highest quality and had been personally handcrafted. It was a unique necklace indeed.

"What else has an old seaman got to spend his money on?"

"Thank you very much! You are not an old seaman," she replied and gave him a kiss. Soon both were embracing lovingly. I began to speculate that there was something developing between these two. When we went back on deck, Natale showed it to everyone else. I found Linda and told her about it. We two giggled, thinking that Henry had fallen in love with Natale. We were both only thirteen and only just beginning to think about such things.

Next, the chores were doled out. However, with such a large crew, in fact none of us had much actually to do. Natale, per her request, was given the cargo hold deck to swab. She convinced Mireio to help her with this chore, explaining that this chore was more than doable for them. Linda and I got to help the cook, primarily washing dishes. Ah well, domestic duties began at last.

That afternoon, I joined Natale who was sitting on the main deck, leaning back against the poop deck walls, watching the ship and the horizon ahead. "Sure isn't much to do but sit and watch," I commented.

"You know, I still owe you so much for the therapy that you gave me after I lost these," Natale began. "Without it, I'd be dead by now I suppose. Thanks to you, I am so full of life that I am nearly bursting with happiness."

"You are more than welcome, Natale. How's everything been going for you? I mean since you left the estate and went into Velona to study linguistics. I rather lost contact with you for a number of years there."

"Oh just fine. No relapses or anything like that. I've had a few embarrassing moments, as you might expect. Nothing major though," she replied. After a few minutes of silence with the warm wind blowing on our faces, she said, "You know, there is one thing that has been puzzling me, Bethany. I'm always right here, above and behind my head down there, never gone back inside as I used to be before your therapy sessions. Yet, many times, I've had a peculiar feeling. Sometimes when I'm about to lose my balance, I sort of feel that I should be able to hold things still, stopping the body from tipping over. At first, I thought I was just trying to reach out with my arms to steady myself. That has happened, you know. Even though they aren't there, sometimes I do catch myself trying to reach for something with my arms — somewhat funny actually, when it happens. But this other thing, this feeling, it's not the same thing."

Suddenly I was keenly curious. It made sense that she should inadvertently try to use her arms. Yet, this other idea intrigued me. "Tell me about this peculiar feeling. What does it seem like you ought to be able to do?"

"Look at that rope there lying along the mast. See, it's flopping in the wind. Bethany, sometimes I feel like I could or ought to be able to reach out and hold it perfectly still. Weird, isn't it? It's as if I should be able to steady it somehow. Another thing, even stranger — when I am translating sometimes I feel as if I can just be inside the other person's mind and read their thoughts! Isn't that just the weirdest idea?"

"No, Natale, neither is weird. You should get Guardian training, because reading other's thoughts is much like what our Communicators can routinely do. It's their specialty. You know we are going to have a huge amount of idle time on our hands this voyage. Why don't I see if Rosina can work with you and see if you can recover any latent telepathic abilities you might have?"

"You mean this is a possible thing? To read other's thoughts?" she asked very surprised.

"Yes, indeed. Yet, the other thing you mentioned, this holding things still. Now I wonder if we could actually get that skill developed. Say, are you willing to work with me and see if we can get you actually to be able to hold things still?"

"You're teasing me? Aren't you? People can't do that," she asked and then declared.

"Yes, people, that is, bodies, can't do that unless they use their hands, for example, to hold the rope up there nice and still. Quite right on that point, but you are a spiritual being, who knows what all a being can do? Shall we give it a try?"

"Sure. How?"

"Well, I think it is going to be just a drill that we do. When mom taught me to move objects, it turned out to be nothing fancier than just routine drilling on heavier and heavier objects. True, all sorts of mental traumas appeared, which I was using to prevent myself from lifting things. Jenna just ran her therapy on those when they appeared, and then we went right back to drilling. Let's see, we started with a dust mote to try to move. Something very tiny and light. We ought to do the same here. I have it. See this bit of your hair fluttering about? I want you to decide that you want to hold it perfectly still and then go ahead and hold it perfectly still."

"Okay!" she exclaimed with a good deal of enthusiasm. Soon, however, her face contorted with an effort to hold it still.

"Are you holding it still or are you trying to make the body hold it still for you?" I asked.

"Oh! I was using the body. Let me try again," she said.

We were off and drilling. After some time, for a brief instant, she did in fact hold that errant bit of hair quite still. "I'm not supposed to be doing this!" she exclaimed, and the hair began to flutter in the wind once more.

"Okay, I want you to take a look and see if you can see any mental picture there where those words might have come from," I asked her, unsure just how to phrase it.

"Oh, you mean like one of those trauma incidents that we ran before! Let's see, I'm not supposed to be doing this. I'm not supposed to be doing this! I'm not supposed to be doing this!" Suddenly, she was yelling these words and was clearly back in some trauma incident!

"Okay, I want you to go through it and tell me what is happening," I said, noticing that I now had a rather large audience. Her yelling had attracted the attention of many of my Circle.

"There is this really bad storm hitting our village. A tree is struck by lightning, and the wind is blowing it over on top of a home, which has a family of ten inside it. I see it is going to strike right where the people are at, in the second floor under the roof. I have to do something. So I held the tree still! Then I am yelling for others around me to get them out of the house. I can't hold the tree from falling forever. I see the ten frightened people running out of the house. The mother is carrying a baby and leading a very small girl. Once they are all out, I let go and the tree smashes into their house, crushing the bedrooms where they had been waiting out the storm."

"Someone calls me a witch. I know I shouldn't be doing this. They are tying me up. They are tying me to a pole and throwing wood all around my feet. God! They are going to burn me for being a witch! A man comes bringing a torch. I hold him still, rigid like a statue. I'm not going to let them burn me. I know I shouldn't be doing this for sure!" Natale let out a scream, passed out on me. A little while later, she came to and said, "Now I seem to be dead. That's all."

"Very good job, Natale! Now let's go through it again. Tell me everything you are seeing, feeling, and tasting." She was off and running through it once more. I noticed now that I had a very large crowd standing around watching our session. I hoped that it would be all right with Natale, but I sure wasn't going to interrupt the session to ask her.

After several more times through, the ending began to unravel, accompanied by heavy yawning. "I am holding the torch man as still as a statue. Suddenly, behind me a man with a sword cuts my head off before I can react and hold him still. Searing pain, cuts through my neck, horrible pain, but it is gone quickly. I'm floating up above the ground now. I think to myself, I should not be doing this. Now I am dead. Now that is an utterly stupid thing for me to decide! I am not dead. The body is." She began laughing, "I am not dead. True, when I did it, holding the tree still, I knew that I should not be doing that, but I wanted to save that family. Once I decided that I was dead, then every time after that when I tried to hold something still, I just knew that I had better not do it and that if I continued to make the attempt, my neck began hurting something terrible, and I just knew that I was dead or would be killed momentarily!" Now she began laughing wildly, and I ended the session there.

Everyone was now cheering her, and we stood up, the wind blowing our long hair around like pennants. Suddenly, her hair froze and became motionless. "Whee, look at this everybody! I can hold my hair absolutely still!" Everyone cheered and clapped. Almost immediately, they all wanted an explanation.

"Well, gang, we have lots of free time on our hands, and I've decided to see what good use I can make of it. Natale is working on gaining some new spiritual abilities. Oh yes, Rosina, will you take Natale to your room and see if she has any latent telepathic abilities? I have a strong hunch that she may just have."

Rosina looked at me, quite surprised. "You mean like an apprentice?"

"Sort of, she has not had any Guardian official training, but I think that she just might have some talents in your area."

"Cool! We could use more Communicators! Come with me, Natale; let's see what we have here."

Natale leaned over, gave me a kiss on my forehead, and said, "Thank you once more, Bethany!"

"Don't worry; we have only barely begun, Natale. We'll work on it some more tomorrow." The two women headed into the poop cabins where the stairs led down to our cabins below deck.

"Okay, the rest of you, you will get your turn one day as well. With all this free time, I've decided to put it to good use. Mireio, it's your turn. Come have a seat here, and let's see what we might do. The rest of you, go find something to do, please." Everyone was chatting about Natale and the offer that I had made to them. Mireio carefully sat down beside me.

"That was pretty darn impressive, Bethany. Just like your mother, I mean, you did the therapy just like Jenna did on me, as nearly as I can remember," Mireio said. Again, the warm wind blew across our faces, fluttering our long hair behind us. I had no proper methods by which to figure out just what skill a person might be able to learn or reacquire. This is a hole in our therapy, I thought. Mireio continued, "Natale really was holding her hair still in this wind. That's really cool."

"It sure is. I can't do it," I was honest with her. "Say, how have things been going for you since your therapy sessions with mom? Have you run into any troubles?"

"Oh her sessions were so incredibly wonderful! I went from near death and utter hopelessness to total, well, I don't have words for it. I just feel so alive, you know. Yes, lack of arms still causes some problems. I sometimes get so annoyed that routine things are so hard to do now. I do get frustrated at times. Roberto is so understanding and so helpful. He's about the greatest man I have ever known." I could tell that she was as madly in love with him, as he, her.

"It's kind of crazy, but every now and when I am not paying close attention to things, I find myself reaching for something with my arms. Silly of me, but sometimes I think I can still feel them. The Healers say this is only natural though. Still, it sure feels funny when it happens," she grinned sheepishly.

"Honestly, I can't imagine how you are getting along so superbly. You are all just fantastic women, that's all I can say." She blushed with the compliment. We chatted some more.

"You know, there is one really weird thing that keeps happening to me. It probably is nothing, but it's strange. I used to be a harpist, you know, before I was abducted and encased. Back home now, Roberto does have a small harp. Frequently when he is out, I sit beside it and look at it. Some days, I have these strange sensations in my arms, as I was saying before, you know, as if I can just reach out and pluck the strings. That's normal, I'm told. Yet, every now and then, I have the darnedest ideas flying through my mind, as if I should be able to pluck the strings without using my hands! That's utterly silly you know, but I have had that feeling a dozen times now, maybe more. Isn't that just the strangest thing?"

"Yes, it is interesting. Say, did Roberto bring the harp along with him?"

"No, he doesn't play it and I cannot any more. Why?"

"Well, come on; let's go find his guitar, Mireio." We went below to their cabin, which was cramped. He had brought along a number of instruments and a mountain of paper and ink. He had a guitar, a mandolin, and a lute.

"He doesn't play the lute all that often," she pointed out.

"Okay then, let's pretend the lute there is the harp. At least it has many strings. Here, come sit on the edge of your bed." Once we were settled, I asked her, "Now I want you to decide to pluck one string, and then once you have made that decision, pluck it."

"You mean with my toes?"

"No, you do it."

"Oh! You think that is even possible? I'm not just wishful thinking? You know, loss of arms and all that?" she asked very curious indeed. I detected a longing hope in her tone as well.

"Sure, why not. Now decide to do it and then do it."

Like Natale, during her first attempt, she was straining her body somehow to make the string move. "Are you doing it or are you trying to make your body do it?"

"Oh, silly. I'm trying to make the body do it! Let me try again." Of course, she didn't succeed. I honestly would have been shocked myself if she had.

We just kept doggedly at it. I explained that this was just a matter of enough drilling on the doing of it. After some time, she began crying, "I don't dare do this! I mustn't do it! They'll kill me!" Immediately I knew that we had just ran smack into a barrier of trauma, which was preventing her from doing this. She was above and behind her head, but some bluish grey mass was now surrounding her.

"Can you see the traumatic images that this is coming from?" Again, I had no idea of the proper way to ask this, I hoped she would spot it.

"Something bluish is here."

"I want you to go to the beginning of it and then go through it, telling me what is happening as you go along."

"I see this fabulous stringed instrument, sort of like a harp, but it is huge, several buildings tall with enormously long, thick strings. It is sitting way up high, far out of my reach. I'm down below. Oh, this is some kind of church, I think. I'm standing there wondering how low the notes would be. I am very curious about it. No one ever plays it. I keep coming to the services there, but I don't ever hear anyone playing it. There are strange carvings or idols around the edges of this massive room. Weird ones, like giants they seem, grey in color, probably just the stone from which the statues are made. No one mentions them either, kind of funny now that I think about it."

"You are doing well, continue," I coaxed her.

"I'm staring at this incredible instrument way up there. I really want to hear how it sounds, you know. Then the whole universe becomes completely scrambled. I'm dizzy, spinning, and don't know where I am at. Somehow, I have lost my body. I'm in a box. I can feel the sides, very, very cold they seem. Long time passes. Suddenly, one side opens and blinding light enters. I cannot see it is so bright. Someone says go find a new baby body and report back here when it dies. I am falling. I'm very scared. After a long time I seem to be floating above the ground near a village, primitive village. I see a very pregnant woman and get a new body. That's all. Boy this is a very strange thing that is happening to me. Maybe it isn't real. Do you suppose I am just imagining all this?"

"Good going. Now let's go back over it again." I had her go to the beginning and run through it again. After four passes, she began to start yawning, which I took as a very good sign indeed. More details began emerging after that.

"This must be some other world that I'm on; it just doesn't look like Tarra at all, so many metal buildings and all. We don't have metal buildings here. Oh, I did go pluck the strings! I got to hear the incredibly low notes. Wow, what a peculiar sound they made. While I was plucking and listening, one of the statues animated? No, that cannot be. Oh, someone walked in! God! It looks like the stone statues! It's not human! It's a giant, grey, huge. He points something at me. I get so confused! Everything begins to whirl and spin around me. I pass out. He is carrying me somewhere. Now some kind of energy overwhelms me. I can no longer feel my body. It's gone somewhere. He's killing me! I can't seem to remember anything anymore. Aieee. It's cold, so utterly cold and black. I touch a side wall and am so cold that I can't even move! I try to remember, but my mind is a complete jumble of images, nothing makes any sense anymore."

"I heard this voice or is it even a voice? It tells me to go find a baby body and to report here when it dies. I'm falling out into the brightly lit world. It's Tarra. It's not where I was. I am completely and utterly lost! I have no idea where this place is and will never be able to return home! I don't dare move things without my body because they will kill me and destroy me. That's the only thought I had throughout this ordeal."

She still wasn't cheerful, so I had her go through it once more. This time laughter began. "I was an artist! A musician, I think. I had to hear this instrument. God, it was just a trap to get those of us who could still do things without our bodies! I fell for it! These giant grey things got me, killed off my body, and dumped me here on Tarra, knowing that I would be completely and utterly lost! I could never find my way back there! I fell for it! Worse than that, it was me that decided that I better never do that again or they would kill me!"

Now she started laughing really hard, "Bethany, I did it to myself! I fell for it. What a stupid thing to have done!" I let her laugh and enjoy her discoveries. I noticed that the bluish mass around her was gone.

Sometime later when she had ceased laughing, I ended the therapy session and asked her to decide to pluck a string and do so. Twang! A note sounded. We both cheered, and she was so excited that she began jumping up and down. I just hugged her. "Super well done, Mireio!" I exclaimed.

"I've got to show Roberto!" she exclaimed.

"Let's call it a day, Mireio. Tomorrow we will drill on this some more."

"Thanks. How on Tarra can I ever possibly thank you, Bethany?" she asked.

"Oh just make music for us. If and when we find other peoples, learn their music so everyone else can enjoy it too," I replied. She leaned onto me, and I knew she wanted to hug me, so I hugged her.

"Thank you, thank you!"

"Come on; let's show Roberto our first step," I suggested.

"Show me what?" he said a minute later. "I'm supposed to tell you two that supper is served."

"Oh Roberto! Watch this," exclaimed his wife. Twang! His lute struck a note. Roberto's mouth opened, but no sound came out. Twang! She did it again. His eyes opened wider than I thought possible.

"That's incredible! You did that! Oh Mireio!" He grabbed her and swung her around in little circles in this small room. I left them in a loving embrace and headed for the dinner table in the aft section of the cargo hold.

Shortly after I sat down, they came bouncing into the dining area. "Wait until I tell you what Bethany has helped me be able to do!" Mireio exclaimed. She told everyone about her newfound skill to pluck a string on his lute. Of course, all talk around the large table focused on Natale and Mireio and what they had accomplished today. Me, I just pondered the horrible significance of Mireio's Grey Creatures. Were they the same ones that Alabaster and I had defeated so many years ago? I had to know.

When we had finished eating and were sitting around drinking our tea, I asked her, "Mireio, I really need to see what your greyish giants looked like. May I take a peek at your images in your mind?"

"Yes, of course, but I don't know how to do that for you."

"All you need to do is just look at one of your images you have of it and I'll see it." I touched her mind and peeked. Bingo, they were identical to the Grey Creatures that we had fought!

"Interesting, most interesting! Thanks, Mireio. I owe you an explanation, Mireio. Gang, the rest of you should hear this too. This is most interesting indeed." Suddenly, I had everyone's attention! You could hear a pin drop.

"Many years ago when I had my first body here on Tarra, Bethany Stanton, I was called. During that lifetime, I discovered some horrifying facts. High in the Appian Way, a group of giants lived. We called them the Grey Creatures, having no other way to identify these beasts. They stood nearly eight feet tall and had three toes. Weird creatures, but horribly powerful. They lived in secret; no one knew of their existence until I came across them. They were manipulating people's lives. When someone's body died, the spiritual being went to their location in the Appian Way. There this tall pole like thing activated, throwing out massive energies on the poor victim. It completely scrambled all their recent memories. Once the person was totally confused, the Grey Creatures ordered them to go and get a new baby body and to report back there when it died later on. I discovered them when I was watching the Centurions exterminate a huge number of Pieta's fighters on the battlefield."

"Later on, I discovered an even more horrible bunch of creatures that were operating out of three pyramids in the middle of the Red Desert. These were ghastly creatures, looking like fifty-foot tall praying mantises! They were doing exactly the same thing to the people who lived south of the Med Sea, trapping them, scrambling their memories, and sending them off to get new baby bodies. In short, I discovered that we were all being manipulated by these vile sets of creatures. Worse, they were playing one side off against the other side, creating the wars!"

"In my next lifetime as Ket Bethany, Alabaster, the founder of the druwid Guardians, and I found a way to exterminate both sets of vile creatures. We ourselves were pretty much powerless against them. So we got them to fight each other, and both sides destroyed each other in one massive battle. As far as we have been able to tell, we got them all. This meddling in our lives has ended. No longer are we being the puppets of these creatures."

Mireio exclaimed, "Well, now it all makes more sense to me! They trapped me and brought me here to Tarra. I'm sure glad that you got them killed off. This is utterly incredible, you know."

"Yes, almost too incredible to believe. However, Mireio, your experiences now make it all begin to make sense. They were systematically trapping spiritual beings and bringing them here, forcing them into fleshly bodies, making them forget about their own true nature and abilities," I replied. Now the talk centered on the Grey Creatures. Many asked me for more details and such. Soon, however, Linda and I had to stop to do all the dirty dishes! With this bunch of people, the dish pile was enormous!

While the others took an evening stroll on deck, Rosina lent us a hand. Actually, she wanted to brief me on her findings with Natale. While we three worked on the dishes, she explained, "You are right. Natale is a latent telepath! Normally, as you know, we train for nine years before we tackle the intricacies of mental communication. However, with Natale, she already is just a hair from actually doing it. Do you want me to see if I can train her?"

"I thought so. Yes, train her. Eventually, she is going to find herself being able to do it, and we don't want a rogue telepath around us. It can cause her too much grief."

"The trick is how to bring her along when she has not yet had all the other formal training, like observing the obvious," Rosina explained. "Is it okay with you if I seek some advice from other more experienced Communicators?"

"Sure thing, Rosina. Find the best way to bring her along. I'll keep her occupied by working her on holding things still, which she very much wants to learn how to do. That will give you some time to work your magic."

Over an hour later, we finally finished all the dishes. Rosina promised to come help us from now on, in fact, and she got Tonia to lend a hand as well. Doing the dishes for such a large bunch of people was a much larger chore than Henry had first estimated.

After taking a walk on deck, breathing in the salty air, gazing at the stars above, it was time to turn in. I made sure that Natale got safely down to our cabin that we shared. It was still overly warm in here for sleeping, so we took off everything — well, I kept on my nickers. Natale wore none so that she could go to the bathroom in the chamber pot by herself. She wanted to be as independent as possible, and I could not fault her for that. I helped her take off her new necklace, which she adored. "I've never been given such an expensive gift before. I kind of wish we were on shore so I could get Henry something. You think he likes me?"

I giggled, "I think he might well be smitten with you, Natale." I couldn't help grinning. She did too. After brushing our hair, we turned in. I helped her get into our shared bed, turned out our lantern, and crawled in beside her, pulling the light sheet up over us.

She whispered, "This bed is much more comfortable than those hammocks we had last time. By the way, thank you ever so much for what you are doing for us, Bethany!" She rolled over awkwardly and kissed my forehead. I gave her a hug. Jenna's therapy process was now progressing far beyond what she had originally envisioned. In a small way, I was now operating like Jes, the Guardian of the Anuir, helping to free spiritual beings, well, helping them regain some godlike skills that they once had had. It was a start anyway.

During the next days, I continued to drill both Natale and Mireio. Yes, as you may be anticipating, more traumatic incidents revealed themselves, as their skills steadily improved. I began to see a pattern developing here. As a being attempted to increase their "lost skills," at each new plateau of ability, a new trauma or series of connected traumas raised their heads. Once those were viewed and wiped out, further drilling raised their skill levels higher. Fascinating, I thought.

By the time that we reached Eyrarbakki, I allowed Mireio to begin working on her own. She was more than able to pluck strings as rapidly as desired. Now she was actually down to learning how to play the lute with its many strings and frets. No further traumas appeared, so I felt I could turn her lose on her own. However, she was under orders to let me know if anything further appeared that needed therapy sessions.

Natale continued to make progress holding things still. By the time that we reached the island, we had run out of things for her to hold still, excepting the ocean. Both of us felt that there was more to this whole thing of holding objects still, and we intended to continue working on it in the days ahead. On the other hand, Rosina had made a major breakthrough with Natale's rogue telepathic talent. She had actually gotten Natale to get across an idea to her and to pick up her thoughts. However, the second that Natale did so with complete certainty that she had just picked up Rosina's thought, another trauma moved in on her, forcing Rosina to bring the crying, semi-comatose Natale to me hastily, for an emergency therapy session.

I won't bore you with the details of that long, slug, slug, session. Instead, I'll tell you the gist of the incident, which had caused Natale to stop using her abilities to communicate directly from being to being. She had made the mistake of trying to communicate to one of the Grey Creatures she had spotted. Her native curiosity about the languages others used had gotten her into big trouble. As soon as she contacted its mind, it had retaliated viciously, blasting her with that same energy blasting device that it had attempted to use on me when I was living in Nuadian and was returning home with Sarah, my daughter. While I was able to dodge its effect, Natale was not and got smashed unconscious. The Grey Creature had killed her body, scrambled her memories, and sent her off to get a new baby body. Ugly, quite ugly. She had decided to never touch another's mind after that. The Grey Creature had been extremely convincing.

Once this traumatic event had been wiped clean, Rosina began to make real progress with Natale. At first, Rosina had Natale make and break contact with we three: Rosina, Sammy, and me. It is far easier to do this with another telepath. By the time we reached the island, Natale was getting good working with us. The next step was making and breaking contact with a non-telepath.

However, during this time, a new situation developed. This was the first time that the twins, Rosina and Renzo had been away from their homeland of Zargarb. While Rosina had kept in frequent touch with their folks, Andre and Lenkova — she was a Communicator after all — Renzo could not. Rosina chatted with me one night while we were doing the dishes. "Boy is my brother ever getting homesick! We've been gone now several months, Bethany. I've been chatting with mom quite a lot, you know. Dad too, but poor Renzo is taking it hard. I've even made Mind Links with him and dad a couple times. It has helped a little bit, but he's still rather melancholic."

"I've seen him practicing with the other Santi fighters on deck, nearly every day," I replied. "He seems okay then."

"Yes, but watch him afterwards, when he thinks no one is looking, when there is nothing for him to do," Rosina explained. "Honestly, Bethany, even his fighting skills are slumping. What should I do about him? Will this just pass away in time? I don't know much about homesickness, really I don't."

"Hum, I haven't given that much thought, Rosina. I think it may stem from a loss of the familiar. You know, what you have around you is not what you are used to having around you; it's all new and strange and not familiar. Let me think about this a bit, Rosina, and see if I can come up with a good way to handle it."

"Oh thanks, Bethany! I am relieved just talking to you about it, you know. Having someone to talk to about intimate things really does help a lot."

After we finished, I wandered on deck to spy on Renzo, to observe him for myself. I found him at the very bow of the main deck, staring off into the distance. "Hi Renzo. Good view?"

"Oh, hi Bethany," he said, rather sadly I thought. "Lots of water out here. Kind of makes you appreciate land and home more, doesn't it?"

"Sure does, pretty amazing that a mariner can travel all this distance and actually get to the island we are looking for, isn't it?"

"Yes, I'm not sure how Henry can figure it all out," he said rather apathetically. After a time, he said, "I guess I am just like mom. Give me a horse and let me ride. Do you think that we will honestly have any real fighting to do on this long trip? I mean I am supposed to be your Protector, but it sure doesn't seem like there is anything from which to protect anyone."

I had been married to a Protector before in my first lifetime. I replied, "Well isn't one of your fundamental rules to expect the unexpected at all times?"

"Yes, sure it is. I suppose I should be thinking about that. Why?" he said rather apathetically.

"Cause it can get you!" I declared and suddenly began to tickle him, relentlessly.

Laughing, he said, "Stop that! Bethany!" I didn't, as he tried to wiggle away, I continued to dive around his defenses and tickle him some more. He was awfully ticklish along his sides. Finally, he began to chase me around the deck, saying, "Okay, Bethany, you asked for this!" Now he was trying to tickle me back. We played around. I ducked his thrusts and countered, tickling his sides relentlessly, which only made him laugh more and try to get me even harder.

Finally, he pulled a sneaky move that I wasn't expecting, and he got me good! Laughing like mad, I called out, "Okay, okay, enough, you win." He was as unrelenting as I had been! At last, he stopped when I was laughing hard; he decided he'd had his revenge. We were both out of breath by this time.

"That was fun, Renzo. I really miss my nightly kick ball games." I explained to him about how every night, Jenna would take all of us kids out onto the lawn and play old-fashioned kick ball with us all until it got too dark to see. We were standing at the side of the deck, leaning on the rail. He put his left arm around my back, beneath my long tresses.

"I know what you mean, Bethany, about missing the game," he said very understandingly. "I miss my horse and going riding across the countryside. You know, wind blowing in your face. It's not quite the same thing here, when the wind blows on your face. There's no horse underneath you."

I'm not sure why, but I liked having his arm around my waist. I leaned my head on his shoulders, and we gazed off into the night sky for a time, without speaking. Just then, the bosun sounded the watch bell, signaling it was time for a shift change and for us all to hit the sack. "Thanks for the chase, Renzo. Want to do it tomorrow night?" I asked.

"You're on, Bethany, but don't feel bad if I always catch you though. I'll be on my guard from now on, so you won't get to tickle me again," he teased. He was in much better spirits as we joined the others heading down into our cabins. Rosina gave me a wink as we passed by each other on our way to our cabins.

After brushing our hair, Natale and I crawled into bed. She just had to tell me all about how her training with Rosina was going. I just snuggled with her and let her chat away. She was so proud of her achievements. The world was indeed becoming better by the day.

Next morning, I took Rosina and Renzo aside, making them sit by me against the poop deck cabin walls. "Gang, I think I have the answer for both of you. What you both need is to just be able to go where you want, like to Zargarb, and have a look around, and see how things are going along for yourselves."

"Yes, but we are out here at sea, hundreds of miles from there. We can't ask you to turn the boat around and take us back to Zargarb," protested Rosina.

I grinned, "That's not what I had in mind. I want you both to close your eyes and relax. I will make a Mind Link with you." They did as I asked, and I joined with both of them.

This is so utterly cool! Renzo thought. *Rosina has done this with me a lot. You are the first person to do it with me other than her.*

Thanks. Now I want you both to come with me. Here's how it works. Decide that we are hovering over Zargarb right now. Yes, make that decision, and here we are. I dragged them both with me as I moved us over their home city.

Oh my god! We really are over home! exclaimed Renzo.

Oh my! added Rosina. *This is so incredibly cool! I didn't know we could do this.*

Look, there's mom! Renzo pointed out Lenkova who was in the courtyard of the Santi fortress tightening a cinch. *Can we say hi?*

I'll do it. Rosina volunteered and made the connection. *Hi mom! It's us. Bethany has brought us here to say hi. We're up here.* I made a little energy flash to help Lenkova spot us three.

Hi! What a surprise. I didn't think you could do this. Are you at sea now? This is cool!

Hi mom. We didn't know we could either. Bethany is doing it really. We are at sea on a big voyage of discovery. Bethany has been doing all sorts of amazing things for some of us while we just sail along. I really miss you and dad, Renzo thought to her.

We miss you too. Have fun and learn lots Renzo, you too, Rosina. I think this exploration thing is a fabulous idea. Just make sure you bring back something we can use here in Zargarb. We have a lot of rebuilding to do. Thanks Bethany; please come by here sometime with your body that is, and visit us. You realize I haven't seen you now that you are all grown up.

Hi Lenkova. I'll take good care of your twins. I think we may just do that, bring the ship by Zargarb at some point later on. We'd better get back to the training now. Bye.

The twins said their farewells. Renzo was definitely in much better humor now. However, I did not bring them back immediately. *Okay you two, this is how it works. You just decide where you are at, and then you are there. I have a line on each of you so you can't get lost. So which one of you wants to go first?*

Let me, please, Renzo. This is so cool!

Okay sis. What do we do? Where are we going now?

All right I want you, Rosina, to decide that we are over Barcella. Make the decision very solid, have no thoughts that are counter to your thought, and we will be there.

She tried and tried. *I keep thinking this isn't going to work,* she said. I kept her at it, but began seeing some mental mass coming in on her. Just as I was thinking that I'd best get them back to the caravel and run a session on her, she did it, well nearly so. A bit wobbly, we mostly arrived over Barcella. I brought Renzo with us. *I did it!* She exclaimed very excitedly.

I let her have her big win for a time, as we watched the city below us. People and horses moved about like ants. Smoke clouds curled into the sky from several chimneys. *Okay, now Renzo, it's your turn. Decide that we are over Velona and take us there.*

He tried. He got the image of Velona in his mind and concentrated. *Imagine that we are above the city,* I suggested.

He worked at it, making the decision repeatedly. Just as we began to move there, a large black mass moved in on top of Renzo. At once, he went unconscious on us. I pulled us all quickly back to the caravel. Rosina opened her eyes and tugged at her brother, who was apparently still unconscious, though now in his usual location above and back of his head. "What's happened to him? Is he hurt somehow?"

"We've run into some trauma that he has suffered, which somehow ties in to his inability to do what we have been doing. It's time for a session. You can watch, just don't say anything. Okay, Renzo, I want you to continue going through the trauma and tell me what is happening as you go along."

After nudging him a number of times, he finally whispered, "I promise I'll never do it again. Please don't kill me, please. No. No! No!" He let out a blood-curling scream, which took everyone on the boat by surprise. Several came over to make sure everything was all right. I just waved them away and had him continue.

He just said, "I'm dead. It's over now. I'm done for." I had him go back to the beginning and go through it again. For three hours, I worked him on the incident and finally got my yawns coming fast and furious. A long time ago, he had a small boy's body in Bonilla. He'd just seen someone die and spied the being floating up and out of the dead body. Curious, he'd begun following the being, which floated up towards the tall peaks of the Appian Way. Renzo had followed him, enjoying the view and the freedom that moving around the world without having to drag a body along with him gave. Then, he saw the Grey Creature doing something horrible to the one he had been following. It saw him and came after him. He raced back towards Bonilla and dove into his small body.

The Grey Creature found him and ignored his promises and pleas. He had used that same energy device on Renzo, which a creature had tried to use on me so long ago. In short, the creature killed his new boy body, transported him to the pole atop the mountain there in the Appian Way nearly opposite from Bonilla, scrambled his mind, and sent him to get a new body. However, so terrified was he, that he flew all the way over to Zargarb before looking for a new baby body. "No wonder I don't dare move about like we did! I got killed for doing it! No wonder I won't go anywhere near Bonilla! I felt creepy even when the caravel that brought us to Velona passed by that sector! Wow!" He began laughing about all this and I ended the session. It was way past lunchtime.

Over lunch, Renzo explained it all to everyone who would listen. Finally after everyone else had left, leaving the dishes to us dishwashers, he said, "Bethany, you are one very hot young woman! Thank you! That was so incredibly interesting, intriguing, exciting — jeesh, I don't even have words for it all!"

I grinned, "But we've only just begun, Renzo." I teased him. After doing the dishes, we went back to our positions by the poop deck walls. "I think I had better work with one of you at a time. Is that all right with you two?" It was, so I worked with Renzo for a while. I had to, actually, otherwise he might have tried it on his own. I was not surprised to find that now he could manage to get us to Velona and back again safely. He was ecstatic when our short trip was done. I ended the day's work on him to let him enjoy his great accomplishment. Now I turned my attention to his sister.

I suspected that some trauma was about to appear, so I had her take us to Velona as well. Once more, I sensed all her counter-thoughts appearing and her monumental struggle to squash them or die trying. That was her attitude. While we made it to Velona merely by brute force, the mass that I had spotted earlier was growing more and more solid. She was unable to smash through it to get us back to the ship. I brought us back and began a session on Rosina.

I worked her for most of the afternoon, before the whole trauma was laid bare. She had also had a violent run-in with a Grey Creature. She'd had a young man's body and had discovered that she could move around without bringing along the body. She loved the freedom to view the countryside and had fallen in love with the Paese di Dio, God's Land, the grassy high plateau that stretched across all the Sea Princes and from which the high mountains of the Appian Way rose. Daily, she visited this region. However, one day, a Grey Creature spied her and tried to capture her. She fought him like the devil. Rosina put up a strong fight against him, refusing to give in to his demands and energy forces. At long last, the creature won by blasting her with the full force of his energy weapon. In the end, swamped with overwhelming black energy, she had decided never to do this again, and her decision had held all these years until today. When she was laughing wholeheartedly, I ended the session, promising more drill the next day. However, I made them both promise not to try going places on their own just yet.

"Land ho!" came the call from the crow's nest early the next morning while we were all eating breakfast. We all dashed onto the main deck to have a look. Sure enough, we had navigated precisely to the island called Eyrarbakki. This proved beyond any doubt that Henry's navigational machines and methods worked perfectly.

After a brief conference, Henry began sailing due west, looking for the island called Vihreä, if it was an island. We only had the vaguest references to this green land. We assumed the green meant either grasslands or forests. Now, however, very careful measurements had to be made in order to properly construct our ongoing map. Since I was more or less tied up with my newest actions, Benet, Emil, and Cedric began taking independent observations, and Henry then compared theirs to his, and then averaged the results. Benet then drew the map based on the results.

Now our speed slowed way down. No longer could we sail at full speed. Running into small rocky islands or submerged or partly submerged rocks would be fatal. Further, we knew not what lay ahead. Stupid me, I did not think of this until Rosina mentioned it when we began our next set of drilling. "Why don't we move on out ahead of the ship and see what is ahead of us?" Duh!

My only justification is that I'm not good with physical distances when I'm out there separated from my body. My perceptions, while improved, are still not very accurate. Of course, the problem with using the twins for this during our training was simply that they had no reference points, no anchor points, to be entirely accurate, by which to locate themselves. I could say, "Be over Zargarb." This they could follow and be certain when they had accomplished it. Saying, "Be two miles ahead of the ship," yielded only more of the vast expanse of sea. None of us could be certain that we had carried out the command. Instead, I altered our drilling slightly. "Okay, gang, let's slowly move on out ahead of the ship for a while, and see if anything lies ahead of us."

Slowly, we three moved on ahead of our caravel, skimming over the ocean waves. Actually, for a time, we all enjoyed this novel way of traveling. *Won't we get lost?* asked Renzo.

Not really. You see you always have a tiny communication line back there to your body. All you need to do is to decide you are back there, and you are. So you can't get disconnected from your bodies, really. I never could.

After spanning a considerable distance, we returned to the ship. Next, I continued the drills of the previous day, having them decide to be at various locations and then do so. Not long thereafter, each had another trauma incident appear, though neither was as massive or bad as the day before. I returned us to our bodies and gave them each another session. Once finished, I worked with Natale, checked on Mireio, and aided them.

That evening, once the dishes were finished, I took my usual stroll on the main deck, watching the early dusk and stars appear. Suddenly, Renzo appeared and began tickling me. "Gotcha! You weren't expecting it this time!" He got me good before I maneuvered out of his reach and began circling him, looking for an opening to retaliate. Finally, I did get even. We both burst out laughing. After that, every evening, one of us invariably would make a sneak tickle attack on the other. We had begun a fun game.

After another week of drilling, the twins were confident enough to move out in front of the ship and see if anything lay in our immediate path. This they dutifully did three times a day. Natale was now stable at holding just about everything in sight quite still. Mireio was even picking out simple tunes on the lute. All was well in the universe.

Chapter 2 The Search for Vihreä

On August 14, 648, dark clouds loomed ahead of us. A storm front bore down upon us. This meant that suddenly the accuracy of our maps would fall off. Who could tell where we would be blown to by the storm? Henry requested that everyone make an attempt to keep track of our location by dead reckoning. Once it passed, we would compare observations. Benet placed a question mark at the location on the map where we were now at, indicating from here on, measurements may well be off.

Next, everyone double checked and then triple checked the entire ship to make sure everything was battened down and secure for the bumpy ride. The sails were lowered and tied, leaving only two steering jibs still in action. Natale insisted that she be allowed to experience this blow, and Henry consented after giving her his usual warning that things could be dangerous up here in a storm. I decided that I ought to stay on deck with her, just in case. The bosun tied himself securely to the aft mast, where he could watch most of the ship and take action if needed. Henry secured himself to the helm, using the post before him, which supported the wheel.

He then had Natale join him, and he tied her around her waist to the post as well. She then stood between him and the wheel. This way, he felt he could totally protect her. Me, I tied myself to the railing behind them and slightly off to their left so that I could see both of them. The seas were definitely getting heavier; the caravel rose and fell much more violently now, even though the storm had not yet hit. When the rains began, Henry said, "Okay, now I'm turning us into the wind. We must always be heading into the winds, Natale. If we don't and we get hit sideways, the waves can capsize the whole ship, sinking us! This is the most important fact to remember always; head the ship into the wind and waves!" He was now yelling to be heard over the thunder and sound of the heavy seas pounding our bow. Soon the waves increased, sending walls of water foaming over the main deck.

"This is really fabulous! What a sight! Wow!" yelled Natale, thoroughly excited and wild with enthusiasm. I realized that I ought to have tied our hair up. The winds blew it nearly straight backwards, which was fine for me, but Natale's blew into Henry's face. Next, the rain pummeled down upon us. Sheets flew nearly horizontal into our faces. I used my hands to cover my eyes, realizing that Natale would not have such protection. Perhaps this was indeed a bad idea for her to be up here.

Nevertheless, the sight was spectacular, wind, rain, and monster waves flowing over the deck. Now the wave splashes even reached us up on the poop deck. We were soaked many times over! Though it was the middle of the day, we could barely see; it was that dark out. The blinding lightning flashes illuminated the ship for an instant, toothpicks waving in the wind or a forest in the dead of winter. Then, it happened. Lightning actually struck the ship, forking in two directions. One of the jib lines broke under the stress, fluttering wildly about the aft mast. The other fork splintered one of the yard arms holding the spanker sail boom. Suddenly, the broken section came falling down upon us. It was heading straight for Henry and Natale. Even before I could act, Natale did. Henry had not seen it coming. Had he been there alone, he would have taken a devastating blow from the broken wood. Yet, Natale had seen it and acted. A split second before it would have smashed into Henry, the broken yardarm piece just froze in mid-flight! It just stayed there inches from Henry's head. The noise was utterly deafening, so we could not yell to each other.

Instead, I now acted. I carefully grabbed a hold of the yardarm piece and pulled it back to the main mast. I made contact with Natale and told her to hold it still right where it was at. As soon as I felt her grasp, I let go and found some dangling rope and began tying it securely to the mast, so it would be out of the way. Then, I looked aft. The bosun was struggling to get to the jib before it was torn to shreds. The storm was so intense that he could not safely get to it, which was plainly obvious.

Therefore, I moved over to the jib, grabbed a hold of the wildly dancing rope, and then pulled it back toward where it had been tied. I then had Natale hold it still, while I undid the broken end of the same rope, tied it onto the other end, which Natale was holding firmly, and finally re-secured the end to its proper place. When Natale let go, I then adjusted its tautness, and the jib was back in business once more. Though we couldn't speak over the noise, Henry gave me a thumb's up sign, and I relaxed once more.

Ahead, I saw a streak of red along the horizon; the end of the storm was in sight. Thank goodness! During the next hour, the storm gradually subsided, until at last, only sprinkles were falling, and the skies coming up on us were crystal clear. The bosun untied himself and sounded the all clear bell. Other crew members came clamoring out of the poop deck doors. I untied myself and went to aid Henry and Natale.

"Bethany, my hands are so stiff I cannot undo these knots. Little help please?" he said grimly. While I untied both of them, the bosun issued orders for repairs, which the crew began executing at once. Another crew member took over for Henry, allowing us drenched and chilled folks to go below, dry off, and warm up.

Once we were in the poop deck hallway, Henry said, "Thanks you two! You saved my life and possibly the whole ship! That was unbelievable!"

"I'm freezing. Let's get dried off before we freeze to death!" I exclaimed and helped Natale into our cabin. Quickly, it was off with the soaked clothing. Our sopping wet hair stuck to everything making a rapid change more awkward. Hastily, I dried her off and wrapped a towel around her head. Then, I dried myself off doing the same with my hair. She was shivering badly still, so was I for that matter. Quickly, I helped her into a warm dress and put on one of mine too. Finally, I wrapped a blanket around each of us, and we headed down to the kitchen.

The cook already had hot chocolate waiting for us; the captain and bosun were already there. Quickly, we two began sipping the warm brew. Henry began, "Which of you did which? You probably saved the ship from a worse calamity! I must admit that you two were invaluable up there. I didn't see the yardarm until it was too late."

Natale said, "I saw it just in time to stop it, Henry, just barely. Bethany then moved it out of the way. I held it to the mast while she tied it up. I can see that I need to learn lots more than just holding things still! I need to be able to move them too!"

"Well thank you two!" Henry gave us both a hug.

"Hey, who fixed the jib?" asked the bosun.

"We both did," I explained, "I grabbed the rope and got it to where it should be, and Natale held it there while I undid the other end, spliced the ends together and re-tied it. We make a pretty good team, don't we fellows?" I teased.

"A darn good team!" Henry exclaimed. "I thought I was a goner there for a second! See, Natale, I told you things could happen in a blow! It can become very dangerous in a split instant up there!"

"Yes, but it was magnificent! The wind in your face, the rain, the waves, the roller coaster ride! Wow! That was the neatest thing I've done in my life! Woo hoo! I've got to do that again!"

"Well, Miss Natale, you can ride any storm out with me after today! You've proven your worth once again!" He gave her a strong hug! She was all smiles. He added, "Natale, you are my kind of woman!"

She replied coyly, "And you are my kind of guy!" She teased, "So what are you going to do about that?"

"This," he said and he put his arms around her and gave her a long, loving kiss.

Just then a crew member came in, spied them embracing, and cleared his throat. "Er Captain Sir. Yardarm's repaired. What course do we sail?"

"Not now, can't you see I have found the love of my dreams?" Henry jested, barely able to pull his head away from Natale's. "Okay, okay. My dear, will you excuse me for a bit? I need to get these swabs back on course." She smiled, but I noticed her cheeks were quite flushed.

I knew that the main questions being asked above decks right now were: where were we and how far off course had we been blown? I hoped that between Henry, the bosun, and our men, they would be able to work it out. I had been very distracted and had no idea.

Natale and I returned to our cabin to dry our hair and hang out our wet things. "I think he really likes me," she ventured. "I sure do like him. What do you think?"

I grinned. "I think you both like each other, but I'm not Beth Ann. I have a hard enough time figuring out these things myself. Love just seems to happen with me. Don't look to me for help on that one! I may need to lean on you, after all, since you are older and more experienced with the men than I am." Actually, I was being quite truthful. I had never really figured this whole love thing out; it just had happened to me.

She giggled and said okay. The only problem with long hair is the incredible length of time it takes to dry out and then to brush. We did not get back on deck for nearly an hour. By then, everything had been repaired, the position determined, and the ship was once more on our original course.

That night, after we finished the dishes and I went on deck, Renzo once more took me by surprise, giving me a good tickle. This time, I cheated. While laughing as his fingers pretended to count my ribs, I just lifted his body up in the air! He yelled down, "Bethany! This is cheating! Hey everyone, Bethany is cheating!" I began laughing so hard that I had to set him back down. He roared with laughter as well. Others who had seen this romp also were laughing. However, out of the corner of my eye, I spied Henry leading Natale below deck. Good for her, I thought.

Still chuckling, I went over to the railing and leaned out, looking at the last of the twilight. Renzo came over beside me and slid his arm under my hair and around my waist. "You got me good tonight, Bethany! Actually, that was fun, you know, being lifted into the air. I heard about how you did that to the assassins that night when they stormed your estate. Incredible thing to be able to do. Is it hard to learn how to do that?"

"Yes, Renzo it was hard for me. I ran into all sorts of traumatic things that I was using to prevent myself from ever moving objects again. If it wasn't for Jenna's therapy sessions, I would never have been able to do this kind of thing. But this ought to teach you a lesson, Mr. Renzo, don't pick on little old me," I laughed.

He squeezed my side closer to him, "Lesson learned the hard way, but, little Bethany, that won't stop me," he teased. "I'll just have to be sneaker about it." Together, we watched the stars come out in their full glory. Sometime later, he admitted to me, "You know, you are the smartest and fun-est person that I've ever met." I thanked him for that. Later when the watch shift bell sounded, we all headed to our cabins for the night.

Natale was not there, I discovered. She didn't come in for over an hour. I had already brushed out my hair and was laying in the bed waiting for her when she finally came into our cabin. Her face was very flushed; her smile was huge. "He took me into his cabin! He held me in his arms. Golly, we talked for hours it seems. He and I, we seem to think so much alike, and we like so many of the same things!"

I grinned and asked, "Is that all you two did in there?"

She blushed, "And then we began kissing each other! I think I am in love! After all these years, Bethany, I am in love with Henry! I think he is in love with me too, don't you think?"

I smiled. "It certainly looks that way. I am so happy for you Natale! You certainly did make a good impression on him today. What better way to get a man's attention than to save his life."

She laughed at my joke. "You know that I would have done it no matter who was there?"

"I know, just teasing you. He is a really good match for you, if my opinion counts for anything in matters of love."

"It does, coming from you!" She leaned for me and I gave her a good hug. Then we turned in, though we continued to chat about it for some time.

Days stretched into weeks and no sign of land. Renzo and Rosina were now very able to move about at will. No longer did I need to watch over them, and I had given them their final pass on this skill. I continued to work with Natale, attempting to expand her hold it still skill into making objects move. However, instead, we ran into an entirely different scenario. It seems that she could more readily throw up barriers to unwanted incoming forces and objects. Interesting idea she had, so we pursued this aspect.

Meantime, I added Linda Sarah to my group. She was a Judger, but had heard of Jovanna's interesting adaptation. In addition to creating illusions that were believed, she had extended it to placing thoughts into their minds along with totally controlling the other person's body. This Linda most definitely wanted to learn how to do! Undaunted by the fact that this was not part of my skill set, I worked with Linda on it. I found it most illuminating that she too had a nasty confrontation with a Grey Creature. She lost her battle with it, however. When the creature had attacked her, Linda had attempted to force the creature to do her bidding and had failed, mostly because she had been blasted by its energy gun. In the depths of that traumatic event, replete with massive pain and unconsciousness, she had decided that she could no longer control others. Once we erased this trauma, Linda was well on her way to doing what she most wanted to be able to do.

Considering that so frequently my friends were encountering that strange energy blasting device of the Grey Creatures, I contemplated training everyone in just how to dodge such energy flows. I was one of the very lucky few whom good old Alabaster, the founder of the druwids centuries ago, had chosen to train in how to avoid being struck by lightning bolts, sheets of fire, and ice. This skill I had already used to avoid being blasted by the Grey Creature's energy devices. Again, that was over a hundred years ago now. Yet we had eliminated all the Grey Creatures, so was this really needed? This was the question that I wrestled with for a number of days without reaching any positive decision.

At last came the call from the crow's nest for which everyone had been waiting! "Land ho!" Everyone rushed to the foredeck, straining for our first glimpse of a virgin land for all us, though not perhaps for those from Volksholm, who had probably sailed here years ago in their long boats. Benet pointed out the occasional shore birds that flew nearby, saying that those were only found on land. Slowly the hilly, green appeared before our eyes. Late that afternoon, we were only a mile off the shore, having begun sailing south paralleling the shore.

The land here was very hilly and densely forested with maple, ash, elm, and scattered oak trees, once more dutifully pointed out by Benet. He, of course, was hoping to find some new species of trees. The shoreline was a bit too rocky to land, but as we went further south, small bays and river inlets appeared, and some looked promising, if we wished to land. Since we were looking primarily for civilizations, we continued moving down the coastline all day. At night, we anchored off a cozy little bay. No longer could we sail during the night, because we ran the distinct risk of missing any coastal settlements.

On September 12, we found a coastal village, the first that we had seen. Our estimates suggested the village was home to perhaps five hundred people. A dozen small fishing boats were out in the sheltered bay when our large ship rounded a bend and entered the bay. While we sounded our way slowly into the bay to avoid running aground, the men in the fishing boats waved and people began congregating on the beach, staring at this unusual sight, a caravel was unknown to these people. In fact, this was the largest ship that they had ever seen. At last, Henry dropped anchor about a half mile from shore. The crew quickly lowered the two longboats, which could seat twenty-one. We were a large party.

The Explorers Circle plus the Santi and Captain Henry went in one boat and the remainder in the other. As we moved closer to shore, Natale suggested, "They look like a hardy, robust people. Good chance that they are Volksholm descendants." I thought so too. The large crowd was talking about us as we landed. After we climbed out, Natale and I took the lead, flanked by Henry, Renzo, and Emil. The others fell in line behind us. One man, who turned out to be the village elder came forward to greet us. I shook his hand, while he stared at Natale, who began working her linguistic miracles with him.

"Yes, Old Volksholm! What should I say?" she told me.

"We are explorers and traders from the Sea Princes," I thought that using such a large country as that might be better known to these people. "I am the leader, Bethany Rose Wilkins."

Our host was named Orlak Olms and this village was called Olmstead. Yes, their ancestors came from Volksholm. To keep this narrative short, they held a feast in our honor. We shared songs and dances afterwards. On the business side, we traded them six new axes for some gold. He told us that there were six inland villages as well and that no ship had come here for years. Hence, arrangements were made for a large delivery of tools, grains, and cloth next spring. They promised to collect a pile of gold nuggets by spring.

More interesting, we learned that winter would come within a month this far north. As far as whether this was really Vihreä or not, the elder believed that this was the name his ancestors gave to this land, but they now called it Grun. Whether Grun was an island or not, none here knew, only that it was large, whichever it was.

The next day, we set sail continuing our southward journey. Henry, Benet, and Emil carefully plotted the location of Olmstead on our map, along with some key details to help others identify its location along the coastline. Mireio and Roberto wrote out the ten new songs that they had learned from the villagers. He had begun making a collection of new songs and dances. I suspected that Bard Tal would dearly love to see this work when we returned.

Once more, days turned into weeks as we sailed past marshes, river outlets, low hills, grasslands, and even a set of low mountains. We found no other villages; however, daily, the temperatures continued to climb, which we all appreciated. The men made careful listings of potential bays, which might be settled later on, should some adventurous folks desire to carve out a home in this unexplored land. Definitely, this was not an island that we had found; it was more like the Southlands with an exceedingly long coastline.

Linda and I celebrated our birthdays; we both were now officially of age. Mireio and Roberto provided the party music, and we held a dance on the main deck in our honor. Renzo had more dances with me than anyone else, which I thought was interesting.

During this time, I continued working away with my friends, helping them regain key abilities that they felt they might have. I continued to use this as my yardstick: what did they dream about doing, have an instinct that this might be possible, that sort of a hunch. I still lacked any positive means by which to determine what skill a given person might be able to achieve.

Specifically, I had both Renzo and Rosina now able to launch their druwid spells, such as lightning bolts while they were hovering miles away over the ocean. Now they, like me, could attack from a distance as spiritual beings. Perhaps even more spectacular, Linda was not only able to place thoughts directly into another's mind, but also to read their thoughts and even control their bodies, much like Jovanna Barcella could do. Now I was ready to see what could be done for some of my other friends.

That was delayed considerably. Henry's estimates placed us nearly two thousand miles south of Vihreä. Still no villages appeared, just a virgin land full of settlement opportunities. However, now the temperatures were very warm indeed, and the vegetation on the land had changed to more like that of the jungles of the Southlands. According to Henry's estimates, if we were paralleling the coast of the Southland, we ought to be near the lower end, where the weather was always warm to hot. We rounded a large outcropping of hilly rocks, and everything suddenly changed for us.

Chapter 3 Wanakan

On October 20, 648, rounding the barrier rocks, we spied a huge bay, filled with countless numbers of strange reed boats. A huge city stretched from the red sandy beach more than a mile inland! Even from this distance, we could see a great many people, like small ants, moving through the streets. No doubt, we had just discovered a major, unknown to us, city!

Around here, the soil was reddish in color, likewise the stone. The multitudinous shades of green jungle foliage contrasted well with the ground and the many buildings. None of us had seen anything like this! Captain Henry spoke first, "Ah, this is what we mariners call a First Contact, rather a huge one at that! Here is a new people, completely foreign to us, with a different language, different customs, different, well different everything. Of course, they have never seen us either. We don't know if they will be hostile to us or friendly to us, but they will probably not be indifferent to our sudden appearance in their world. It's a whole new culture that we are staring at, gang."

"Bethany, I need you to work with me," Natale asked with a note of concern in her voice. "These people will have a totally foreign language. As I get a word figured out, will you write it down, you know, write how it sounds and then what it means. Then, everyone can benefit from it as I get their language figured out." I wholeheartedly agreed and made sure that I had the needed supplies with me.

As we turned into the bay, the crew was sounding once more. Captain Henry wanted to take no chances of us running aground in a shallow bay. If these people were hostile, he claimed that we might need to make a fast getaway. Benet counted forty-five reed fishing boats out in the bay, with more onshore. As we drew near, some of the fishermen began to wave back in response to our waving hello to them. Within a couple minutes, all the fishing stopped, and the reed boats moved in around us, the men looking us over. One was close enough to talk, so Natale began her enormous task of figuring out their language. I didn't envy her one tiny bit; each word was a struggle to obtain. This language was very different from anything that we knew.

"Ah, this is the city of Wanakan," Natale finally proclaimed. A little later, she decided that these people were known as the Acalans. Now that we were closer, we began to get a good view of these people. Their skins were brownish in color, with oval faces. Dark hair predominated with black eyes. The men wore their hair shoulder length, while the women's hair generally reached to their hips. With both sexes, the hair was thick and uniformly straight. They all had comparatively thick lips and slightly flattened noses.

Clothing was very exotic from our viewpoint. Men wore loin cloths, reminiscent of the Highlander kilts, only these were made from some unknown material, woven in deep reds with blue and green and yellow bands, quite colorful indeed. The women wore dresses of a similar make, which had wide neck openings and stopped just above the knees. Shoes were similar to our leathers, only they had an exaggerated pointed toe.

However, the personal ornaments were lavish, from our standards. Men wore gold and jade necklaces complete with long jade earrings. The women wore even fancier necklaces, which flared out fan shaped over their chests. Gold and jade were interspersed. Their earrings were very large and probably heavy. Upon a closer examination a little later, we saw that a hole had been made in their ear lobes and a gold disk inserted. Typically, these disks ranged from a quarter of an inch to an inch in diameter. From a central hole, the heavy earrings dangled. Additionally, the women wore arm and wristbands made of gold as well.

By the time that Henry lowered the anchor, we were about a thousand feet from shore. Hundreds of people were lining the red sandy beach watching us closely. They watched with keen interest as we lowered our two longboats. As we began rowing the short distance, the crowd backed aside, allowing some others, rulers perhaps, to come to the front. These were very differently garbed. In addition to the usual clothing, these men and women wore enormous head pieces made from feathers of nearly every color in the rainbow! Spectacular indeed, these men and women certainly stood out. A few held some kind of weapon that looked like a rock affixed to a three foot piece of wood, an effective club perhaps.

By the time we landed, Natale already had over a hundred words figured out! I was writing them down carefully. I will make this narrative as smooth as possible; just realize that we needed some things said several times, with lots of gesturing and drawing in the sand. Upon landing, we formed up around me, since I'm our leader. Natale was on my left and Emil, my right. Henry was beside Natale and Renzo was behind us, between Natale and me, Protectors on all sides. The others fell in behind us, with our musicians in the rear along with the crew members. We all wore our Santi tunics, but not the heavy chain mail.

The tall man with the fanciest headdress spoke first. "Welcome to Wanakan. I am King Matial. This is my wife Amihan, my daughter Teyacapan, my son Coatl."

I introduced many of us, identifying us as Santi del Dio and that we came from far across the ocean from a place called the Sea Princes. We came to make new friends and make trading arrangements. This he really thought highly of and became very animated about making trades.

It seemed that he needed things, but as yet, we were not quite sure what his people needed.

However, as I did the introductions, many were pointing to Natale and Mireio, undoubtedly wondering about their arms. However, before we could make some explanations, two other men wearing ornate, heavy robes, again made of the same material as the other clothing, stepped up to the King's side. One robe displayed a golden sun, which we learned was indeed made from gold thread! The other bore a strange black stick like creature on its front. King Matial spoke, "This is our High Sun God Priest, Itzli. This is our Black God High Priest, Ajacopa."

Ajacopa looked at Natale, who was translating away. "You worship the Black God too I see. Yet, you allow two of your Holy Touched Maidens to walk among you?"

Natale had no idea what he was talking about, but took this as a compliment. "Yes, our Holy Touched Maidens are always with us. Where we go, so they go." She and I thought this was a reasonable reply.

High Priest Itzli frowned, "You worship the Black God?"

I detected some animosity between the two priests, so I had Natale explain that we worshiped Nature, but that came across as the Sun, when I pointed up to the sky. He seemed to relax, accepting what must be a duality with us as it was with them, two religions co-habiting. High Priest Itzli now smiled and said, "You must come and visit our Sun Temple. It is the finest in all the land!"

Not to be outdone, High Priest Ajacopa said, "And you must come and visit the Temple of the Black, especially your Holy Touched Maidens. They will be very much welcomed by our followers."

"Yes, yes, but first, they must come to my palace and dine. We have so much to show them and to discuss. Trade is more vital than priestly matters at this time, as you both well know. May I ask, is it usual among your people to have a woman leader? Here it is the man's role."

Being diplomatic, I replied via Natale, "In our land, more men are the leaders than women. Yet, within the Santi del Dio, we have found that often women make better leaders." Amihan and Teyacapan both smiled and nodded. I took an instant liking to these two women. The king and his wife I estimated to be in their thirties, while Teyacapan was probably sixteen. Coatl was likely eighteen.

"Come, let us show you our Wanakan," the King said, and we fell in beside him and his family. Once more, the large crowd parted so that we could walk into the city from the beach. We learned that there were perhaps five hundred thousand people in the city and immediate outskirts. Actually, Wanakan was the name of the state. There were six Acalan city-states all told. Further south lay another port city called Timuan. Inland city-states were Topikan, Malu, Chuchuan, and Alakan. All held about the same sized population. Wanakan and Timuan exported fish to the other city-states, which sent them grains and other edibles, primarily fruits and vegetables.

As we walked along the streets, Cedric pointed out the architectural details. All buildings were made from red stone, durable and solid. Most were single storied. Deeper into the city, the homes became two-storied, with various shops and markets on the lower floors. We passed by many shops offering everything from foods to clothing to jewelry to animals to exotic animals. Okay, all the animals were exotic as far as we were concerned. Their chickens had multi-colored feathers, browns and yellows predominated, and they laid brown eggs. On the exotic side, one shop had a black jaguar for sale. The King said that it had been raised from a cub and was quite tame, for a wild beast. However, the owner wanted an exorbitant price for it.

Deeper into the city, we spied the Royal Palace and the two Holy Temples. They were impossible to miss. The palace had a red stone wall around it, with three story buildings, rising above everything around here, except the temples. The Holy Temples were giant pyramids in shape, made from red stones. Hundreds of steps led up their enormous sides, rising at least a hundred feet above the ground. Each complex structure was hundreds of feet long; its base was square in nature. Ornate stone heads adorned rows of entrance steps, hundreds of them to be precise. We suspected the entrances to the temples were at the very top, where we saw what appeared to be some kind of entryway.

Inside the Royal Palace, the King took us to this Throne Room, where he customarily held court and well as royal banquets. A huge polished teak wood table with matching chairs occupied the right quarter, capable of seating all of us. His throne was made from polished red stone and heavily adorned with gold and jade, worth a fortune, we guessed. He bade us sit, while they removed their ornate headpieces. He clapped his hands and a number of serving maids entered bringing refreshments, none of which we had ever seen or tasted.

For some time we indulged ourselves in a culinary taste treat. I fell in love with the wild berry juice they called juju. This I insisted we needed to import somehow. As you might expect, the men began talking with the other men, while we women talked among ourselves. Poor Natale tried to handle both groups, and I kept adding more words. Linda hastily copied them so that the men could have a set. I knew that at night, I was going to have to make copies for everyone.

Later, I found out that the King, having examined Benet's short sword, greatly desired to trade much for many blades. He claimed that they would be vastly superior in hacking the dense jungle vegetation than their blades. Later on, he tested our rigging ropes and found them to be vastly superior to their ropes. He placed a large order for rope as well. Grains were also much needed here, we discovered. Why, we didn't learn for several days.

"Teyacapan, I must say that I love your jewelry. It is exquisite!" I complimented her. I was being sincere; she wore what might sell for a hundred thousand gold coins back home. Her heavy gold and jade earrings touched her shoulders, while her necklace was covered nearly all of her chest above her breasts. Her mother's was similar, though larger.

She smiled and blushed. "Here in Wanakan, all women adorn themselves as you have seen. The length and size indicates a woman's status. If her earrings touch her shoulders, everyone knows that she is a very important woman indeed. You all should have some like ours, shouldn't they mom?"

Amihan agreed, "Oh yes, yes indeed! Very much so, since you are the leader. While you are among our people, if yours are as long as ours, then everyone you meet will know that you are the leader and a very important person. You must let us so adorn you all! Please, we insist. Never have we had such important guests and never from across the wide, flat ocean. Please, allow us to so honor you."

"It doesn't hurt," Teyacapan added, sensing that we may be hesitant for that reason.

"Where we come from, this would be an enormously expensive gift that you are offering us," Natale tried to explain. "We would be very honored to accept your fabulous gift, only we feel that we need to give you something you consider as valuable in exchange." I nodded my agreement; she had stated it well.

They agreed to this and were quite excited to see what we might have that they desired. Our talk then turned to clothing, customs, and life. After touching their clothing and finding the cloth unbelievably soft, we found out that the wool came from an animal called a paca, which looked something like a fuzzy donkey. This was their domesticated beast of burden, we learned, capable of carrying a heavy load a long way. The paca ate grasses. I wondered if they would do well in our land.

They, on the other hand, were intrigued with our soft, supple leather clothing as well as our lighter cottons. Yes, we talked about things for hours. Finally, we all agreed that we needed to take them onto our caravel and show them our trading goods. Words were becoming difficult to describe everything. Thus, in the mid-afternoon, the King and his family and a half dozen bodyguards joined us on our ship. Henry gave the guided tour, and then the men split off to examine the cargo, while we women began discussing cloth and what we imagined they might be interested in having for a trade.

Leather and cotton cloth bolts were greatly desired along with hairbrushes and combs. Coming a close second was our tea! Both women loved it as much as I did their berry juice, juju! Our wide selection of grains also interested them, especially after they sampled our bread made from some of the grains. While we were sampling the tea and breads, Roberto and Mireio entertained us all with a number of songs. This was an instant hit! Both Matial and Amihan insisted they play for everyone this evening after the feast. They promised that their musicians would play as well, which made Mireio's eyes light up like a lantern!

King Matial lost no time in placing an order. As soon as he found out that we had many ships like this one and could send one fully loaded to here fairly soon, he began listing what he greatly desired. A hundred short swords for jungle clearing, all the rope we could carry, numerous metal pots and pans, and many grains, topped his list, which was then modified by his wife. She added cloth bolts, leather, and many combs and hairbrushes. She also wanted all the tea the ship could carry! It seemed that this culture lacked much in the way of worked metals, other than gold. Most everything was stored in clay pottery vessels. Both Henry and Matial were most excited to have the means of exchange be gold and jade. It seemed that these were rather commonplace around here, but would bring a fortune back in our countries.

Back at the Royal Palace, Henry and Matial finally created the King's first order, but he had to modify it to accommodate his wife and daughter's wishes. Henry said enthusiastically without thinking about what he was saying, primarily because he had just made the trading deal of the century! "Okay. King Matial, I will have the order sent home tonight. Sammy here will relay it and tomorrow, the shippers will begin to start collecting it together. Within a couple weeks, you can expect the caravel to sail, though it will probably take the ship a couple months to cross the ocean to get here. We've made detailed sailing plans, and with our new instruments, they ought to be able to find this city fairly easily."

The King looked at Sammy and then at Henry. His wife did as well. "How can this be? You are a couple months away. Does it not take a couple months for you to return and give them this order?"

Natale had to step in and explain, "King Matial, some of us can use our minds to communicate across vast distances. We call it telepathy. He is right, Sammy will relay your order tonight, and another ship like ours will be here with it in a couple months."

"Are you then gods?" asked Teyacapan, who had listened in to her explanation. Indeed, she had taken the words right out of her father's mouth.

"No, not gods," Natale blushed, unsure how to handle this one. She decided the best way was to reverse it. "Do not you have such people among your city here, people who can communicate with their minds across space?"

"No! Not even the High Priests can do that!" exclaimed Matial, highly impressed with this unexpected discovery. He had made new allies today, only he was now just discovering how valuable these might be.

"Well, only some of us Santi can do this," Natale explained. "In our normal cities, no one else can do this, only some of us Santi. We have to study and work long and hard to learn how to do this, and only a very few can master it. So we are not as unalike as you might think." She smoothed Henry's blunder over rather well, I thought.

Amihan suggested, "Matial, there is yet time before the feast for us to adorn their women as befitting their high status. You could also so adorn the men, while we women prepare ourselves for the feast. It is only fitting and proper that Bethany displays her proper status while she is here with us."

He smiled, "Ah yes, Queen Bethany, please accept the gratitude of people for your great kindness and trading. Allow us to present you with a small token of our eternal gratitude. When you walk among our people, your adornments will speak of your Highest Status. Oh yes, it does not hurt, I am told. Please, this is the least that we can offer you." You know women, how could we refuse an offer of very expensive jewelry? The men were not so keen on getting earrings, however, and declined, which did not offend our hosts, fortunately. We nine women left them still discussing future trading plans, and followed Amihan and her daughter into another room.

Mary Beth and Angel, our two Santi sergeants, while more than pleased to be given such expensive gifts, expressed the idea that the long earrings might get in the way of their performance as fighters. I had Natale explain this to Amihan, who smiled and suggested that shorter ones would be fine. Next, in came a dozen of her staff, who took our measurements. Natale had a hard time translating the words used in their measurements, however. In the end, Teyacapan brought in some samples.

"These small ones will be for Angel and Mary Beth," she showed two beautiful earrings that were about two inches long. "These will be for most of you," she showed another pair that was four inches long. "As befitting the leader and the Holy Touched Maidens, yours should be the longest." She didn't have those to show us yet. We asked about the golden disks in her ears.

"Oh no," she giggled. "I have worn these since I was a little girl. It takes many, many seasons for you get be able to have such big disks as I have. Even longer for mom. No, yours will only be little disks." She indicated something small with her fingers. "Now lie down on the reeds upon the stones and we will begin. It won't hurt, just a little sting at first. We know what we are doing; well, rather I should say that they know what they are doing. I've never done it myself." She chatted away while her mother's staff pricked our ear lobes with a thin needle from some kind of tree. I noticed the tips were dipped in some kind of liquid. I felt a prick or two, but that was all. The substance numbed my lobes.

Tonia said, "Bethany, this is numbing the skin. We should get some samples of this stuff. Think how useful this would be in healing!"

"Please hold still, Tonia," the woman working on her insisted.

"Sure, it a common jungle plant. Perhaps we can take a walk tomorrow, and I can show you," suggested Amihan. "Of course, we will have to have a lot of bodyguards when out in the jungle. I'll speak to Matial about it tonight."

A half hour later, we were done. "Whoa! These are heavy!" I exclaimed. My set touched my shoulders! I was wearing perhaps a ten thousand gold piece set of earrings, if not more! We all began looking at each other's earrings, admiring their great beauty and artistic designs. Mine looked like a pair of intertwining jaguars. Natale and Mireio had intertwined serpents of some kind as the motif. The polished jade formed the shapes of the creatures. "How do we get them off?" I asked.

Teyacapan laughed and giggled, "You are not supposed to take them off, silly. We wear them always. Now do you want to change into our style dresses before we put on your necklaces? I'm afraid that they will lie on top of your leathers, unless you wear our clothing."

"Oh please, let's do. Your cloth is so soft and luxurious compared to ours," I replied. Quickly, we all began to change, with several of us helping Natale and Mireio. Another half hour later, the soft, supple textures of our new outfits were being touched by many hands. It was an incredible feel that we had never experienced. After putting our old clothes into several large sacks, their staff returned with our necklaces.

"These you can take off when you want, see the strong clasp here," Teyacapan showed us. "Normally, we wear them all the time too, except when bathing or swimming. Again, mine was the largest of fans, resting atop my small breasts. Natale and Mireio had a pair that was only slightly smaller than mine. The others were significantly smaller, nonetheless regal and fancy, however.

"Thank you, thank you! This is a kingly present indeed!" I thanked our hosts and gave both women a good hug, which they really enjoyed. One by one, the rest of us did the same, only they had to hug Natale and Mireio.

Looking like a million, we women rejoined the men, just in time for the big feast. Yes, we received numerous compliments on our new native look. The feast was an understatement. The room with the teak table was filled with the King and his court. Everyone wanted to meet with us and thus the feast provided the mechanism. Food and drink was mounded high on the table. All of it was exotic to us, completely unfamiliar, except the juju juice which I now just loved.

"Ouch! That one is a hot one!" exclaimed Benet fanning his

mouth. Indeed, many of the dishes were incredibly spicy for our palates. Natale quickly discovered from Teyacapan which ones were hot and which were not. Most of us ate the cooler ones, which I still found more than a little hot. Some of the meat came from a wild pig creature, some from various birds. The real delicacies we didn't try. Snake, eel, snail, and various bugs did not appeal to us.

Yet, the various melons and vegetables were well liked by us women in particular, while the men preferred to sample all the different meats. "Hey, this snake thing is pretty tasty, Bethany," Renzo called out to me. With a big grin, I turned up my nose at him.

During the meal, many different conversations took place on all sides of me. I lost track of them all. However, I suddenly thought of something that we could do for these gracious hosts. "Say, King Matial, we Santi are known as great Healers in our land. We have great skill in the healing arts. Do you have any sick or injured people that we might bring our skills to help?"

"Healers? That is the province of our High Priests," he said sternly, as if he were reciting the "party line." After a moment, he said, "Well, I have some twenty men that were injured on their last hunting expedition into the jungle." He leaned close to me, clearly worried about being overheard. He whispered, "They are not doing so well when I visited them yesterday. If you would like, I can take you to them tomorrow. You must deal with the Priests; if they will allow you to heal, then you may do what you can for my men. In this arena, I have no authority, you see." I didn't see, but agreed with him anyway.

After the meal, I was stuffed! Quickly, the meal and golden plates were removed and some form of mead served. At this point, the Royal Musicians entered, dressed in all sorts of wild costumes, resembling exotic birds and animals. Their instruments looked like the panpipes that Bard Tal had discovered in the Southlands. Others were flutes, but of a kind that I had not seen. Drums were universal, I thought. Plus, they had some stringed instrument that rather resembled a cross between a guitar and a lute. I glanced at Mireio. The shine of her eyes, the glow on her face, told me that she was in heaven! Roberto too.

For an hour, they played and danced. Some songs were slow and hauntingly lyrical, others, fast and warlike. Teyacapan whispered to me that they were acting out a historical play of the great Sun God's visit to Acalan. However, I did not understand most of the words that they sang. Still, I thoroughly enjoyed the music and dance. I wished that Bard Tal were here with me! One day, I would send him here, that I knew! Yet, Mireio was with us. She had a photographic memory for music. If Roberto could somehow notate all this, perhaps Tal could reproduce it in some way.

When they finished, we clapped and cheered loudly, which was universally, I discovered, accepted by musicians everywhere as a sign that they had been greatly appreciated. Next, Roberto and Mireio gave a half hour performance to our hosts, who also seemed to enjoy the novelty of hearing strange music. They also received a hearty round of applause when they finished.

Mireio leaned over to whisper into the King's ear. He smiled and said, "Of course, what is a meal without good music!" I figured that she had asked him if we could have more music later on.

It was late by the time that we all got back on board our ship. For safety reasons, we turned down our host's offer of spending the night in his palace. He did, however, send a large number of guards to escort us back to our two longboats. They did not return to the palace until we were climbing aboard our caravel. We were all too tired to do much talking, and we went to bed right away, but not before Henry posted four guards.

In our cabin, I helped Natale out of her new dress. "Should we try to take these necklaces off?" she asked.

"No, I'm too tired to try, and I sure don't want to accidentally break them. Teyacapan said she only takes hers off when she goes swimming, so I guess we sleep in them."

"My ears hurt a little, does yours? These are so heavy!"

"Yes, mine do too. I guess it takes a little getting used to."

"These are worth a fortune, you know," Natale added. "My earrings are so incredibly beautiful! Yours are too. They are sure generous aren't they?"

"Yes, they sure are. Either that or gold and jade are incredibly commonplace around here." We climbed into bed. It was so warm, that I took off my nickers joining Natale, who always slept in the buff. Only tonight, we slept in our fabulous new jewelry.

I whispered, "Natale, I cannot find the words to thank you for what all you have done for us today! We would still be fumbling with a few words if it wasn't for your fabulous linguistic skills!" She rolled over to give me a hug, but I hugged her instead.

That night, I awoke in a sweat. I had a nightmare. I never have nightmares! I was back more than a quarter of a century ago when my Lightning Circle first encountered the black praying mantis creatures out there in the Red Desert. I was helpless, and the slavering, fifty-foot tall creature was coming for me, drooling over my prone body. It lowered its head and began nibbling on my arms! I awoke with a start. Natale was still sleeping, thankfully; I had not awakened her. My ears stung. The weight of the necklace on my chest seemed oppressive at this moment. Carefully I got up and wiped off, got a drink, and went back to bed. Maybe it was just having my ears pierced.

Next day, we all had breakfast together, discussing our plans for the day. We needed to check on his wounded men, and Teyacapan had promised to take us to find this liquid, which anesthetized our ears. For the Healers, this promised to be an extremely valuable find. Roberto and Mireio added another suggestion to the pot; they wanted to meet with the musicians and exchange songs.

"Also, I suppose that we should make an appearance at the two temples," I added, remembering that the High Priests had asked us to do so.

"I'd like to find out more about their political organization and how the people are governed," Linda Sarah added.

"I'd like to wander about and see what other things we could trade for," explained Henry. "Who knows what other useful things these people might have here that we could use?"

Benet spoke up, "I'd like to see all their domesticated animals and don't forget me when you all go off into the jungle. This is a Loremaster's paradise!"

"Wait a minute, gang," Emil broke in. "I don't think it's wise of us to split into so many different groups. We've only been here one day. Who knows what troubles are just under the surface? Besides, we only have one translator."

"Okay, while we Guardians are looking into the healing, why don't Natale and Linda see what they can discover about the politics and such? Further, Roberto and Mireio can't get into too much trouble sitting around making music. Take a couple of bodyguards with you two. Once we have the healing handled, perhaps we should, as a group, pay the High Priests a visit. Then, we can see about going hunting for the anesthetic herbs, and Henry can take his bunch in search of other finds. How does that sound?" Yes, it was a compromise, one that Emil and Renzo liked. We would only be split in to a few groups at any one time.

A half hour later, we climbed out of our longboats onto the beach. The people were very friendly, and we noticed that many stared at our earrings and necklaces, recognizing our high status. Teyacapan had not been wrong in her statement of that fact. We walked through the streets heading for the Royal Palace. The city folk were courteous, often bowing to Natale, Mireio, and me. As we walked into the huge palace complex, Amihan was there to greet us, along with her daughter, Teyacapan.

"Welcome Great Travelers. You look well today. My husband is in court, and I have been asked to greet you. He will be with us shortly."

I explained that Mireio and Roberto desired to meet with their musicians, and Teyacapan cheerfully led the two with their two bodyguards off to find them. While we waited for the King, I was able to get another cup of juju juice. Meanwhile, Natale was going over the many copies of her first linguistic dictionary with Henry and several others who expected to be out on their own later today. She made each of them practice saying all the words.

"Ah, good morning," said King Matial, coming into the room and taking off his heavy, feathered headdress.

"We should examine those wounded men of yours first thing," I explained. "Healing may take a while."

He snapped his fingers and his own group of bodyguards came running into the room. "Follow me then." As we walked through the city streets, drawing ever closer to the two tall, imposing temples, he explained, "These are my men that you are going to examine. However, healing is specifically part of the High Priests' responsibilities. I'm not sure how they will take to your apparent meddling in their realm. However, they are my men, and I want them healed, if it is possible to do so."

"I take it that your priests are not often too successful at healing your wounded?" It seemed a fair assumption, given his remarks thus far.

"True. They claim it is because insufficient sacrifices have been made, but they have always said that no matter what the problem actually might be. Between you and me, don't breathe a word of this to the priests, but I don't think much of their handiwork. Ah, here we are." We stood outside a single story, red stone building with a pair of protruding, carved, stone heads mounted on either side of the door. The King knocked on the door. A man in priestly robes opened the door.

"We are here to see my men. I've brought our guests who claim to be Great Healers in their own lands," Matial said to the priest.

From the grimace on the priest's face, I surmised this was a highly unusual move. His robes had a golden sun woven into its front side. After a slight hesitation, he opened the door and asked us to follow him. We entered a room in which fifteen men lay on various mats. Many were still in great pain. Another priest was standing over one man, waving a smoking incense pot over the man's body, while chanting some prayer. This man wore a black circle on his robes.

"What is the meaning of this intrusion?" he said coldly. King Matial explained what he was doing. "This is highly irregular of you, King. When Ajacopa hears of this, surely he will determine that all the good work that the Holy Sacrifices, which have been made, have been compromised. He will seek to begin anew with additional Holy Sacrifices."

Whether this would be a problem, King Matial didn't let on, saying instead, "Allow these Healers to examine my men, Priest."

Cathy was seven years older than Tonia was, so she was our senior Healer. I allowed the two of them rapidly to survey the fifteen men. While they were doing this, I let Natale and Linda chat outside the room with the King. I figured that they could begin pumping him for political matters, while we Guardians did our thing. The rest of our Santi group milled around outside the building.

A half hour later, Cathy took me aside. She had just finished looking at the last man and compared notes with Tonia. "Bethany, these men were in a battle. These are war wounds, not wounds made by attacking wild animals."

"Interesting. How bad off are they?"

"Well, there are a lot of blunt force trauma wounds, but some have nasty cuts as well. Given the primitive care that they have been getting, I would guess that over half of them won't make it. If these were our patients, then most would recover, given our proper care. What should we do?"

"I'll get Matial." I stepped outside and asked him, "King Matial, your men are suffering from battle wounds, not animal bites."

"Well, yes, while out hunting, they ran into some party from another city-state. They defended our hunting territory."

"I see. May I ask you a probing question?" He nodded, showing concern for his men I thought. "If you continue to allow your priests to heal them, out of the fifteen men inside, how many would you suspect would be returned to you cured? Please be honest with me on this point. The conditions of their treatment are absolutely deplorable."

"This has happened before. Last time, only two survived, though the High Black Priest stated that the Black God felt offended by the poor quality of our sacrifices. Can you save them?"

"We've handled combat wounds far worse than these. If these were under our care, perhaps one or two might die from their wounds, certainly no more than that."

King Matial reacted as if someone had just offered him something of immense value. "You can cure so many? What must I sacrifice to your god for this healing?"

"You must sacrifice nothing, King. We just need to be allowed to work our healing on your men, without intervention from those priests, who really don't know as much about healing as we do. Is this possible to do without getting yourself into trouble with the High Priests?" Not knowing their political situation, I wanted him to have a way to refuse our services.

A sparkle illuminated his eyes. "Ah, then leave that to me. I will place my men under your care. Priests, yes, you two. Go tell your High Priests that King Matial has hereby placed my men under the care of our Honored Guests from Across the Ocean. We will see how well they do. Mark my words, if they heal my men better than you have done, we will have words!" Both priests looked at the King and then each other. Hastily they left to notify their respective High Priest. "Now they are all in your hands," he said formally to me. I relayed this to Cathy and Tonia.

"Send someone back to the caravel to bring our healing bags. We need boiling water. For heaven's sake, can we get some real light in here so we can see what we are doing? You all can be our assistants. Only a couple is in a really bad state," Cathy ordered.

We worked on these fifteen men for three hours, cleaning the wounds, sterilizing them, getting the infections out of their cuts. Two men had taken some kind of blunt blow to their heads. These we could do little for and Cathy did not hold out much hope for them. When King Matial returned at our request, he saw a well-illuminated room, which now smelled healthy, not slightly rotten. Further, he could see that his men at least looked better. He was most gratified and very pleased with our results thus far, withholding a final opinion if his men actually did recover.

Since it was well past lunchtime, we again dined with the King. After lunch, I suggested we should pay the High Priests a visit. The King explained that he was not allowed in their temples, but he would send an armed escort with us to see us safely to the temples. He suggested that we visit the Temple of the Sun first. He was most hesitant about whether the Black Temple High Priest would show us around their holy mound.

We walked the mile to the Temple of the Sun, while six armed escorts led the way in a ceremonial manner. We guessed they felt honored to lead us to the temple. When we arrived, the High Priest Itzli stood high atop his temple, welcoming us warmly. "Come on up," He called out to us. We looked at the relatively steep climb up some five stories. No guardrails. I bet coming down would be even trickier.

Huffing and puffing, our large group finally reached the top. "Welcome to the Temple of the Sun, the oldest temple of the Acalan. The view," he gestured, moving his arms around the city. We turned slowly in all directions; indeed the view was spectacular. Before us, the whole city was laid out like some child's toy world. As we were standing there, I noticed two things. Each of the Sun priests had a circular burn mark on their foreheads, and a golden disk with a two-inch hole in its center hung down over their foreheads, outlining the burn mark. I also noticed the glass lens sitting here high atop the mound. It cast light to somewhere far below.

"Allow me to take you on a tour of the common areas. Mind you, some of the holiest rooms will be off limits. I heard that you have been healing King Matial's men. Are you also great healers among your people?"

We needed no further invitation; we chatted away as we began descending into the pyramid. It was hollow, but how many rooms and side tunnels were concealed beneath the huge stone mound none could tell. I noticed many paintings along the hallways. He explained these depicted the history of the city. "The Acalan have been here for nine hundred sixty-four years now. This series here depict each of the many kings of Wanakan. Sun Temples in the other city-states depict their rulers as well. The Sun has every played a prominent role in our society. For without it, the jungle would die; the animals would then die, and we would die. All life is an interrelated whole. We must study the Sun to know its moods. Let me show you. Here is our chart," he pointed to another strange painting covering one wall. Did you know that Tarra's Holy Sun goes through periods when it is cooler? There is an eleven-year cycle and an eighty-four-year cycle that we have carefully measured. Certain crops grow better when the Holy Sun is warmer, while others do better when the Holy Sun is cooler. We must know what these times are, for the King depends upon us for his crops."

The Wid in me kicked in hard. Here was information that we did not know! I asked, "How can you tell if the Holy Sun is hotter than normal or cooler than it used to be? This is incredible knowledge that you have here. Say, what is this really deep line mean?" I spotted a line that extended nearly to the floor.

"Ah, that was three hundred years ago when Xochitl, Lord of the Underground, broke his chains and tried to escape above ground. He blew a huge, dark cloud of earth high into the sky, nearly obliterating our Sun God. Rivers of hot liquids poured out of the fuming earth, forming a tall mountain in honor of Xochitl! Crops died; even the jungle, our life's blood, withered and died. That was the gravest year in Acalan history. Half of our people perished from lack of food and water. So grave was the battle between Xochitl and the Sun God that we even resorted to human sacrifices to convince the Sun God to triumph! That is the only period in our history when we sacrificed maidens. Normally, we accept well-prepared meals, fit for our Sun God. That is the usual sacrifices we ask of our faithful. Only after that were our prayers and sacrifices accepted, the next year, heavy rains returned and the Sun God re-emerged, victorious over Xochitl, driving him back far underground. Some day if you like, you can journey to that mountain and see for yourselves how powerful Xochitl actually is."

"Amazing!" I relied. Half of this had to be superstition, the other half had elements of truth in them. "What are these little marks across the top?"

"They denote the passing of a year."

"And these black lines?"

"Ah, our enemy. See here," he pointed to the first of the black lines, which appeared shortly after the recovery from Xochitl disaster. Some three hundred years ago, the Black God first appeared in Acalan. Soon, they wrestled control over our people from us. Always, we have been at war with the Black God. Then, our continued prayers, year after year, our continued vigilance finally paid off. See here, no black marks! Twenty-six years ago, the Black God vanished completely from all their temples here in the Acalan!"

"Oh, you should have seen how their priests prayed for their evil god to return! The Sun God once more triumphed!"

"Wait a second, there's another black mark right here; this is supposed to be this year?"

"Ah, alas, it's true. Four months ago, the Black God has returned to Acalan. Dismayed, we sent out runners to the other city-states. However, the Black God has only returned to Wanakan! Thus far, the Sun God has prevented the Black God from returning to the five other city-states, thankfully."

"The Black God is evil! I know that High Priest Ajacopa has invited you to visit his temple, but I urge you do not go there! You may never return from within its mound." What happened twenty-six years ago, I wondered, that could have eliminated their Black God. How could he have returned now? It didn't make a lot of sense at the time.

"Come, let me show you our Holy Room. He led us into another room, which was directly underneath the lense on top of the pyramid. We saw a red stone altar in the middle of the room. It had a shape carved into it, fitting the human body. "Ah, now I see, Itzli. The lens up there brings the Holy Sunlight down here. Your new adepts probably lie there on the altar, and the Sun God burns his mark onto your foreheads!"

"Ah, you are very wise indeed! Yes, that is so. Only those worthy of the Sun God can manage the ceremony. Only those who can become one with the Sun God survive the ceremony. These marks mean the man has been found worthy by the Son God himself!"

Surprisingly, Linda spoke up, "High Priest Itzli, I was wondering if sometime some of us could come and study your records here on your walls, learn the history of your land? In return, we could trade something that we have that you might desire." Ah, the Judger is ever vigilant in acquiring information.

"I am so honored that you find our Sun God so interesting that you wish to learn more. Yes, you may, but first, I must ask you about the King's men. I know that he sent the priests away and turned his men over to your healers. I will be honest with you. We know that most of those men suffered fatal wounds and will die in time. Do you not agree?"

Cathy answered that one, "No, on the contrary, most will live and be perfectly fine in a few weeks. Only the two with the terrible head wounds are beyond our skill to heal."

"You jest with me?"

"No, I speak the truth. See for yourself in a few weeks," she replied, uncertain how else to convince him.

"Ah, then I shall wait and see. If, Linda, they are indeed healed, can you teach us how to work such miracles? If so, we will have a most fair bargain."

"Tonia and I studied long and hard for ten years to obtain the knowledge and skills we possess as Healers," Cathy replied, since this was her specialty. "However, there is much that we can teach you in a shorter time than that. The world always needs better healers. We would be honored to teach your priests."

Itzli smiled; he'd just make a fabulous bargain. If he could learn even a small amount of healing, then his priests would become even more powerful, more so than those in the other city states! He shook hands with Linda, sealing the bargain.

With that done, it was time for us to take our leave. He had some official duties to perform, and we wanted to go and try to find these plants that Teyacapan had told us about. None of us desired to visit the Temple of the Black God today.

When we returned to the palace, we found that Amihan and Teyacapan were waiting for us. They had six other women with them and a dozen guards. Teyacapan was excited, "We've got everything ready, sacks and tools. We can go just as soon as you are ready." Plainly obvious was her sincere desire to help us.

I knew that Henry would not want to go traipsing through the jungle in search of plants. "Okay, Henry, you take half of us with you, including Natale to translate, and the other half with me into the jungle. See what all you can find, Captain." He grinned from ear to ear; this was his big chance to explore. He needed no coaxing.

We Guardian women, accompanied by Benet, Emil, and Renzo, along with a half dozen Santi fighters, followed Teyacapan and her mother. Their helpers and dozen bodyguards fell in behind us as we walked through the street. "See how everyone notices your earrings, Bethany? They know you are a very important person now!" I didn't have the heart to tell her that we were in the company of the King's wife and daughter, which probably carried a whole lot more weight than our long earrings did.

She chatted about many things as we walked through the rest of the large city. "Often we go out hunting for the aruiba plant. It grows all over the jungle, you see. Now you do have to be careful with it. If you make it too strong, it can make a person unconscious. Mom told me once that it was even used as a poison! But that was a long time ago. After we get some, I'll show you how to mix it properly, right mom?"

"Yes, dear, you can show them," she winked knowingly at me. I believe that she was actually testing her daughter's knowledge, probably part of her training. Once we reached the edge of the city, six guards moved out in front. Each carried a crudely made blade. A well-marked trail led out of the city and into the depths of the jungle.

Teyacapan called out to these men, "We are searching for the aruiba plant. Take us where some might be found, please." She added,

"This trail here leads to Topikan city, but that is at least a hundred miles, I'm told. I've never been there, personally, you realize, but dad sends communication runners there sometimes." She chatted on and on.

After a few miles, the six men stopped and turned to the right, into the dense jungle. Now I saw what the crude blades were for — hacking a pathway through the dense foliage. We followed along now only two abreast. Soon, it was single file. Teyacapan suggested, "Do keep a sharp eye out for jaguars and snakes! They live out here, though I don't suppose that we will see any today, not this close to the city. Some have been seen around here, from time to time. We are supposed to make noise so that it will frighten them away. That's what dad says. I've never seen a jaguar in the wild though, only that one that was raised from a cub in the city."

Angel and Mary Beth, together said, "We should've brought our longbows!" I agreed with them on this point, hoping we wouldn't see a jaguar, but Benet, of course, really did want to see one in the wild. He was the Loremaster. We hiked for some distance. By now, sweat was pouring off all of us, particularly those six doing all the work up front. After a time, six others took their place, giving them a breather. Now I could see where our short swords would be quite useful.

Just then, a giant snake dropped from the dense tree canopy onto one of the leading hackers. Instantly confusion broke out; the snake was a constrictor. Quickly, it began coiling around the poor man. While his companions wrestled with the snake, trying to uncoil it from their friend, Benet rushed to their aid. "Let me at it please. Bethany, tell them to let me handle the snake!" I tried to calm the growing panic. When he got to the snake, the others backed off slightly. He could see the terror in the man, who had his hands around the snake's head.

Benet began talking gently to the snake, petting its head, and stroking its long body. Slowly the snake began to release its hold on the man. As soon as he could, the man wiggled free from its grasp and ran back to where we all stood watching Benet, who continued petting it for a time. At last, the snake slithered on off into the dense brush. Benet held out his hand cautioning us from approaching him. He poked around the brush a bit. "Ah, here is its companion. I think it might be poisonous, given its fangs. Let me shoo it away. There, it's gone. It's safe now." He walked back to us.

"How did you do that? You saved his life!" exclaimed Teyacapan.

"I just convinced him that all was well in his world. Really, the man was too big for its dinner. It was just frightened that's all. Snakes often travel in pairs; there was another one, a small viper of some kind, probably looking for a free bit of dinner, compliments of big boy there. It sure was a fine specimen. I've never seen one that big."

"Oh, well, sometimes they can weigh more than a man," Amihan explained. "For very special celebrations, we sometimes catch a really large one. Their meat is considered a delicacy, though I personally don't care much for it. Matial does, however. Come on, we should be getting close. I hear water ahead and that is a good place to begin looking."

The guards took point once more and hacked ahead to a bubbling stream. "Careful of snakes," cautioned Teyacapan once more. She began searching the area, along with the six women companions that came with her and her mother. One called out to her, Teyacapan verified it and called for us to come over. "This is the plant that we are looking for. We must very carefully dig it up, roots and all, you see. Be very careful not to break the stem, because the juice is in there, and if you get it on you, you will become quite numb in that area. See — as she is doing. We need to get these sacks filled. Start hunting. When you find one, yell and we will make sure it is the right one." We scattered about, searching for a matching plant. The dozen guards merely washed off their sweat in the brook and then laid down, waiting on us.

After a half hour of searching, we had half of the sacks filled. We were now rather scattered about the area. I was staying near Teyacapan and Renzo was near me. Suddenly, a snorting broke the stillness, followed by a crashing noise. A large wild boar with the largest tusks I had ever seen came charging at us. Teyacapan froze; there was little time to react. No time for Renzo to do anything with his sword, though little would that do to this several hundred-pound boar.

I acted. I reached out and simply picked the boar up into the air, holding it still. At once, the others came running to our rescue. "Wow, Bethany has a wild boar!" exclaimed Benet.

"Yes, I got it. Now what do I do with it?" It was squealing like mad, squirming around, and legs flailing in the air. "If I put it down, will it charge us again?"

"Dunno, probably you are giving it a good scare," he replied. Slowly I moved the pig through the air, smashing through the dense foliage with it. When I was several hundred feet away, I carefully set it back on the ground, hoping it would not return to us. It was so spooked that it fled in the opposite direction from us.

"Okay, boar has left," I announced.

"How did you?" asked Teyacapan, who could not figure out what to actually ask. "Lifted it in the air? You must be a goddess!"

"Not a goddess. I just lifted it and got it out of our way. Come on, let's get the rest of these bags filled," I tried to change the topic.

While we resumed our hunt, I could hear the others discussing what they had just seen. I hoped that my defensive move had not scared them. Seeing such powers at work could turn them against us. I hoped this would not be the case. An hour later, the bags were stuffed, and we headed back the way we had come. The return trip took far less time because we now had a path.

"Don't worry, the path will disappear in a couple of days," Teyacapan explained. "The jungle grows fast. Now tonight after supper, I will show you how to prepare the juice."

"Once it is made, how long does it keep? I mean, if we don't need it for say a month, will it still be okay to use?" I asked.

"Sure, it keeps for a very long time," Amihan answered. "We've kept some for well over a year with no loss of effectiveness. However, you need to keep it from slowly evaporating, though."

A short while later, we arrived back in the city. After dumping off the sacks, Teyacapan gathered up a whole bunch of clean clothes and took us to the beach where we all took a much-needed bath. This was rather like our public baths, everyone washed off in the warm seawaters. Dozens of others were doing likewise while we were there. I did catch many of the locals looking at our particularly white bodies, compared to their rather brownish hue. Teyacapan told us, "Don't worry, you can keep these clothes too. I will have the others washed tomorrow. Then you will have two sets!" She seemed glad that we would have two sets, and I certainly did love the soft feel of these dresses!

Once more, we had a splendid dinner with our hosts, who continually thanked Benet and me for having saved his daughter and his guard from eminent danger. I had to explain that I could lift and move objects. Still, I doubted that he honestly believed such was possible.

Roberto and Mireio were ecstatic, they had heard over fifty songs and shared many that they knew. He had written down their names and the first couple of notes, hoping that would be enough for his wife to recall the rest of the tune so he could write it down on our long voyage home.

Natale was equally pleased, having now added another two hundred words to her ever-growing dictionary. Henry had found numerous other items that would be very usable back home. In fact, he now had a pair of paca's to take back with us! They were a breeding pair, so he hoped that we would be able to begin a small herd of these amazing creatures, perhaps on Jenna's estate. "If so, think of the wool that can be harvested, they are like sheep back home!" his excitement shone through.

Renzo asked, "Hey Henry, how about getting a couple for us to take back to Zargarb? Maybe they will thrive there too? Lady Ariana could really use the assistance." Henry agreed to get another pair tomorrow.

"I think mom will really like the feel of these clothes," Rosina said to Renzo. The both agreed on that point.

Tonight, while the others enjoyed the musicians, many of us followed Amihan and Teyacapan into another room. Here their six helpers were already getting started on the plant preparation. "You see how they are carefully smashing the plants, being extra careful not to get any of the juice on their hands? We let them drain into these pots, one plant per pot. Once all the liquid is out, you can also grind up the stems and get a little more juice in the pot. Then we add water, filling it to the top and seal the lids on tight. You let everything settle for maybe a week. All the junk sinks to the bottom, and it's ready to use. We just dipped our thorns into the pot and then pricked your ears in several places when we did your ears the other night. A small amount goes a long way. In a couple hours you should have a couple dozen pots to take back with you." She was extremely proud of her donation to our healers. I could tell that this was her way of thanking me for rescuing her today, if nothing else.

Well, her timing was a little off. It took us nearly two hours to finish making the anesthesia. However, Matial brought us a small pushcart with which to transport the two dozen jars safely back to our ship that night. While the Healers spent an hour safely packing these precious jars into watertight and break proof packages, Natale had me sit down and copy out all of her new words onto everyone else's copies of her new dictionary. That took me the rest of the night! Meanwhile, the men dealt with the problem of how to safely transport the pair of pacas, making space for the second pair Henry would get for the twins tomorrow.

Finally, more than tired, we all turned in for the night. In our cabin, Natale chatted with me, while I brushed out her hair. She wanted to talk, so I let her. "How are your ears doing? The sting is gone from mine now. They are still very heavy though. That takes some getting used to, I'm told. When we were out around the city today, I noticed that I did get an awful lot of stares. It wasn't my arms that they were looking at. I watched their eyes. Teyacapan is right; they see these and know that we are very important people. The other women that I saw also have similar earrings, but theirs are only a few inches long, mostly, and nowhere near as fancy. It is interesting how these people use jewelry to help identify which person is more important than another is. We do it in other ways, back home. You know, you see our black tunics with the red cross, and everyone knows there goes a Santi. You see Elona's royal guard's tunics and know who they are. We identify by wearing different clothing, but these people here all have the same type of clothing, so I can see how earrings can help. Yet, it sure is a strange way to do it."

"Yes, it certainly is, but then I wonder why they never thought of having different clothing, perhaps because it is so warm here. Oh, I see, this is their winter. Golly, I wonder what their summertime temperatures are like? Maybe they have something with all this." I yawned, "There, your hair is done, mine too. I'm falling asleep on me feet. Come on, we have another big day tomorrow." I helped her into bed, blew out our

Vic Broquard

lantern, and crawled in beside her. Again, it was so overly warm here in the enclosed cabin that we slept with no clothes on, only a thin sheet covering us. Back home, it was nearly winter, and we would have lots of warm clothing on while sleeping. What a contrast. Here, in the summer, the heat must be unbearable. How could anyone sleep then, I wondered.

Chapter 4 The Temple of the Black God

Over breakfast the next morning, we decided to spend the day wandering the city, examining the numerous markets that Henry and Natale had seen yesterday. We landed our two longboats and walked up the beach, unprepared for what happened next. Suddenly, we saw many people running our way. Out in front of them was Teyacapan! Even from this distance, she looked terrified!

We began running towards her as fast as we could go. Behind her, we could now see a number of priests wearing the robes with the black circle on them. No doubt, they were from the Temple of the Black God. We noticed that her hands were tied in front of her, which was why she was running so awkwardly. Terror was in her eyes, radiating from her as we got to her. The six priests were only ten feet from catching her when I put my arm around her and faced these men, a steely glare in my eyes and on my face.

One priest spoke, "Give her to us. She is to be sacrificed today to the Black God. She will become a Holy Touched Maiden by tonight."

"Don't let them take me!" Teyacapan cried, "I don't want to die for their god. I want to live. Please don't let them take me," she wailed. Benet quickly cut the ropes binding her hands and began rubbing the life back into them.

"You heard her; she doesn't want to be sacrificed!" I glared at the priest.

"She has no say. It is ordained by the Black God. She is the Chosen One. The King has given his consent. She is to become a Holy Touched Maiden. Now give her to us."

"I will not! Go sacrifice yourself to your Black God!" I spat back at him.

"You do not understand. You are foreigners. When the High Priest of the Black God decrees that a maiden be sacrificed, none is allowed to counter his order, not even the King has that right. She is the Chosen One, you must hand her over to us now."

"I said I will not. She is now under Santi protection. Go sacrifice yourselves."

Clearly dumbfounded, he tried to explain further, "You don't understand. We would gladly sacrifice our lives for the Black God, but the Black God only desires the purest of maidens. We would never be accepted. She has been deemed the best maiden in all of Wanakan. This is the highest honor the Temple of the Black God can bestow upon a maiden, to be the Chosen One, to become a Holy Touched Maiden."

"Please, don't let them take me. I will be killed, I know it. No one ever sees a Holy Touched Maiden ever again! I don't want to die," Teyacapan wailed, afraid that I might consent. She need not have worried; there was no way I was going to let her be taken.

"You heard her; she does not want to be taken. Go back to your temple and leave her alone. She is under our protection now. She will never be one of your Holy Touched Maidens!" I was resolute. Evidently, the priests now thought so too. I expected some curse, some overt threat, some veiled warning, but they said nothing, just turned around and left.

"There now, you are safe, Teyacapan. Tell us what happened?" I asked.

She hugged me tightly for a time. "Early this morning the priests came to the palace, requesting to speak to dad. They told him I was now their Chosen One. He cried. I know he didn't want this to happen to me, but by law, he can't do anything about it. No one can; the law of the High Priest is sacrosanct. They tied my hands and began leading me to their temple. I tricked them and pretended to walk along peacefully. When they relaxed their grip on me, I bolted and ran here for my life. Of course, if you were not on shore, I don't know what I was going to do, maybe try to swim for your boat. Now I have really gotten you all into very big trouble. Not even dad can do anything about it!" She began crying again.

Everyone was looking at me for guidance. "Okay, take her back onboard the ship and guard her as you would me. I think it is time that we go pay this Temple of the Black God a visit. Are you all armed?" Many wanted to retrieve more and better weapons. "Teyacapan, you go stay on our ship until we get this whole thing settled. There is no way we are going to give you to these evil priests. You should be safe on the ship until we get back."

It took a few minutes for the longboat to reach our ship and return with our weapons. I left the young girl under the protection of Cathy and a half dozen Santi guards, along with the crew. Henry insisted on going wherever Natale went. I couldn't blame him; he was totally in love with her. Everyone else fell in line, and we headed to the Royal Palace.

When we got there, things were strangely silent. Gone were all the many people that usually were about at this time of day. I suspected the King had cancelled all his meetings. This was the case; we found the two of them sitting alone in their throne room, crying and holding each other. His son was nowhere to be seen.

"I had no choice," he cried when we entered. "My only daughter is now lost forever!"

"No, she escaped and is now safely on our boat under our guard and protection. I told their priests that I would not allow her to be sacrificed to their god," I stated flatly.

"She's alive?" Amihan cried out and hugged her husband tightly.

"Alive?" he repeated stunned by the unexpected news. "Oh what have we done now?" he sighed. "The Black God will demand vengeance upon all of us now!"

"We'll see about that," I stated coldly. "We are going to pay these priests a visit right now."

"Oh no, they will kill you all! I know it! The Black God is all powerful! If you go into their temple you will never come out again!"

"King Matial, we are all Santi del Dio, the Knights of God; we cannot stand by when evil threatens. It is our sworn duty to put an end to this evil sacrificing of human lives. I am going to leave Roberto, Mireio, and a couple Santi guards here with you. This way, I can contact them if need be. By the way, where is Coatl? We haven't seen him."

"He swore that he would not let them take his sister. I fear he is doing something foolish, like attacking the priests. I fear that he is already lost to us as well. This is a black day for our family."

"Come on, then; there might not be time. We'll stay in touch with you, Roberto, Mireio; keep the King and Queen safe." Hastily, we all left the palace and began jogging toward the Temple of the Black God. I had intended to leave Natale behind too, but she would have none of that; we might just need her services translating with these priests. I could not discount that likelihood, so she jogged along with the rest of us. By now much of the city already knew what had happened; most felt horribly sorry for the royal family. Some of them had lost their daughters in the last few months. The folks on the streets just stopped and stared at us as we jogged to the temple.

Linda yelled, "We should attempt to reason with them, find out exactly what they do. Slay the women? That sort of thing. We need basic facts before we can take appropriate action."

"I know. Let's see what they have to say," I yelled back.

Shortly, we arrived at the base of the tall Temple of the Black God. We stopped to catch our breath. Coatl lay in a heap on the ground. He was beaten but otherwise okay; he'd tried to rescue his sister. Several priests stood atop the pyramid. I didn't see any weapons in their hands, which we took as a good sign. Shortly, the High Priest himself appeared, Ajacopa. He waved to us and called out, "Hello! Please come to our temple for a visit."

"I don't trust him," Emil said.

"Neither do I," Renzo added. "We could be walking straight into a trap!"

"But we must confront him and find out what is going on," Linda replied.

"Okay, everyone, be on guard. Let's go have a chat with him." I began climbing the five stories of steps, Renzo and Emil fell into line on either side of me. Other Santi fighters fanned our protecting our flank and rear, where Henry and Natale were located. Damn these steps! We were all out of breath by the time we reached the High Priest.

"So glad you could come. I would like to personally show you around our magnificent Temple of the Black God."

"What's all this about making Teyacapan a Chosen One and making her become a Holy Touched Maiden when she does not want to be one?" I asked directly. I didn't want him to entertain any other ideas about why we were here in force.

His voice was cold and covert. I ought to have known something was amiss. "Ah, that is but a small misunderstanding. To be selected as a Chosen One, to become a Holy Touched Maiden by the Black God personally, is the very highest honor that any maiden of Acalan could possibly have! Come, follow me. Inside our long halls, which are similar to those of the Sun God Temple, we have our long and illustrious history documented. Soon you shall see for yourselves just how high an honor it is to become a Holy Touched Maiden, just as your maiden there in your rear instinctively knows." He must have been referring to Natale, though I had no idea what he meant.

He led us down a long set of stairs, similar to those in the Sun Temple. After a time, we entered a long hall. Many paintings were drawn upon the walls. Just as we all were in the long hallway, six priests suddenly stepped out of some side passages and lobbed six gourds our way. The gourds shattered when they hit the stone floor and released some form of gas. Quickly, we were choking. After inhaling one breath, my body began to feel numb. We whirled to face the attackers, but they had fled from the tunnel area. Coughing, one by one, our bodies went completely numb and slumped to the ground. Then, everything went black as my body went unconscious. We had been ambushed!

How long I was unconscious, I cannot say. I was swirling in some kind of greyish black mass, the effects of the gas drug upon my body and mind. Suddenly, I heard Natale screaming at me. No, my body was still unconscious. *Bethany! Help me! I can't hold it off much longer. They are coming after yours too! Help! Wake up, please Bethany!*

I pulled out of the black mass by moving upwards. Now I could see where we were at; lanterns on the walls illuminated this large room. There was my body lying chained to some stone altar kind of thing. My arms were chained out beyond the edge, dangling in empty space. My other companions were similarly bound and unconscious. Natale was chained below my feet, and there leaning over her legs was a small, black praying mantis!

It was just like the giant mantises that Alabaster and I had eliminated a quarter century ago! It was salivating over her legs, its mandibles clicking together as if it was ready to dine on her legs. Yet, she was holding its body still, preventing it from its meal. Worse still, four more were slowly making their way towards all our unconscious bodies! These were just like the giant, fifty-foot tall mantises that we had killed — the ones who were controlling the lives of people in the Southlands, only smaller. Oh god! I realized what these were, baby mantises!

I'm here. Hang on, Natale. I picked the creature up and flung it back down into the dark hole from which the other four were slowly crawling towards us. Perhaps down there was their nest?

It's trying to eat my legs! shrieked Natale into my mind. She was tremendously terrified.

Good thing you got my attention, Natale, I was really zonked with that drug. See if you can get the other's attention. I'll hold these mantises off.

I can't! I've already tried!

Okay, you hold them off and I will.

A cold, inhuman voice entered my awareness. Oh, no you won't. We are in total control of you now. First, we will dine on the exquisite delicacy of your arms. Don't worry; you won't feel a thing; our saliva paralyzes your body's nerves. We are very humane with our dining. We will only eat all of your arms today. We are not greedy; we will eat your legs another day.

A second cold voice interrupted the first. *Iee! Look, this is one of those who killed our mother!* I felt my mental images of a quarter century ago being replayed, my attacks against the mantis in the Red Desert, my subterfuge in getting the Grey Creatures to attack the mantises, destroying them all utterly. It was weird having my own memories being controlled and replayed by another.

The first creature shrieked. *Mother killer! Damn you to eternal suffering! We will have our revenge for our mother! Eat half her arms and half her legs! Keep her alive for a long time! She must be made to pay for our mother's death and all the others! Get her now!*

Natale shrieked. *I cannot hold off five of them!*

I reached down, found Renzo, and pulled him up and out of the grey-black drug mass, leaving him to begin to see what was happening. I grabbed Emil and did the same with him. Natale screamed again. *He's trying to eat your arm!*

One had gotten past Natale. Dribbling saliva onto my arm, its mandibles were just about to take a bite when I grabbed it and threw it far back down the dark hole from which it had crawled. I began yanking others out of their drug obscuring masses, bringing the room into their consciousness. I knew that this would be terribly disorienting to them, but I had to have help; there were too many of these mantises.

Natale hollered again, and I threw yet another mantis off my body. Soon, I had the entire crew out of their bodies, struggling to grasp what had happened to us and what was going on in the present. Most were terribly groggy, as I had been. *Mantises, like the giant ones Alabaster and I destroyed. Try fire, I hurt one once that way.* I now had everyone here in one giant Mind Link, which only created major confusion as everyone's thoughts came flooding into everyone else's minds. Fear and terror only added to the incredible mixture. *Fire, shoot fire!*

Renzo reacted first; he pitched a flaming sheet at two who were farthest from us, while I tossed another back down into their hole. Natale kept another from advancing. Now another attempted to bite my arms. I pitched it as well. The two hit with the flames screeched an awful sound, but quickly came up with a counter spell of some kind. Now Rosina added her flames to her brother's, and then Emil launched a third set. I threw the last one off Natale and me.

You cannot stop us with petty flames. We are on to that trick! For that, we will also make you three pay dearly. We will eat half of your arms and half of your legs too. You can then life long as a half human! This was followed by some sound, which we interpreted as laughter or a sneer.

Blast them! The first inhuman voice ordered. Wham. Some kind of energy beam arced out and smashed into the space that Emil was occupying, sending him into a confused mass of grey energy. Emil was now out of the battle for a time, lost, confused, and dazed. Wham, another knocked out Renzo. Wham, another knocked out Rosina. Wham, another came at me, but my training with Alabaster kicked in, and I dodged it and pulled Natale out of the way of a fifth blast.

Linda said, *Oh no you don't!* They began launching their next volley at us. As one creature began to fire off its energy blast, she dove head first into its body, knocking it over. Its blast smashed into the ceiling, knocking off bits of rock, which rained down upon the mantises. She began moving about as fast as she could.

That's it. Everyone else, move around like crazy! While this was not exactly what Alabaster had taught me about avoiding energy blasts, such as a lightning bolt, Linda's solution gave us a chance. What a sight, spiritual beings flying about the room like mad, five mantises firing off their energy weapons attempting to knock each being into an unconscious state, bits of rock falling down all around us, and even onto our unconscious bodies below.

It did give me time to observe them. Their energy weapons did not come from the spiritual beings that occupied the mantis bodies! Rather, it appeared to come from some organ near their multifaceted eyes! After each blast, each mantis needed some time to recharge its energy producing glands.

Natale was a good pupil of mine. While the others frantically moved about at random, she noticed that I did not. She watched what I did and emulated it. I prompted her, *Wait until it starts coming at you and then just push it aside.* She caught on quickly, deflecting another beam sent her way.

However, things were not going our way. One by one, my companions eventually were hit with an energy beam, knocking them unconscious. Finally, it was down to Linda, Natale, and me. I had shown Linda how to avoid the beams as well. Because in her last lifetime as Sarah she had been similarly attacked when we were on our way home, she was better equipped to deal with them.

The first inhuman voice spoke, *Now then, Bethany, Mother Murderer, you see we are invincible. All your petty companion beings have been eliminated. Only you three remain, so while you dance about, we will begin dining on our delicacy, your arms. We have been fed only fingers for far too long a time. Now our bodies demand better nourishment. You should be honored that we have chosen you. You all will become Holy Touched Maidens, except for the male bodies. Those we will just kill. They taste bad.*

Why are you doing this to us humans? Where do you come from? Why are you here? Can't you at least answer your Holy Touched Maiden's questions? I tried to stall and get information at the same time.

The second inhuman voice spoke, *We should answer the Holy Touched Maiden's questions.*

The first said, *Long have we raised your bodies to feed ours. You see, your Holy Touched Maiden bodies provide certain nutritional needs that we cannot get otherwise. For hundreds of years, we have been raising your bodies. It is very unfortunate that the grey giants intervened. We have you to thank for eliminating our powerful foes. Hence, we are giving you the highest honor that we can bestow on humans, making you our Holy Touched Maidens. Your bodies will live a long life, a healthy life with none of the diseases your species tend to get, albeit without your silly appendages to get in the way.*

But we need our silly appendages! Natale protested.

Holy Touched Maiden, you do not need them. You only need to eat and excrete, nothing more. This way you will live a very long life indeed. Periodically, we will suck a bit of your juices out and infuse you with the elixir of life so that you can remain healthy and live long. See, you are most honored.

I'd like to pull your appendages out and see how you like it! Natale declared, as she deflected another energy blast.

With three creatures keeping us occupied, two advanced upon my unconscious body. It would have made little difference had it been conscious, however. It was securely chained to the stone altar; so were my companions. I was rapidly running out of ideas.

They effectively countered our fire spells, ice they enjoyed eating, and there was no way to get a lightning bolt down here so far underground. How long could I continue to pick them up and pitch them away? Eventually, they might overwhelm me, and then we were all doomed utterly! There had to be another way to defeat these monsters! I began looking around the room.

It was empty except for the huge altar stone and the dozens of lanterns. Our weapons were nowhere in sight. There was nothing but this giant altar stone and the walls. Two were now closing in on my helpless body. The walls! They were made of stone blocks! I shoved the two back from my body, buying me a small amount of time. I latched onto one stone block in the side of the room. I pulled and pulled.

Now the two were once more closing in on my body. Thankfully, these creatures moved slowly when they were not flying! I pulled and pulled. Just as one was leaning over to bite into my arm, I heard the grating sound of stone upon stone. I had at last overcome the friction between the stones. I pulled even harder.

I wasn't prepared for the moment of release, however. Pulling so hard against the friction between the blocks, the instant it slid free from the wall, the stone block went flying across the room. It hit one of the mantises who was about to bite into my arm, slamming its body against the other wall. An awful squishing sound echoed in the room along with a weird noise, which I took as a cry of pain. I moved the block, and the mantis head was completely flattened, goo oozing out all over the wall. Its dead body slowly slid onto the floor.

I threw the block with all my might at the other mantis who was about to bite into my other arm. The flying block caught it off guard as well, sending its body smashing into the other side wall. Once more, that weird scream echoed, and when I moved the block away, the second mantis slid down to the floor, its head similarly squashed. Now I had a weapon that worked.

Okay you vile creatures, Bethany is on the move! Two down, three to go. It's bug squashing time in the temple! Natale and Linda cheered me on.

Damn you Bethany! You killed our sisters! Now we must kill you! screeched one of the remaining three. It lunged for my body. Ah, a new tactic came into play. They were now going to attack my defenseless body, not me. As the creature dove for my body, intent upon landing upon it and ripping its head off, I swung the stone as hard as I could and hit it squarely in its head.

That same weird scream told all; I had smashed in its head. Ah, their bodies were actually quite soft and very vulnerable to physical damage! Now it was kick ball time! The other two tried to back away, heading back into their hole. I threw the stone at them. All my many hours of playing kick ball came into play. While they might be able to dodge one toss, they could not dodge them all. The hundred pound stone block was my ball. I pitched it, retrieved it, and pitched it repeatedly. Wham! I connected to the fourth, only the stone completely severed its head this time.

The last was escaping into its hole. I grabbed it by its tail and pulled it out into the room. Hey, I'm not done playing kick ball with you creatures. Now you have to avoid being hit by the ball here. Look out here it comes again! Once more, I threw the stone around as rapidly as I could, the creature doing its best to dodge it, leaping high into the air, flapping its wings for stability. The only caution I exerted was to avoid having the stone get anywhere near the altar stone where our bodies would be smashed as well.

At this time, Renzo, Rosina, and Emil pulled out of their grogginess. Emil had played many hours of kick ball at Jenna's estate with me. He saw at once what was happening. He told the other three, *Distract it any way you can.* All three began shooting flame sheets this way and that, designed to get in the creature's path as it tried to dodge my stone ball. At last, confused by so many flames, my ball throw connected, sending the creature smashing into the side of the room, its guts sprayed upon the wall, its eyes drilling into me. Then, it was gone.

Well done Bethany! exclaimed Renzo. *Remind me never to get into a kick ball game with you!* He was recovering his sense of humor.

Now what do we do? asked Natale. *My body is still out of it.*

Heck if I know. Renzo, Emil, you are on look out. Rosina, Natale, you are with me. Let's see if we can find a way to wake bodies up. We didn't. We would just have to wait it out until the drug wore off. One by one, the others came out of their confusion masses, none the worse for the energy blasts. Yet, we were helpless while our bodies down below were so unconscious. Of course, then there was the matter of the chains holding them to the altar stone. In the end, all we could do was wait.

After some time, our bodies awoke. We checked on them, but they did not seem to have been injured or hurt. At last, I let go of the massive Mind Link. "Okay gang, now what do we do? I can't budge my chains," I said.

"I've got a chain around my waist," explained Natale. "Maybe I can wiggle out of it." After some time, Natale was free, standing there looking down at us. "Now what do I do? Damn this having no arms thing! Here I am free and can't do a darn thing to free you men."

"Yes you can," Henry replied before I could. "Honey, look around and see if you can find any keys to these locks!"

"Oh, right. I never thought of that!" She began wandering around the large room, looking for keys. After a long search, she sat down beside Henry, a forlorn look on her face. "No keys. I guess it doesn't matter that I don't have arms now. Even if I had them, I couldn't get you out of these chains."

"Well, eventually, the High Priest will come to take all us Holy Touched Maidens away. He must have the keys. We'll get free in a while," I suggested. Again, we all waited.

Some time later, we heard a key moving in the door. Linda was instantly alert; she was determined to put her newly learned skills to good use. In a moment, the High Priest Ajacopa opened the door and came inside to examine the newly created Holy Touched Maidens. "What's this? Oh my god! What have you done?"

"Shut the door and lock it," stated Linda with a powerful command tone in her voice. He tried to resist her command. She merely moved his body to carry out her command, just as Lady Jovanna had done with the Holy Paladins and priests of Jehosanity in Barcella!

With the door secure, she commanded, "Now unlock all these chains!" Again, he resisted, but again she forced his body to begin carrying out her orders. Within a few minutes, we were all rubbing our hands and legs, getting the circulation going once more. Meanwhile, other priests were pounding on the thick door, but we ignored them for the time being.

"Now then, tell us how did you get those five mantis creatures and are there any more of them around?" Linda asked him. I left his interrogation to our Judger. "Speak, or I will force it out of you!"

"You killed them! You fiends! You killed our Black Gods!"

"Okay. Now how did you get them? Where did they come from?"

"I won't tell you! You evil fiends!" He became utterly defiant.

Linda looked at me, and I made the Mind Link between the three of us. Linda commanded, *How did you get them? Where did they come from?* He tried to hide his memories, which came flooding into his consciousness in response to her questions. We viewed his memories as they flashed by. Apparently, the priests had been searching all along the coastline looking for nests made by the now long dead mantis creatures. Evidently, they laid a batch of eggs when they reproduced. After nearly twenty-five years of searching, they had located a clutch of eggs. Not knowing how to hatch them, they began experimenting. Finally, five hatched, and they had their Black Gods back!

How many eggs are left and where are they? A dozen remained in the hatchery room here within the temple.

Just then, the door opened. Worried priests had gotten a second key, and seven came barging in. Natale was prepared for them, one by one, she forced their bodies to stand rigidly still just after they entered the room. No way was she going to let these men interrupt Linda or me. Quickly, the men carried the stiff forms over to the altar and chained them where we had recently been tied up.

How many more priest are in the temple? Six more were about.

Where are our weapons and things? Linda obtained a location, which she relayed to Emil.

"Emil, you take the other Santi and go and see if you can find your weapons. Report here when you're armed once more. Then, we will set about capturing the remaining priests," I requested. A dozen took off with him. I broke the link, since Linda had finished with Ajacopa.

As Renzo was chaining Ajacopa to his own altar, Linda told him, "You sir, are under arrest. You will stand trial for committing high crimes against your fellow human beings. You have been aiding and abetting an enemy race, bent on the destruction of humans."

While we were waiting for the others to return, I contacted Roberto, Mireio, and Cathy. It took me some time to describe what had happened to us. All three were very concerned, since it was now nearly dawn! We had been out nearly three-quarters of a day!

Soon, Emil returned. Not only did he have all our weapons and gear, he had also captured the remaining six priests. "Ah, we found them nearby our weapons stash. We had to play a bit rough with them," he grinned. Most of the priests had red swellings on their faces, and I suspected they had used their fists on them.

Once these men were chained, I said, "Okay, now let's thoroughly search this entire temple. Somewhere we should find their captured Holy Touched Maidens. I have a really bad feeling about their condition, however."

"Perhaps they will also have some treasure that we can confiscate," Henry suggested hopefully. He had his arm around Natale once more, and she was leaning her head on his shoulders. Off we went doing a thorough search of the entire temple complex. Indeed, we soon discovered their treasury, which Henry dutifully confiscated. He had not yet decided whether we should keep it or to whom it should be given. He only knew that these priests were losing it!

Most of the rooms contained mundane items, which we ignored. At last, deep inside the temple, we came across another locked room. "Allow a Planner to do his work," teased Cedric. He finally had something of value to contribute. In less than a minute, he had the lock opened, and we all entered. Yes, we had found all the Holy Touched Maidens!

"Oh no!" exclaimed Natale.

"Good god!" added Tonia.

"Here we go again," I put in. The others gasped, holding their hands over their mouths.

The room contained two dozen women, mutilated women I should say, though perhaps mutilated is the wrong word here. The mantis creatures had their delicacies from these women. All twenty-four women were in a sort of drugged daze, feeling no pain or sensation. All were totally docile and obedient.

Quickly, Tonia went from woman to woman, sizing up the grim situation. "Twelve have lost all their fingers," she announced.

Hearing this, one of those women spoke, "We serve the others." It was as if she were rattling off some hypnotically given command.

"We've four with arms at least to their elbows; four more have no arms left at all. Damn, we've t two who have only half their arms and half their legs left! Oh no, these two have nothing left at all! God, Bethany, I don't know what to do!" Tonia was shocked beyond words. Nothing in her training had prepared her for this situation. "They are all drugged, I'm guessing."

"Are their wounds bleeding or infected, requiring immediate treatment? Any lives in dire jeopardy?" I asked, trying to get her to focus on the immediate situation.

"Ah, no bleeding. In this poor light, I cannot tell about infections, but we don't smell that rotten odor, so maybe we have a break on the infections," she replied, regaining some of her composure.

"Okay, Bethany," Linda scratched her head and spoke what she had been calculating. "We know that the King has no jurisdiction over the priests in this society. However, the priests do. I would suggest that we contact High Priest Itzli and have him adjudicate these priestly crimes. He should know what would be the best way to handle the situation. As far as these women go, we should get them moved up to the entranceway. You are going to want to do your therapy on them after Tonia and Cathy pronounce them fit. The real question is where to house them. They are part of this society, not ours. Yet, they may feel more at ease on our ship because they would not have to face their families, friends, and neighbors just yet."

"You are right. We should get in touch with Itzli at once. Emil, take some Santi with you and go fetch Itzli at once. The rest of us will begin getting these women up to the top, along with the treasure," I winked at Henry. He smiled back at me.

Emil and six Santi left at once. I walked over to one of the women who was in the worst situation. Indeed, she had neither arms nor legs. She was definitely drugged. I picked her up like a baby and headed out and up. Tonia carried the other similar woman. Other strong hands carried the four who could not walk. The rest of our party assisted those who could walk. The going was slow; the drugged women moved excruciatingly slowly! It was also a long way up to the top, what with all the winding corridors. We placed them in a long line just inside the temple entrance. While Natale, Linda, Tonia, and I stayed here, the others returned to bring up the treasure. Here the lighting was better, so Tonia began to examine the two worst cases.

"Look at this, Bethany," Tonia said. "I've never seen anything quite like this. See, the bones have been removed from their sockets! Yet, the skin shows no sign of suture marks. It has grown over smoothly, as if she was born without legs or arms. Weird indeed, but she does have bed sores, look at her back. The other woman does too. They need to be moved far more frequently than they have been, that's for sure."

"And look at these here. The lower leg bones are neatly removed along with the knee caps and the skin regrown as if she never had lower legs," Tonia commented.

I added, "Her arms are the same way, as if she never had arms below her elbows." Quickly, we examined the others and found them in precisely the same condition. "It does look like every one of them is perfectly healed! Amazing."

Now we examined the ones without fingers. It was the same story with them. Their hands appeared as though they had been born without any fingers or thumbs. How ever these mantis creatures performed their surgery, they were certainly good at it. Next, we both wondered how long it would take for the drugs that they were under to wear off. We decided we hadn't the slightest idea.

The others began arriving with the many sacks of treasure, piling them us, after the line of women. At last, Emil arrived with High Priest Itzli. Linda took charge at once. "High Priest Itzli, we are bringing formal charges against all the Black God priests. They have been systematically taking women from your city and feeding their body parts to evil creatures, which they call their Black Gods. First, I want you to see the condition of their so-called Holy Touched Maidens. Look at them, please."

"Oh dear god! Oh my. This is utterly horrible." He could say no more, holding his hand over his mouth.

"Now come with us to their sacrificial altar room. We will show you the bodies of the creatures that they fed these poor women's body parts to, inhuman creatures. Bethany killed them. These Black God priests knocked us out with some kind of gas and chained us to their altar, intent on feeding our parts to their vile creatures. Bethany killed all them and freed us. Come, but prepare to be shocked, however."

Linda and I led him down into the altar room. When we entered, Ajacopa hollered, "Itzli! Rescue us! These vile foreigners have captured us and. . ." He chose not to finish his sentence. Itzli ignored his rival, following us to the other end, where the squashed bodies of the mantises lay, greenish ooze creeping across the floor and down the walls.

"He fed these with those women?" Itzli vomited. We gave him a minute to recover. When he felt a bit better, he walked over to Ajacopa and spat on the man's face.

While we were walking back up, I suggested, "You know, Itzli, I really want this Temple of the Black God destroyed utterly, once and for all time. I do not want them ever to be able to reuse this temple for such wickedness. However, I suspect that there are some in Wanakan who are believers and followers of this Black God, correct?" He agreed, nearly half of the city either worshiped the Black God or were ardent followers.

"What we need here is a display of the true power of your Sun God, a display that everyone can see, in which the Sun God destroys utterly this temple."

"Yes, but Bethany, this temple took at least a hundred years to build. Many, many years will be required to destroy it."

I grinned, not if I have any say in the matter. "Here's what I want you to do. Bring some of your men to take away these evil priests. They should be held accountable for what they have done. Meanwhile, we will take the women down to the King's palace. There, I will set about healing them as we can. I want the city to see the horrid condition of these supposedly Holy Touched Maidens. Then, I want you to focus your Holy Lense over onto this temple. Let the light of the Sun God shine on this black temple, and it will be destroyed. I will see to it personally, and everyone in the city will see it as well. That should put an end to this Black God cult. Will you do that?"

He didn't understand why, but agreed to do it. As we rejoined the others, Henry pointed to the treasure sacks. He'd forgotten to ask Itzli about that, so I did now. "We recovered quite a lot of gold and jade that these priests had collected. What should be done with it all?"

"Ah, it has been touched by evil. None of us should ever be allowed to touch it. It is yours to dispose of as you wish. I must make the preparations. As agreed, then, our signal will be the Holy Light of the Sun God shining upon this temple of wickedness." He bowed to me and left rushing down the steps as fast as he dared.

"Okay gang, we are going to take these women through the city to the palace for now. Henry, you bring along the treasure," I grinned at the mariner. Slowly, our small parade made its way down the long steps. By the time that we reached the streets below, people had seen us and crowds began to gather. As expected, we heard numerous gasps, shrieks, and curses as we ushered these poor women through the streets toward the palace.

When we arrived there, Cathy and Teyacapan were already there awaiting our arrival. While Cathy was somewhat prepared for the sight, Teyacapan began crying, "That's what they were going to do to me? Oh my god! Those poor women. Oh god, there is my friend, Teiuc! God, she has lost half her arms and legs! Teiuc! Teiuc!" She tried to talk to her girlfriend, who had been abducted about a year ago. Unfortunately, the drugged woman did not respond to her friend.

Cathy explained, "Teyacapan, they are all drugged senseless. She needs time for the drug to get out of her system." As we entered, there was a flurry of action, as Amihan directed her staff to fetch blankets, food, and drink for the women. We put them all in the main throne room for the time being. I sent Emil outside to watch for the Sun God sign.

"King Matial, we have destroyed the evil creatures that were fed these women's body parts. Itzli has arrested and will probably execute all the priests of the Black God. However, the true power of the Sun God is about to be shown. Emil will let us know when the show is about to begin."

Linda then began telling everyone the full story of our encounter. She was only halfway through when Emil came running in, "Hey, the Sun God is shining on the Temple of the Black God!" I raced outside and began to concentrate.

One stone block at the top floated up and off the temple, landing in the jungle behind the temple. Another stone, and another stone. Soon everyone began to see the "power of the Sun God" in action. Not to be left out, Renzo, Rosina, and Linda added some fireworks of their own, flames shooting skyward and such. Now Natale joined me, experimenting with moving objects. Yes, we all had a release of our anger. Everyone in the city got to witness the utter and complete destruction of the temple. The King even brought the Holy Touched Maidens out to watch it, though we didn't know if they could even appreciate what they were seeing.

Towards the bottom of the pyramid, I was throwing away stones like a dog digging into a fox burrow! Linda guessed that the King had finally figured out that we were doing the actual destruction of the temple, though he did not ask. Clearly, from the wild antics of the Sun God priests, it was the work of the Sun God. Around suppertime, as the sun set, only the roofless tops of some underground tunnels remained.

Now it was suppertime; we had not eaten much in nearly two days and were starving. Unfortunately, the cooks had also been watching the spectacle, so supper was delayed a bit. Cathy reported no change in the drugged state of the women, so we listened to the King's musicians play while we waited for dinner. After we were all stuffed, again, we checked on the patients. Still no change.

I decided that in case the drugs wore off during the night, we should stay here with them. Amihan and her daughter brought us many reed mats and some blankets. Meanwhile, Henry and the men transported the treasure to the caravel, returning to be with us. Finally, tired, we all turned in. The men slept in a nearby room, while we women slept in with our patients. Teyacapan insisted on sleeping with her friend, Teiuc.

By now, we had made another discovery about the twelve women who had only lost their fingers. Like one of Henry's shipboard clocks, every three hours, they arose and went to the other twelve women. They would lift the two who were in the worst situation, hold them over one of the chamber pots, and wait for the woman to go to the bathroom. The others did similar actions for the other women who were not as bad off. Somehow, these twelve had been indoctrinated to care for their companions. During the night, they continued to follow the same pattern, waking from sleep and performing their ritual.

Around midnight, it began; the drugs started wearing off, not uniformly, but a woman here and there. We concluded that the drugs had to be administered every other day somehow. Suddenly without any warning at all, Teiuc began screaming at the top of her lungs! Startled out of a deep sleep, we jumped up, expecting an attack or something. There was Teiuc rather propped up against the wall, looking at what remained of her arms and legs, screaming as loudly as she could.

Teyacapan rushed to her friend and put her arms around her, talking soothing words all the while. "It's okay, Teiuc. You have been rescued. The evil creatures that did this to you are dead. The priests have been arrested and are probably dead by now. You are with me in the Royal Palace. You are safe. It's okay, Teiuc. It's going to be okay now. Really it is, Teiuc, really it is."

She stopped screaming and looked at her friend, finally recognizing her. Then, she started crying heavily. Teyacapan continued to console her friend. "Look what they've done to me! I've no arms or legs anymore," she wailed.

Trying to be comforting, Teyacapan replied, "Yes you do. They are only half gone. Those two over there, they really have none left. At least you have half of them left. I know it's not much, but at least it is better than those two. Don't worry, Teiuc, I will always look after you now. You are my best friend still!" The woman continued to sob on Teyacapan's shoulder.

Of course, when the screams began, everyone came running in, including the King and his wife. Everyone saw the wild reaction the woman had as she came out of the drugged state that she had been in for the year since she had been taken. The King and his wife cried to themselves as they left to return to bed. I knew that they had never seen such a helpless mess.

Throughout the long night, we were treated with random screaming sessions, as one by one the women came out of their drugged states. None was worse than the two who had lost everything. Their screams were the most pitiful and sorrowful of all. Poor Teyacapan went to each woman who awoke, doing her very best to console them until they stopped screaming and their subsequent crying had subsided. I was thankful for her efforts, had we been the ones, only more trauma would have been felt by these women, awaking to find a different race of people looking over them. We barely spoke their language.

The next morning over breakfast, I needed to discuss the situation with our patients. King Matial began by saying, "I don't know how to thank you for all that you and your people have done for us. I am the luckiest father in the world! To think that my little Teyacapan almost ended up like those poor women!"

"I'm glad you brought up this situation. Back in our lands, a group of evil men brutalized some women. Natale and Mireio are just two of those that they mutilated. We have developed a therapy, which can erase the horrible trauma that your women have endured. When done properly, they experience a total relief and a new lease on life. Then, there is all the special training that we have. You've seen how well Natale does; she is but one example. I would like your permission to use my therapy on these women. It is the least that I can do for them, to help restore some life into them. Further, when that is done, I would like to extend an offer to take anyone of them who desires it back to our headquarters for several years, so that they can get the special training that only we can give them. Once they have learned all that they desire to learn, we will bring them right back here. However, I most certainly would need your official permission to do so. They are your people."

"You would do this for our women? What would it cost us?"

"Nothing. We have an entire foundation setup to help women who have been brutalized by men, such as these women have. I suspect that those who have only lost their fingers will probably adapt well and may prefer to rejoin their families, once their therapy is completed. However, I will be honest with you. The two who have lost everything, I don't know if there is anything that we can do for them, other than erasing their traumas. We might be able to somehow make their lives more endurable."

"Like a paca with a broken leg, we would just put them out of their misery. Yet, if you are willing to train them, then if they should desire to go with you for a time, you have my approval," the King replied. "However, if I should find myself as many of they are now, I should wish myself dead. Yet, they are even denied the means for that, those wretched, poor women."

"What do your people believe about bodies and your true selves?" I asked curiously.

"That is a matter for the priests, Bethany. Yet, myself, and many others believe that we are all children of the Sun God and that he has given unto us this brief time in these mortal bodies. I do not believe that I am this body you see before you, but what more I may be, I cannot say."

"You have the wisdom of a priest," I complimented him.

Just then, Cathy entered, "Bethany, they have all been fed. I've examined each one very carefully once more. Physically, they are healthy and have not been molested; many still have their maidenhood intact, which I found quite surprising. However, their trauma is monumental;

perhaps it is far worse than what we have found in the Sea Princes."

"Excuse me, Matial. I must begin their therapy sessions. If you could search out their remaining family members or perhaps husbands, if they were married, I would appreciate meeting with them here at suppertime. If you hear screams today, do not be alarmed; they will be erasing the trauma that they have been suffering all this time."

I followed Cathy into the side room where the twenty-four women were now being housed. I brought Natale with me. On our way, Cathy pointed out one interesting detail: the twelve, who had been caring for the others who were in worse physical shape than they, were no longer doing so. The mental commands to do so every three hours had gone away, along with the effects of the drug.

"Hello everyone. My name is Bethany. I come from a land far across the ocean. We came in a big ship. We are called Santi del Dio, the Knights of God. Among our people, we are known as great healers. I know that your bodies are healed, but you still bear the mental scars, the trauma of your ordeal. Know this: you are now safe. The Temple of the Black God has been destroyed, and the black creatures are dead."

One woman asked, "How could they be killed? They are so strong? Are they really dead?"

"Yes, I killed all them myself."

"But how did you do that?"

"I smashed their heads in with a heavy stone — squashed their brains all over the walls. Come, let us show you where their temple used to stand. It was destroyed yesterday. Will you help me carry those who cannot walk? We'll go outside and look." I leaned down and picked up one of the two who had nothing left. Teyacapan carried her girlfriend; Cathy, the other one in bad shape. Tonia and the others helped the rest. We walked outside and looked toward the temples. Only the Sun God temple stood tall and imposing. Empty space indicated where the evil temple had stood. This did much to convince them that indeed it was permanently over.

Back inside and comfortable once more, I continued. "As I said, I'm a great healer. In our land, some women have been horribly mutilated as some of you are. Natale here was one of them. I worked my therapy on her, and she has her life back. We are also great teachers, and there is much that we can teach you, if you decide that you might be inclined to come and learn from us. Now then, I promise each and every one of you that I will help you erase the trauma that you have undergone, but it takes time."

"I have asked your King Matial to find your relatives and husbands. I will speak with them tonight. I know that for some of you, facing them as you are will be very hard indeed. If you do not feel up to facing them right now, I'll see that you do not have to do that until you are truly ready."

"I'm not very fluent in your language yet. Natale here knows it the best of us and learns new words quickly. So if you don't understand something I say, let me know. Natale and Teyacapan will help get the words figured out for you and for me. Is that okay with you?" It was. Now came the tricky part, especially for me.

"Because there are so many of you, I'm going to have some of my friends help me with your therapy. I'll be back in a short time, and we will begin. Okay?" Again, they agreed, but were mostly apathetic about it.

I got Teyacapan, Linda, Natale, Tonia, Cathy, Rosina, and Mireio together for a conference. "I'm going to show you how to do the therapy sessions. Natale and Teyacapan are going to watch over all six sessions at the same time, looking for anything that is not understood. Between them, they'll get the words sorted out. Expect the women to use words that you don't know. I know none of you have done this before, but we have two things in our favor. One, the technique is easy, and I will be watching over each of you at the same time as I am running my session. Two, all these traumas will very likely be quite similar in nature, if not exactly the same — the creatures just nibbling away at their limbs, so I think that we can get away with this method. I will have you five working on those who only lost fingers, while I work the harder cases. Questions?"

"Please, Bethany, please do Teiuc first, please," Teyacapan begged me.

I agreed, how could I not? "Do you think that we can do this?" asked Cathy.

"Yes, I'd ask the men to help, but it was men who held them captive. That might not be a wise action to take. Besides, having Mireio and Natale present will only help them. Did you see the way that they have been continuously watching those two?"

"They can't take their eyes off of me," Natale grinned. "Besides, more than one stared at my earrings."

"Yes," Teyacapan agreed, "they see you as a very important person. Only mom and I have ones as long as Bethany, Mireio, and you, Natale. They know that you three are very important people."

Next, I explained in detail what they needed to do. I also told them that I would be the one to let them know when they should ask for some earlier trauma that might be similar to this one. I didn't expect to run into that situation in this case. The traumas were right here and now. I thought it unlikely that they would have experienced anything similar. Satisfied they were ready, we went back into the room. The King had made the next room available to us to use. It had been a storage room, but was large enough to fit us all in. Teyacapan carried her friend, while I helped choose the five for the others to treat first.

We got them all settled down, and I explained to the women what was going to happen and what they were to do. Satisfied that they understood, I had each of my helpers get their session started on the right foot, so to speak. Finally, with five women returned to the start of their nightmare, I asked Teiuc, "Are you thirsty or hungry or need to go to the bathroom before we start?"

"I am thirsty," she said meekly.

Teyacapan hastily brought her a mug of water. She was going to hold it to her lips so she could drink, when I intervened, taking the cup from her. "Here, you have arms yet. See if you can do this for yourself." I was nudging her into attempting not to be so completely dependent upon others. I held the cup so she could clutch it in her arms. She tried and managed to hold it. Leaning over, she drank her fill. "There now, all set?" She was. I began the session by having her go back to the moment when she found out that she had become a Chosen One. Teyacapan was right there listening in, though she soon had to lend Cathy a hand with a word that Natale didn't know.

While I had complete attention on Teiuc, I also overheard the others close by, so it was not too difficult to monitor them as well. Occasional screams broke the otherwise quiet of the sessions, and we all knew what happened during those moments. Uniformly, the other five women's trauma incidents were very similar, as I had expected. They had been drugged as we had, chained to the altar stone. While they were mostly unconscious, one or more of the creatures had come and nibbled their appendages. The effects of the drug made everything go excruciatingly slowly; the poor women were constantly kept in a sort of sub-apathy trance. By the end of the day, the five had finally broken through the heavy drugged state and had begun to see what had actually happened to them while they were unconscious. Even though more days were needed to totally erase the trauma, by suppertime, all five were feeling a whole lot better about it.

Teiuc, on the other hand, fared far worse, as I had suspected. She'd been under that drug for nearly a year now. Imagine her horror, as she would open her eyes one morning only to find more parts of her body gone! They just kept on disappearing, until finally she found herself as she was now. By suppertime, we had only gone through the incident two times. It was very tough going, due to the drug's effects.

After supper, the King's meeting room filled up with all their relatives. Naturally, they all wanted to know how their loved ones were doing and when they could see them. The King introduced me, and I explained the situation to these people. I added, "Prepare yourselves; their condition is horrible. Twelve women have no fingers left; those are the lucky ones." I had the King call off their names, and I listened to the cries and gasps of their relatives.

"Four have lost their entire lower arms." Again, the King called off their names. "Four have no arms left at all." When he called off those names, the relatives really reacted badly. "Look, two of our own companions have lost their arms and are still totally fit to have traveled clear across the wide ocean to be here and help. It isn't the end of the world for them. We can help them learn new ways to do things." They calmed down after staring at Natale and Mireio.

"Four more are in worse shape. They have lost the lower half of their arms and the lower half of their legs." Matial called off their names. Shrieks of anguish filled his throne room. I did not know what piece of optimism to share and so said nothing.

"Finally, two have no arms or legs left at all." The King did not need to call off their names. Their relatives knew who was left. One mother fainted. It was a grim sight to see these families reacting to such horrible news of their precious daughters. "Before you say to just put them out of their misery like a paca with a broken leg, please let me work my therapy on them. Then allow them the dignity to decide their own fates, please." That seemed to pacify them somewhat.

"Now that you all know what to expect, it's time for you to meet with them. We have begun to do our therapy on them, but it will be some days before they can be sent home. Because there are so many of you, let's do this in smaller groups. Remember that your loved ones are right in the middle of a horrible trauma; it is still very real and vivid to them."

Now came the horrid part, watching the reactions of these parents as they met with their daughters. I hated having to go through this part. Yet, seeing the love their parents still had for their daughters partly made up for it. None of the women had been married, I discovered, although I ought to have deduced that fact, because they were all maidens. Still the shock of seeing what the true state of a Holy Touched Maiden actually was, in contrast to what the priests had exalted as this holy blessed state, raised their parents' anger to a fevered pitch. I thought about warning the King about possible retaliations against the Black God supporters, but didn't.

The next day, we learned that the severed heads of all the Black God priests' heads were lined up neatly on public display along the foundations of their destroyed temple. Their bodies had disappeared. All over the city, this was a day of retribution. Over breakfast, King Matial told us the fate of the Black God priests and warned us not to travel in the city alone today. "Many will be seeking retribution, including my own soldiers. If you need to travel, I will send along a substantial bodyguard. Word of the plight of the women has spread to everyone. Those who supported the Black God must answer the pan piper today."

It was not our place to intervene in local politics. I asked, "Is there any way that you can find out if the Black God cult is taking Holy

Touched Maidens in other city-states? You see, if there were more of these black creatures, they would be feeding off humans. This will provide us with a good way to hunt them down and eliminate any more of them. My biggest concern is that there may be others in some other city-state, who may opt to come back here and try to re-establish their hold on Wanakan."

"I see your point. I will send out runners today. Until now, we have not heard that the other city-states have been taking any Holy Touched Maidens, but now that we know what to look for, we will investigate. Already runners have been sent to the other kings about what has happened here. It will be several weeks before we hear back, however. A month is likely for the two furthest ones."

Breakfast done, it was back to therapy for us. Today, there was no screaming, rather, the five women began running through their trauma much more quickly. By the end of the day, three women were now laughing about the silly decisions that they had made while under that heavy duress and drugs. One was as silly as "I will never be able to scratch my nose." I was beginning to see the awful impact of undergoing such traumatic events while heavily drugged! True, the pain and unconsciousness had been masked, but it was still there to be contacted and released. However, due to the drug's impact, their thinking and reasoning powers were drastically altered. In this case, the drugs made them think rather silly thoughts in contrast to heavy one such as "Life is not worth living anymore."

The three who finished today, chatted enthusiastically to the other women, praising the results and us. Indeed, they had become cheerful about life, though not necessarily about how much more difficult their lives would become. The next day, these first three were allowed to go home to their families, who were quite surprised to see how much better their daughters were from that first night's visit.

With Teiuc, things merely ground on slowly. However, the beginning months of her ordeal began to lighten, as similar silly decisions began to come off as her fingers were eaten. "Now I cannot comb my hair. Now I cannot take off my necklace. How will I ever pick up the garbage on the floor?" Yes, it was the effects of the mantis drugs. Then, we hit the heavier stuff, the day when the creature ate her left arm up to the elbow. Now real shock set in. She became nauseated as she had that same day it happened. A week later, she had lost her other arm at the elbow. Heavy shock accompanied these two along with a real feeling of hopelessness that even the drugs could not completely mask. She sat in an apathetic state for several months before they once more began devouring her legs. At least they took both of them off at one time, she only had one horrific wake up shock to re-experience, not two as she had with her arms. By the end of this second day, Teiuc had gone through the whole thing three times and felt some relief from the loss of her fingers.

I felt sorry for Teyacapan, though. She had sat close to her friend nearly the whole day, only leaving her side when Natale needed some help with a few words. I could tell that she was visualizing what her dear friend had endured as Teiuc told me about it. This was making a lasting impression on her. Just how much I did not find out until the next day.

On the third day, three new women began their therapy, while the other two finished theirs. Yes, as I had anticipated, those with only finger losses came through rapidly. With Teiuc, today we made much faster progress. She had blown through the drug's effects and now contacted the underlying pain and unconsciousness that it had masked. She did very well; we had gone through the heavy stuff five times, and nothing new had been uncovered. However, I noticed that Teyacapan was herself now surrounded in a blackish mental mass. Her sitting here and listening to every word her friend said had somehow re-activated some trauma that she had some time in the past! She was not conducting the session, merely watching. Well, she had a stake in it; this was her best friend.

I needed to search for another trauma in Teiuc that was both similar and happened to her earlier. From the age of the young woman, perhaps sixteen, it would have to have been in a previous lifetime. I had not yet given them my usual speech about spiritual beings being immortal and that we have had many previous lifetimes. Still, if I were to stay true to Jenna's methods, I had to ask. "Teiuc, I want you to look and see if there is some similar trauma that happened to you long before this one occurred. Can you see any other images in your mind?"

She yawned, Teyacapan yawned. "I see some blue sky. That's all I see."

"Me too," whispered Teyacapan. I looked at her; she had her eyes closed just like her dear friend. Suddenly, I realized that Teyacapan was also following my commands! I was now giving two sessions at the same time! Nothing that Jenna had taught me fit this unusual situation. Since Teiuc was waiting for her next command, I gave it to her, and both women followed it.

"I want you to go through the incident and tell me all about what is happening as you go along, what you are seeing, what you are feeling, what you are tasting, all about it."

This was very weird! Both women were speaking at nearly the same time. If this was not sufficient to confuse me, both were saying pretty much the same words, describing pretty much the same thing! What was going on here?

"I see a lake and another young girl. We are sixteen. We are best friends. We are taking a bath, washing each other's backs. Suddenly these priests come and tie us up. You are now the Chosen Ones. You must come with us. We scream. No one comes to help us. We are led up these tall steps, oh so high. We are terrified. From the top here, I can see for miles. Our city is beautiful, but I am scared to death. I pee down my legs. My friend is frightened too. Down, down we go into the darkness of the tunnels. I am lost now. I know I can never find my way outside."

"The priest wears a robe with a black circle on it. He makes us drink this juice. I don't want to; he forces it down my throat. He leaves us alone. My friend tried to undo her ropes, so I do too. My body feels strange. It's getting numb. My teeth won't bite hard enough to undo the knot in the rope. My arms feel heavy. I feel so heavy. She lays down. I do too. All goes black."

Both women went unconscious on me at this point. I coached them on with "Okay, then what happens." After a bit of nudging and some time passed, they woke up a bit, and then screamed wildly. Of course, the others doing their sessions looked over at us. Natale was very concerned, and I pointed to Teyacapan, indicating that I was running her too. She relayed this to my friends. We hoped that we would not need Teyacapan to help Natale translate today!

Both women were now talking nearly in unison. "I wake up. I am sitting up looking at my friend. She has no hands, nothing below her elbows! She is looking at me. I look at me. I have nothing there either! We screamed and screamed, but no one came. We were not bleeding. I wasn't in any pain. I reached toward her and she reached toward me. We touched each other with what was left of our arms. We scooted close to each other and hugged each other and we cried."

"Then, we looked around. We were in a small room. I see a large, reed bed. There is a table with mugs and a plate on it. She said, 'There are no wooden forks.' I said, 'There are no wooden spoons.' We both said, 'How are we supposed to eat?' We looked at our arms and laughed. We are both very hungry, and we sit down. We manage to get the mugs up to our mouths. I take a little sip and spit it out. She does too. We both say that it tastes like that awful stuff that put us asleep. We lean over the plate. Eat like a dog, she says to me. We try. It doesn't have that awful taste, so we eat it."

"My friend says to me, 'I have to look after you now.' And I say to her, 'I have to look after you now too.' We laugh. She says, 'We have to get out of here.' I say, 'Let's escape!' We hear footsteps coming our way. I say, 'Let's lie down and pretend that we are unconscious.' She says, 'We must dump out our mugs so it looks real.' We dump the poison and lie down just in time. I lie very still. The person takes our plates and mugs away and shuts the door. It is working."

"We are naked and I cannot see our clothes. We go to the door but it has a latch." Both women began yawning heavily at this point. "I try to open it. She tries to open it. We cannot open it. I look at her and she looks at me. 'I have to help you now,' I say, and she says it back to me. We grin. We both work on the latch together and it opens!"

It is dark, but I can see a little. We listen for a long time. All is quiet. We sneak out and decide to walk in the direction that goes up. I whisper, 'We'll never get out of here!' She says, 'Yes we will. Keep on walking!' So I do. Tunnels go on forever! Finally, I smell fresh air, not the stale, damp air. We are near the top! Now I can suddenly see the stars! We are out!"

"Now we climb down the long steps. It is hard to do at night. I stumble. She catches me. She stumbles; I catch her. We are a team now. We get to the bottom. Now we don't know what to do next. We have no clothes. It is chilly. Where do we go now, I ask her. We can't go home; that's the first place they will look for us. We cry about that. 'I promise I will always look after you now,' I say. She says the same thing to me. We hug each other."

"'Where can we go,' I ask? She says she has an uncle in the next village, maybe he will take us in. We sneak through the city and head out down the path to that village. 'How are we going to live like this,' I ask. She says. 'We just have to help each other somehow.' I swear that I always will be there to help her. Then, we come to a small stream. We are very thirsty and stop to drink. The sun is coming up now." Both women began yawning very heavily now.

"We hear footsteps. Someone is running after us. They are coming to capture us. I don't ever want to go back there, I say. She says the same thing. We run off into the jungle. Brush slaps us in the face, but we don't care. We have to get away from them."

"I hear this noise overhead. We look up and see this huge black flying creature! Oh god! It's the thing that ate our arms! We run faster now. Finally, we have to stop. I am standing at the edge of a big cliff. The black thing hovers over us. It speaks into my mind. 'You are my Holy Touched Maidens. You will return with me now.' I scream out, 'No I am not! I will never go back there!' She says for him to go eat himself! I laugh. It seemed so silly."

"Now a lot of men are getting close to us. The creature is coming down for us too. She says, 'Let's jump for it. I'm not going back there.' I say, 'Let's do it.' We jump. I'm falling. I have a funny feeling in my stomach. My leg hits something. I am spinning. I don't like the spinning. I hit something hard. I get a huge flood of pain in my head and all goes black. I just do nothing. Pain goes away. I can see now. I am above my body. It lies smashed upon a rock. So is my friend's body. I see her now. She sees me. We laugh. I don't know how we can laugh, but we laugh. I get her idea that we did it. We are not going to have to go back there with that horrid creature and let it eat more of us. We laugh. Then, I follow her. We are going to her uncle's village anyway."

Both women open their eyes at the same time. Both stared at each other for a moment. They both began laughing. "It was you!" They said in unison and hugged each other, all the while laughing like mad. Teiuc said, "We did it! We escaped, and it didn't get to eat us anymore. We actually did it!"

"Yes, we did it! We helped each other and got free! I promised you that I would always look after you," Teyacapan exclaimed.

"I know, and I promised to always help you. We did it together! We were a team then!"

"We still are a team now!" declared Teyacapan. "I won't leave you ever, Teiuc, never! Only just don't leave me."

"Oh I promise I won't! We actually got away from that evil creature, didn't we?"

"You bet. We are a team!"

"Boy do I ever feel alive, Teyacapan! Things are so vividly real to me!"

"Me too. I'm so happy that I could dance around."

"Me too, but you are going to have to help me dance, that is if you are still going to be helping me out."

She picked up her friend and began twirling around the room. "We are a team! I promised you then and promise you now. I won't ever leave you. Just don't go leaving me!" Both laughed. I quietly ended their therapy session.

Suddenly, Teiuc exclaimed, "Teyacapan! We've lived before!"

She stopped twirling the two of them around. "Oh my! You're right. We lived before, together. Bethany, what does this mean?"

I had to give them my usual speech about spiritual beings and lifetimes. "If you two will come back with us to our headquarters across the ocean for a few years, we can teach you many very useful things." We discussed this at length over supper. Teyacapan insisted that Teiuc join her at her father's table for supper that night. They were two chattering young women at the dinner table. Even King Matial noticed the dramatic change in his own daughter.

However, I had to caution Teyacapan to allow Teiuc the opportunity to do some things for herself, such as drinking from her own mug. Yes, she could feed her, but let her handle her own mug. "Always allow Teiuc the opportunity to do something for herself. Only be there to help her when she asks for help."

That night, I contacted mom to tell her about this most unusual therapy session. Sammy had been keeping everyone up to date on the happenings with us. Jenna said, *I was going to contact you and read scold you about getting everyone in dire trouble, Bethany, but then I realized that was just the mother in me coming out. So how has it been going? Sammy suggested that we not directly contact you because you were doing many therapy sessions.*

Thanks mom. I have two dozen to handle, though I have five others helping me with the easy cases. You'll never believe what happened today! I related all that had occurred. She was very impressed with how I was handling it and most intrigued about the dual past lives.

What we really have to worry about is the reappearance of these mantis creatures. These were babies or young children. They were almost too much for us. I now know that they are hatched from eggs. Much of their powers stem from their physical bodies, not themselves. We need to be on the alert for the reappearance of these nasty bugs, mom. Probably in the Southlands would be my guess, since they had their base in the Red Desert. I'm going to find out all I can about them around here before we sail for home.

We chatted a while longer, before she said, *It's a shame that those priests were beheaded before they had the opportunity to get therapy. In their next lifetimes, they will have to be handled. We are making tomorrow's problems today.* I thought that was a profound statement of the problem. It was becoming abundantly clear to me that much of what was wrong with people in today's world came from unhandled trauma of the past.

Oh yes, Hank wants a word with you. Hank joined the Mind Link.

Hi, honey. Say, I've been thinking about the situation you have there. Sammy has been keeping us posted. Well done on the bug smashing, by the way. I got to thinking about Teiuc and those like her. I believe I have invented a way that they can move about somewhat. We both know that a person really has to have some mobility on their own, that is really vital. Here's a picture of my invention. He sent me a series of good images and instructions to follow. I promised I would see if it would work.

That evening, I first found Teiuc and carefully measured the bottom of her short legs. Then, I went back to the caravel to see if we could make a pair of these special shoes, booties really. I sketched out dad's design and set everyone scrambling to find the necessary materials. Two hours later, we had finished making our first pair. I went back to find Teiuc. Of course, she was with Teyacapan in her room. They were making a second bed up for her friend. From now on, Teyacapan insisted that Teiuc stay with her here.

"Hi, I've got something for Teiuc to try out. These booties are my dad's invention. He thinks that you will be able to walk upright on your own with these on. Let's see if they really do work."

"You're teasing me?" she asked more than a little confused. She had already accepted the fact that the only way she could get around was sort of walking on all fours like a paca.

They slipped on well, and I tied them at the top with the drawstrings. "They have a wooden base for support and are very well cushioned. I think you can stand in these. Might take some getting used to, though. Let's try them out." Teyacapan helped her friend stand up and helped her keep her balance. It was an awkward motion, but Teiuc took her first steps as a person again.

"It works! I can walk again!" She shouted for joy. "I'm really wobbly. It's very slow, but I can do this! Look at me, Teyacapan! You don't have to carry me everywhere anymore!" She was elated, and that was an understatement!

She insisted on walking out into the main throne room. Then, she insisted on walking to the room where the other women were staying. She just had to show the other three that this would work for them too! I took careful measurements of the other three women and promised that by tomorrow night they would have a pair as well. It did bring a small spark of life to their eyes. Therapy would do the rest, I knew.

Back in their room, Teiuc gave me a big hug. "Tell your dad thank you for me! Between both of you, I have a new life. I was ready to just die before, now I can live again!"

"You are most welcome, Teiuc. I do hope that you will come back to our land with us and stay for a few years so we can teach you how to do many other things."

"I should like that, but I have so little gold. How should I pay for it?"

I grinned, "You don't have to pay for it like you think. We will only ask you to help out around the place and help others as you are able. I think that you will be amazed at what may well be possible."

"Hey, if she goes, so do I!" insisted Teyacapan.

"Your dad has already said so. How could I possibly separate you two anyway? I don't want you two to go jumping off any more cliffs!" All three of us roared with laughter.

The next day, while the men were making more booties, it was therapy sessions for the rest of us. I tackled the next woman who was like Teiuc. Her name was Cazamel. My five helpers continued with the easier cases.

A week later, all the remaining fingerless women were finished and had left, choosing to rejoin their families. Cazamel was also done. She too had been an earlier victim of the mantis creatures, some hundred years ago. I was now halfway done working with Iacotl. Xilonen was patiently waiting her turn, though all three were now walking rather well with their new booties.

Hence, I decided to let my helpers tackle the four armless women, knowing that these may well run into previous traumatic incidents. Chica, Meloa, Malotl, and Mecoa began their sessions now. Going along with the pattern, they were also sixteen. I paired one with Mireio, with Natale continually hovering between sessions, hoping that they would instinctively see that their condition was not hopeless. Only the two in the worst shape remained. I knew these last two would pose the greatest challenge for us. I wanted to work them personally.

Eight days later, all five finally had their traumas handled, along with Xilonen with consequent renewal of life and vigor. We were all elated with our successes. However, the two worst cases remained. During this time, I missed an event that I wish I had not. Teyacapan helped Teiuc walk all the way to the beach and take her first real bath in well over a year. A large crowd of people cheered her all the way to and from the beach. Yes, it took her a very long time to navigate the distance, but she did it herself, and that made all the difference in the world to this young woman.

Down to our last two, I relented and let Mireio handle Moca, while I worked Itha. By now, we had not come across any more words that we didn't know, so I let the others have some welcomed time off. My guess was that these two cases would be similar. I was not far wrong. It took a week for us to just get the lighter portions of their trauma reduced! This was the worst going I had yet handled. Both women were now eighteen, and that meant that they had been under the influence of the drug for well over two years! Oh, was this ever slow going.

The next week brought faster progress and by the end of the week, Mireio and I had the two women viewing the deepest, roughest portions of their horrid ordeal. As I suspected, neither one's trauma erased. We had to go earlier, no choice in the matter. Moca found hers relatively rapidly. She had also been a victim some hundred and fifty years ago, only she had died at the hands of the mantis creatures. It seemed that the next stage of their nibbling, they ate their vital organs, killing the woman. Once this was completely re-experienced, Moca realized that she had actually gotten her wish; she had finally died, rather her body had. For nearly two years during that time, she had been trying to die to get out of it, but without the means by which to do it. She had actually welcomed the beast's last feast! Laughing wildly, she blew off all of her accumulated lifetimes of trauma.

Itha, on the other hand, had a most difficult time trying to find something earlier. "I don't see anything, just this priest," she kept insisting. When I would try to have her see what was happening with the priest, she would refuse. "It's not me!" she declared flatly. Suddenly, I realized what was happening. I had her say those very words repeatedly. "It's not me! It's not me!" Wham! She was suddenly smack into another incident.

Only this time, she had been one of the Black God priests, the High Priest at that! After assisting the twenty-fifth young woman back into their Keep Room after the mantis had eaten its desire, he had stared at the room of limbless women and had finally woken up to what was really happening here. He had vomited in the room and fled to his own chamber. "Oh my god! What have I done here? I am sick for days after that." She began yawning extremely heavily.

Suddenly she opened her eyes and stared at me. "The only way out was for me to deny myself, by saying it's not me! But it was me! I did that or rather helped do that to all those women!" She began laughing heartily. "It's not me! But it is me! Payback time! Good god! That's what has held this so tightly to me! Payback time! I made myself suffer like those I made suffer. Now that is really stupid!" She roared even harder, and I ended this last session.

Next, I had to do the hardest thing that I have ever had to do. I got both Itha and Moca together, just the three of us. Both were now cheerful. They too instinctively knew what I was going to say. Itha broke the ice, for which I was grateful. "So what do we do now? The trauma is gone. We both feel like a million. But we are like this, completely and utterly dependent upon everyone else for absolutely everything in life. What do we do now?"

"Itha, you are right. That's what I want to discuss with you now, your future. We Santi have done a huge amount for the others who are not as bad off physically as you two are. I'll be bluntly honest with you two. You deserve this at the very least. I really do not know. You are very correct, without any limbs at all, you are facing a very grim lifetime here. You will have to live with others doing nearly everything for you and that is an awful way to live. We Santi believe in reciprocal help. You help me with something that you can do that I need, and I help you with something that you need."

"We have seen that with the others, you know, with Natale and Mireio, but we can't do anything except lay here," Itha replied.

Both women were still residing in their heads, so probably advanced Guardian training was out of the question. "Let's see what things you still can do. For one, you have sharp minds. Your reproductive system is intact, so you could bear children and raise a family. You have a voice, so perhaps you could sing or become a storyteller. I believe that I can find a way for you to be able to sit up like a normal person for a time. That would go a long way to end the ceaseless boredom of always lying down."

"Yes, but what man would want us as a wife? Tell us that. I always dreamed of having my own family and many children, but this way? I couldn't take care of any of them, and no man in his right mind would want us, now would they?" Moca said.

"Well, we were both promised and in love before we were taken, but that's been years now. I would imagine our boyfriends have found someone else by now. Yet, it would be nice if we could sit up, once in a while at least," Itha suggested. "Maybe we could sing, Moca; we used to sing to ourselves while we did chores."

Just then, Henry came knocking. "Am I interrupting? I've got a surprise for you two here."

"What?" asked Itha, so I motioned for him to come on in. Actually, Henry, Natale, and Emil came in carrying two special chairs.

"Ta da! We have fixed up two chairs especially for you two ladies. Soft cushions on the bottom, lots of padding. We put wheels on the legs so they can be moved around fairly easily." To me, Henry added, "We were a little bored so we decided to see if we could fix up something for these two ladies."

We gently lifted each and put them into their chairs. Henry had a strap that secured them to the back. He was right about the padding. "We are actually sitting up!" exclaimed Moca.

"Oh, this is wonderful! I feel like a human again! Thank you!" Itha said.

"Yes, thanks a hundred times! This means so much to us, to sit up," Moca added.

It was getting along towards suppertime, so I suggested that they wheel them into the dining room so that they could eat with the rest of us for the very first time. Besides, they could surprise everyone with their new chairs. Meanwhile, I went to find the King.

When everyone gathered for supper, they got a pleasant surprise. There were both women sitting up proudly in their new chairs; in this small way, they felt a part of their society once more. They received a round of clapping for being so brave and making this attempt to dine with us. Over the meal, King Matial announced that Itha and Moca were appointed to his Court Musicians as singers, if they so desired the position, which came with a substantial monetary stipend as well. After dinner, the musicians arrived and rolled their chairs into another room. It was try out time. I really wanted to go with them and see how it went, but I had to allow them to fend for themselves as much as possible. Instead, our two musicians entertained us.

Much later, the two women were wheeled back into the main room, beaming from ear to ear. The head musician stated, "King Matial, both women have excellent voices, and we are confident that they can learn our music. We accept them into our group." Everyone clapped and cheered, while the two young women just grinned.

The next morning, two young men arrived to see the king, who sent for me. "These are the two who were to marry Itha and Moca. Neither has taken a wife as yet. Perhaps you should hear their story before we continue."

Both men had scars on their faces. One said, "We tried to come earlier, but were turned away; they said only immediate relatives were allowed in."

"Yes, they were pretty traumatized at that time. Thank you for being patient," I replied.

He continued. "After they were taken, we tried to figure out ways to rescue them — to get them back. Twice we tried to sneak in to their temple. The last time, this is what we got for our attempts," he pointed to the two nasty scars on their faces. The priest told us that if we came back again, they would kill us. We had to obey, but we kept trying to figure out a way to get in there. We even tried to dig a tunnel underneath their temple, but it collapsed on us, and we had to give that idea up. We know that they probably will not want us anymore; our faces look awful. Everyone stares at us, but could we please see them, that is, if they still want to see us? Even if it's only for a minute, please, King Matial."

The King looked at me. "Do you know what their condition is like?" I asked.

"They said they have no arms or legs. How can that be without them being dead?"

The other man, who had been quiet up to this point, broke in, "Please, don't kill them as we do with pacas that have broken a leg. I know that you probably will put them out of their misery, and when you do, please do it to me as well. Then, Itha and I can be together at long last with the Sun God."

"Wait a second here, men. I have no such intention to put them out of their misery. For one, thing, Bethany's incredible therapy has gotten them out of their misery. They are like two happy birds at supper last night. I've appointed them to my Royal Musicians as singers. Let's not hear any more of this putting them out of their misery. But, yes, if it was not for Bethany, I would have done just that. Without her intervention, that would have been the kindest thing I could do for them. However, if they should come to me and ask that I do it, I will not hesitate. They deserve all that we can do for them."

"Please let us see them."

I went to check on them and see if they were ready for visitors. The King's staff had both women up and were putting them into their chairs as I entered. "Good morning you two. You look good today." I noticed that both had their hair combed nicely. "Are you up to having some visitors? Two are most anxious to have a visit with you, if you are ready."

"Sure, but who? The musician said we would begin practice just after lunch. It isn't that late already," Itha asked.

"Okay, I'll send them in. If you need anything, just holler, I'll be not far away."

"Yes, but who is it?" Moca asked. I didn't answer her, instead I motioned for the two men to enter, while I stepped out. This was a very private meeting. From my point of view, much hinged upon it.

"Citlali!"

"Tlaloc!"

I left them to themselves. While I was patiently waiting not far away, Emil came up to tell me that some of the runners had returned. In the three nearest city-states, the Black God was definitely not active. No one could remember when the last Chosen One had been abducted; it had been so many years ago. We took this as a very hopeful sign. However, the other two more distant city-states had yet to report in, we kept our fingers crossed. Emil stated the obvious, "Bethany, we cannot leave for home until we know for sure about those other two." I agreed.

An hour later, the two men wheeled their loves out of the room. "We are going to see the city a bit, kind of like a walk, if that is okay." All four looked extremely happy. I watched them heading outside and went to let the King know how things were progressing.

"I am so glad that I do not have to put them out of their misery. I have had to do it to a few paca's in my life, and even with them, it is so hard to do. But with women, oh, I would have had nightmares for the rest of my life, though I would have known it had to be done. Thank you once again, Bethany!"

Finally, I had free time to stroll the city! For the next two weeks, I visited shops and even purchased a number of instruments for Tal. I picked out a rather lot of paca clothing for everyone back home. Henry had also stocked up on a number of their domesticated animals, including their multi-colored chickens. Our rather empty cargo hold was filling up rapidly with our acquisitions.

Interestingly enough, one day the gold disks in my ears were very loose. Teyacapan giggled. "I told you they would. Now you need to insert the next size disks." She helped me do it, and once more, I liked the result. Once done, she said, "I've talked to dad about this, and he had given us permission. This afternoon, Teiuc and I have a very big surprise for you. It's a present. She wanted to thank you for all that you have done for us. Dad agreed with her idea. It's a surprise, but I know that you will love it. I hope you don't mind if Teiuc comes along with us. I know she goes awfully slowly, but this was her idea; she made it happen."

"Sure, I have all the free time in the world right now. This is a good time for shopping. You have so many interesting shops here in Wanakan. When you two are ready, come get me. But won't you give me a clue what the surprise is? Maybe a tiny clue?" She only giggled, saying that I would love them. Ah, now there were more than one! She had me wondering all morning long!

After lunch, the two young women, only a year older than myself now, came to get me. Teiuc was grinning with childish delight. "I have a big present for you, Bethany. I wanted to thank you on behalf of all of us. I hope you will like them."

"Thanks, but what are them?" I teased.

"Oh, you will see. Come on. I know I go slowly, but thanks to you and your dad, I can go! And that is something really important to me."

"I don't mind how slowly you go, Teiuc, only that you go. Besides, it is a pretty day, not too hot, and I love getting surprise presents, only I cannot figure out what it might be. Clue perhaps?"

She giggled, "Nope. You just have to wait." She waddled along, and Teyacapan and I strolled on either side of her. I could tell the Teiuc considered this to be incredibly important to her. Still, what could the surprise be?

"Here is the place," Teyacapan announced. Unfortunately, I discovered that I could not read their language, only speak it.

"What does the sign say?" I asked.

Both women giggled, but refused to answer. I opened the door, and the two walked in; I brought up the rear. Ah, ha! This was a jewelry store, rather the shop of a jewelry smith or gem cutter, I couldn't tell which. The man behind the workbench got up as we entered. "Ah, Teiuc, Teyacapan. You've come for them. And this must be the Bethany that we've heard so much about. I am Calan, the Royal Jeweler for the King. If you will have a seat, Teiuc, I will bring them out." She raised her arms so that Teyacapan could lift her up onto the chair. I took a seat beside Teyacapan. Had they made me a broach? A necklace? A pendant?

He came out with a tray that held a magnificent pair of earrings! These were so long that they would ride upon my breasts! Gold and highly polished jade intertwined. At the top of each was a pair of Jade jaguars, intertwined, which Teiuc explained represented love. From these descended seven gold and jade snakes, which represented the Seven Aspects of Life that I had so laboriously explained to them. "See, you carry and display your Seven Aspects with you now at all times!" Teiuc excitedly explained. "And they are three inches longer than the King's! He gave us permission to honor you! Never in our history has anyone had such a high honor! I do hope you like them!"

"Teiuc! They are magnificent, so beautiful, so gorgeous. The Seven Aspects, wow! This is the nicest surprise I have ever had! Thank you ever so much!" I gave her a big hug, and she, me.

"Come on; we've got to see them on you!" Teyacapan insisted. Carefully, she undid the fastenings on my earrings and put the new ones into my little gold ear disks. Yes, I noticed the weight difference at once. They dangled down and lay on my chest, a little above my breasts.

"Let's see!" Teiuc insisted, so I turned so she could see how they looked. "Wow! They look better than I imagined they would." I pivoted so Teyacapan could also get a good look. Then the Royal Jeweler pointed to a mirror, and I walked over to see for myself. They certainly were big, but exquisite, gorgeous. I beamed and thanked them repeatedly. At last, we left to head home.

I received an many comments on my new earrings when we got back. All the women just had to see them. Teiuc was very pleased indeed that her special gift was so well admired. She had found a way to thank me, as befitting the customs of her people. Now I had two fabulous sets of earrings!

Finally, December 10, 648, the Lucky Dog sailed up alongside the Sleepy Hollow. The first of our many trading voyages to Wanakan had arrived. The King was ecstatic about all the cargo, delivered just as he had ordered. Natale gave its captain, James Dog, yes he named his ship after himself, two copies of her dictionary and drilled him and his bosun in how to use it.

It took a week to unload and load all the incoming and outgoing cargo. Interestingly enough, they brought two other passengers along with them, the two that we had not thought about: a pair of artists! Isabella, the Chairwoman of the Laird Foundation, had sent along Tom and Luciana Whitehall. She was one of the armless women whom I had helped and later had helped regain her ability to do art, following the guidelines relayed to me from Zargarb.

Teyacapan, Teiuc, and I met them as they landed. "Wow! Wow! And oh wow!" exclaimed Luciana as she saw us and the incredible city. "This city is so beautiful!" I quickly translated for my two companions, who smiled, proud of their city. Then, she saw their earrings and mine. "Oh my, those are just fabulous earrings! Does everyone wear them?" After translating, Teiuc really broke into a smile. I explained their use and function here. Finally, we hugged a warm welcome. Tom shook hands with everyone, including Teiuc's arm. I explained to Teiuc that men always shook our hands and she grinned even more broadly, placing her other arm over his hand adding to the shake. A good sign I thought; she was adapting well.

Luciana explained that they had worked out a system for their art. She would do the rough sketches, and he would then lay down the oils. This way, they were sure to capture the closest approximation to the reality of this beautiful new city. Natale gave them a pair of copies of her dictionary as well. They would need it. Additionally, four Santi, one was a Communicator, would stay here with them. Jenna had though ahead once again, good old mom!

When Luciana saw Natale's earrings and Mireio's too, she just had to get some like theirs as well. Once more, Teyacapan was very eager to assist, and that very night Luciana was sporting the little gold disks with the magnificent long earrings, similar to those of Natale and Mireio.

During this time, the last runners arrived with word that no other

Holy Touched Maidens were being made. It seemed that the Black God was only operating here in Wanakan. Hence, we began to arrange for our return trip home.

Eight of the women decided to accept our offer for training. Teyacapan, of course, accompanied Teiuc. They simply could not be parted, so strong was their bond now. Cazamel, Xilonen, and Iacotl came as well; all hoped that somehow they could learn how to survive better with only half arms and half legs. In addition, the four armless women, having seen how much Mireio and Natale could do, insisted on coming as well: Chica, Meloa, Malotl, and Mecoa. However, we had yet another surprise.

Three young men came to see the King, who in turn called for me. "Bethany, these are Yaotl, Zolin, and Matlali. They are the betrothed of Chica, Mecoa, and Matlali, respectively. They are insisting that they be allowed to accompany their fiancés to your land. If you will permit them, I would like to send them along to learn of your country and ways. They will be the sworn protectors of my daughter and the eight other women."

"Sure, they are welcome to come and learn all that they desire. Besides, I think that Chica, Mecoa, and Matlali will really love to have them along! I know I wouldn't want to be separated from my fiancé, if I could avoid it." All three men bowed to me and thanked me profusely, which I didn't particularly like, but accepted their thanks.

Henry and I went over what all the men should bring with them, as well as our women travelers. He made sure that everything got aboard just fine. Once more, I had not thought far enough ahead. We were now running very low on food for the return trip. Good old mom had not. She'd sent along another batch of supplies, sufficient for two more months of sailing, more than enough to get us all home. So finally, we set sail for home on December 14.

Chapter 5 Home Again

New cabin arrangements were made, dictated by the four with short legs. They needed to stay in the cabins in the cargo hold so that they could walk around the hold and get to the table. Four men vacated their cabins, taking over two of the Santi crew cabins, who moved below deck into the cargo hold. The other Guardians also moved below decks, giving us another two cabins. We then split up so that each woman was paired with one of us with hands.

Natale and I still bunked together. Now Rosina bunked with Cazamel; Linda, with Xilonen; Tonia, with Iacotl. Of course, Teyacapan stayed with Teiuc. The armless women were paired up as well, with Cathy bunking with Chica; Angel, with Meloa; Mary Beth, with Malotl. I asked one of the Santi fighters, Jenny, to bunk with Mecoa. Thus, I was assured that someone would be watching out for each of our guests.

All of us were on deck as we set sail, waving goodbye to everyone on shore. Captain Henry was most concerned about the safety of the women without feet. While they could manage to walk on land, on a moving, rolling ship, they would have an awful time. Further, if anything went wrong, they had no hands to grab a hold of something. He insisted that they have a lifeline tied to their waists while on deck. I complied, but there was no way I was going to have these women miss the spectacular view of the ship departing. After all, ahead lay weeks of open sea.

A few hours later, we were far out at sea. Tea and herbs were dispensed. Cathy wanted no seasickness aboard her ship. Then, it was down to business. During our long voyage home, Natale insisted that our guests learn the Sea Prince dialect so that when we arrived they could understand what was being said. Plus, the never ending chores were doled out again. However, this time, I had more assistance on the dish washing duty.

On the way back, while the others were getting language lessons, I spent time with Benet and Emil, working half a day with each one. In the mornings, I drilled Benet on what he had always suspected he could do. He had a knack for sensing weather conditions, but he wanted to be able to move far away from his body and sense there. His reasoning went like this. "If I am to be a good Loremaster and am leading a party, I need to be able to move out many miles ahead and know what the weather that we are heading into is going to be like. Here at sea, if I could go off that way for say a hundred miles and check on the weather there, I could come back and steer us around squalls, blows, or even typhoons. This is typhoon season in these southern waters, Bethany. Just ask Henry if it isn't."

First, we drilled on moving away short distances and slowly increased the amount. This he caught onto extremely well. It was just a matter of drill and practice, especially with someone there to coach him along. Only when I then added the command to detect the weather there did we run into a barrier. A deep blue mass came in on him. Therapy time once again.

I'll spare you the lengthy details and summarize what had happened to him. Several hundred years ago, as a Sea Prince mariner from Velona and captain of his own ship, he had this very skill. He had run into a storm and had moved out in several directions trying to find the optimum route out of it, when he ran smack into the Grey Creature's flying boat craft. He'd been zapped by their energy beams and sent off to get a new body. His captain's body was found dead at the helm. The conclusion he reached at that time was that you would be killed if you did this. Once that was blown, he began picking up the weather at a distance quite easily.

Emil, our Protector, having seen the incredible value in being able to move heavy objects without needing a body, was determined to learn how to do this. However, I found that on his part, this was wishful thinking at this time. Try as he might, he could not move a dust mote! Worse still, from my point of view, no mental barriers appeared that we might eradicate so that he could regain that skill. At last, I had to tell him that he would need to journey to the Red Desert and train with the Guardian of the Anuir, Jes Amir, to learn how to do this one.

However, in working with him, I did discover something of interest. He had some suppressed instincts that would tell him what an opponent would do next, rather like reading a mind. Instead, I began working him on improving this skill. With a Protector, this was doubly difficult because they are highly trained to spot the tiny muscle motions that precede a major movement. I had to be very tricky. I got my body ready to launch a specific attack, such as poking him in the ribs. Just as I began to execute it, I swung my hand to hit him in his head. His fighter training picked up on the motion towards his ribs, but his instinct told him his head was the actual target.

After the first few times, I saw that he was ignoring his instinct and going with his fighter training. Now I worked him on going with what he actually sensed in his opponent. We began to make real headway. Then he started complaining, "Bethany, I just cannot trust my instincts." Had he said it once, I would have ignored it, but every time I got by his defenses, he said it.

About the tenth time he used that line on me, I asked him, "Okay, Emil, where is that coming from? Do you see a mental image or something from which this might be coming?"

He yawned and I knew I had it. "I see something, probably just nothing." I began therapy on him. Sure enough, two hundred years ago, he had been in a major battle with a Grey Creature! He was a druwid Protector then and had run into one of these creatures while hiking in the Appian Way. He had launched an attack at it, after it had attempted to blast him with its energy weapon. For a time, he had actually been very successful at dodging its strikes and energy weapons. He had even cut its legs twice! Of course, the creature was nearly twelve feet tall; its legs were about all he could reach with his sword. Emil was being successful solely because he went with his instinct. The creature did not use any of the usual fighter patterns in which he had been trained, so he had no choice but to trust his instincts.

Just when he thought he might defeat this strange creature and bring back news of its existence to Alabaster, who was the druwid leader at that time, an energy blast took off his head. He had decided right there that he could not trust his instincts. However, as we ran through this trauma the sixth time, he suddenly realized that the shot came from another Grey Creature, who had appeared behind him. His intuition was not faulty after all! Once he spotted this, the whole thing blew off. Now no matter what I or anyone else attempted, Emil was right there countering it. None of us could get through his defenses. He was one very pleased Protector!

Three weeks out, Benet proved his worth. He detected that a typhoon was headed our way. Henry followed his suggested course, and we only had a big blow from it, nothing serious. However, Natale and I rode it out on deck with the bosun and Henry. Below, the others kept our guests calm, while the boat pitched and rocked violently. They had their hands full with that chore. Of course, the eight women were most impressed with Natale, who had been topside through it all. Cathy explained to them what Natale had done on our last voyage, so they were doubly impressed, which I though was a very good sign. If Natale could do things, so could they, perhaps.

Another small event perked the eight women's interest as well. One day they heard a beautiful duet, guitar and lute, coming from the cabin of Roberto and Mireio. Chica decided to ask them about it, after seeing only those two coming out of the cabin later on. "Excuse me, Mireio, but we all thought we heard two different stringed instruments playing. Can Roberto play two at one time?"

Mireio's face flushed; she had been caught in the act. "No, you heard us. Roberto plays the guitar, and I play the lute."

Chica said, "But you can't play the lute. You have no arms like me. It is not possible. You are teasing me, no?"

"Honey, I think you are going to have to demonstrate this one," Roberto nudged her and went to fetch the lute.

"I can't carry it, no arms, but Bethany has taught me how to play it. I'll show you when he brings it back." A minute later, Roberto returned, lute in hand. He sat it on the deck, and she sat down and leaned against the side of the hull, holding the lute steady with her feet.

"Not much to see, really, but here goes." She closed her eyes and moved over the strings. The sweet sounds of the melody they had heard before coming from their cabin echoed here in the cargo hold.

The eight women and their three protectors looked dumbfounded, and some even gaped. When she finished, Mireio said, "Bethany taught me how to do this while we were sailing towards your land. Perhaps she or another will be able to teach you how to do things like this." If Chica was convinced she needed to go with us before, now she was utterly convinced! Mireio had to answer many questions for the next hour. Plus, she ended up promising that she and Roberto would play for everyone after dinners.

The next weeks I spent working with Tonia and Cedric. His sessions were easy. When I asked him, he explained that he always had the sense that he ought to be able to pervade into a solid object and sense it structure and any weaknesses it might have. "Like this boat, sometimes when I am lying in bed, I think I can almost feel into the hull and sense where the wood has weakened, where it needs to be replaced. Do you think that is possible?" Off we went, again, I found out that it was just a matter of drill. We began by working with a small piece of rotted wood that we found lying around in the bilge. After three weeks of this, he had become quite good at it. No traumas appeared. However, there were so many more possibilities on land that we agreed to continue this sometime when we were on shore.

Tonia, on the other hand, was more difficult. She felt that as a Healer, she ought to be able to sense what was wrong with someone internally, when she could not see inside them with her eyes, or when they were unconscious and could not answer her questions. "Like when mom was attacked by the Holy Paladin assassins and was stabbed. She was unconscious. I thought I should still be able somehow to see inside her body so I would know what needed to be fixed. Thank goodness she was taken to Jenna's and got good care."

Now I had really gone and done it! We were all quite healthy; I was dooming myself to be stuck in an infirmary when we landed! Instead of having a good time, I'd have to help her with lots of sick people until she worked all this out.

"Well, let's go around to everybody and see if we can get this skill going," I offered. I knew she was about to say that everyone was well. "Come on; let's give it a try. You can start with me. I want you to sort of pervade into my body and see if anything is wrong with it. You can do it."

I caught her straining with her body and got that corrected. This was a purely spiritual action; nothing involved the use of her body in any way. Soon, I could detect her presence looking in at my stomach. "I can't! I can't! I'll be killed! I can't!" she shrieked, startling even me! I had her sit down and lean against the poop deck walls, and we began therapy at once.

Two hundred years ago, Tonia had been a Healer with Alabaster, shortly after he had begun the druwids. She was a darn good healer because she natively could sense what was precisely wrong with someone's body and then work to correct it. One day while out in the field at a small village, she came across a man lying in a field. She stopped to render assistance. He seemed unconscious, so she had used her pervading ability. Only she detected an alien body! It was a Grey Creature using its ability to disguise itself as a human! The creature was on his way back to the Appian Way when he became tired and lay down for a nap, then she came along. Naturally, she was killed, because the Grey Creatures were keeping their presence here on Tarra a total secret. Her conclusion was the obvious one: if she actually used her skill, she would be killed. It made perfect sense at that time, but not now. She roared with laughter as her decision sprang into view and evaporated.

Now we went from person to person, and Tonia had no difficulty pervading their bodies and sensing their state of health. When she got to Mireio, she said, "Oh. Mireio! I didn't know. You are pregnant! Why didn't you tell us? When is it due?"

"What? I'm not, am I? I mean I'm not due for a week yet on the bloodletting. How can you tell so soon? I'm going to have a baby? Wow! Fantastic! Thanks Tonia! I have to go tell Roberto! We're going to have our family at last!" She was elated and so was Roberto when he found out. Tonia smiled, confident she had recovered her long lost skills as a Healer.

It took us six weeks to sail across the wide ocean. In the evenings after supper, as usual, I missed my kick ball games. However, the first evening when I went on deck after eating, Renzo got me good. Out of nowhere, he appeared, tickling my sides. "Gotcha, Bethany! You can't get me!" Our tickle game was on again! Chasing him around the deck, I suddenly realized just how much I missed our little game while we were on land in Wanakan. We dashed about the main deck, my earrings flying about wildly, until we were out of breath. At last, we stood at the edge, leaning on the deck railing as we used to do. He slid his arm around my waist and under my hair. I leaned my head on his shoulder.

I whispered, "Thanks Renzo. I really do enjoy our playful romps. No matter what happens, I always seem to have pure fun when I'm around you. Thanks." He kissed my forehead, and I put my arm around him too.

He whispered, "You are also the fun-est person I've ever met, Bethany. I've never met a girl quite like you before. Can we play your kick ball game when we get to your estate? I mean they won't think we are being childish or anything will they?"

"Heck no. Mom always devotes each evening to playing kick ball with anyone who wants to play. Usually, it's the children, but sometimes many adults join in. I once remember having a massive kick ball game. All the armless women ganged up on little old me. I must have been seven or eight. They were all laughing and getting me good. You are on, Renzo."

He teased me, "So what do I get if I win, if I beat you?"

I teased him back, "A kiss. I'll give you a real kiss. How's that?" He squeezed my waist, and I, his.

On January 28, 649, the cry we all were waiting for came at last, "Land ho!" Ahead lay the huge harbor of Velona. It was the middle of winter, yet still a dozen ships were docked, either loading or unloading, another one was tacking out towards us. Quickly, we got everyone on deck to watch the tremendous sight. Our guests were impressed with all the large caravels, but I had to explain that another hundred or more were off sailing to other places.

As the land slowly drew closer, I went up to Henry. "Thank you, Henry. Your new navigational equipment and skills are perfect. You sailed us directly home. That in itself is an impressive feat! Well done indeed." Natale, who was standing beside him, smiled.

"Yes, it is pretty impressive. Ten years ago, this would not have been remotely possible — to sail directly across empty ocean for six weeks without becoming totally and completely lost!" After a pause, he asked, "Do you suppose that your mother or Elona Po could marry us right away? Natale and I want to get married first thing, so we can have time together before we set sail again."

"Congratulations you two!" I hugged them both. "I'm sure that I can get Elona to do it. Like today even?" I teased.

"Well, tomorrow at the latest," Natale giggled. "We want some time when neither of us have obligations to fulfill — you know private time." He flushed slightly, holding her tightly with one arm while holding the helm with his other.

"I'll see to it. Big wedding or small one? Lots of us would like to get you presents and maybe throw you a party. We need some time to buy things."

"Can we keep it to just the Explorer's Circle, for the ceremony, that is? You can always throw us a party afterwards, maybe next week," Natale suggested. After a pause, she added, "Will you be willing to be my maid of honor? The bosun will be his best man. I'll wear my fancy dress. You can too, if you like. Please?"

"You don't have to ask twice! You got it. I'll see when we can schedule a big wedding bash, but I'll see if Elona can do it tomorrow and let you know. Congratulations!" They smiled and thanked me.

Of course, I just had to go tell Linda, and we just had to tell all the others about this! Ten minutes later, the whole ship knew about their wedding plans! The two were besieged with well wishes, so much so that he had to order us all to stand down so he could dock the boat!

Once we docked, I saw mom, Hank, Lilly Ann, Beth Ann, and all the others standing waiting for us. Even Bard Tal and his ever-growing group were there. I spied Elona Po and her bunch waiting for us. Also, there were a lot of coaches lined up as well to take us all to the estate.

Once the gangplank was lowered, Bard Tal struck up a lively tune, welcoming us all home from our record setting voyage. Our guests were quite surprised at the reception they were receiving as well. They and we women were still wearing our Wanakan super soft clothing, so we were quite a sight as we disembarked. Henry stayed behind and to see to the unloading of our precious cargo and bring it all to the estate later today.

We carried the four with the short legs down the gangplank, but they insisted on walking, waddling to be more accurate, alongside of us. Teyacapan and Teiuc were chatting about everything. All this was very new to them, as it had been for us when we first found their land. Fortunately, Tal stopped when we drew close to Elona. It was her position to speak to us first.

She spoke slowly and clearly, trying to use simple words so that our guests could understand her. "I am Elona Po, the ruler of Velona. On behalf of all our people, let me be the first to welcome our honored guests from the new land of Wanakan!" The large crowd cheered and clapped. Angus played a little drum roll for emphasis. "You are welcome to stay here as long as you desire. If there is ever anything that you need, simply let me know." Next, she looked at us, "And a mighty fine welcome to the Explorers Circle. Today is an historic day, you have proven our caravels can sail across the vast ocean, and you have discovered a completely new land full of wonderful people! Please accept my most heartfelt thanks for a job more than well done! Now, I know you want to greet your families, so get on with it!"

That was the signal for us to continue forward to where mom was. I rushed to her and dad and gave them both a big hug. I didn't care that it might seem childish to me. I had missed them both. The others came up and now I began the long introductions. Gang, this is my mom and dad. Jenna Rose Weston, the Supreme Commander of the entire Santi del Dio. Hank Weston."

To our surprise, Teiuc waddled up to dad and put her arms around him. "Thank you for helping us. These booties do work. We can now walk!"

He took her arm firmly, bent down closer to her head and said, "Teiuc, you are more than welcome. I am glad that this little invention works so well for you. While you are here, I'll see what else I can invent to make your life easier." He gave her a kiss on her forehead; she blushed.

Once all the introductions were done, we all got into the many coaches. I sat with mom, dad, Lilly Ann, and Beth Ann. Roberto and Mireio were also with us. They all had to feel our dresses! "My but you have all gone native," mom teased. "I bet those earrings are heavy!"

"Yes, but among the Acalan people, they use the length of the earrings much like we use our uniforms and tunics, to tell who is who. Boy do we ever have stories to tell all of you!"

When we got to the estate, our guests were even more impressed. They had never seen horses before, but the sheer size of the manor house was staggering to them. The twin palaces of the Laird Foundation took their breath way. However, when we all entered the manor house and they saw the countless foundation women who were just like them, they were nearly speechless. Now they knew that real hope lay ahead of them, that their lives could not help but become far better than they had ever dreamed would be possible.

As usual, once we were all inside, Jenna gave her usual speech, telling our guests that none of the doors anywhere on the estate had knobs, that they only needed to push to open a door. However, if they wanted their privacy, they could move a sliding bar with their feet or arms. The first action was for all of us women to change into something warmer. It was the middle of winter here and our Wanakan dresses were made more for summer. Each woman got several sets of warm clothing, sized properly for their situation. All had rooms here on the first floor. Jenna arranged for three to be in each room, two guests, and one of the foundation women. She figured that with so much in common, the women would bond rapidly.

While everyone was scampering about getting settled in, I asked Paulette, mom's Communicator, if she would contact Elona Po about marrying Henry and Natale. Shortly after that, Paulette replied, "Elona is very excited about their getting married. She said she would love to do it. Just let her know when they want to do it and to come by her Rose Cathedral."

It was controlled chaos those first few days back. After changing into winter clothes, our guests were taken on a complete tour of the twin palaces of the Laird Foundation by Isabel herself. One by one, they were introduce to the directors, none of which had any arms, a fact not missed by our guests. Then, the large number of artists in residence were introduced, as they toured each section of the foundation. This way, the guests were somewhat able to relate the person to the type of art they did. Now they also saw many normal folks, that is to say ones with arms.

While they were off touring, Henry arrived with our many

packages. It was presents time all around. Everyone loved what they got. However, Bard Tal and his group were stunned with all the musical instruments I had brought back for them. "You need to ask our guests and Mireio and Roberto how they are played, and they have a whole stack of songs for you to try out! She has an incredible memory for tunes, and his system somehow puts music onto paper. If I have time, I am going to try to learn how to read them myself." He just gave me a bear hug and swung me around in little circles. I had made his year!

He then said, "Bethany, do you realize that you are wearing at least twenty thousand gold pieces worth of earrings there? Those are absolutely breath taking!" I grinned and said that I did and that I had a slightly smaller pair as well. He just shook his head in disbelief. He teased me, "Gang, we send off little Bethany here to go sailing and what does she do? Why she comes back fabulously wealthy and even discovering entirely new lands!" Everyone laughed.

Later at supper, I noticed that all the high chairs for the armless women now had sloped backs. Hank explained that he discovered that this gave them more support and made it a whole lot easier for them to manage. It was fun seeing so many people gathered around the huge table for dinner once again. Natale and Mireio had been working with four of our guests and everyone was very surprised and pleased to see how well Chica, Meloa, Malotl, and Mecoa had adapted. They had only a little trouble handling their mugs. At least the other four could handle their mugs, but that was about all.

When the feast was done, Jenna stood up to speak. "After dinner is when I usually take all the children outside for a kick ball game. However, tonight, we are forgoing that. Instead, Bard Tal and his band of musicians, singers, and dancers wish to give you and our guests a sample of their song and dance. If you feel so inclined, they wish you to dance to your heart's content as well. Kids, kick ball resumes tomorrow night!" The many children laughed and giggled.

We adjourned to the huge sitting room, where Tal had everything set up. Our guests had front row seats and the show began. I sat not too far behind our guests in case they needed anything. Renzo sat with me. Indeed their performance had grown in stature beyond anything I had ever seen. The interpretive dances done by so many armless women enthralled our guests, but the Greenway jumping dances, in which all the dancer's arms were entirely motionless at their sides if they even had them, especially excited our guests. They had never seen anything like this at all.

After an hour, Bard Tal announced, "And now it's slow dance time. We invite you to grab your partner and enjoy the next half hour." Now they did play slow tunes, Renzo took my arm and we began to dance. He smiled at me and I put my head on his shoulder. It felt so wonderful to just relax and dance, without any cares in the world. A bit later, I saw other fellows, art students I suspected, dragging the four women on to the floor, showing them how it was done. They had been observing the other women and were quick to catch on.

What surprised me the most was dad. Hank walked up to Teiuc and said, "May I have this dance, Teiuc?"

She was shocked. "But, but I don't have any legs. How?"

"Ah, like this." He got down on his knees and was magically at her height. "Now put your arms around me like so. Yes, and I put mine like so. I know this is not exactly like they are doing it, but let's give it a try, shall we?" With dad supporting her and helping her maintain her balance, she was able to move about, imitating the others. The grin on her face told all. Soon, several other art students followed dad's lead, in fact one even cut in on him.

Renzo and I danced over to him. "Way to go dad!"

"Kind of hard on an old man's knees," he smiled. "But sometimes we got to teach you youngsters a thing or two." Mom just whisked him away after that.

A little later, Tal announced, "Okay last dance of the night. Jenna wants all you children in bed shortly. Dim the lights please; here is a really slow one." He actually meant a romantic one. I knew what he intended!

The lights were dimmed, and we all enjoyed this last one. When it was done, Renzo leaned over and gave me a loving kiss on my lips! I felt chills and tingles I didn't know I could feel. I responded back with another of my own. "Thanks for a wonderful evening, Bethany." I couldn't think of anything to say back. I was tingling all over, wishing I was like Beth Ann, who would know just the right thing to say to Renzo.

I mumbled, "Thanks, that was really fun for me too." Then came the helter-skelter dispersal, with everyone heading for their rooms. I made sure that our guests all made it to their rooms.

Teyacapan and Teiuc came along near the rear; both looked radiant. "You never told us that your place was this incredible!" Teyacapan exclaimed.

"I can dance even!" added Teiuc. "Well sort of anyway. What fun! Do you do this often?"

"We have public dances, with thousands of people, at least twice a week around here. We young folks love to go to the dances. You can see why. You two sure have attracted the attention of a lot of young men tonight!" Both giggled. I made sure that they were okay in their room. Chelo, the Director of Dance, was staying here with them.

She said, "Okay Bethany. These two are in my capable feet now. You can go to bed." Both guests laughed at her joke. Chelo ushered them inside and chatted away. Yes, these two were in good feet; I chuckled all the way to my room. I plopped on my old bed. I had forgotten how soft it was. After a time, I couldn't sleep, so when all was quiet, I stole out to the panty to grab a snack.

Mom was there waiting for me, hot cocoa and biscuit at hand. "Wondered how long it would take you to wander in here, Bethany," she teased me. "You know you have opened up vast new doors on Tarra?"

"Yes, but we forgot to bring along artists who could bring back paintings of what it was like there. It is so very different, yet so incredibly beautiful in their own way. So many different customs, though, takes a bit of getting use to I discovered." We hugged long and then I drank my treat. Finally, I was tired enough to sleep.

In the mornings as usual, Jenna held her Santi meetings with her Circle. I attended so that I could give them a full report and get an update on how things were going around here. First, mom gave me a short briefing. Around this area, all had been quiet, which, while greatly appreciated, left us wondering why. Not much news. I then related what I considered the most urgent.

"Before I launch into a detailed report on Wanakan, I want to tell you what I have found out that may be vastly more crucial. During the long voyages, I experimented on many of my Circle. I was interested in seeing if, by means of Jenna's therapy, some of their native spiritual abilities might be regained. I am pleased to report it had been a smashing success."

"Renzo and Rosina are able to move out of their bodies and travel nearly anywhere they desire and are able to launch our druwid spells while at that distant location. Linda is now able to control other's thoughts as well as their bodies, much like Jovanna, but also she picks up their thoughts, rather like reading their minds. Benet is able to move off to far distances and see what the weather is like there. Emil is able to intuitively know where another's next attack is aimed and so counter it. Tonia is able to pervade bodies and know what is wrong inside them. Cedric can pervade objects and tell the nature of structural weaknesses. Natale can hold objects still, can throw up a resistance field against incoming forces, and even has begun to move objects." I received quite a lot of comments and questions about all this; I expected that I would.

"What I found fairly uniformly among our people is that they all had nasty encounters with the Grey Creatures in their past lives. These encounters, which had not been known before, put a stopper on these skills. It literally caused them to shut down using these skills."

"In Wanakan, actually all of Acalan really, the giant mantises reigned. A religious cult called them the Black Gods. I now know a whole lot more about these creatures. Unlike the Grey Creatures, which use some kind of technology with their energy blasters, the mantis creatures have glands behind their multi-faceted eyes, which shoot out energy blasts. This makes them more dangerous because they have a native weapon. Apparently, when Alabaster and I got them to destroy themselves some twenty-six years ago, all the mantis creatures in Acalan went off to the battle and died. For a quarter century, this Black God cult there was dormant. However, recently, the priests in Wanakan discovered a clutch of mantis eggs and succeeded in hatching five new mantis creatures. When we ran into them, they were only about six feet long, not fifty — babies would be my guess. Even so, they are terribly difficult to defeat. I killed them by squashing their heads with a large stone from the temple walls."

"These mantis creatures consider dining upon human arms, legs, and fingers a great delicacy! Hence, the condition of those I brought back with us. However, in running out their traumas, I discovered that many had been similarly victimized hundreds of years ago by these creatures or had been part of that priesthood."

"Conclusions. Okay, it has become abundantly clear to me that such traumas in one lifetime come back to harm us in the next lifetime, either decreasing our abilities or enforcing certain behavior patterns on us. Secondly, I believe that the origin of we in the north having lost so many of our natural spiritual skills lay at the hands of trauma delivered by the Grey Creatures, who were manipulating the people up north. Similarly, the mantis creatures and their habits are very likely behind this rash of armless-handless women victimizing that we have been seeing over the years. My guess is that this is the real reason why the Megalos Church of Jehosanity has been so keen on the removal of women's appendages. They are simply acting out the mantis obsession in which they have been somehow been involved."

Lilly Ann commented, "Well finally all this stuff makes some intelligible sense! Megalos is in the south where they mantis creatures lived. It makes sense."

"Yes, but two major questions arise immediately. Are there any Grey Creatures left roaming around up here in the north? Are more of the mantis creatures still alive in the south? And are there more of these undiscovered mantis egg nests? Personally, I am concerned about these last two points. If these creatures still exist, humanity is in big trouble."

Jenna decided, "Well, Bethany, we can send out many scouts into the Appian Way. It is winter and if any of these Grey Creatures are still around the mountains, they surely would leave tell-tale three toes foot prints. Let us check on the Grey Creatures. Perhaps on the next explorer voyage, you could search the southern portion of the ocean, say between Acalan and the Spice Islands. If there are other landmasses between there, surely the mantis creatures would have been there." I agreed with her. Then, I proceeded to relate the whole adventure that we had.

Just after lunch, my Circle began to get dressed up for Henry and

Natale's wedding. Mom had found me a new white silk dress that fit me very tightly, showing off my ever-increasing curves. She had a hunch about Natale and had taken the initiative, mostly because she now had so many seamstresses living here at the estate. The white dress billowed out at my waist and had a very low, scooped neckline, so I decided that I could also wear my new necklace from Teyacapan.

Teyacapan and Teiuc had followed me into my room to help me change, asking many questions about Natale's wedding. I explained that they wanted the ceremony to be very small and private, but that in a week or so, we would throw them a really big wedding party. I appreciated Teyacapan's assistance in getting into this new tight fitting dress. I could not manage the back buttons by myself. She also insisted on brushing out my hair and adjusting my gorgeous necklace. When I was all set, I planned to go aid Natale. But I had Teyacapan here with me and something had aroused my curiosity, Renzo's passionate kiss last night. I didn't know the right words in her language and dared not bother Natale. Oh, if I only had Beth Ann's knowledge about such things. "Teyacapan, there is one thing that I have been wondering about these magnificent earrings. Do you take them off when you, I mean, when you are married and you are going to, ah, well, go to bed with your husband and, ah, well, you know, kiss and all that goes with it?"

She and Teiuc both giggled at my embarrassment. "No silly. You almost never take them off, especially when you are in bed with your man! They can touch his body, and it drives our men back home wild with excitement, though neither of us has firsthand knowledge of this just yet. Our mothers have explained all this to us, though."

"Thanks. I'll let Natale know too."

"Besides, Bethany, they are almost impossible for you to take off by yourself, if you hadn't noticed. We always help each other with that when we need to put in a bigger disk and such." That was true, I had observed already. Then, we three headed off to assist Natale, I was her bridesmaid and this was my task.

"Oh look at what Jenna has given me!" exclaimed Natale when we three walked into her room. She had laid out a new white silk dress, similar to my new one, only hers had no armholes, and her bottom puffed out about twice the distance that mine did. "Oh, you have a new one too, quite like mine! How did your mother know about this?"

"Sometimes mom is way ahead of the rest of us! Come on, let's get it on you, and see how you look in it. You will be able to wear your fancy necklace too." A half hour later, I had her all dressed in her new gown. "Natale, you are a knock out in this dress! You are going to drive Henry wild, out of his mind! Wow!" She blushed.

While Teyacapan brushed out her very long hair, I fiddled with her heavy necklace, which was similar to mine. She and I discovered that she could wear both the one from Teyacapan and the Santi pendant that Henry had given her. I shortened the chain of Henry's gift so that it rode high on her neck above the fan shaped jade and gold necklace of Teyacapan's. At last, we three were satisfied with Natale's looks. "Go take a look in the mirror," I suggested.

Natale did so and began crying. "I do look so beautiful! I didn't realize that I looked so good. Thank you three!" She was incredibly happy! Now we were ready to go. As we walked out, our other guests had come by to see her and wish her well. Uniformly, these women from Acalan were astounded to see how gorgeous Natale looked.

Natale could not resist explaining a bit to the four women who were like her. She had taken them under her wing, so to speak for the last six weeks. "You see, when I get all dressed up like this, with the tight fitting dress that shows my body's form, these underclothes and shoes that tie, I am now nearly helpless. I can't feed myself or even go to the bathroom. I am dependent rather completely on others when I dress up like this. When I do dress up like this, I am knowingly making my Henry look after me. Instead of looking at it as if I am now helpless, I look at is as now I am controlling Henry, making him look after me. Kind of sexy, I think."

Chica giggled, "I see, make your lover really desire you. I get it. Can you help me look like you do sometime? I want to surprise Yaotl!"

"Me too," put in Mecoa. "It'll drive Zolin mad!" She giggled.

"You got it. We'll do it for the next dance!"

"Hey, time to go. Carriages are here, Natale," I interrupted. "Now we must make sure that Henry doesn't get a peek at you until the ceremony! Come on." We headed out to the carriage and the other women of our Circle joined us. We filled two carriages. After we left, the men came out and filled another two carriages.

At the Rose Cathedral, Elona met us. She ushered Natale and me into her side room, while the others went into the chapel, sitting in the front row of the pews. Elona looked Natale over and said, "My, oh my, Natale! You look fabulous! You are going to drive Henry mad with your looks today! You are one of the prettiest brides that I've married."

"Thanks," she blushed. "I'm so nervous!"

"Don't worry. I've never known a bride who wasn't nervous on her wedding day! Here's how it will go." Elona explained what was about to happen. We waited patiently until the chimes sounded. Elona walked in front of us. I put my arm around Natale, and we followed her into the massive cathedral. Henry stood before the altar, with bosun Thad at his side, the best man. Henry wore a new white silk suit. I'd never seen him look so good.

When I moved Natale beside him and stepped back, his mouth opened involuntarily. "God, you look beautiful!" he exclaimed. She blushed. Elona Po then conducted the ceremony. Henry had gotten a simple golden ring for her, inscribed with their names. Carefully, he put it on a chain and fastened it around her neck, allowing it to join her other prized jewelry. I cried a little when they kissed; they looked so happy!

When it was over, we all went up and congratulated the loving couple. Shortly after that, Henry whisked his bride out of the church and into a waiting carriage. They had private plans for the next few days at least.

Renzo came to my side, "Bethany, you look fabulous today!"

"Hey, so do you. New suit?"

"Yes, Jenna had it made. Rosina has a new dress too. Your mom thinks of absolutely everything! Say, would you care to take a walk about town with me for a while? I have brought us each a jacket, hoping you would say yes."

"Well, I am all dressed up. It seems a shame to go home and undress after so short a time. I'm really glad that you asked me." I blushed when I said that last.

He helped me slip into a new white jacket; my tight dress made it more difficult for me to move my arms. "Thanks."

"Hair out or hair under?" he asked, adding, "My, this dress feels so good! I could run my hands over this all day!"

"Out please," I discovered that in this form-fitting dress, I could not easily reach up to flair my own hair out. He gently did it for me. I don't know why I said what I said next, but I said, "Sometime I would really like you to run your hands all over it." I blushed, and wondered what I was doing!

He blushed too, so I didn't feel so bad. He slipped on his new black jacket, took my hand, and we left the cathedral. We walked the streets for a while, neither saying much. I was still wondering why I had said what I had said. Renzo said, "I'm actually taking you some place special, at least I think that it's special, maybe for you and me. You like kick ball, right?"

I squeezed his hand in a tease. "Of course, silly. I've grown up with it nearly every day of my life. Honestly, Renzo, I just love playing games and having fun; you know, discard all responsibilities for a short time; go out and just play and have fun."

He blushed and said, "I know, Bethany. I have, er, been watching you. I know that you think of me as a Protector and all that. Yes, I have been trying all my life to live up to the legends of both my parents. That's a tall order, you know. Lenkova and Andre are absolute legends in Zargarb. I've worked so hard at everything, but really, Bethany, I always just longed to forget it all and just play for a while. I couldn't do it while I was growing up. Now that I'm mostly on my own, I have been taking time to just play and have fun, even if it's only for an hour or so."

"I'm sorry, Renzo. I hadn't thought about what it must have been like to be around your parents. I know them both; they are terrific people. How awful that you never got to just play!"

"Then, I came across you and your mother. Anyway, I have a surprise for you. I found just the place for us to come and play, even if only for an hour."

Now my curiosity was really pricked. "Whatever do you mean? What have you found?"

"It's a secret until we get there. We are nearly there now. Just remember, if you don't like it, and you don't have to like it by the way, just because I like it, I mean, we don't have to come here and play."

"What is it?" I begged him.

"A new game, just been invented, I'm told. You do get a good work out playing it. Here we are; this is the building." He opened the door and we went inside.

The attendant recognized Renzo. "Ah, Renzo, haven't seen you here for several months. Come to play again? My, what a beautiful lady you have with you!"

"Not today, er, right now. I came to show her around. Is that okay?"

"Certainly, anything for one of my best customers!" he chuckled.

"Here, the viewing galley is up these steps." We climbed a series of steps and came out onto a balcony overlooking a well-lighted room. Two men were currently playing. "It's called Torque Ball. Normally, two players. One hits the ball with any part of their body. You have to make the ball hit the wall there above the white line. It bounces back. Your opponent must hit it back to the wall above the white line on either no bounce or one bounce. If he doesn't, then you get a point. First person to get to fifty points wins."

We watched, and yes, the players certainly got a work out. They had to run like mad to get to the ball and thump it back. I could see all sorts of strategies at work. Hit it so that it rebounded far from where your opponent was located. If he ran fast enough, then the next bounce, try to make it rebound where he used to be. It was exciting just to watch!

"Renzo! This is so great! I could just kiss you!" In my enthusiasm, I leaned over and did kiss him. Oops. "We just have to get away and play this. Of course, you must give me a little while to get the hang of it."

"Great! Let me know when you are free and can come! I'm so glad that you like it. I hoped you would. I've spent many hours here playing, often by myself, whenever I had any free time. Rosina doesn't see why, though." We chatted for an hour about how to play the game, tactics to use, and such. Finally, we decided we'd better be getting back to the estate. He helped me get my jacket back on. Only this time, as he did, he slid his hands along my sides, upwards from my rear. Oh, did that ever feel good. What was happening to me, I wondered. Even more surprising, he gave me a kiss. I responded by throwing my arms around him, returning his kiss.

A short while later, we were back at the estate. After changing clothes — borrowing Teyacapan to help me get out of the new dress and telling her and Teiuc all about the wedding, I then got word that Isabel, the Laird Foundation, wanted to see me.

I headed off to find her. I found her watching several artists painting away. "Oh, Bethany. So glad you could see me. My, your earrings are just fabulous!"

"Thanks, you needed something?"

"Yes, it seems you and I have overlooked something that is important with your explorations."

"Artists?" I hazarded a guess.

She grinned. "Yes, thankfully your mother didn't. How are the two that I sent working out?"

"Terrifically, but I only got to see them for a few days. Yet, I think when you see what they paint you'll be astounded. You are very right. We should have taken along some painters at least. Truthfully, I didn't think that we would need painters. I never dreamed that we would have discovered a new world or civilization! We might sail for another two years and see nothing but ocean. That's partly why I didn't think about bringing along artists. What would they do for a year with nothing going on but the sailing?"

"I agree totally with you. That is also why I did not mention it when we sent along Mireio and Roberto. I think it prudent to send out good artists to locations where you have discovered something worth rendering, as we have done with Wanakan. However, would you come with me? I'd like to show you some paintings."

I followed her into the huge gallery display room. Here the artists put their works on display, and often the public would come and purchase them. "Here we are. What do you think of this artist's works? These twelve here."

"Hey, they are good, really realistic. Well done paintings. I'd say the person has a fascination on ships and the ocean. Why?"

"We have an artist in residence here that is in love with the sea and all aspect of it, perhaps, once a mariner, who knows. What would you say if we sent along this artist, who could paint to their heart's content while at sea, but could also render anything that you discover? If the find is like Wanakan, then we can send in a team of artists. Yet, if the find is smaller, this artist could capture it for us."

"Hey, I like that idea. At least the person would not get bored at sea, but would they have enough painting supplies? I don't know a thing about oils and pigments. If they run out, I'd be at a loss on how to get more."

"Leave that to us and the painter. I'll make sure that ample supplies are sent along with the painter. If they run out, painters are very creative and inventive, you know."

"Okay, you have a deal. Say, who is this painter anyway?"

"Come, I'll introduce you." We left the display gallery and climbed up to the second floor, where the huge painting studio was located. Here, Allan had installed mostly glass windows on three sides, so the huge room was very well lighted. Pungent odors impinged upon my olfactory senses as we entered the room. Linseed oils, thinners, and other unrecognizable smells assaulted my nose. Dozens of painters were hard at work, some doing portraits, some landscapes. We walked across the room to the far corner, where I could see several more seascapes in progress. The long brown hair told me the painter was a woman.

"Michelle Millene, may we interrupt you for a moment? I have someone who wants to meet you." Isabel said. The young girl pivoted on her painting stool, which had lazy-Susan type rollers under the seat allowing easy turning. I was not expecting what I saw, though. She had long curly brown hair, deep blue eyes, and a very roundish face, with an enchanting smile. However, the paintbrush was attached to a long metal rod, which was in turn attached to a metal sleeve around her upper arms. She had lost her arms below the elbows.

"Oh, it's you, Bethany! Pleased to meet you. Excuse the brush." She extended her left arm, which I took in both hands and shook. "Heavy crate fell on them. Lost them both. First thing everyone wants to know. Nothing very exciting. Thank god for the Laird Foundation and Jenna Rose Weston! But then you know all that. I'm babbling. So pleased to meet you, Bethany."

"Pleasure's mine. I've seen your paintings. You like the sea?"

"Oh yes, dad's a warehouse boss. Been living on the docks all my life. I've always dreamed of going to sea, but they don't take girls."

"Well, we take girls," I teased. "Isabel and I have agreed that we need a painter to join the Explorers Circle and to paint whatever we find or come across. You are the candidate. You interested in going on long sea voyages and painting to your heart's content?"

"You, you are teasing me?"

"No, I am quite serious. It will be long voyages, many days spent at sea. We might not find anything on land worth painting. Yet, we didn't expect to find the new world either, for that matter. I need someone who can be perfectly content to paint sea life, because for the vast majority of the time, that is all you see, the boat and the ocean. You game for it?"

"Wow! Oh, wow! You bet! This is the best news that I have ever had in my life! I get to actually go to sea and paint it firsthand — I mean first-arm really." We chuckled. "How soon do we leave? I mean how long do I have to prepare and all that?"

"Don't know; we just got back, so it will be a few weeks at the earliest. How about coming round to the estate after supper tonight, and I'll introduce you to the rest of the Explorers Circle of which you are now full-fledged member."

"Really, a member of your Circle? Oh my! Yes, yes, right after supper! I'll be there!"

"Say, are you going to be here painting for a while longer?"

"Sure, until around four, when I ride back home for supper. I still live with my folks. We have a house near the docks."

"Great. I have four guests that I would like to bring over and show them what you are doing." She smiled, and Isabel and I left. Isabel said that she would see to all the necessary arrangements for her artist in residence, so all I needed to do was make sure we had a cabin for her and that we had food for another person.

I found Teyacapan and Teiuc busily explaining their daily life in their land to a group of us. I borrowed them, and picked Cazamel, Xilonen, and Iacotl along the way. As they waddled along, Teiuc asked, "Where are we going?"

"First I want to show you some finished paintings that are on display. Then, I want you four to meet the artist personally. You'll see why later on." Sometime later — they moved slowly — we six stood looking at the really well done sea paintings.

"These are really nice paintings. It looks like the sea off our beach, if only the sands were red," Iacotl said.

"How is it done? I mean how is it made?" asked Teiuc.

"Come, I'll show you. They use oils and canvass. Me, I can't draw anything; no talent in that area." A short while later, we wandered through the huge painting studio. Now the five could see how it was done. We passed by many painters hard at work, and the women were indeed interested in seeing all this, I noted. At last, we got to Michelle's small corner. I wondered why she was in this tiny corner and not out in the wide open areas where the lighting was better.

As expected, Michelle's back was to us, her long brown hair draped over her chair back. Several seascapes lined the walls beside her. "There's the painter that I wanted you to meet. Excuse me, Michelle. I've brought the people that I wanted to meet you." She pivoted in her chair, recognizing my voice this time.

Teyacapan gasped, the other four stared in disbelief. "This is Michelle Millene, painter of seascapes, and the newest addition to our Explorers Circle. These are some of our guests from Wanakan. The tall one is Teyacapan; that's her dear friend beside her, Teiuc. These are Cazamel, Xilonen, and Iacotl."

"Hi all. I'd shake hands with you, but we both would have big problems doing that!" Michelle said cheerily. She fiddled with the contraption on her arm, set it down on her workbench, and hopped off. She gave each one a little hug. "Oh, a crate, a big heavy box, fell on my arms. Lost them both."

"Oh, did that hurt?" asked Teiuc, sympathetically.

"Yes, really, really bad! How did you lose yours?"

"A bug ate ours," Teiuc replied. "But we didn't feel a thing. We were drugged somehow."

Michelle's eyes popped out. "Let's sit down on the floor here. Tell me about this. I've never heard of anything like this before." I saw that Michelle was very observant. She saw that it was difficult for the four to continue standing, so sitting was perfect for them. Teiuc was more than pleased to tell Michelle what had happened to them. The others kept adding bits here and there.

When they finished chatting, Michelle replied, "Well ladies, you have certainly come to the right place! Around here, our saying is nothing is impossible! Sometimes it just takes a whole lot longer to accomplish. Like my paintings. I am really, really slow compared to those out there. Yet, I keep at it and get my paintings done. People do like them enough to buy them. I've sold twelve already!"

"Thanks Michelle. We had better be getting back. I stole these five away from some others, and I had better get them back." She smiled and suggested that they could come back and visit her any time during the daytime.

On our slow way back, the four chatted fast and furiously; I could only catch a word here and there. Teyacapan told me that they were saying they had found Michelle nearly unbelievable and that if she could paint like that, maybe they could too. Opportunities, yes that is what I wanted them to see for themselves. Here, there were opportunities. I had no idea whether any of the four were even remotely interested in painting, but they had seen things they had not dreamed possible, that was my point.

After supper, I introduced Michelle to our group, all except Henry and Natale, that is. Everyone wanted to go see her works, and I left them with her, while I joined mom outside in the cold to play kick ball with over two dozen children. As I stepped out, there was Renzo waiting for me. "Mind if I play too?" he teased. We joined in the fun with the children, who decided to gang up and get me, since I was the relative newcomer.

The next afternoon, a Friday and a dance night, I had nothing else that I had to do. I found Renzo, and we took a coach into town. Yes, this would be my first taste of Torque Ball. We had the court all to ourselves. At first, he took it easy on me, showing me the best way to serve the ball. Slowly but surely, I caught on to how it was played. "Okay, now you ready for that challenge? If I win, I get that kiss you promised me," he teased.

"Okay, play boy you are on. No, wait a minute. What do I get if I win?"

"Hum, what do you want?" he asked bashfully.

I thought a second, "Ah, I win, you take me to the dance tonight and rub your hands all over my silky dress." I blushed, now why had I said that! I was so embarrassed that I couldn't concentrate, and he scored five quick points on me! Then, the spirit of play kicked in. I was not about to let him beat me! I earned my five points back fairly quickly.

"Okay lady, kid gloves come off now!" Renzo teased. "Now watch these moves!" Wham! The ball hit the wall all right, but he had put some kind of spin on the ball, and it rebounded not where I thought it should have!

"Hey, that's a pretty cool move there, but I've figured it out now. Look out buddy!"

An exhausting hour later, we were neck and neck, forty-nine each! He looked determined to win. "It all comes down to this final point!" he pointed out, as if I didn't know. Wham! He pounded the ball hard into the wall. I had to dash way back to get it and smashed it back to the wall, giving it a little spin so that it rebounded slightly differently. Now he had to make a mad dash, since he was taken off guard. He slammed into the floor at the last instant, bouncing the ball barely above the line. I had to run at top speed to get to it before it hit the floor the second time. I made it barely and just got it into the wall. He had recovered and sent it back with a mighty slam. The rebound arced high over my head. There was no way I could get my body back there in time.

Okay, so I cheated, but just a little. I moved myself and used my spiritual skills to bounce the ball back to the wall above the line, but very softly. It rebounded and hit the floor only three feet from the wall. No way could he get to it before it double and then triple bounced. "I win!" I announced.

"You cheated!" he teased back. "That's not fair."

"But you didn't say you had to hit it with your body, now did you?" I teased back, knowing that he had not said that — it was implied, but not officially stated.

"Darn, you are right! Only with you would I have to remember to say you have to hit it with some part of your body!" He began to laugh. I laughed along with him and gave him a hug.

"That was terrific fun, Renzo! We have to do this all the time! I haven't had so much pure fun in I don't know how long!"

"Me too, you are an exceptional player, Bethany! I've seen many players here, but no one has ever caught on and gotten as good as you have in just one game! You are one hot player!"

"Thanks, you are almost too good for me. You should have won, you know." I gave him his passionate kiss anyway. He blushed and smiled.

"I was going to take you to the dance anyway," he added.

When we got back at the estate, I was surprised to see Henry and Natale there. She said, "Bethany, can you help me with our four guests? I promised them that I would dress them up fancy for the next dance. That's why Henry and I are back, so I can do this small thing for them.

"Sure thing. You look radiant, Natale. I take it married life is going well for you."

"Super, I have never been happier in my life! I'll tell you all about it later when we can't be overheard. I've located some silk dresses for the women, but I'll need help getting them into them." She already wore her fancy party dress so we draped the dresses over Natale's shoulder, while I carried the shoes, underclothes, and hose; we headed off to find the four women.

"Nope, nope, you are not going to the dance in those everyday clothes," Natale announced, as we entered the room in which all four had gathered. "I promised you that this next dance you could wear fancy dresses like mine, and here they are." They oh'ed and ah'ed over the dresses, even rubbing their cheeks against the slippery fabric. Meanwhile, we began dressing them up. Lilly Ann and Beth Ann heard from Henry what was up, and they showed up to lend a hand. Soon, we had all four looking just like Natale — knock out women. It did wonders for their morale, I might add. We three left Natale with them and went door to door, seeing who else needed help dressing up. This was the normal routine around here; so many women wanted to go to the dance wearing their trademark style, sleek, form fitting, slim-line dresses with no armholes. We also had to brush out their exceedingly long hair, so that it flowed over their sides and backs. It was our job to see that they looked fabulous. Thankfully, well over half had already married and their husbands now handled them.

Then I hastily changed into mine, fixed my hair, and stood for a minute looking at my appearance in the mirror. I definitely was filling out, but would mine be as large as mom's I wondered? Ah well. The coaches were arriving, time to go. As I helped get our guests into their coaches, I noticed that Zolin and Yaotl could not keep their hands off their fiancés! Chica and Mecoa were smiling broadly and look just radiant, I thought. Once they were off, I felt a hand slide around my waist. I turned; there was Renzo.

"Ready for the dance?" he asked. I let him usher us into the next coach. I was more than ready!

During the slow dance section, I noticed that many of the men were sliding their arms up and down the sides of the women in their silky dresses. As if reading my thoughts, Renzo whispered in my ear, "Were you serious this afternoon about wanting me to slide my hands along your silky dress?"

I blushed. I wanted to scream, yes, yes, but I managed to whisper, "Oh yes, please. Like the others are doing it."

He whispered back, "You know that once I start, I might not be able to stop," he was teasing me again and I smiled. For the next few minutes I had what must have been electricity running up and down my body. My legs nearly gave way. I now knew what these other women had known for years now, and I didn't want him to stop. What was going on with me?

As the last dance of the night ended and the lights were quite dim, on impulse, I gave Renzo a very passionate kiss. "Thanks for a wonderful dance." He flushed and could say nothing, just a broad grin on his face.

Once we were back at the estate, I immediately had to help our guests out of their confining dresses. They were so happy, so excited, that they were talking so fast that I couldn't get but every fifth word. Yet, I knew that they had just had a night to remember. Once I had these four handled, I went to aid our other women, catching up to Beth Ann and Lilly Ann. Together, we made rapid work of the task. There is one thing that I know firsthand: we women just love the dances!

Quite some time later, I finally entered my room to change. The estate had finally quieted down. I didn't want to change just yet. I found my own hands running up and down my sides. While there was tingling and a silky sensation there, it paled compared to his touch. Why would his touch be any different from mine, I wondered? I had no answer, except that I was hungry. Instead of changing, I wandered down to the pantry. I knew that mom and dad would be in bed, probably kissing like there was no tomorrow. They always did so after a dance. Hence, I expected to find the pantry empty.

"Oh, hi, Beth Ann. I didn't expect to see you still up."

"I was looking after our guests so much tonight, that I didn't get much chance to snack. I can see that it is going to be hard keeping all the local men in line. Did you see the way that they went after our guests tonight? And that Shorty Phil, the small sized painter, he couldn't keep his hands off poor Cazamel. Well, they are about the same size. He's so short you know. He about wore her out with all that dancing, and her with no legs. He ought to know better!"

"Did she enjoy it? I know the Chica and her group were absolutely ecstatic when they got back tonight."

"Oh yes, yes, I think she is quite smitten with him. Poor thing, I suspect her legs will ever so sore tomorrow. I noticed you danced every dance with Renzo. Say, you haven't even changed yet."

"No, helping others change. Got hungry. Beth Ann, can I ask you something?" I decided it was now or never. I blurted out everything that had been happening with me, including how great it felt when Renzo slid his hands over my dress, and it wasn't the same thing when I did it to myself. "What's wrong with me?" I asked.

"Oh good grief, Bethany! There is nothing wrong with you." She chuckled at an unseen joke, and then said, "How many lifetimes must I keep on educating you about the birds and the bees?" I turned beet red. Beth Ann and I had been dear friends across several lifetimes now. I first met her when she was part of my Lightning Circle so long ago. She let me squirm and fidget for a time, before she answered me.

"Bethany, there is nothing wrong with you. You are simply in love, that's all. I guess Renzo is the lucky man." If I was red before, now I was burning up. "Haven't you seen how he's always around you? I think that he is madly in love with you as well, if I know anything about men." That was one of her specialties, always had been. She was the biggest flirt that I had ever known. Give her five minutes with a man, and she'd have him bending over backwards to help her.

All I could manage to say is, "Really?"

"Really!" After a pause, she added, "He is rather handsome too. I'm surprised the other girls around here aren't all over him, but I suppose that's because he's been off exploring so long. What do you want? Cocoa?"

"Yes, please. Thanks. But what do I do now? I mean about Renzo?"

"Silly woman, don't do anything. Just live your life normally and see what happens, unless it's your idea to hook him and reel him in quick like. Hum, is that what you want to do, get him to ask you to marry him right away?"

Now I was on fire, not merely hot. I wanted to scream Yes! Instead, I muttered, "Normal huh?"

"Well, that's the sensible approach. You are only fourteen after all, plenty of time to worry about getting married later on. First loves can be so emotional, you know. Give it time; who knows, Renzo might turn out to be an ogre or a womanizer or a drunk. Yes, give it time; that's the sensible approach."

I sipped my cocoa. I wanted to say the devil with sensibleness, but I dare not. She was right. What if we really didn't get along all that well? I returned to my room chanting, "Be sensible, Bethany, be sensible." Somehow, I didn't feel at all like being sensible. I plopped down on my bed still chanting it. I awoke in the morning, and I still had on my party dress!

I hastily changed and headed down for breakfast, trying not to look at Renzo. It didn't work. As we were getting up from eating, he whispered in my ear, "Torque Ball this afternoon?" Of course, I instantly said yes.

This morning mom gave the situation reports on our new guests. "Bethany has done a perfect job with the handling of their traumas. Further, all of them, including surprisingly enough their three escorts, are all outside their bodies, prime druwid candidates. I am confident that they can learn as much as they desire from us here. In fact, the three men have already discovered what they most greatly desire to learn. Matlali is a natural Protector material. Both Yaotl and Zolin are keenly interested in all the engineering and architectural projects. Plus, they have been hounding Allan nearly every day."

"The women are adapting fabulously to our culture, better than I would have expected, due in large part, I suspect, to Natale having educated them during the six weeks at sea. We are not yet sure what these women will ultimately excel in just yet, but I'm sure they are all willing to learn. So the report is all of them are fully accepted here. That means, Bethany, the Explorers Circle can begin to make preparations for sailing."

"While we aren't going to order you to sail anywhere specifically, based upon your recent findings, the Santi would like the southern area of the ocean between Wanakan and the Spice Islands searched, just in case there are more of these mantis creatures lying in wait to get us." I agreed that would be our next voyage. We set the date for March 1, 649. However, no sooner had we set the date when Henry changed it to March 15. He wanted the caravel's bottom cleaned. It seems that we had picked up too many barnacles on our bottom. We now had four weeks to kill.

While playing Torque Ball with Rezno that afternoon, I got a wild idea. When we were done, I said, "You know, we've got nearly a month before we sail again. Why don't we load up the stuff for your folks and take a quick trip to Zargarb? You two will get a chance to see your folks again. What do you think?"

"Wow, yes, I'd love to visit home, even if only for a week or so. You mean you'll be coming with us?" He blushed.

"Certainly, I've got nearly nothing to do here. Besides, with my Torque Ball player gone, there is next to nothing at all to do!" His grin spoke mountains.

When I told mom of our idea, she was delighted. "Actually, this works out perfectly. Elona has two new caravels to be delivered to Ariana. You can hitch a ride on their maiden voyages. They will be empty and can make the run swiftly. It won't be too much to ask to have them bring you all back. Who all is going?"

"The twins, of course. I'm going too. I'd like to see Lenkova and Andre. Oh yes, Cedric asked if he could come along too. I think he likes Rosina, just between you and me."

"Oh, I see," she said with a covert smirk on her face. I flushed.

"And you, you certainly don't have a crush on Renzo, now do you?" I turned beet red.

"It's that obvious?" I wailed.

"Dear, how could I possibly have missed it? You two have been nearly inseparable all the time you have been back here! Oh!" she suddenly realized something. "I'm sorry, Bethany. I didn't realize that you hadn't realized that you had a crush on him."

"Well, I didn't. But I do. Is it okay that I do like him?"

"Of course it is! He's a fine lad. Just don't rush things. Let nature take its course. If he's the one for you, you both will know it in time. Now you had better go get packed. Boat is supposed to leave this afternoon!"

"Thanks mom! Can we maybe delay Henry and Natale's wedding party until we get back?" She agreed, I gave her a hug and rushed to find the others. Hastily we packed everything, carrying our sacks to the front door. Renzo discovered that a Santi had already hitched a buckboard wagon. All hands began loading in the boxes of presents the twins had gotten for their folks, including the paca's, which had to be rounded up. They were out running in the fields of the estate. Once we had everything loaded we were off to the docks, a Santi came with us to drive the wagon back. We were just in time.

The captain welcomed us aboard and wanted to know what cabins we desired. Again, I did not want to force anyone out of theirs, but four cabins were vacant. It was a skeleton crew manning the ship. An hour later, we were on our way. As we four stood on the deck watching the caravel slip out to sea and Velona dropping behind us, I noticed Cedric and Rosina for the first time. They were holding hands. How had I missed all this I wondered? I'd only seen them close a few times, but then I was always so busy on the voyage. Renzo had his arm around my waist as we leaned on the railing. It felt very comforting to me.

Once we were at sea, sailing along at top speed, I took Renzo below into the cargo hold. "I've got a surprise for you."

"Down here? The place is empty except for our few boxes and the pacas."

"Close your eyes and don't peek. I'll be right back." I ducked into my cabin and grabbed the kick ball. I had borrowed one of mom's spares. "Ta da!" I exclaimed. "Kick ball time. You're it!" I pitched the ball at him. For the next five days, we had ourselves a blast. We played kick ball and then turned the cargo hold into a Torque Ball center as well. After we were both exhausted, we found ourselves passionately kissing each other.

Zargarb came far too soon for my liking. As we were playing our last game, Cedric and Rosina came into the cargo hold. Rosina had the biggest grin on her face that I had ever seen her have. We stopped. She giggled. Cedric announced proudly, "I want you to be the first to know. I have just asked Rosina for her hand in marriage, and she has agreed! I'll ask her father and mother for permission when we land."

"Wow! Great, congratulations!" I exclaimed and gave them both a hand.

"I'm so excited!" she said. Then she winked at Renzo, who flushed.

He was very bashful all of a sudden. "I was going to do this later, but," he got down on one knee and said, "Bethany, I am madly in love with you. Will you marry me?"

Now I did have tingles, my knees barely held me up! "I thought you'd never ask. Of course, I will. I'm in love with you too!" He got up, and we embraced passionately again.

"There, I told you so," declared Rosina. "You owe me a kiss!" Cedric must have lost some bet, because he gave her a loving kiss as well.

"Now we can really surprise mom and dad," Rosina told Renzo.

Ever practical, I said, "I wonder when we can get married? We are supposed to sail again almost as soon as we get back. I won't be fair not to let all of or friends have a big party and all that. Besides, I certainly want your parents and friends to be able to come to the weddings."

"No problem. We can get married when we come back from the next trip. By then, everything can be already arranged and all that," Renzo suggested.

"Land ho!" ended our discussion. We rushed on deck to watch our arrival in Zargarb.

Soon we were walking down the gangplank onto the docks. As expected, there was Lenkova and Andre waiting to greet their twins. I also saw Lady Ariana Zar Wilkins, the monarch of Zargarb, along with her husband Ben and her inseparable assistants, Julianna and Rachele. Then, I saw so many others that I knew, dear friends of mine that I used to play with as a little girl back at Jenna's old estate.

The twins ran up to their parents, while Cedric and I walked more slowly. Andre and Lenkova Pazzio le Gouer were now much older than I remembered. He was forty-eight and she, sixty. Her long hair had now turned quite grey. In fact, I was stuck with how old all my friends were! As we reached Andre and Lenkova, she said, "What's this? I send my twins out to explore the world and broaden their horizons, and they come back with fiancés instead?"

"Hi, Lenkova," I grinned. "I haven't seen you in so long! I hope you don't mind having me in your family?"

"Mind? Oh, there couldn't be a higher honor possible! Not only does he go off and help discover a completely new land, he comes back with the future Santi del Dio leader as his fiancé! Oh my, where did you get those incredible earrings?" I gave her a big hug and told her we'd explain later. Andre also gave me a warm hug welcome as well.

"And Cedric, so you've stolen the heart of my Rosina."

"Yes, ma'am. She's just about the greatest person I've ever met!"

She gave a warm welcoming hug. He looked at Andre and said, "This wasn't the way it was supposed to work. I was supposed to ask both of you for her hand in marriage."

Andre chuckled. "Consider it done, my lad. It's just faster this way. Rosina never could keep a secret." We all laughed.

Next, we met Lady Ariana and Ben, whom I'd played with when I was a little girl. He was now forty-two and she, thirty-four. She, of course, had lost her hands to the Holy Paladin general when she was just a young woman. I gave them both a warm hug welcome.

"Golly, you have grown so, Bethany!" exclaimed Ariana. "What's this we hear about your marrying Renzo? My where did you get those earrings? They are incredible!"

"Explain later about the earrings. Yes, he's just asked me and I said yes!" We hugged again. Ben also gave me a good congratulations and warm hug.

"Don't forget us," chorused her assistants.

"I certainly will not! Come here Julianna and Rachele. You two look great!" I hugged these two armless women on whom mom and I had performed their therapies.

"You are so grown up!" exclaimed Julianna. "You were just a little girl when we last played kick ball! I do like those earrings!"

"Are you really marrying Renzo?" asked Rachele as I hugged her.

"Yes, you will hear all about it in a bit. You two look good! Life here in Zargarb must be agreeing with you."

"Yes, we are both very happily married, children and everything," Rachele replied.

The other members of Ariana's Circle pressed forward to meet me. These four had been with me at mom's estate. Sarah Amber, Lilly Ann's daughter, was now twenty-one; Donata Weston, my older sister, was twenty-two; Cory Amir was twenty-four; Sedwick Alyster was forty-nine, but he I had not yet met.

Donata gave me a long hug. "God, I have missed you little sister! You are all grown up now. Will you look at those earrings? They must be worth a fortune!"

Then, I had to meet the Fortress Zargarb Circle, the rest of Andre's Circle. Fred and Ann Waterton were both fifty-four and greying. Tom and Mary Bridgeport were both sixty-five and really showing their age. Art and Le Ann Weatherby were two years older and greyer still. It was good to meet these legendary Guardians as well.

As we rode to the Palace, which was the old Sisterhood inn, I was floored at how deserted the city was, compared to the last time I had been here so many, many years ago. The decimation of the Holy Paladins had nearly wiped the entire population out! Lady Ariana had turned that all around now, and the people were prospering and thriving.

Lenkova loved the new paca clothing the twins had brought back for her. Andre didn't quite know what to make of the pair of pacas. However, Ariana, Ben, Julianna, and Rachele were nuts about them. Hence, I suggested one of their first voyages of their new caravels might be to take a bunch of goods to Wanakan and acquire more pacas. Ariana jumped upon this idea!

During our all too brief stay here, I spent a lot of time with Donata and with Lenkova, although I did meet everyone's spouse and the many children. We had a rapt audience for hours as we told them all about our first voyage. Finally, the meaning behind the large earrings that Rosina and I wore was understood. Lenkova and Andre were exceedingly pleased that the twins had regained such new skills, abilities that neither of them possessed. Both thanked me repeatedly for what I had done for their twins.

On our last day before we had to sail back, Julianna and Rachele asked us if we wanted to go for a horse ride. We four jumped at the chance! When we met them at the stables, the two already had their horses ready to go and were waiting us. Several Santi saddled up four for us, and I went to help Julianna and Rachele mount.

To my surprise, Rachele said, "No thanks, Bethany. We can do it ourselves. Watch this." Both women were able to mount their mares easily! Their reins were tied to a wooden mouthpiece, which they leaned over and took between their teeth. "Can't talk very well though. Come on." I kept saying this is amazing. They both grinned.

They took us on a two-hour ride around the countryside. Both Renzo and Rosina were born to the saddle, I discovered, though with Lenkova as their mother, I was not surprised. When we got back, Julianna said, "See Bethany. We both wanted to show you just how far we have come. We are both full Loremasters and very capable riders. We owe you and your mother so much that we don't have words to thank you properly. Rachele and I thought this little demonstration would speak louder than words."

"It has, you two are fabulous!" I gave them both a long, hearty hug. Then, I had an idea. "You know, I think that you two and Ariana and Ben have earned a little trip. How would you two like to visit this new land of Wanakan and see the sights, maybe even get yourself a set of these cool earrings and paca clothes?"

"You're kidding?" Rachele's eyes opened wide. I knew this was a Loremaster's dream trip.

"Come on; let's go talk to Ariana and Ben."

A little while later, Ariana said, "You are teasing us, right, Bethany? Us all go to this new world ourselves?"

"Yes, you have the new caravels with the proper navigational instruments. Just get packing, and we can sail there together. I can even introduce you all to their king and queen. Takes about six weeks to get there and another six to get back. So even if you stay there for a month, you would only be gone four months at most. I know there is not much time, but I can hold off our departure date a few days until you get to Velona. What do you say? I guarantee you that this trip is a Loremaster's dream trip. Trust me. Besides, then you too can get fabulous earrings like Rosina's."

They decided to do it! They brought their spouses and all of Ariana's Circle and the four Santi Guards. Only Sedwick decided to remain and help the others manage the country during their absence. I changed our sailing plans. By delaying a few days, we managed to get all the cargo for trade loaded, along with sufficient provisions, and their personal gear. We sailed for Velona five days later than I had planned.

When we arrived in Velona, Ariana and her whole group followed us to the new estate. None of them had seen it. Boy, were they ever surprised and shocked to see such a fabulous set of buildings. Mom really did love to see Donata again as well.

However, when I got back, mom teased me, "I sent you on a simple task to take these homesick twins to visit their parents, and you come back engaged!" I grinned; so much for going slowly.

"Don't worry, mom. We cannot get married until we return from this voyage." She laughed and gave me a big hug.

I introduced Ariana and her party to our guests from Wanakan. Natale gave them several of her dictionaries, and Teyacapan and Teiuc spent much of the days before we sailed helping Ariana and her bunch learn the basics of their language. By now, Ariana, Julianna, and Rachele saw what we meant by the length of the earrings denoting status, much like our uniforms and tunics. Natale, Mireio, and Teyacapan had identical long lengths, only my special set was longer. The other guests wore earrings of different, but shorter lengths. Different customs for a different culture.

The next day was the big party for Henry and Natale to celebrate their wedding. Neither was offended that it had been delayed so long. Bard Tal provided the music and literally blew Ariana and her people away with his group's performance! We all enjoyed the party.

Finally, on March 5 we set sail, two caravels bound for the new land of Wanakan. We, of course, had a new member of our Explorers Circle, Michelle Millene, our painter.

Chapter 6 Into the Southern Ocean

With Natale now staying in the captain's cabin, I took Michelle on as my cabin mate. As we were stowing our gear in our cabin, Michelle said, "I do hope that you won't find me too big a burden. I try to do as much as I can on my own, but some things are just beyond me. Mom and dad always helped me with them. This is the first time I have been away from home. I really don't know what to expect either, only that I am so happy to come along. Do we share the bed?"

She finally ran down a bit. "Yes, Natale used to sleep with me, now it's your turn. I really don't know much about you, Michelle, so I will have to rely on you to let me know when you need some assistance. Is that okay with you?"

"Sure thing. Not too much to tell about me really. I used to sit and paint every day at the docks. Often I would help dad around the warehouse. Then, one afternoon, a weak box on the bottom just broke, and the whole stack fell down. I just happened to be at the wrong place at the wrong time. A heavy crate crushed my arms. After I passed out, dad took me to Elona's place. Mary Dietz, Cedric's mother, she fixed me up. Once I healed, she sent me to your estate and your mom gave me her therapy; it sure did work wonders on me. I was so depressed after the accident, you know. I'd never get to sea because I'm a woman. Now I could never paint the sea cause of no arms. Well, after the therapy was done, I felt so alive and happy I could burst. Jenna then sent me over to the Laird Foundation."

"At first, they taught me so many useful things, so that I could get along by myself, well mostly anyway. That took some time. After that, the Director of Painting, she took me under her wing and helped me learn new ways to paint. I've finally gotten back as good as I used to be, although it is now much slower in the doing."

"I still cannot eat all that well by myself. I always need help with my privates and after going to the bathroom, you know what I mean?" I nodded. "And I love my long hair, but still have a devil of a time trying to brush it out. If all those women who are in worse shape than I am in can do it, then I sure am going to keep working at it!"

"You will make a good cabin mate. I love long hair as well! I'll keep my eye on you and see if I can figure out anything to make life easier for you. Just remember to ask me when you need some help, all right?"

"Sure. Can I ask you something?"

"Michelle, you can ask me and anybody else here anything you want at any time! You are one of us now."

"Was Natale really up on deck with the captain during one of the really big blows?"

"You bet. She loves storms. I was there with her, just in case of trouble."

She smiled. "Do you suppose that I could be allowed on deck during a blow? I want to paint some blow paintings, but I have to see it for myself. Is this possible? I know it is dangerous up there in a bad storm, but I need to see it firsthand."

"Certainly. We just tie ourselves to the ship, because at its height, we can hardly stand up! I will caution you, once tied on and the blow starts, there is no turning back. You have to ride it out. There is no way to get back inside; the waves and the lurching of the boat make walking impossible, even for those of us with hands."

"Okay. I'll do it. Should I speak to the captain about it?"

"We'll do it together when we run into a blow, how's that?" She agreed and smiled. Gear stored, we went on deck to watch our departure.

Since this was the maiden voyage of Ariana's new ship which she named The Shining Lady, Captain Henry decided to have Emil travel with her crew to make sure that they did the navigation correctly. Further, for a time Natale wanted to travel with them as well, so that she could get everyone's language skills as good as possible. Also, I wanted to spend some time with my sister, Donata, so she stayed with us for a time. Since Linda also wanted to spend some time with her sister, Sarah Amber, she came with us as well.

Slowly the two ships tacked out of the harbor and we were underway at last. Renzo, as usual, had his arm around my waist, as we leaned on the railing watching the city shrink behind us. Only this time, I knew why I really wanted his arm there! Then, I remembered my charge and looked around for Michelle. I saw her up on the poop deck near Captain Henry. We moved closer to them so I could eavesdrop.

"I know the names of all the ropes, sir, and the proper way the sails are to be trimmed."

"What's the name of that one up there?" he asked, pointing out a line way up.

"The main topsail lanyard, sir. It ought to be slightly tighter once you set the tack."

"Right you are lassie. You do know your ships!" He tested her on a whole bunch more lines. Suddenly I realized that I knew next to nothing about the physical ship! "And that one?"

"Spanker led line, though it used to be known as the dead line, before the caravels came."

"You are good!" He quizzed her about other lines, rope coils, and any number of other items of which I had no idea what he was saying. She got them all correct. "Damn, you are going to give the bosun a run for his money! He still doesn't have them all down pat. Got to, in a blow."

"Yes, sir, you've got to know in a blow because the safety of the ship can hang on getting one specific line handled immediately," she replied, finishing his sentence. He stared at her for a moment.

"How about that school of fish there?"

"Sorry, sir, those are not fish; they're dolphins, mammals, sir."

"Oh you are good, lassie, very good! Welcome aboard me ship!" She smiled. "Where'd you learn all this? You have the ship down better than Bosun Thad!"

"I don't know. I just know it, sir. Been painting sea and ships all my life. Lived on the docks of Velona."

"How about just Henry, not sir."

"But sir, you are the captain."

"Yes, but we are all Santi Explorers Circle members, so just Henry, okay?" She agreed.

I turned to Renzo and challenged him. "Okay buster, what do you make of that?"

"Michelle sure knows her ship inside and out! No hesitation to think of the answer — right there with each one. Her father's a dockhand, not a captain. She's definitely got captain type knowledge. So where the heck did she learn it?"

"Good observations. That's exactly what I saw. Now, any speculation on how she comes by this information? You are going to have to stay sharp if you are going to marry little old me," I teased him.

"Even if her father had been a sea captain, she would have had to be at sea working with these terms to know them instantly. Besides, landlubbers have never seen a dolphin. Some Loremasters know about them, but not ordinary folks. She barely glanced at them."

"So big boy, your conclusion? She gave us a big clue."

"Hey, even she said that she didn't know how she knew it all," he protested. I didn't relent, but kept him thinking. At last, Renzo said, "Okay, Bethany, don't laugh at me, but maybe she was a sea captain in another life and that's how she knows it so well."

"Excellent, Renzo. I will let you marry me," I teased him. "Exactly what I am thinking. That would explain it. I'm not sure just yet where this leads, but it gives me some ideas."

"Now do I get my reward kiss for getting it right?" he teased me back. I gave him his reward.

Later Donata and I sat with our backs to the poop deck walls, my favorite resting place. We were chatting about this and that, sister things. She was telling me about her boyfriend and Sarah Amber's. Both women were planning to get married later this year. Somehow, our conversation got twisted into the past. She said, "You know when you were off looking all over the Sea Princes for Alabaster?" I said yes. Donata asked, "Was it hard to try to locate him? I mean is it very difficult to actually move across space and find someone? Is that hard to do? I sometimes have dreams that I can do that with mom. I know I can just make the mental connections as a Communicator, but in my dreams, I can find someone without making the connection, find them, and then look at them as if I were there with them."

I was given a gift horse! "Okay sis, close your eyes. It is all just a matter of drilling. I want you to be up at the top of the crow's nest." She didn't succeed. "Okay, be right up there at the bottom of this lower sail." This she could do, it was very close to where she was.

I began to drill her, moving her farther away and closer, to the left and right. She kept getting better and faster at it. "Okay, now let's be over Velona." She did and then let out a terrifying yell. Of course, everyone noticed, but by now, they all knew what that meant. Bethany was about to do her thing!

"Okay, Donata, I want you to go to the start of that trauma that you are sitting in. All right." I proceeded to give her one of my therapy sessions. By suppertime, she was laughing wildly. Her story was simple. She used to do this all the time. She had actually been one of Alabaster's first druwids! One night while out in the woods on a short trip and while her body slept, she had been out roaming the countryside and ran into this strange grey giant. You can guess the rest. She too had been victimized by the Grey Creatures. At the bottom of that entire trauma lay her decision to never leave her body again and go roaming. By the next evening, she was bouncing all over Tarra, even standing above the estate watching Jenna play kick ball with the kids right after supper before dark!

Unknown to me, Michelle had been watching us, ever since she heard Donata scream. Of course, she came rushing down to find out what horrible thing had happened. Renzo explained to her what was happening, and she had sat down nearby to listen in on the whole session. That night when we were in our cabin, after I had helped her brush her teeth and was gently combing her long, shiny, black hair, she asked me, "I heard your session with your sister today. Renzo told me what you were doing. It's just like what your mom did for me isn't it?"

"Yes, I learned how to do it from mom."

"I was wondering, is she really able to move about like that? I mean can I just leave my body and go all around out there somewhere, look around, and then come back? Is that really possible to learn how to do?"

"Yes, several of us can do just that, why?" I wasn't being mean; I just needed her to say it.

"Well, I sometimes have dreams that I'm doing that. It's weird, really. I know that I'm asleep, but I'm off out over the sea, just looking around. I see the waves, the crests, and the fish. I smell the sea air, feel the breezes, everything. It is so real sometimes."

"Well, once I get my sister handled, we'll see about it, how's that? Now we ought to get to bed. Natale always slept against the hull. I'm not sure why, because it's easier to get out on my side."

"That's fine with me, because I can smell the wood. I love the smell of the timbers." We climbed in, but the bed was quite chilly; it was wintertime still in the Velona area. We snuggled close to keep each other warm. Curious about what she had said, I stayed awake and watched her fall asleep. Sure enough, once her body was asleep, she drifted up and out over the sea! I let my body drift into slumber, but kept my spiritual "eye" on her to make sure she got back safely, which she did.

Benet continually explored the weather out in front of us as he now routinely did. This way, he helped us avoid the frequent squalls and storms. This next day, he did just that, requested a slight course change to bypass a late afternoon squall.

After I had my sister finished up, I decided to tackle Michelle next. The third day out, I had Michelle sit down with me in my usual place. "I've been watching you at night after your body is asleep. You are not dreaming; you are actually moving out over the sea. We are going to get this skill more under control, okay?" She agreed. I had her close her eyes and then begin moving about.

"I'm doing it, but I shouldn't be doing this, you know." I kept her at it. She had little resistance to moving about over the sea, I discovered. However, she constantly kept saying that she shouldn't be doing this. Finally, I had enough of this phrase and asked her if she saw where that phrase was coming from. I had her repeat it several times and we had the trauma located. Fortunately, this one was not a nasty, heavy one. She had been a ship's captain and had often wandered off, especially at night to observe what lay ahead. Much like Benet, he wanted to avoid trouble ahead. One night while he was off scouting ahead, someone on his ship attacked his body, cutting his throat. He dove back to find out what was happening. One of his partners had gotten greedy and wanted to take over his ship for himself.

Once she had it well viewed, she yawned a lot and started laughing. "Oh my god! No wonder I know so much about the ship and sea! I was an experienced sea captain! Oh no! I just spotted who I was — I mean my name, what they called me. I was Antonio Zar. God I founded Zargarb! My partner, the High Priest, stole it from me that night. That means Ariana Zar over there is my descendent. That is weird!" I ended the session.

That night as we climbed into bed, I told her that it was okay to go out and look about and all that, only when she did it, she was to let one of us know that she was doing it. She readily agreed to that.

At breakfast, Michelle was gaily telling everyone about her discovery, "Antonio Zar! So that's why I know so much about ships and the sea. Now everything makes so much more sense! I used to go off flying out ahead of our ship and look for storms or troubles ahead. Then, I'd come back and steer us around them. Sure made for better sailing that way. Bethany said I can still do it, only I have to let one of you know when I'm doing it, just in case I get into trouble or something, though I don't see how I would get into trouble anymore; it's not like one of you are after my ship or anything. I promise to always see if there is any way around bad weather so we all have a good sail, but then I would like to run through a good blow, maybe just once, you know, so I can paint it and all that, if you don't mind the rough ride."

When she finally ran down a bit, Henry asked, "Say, if you were old Antonio Zar, why did you chose that location, where Zargarb is at, instead of Velona's location? I've always wondered how the founders chose what they did."

Michelle though for a moment, looking at her old memories. "Old Pet, that's what we called Pietro Velona — he and I fought over the two locations. I believe I thought I was getting the better deal because my spot was right at the crossroads of civilizations at the time. I guess my choice wasn't that good. Zargarb keeps on being overrun. So old Pet, he got the better deal after all. I wonder where old Pet is at these days? If he's like me, he'll never be able to get the sea out of him. Has anyone come across old Pietro Velona?" No one had.

Benet asked, "Say Michelle, can you really go out there and check on the weather? I mean like say a hundred miles ahead?"

"Yes, I've been doing in even in my sleep, though until now, I didn't really believe that I was actually doing it, you know, sort of thought it was just me dreaming I was, but I really was doing it."

Benet grinned, a sly look on his face. "Since you're done with breakfast, how about coming on deck and lending me a hand with the weather checking? Bethany, we're doing the daily morning check now."

I chuckled, "Go ahead, have fun."

She didn't quite know what Benet was about to do with her, but she followed him out of the cargo hold dining room area and up onto the main deck. He preferred to sit quietly near the bow anchor area, out of the way of everyone. "Here, make yourself comfortable." She did and looked at him expectantly. "Okay, here's what I do a couple times a day. I sit here and move out a hundred miles or so, checking on the weather. Ready to come with me?"

"Wow! You mean we go together? I've never gone with anyone before. How do we do it?"

"Well, just get up here with me at the crow's nest first and then spot me and away we go."

Okay, I see you. Now what do we do?

What? You can talk to me? I mean I hear you in my mind, just as I do the telepaths! Are you also a telepath?

Please stop shouting! No, I don't know what a telepath is. Are we not supposed to be talking to each other? I mean when we are doing this?

Er sorry. I'm not a telepath. I just think my thoughts when a telepath is talking to me. I think that you can talk with me is just super! Come on; let's go see what's ahead.

Oh, this is so much nicer going out over the sea with someone else with you! Wow, this is really great! Look, I love to buzz the water.

After doing the dishes, I wandered up on deck to take in the early morning fresh air. I saw our sister vessel a mile astern. It was good to have company, at least for a while. I noticed the two forms of Benet and Michelle sitting as if asleep way up front. I sipped my tea and watched the waves break against the hull.

I heard them return. Michelle said, "Golly Benet that sure was fun wasn't it? And those dolphins sure liked us playing with them, don't you think?"

"You bet, yes, that's the most fun I've had zipping along out there. I don't know why I never thought of buzzing things as I move along. Sure was cool. Say, let's see if you can send me a message now. Go ahead, say hello or something." He waited, looking at her. "Go ahead, just say something."

"Darn it I am, but nothing is getting through is it? I don't sense you either."

"Weird. Well, how about sitting up there on the crow's nest and trying it?"

"Did you get it?" she asked.

"Er, nothing. Well, let me sit on the crow's nest and you try it from here."

"Darn strange. Nothing again." He saw me and got my attention. I walked over. "Bethany, this is really strange. When we are both out of our bodies flying over the sea, she can talk to me, and I, her, as if she had telepathy or something. Yet, when either one of us is not out there, nothing. How can a telepath only do stuff when both are way out there? Is that normal?"

Michelle had an awful look on her face. "Is there something dreadfully wrong with me?"

"Oh no not at all. You are just fine. Can I see this in operation? Let's both go sit on the crow's nest." *Can you hear me now?*

Oh sure, loud and clear.

I zipped back into my body. *Can you hear me now?* Silence. I got her back into her body, well around its head anyway.

"What's this mean? Am I somehow broken? Maybe I shouldn't be doing this?" Michelle still looked worried.

"Oh no, Michelle, you are just great. I believe you may well have some telepathic abilities as well. That's rare and fabulous, you know. I am going to have Rosina, our Communicator, examine you. She is the real telepath and knows all about it. Come on, let's go find her; she's probably somewhere below kissing Cedric, if I know her. We went below deck, and interrupted the two lovers.

I explained what we'd discovered about Michelle and asked her to check her out fully. I went to chat with Sarah Amber, Ariana's Healer. She and her sister, Linda, were chatting away still catching up on all the news. Linda was telling her all about Bard Tal, their older brother.

I borrowed Sarah and we sat in my usual spot. "I've heard that you've been quizzing Tonia about how she can sense what's wrong with a patient."

"Yes, that is a fabulously useful skill that she's learned. Often sick or injured people cannot tell you what is wrong. To be able to just know would be of immense help to we Healers. Is it hard to learn? How does one go about it?"

"It's just drill and practice. Tonia figured it out. You just pervade the patient's body and sense what's wrong, if anything. Try it. Pervade my body here and see if you can sense what if anything is not quite right with it." Once more, I caught her trying to use her body and somehow effort it into mine. After I corrected that false start, I felt her moving into my body.

A while later she said, "Nothing wrong, except your ears feel funny, guess it's those heavy earrings you are wearing. Say this is actually very easy. I wonder why none of us ever tried this before?"

"Don't know. Come on. Let's check out Mireio; she's pregnant. Let's see if you can detect that." A while later she was ecstatic.

"Bethany, I can sense it! Mireio, you really are pregnant!" Mireio smiled; she knew physically this was true now. "There are two heart beats going! Terrific!"

We found Tonia and I told her what Sarah Amber was now doing. I sent the two off to go check up on everyone on the ship, one by one. It would be good practice for Sarah. I cautioned them both to get me at once if any signs of trauma should suddenly appear in Sarah Amber.

The morning was only half over and now I had nothing else to do. I wandered the main deck. Suddenly out of nowhere, Rezno appeared, his fingers tickling my sides. Laughing madly, I twisted out of his reach. He called out, "The game is afoot!" I charged after him. We had a good romp all over the main deck. Quite a few of our friends called out, either cheering him on to get me or cheering me on to get him. We stopped and kissed once we were both out of breath. Our scores were about equal.

The next day dawned gloomy, as predicted by Michelle and Benet. A typhoon was raging to the south of us and we dutifully followed their suggestions to sail northwest. Both said that we would not be able to bypass the entire storm, just the brunt of it. Rosina relayed the information over to Natale, who relayed it to those on her ship. Midmorning, we battened down all the hatches, and rigged our ship for the approaching storm.

Henry allowed Michelle and me to tie ourselves up on the poop deck just behind him so that she could observe the storm and then paint it. On the other ship, Natale also was tied to the helm in front of their Captain. She insisted that she be allowed to be there in case of trouble. At least, she could hold things still that might break loose in the storm.

For several hours, we had nothing but rain, and the captains continued to sail using the two main sails, but no top sails, lowering them in the wind would be too risky for the crew members. Finally, the blow strengthened, and the captains ordered the main sails down, the two steering jibs up and the crew below deck. As usual, the bosuns were secured to the bow mast, ready for any trouble that might appear.

"Isn't this just great!" yelled Michelle, barely able to be heard over the howling winds and the sheets of rain that now were almost horizontal. I nodded, our hair blowing behind us nearly parallel to the deck. I made a Mind Link to Natale and picked up her excitement. All was well on her ship. We just had to ride it out.

The Sleepy Hollow rose high into the air, pitched wildly to port, and came crashing downward. We pitched and rolled with abandon, but she was a sturdy ship indeed. Actually, I was beginning to enjoy this incredible ride. Because of the noise, I joined Michelle into our Mind Link so we could talk. It was good that I did.

She had been trying to tell me something. She sent, *A big wave is headed our way!* Whoosh, the wave broke over the bow, an avalanche of seawater buried the bosun, and came swirling up towards us. *Woohoo!* Michelle exclaimed, thoroughly enjoying this. The wall of water swept over us, completely drenching us, though we were already quite soaked! Wiping the water off our faces, we saw that Henry had been smacked in his head by a fish that had been caught in the wave and thrown on deck. It flopped around, but was unable to get back into the sea. However, Henry was out cold, and the helm was beginning to spin like mad, causing the boat to turn. *Bethany, untie me! We have to get the heading back into the waves or we will be sunk!*

I struggled with the wet rope and got one end undone, leaving the other end still around her. She got down on her knees and crawled across the poop deck, working like mad to be not thrown overboard. At last, she stood up beside the helm. Henry was leaning off to one side, out cold. She put her legs over the rope that held Henry fastened to the helm. Now she was more or less stable, and she began to use her arms to turn the spoked wheel back to where it belonged.

Seeing that she was secure, I then tied her line off. Even if she was swept overboard, I could reel her in like a fish. I then untied my line and retied it, giving me enough play to get to the helm. I sent the bosun the okay sign, as he was attempting to make his way from the bow. Now I could examine Henry, worried that he had really been hurt. He had a small cut on his forehead. Natale was quite frantic about his welfare, but I sent her the okay message as well. He was just knocked out cold. He started to come around.

Have to get the ship back on course! He thought as I now linked with him.

We are back on course, sir! sent Michelle. *I got her going right now. Are you okay?*

Dear are you okay? You are giving us all a fright! Natale sent.

I'm okay, bang on the head. What hit me?

You caught a mackerel, sir. On your forehead.

That's never happened before. Damn fish nearly sunk us! Want me to take over now?

I have her, sir. Just take it easy; the blow is nearly over. Calmer waters are coming up fast now, sir.

Will you stop calling me sir? It's Henry. Natale roared with laughter from her caravel.

Sorry sir, I mean Henry. Bit excited here. Forgot. Woohoo. You enjoying this too, Natale?

You bet! Can't get this on land ever! Say are you really steering the ship by yourself?

Yes, I still got arms, more or less. Fun, great fun. Bit hard though to turn her against the wind. Here comes the calmer water. Indeed, almost at that instant the lurching subsided. The winds lessened and the waves, smaller. We had passed through the worst of the blow. *We'll be out of it in a few more miles, Henry.*

She was right. A few minutes later, the sun peaked out of the distant clouds. The rain dwindled to light showers, and then to mere sprinkles. The bosun began untying himself, so I untied all of us. "I'll relieve you now, Michelle. Go below and dry out. I'll be relieved myself as soon as the crew gets up here." Reluctantly, she let go of the helm.

"Captain sir, what do you want done with your catch here?" The bosun was standing over the flopping mackerel. He told him to pitch it back into the sea.

Michelle and I headed down to our cabin, passing the crew who were coming topside to relieve the captain and bosun. "Have fun?" one asked Michelle as we passed.

"You bet!" she replied, though we were both now starting to

shiver, soaked to the bone and then some. Once in our cabin, I got her out of her wet clothes, and then out of mine. I draped a towel around me and took another to dry her off. "Thanks, it is rather hard to dry myself off." Once we were dry, I wrapped our hair up in the towels, and we changed into dry clothes. She insisted on dressing herself, so I let her. Then, we headed to the galley for something hot to warm our insides.

Henry was already there. "You handled the helm like a pro, Michelle. Thanks."

She smiled, "Had to, we were turning sideways to the waves, a recipe for a swamping."

"How would you like a watch at the helm, Michelle?"

"What? You, you'd let me take a whole watch? Me, a woman?" I noticed that her surprise and hesitancy was not because she had nothing below her elbows, but because she was a woman! Now that she mentioned it, I'd never seen a woman sea captain before.

"I don't care if you are a dog! You handled that helm like a professional captain. You can have the early evening watch, if you want it."

"Thank you sir! I mean, Henry!" she was so elated, so excited about this.

Bosun Thad added, "Nice fast reaction, there Michelle. I was heading to the helm, but it would have taken me quite a while to reach him. Good show!" She beamed.

A crew member came to report that there was no damage, and that the other caravel had signaled them that there was no damage there either. Now it was back to smooth sailing once more.

The next day, Benet and Michelle came up with an interesting idea. We were on the backside of the typhoon with strong tail winds. If we could rig up another pair of outer jib sails tied to the fore-mainmast, we could gain a great deal of speed for several days. "That's how I used to out-sail the other Sea Princes," Michelle explained her idea to Henry.

He liked the idea, and in an hour, we had two more large outer jibs rigged up. We relayed the idea to the other ship, and she followed our lead. Quick estimates suggested that we were adding another ten miles per hour to our speed this way!

I helped Michelle set up her painting studio on the main deck. She and Benet predicted smooth sailing for several days, so she wanted to take advantage of the weather and get a start on her paintings. She had collected many ideas for paintings. She explained that it was hard for her to do good, detailed work on the moving ship, but that she was going to sketch out a number of rough images that she could then finish when on land.

Three weeks out, we switched passengers back to their right ships. Natale was very glad to be with Henry once more, staying at his side for days, sneaking kisses whenever she could. As it turned out, that was our only blow. We had a few squalls, true, but nothing serious. Our two weather people were doing their jobs very well indeed.

We made exceptionally good time and made landfall four days earlier than expected. Congratulations were given to the two captains, because we arrived only five miles north of Wanakan! This kind of accuracy had never before been possible, truly an impressive feat of navigation.

Yes, Ariana and her group were utterly amazed at the sight of Wanakan and its people and culture, so vastly different from ours. I introduced them all to King Matial, Queen Amihan, and their son, Coatl. Indeed, the King was exceptionally pleased to receive all the items that Ariana had brought to trade for pacas. They would return with the cargo hold full of the creatures and fodder for them. As soon as I introduced our newest member, Michelle to them, Amihan asked her if she wanted earrings befitting the others in our group. When Ariana and her group saw the new look for Michelle, they too just had to get some as well. Amihan was very pleased to give them all fine sets of earrings as well.

I took a little time to tell them about how Teyacapan was doing and how well and excited all the people were to be at our estate. Further that the three protectors were also being trained, one to be a fighter, and the other two wanted to be engineers, builders of things. He was impressed. What really impressed them the most were the presents that Teyacapan had sent back for them. Her father received a huge two handed sword made in the Highlands, a fine blade. She said the King needed the biggest blade, and he laughed when I told him her words. She sent along another nice blade for her brother. For Amihan, she send bolts of silk and sewing gear, along with one already made dress so that she could figure out how it was done. Ariana and her group gave her sewing lessons before they left.

On the third day, we said our farewells to our new friends. Ariana and all her people accompanied us to the longboats. Julianna and Rachele giggled as she proudly showed Natale their new earrings, which were as long as Natale and Mireio's. Indeed, they just touched their shoulders. Ariana's were similar. I teased everyone, "See, we've all gone native." They just could not get over the fact that in this land, gold and jade were commonplace, that the means of exchange was grain and pacas!

Once more we stood on deck watching the city of Wanakan drift behind us. "Orders, commander?" Henry teased me.

"Due east, Captain Sir!" Nearby, Michelle giggled at my reply.

I added, "Okay, everyone to the galley. It's meeting time." The bosun took over for Henry.

Over tea all around, I began our meeting. "Our objective this trip is to explore the southern waters between here and the Spice Islands. To my knowledge, no ship has ever sailed here. As you know, we are to keep a very sharp eye out for more mantis creatures, these Black Gods of the Wanakan. Also, be alert for possible locations where they might have laid their eggs. We already know that the eggs can lie dormant for a quarter century and then be hatched."

"Our biggest fear," Emil added, "is that there are either other groups of mantis creatures being raised or that their nests may be found. If we could barely kill the babies, think of how formidable an adult mantis creature would be."

"Question, are we to take a large zig-zag course across the southern ocean?" asked Henry. "Sailing straight, we might miss islands even as large as West Reach. We could set the offset to span a hundred miles or more."

"I like that, plus, let's have Benet and Michelle search as well. Show them the daily charts of our path and they can extend the search area further. I don't want to have to just sail back and forth across the whole ocean three or four times."

"Good plan," said Henry. "Now when we draw near the Spice Islands, I expect to find a whole lot more of them. Mariners are still discovering new islands and natives there, opening up smaller trades."

Thus began our systematic search of the southern ocean. Days later, we discovered an uninhabited island, about twenty miles around. It had a fabulous beach, so we spent a day taking a swim and relaxing. Michelle named this island the Vacation Island, rather appropriately I thought.

April 5, 649, we found a large island, a strange one. We sailed around it first, estimating it to be a hundred miles in circumference, but not quite circular, some thirty-two miles across. A mountain rose high in its center. Much of it was full of waving grasslands. What caught our attention immediately lay on the southern coast, where the best porting beach lay. Twenty-four giant stone statues, twenty-five feet tall, rose from the ground, staring out to sea at us. Spooky.

Seeing no telltale smoke clouds or any signs of habitation, we lay anchor in the bay and took our two longboats to shore. We stepped onto the white sands of a virgin beach. I let the Loremaster take the lead, though Michelle followed him closely, asking him many questions as they went. Emil was nearby in case of trouble. The rest of us followed behind the three.

"Sea turtles crawled up here, Michelle. See their unique trails here and here?" She observed carefully the patterns. "No signs of any people, Bethany," he called out. Soon we left the beach area and climbed onto the main land, where the tall grasses rose above our waists!

"Scary not being able to see where your feet are going," Michelle commented. Natale and Mireio seconded her observation. A half hour later, we reached the statues. Up close, they were even more impressive! Standing twenty-five feet tall and four to five in diameter, these monsters were hewn from a single solid stone. They wore some kind of hat or helmet of a different kind of stone. All were carefully carved to represent figures. Their faces were long with thick lips and big eyebrows. Their ears appeared to be wearing earrings similar to those that Natale, Mireio, and Michelle now wore or my other original pair.

Moss grew at their bases, while lichens covered much of their bodies, along with many bird droppings. They had been here a very long time indeed. But who made them and why? We were all asking that question. Cedric, our Planner, pointed out that each must weigh in the tons and that they were not made here, but somehow transported. How could this be? After spending several hours here and finding more questions and no answers, we decided to hike on up to the mountain. Perhaps the rock came from there and maybe we'd find a village or two.

Four hours later, we were climbing among the rocks of the mountain, having left the grasslands behind us. "Here's where they were quarried," Benet pointed out. It was very clear to me he was right. Long, rectangular chunks of the stone had been systematically removed. We could even see the drill marks at regular intervals along the backsides of a ledge.

"Hey, I found a cave over here," Emil called out. Everyone rushed to see. It was a huge natural cavern. "Look out for the three dead bodies," Emil warned us as we entered. Three skeletons lie near the entrance. "It's too dark in here without some lanterns," he added coming back to where we stood.

"Hey, look at them! They are missing their arms!" declared Natale. We looked closer at the bones.

"You are right. Legs, ribs, chest, backbone, skull, all there," Tonia stated, as she bent low to examine them. "I'd say these were women, see their pelvis region? Childbirth, men." I chuckled. "I wonder how they died." She looked the skulls over and found nothing to indicate that they had sustained head injuries. Their long leg bones were intact. Nothing seemed amiss.

"There is only this jade knife, if that's what it is, lying there between the toes of this one," Tonia observed. She began moving the piles of dust about. "Hey, got something here. Well look at this!" She had uncovered a set of gold and jade earrings, not too dissimilar from the ones we now wore. Shortly, she found two more pairs by each of the other two skulls. She collected them.

"Perhaps we should start an artifact collection, in case we find more stuff," Benet suggested. We all agreed. Due to the hour, we hiked back to the ship, making plans to bring lanterns, food, water, and blankets with us tomorrow so that we could explore more fully.

Most of us spent the day packing gear up to the cave. Benet assisted Michelle, who set up her painting station so that she could sketch out the statues. "You have to go stand by that one for me, please. I really want to get the scale right, otherwise the viewers will not appreciate just how big these really are." The two joined us at noon for lunch, she had six canvas sketches roughed out already, but they wanted to be part of the cave exploration after lunch.

Armed with a dozen lanterns, the Explorers Circle walked deeper into the cave. Benet pointed out several fire circles, where rocks were arranged in a circle, their inner sides blackened from fires from long ago. Further in, we found what must have been grass beds. Long bundles of the grasses had been tied into bunches, but now they were nearly dust, though their shape was still visible. Michelle counted fifty such beds. "I hope we don't find fifty more skeletons in here," she commented.

Next, we found hundreds of clay pots; their lids were off and all were empty. Benet hazarded a guess that they may have held the people's food. It seemed a reasonable assumption. The walls were definitely getting closer together now; we must be reaching the end soon.

Emil called out, "Found something, several somethings. Boxes perhaps?"

We squeezed in around him. Five boxes, about three feet long, two high and two deep lined the sidewalls of the cavern. "Shall I open one?" he asked. Several of us positioned our lanterns so that everyone could see. Carefully, Emil began to open one lid. As soon as he put pressure on it, the wood crumbled in his fingers. As he jerked from the surprise, he bumped the side of the box, and it crumbled as well. Like a small avalanche, the box disintegrated, and its contents flowed out onto the floor.

We stared at hundreds of these same earrings! Emil teased, "I hope you don't take this as a sign that we men should be wearing these too." Everyone laughed. Cedric held a sack, and we formed a human chain, moving the earrings into the sack. "One hundred pairs," Emil called out as he passed the last two to me.

Natale said, "A jeweler said that my pair would sell for twelve thousand gold pieces, mostly because of the jade in them. This means that we have just found about one hundred twenty thousand gold coins worth of treasure. Incredible!"

"Hey, these are longer than mine or Linda's or Rosina's," Tonia stated. We compared them to Natale's. Sure enough, they were the same length, just very different motifs.

"Why don't we each take a pair," I suggested. "Tonight we can try these new one on you three and see if you like them. I think yours ought to be as long as ours are. Maybe Cathy, Angel, and Mary Beth will want some longer ones too." The women grinned; they liked my idea.

"I'm going for the next one," Emil called out. Like the other, the wooden box had dry rotted and fell to pieces when he touched it. Two hundred golden necklaces spewed out on the floor. These were very strange indeed. Each necklace was formed from five long bands of gold, each about one and a half inch wide, with each successive row much longer than the previous one. The top three rows fastened together around the neck. Golden chains held each row or layer in place. Bits of jade beads were strung along these chains. Each was relatively heavy. Soon each of us had one in our hands examining it closely, particularly how they were fastened.

"Oh I get it," I announced. "Who wants to try one on so we can see how they look?"

"Women!" teased Emil.

"Please, don't make us wear them," pleaded Renzo, teasing me.

"But look there are two hundred of them, but only one hundred earrings. Obviously, the men here wore these as a fashion statement, Renzo." Everyone laughed.

"Try one on me," declared Michelle.

"The way these work, they are going to be easy to get on, but hard to get off. They have a sort of twisting metal lock so that they cannot easily fall off." She held her hair back to one side while I began fastening one on to her neck. The three top bands went around her neck with the top one near her chin. The bottom two semi-circular bands rested across her upper chest. Once I had it securely on, I straightened out her long black hair. "Guys, what do you think?"

"Well, actually, now that I see one being worn, they do look really beautiful. It does add to your beauty, Michelle," Benet said. She flushed.

I set to work putting one on the rest of us, Linda finished up with mine. "Our earrings keep banging in to the necklace, rather interesting," she commented. "There, my, they do look good on us, don't they? These people certainly had a sense of style and fashion."

By now, the fellows had all the others safely stowed in two more sacks. Emil tackled then third chest. This one contained various bits from which more necklaces and earrings could be put together. Piles of gold chains, jade beads, gold strips, and heavier jade pieces littered the floor. This took us nearly an hour to retrieve, since we didn't want to miss any of the tinier jade beads.

The next box contained hundreds and hundreds of the little gold disks that we put into our pierced ears to support the heavy earrings. Some were small, similar to the ones we had when we first got our earrings from Teyacapan. Various sizes ranged up to nearly two inches around. Again, we spent an hour making sure that we had retrieved all these pieces.

The final box crumbled in Emil's hands. Out rolled over a hundred jade knives very sharp on one edge with beautifully carved handles. These were more difficult to transport, they kept cutting into the sides of the sacks. We ended up putting only a few in each sack.

While the rest of us spent a couple hours getting all this back to the ship, Michelle continued making her rough sketches of the island and its statues. She insisted that Benet stand as a yardstick once more. I passed them by several times, glad that I didn't have to stand there. However, I saw that he was really looking at her. Interesting, I thought. On my last trip past them, I overheard him say, "That necklace does look really good on you, Michelle."

That night, Cathy, Angel, and Mary Beth tried on a new set of earrings and kept them, as we had. I helped each into one of the gorgeous necklaces as well. Now we all looked similar. At dusk on the deck, I asked Renzo, "So how do you like my new look?" He smiled and gave me a very loving kiss. I guess he liked the new look!

The next day, Michelle stayed behind in the company of Cathy and the Santi to paint, while the rest of us went to explore the island further. Benet promised to come get her if we discovered anything else noteworthy.

We found another cave with a cache of stone cutting and carving tools in them. Late that afternoon, we found many small caves on the northern side of the island. These, we quickly discovered, were burial caves, which we left untouched. However, Emil suggested that we do a quick head count to get an estimate of how many people had died here.

After an hour, we gave up trying to make an accurate count and simply did an estimate. Based on the number of caves and what we found in the few we examined, we guessed that over five hundred people had died here. Presumably, that also meant that they lived here. "But who buried the last one?" asked Linda. We could not answer that one or what had happened to all the other people who had lived here.

Cedric made an estimate and stated, "Gang, by my calculations, at least a thousand men must have worked to make one statute. There are twenty-four of them. Either they were at it a very long time or there were lots more people here. Where did they all go? Why would they build these incredible statues and then leave them here, abandoned?"

"More important than that," Benet stated, "what would they eat? We've seen a couple freshwater streams, but unless there were pacas, there's little here to eat, except mice in the grass."

We camped overnight, and by the middle of the next day returned to the ship. Michelle had one painting of the statues done. We all had to peek and I was floored! It was a perfect likeness, down to the lichens growing on it, complete with Benet standing beside it, as a tiny figure." Everyone praised her work, and she asked that we stay around for a few more days so she could get several more actually done.

"Shore leave for everyone," I announced. Renzo and I went for a long walk in the tall grasslands. Eventually, we stopped and lay down on the soft grass. Yes, we kissed and held each other for a long time. Until now, we really didn't have much private time, you see.

On April 11, we weighed anchor and left the Island of the Statues behind. Again, Michelle named it for us and Henry very carefully drew its location on our map. It was a hundred miles or so from Wanakan. We speculated that perhaps some ancient Wanakan's had come here and created the statues; it would make some sense, well at least from the earrings. However, we'd seen nothing like these necklaces in Wanakan, nor the jade knives, for that matter.

As we began sailing again, I wanted to work with Michelle on her telepathy situation, but she spent most of her time either painting or out scouting ahead with Benet. That would have to wait. Now came the long days of swabbing the deck and the endless piles of dishes. Steadily, each day became warmer than the last. I began to dread how hot the summers must be down here.

The next day, we received word that Ariana had set sail for home, loaded with two hundred pacas! Good for her, for soon she would have the only large herd in the Sea Princes, and after that, she'd have the market cornered on their fabulous wool! Shortly after that, Donata made a big Mind Link with me. All of her gang was joined up. Everyone wanted to thank for having convinced them to take this trip! They were, as I thought, in seventh heaven, so to speak. They learned so much, made so many new friends and trading partners, that Ariana couldn't keep track of them all. Julianna and Rachele could and did, however. Rachele added, *And we are all coming back in native paca clothing! You are so right; this wool is super soft to the touch, just a fabulous find! Thank you, thank you, thank you!*

Donata, as she signed off, said, *You did good, little sister, really good! Thanks, I owe you a big one.* I felt happy the rest of the day. Plus, I didn't have to worry about them running into major storms, because Benet and Michelle were looking out for them each day, while they were out searching for us.

By May 15, we had covered nearly half of the distance across the southern ocean. Only a handful of widely scattered islands had been found, all uninhabited. No, the problem was the heat! This far south, we were rapidly approaching the summer season. Already, in the daytime the temperatures reached nearly a hundred degrees. The men stripped down to their undershorts, but still the sweat poured off them when they worked much on deck. We women now had a problem. While no one thought anything of going nude in the public baths or on the public beaches, which were used in place of a bathhouse, we were not used to being naked elsewhere. Yet, we were melting in our clothing.

Linda suggested that we take everything off but our undies as well. Normally, that would have worked out, except for Natale, Mireio, and Michelle. In order that they could handle going to the bathroom by themselves, they wore no undergarments. They would not be able to get them off themselves if they had worn them. We held a women's conference in the broiling galley. "But if I take off the dress, I'll be parading around naked and this isn't a bathhouse," declared Natale. "I can't leave the dress on much longer. I am melting to death!"

"I see why women don't go to sea," Michelle added. "Men can take everything off, mostly, but we are stuck, unless it is an all-woman boat, that is." We laughed at that idea.

Linda said, "Look, if these three have to go around naked, then we ought to too, just so they don't feel totally out of place. It isn't fair to them, if we don't."

"I don't mind being naked in the bath house, but on deck, I'd feel a bit funny," I added. "Of course, I wouldn't mind being like that in front of just Renzo." Everyone laughed, knowing what I meant by that.

"Then, as I see it," Linda replied, "there is only one thing we can do. We must agree to look after the three here, you know, take away a bit of their independence for a while and be vigilant to their needs. We wear only our undies, like the mem are doing. But I think we ought to leave it up to those three. It should be their decision: we all go naked so they can continue with their independence or we take away a bit of that and we wear undies. What do you think?"

They voted to lose a bit of independence. After that, we all took turns looking after their needs. Now we found the temperature a lot more tolerable, though we all quickly began tanning like the men. That evening, when Renzo and I were along on the deck, he commented, "Bethany, you look absolutely gorgeous like this. The earrings, necklace, bare chest, it looks fabulous. I am the absolutely luckiest guy in the whole wide world! I love you so much I can hardly stand this long wait to get married."

"Me either," I whispered back and we held each other tightly and embraced.

That night, as I brushed out Michelle's long black hair, she confided in me. "Bethany, mom's not here and I am awfully confused about some things. Can I talk privately with you? I know I am older and should know these things, but..." her voice trailed off.

"Sure, there, all done. Shall we talk in bed?" I killed the lights, figuring that might ease her embarrassment. We had the porthole open, but it didn't do much good. Not until late at night would a cool breeze trickle down on us. We had no covers on either, just too darn hot. I dreaded what it must be like in August! We crawled into bed. She rolled over to face me, lying on her side. She put her arm on my side and began.

"This afternoon, Benet kissed me. I mean really kissed me. I've never been kissed like that before, you know as lovers might kiss, not a good night kiss or you did good kid kind of kiss. My body had all sorts of reactions that I've never felt before." She rattled off a number of very private things that I won't mention here.

"Could it be that you are starting to fall in love with Benet? I think that he may well have fallen for you." I tried not to evaluate for her, but perhaps nudge her in the right direction.

"Oh!" she replied startled.

"Is that the confusion you were mentioning?"

"Er, no, no it's not that, well yes, sort of, but not really, but somewhat it is," she was really having a hard time with this.

"Well, why not just come right out with it, I promise that it will be just between you and me. No one else needs to know about it."

"I, ah, I, well all right. I have always been a man. I mean, I've always had male bodies. I know how to be a man. I mean, it has been so hard for me to lie here beside you and not, well, you know, do things that would give you great pleasure. I don't know how to be a woman. I am completely lost. What do I do when Benet kisses me like that? My body felt like it was on fire in all sorts of places."

"Michelle, you are not alone with this problem! I'm the opposite. Let me tell you a bit of my history. I first had two female bodies and had the role of being a woman down really good, except figuring out when I was in love and all that. Then, last lifetime, I had a new female body all lined up for me to get. Only I got messed up on the timing. My future mom was pregnant with a little girl body that I intended to get, but I got zapped by a Grey Creature and when I recovered and took the new born baby body, it was years later and it was a boy body. I had no idea of how to be a man! Just the opposite of your situation. It was a most embarrassing situation for me for so many years. I love long hair and insisted on that body having long hair. I love the name Bethany, and insisted Bethany be part of my name, duh. I even for a while masqueraded around as a woman for a time, but well I had a valid reason for doing so, because they were after a male. Anyway, I was most confused until I found the right woman for me. Good old Caitlyn, she helped me get things figured out properly, my first wife, Tal's mother. She was assassinated right after giving birth to our twins, you see. After that, I was completely lost once more. Then, Lilly Ann straightened me out; she was my second wife. Thank god I've a female body this lifetime!" She giggled and understood completely.

"So you see, Michelle, I really do understand your situation. It is nothing at all to be ashamed of, not the least bit, perfectly natural. As far as guidance is concerned, I am not very good at match making. My advice is to find a man that you truly admire and respect. If your body agrees with you, it will respond just the way it has been responding, only more intensely. How's that for complete vagueness! God, I am no good with love advice am I?"

"No, I think I see what you mean. I really do admire Benet. We get along so well. He's like perfect. I mean, if he had my body and I his, I don't mean that he has to be minus his arms like I am, I mean if he was female and I male, there that sounds lots better. If we were switched, I'd be wooing him, er her, like mad, my dream person."

"Well, then that's settled; you are in love with Benet."

"Yes, yes I am, but I still don't know what to do. I mean how do I respond? How am I supposed to act? I don't want to turn him away from me because I am so ignorant of things."

"Hum, can you remember some of your wives?"

"Sure, why?"

"Let's pretend that I am one of your wives and we are in bed. What would you be doing? Let's act it out, shall we?"

She stroked the side of my head slowly moving down my neck out onto my chest, finally ending up on my breast. God, I was getting aroused! I cleared my throat. "Okay, now can you recall what she did when you did this to her?"

"Hum, she moved her pelvis like this, put her arms around me like this, and kissed me passionately. God, my body is being turned on when I do this! Should I do these things to you?"

"Er, no. There you have it, Michelle. Just do what you feel you want to do, respond how you personally want to respond. You must always be true to yourself in any relationship. Only to do what someone else says to do or to do just what you have been told to do is deadly to the relationship. If Benet is the one for you, he will rejoice in how you respond to him, as he will freely respond to what you do to him. For example, when he kissed you this afternoon, what did you really feel like you wanted to do?"

"I felt so light! I wanted to throw my arms, or what's left of them anyway, around him, hold him tightly, and kiss him back for hours!"

"I suggest the next time he kisses you, go with what you feel you want to do at that very instant and you should be just fine. If you are at a complete loss, look back on your wives and remember how they responded, though I would suggest you go with how you feel first."

"Thank you ever so much!" she gave me a hug. "I'll do it. I wonder if he will ever kiss me again, because, well because I didn't know what to do?"

"Okay, tiny bit of advice. Tomorrow morning when you two go up to the bow, before you sit down, stand right in front of him, smile, and open your arms wide. He'll get the message."

"Oh yes, she used to do that to me. I'd come home, and she'd stand right there in front of me, arms spread. I can't wait til morning!"

The next morning after breakfast, I sneakily followed the two up on deck as they headed to the bow. They planned to spend the morning searching a wide path on either side of our heading. She did as I suggested. Benet reached over and began to kiss her; her arms went around him. Smiling, I went back down to tackle the mountain of dirty dishes.

That night when we were in bed, she bubbled, "It worked fabulously! I don't know how to thank you! Does your body get so tingly and like electrified when Renzo kisses you?"

"My legs almost buckled under me the first time he kissed me passionately." She giggled.

The next morning, Benet and Michelle came back from their sweeping pattern way early. He yelled, "We found an island. We think we saw people on it. It's that way about twenty miles or so. Just remember we are not so good on distances."

Chapter 7 Isle of Loving

May 17, we found a new, unknown island — a large one at that, rugged in places, with many dense stands of trees. As usual, we circumnavigated the island, estimating its circumference as at least three hundred miles around, making its diameter something like a hundred miles across, quite large enough to sustain a population, we all concluded.

We saw no telltale smoke clouds, but perhaps no one wanted a fire in this heat! The southern shores were a bit too rocky for a safe landing. On the northern shore, there was a wide bay, with a white sandy beach, the best landing location the island offered us. Mid-afternoon, we sounded our way in, carefully, anchoring about a quarter mile from shore. While we were lowering the longboats, I thought I saw a person in the palm trees just beyond the beach, but only a fleeting glimpse.

Slowly we sailed towards the beach. "Looks like a really great beach; the waters are so clear and blue, so perhaps this is another vacation island," suggested Michelle, who sat behind Natale and I. "I sure could go for a swim just to cool off," she added. We all agreed with her.

When our longboats were about a hundred feet from shore, suddenly the people began appearing. Women actually, lots of women, naked women at that, came rushing out of the trees onto the sands. They were obviously very excited and were jumping up and down. "Good god!" yelled Natale. "None of them have any arms! Not a one!"

"What have we gotten ourselves into this time?" I said aloud, very exasperated with this whole concept of mutilating women!

"Some are but little children!" added Michelle.

"They all are wearing earrings similar to yours," Renzo commented from behind me. "They do seem very excited to see us. Where are all the men?"

"Look, more keep appearing from the trees!" Emil yelled from the boat beside us. "I don't see any men or boys. Do any of you see any?"

"Not a one," I replied. "There must be over a hundred women there of all ages. What have we run into anyway?"

Thud, our boats hit the beach and quickly we all climbed out, forming a line with Natale and myself in the front, ready to meet these new people. None of us was prepared for what happened next! Not in a million years!

As soon as we lined up the older women, not the children, ran up to us and began sexually attacking us! One woman began rubbing her breasts against mine; her tits became erect. Another attempted to give me a passionate kiss, while another squatted down to lick, well, I won't say what she was attempting! It was the same with all of us, man or woman. Each of us found ourselves with three women on them, each one trying their best to be the most passionate of lovers!

They had no arms. I felt guilty trying to push them off me; I surely didn't want to knock them to the ground. We yelled "No! No! No!" in an attempt to get them to stop. Natale and Mireio had it the worst, for they didn't have the means of pushing the women back. At least Michelle did her best to try. Roberto, grabbed his wife by the waist and turned her around to face him, putting their backs to the well-wishers, still the women tried to kiss them. They ended that by kissing each other. Well that was one way to stop the love attack!

Henry followed Roberto's lead and soon had Natale rescued, not minding at all kissing his wife. Quickly, everyone else follow their plan. Renzo rescued me and we began embracing. Benet took care of Michelle and so on down the line. I saw Emit passionately kissing Tonia, and she loved it. Those two, I thought to myself. Boy had I ever been blind to love on this trip!

Finally, with all of us making it abundantly clear that we did not want their love making affection at this time, the women stopped and backed off a bit. Quickly, Natale began to speak for us. "Leader? Leader?" she asked in several languages, but the women look at her strangely. Finally, one said, "Ah, leader!"

Natale caught on rapidly, "It's a form of Wanakan, some dialect. Let me find out what's going on here." She began talking to whatever woman was closest to her, quickly working out their variations. Then all of a sudden, the women backed off, making an opening for another woman to approach us, well six of them. One had long greying hair, the eldest I guessed. One woman called out to Natale, "Leader."

All these women had darker skin, somewhat browner than those in Wanakan. All had thick lips and oval faces, pretty to look at I thought. They all wore long earrings, very similar to ours, just touching their shoulders. Every woman had very long, thick, straight black hair, except for the grey that six had streaking theirs. I envied them for a moment, for their hair reached their upper thighs while mine was only down to my bottom.

Tonia brought me to the present, "Bethany, they are all awfully thin, especially the children. Look how thin their legs are. I wonder if they are getting enough to eat?"

Natale called for me to join her. "If you stick a 'th' sound at the end of many words, their speech is nearly the same as Wanakan. This is their leader now. Hina. She's fifty-six. She says that there are no men anymore. I haven't figured out what that is all about yet. However, she says that they are all starving. Already twenty have died. They are having an awful time trying to get food for a year now, if I understand her right.

She wants to know if we can help make food for them."

"Okay, tell her if her women will not try to make love to us, we will make them a lot of food."

Natale grinned, "Thank god for that! You know these women are very good at it. I got really aroused there!" She returned to the leader and relayed my request. I admit that the women looked forlorn when they heard no love making. However, the mention of food brought on tremendous excitement; they all began talking at once, even relaying to the children who were behind them.

I ordered the men to go back to the ship and bring a feast back with them. "We should find out where they are living and what cooking facilities they have," Renzo suggested to me. Shortly Natale said that they will lead the way to their village. As we walked following the horde of women, Renzo had his arm firmly around my waist. No way was he going to let them attack me with their love! Ah, my Protector!

I teased him, "Bet you never thought that you would have to be protecting me from a bunch of love-starved women." He roared and squeezed me tightly.

We walked through a grove of coconut trees and other fruit bearing trees. Ahead lay their current village, some fifty thatched huts in bad disrepair encircling a communal fire pit, long unused. Children's footprints were all over the ashes in the center. A small freshwater stream flowed nearby, their source of drinking water.

The leader suggested, "Start fire, roast meat, please, we are starving." She then lay down, and Tonia saw at once that she was really slowly starving to death, which was why her body was so weak and fragile. I ordered everyone to gather up firewood and to set a cooking fire. By the time that the others arrived carrying boxes of food supplies, we had the fire going. Next, we all set to work preparing a large dinner for something like two hundred.

Meanwhile, I had the group line up so that Tonia could check over their health, just in case we had some infections or diseases to handle as well. As she went from woman to woman, Tonia commented, "You know they lost their arms a very long time ago. None of their surgeries is at all recent, not even the little girls. At least we don't have infections from that to deal with here. They are all malnourished. Protein appears to be the single biggest factor so far. I'll keep you posted, Bethany. My new skill is coming in very handy indeed!"

Tonia went on, "Ah, this woman needs treatment for a knife wound on her feet. Says she cut them trying to open a coconut for the kids." She got her bag, and she and I went to treat the woman. The cuts were not deep and only had a tiny bit of infection. She got her patched up, wrapping her feet with lots of binding to protect them. Everyone here was barefoot. I could see why, since they only had their feet to work with in an attempt to live.

By the time that Tonia and I finished up, the smells of food filled the camp. The leader said something, and everyone went into the various huts and came out with a bowl, holding it between their head and shoulders. I say bowls, but really, they were the bottoms of coconuts. We all lent a hand going from person to person, filling their bowls. Each thanked us and leaned over, carefully lifted the bowl to their mouths. Whoever figured out what to cook sure thought ahead. They had no silverware, and the semi-liquid paste was thus easily eaten from the bowls. We told everyone that they could have as much as they could eat. Most took seconds. We had not enough mugs, but that was not a problem. When they wanted a drink, they went over to the stream.

After everyone was done, I had Natale ask Hina if she was strong enough to talk with us. She looked very tired. She asked her daughter, Hinatea to speak for her. In fact, the six older women went to take a nap. Hinatea was thirty-three, and I couldn't help but notice that she had very beautifully formed, full breasts. Ah, woman envy here.

We sat in a semi-circle around Hinatea. First, she asked Natale, "You Old Way too, like us, she too?" she indicated Mireio. "They New Way?" she pointed her head to me and the others. Natale said that we did not understand and asked her to tell us the history of her people. This she could do.

Slowly the picture began to emerge, but not without numerous interruptions when Natale didn't understand something and the two women had to work it out. These people considered themselves the Children of the Black God. That was what they had always called themselves. There used to be a thousand or more men, women, and children living in the main village, further inland. The Black God lived on the mountain behind the village. Always, the Black God provided for the villagers, bringing food and strange metal tools, gold, and green stones to the people. It was said that the Black God loved all of his people.

However, the Black God demanded only one thing from his followers, only one thing. When female children were born, its arms were to be removed along with the mother's cord and given to the Black God. It is said that by the female baby arms the God survived. Gladly did the women offer unto their all-powerful, all providing, all loving god the tiny arms of their female babies. It was such a tiny offering for all the greatness bestowed upon the Children of the Black God.

The women were all loved and well cared for by the men of the village, and wanted for nothing. In return, all the women were trained from childhood that their dual purpose in life was to bring forth new life and to always provide love and great pleasure to both men and women. Their highest purpose was to pleasure both sexes at all times. Should they become with child by this, then the Black God would reward them with love and presents. This is now called the Old Way.

The village thrived and grew to over a thousand before the Black God vanished. His absence was first noted something like twenty-seven years ago. At first, no one thought much about it, life continued on it usual path. When girls were born, their umbilical cord was cut and their arms very carefully removed, before it was given to its mother to suckle. The offering was then placed on the high altar for the Black God to dine upon. Yet, he did not come. Small baby arms rotted on the altar and eventually had to be discarded.

"Now all the men began wondering what they had done wrong to so displease our god. Even we women searched our souls for our failings. Had we not pleasured others enough? Had we not conceived enough new life? Women vowed to increase our pleasure making to make amends for our short comings."

"Still the Black God did not return. Some ten years ago, some fathers began to say that removing their baby's arms was wrong and they began to refuse to do this deed! These became known as the New Way. Over the years, more and more men began to desert the Old Way, joining with those of the New Way. Always they fought and argued over who was right and who was wrong."

"Then, last year about this time, those of the Old Ways saw that too many were drifting over to the New Way. One night, they slipped into the houses of the New Way women and killed every woman who retained her unholy arms! The next day, all the men began a great battle! We women of the Old Ways huddled in our huts, fearing those of the New Way would come and kill us too!"

"At night, everything became quiet, but we stayed inside, not daring to go out, for fear that a New Way man might kill us. When morning came, we were very hungry and had to go outside. It was very quiet. We began looking around; dead bodies were everywhere. Only one man of the Old Way still lived, but his blood was oozing out of him. We could do nothing to save him."

"We began to panic! Always our men provided for us. We could not start the fires of life, nor fish, nor spear the wild pig. We could not plow the fields nor grind the grain. Worst still, we could not cook, even if we had these things! A simple thing as a drink of water we could not get. For days, we tried to work the well that the men always used to draw up cold spring water for us, but not a drop could we manage to bring up. Then, we could no longer stand the stink of so many bodies. We could not bury them either. Alas, we had to leave them to the scavengers. What else could we do?"

"That's when mom, Hina, said that we must move to where we can find water and something to eat. We came down here. Water always flows and is clear and good. Every day, we go out in search of something for us to eat. It is hard. We can only gather what has fallen from the trees and the berries on the bushes. Occasionally, we did catch a fish, but we have no way to cook it, so we ate it raw. Not very often though, very hard for us to catch a fish and so many of us to feed. Already, twenty of us have died from hunger. We push their bodies away from our huts, but have no way to bury them. Today, we see your ship. Some say we will be killed. Some say we will be rescued."

"So are you, Natale, Old Way woman?"

"No, I ran into some very bad men who cut them off of me, painfully. Same with Mireio. Michelle had some heavy boxes fall on her arms and crushed them. I guess you would say that we are all New Way people from a distant land. Actually, this might come as a shock to your people, but there is a huge, huge world out there across the sea. It is full of New Way people."

"But New Way people help us? Not kill us?"

"Yes, we have come to help all of you. We swear to protect you from all harm, right Bethany?"

"Absolutely, Hinatea, we have come to rescue all of you and to see that you can once more live life to its fullest. You have my word on that. I am their leader."

"Thank you, Leader Bethany. Truly, you are saving our lives. Thank you. But we are trained to always give back something in return. We only know how to do one thing, give others pleasure. If we promise not to do that which creates more new life, can we be allowed to give you all back in return the only thing that we know how to do? We feel so badly that we cannot give back something to all of you who are saving us from starving to death. Perhaps I am too old for you. You are all so young. We have many young about your ages who would give anything to give you pleasure to thank you for all of us. Please let us do this simple thing in return."

Lilly Ann I need you! I wanted to scream for her, mom's Judger. Instead, I screamed for Linda, my Judger, okay, I didn't actually scream. "Let us discuss this among ourselves. I will let you know in a few minutes."

"Thank you Leader Bethany. Thank you so much for saving us all!"

We got into a small group, I said, "Well, Linda what do we do now?"

She said, "Scream for mom, that's what!"

"I already thought of that! Where's Lilly Ann when you really, really need her!"

She chuckled. "Okay, we've got a big problem here. They are very right about the principle of exchange, Bethany. We all know that the route to criminality lies in not being able to contribute back. Here we are literally saving nearly two hundred of their lives. They are slowly starving to death. They also know that they must contribute something of value back, Bethany. Can you imagine how they will feel if we save them and do not let them return something of value back to us? Surely, we are bigger than that!"

"Look, she has already said that they would not do what is needed to create more babies. That is very key here, I think. They are only looking to pleasure us, not have sex with us. That is one huge difference! However, I, for one, would be very embarrassed to have them, well fondling me in front of all of you."

"Same here, same here," everyone else agreed with her.

"She's volunteering women our own age. I don't think that we honestly have much choice today. We have to let them do this at least once. Maybe tomorrow we can figure out something else for them to do in exchange. Let's do it after dark and let's scatter all around. I'll find it less embarrassing that way. What do you all think?"

Renzo put in his ideas. "She's got a seriously valid point. We have to let them contribute something. Until we can figure out something more palatable to us, we ought to let them give us what they consider of great value. However, can we somehow explain to them that it is our custom only to be doing this to our spouses and not to strangers? I am going to feel very funny — well embarrassed is a good word, Linda. Explain that we consider this a very private thing, the giving of such pleasures only to our wives and husbands."

"Okay, still, I cannot order anyone of you to go through with this. So anyone who does not want to do this, quietly take one of the longboats back to the ship. If anyone asks, I'll say you have a stomachache. Are we all agreed?" I asked. We were.

I had Linda explain all this to Hinatea, three times, just to make sure that she understood us properly. She beamed with happiness and went to tell the others. Meanwhile, Cedric remarked, "No wonder these huts are in such disrepair. In fact, they are not in disrepair; they were built by feet only. Now I understand. These women have been resourceful. What say we spend what's left of the daylight to fix up their huts a little bit?"

"Sounds good to me. Some of us will need to work on fixing supper though. I guess I am still on dishwasher duty," they laughed. While we wanted to go exploring, insufficient daylight remained. Linda came and lent me a hand with the dishes.

She said in a low voice, "You know that we are going to have to take them back to Velona pronto don't you? We can hold them all in the cargo hold, perhaps in hammocks, but I doubt that we have enough of hammocks to go around, there are hundreds of them."

"Yes, I know. We have ourselves one big problem. Linda, I have to take some responsibility for all this; after all, it was Alabaster and me who caused the destruction of their god and ultimately led to their current situation. Don't misunderstand me here. I'm not casting blame around, just that I need to be responsible for what I have done and see that they are well handled."

"Of course, Bethany, we all do."

Around sunset, we once more doled out a healthy meal. These women had not had two full meals in over a year. I felt good about helping them get their bodies recovering once more. Then came another pile of dishes. At last, we could put it off no longer. It was dark now. We spread out over the perimeter of the village. As I got to a likely spot, three young women in their early twenties came shyly up to me.

"I am called Gesa; this is Emiri and Amiria. On behalf of all of us here, we want to give you thanks for saving our lives the only way we know how. Please accept our thanks."

"Hi, Gesa, Emiri, Amiria. I'm afraid I don't know what you want me to do."

They giggled. Emiri said, "But you have even longer earrings than we and you do not yet know their purpose? Come we will show you. It takes three of us to do this because we have no arms. Relax, enjoy, feel; we know what we are doing." An hour later, I could not agree more fully with her statement. I had learned a few erotic tricks that I intended to use with Renzo, once we were married. I actually got quite an education, one that I never had had before.

The next day, none of us spoke openly about the night's experience, but from the looks on everyone's faces, I knew that each had learned quite a bit. Interestingly enough, Gesa, Emiri, and Amiria now hung around me. Likewise, three women hung around each of the rest of us. While we were combing our hair, Gesa explained, we will be with you today to help you anyway we can. Hina has said that we must learn new ways to thank you. We promise to do so, just let us know."

"That's really good news to hear, Gesa. Thank you very much. After we get everyone fed, we want to go have a look at your old village. Perhaps we can properly bury you dead."

Hina made her way over to me. She was still very weak. "Bethany, I have told everyone that we must now learn the New Ways. If we do not, we shall die. They are all very willing to try. I am still too weak to do much. I gave much of my food to the children. Better that they live than I."

"I understand. Thank you. I would have done the same thing. Children are our future and yours. You rest up and get your strength back." She smiled and went to lie down once more.

While I was washing the dishes, I had my three helpers put the dried dishes into the boxes. I would stick a plate between their head and shoulders and they did their best to put them where they went. With metal plates, they could do no harm. As I was washing, Emiri said, "Now you see what the earrings are for?" I grinned and said that I did. She looked pleased.

She then asked, "Some of us are in need of larger little disks. You know about this, I see you have larger ones than Michelle. Can you please help us with bigger disks?"

"Now that one we certainly can!"

She smiled. "Thank you. I will show you where the men keep them in the old village today. Mine are getting way too loose."

A little while later, we all tromped through the trees, following a well-worn path inland. Gesa told us to make noise to frighten away the wild boars, unless we wanted to catch one for supper. Emil thought that would be ideal and promised that on our way back, he would take a small expedition off in search of boars. After an hour of nearly steady upwards hiking, we came to their old village, set against the rocky sides of the central mountain of the island.

She was right, the remains of dead bodies lay everywhere in various states of decomposition. Daggers and knives had been their weapons. The men formed up a burial detail, while we began searching each wooden building, looking for something with which to dig. Gesa suggested that the men kept such tools in their work shack. Shortly, I handed out many shovels.

Their village was well made. Wooden buildings were laid out in a large semicircle around the base of the rocky mountainside. Most of these were similarly made and had housed the women. None had doorways. Emiri showed us what used to be her family's home. Inside were well made beds, some light blankets, and some personal items, which they were unable to carry to their new homes by the stream.

A central water well beckoned. It had a stone base, circular in shape and well crafted. Buckets attached to ropes could be lowered to draw up the cool, clear water. Several buckets now sat on the water at the bottom of the well, a result of their frantic, but unsuccessful attempts to get water for themselves.

Six large, permanent campfire rings held huge pots. Here was where the cooks had prepared the meals for the whole village. We guessed mealtime here had been a communal affair, as opposed to a family dinner. Since we now had to feed so many, these large metal pots would be most welcome.

What caught my eyes next were the steps carved from stone that led upwards to the homes of the men. At least fifty wooden buildings were precariously lining the sides of the rocky cliff. Wooden walkways connected these to the winding stone stairway, whose end I could not see. Gesa explained, "That first building is where they kept our earrings and disks. When we needed them, they would take us up to that first one there. Women were never allowed beyond that first building,"

"Okay, I'm going to go have a look and see if I can find all that we need to fix up your earrings. Do you want to come up there too? It is a steep climb," I suggested, giving her a way to refuse if she didn't think she could easily make it.

"We are always scared to go up there. It is so high and we have no arms, scary climb for us, but if you need us, then we will go with you."

"Okay, you can stay here. If we need you, we'll come and get you, how's that?" She smiled, relieved not to have to make that climb. I took Linda and we climbed up the steps. While they were broad enough, the exposure began to tickle our stomachs by the time that we were fifty feet above the ground. Walking the rope-held wooden planks from the steps to the building was tricky, even with hands.

Inside we found a bed and a large cabinet with many drawers. I opened the top one, figuring to be systematic about this. In the top on were large thorns and many glass vials with a liquid in them. I took a sniff from one and recognized the same anesthesia that we had gotten from Teyacapan! Yet we had not seen any of those plants around here yet.

"I'll make a note to keep our eyes open for those plants, Bethany. Do you suppose such plants do not exist on this island? If so, where did these come from? And what craftsman made such intricate, useful vials?" Linda commented. "They are much better than the pots of Teyacapan."

The next drawer held trays of the gold disks, ranging in size from very tiny ones, which could be used perhaps on a baby, all the way up to ones nearly three inches in diameter. There were only a few of these however. All were methodically organized. Someone had taken great pains to make this a well-organized setup. The remaining drawers contained the earrings. Again, they were graded by size, some for small children. Most were for adults. If one counted only the gold and jade values here, ignoring the jewelry sale value, one would have been fabulously wealthy!

"Who made all these and where and how? Where did the gold and jade come from?" Linda pointed out the most significant details. We had thus far seen no signs of gold or jade on the ground. Perhaps they had a mine nearby?

"Say, I have an idea," Linda perked up. "These women need to exchange something of value, well, how about all these? There's enough value here to provide for them in Velona for the rest of their lives and then some!" I hugged her! "What's that for?"

"Rescuing me from their eroticism! That's what." We both chuckled.

Together, we carried the drawer with the disks back down to the ground level. Then, we went to help the others with the massive burial project. Emil had chosen a spot by a gully where with only a small amount of digging, we could cover up the hundreds of dead bodies. It took us all day to do this grim action. Finally, with a mound of dirt covering the mass burial site, we carried the cooking pots and the drawer back to the main campsite, where the cook kindly had dinner waiting for us.

After dinner, I took Hina and Hinatea aside. "Ladies, we have found something that holds great value for us that you have. In the men's hut, we have found many hundreds of these gold and jade earrings. In our world, gold and jade are very rare and are very valuable indeed. If you wish to trade the stash or part of the stash, it would be so valuable to us that your people would be very well cared for their entire life! In our world, this means you are very rich and wealthy. You could get anything that you desired by trading these for them. You no longer have to please men; you can hire men to please you!" I thought I'd try twisting it around and see what reaction I might get.

"We would need some for our future children," Hina said hesitatingly.

"Of course, but there are so many, even allowing for that, you would never again have any worries at all, believe me."

"Then, that is what we must do, Leader Bethany. You talk of this world of yours. Where is it? Is it larger than our land here?"

"It is a long way across the sea. Yes, it is very, very big. Let me talk with my mother and see what arrangements we can make for you. Your people now have more than enough to trade for absolutely all your needs."

"We are forever in your debt, Leader Bethany. We were never allowed into the men's houses. Perhaps there are some things there that you might deem valuable as well."

"Thanks, we will check everything out. All your dead have now been properly buried, except for those who have died here recently. We'll bury those tonight."

"Thank you for such kindness." She smiled. Though she was regaining strength, I didn't want to tire her further.

While I did the dishes and the men finished up with the last of the burial duties, Linda and Tonia went from woman to woman, replacing disks as needed. By nightfall, all had been handled, and we headed for the beach to take a much needed and deserved bath!

When I finally lay down for the night cradled in Renzo's arms, I had to contact mom. I couldn't put this off any longer. *Hi mom. We are all fine. Discovered a new island. Got a new problem for you. We have just rescued one hundred eighty-three women between fifty-six down to three years of age, all armless since childbirth. All the men on the island* killed each other. We found them slowly starving to death. They have hundreds and hundreds of these gold and jade earrings that they will trade for living accommodations. No traumas, thankfully. Help!

God! One hundred eighty-three! I send you off to explore, and you keep on bringing me back armless women! Maybe I should recall you! She was teasing of course. I then related the entire story, as we knew it thus far.

We have a real problem here. We don't have enough food for this many for very long and have insufficient capacity to transport that many back home. Help!

Okay, I'll send some caravels as soon as possible. Allan can get to work making a new building to house them all. Please search the island carefully! If the mantis lived there, who knows what useful information you might find, even their eggs. I'll have Paulette get back to you, as we know more.

The next day, I sent Emil out with a hunting party to get fresh meat. Henry had his crew out fishing. We women, along with many of the younger women of the island, went on a foraging outing to bring back as much fresh fruits, berries, nuts, greens — whatever we could find. I knew that it would take weeks before mom's caravels arrived, and we had to make our provisions last until then at the very least.

Two days later, I was satisfied that we had increased our stockpile of foods sufficiently, especially since the mariners would continue to fish each day. Thus, it was back to exploring the old village once more. Several of the women came with us. Gesa, Emiri, and Amiria had constantly been following me wherever I went and today was no exception. "You are going into the men's huts, right?" Gesa asked as we walked to the old village.

"Yes, perhaps we will find more useful things that you can trade with us."

Emiri timidly asked, "And Natale and Mireio — they go with you too, up into the men's huts?"

"Probably they will. They don't want to miss anything either."

"Then we come too!" she said bravely. "If Natale can do it, Emiri can do it too. We have always been curious what the men had in their huts. Now we can see for ourselves."

At the edge of the village, we stopped while Renzo and Benet gathered up the pile of jade knives and the metal daggers they had collected the other day. They filled three sacks. I told the women that these were valuable as well. Then, it was up the first set of stone steps to the building where they women went to get their earrings adjusted. We filled many, many sacks with the valuables in this room. Renzo and Benet also carried the wooden cabinet down as well.

Next, we climbed up to the next level. Now we were a hundred feet above the ground. Rope and wood bridges ran off in many directions here, going from hut to hut. Most of the huts were at this level, however. These were the primary dwellings of the men, we discovered.

Walking on these wobbling bridges was a challenge even for those of us with arms. Each of us took charge of one woman. I had Natale in front of me. More than once, I had to steady her as she lost her balance on these bridges. I now realized that the main reason they were off limits to the women was just the simple fact that it was very difficult for them to manage without constant assistance.

What did we find for our half-day troubles? Virtually nothing of any value, loincloths, bedding, blankets, things like that. Still, the stone stairs beckoned ever upwards. At noontime, up we went to the next level, which had only two buildings, both quite large. These turned out to be meeting rooms. However, from Mireio and Roberto's point of view, we hit the jackpot. Ten different sizes of drums, two strange looking stringed instruments, a set of musical shells that made beautiful sounds when tapped, and three flute-like instruments lined one wall. These, the two confiscated immediately, along with several scrolls with strange markings on them.

Undaunted, the stairs led still higher up the cliff; it looked like a cavern possibly. Up we went, now nearly three hundred feet above the ground. The view was spectacular from here, however. The steps ended in a cavern, whose opening was huge. "Large enough for a mantis to get in here," Linda noted. I concurred.

Just inside the cavern, we found a jackpot of treasure. Here was where the jewelry had been crafted. Against one wall was a very large bin containing piles of gold nuggets. On the other side was a similar bin filled with jade stones of all shapes and sizes. The quantity staggered the imagination. "Gesa, forget trading your earrings stash. The treasure here in these two bins is enough for all your people to live like queens for the rest of your lives! This is incredible!"

Four jewelry workstations stood nearby. A small melting furnace allowed the smiths to melt the gold. We found the forms into which the molten gold was poured to make the various parts and chain rings. After examining everything here, we walked deeper into the cave.

"What is this?" asked Natale. We stood before what could only be described as a desk perhaps, but for a giant. We could just barely see the desk's surface. There were strange metal slabs on the desk, like paper, only metallic in nature. Emil, the tallest of us, reached up and brought one down for us to examine. Strange symbols covered the sheet. "Writing perhaps?" Natale suggested.

After bringing several jeweler's chairs over, we climbed up to have a better look. Six more of these unique slabs were there, along with a metallic pen of some kind, which made the marking on the slabs. Two of the six were blank, however. Nothing else was on the desk. Natale requested that we take the slabs. Perhaps one day she could decipher the symbols.

Further inside, we found what could only be described as an insect nest, one of enormous proportions! None of us had any doubts now that at least one of the mantis creatures had lived here. Worse, we found a clutch of twenty eggs! These we knew that we would have to destroy, but not in front of the women.

The next three days, we all worked hard bringing down all that gold and jade, along with the equipment with which to make the jewelry. Up and down all those stairs gave us all quite a work out indeed. The first day, however, we brought shovels with which to smash the eggs. Two had small embryos, which looked like small, black, praying mantises!

During the process of removal, Cedric began toying with the giant desk. He was using his heightened sense of pervasion looking at its structure. "Hey, Rosina, come here a minute, I think that I've found something. There is a hollow spot behind this desk somehow. Listen to this." he tapped here and there, she also heard the distinctive hollow sound.

"Wonder what's back there and how we get to it?" she said, very curious now. "Hurry up and figure it out, dear."

Cedric climbed onto the desktop and began looking for some mechanism that might open it. Soon he found a tiny button and pressed it. Slunk. A metal plate slid open, revealing the secret compartment. "What's in there? I can't see from down here!" Rosina exclaimed, jumping up and down, trying to get a peek inside.

"More of those books, lots of them. Here, I'll hand them down to you." A little later, the two proudly showed the rest of us the three dozen "books" of the metallic pages, if book is the right term. Natale was quite excited about the discovery, whereas the rest of us didn't think much of it at the time. If they could be somehow read, that would be something else again.

With the treasure safely stacked near the new village huts, I decided to see if the women wanted any of the belongings, which they had abandoned when they moved here close to the fresh water stream and beach. Many wanted some small items, so another couple of days passed while we went with them to search and recover what they wanted to bring with them.

To keep the men from utter boredom, I sent most on a search mission: search every inch of the island for anything that might be relevant. It took them nearly a week to circumnavigate the island. They had found the former crop fields and the remains of some kind of domesticated chicken coop. However, the chickens were long gone. They either escaped or met with some predator. All they had to report was that the island was nice but with a fair number of wild boars roaming on the opposite side.

To help with my own boredom, I brought a kick ball from the ship and started up a never-ending kick ball game with the children and a few teenagers. They caught on quickly, especially when Natale and Mireio joined in with me. "Let's get Bethany," Natale said to a five year old girl named Arihi. She giggled and tried to kick it at me.

"Whoa," I made an effort to get out of the way, but let the ball hit me so that I was now it. "Oh, now I'm a going to get you, Arihi!" She laughed and ran all around. Later, more joined in, and soon I had fifty of us running around, laughing like mad. This was the first fun thing the younger kids had done in over a year. It brought a big smile to Hina's face, seeing them run and play once more.

Later that afternoon, Roberto and Mireio closely examined the instruments. Emiri got my attention and said, "Those are what the men used to play while we sang and danced." Mireio overheard that and ran over to us.

"Emiri, you never said that you all sang! Do you remember any of the songs or dances, how they go?"

"Sure, we all do, excepting the little ones. The men would look at those papers there when they played. We thought the papers told them how to play, but we don't really know if that's true."

That was all Roberto needed to know — that these pages somehow held the key to the music. Now he began sorting them out. "Look, Mireio, these look like a percussionist's markings, while these are quite different. Three distinct types here. How do I determine which are for the flutes and which are for these strings? Ah, I know, the strings have a wide range. These pages have more markings and over a big space.

After supper, the music session began. Roberto began by trying to play the basic rhythm on the largest drum. Catching on to what he was attempting, several women came over and set him straight on what it was supposed to sound like. He went from drum to drum, with the women telling him how it should be sounding. He commandeered Linda, Tonia, and me, showing us what and how to pound three of the drums, while he took the more complex ones. Me, I had the large drum, which simply went boom, boom, boom, boring really.

Next, all the women, except the six older ones, lined up in four rows out in front of us. Roberto started us going and the women made all sorts of suggestions until we had it right. Then they began to sing their first song that went to this one. After several choruses, the four lines began to dance to their singing. As one group, they danced, following complicated foot patterns, which many of the youngest had not yet mastered. Occasionally, the lines would move forward and backward as well. Then they swayed in place, which was followed by lowering their heads and swirling their long black hair in wide circles about themselves, twirling their bodies as well.

Conclusion: these women had a very sophisticated series of songs and dances. Bard Tal would certainly find a use for these women, of that I was certain! Roberto and Mireio were happy as a pair of larks on a springtime morning!

I also took time every early afternoon to explain in more and more detail what was going to be happening to them, that three more large ships would be coming to take them to a new home, where they could learn many new things that would help them lead a happier life. Additionally, we all worked on helping them learn the Velona Sea Prince dialect. We all knew that knowing how to speak our language somewhat would greatly ease their transition after the long ocean voyage.

Thus, from now until the caravels arrived from Velona, mornings were spent foraging for food, early afternoons dealt with language and descriptions of Velona life, late afternoons sported the never-ending kick ball game, evenings were filled with song and dance. The women of the Isle of Loving, so named by Natale, came alive once more.

On June 20, 649, three caravels arrived, anchoring near ours. One caravel had brought us a new set of food supplies; mom didn't want us returning anytime soon! It took us a week to load the women's treasure onto the ships and to transport the women there by longboat. Finally on the June 27, we went from ship to ship to say farewell to our new friends. We promised them that we would visit them just as soon as our long trip was done. This, I believe, bolstered their courage. Each ship carried about sixty women. Make shift beds filled the sides of the cargo hold, while the provisions were tied securely in the center. Twenty additional Santi were along to help the women with daily life. I knew they would be safe. We waved until the ships were but small dots on the horizon, sailing northward.

An hour later, we had gathered up all of our gear, transported it to the Sleepy Hollow. We all took one last swim in the blue waters off the beach. Now it was back into the sweatbox for us once more. While on the island, whenever we were hot and sweaty, we just took a dip. Ugh, sweat box for us now.

"Heading, Leader Bethany?" Henry teased me. I never could get Hina and the others to stop calling me Leader.

"East, Captain Sir!" I teased him back. Michelle giggled as she and Benet walked on up to their usual spot way aft. We were under way once more in the stifling heat. Once the two returned with the all clear for the next fifty miles, Henry allowed Michelle to take the helm once more.

Chapter 8 Flying Death

"Why do you suppose that the mantis creature was taking care of all those people on that island?" Michelle asked me. We were lying in our cabin bed this first night after leaving the Isle of Loving behind. The daytime temperatures had soared into the hundreds. All of us had stripped down to only our undies, yet still sweat rolled down the men's chests and ours too. Our long hair didn't help matters either. The island's blue waters called for me to return and go for a swim. We had our porthole open, but only hot air entered. "God, I am so hot, sweat is sliding down my breasts! How can we ever sleep in this heat?"

"I'm wringing wet too, Michelle. It sure is a strange situation, a mantis creature on its own private island. Maybe it was just trying to raise its own crop of arms? They seem to have liked to dine on them."

"But a baby's arms are so tiny," she countered. "Do you really think all this perversion among so many different people all stems from the mantis creatures and what they did?"

"Michelle, people are basically good, and they don't go around cutting off people's appendages. Well, in a war, they kill and maim with abandon. What bothers me the most is that all one hundred eighty-three of those women thought absolutely nothing about having no arms. Women are supposed to be like that! In fact, they really were just made into sex slaves, if we are totally honest about it."

"Like the toys of a man?" she asked.

"Yes, good way of putting it. In the lands of the Greenway, women used to be treated as equals to men. Now however, the influence from the south has been creeping its way northward. We've already seen some of the eastern kingdoms of the Greenway begin to mistreat their women. You know, that island was almost like some kind of hideous experiment on humans, to see if it could create a whole society in which all women were the armless, sex toys of men."

"Well, that's awful. Yet, it did apparently work out for a long time, that is, until the men were lost. If those women still had their arms, they could have survived well on the island. Oh, no men, no more babies. Even they too would have died out," Michelle replied.

"Maybe the island was their prototype for all of Tarra? Maybe that was their plan all along and the Grey Creatures were trying to stop them from doing that."

"If the island was the prototype, what then of Wanakan? How does that fit in? They ate young women's arms, but only a very few at that," Michelle countered.

"And the Holy Paladins and their priests either cut off or encased the arms of women, but mostly the women were the artists and the most intelligent beings of the countries. Now that I think about it, you know, we did not get a single peasant woman at Jenna's who had lost their arms in any way. The Church of Jehosanity struck out against only those women who could counteract or potentially cause them difficulty in their overall plans for subjugating women. I will be very curious indeed to find out what natural talents the Wanakan women end up showing. Michelle, I'll bet you anything that those women whose arms the Black God ate are the higher powered women artists and great thinkers of Wanakan!"

"Ah, I am beginning to see, but was it their plan to turn all the women of Tarra into armless play toys? That's at least half of the entire population of Tarra, but then you said they were only able to operate here in the southern part. Do you suppose that if we go further south we will find entire countries with armless women?"

"Lord I hope not! Mom and I have done an awful lot of therapies now and we've not come across anyone who has led such a lifetime. Doesn't mean they don't exist. We had no idea this island existed. It may well be that the mantis creatures were stopped before they could implement their grand plan for Tarra."

"That would mean that we are now cleaning up their messes," she concluded. "I much prefer that point of view. Damn it's hot. I could use another drink. Would you please lend me a hand with it?"

Four weeks passed us by. We'd discovered another twenty smaller uninhabited islands. Each time, we spent some time cooling off on their beaches. Some were habitable, though we found no trace of any settlements from bygone days. It was now July 27, and we were a hundred miles from the collection of islands known as the Spice Islands. We were way east and somewhat south of that group, when Michelle and Benet reported another island, this time with people on it.

Following our usual procedure, we circled the island. This one was twice the size of the Isle of Loving with a heavy forested central hilly region. The northwestern side had the best bay with a brown sandy beach. Here we chose to land. Also figuring into our planning was the fact that there was a coastal village here with numerous fishing boats. Strangely, none was out on the water. It was around noon.

We sounded our way in as close as we dared and set our anchor. Henry stated the obvious, "Spice Island terrain and vegetation, but where are all the villagers? All these boats should be out fishing. People should be on the beach. I say, rig for trouble!"

"Dear, does this mean that they will likely speak Thundercanand?" Natale asked. This was what we called their melodious dialect, full of long musical sounding words. He nodded. Others broke out their longbows and strapped on their swords and daggers. Chain mail was out — too darn hot! The crew sweated profusely as they lowered the longboats for us. However, we all knew that once we were on our way, they would dive overboard for a cooling-off swim.

We had gotten within a hundred feet of shore when around fifty men, women carrying their babies, and children came running out towards us, yelling loudly. The men were also making signs telling us to go back, go back. Natale did her best to understand them. She said, "It sounds like they are saying take us with you and go back. Or perhaps take us and get away from here. I don't understand this."

As we rowed in towards them, I got my first look at a Spice Islander. These people had dark brown skin, probably an adaptation to the extreme sun and heat. All had black hair and black eyes. The women, like those on the Isle of Loving, had never cut their straight, thick black hair. The men wore theirs rather long, but most had moustaches. Like us, all wore only a loincloth, made from a blood red dyed silk. Henry had told us that in cooler weather, the women wore a loose fitting dress called a sarong, held up over one shoulder.

We beached the longboats, surrounded by fifty or more rapidly talking people, some of whom were actually trying to get into the longboats. Emil had to bring order. He yelled loudly, "Stop!" That got everyone's attention.

Natale took immediate advantage of the moment of silence. "Hello. Please, only one person talks at one time. I can barely understand your language. Please speak slowly."

Several looked at each other and one man began to speak for the group, "You must take us away from here. You must leave at once, before the black devil comes again! Please, you must take us, save us we beg you."

"We do not know what this black devil is. Can we go into your village, meet with you, and have you tell us about this devil? We are Santi del Dio from Velona, Sea Princes. We promise to do what we can to protect you from this devil. We are powerful fighters. Please, we must meet with you where it is safe. We do not understand. Are any of your people injured or wounded? We have great Healers among us."

One woman echoed, "Healers! They have healers. Please bring them back to the village, Thainanonian. Think of the others."

"Okay, follow us, but be quick before the black devil sees us and dives upon us again." Clearly the man was very frightened indeed. Hastily, we pulled the longboats securely onto the beach and followed the fifty as they ran back into their village. One large hut made from bamboo poles and perhaps palm leaves was the village meeting hall. We followed them inside. Normally, the flimsy building would have its many windows wide open to allow the sea breezes to pass. However, today, the reed mats, which served as blinds, were lowered, as was the reed mat door. The building was anything but secure!

You can smell death and dying a mile away. The odor is unmistakable. "Show us the injured right away," I said, but I forgot that they didn't understand me. Natale quickly translated.

The woman, still carrying her year old infant, led us to the back of the room. There lying on reed mats were four women of varying ages, from ten to perhaps twenty. I might have guessed it; appendages were missing! One woman was missing her right leg below the kneecap. Another was missing her entire left leg. A third had lost her left arm at the shoulder. The fourth, who was only ten, had lost both her arms below the elbows. Worse, some kind of clear, gooey substance covered the amputated ends, a small amount of blood oozed out. Several were running a fever, including the child. The four were uniformly delirious.

Tonia had come prepared for action. Via Natale, she asked for some boiling water, while she opened up her healing pouch and began taking out what she might need. Cedric offered his help as her assistant. Meanwhile, I asked Natale to ask someone to explain what was going on here. We needed facts fast.

Natale did her best. "They call it the black devil. They don't have any other word for it. Apparently, it flies. Some are saying that it is a hundred feet long; some say it's but five feet. I have all sizes in between. At least they all agree that it flies, swoops down on unsuspecting people, and begins devouring parts of their anatomy. Several men have been eaten alive, with nothing but a carcass to bury. These women were luckier. The villagers came out as a group waving whatever they could find as a weapon and frightened it off of them before they were entirely eaten."

Just then, the reed mat door opened and a tall man, wearing a red sarong entered. At once, a hush came over the people. One man whispered to Natale, explaining that he is the Sik, the village leader. He spoke in a commanding tone, "I am Sik Anethion. Welcome to our humble village. Forgive these frightened people; they know not what they do. Who may you be and where do you come from and what do you want here?"

Natale and I stepped forward. She said, "This is our leader, Bethany." She gave her usual opening speech.

He looked at her with a great sympathy. "I had not known that these black devils attacked ships at sea. At least you live, Natale."

"Oh no. We were not attacked. You must mean my arms. I lost a fight with some very bad men, that's all. No, we do not know what this black devil is. We are also Healers, and two of us are working on the four wounded women back there." Just then, two men came in carrying a large copper basin. Steam from the boiling water rose, adding to the heat and humidity in the room.

Via Natale, I asked, "Is there someplace less crowded where we may go and discuss what has been happening around here? We are Santi fighters, and perhaps we can slay this devil for you."

This, as I expected, got his full attention. I suspected rightly that he had been powerless to stop this devil and his people had paid for it dearly. I left Rosina with Tonia and Cedric. In case of trouble, she could contact me, though I didn't expect any.

"Ah, yes. Follow me to my business quarters." We followed him outside. I noticed that he carefully scanned the skies before moving rapidly through the red dirt streets of the village. At the far end on a rise stood the only stone building in town, his quarters. Inside, his wife, also wearing a red sarong, bowed to us, but said nothing, bringing a decanter of water and a number of copper cups to his meeting table.

He sat at the end of the table in a mahogany chair, whose back was intricately carved with intertwining motifs, which I did not recognize. After pouring her husband a glass and accepting his nod, she poured a copper glass for each of us, although she hesitated before Natale, Mireio, and Michelle, uncertain. Natale just said, "Yes, please." She smiled and sat a copper glass for them as well, bowed and left the room.

Sik Anethion began, "Now then, I should tell you about this thing the villagers are calling the black devil." In order that Natale could concentrate fully on the translations, I held the cup for her occasionally to sip, since she was doing all the talking. Apparently, this flying devil first made its appearance near the village of Ramadanon, near the center of the island about two months ago. He told us that the island had ten villages, one here on the coast, one near the center of the island, and the others at locations, which were ideal for their crops and water supplies. The other Siks had sent word of this flying menace to him periodically for the past two months. Only in the last ten days had the devil creature flown over his village. Six men had been killed and their bodies mostly eaten. Four women had died as well. The four that we were treating somehow had survived their attacks, though the fever was taking them, one by one. He'd convinced their families to move them into the meeting hall, confiding in us that he was mostly concerned that they might cause disease among the others.

Next, I inquired about how frequent the attacks had been and if he had noticed any pattern in them, such as always in the afternoon hours. His reply was vague, "You are safe from a couple hours after dark until the morning twilight hours. It does not come every day. Random, so it would seem to me. While I am expected to enforce our laws equally and fairly, my spear, effective against a man, is useless against a flying beast. In this matter, I am powerless. I have prayed to the golden Huwan for divine intervention as my people desire. Perhaps, Lord Huwan has sent you to rid of this devil, that is what I think when I first heard your words."

"Ah but then I see that you have no arms, and your leader is also a woman, and so many of your party are women, yet another without arms and one without hands, so I realize the folly of my first impressions. Please accept my humble apologies." He bowed to Natale and me.

Good old Natale, feisty Natale, she beat me to the reply, "Ah Sik Anethion, looks can be deceiving, deceiving indeed. If we say that we will fight this devil, then either we are foolish or we are more than meets your eyes. Now then, has it attacked other people in the other villages?"

"Yes, the other Siks have reported many dead, many wounded, although wounded seems not to be the correct word. We have no word for what it has done to those who yet live for a while."

"Say, have you ever had any kind of thing like this occurring in your past history?" I asked, wondering if there was some kind of repeating history, as there had been elsewhere.

"Our people settled on this virgin island twenty-five years ago. We built our villages with our own hands. This is very fertile island, and our people are earning a good living here, until the last two months. Perhaps it is as some say: we have done something to upset Lord Huwan, though none can say what that might be. Yet, gods act in mysterious ways as we all know."

Via Natale, Renzo asked, "Do you have contact with the other islands? Has this black devil been sighted on other islands?"

"Four times a year, the supply boats come to us, and we make our trades. The next one is not due for nearly a month. We have not heard anything about this black devil being on other islands, but as I said, it only appeared here about two months ago. Who can say? Many villagers want to flee our island, forsaking all that they have done here. Can we blame them? No. Yet, I know the supply boat can only carry a few that may want to leave. I expect that our poor village will be overrun with our people fleeing from the other nine villages when the supply boat comes."

"Let's hope that we can eliminate this devil long before then," Emil said, via Natale. "Say, when the devil attacks your village, where do the attacks occur? Is there any one particular place?"

"No, it sweeps in from the middle of the island, flies overhead looking for those outside, perhaps in their fields or on the streets. I'm told that it sweeps down and pounces upon its victims, though I seem to keep missing its attacks. I've only seen a black shape flying back toward the center of the island twice now. For the last many days, everyone is too afraid to work out in the fields, and people run from place to place when they have to be outside."

"Okay, Sik Anethion. Unless you have any objections, we will setup our attack formation in the village's large central area by the well.

We have a wide field of view there and our combat will not be close to the villager's homes."

"Yes, yes, by all means do so." We thanked him and returned to see how Tonia was doing with her four patients.

She, Cedric, and Rosina were busily at work. They had finished washing off the gooey substance and Tonia was carefully inspecting the damaged areas. I explained that we were going to prepare to do battle outside with this creature the next time it showed up. "Rosina, you are to stay here and protect these two. If you get a chance to launch a long-range strike to help the rest of us, do so. Primarily, I want you to look after these two and help get any of us that get wounded inside here fast."

I ordered Roberto, Mireio, and Michelle back to the caravel. There was little that they could do if we had a battle to fight. Two of our spear shooting ballistae were brought ashore and set up on the beach, where they would have a clear line of fire at any incoming flying devil. On the ship, the other two were made ready to protect the ship. We could not use the flame throwing devices because we'd be more likely to burn down people's homes than hit a flying creature. Sergeants Angel and Mary Beth commanded the two onshore ballistae with Captain Henry overseeing them, while Bill handled the ship's defenses.

With those preparations set, the rest of us took up our positions near the southern end of the large open central plaza of the village. Natale and I took the point position. Renzo and Emil stood behind us at my request. I wanted them to have the best chance of attacking the creatures, since she and I were playing bait. Benet and Linda were behind them. Benet was charged with evacuating anyone who got wounded into the hut where Tonia could deal with their injuries immediately.

Now we waited. From time to time, I saw Sik Anethion peering out a window at us. He probably thought that we were doomed — six of us, half women, standing in the open like sitting ducks. Yet, the two ballistae looked impressive, for a land or sea battle, that is. Against a flying target, ah, I had my doubts that they would be able to hit it.

"I need something big and heavy, if this devil turns out to be one of those mantis creatures." Although we looked, there were no big stone blocks of which the Wanakan temple had been made. In fact, the only stone work, other than the Sik's house, was the village well, and those were all smaller blocks.

Now we sweated in the hot sun and waited. We got only a small relief from the well, frequent drinks and water dumpings. That is, I'd fill the bucket and dump it over Natale and me. The others followed our example. We waited. Supper was brought to us from the caravel. Still nothing, except that I got out of having to do the dishes, along with Linda. At last, we headed back to our caravel to spend the night, leaving the ballistae ready for action the next day.

We ate an early breakfast and took the longboat back to the village. We took our positions, while Tonia checked on her four patients. One woman's fever had broken, which she pronounced was a good sign. The older women who had lost a leg or part of one were now conscious and eating, but were in despair over their loss, naturally. The twenty-one year old woman, Minanan, had no fever this morning, but had no appetite as yet, barely drinking. The child was still fighting a raging fever.

At least the morning hours were relatively cool, if ninety is considered cool. The waiting was beginning to take its toll on our alertness, however. A spear from a ballista whizzed over our heads, waking us up to action. The spear missed the flying target because it veered out of the way, proving it had intelligence. Sweeping in with the sun at its back, we could not see exactly what we were about to fight. Altering its flight path, it had obviously seen us and was coming for us.

"Remember kick ball, dodge, Natale. Here we go!" I called out. A few seconds later, we knew what we were facing. Yes, it was another young black mantis creature, nearly twelve feet long! As it homed in on our front, it made contact with Natale, sending, *Ah, I see we must have met before. You must therefore be quite tasty. I'll have a serving of legs this time, before moving back to her arms.*

Natale sent, *Prepare to meet your doom, bug. We are the Bug Killers!* She concentrated and achieved her desired effect. The mantis froze in mid-flight. Its wings stopped mid-flap; it hung as if suspended by some invisible thread! Twang! Twang! Nearly simultaneously two giant quarrels flew overhead, piercing completely through the belly of the mantis; greenish ooze began dripping onto the ground.

Yet, it was not helpless, mostly startled by such unexpected resistance. Immediately, it launched an energy blast, which Natale was unable to completely dodge; part of it hit her body, knocking her off her feet. She hit her head hard on the ground and lost consciousness, freeing the creature from her grip. Although it was flying once more, three walls of fire now appeared in front of it and on both sides, rapidly closing the distance to its body.

It dropped like a rock, avoiding the collapsing flames, and emitting another blast, which sent Emil flying backwards, knocking him out as well. During this time, I took a brick from the well and moved it high into the sky. Wham. Renzo dodged an energy blast from the creature as it swooped over us, but it took a long distance quarrel hit from the ship this time — again so powerful was the force behind the spear-like bolt that it went completely through its soft abdomen, leaking more greenish goo onto the ground. It arced around and swopped down towards the ground close to Natale, intent on taking a nibble. Just as it opened its mandibles, wham, my stone hit it in the head, sending it into a roll across the ground.

Some of its arms rubbed its head, while its eyes sent a heavy energy blast my way. I did a roll and dive to get out of the way, grabbing up the brick and pulling another one loose from the well. Renzo bought me some time by placing a wall of fire right in front of the creature, forcing its attention off me and onto the flames and him. Benet was now dragging Emil away towards the hut where Cedric was waiting to take him from Benet. I regained my feet, close to where Natale lay.

Once more, it avoided the flames, this time by making an enormous leap up and over the flames faster than Renzo could move them. Renzo was forced to do a tuck and roll to get out of the way of its retaliatory energy blast. Now the creature had a chance at Benet, and it took it, knocking Benet off his feet, sending him sprawling. A quarrel from the ship flew past its previous location, missing it. Only Renzo and I remain active, immediate opponents. Apparently, it was not concerned about the ballistae, even though it had been pierced three times now. It certainly did not seem weakened much by the puncture wounds. Cedric now ran to get both Benet and Emil out of harm's way.

Renzo yelled, "Toque Ball, Sucker Roll. Signal when ready."

Oh no! He was going to make himself the target, drawing the full attention of the bug so that I would have the perfect shot at its head! That was a very dangerous move, because if anything went wrong, he was going to be in big trouble! I got the two stones far apart and yelled, "Execute!" This kind of play can only be done by players who have total, complete confidence in the other. One tiny miscue and Renzo would be done for!

He ducked and rolled right under the head of the mantis! Simultaneously, his feet plunged upwards, delivering a very solid blow to the lower jaw of the mantis. A human would be knocked out by this move, but not the mantis. Its head thrust upwards violently, nearly cracking the neck casing shell. It was stunned. Now was my chance.

I brought the two stones together as hard and fast as I could. Both smashed simultaneously into opposite sides of its head. It shrieked in terrible pain, but the stones did not have enough mass to crush its head, unfortunately. Yet it was stunned, momentarily doing nothing. Renzo was pinned down by one of its feet and could not get free. I had to do something else. Ah, another idea formed.

Since it was motionless, I grabbed onto its rear leg and began swinging it in a circle, and every few passes, I smashed its head into the ground. Around and around and down. To the many people watching, this must have been a wild sight. There was the mantis just being thrown around as if by magic. No one was apparently doing anything to it. Renzo leaped to his feet and created a sheet of flames where I was forcing its head repeatedly to hit the ground. On the next bash, the flames began searing its head as well. Again and again, I bashed its head into the flames and ground. Finally, the last time I forced its head into the ground, creature's head broke off from its body! I dropped its body at once and it fell to the ground with a thump.

Renzo shook my hand, "Nice move, dear. I wouldn't have thought of that one. Stones not heavy enough?"

I grinned, "Yes, not heavy enough. If you hadn't stunned it, I couldn't have swung it around like that. Instead, it would have blasted me where I stood. Good teamwork. Better check on Natale."

We lifted her up into a sitting position and she came to, "Oh my head! Do I ever have a headache! Oh, did we get it?" I pointed out the mess. She smiled and asked us to help her up. The others came out to check on us and the ballistae crew came up just behind them. We all stood around the severed head and body, which still quivered a little. Angel stabbed it a couple more times with the spear-quarrel, taking no chances. She was trained to make sure the dead were dead.

Natale managed a smile, "Well, I did tell him that we were the Bug Killers; he should have listened to me." We chuckled. Emil and Benet were both rubbing their heads. Emil had a very bloody nose, however.

"Gang, go get Tonia's four patients, bring them out here. I want them to see that the creature that harmed them is really very much dead now." Several went to bring them out. As I suspected, staring down at the remains of the creature, which had harmed them, did wonders. Since they all had feet, I had them kick the carcass repeatedly until their anger waned. By now, all the villagers came out, and some of them too had to kick the carcass.

Sik Anethion joined the throng, "Hail our heroes. We thank you beyond words. A feast for all shall be held tonight in your honor. Please ask some of your wives to help mine prepare the feast. The black devil is dead! Musicians, please entertain our heroes this afternoon while the preparations are made. Tonight we celebrate as we have never celebrated before!"

The villagers yelled and cheered. Later, we discovered that seldom had their Sik held such celebrations. Several villagers wanted to dispose of the remains, so we let them. The rest of us took a much-needed swim to wash off and cool off. The equipment was ferried back to our ship and stowed. By the time that we returned, only one patient remained, the small ten year old girl. The husbands had come to take their wives home. Tonia and I went to check on them, because I had not yet given them therapy.

Uniformly, the three women declined saying that they were all right, that their Lord Huwan would see to their needs. I discovered that you cannot force a person to accept therapy. A bit annoyed, we returned to the others. The little girl's fever had broken, and she said her name was Alwanianon. She asked about her mother and father. Since we didn't know, Natale and I went to try to find them. The Sik was very apologetic. "Both of them were killed trying to get the devil off her. She has no other relatives here. Perhaps you would care for her? We do not have the facilities to properly care for her needs here on this island."

I readily agreed. On our way back, I spat, "What a creep, Natale! He didn't have the balls to come right out and say that he didn't want a cripple such as her to care for. Can you imagine abandoning a young girl just like that? Of all the nerve."

"It's good that we are here, for her sake. They might have just let her starve or worse. Can't say much for their humanity around here," Natale answered. "What will we tell her?"

We found her sitting up, accepting a long drink of water from Tonia. "Hi Alwanianon. My name is Bethany and this is Natale."

"Hello, Bug Killers," she grinned. By now, the whole village had picked up Natale's name suggestion.

"Honey, I'm terribly sorry to have to tell you this, but your mom and dad died trying to save you from the black creature."

"I know. I just remembered. Now I have no one to live with any more. Like this, the villagers will just leave me alone. I know, I saw it happen to one man who got his arm cut off in the fields last year. They just let him be until he didn't move anymore. Then they put him under the ground. I don't want to be under the ground, Bethany."

"Well, honey, I don't want you there either. From now on, you will be living with us. All of us will share being your replacement mom and dad, how does that sound?"

Her eyes lit up. "You mean go away on that really big boat?"

"Yes, how does that sound? You aren't afraid of riding on the sea in a big boat are you?"

"Oh no, Bethany! That sounds like a lot of fun! Thank you for saving me from being put under the ground." I hugged her and then asked how soon she could be up and around. Tonia wanted her to rest up at least another day, to make sure the fever stayed down and she began eating regularly once more.

Shortly after this, the musicians began to play. I brought Alwanianon outside into the shade so she could watch them too. Roberto and Mireio agreed to babysit her, while she memorized the music and he made initial notations. She asked what they were doing, and when she found out, she said, "Oh, I know all the words to their songs. I used to sing them quietly to myself when they played. It isn't polite to sing along with them, you see."

"That's the best news I've heard in a long time! Hey, when I lean to you like this, I'm trying to hug you, so you have to help me out a bit, okay?" She put her arms partway around Mireio.

She then said, "Oh, you are going to have a baby soon aren't you? Mommy told me about that. Someday I am going to have many babies, not just one like my mom. I want lots of them."

"Great! When this one comes, I'm going to need a lot of help. Do you suppose that you can help me with the baby?"

"Oh sure, you don't have any, but at least I got this much left. I suppose that we will need the other's help too."

Henry came by to tell our two musicians that the instruments were the usual ones found here in the Spice Islands and that better makes could be purchased elsewhere. They appreciated the information, and Roberto decided not to ask about buying some of these.

They roasted a pig in our honor, but boy were the spices ever hot! Henry cleverly "forgot" to mention this minor detail. Natale gave him a hard time after that. Later that evening, I got the opportunity to talk with the Sik once more. He agreed to send out messengers to the other nine villages telling them that the devil had been killed and that we, who had done it, would be visiting their villages during the next few days. I wanted to see how many others might need healing, but we needed to track down where this mantis had come from, because there could well be more of them just waiting to appear and attack these unfortunate people.

The next day, we took our adopted little girl out to the ship, where Mireio and Roberto could look after her, putting her up in their cabin. Henry stayed behind to work on trading deals with the Sik. The rest of our group plus six of the Santi, including Angel and Mary Beth, went with us on our tour of the island and its villages. Along the way, we passed many neatly tended fields, and Benet pointed out the plants from which we got many of our staples back home, such a tea and coffee and even cocoa, to say nothing of all the spices.

One by one, we discovered that the other villages had been even harder hit. The closer that we got to the last village that sat near the tall hill, which marked the center of the island, and where the best tea leaves grew, the more the dead body count grew. We added ten more victims to our group; we just could not abandon them, knowing that the villagers would just let them die slowly! By now, I didn't think much of their Lord Huwan or their religion.

Two days after we began going to village after village, we arrived at the last village. We had rented a donkey-pulled wagon to carry the women that we were adopting along with us. As with the other villages, when we arrived, the local Sik welcomed us warmly, thanking us profusely for having slain their devil. Here at this village, we allowed them to hold a feast in our honor. Why? Because we intended to explore this area for several days, looking for the origin point of the mantis.

We asked many questions until at last Natale asked the right one, which got us on the right path. She asked, "Who was the first person to be attacked and where had he or she lived?"

The next morning, we left Tonia in charge of her patients, while we hiked up the side of the steep, rugged hill. It was still in the relative cool of the morning, in the low nineties. Dripping wet, we found the tea plantation that had been hit first. It was the last homestead plantation on the hill, which rose several hundred more feet above here, rocky and foreboding.

Soon we found the man's home and entered to search it. Benet found it first, though Michelle was almost as fast. "Look here, this looks like a large mantis egg. See, it looks like the stupid man was trying to hatch it! Boy I bet he was surprised when it hatched!"

"Maybe he thought it was some kind of bird, something that would be useful to him?" Michelle suggested.

"Yes, but where did he find it? Now that is what we need to figure out. Search thoroughly and see if you can get any clues," I countered. We rummaged through everything, but found nothing that might shed light on where the man found the egg.

Benet and Michelle went outside to have a look around the place. I noticed that they began walking in semi-circular arcs, each one more distant from the cabin. I followed them from a distance, listening to them chat. Benet was pointing out the signs, "See here he walked out to the tea field and here he is coming back."

"So that means this one in the center here is the most likely route?" Michelle concluded.

"Yes, the others are all going into his fields. I don't see any fields up there, so that's where I would head next. Let's let Bethany know."

We all followed the two as they carefully followed the single trail, which led first up and then back down the steep hillside. Evidently, the man had gone exploring. At times, we halted because the trail went over a very rocky section, making the tracking far more difficult. Still, Benet kept doggedly at it. This was his specialty, tracking, part of the Loremaster's special skills. Now the day turned hot once more, sweat really poured off our nearly naked bodies. More than once, we had to stop to cool off and drink more water with a pinch of sea salts.

At last, near the craggy peak, we found what we had been looking for, a cave entrance, barely large enough for a person to crawl through. Poor Emil, he was just a bit too large to squeeze through. There was no way for Natale to make the crawl, and she was upset that she had finally encountered something that she couldn't handle, crawling. Emil consoled her, explaining that perhaps he ought to lose some weight. Even Michelle found it tough going, but she made it, doggedly following Benet.

Benet kept pushing his lantern in ahead of himself. Once inside, the rest of us lighted several more lanterns so we could get a good look around. This had obviously been the home of a large mantis a long time ago. There was a circular opening in the very top, large enough for an adult to enter. 'What's in there?" called out Natale; the disappointment was plainly evident in her sad tone. This was quite a find, and she just had to be a part of this, I decided.

"I'm bringing you inside another way," I called out. I slipped up and out of the top hole, down to her, picked her up. Everyone looked up in total surprise to see Natale floating down from the large roof opening, grinning like mad!

"Now that is a great way to travel! Thanks Bethany. Oh! Look at all this stuff!" Our sentiments exactly! I then did the same with Emil, who was very glad not to be also left out!

The disturbed nest got our immediate attention. Benet and Michelle were examining it carefully. "Look, most of the shells dried out and cracked. I can see footprints around here. I'd say that the man came here, found the nest, and took an egg back with him," he commented.

Michelle added, "Good, all the other eggs are long destroyed! That means no more of these are around here. That is, if he only took the one egg." Since we had not found any traces of a second egg in the old man's hut, we relaxed considerably.

The cavern was rather large and a number of items got our interest. We found a large stash of gold and silver ingots, nicely stacked. Each weighed ten pounds. There were hundreds of these ingots. We had a good idea now where all the gold found at the other locations may have originated. Either that or the creature here was mining the stuff for its own use.

A workbench caught our attention. Here a large number of very strange tools were stored neatly arranged on hooks. However, we could see no "works in progress." Some of the tools certainly were for the making of the ingots. A small smelter sat in one corner, along with the molds for the ingots. Just how the furnace was fired, we could not guess.

Natale discovered another writing desk with at least a dozen of the metallic books, over which she was very excited. "The more samples of their writing we have, the better a linguist has to identify the symbols and translate it, you see." We didn't, but took her word for it.

What captivated my interest was the large metallic wall hanging. It looked to me like a map, with strange markings on it, very strange indeed. Near the top, a number of vertical lines originated from a point, expanding outward uniformly as one approached the lower third of the map, where they began shrinking once more. These were placed at uniform intervals all across the map. Other lines ran perpendicular to these, going uniformly spaced from top to bottom. Taken together, these formed some kind of grid over the entire map.

I say map loosely because at this point, I had not decided just what this represented. One by one, the others slowly joined me, also staring at the map. "What is it?" asked Natale, "A map perhaps?"

"Well, it could be," Benet suggested. "Up here, this looks like the Med Sea, the Sea Princes, and West Reach."

"If so, this would be the Southlands. Gosh, it sure is huge," added Renzo.

"Hey, then this is Megalos," I pointed out the island cradled between the stem of the dog bone of landmasses.

"Does this represent Wanakan way over here?" Rosina indicated the landmass on the far left side.

"Hey, this is starting to make sense to me," I declared. "This is a map of parts of Tarra! Look, the islands that we discovered between Wanakan and here are on here too!"

"Yes, but what do these symbols and markings mean?" Natale asked what turned out to be the most important question. "See there is a star thing where I kind of think Wanakan is at, though we ought to get Captain Henry's view; he's the expert, but there are five other stars here too, maybe these are the six city states. Then, there is a star on Island of Giants and also one on the Isle of Loving."

"Where, I've got to see these," Benet exclaimed, hastily looking where Natale pointed with her foot. "You are right. They all have a star there. I wonder where this place is at?"

"I'll bet Henry could tell us pretty exactly, but here is a likely spot with a star," Natale pointed out. "Hey, gang, look there are two more stars in the Southlands!" We looked where she was pointing with her toes. One was in the middle of nowhere in the southern portion of the Southlands. The other, I recognized instantly.

"That one there was where the three pyramids were at, where Alabaster went. That was the place that was destroyed during the Grey Creature-Mantis battle that night. We can forget about looking for anything there; even the pyramids are gone now."

"What about this other one?" asked Michelle.

"No clue. We've never been anywhere near the interior of the Southlands. Perhaps the Centurions have, but I just don't know," I answered.

"Let's all look and see if there are any other stars on the map anywhere?" Natale suggested.

"Hey, look, there are islands south of the Southlands that we did not know existed!" I pointed out. Two have stars on them, here and on this really big island." Indeed, it was twice the size of Megalos, located directly south of the bottom of the Southway. How far, we could only guess roughly, having only an idea of scale. Henry probably could give us a far more accurate idea. Perhaps it was two hundred miles south?

The other island with a star was closer to us, but west of this big one. It was nearly due south of the collection of Spice Islands. Although we had no idea if the islands and landmasses were drawn to scale or not, if they were, this island was about the same size as the one we were on right now. "What's that big X symbol doing up in the Appian Way?" asked Michelle.

"Ah, now that looks like where the Grey Creature base was located. Look over the map, everyone, and see if you can find any other X symbols. We might have some clues where their bases were located," I replied. We didn't find another single X symbol, only the one. I felt a surge of hopefulness. Perhaps we had gotten them all afterwards and only the previously laid eggs were now causing the various problems in today's world.

"Bethany," Cedric commented, "this map is the most important find that we have made, I think. It shows us new places to explore, and where the mantis creatures used to dwell. We should get this most valuable map to Henry, because he has more knowledge about these matters than the rest of us. If it is truly a map of Tarra, or part of it at least, we need to get a copy of this to headquarters, in case something bad happens to this one. Although it is made of some kind of metal, still our ship could be sunk or something. We cannot let this map get lost."

"That will be easy for me to do," Michelle commented. We all looked at her, expecting an explanation. If I had to make a copy of it, I would need weeks to be sure I had not missed anything.

"See, the lines and writing, everything on it is etched into the metal. I put a paper over it and can quickly make a mirror copy of everything." Ah, simple if you are a painter, I thought.

"Okay, then let's get all this stuff out to the donkey wagon and head back to the ship."

"This will take us forever, crawling through that small hole," Cedric complained.

I laughed, "So you all want it all left to your leader to do, is that it? Lazy's," I teased them. One by one, I lifted each person out. Then I brought out the map. It took some time to move the pile of ingots, however. At last, I sent out the books and the tools. After making sure that we were leaving nothing behind, I lifted myself up and out. "Say, Natale," I said as I gently sat my body back down outside, "this is a really great way to travel. I've never done it to my own body before. Pretty neat experience." Everyone laughed.

They had not been idle. All the cargo was loaded onto the little wagon, which was now very overloaded. Still our nine adopted women did not complain. I hoped the wagon would make it to the village, where we could rent a second wagon. It did thankfully.

Four days later, everything had been transported onto our ship.

Henry had the map laid out on his navigation table, and many of us crowed around him. To say that Henry was excited would be a gross understatement! "Do you realize the magnitude of this discovery? This is revolutionary! Even shows new, unknown islands and landmasses way down south! This grid system is undoubtedly a navigational grid, only we need to work out how it is devised and is to be used. Yes, the landmasses are drawn to scale, as near as I can tell. Proportions across the ocean here seem right, and the placements match fairly well our maps that we've been making."

"We need to find this island next, and then tackle this large one. However, Michelle must make a precise copy, and we must get it to headquarters," he stated. We discussed the map for some time. At last, he allowed Michelle to work her magic, only he insisted that he help her. He was not about to let this out of his sight!

While we were studying the map, Cedric and Tonia were making our newest nine women comfortable in the cargo hold, fixing up hammocks and such, familiarizing the women with ship life. I would have to deal with their traumas soon.

Henry said, "Oh, by the way, while I was making trading arrangements with the Sik, I discovered something about their earrings. Recall that the Sik's wife had three in each ear, one was really a very large circle, perhaps four inches across, one was two inches, and the third was about one inch?" We said that we did. "You've also noticed that nearly none of the other women had three such earrings. Many of the village women had only the two smaller sized ones or just the one small one. All the women you've brought on board have only the one small pair."

"Yes, yes, but what's it mean?" I asked, wondering what he'd found out.

"It's a caste system. The Spice Island people have a caste system. The highest caste are the wealthy, well-to-do people; they are the only ones who wear the three earrings. Then there's the middle caste, primarily the musician, trades and crafts. Finally, there is the lowest caste, the ones with the single pair. Their religion defines these three castes, and each person is born into their caste and cannot ever change it. Those of a caste do not socialize or marry outside their caste. It is a very rigid system. That's why they villagers were going to allow these ten women we brought onboard to just starve and die; they are the lowest caste, not worth saving, according to their religion."

"Nasty religion, if you ask me," I retorted. "We really are saving their lives. So be it."

Natale laughed, "Notice that not a single woman of the other two castes accepted your offer of assistance and trauma therapy. Only these ten will get it. Serves them right for what they intended to have happen to these ten!"

"Thanks, Henry. Now we must decide what course to take. Suggestions?"

"Well, there are clearly more Spice Islands marked on the map here on the far western edge that we do not know about as yet. Perhaps, we should visit them and open up trading arrangements with them on behalf of the Santi. That will take at least a month to do, maybe more. We could have a caravel meet us at say here, the first big Spice Island, have them bring us additional food supplies, take back our finds, and a copy of our precious map and even the new guests, assuming they have had their therapy sessions finished by then. Once that transfer is finished, off we go exploring again."

"But that means we will not get back to Velona for even longer, and Bethany and I will have to put off our wedding further," complained Renzo. "Rosina's too," he added, as if that would make a difference. It didn't, the proposed exchange was quite sound. Besides, we were only a few hundred miles from the new "starred" locations, which had to be explored. His plan was common sense. I had Rosina make the arrangements, with Henry's input.

On July 1, 649, we weighed anchor and set sail once more, visiting some dozen more new Spice Islands. I now began to do therapy sessions on our adopted ten women. Mireio took me aside, when I announced this was my plan at breakfast on the day that we set sail. "Bethany, Roberto and I have decided that we want to formally adopt Alwanianon as our daughter. How do we do this? Also, could I ask a favor and have you do her therapy sessions first, as a favor to me, please?"

"What a fabulous thing to do for her! What does she think of this?"

"Oh, she's very excited about it. We've been learning each other's language some these past many days."

I went to their cabin, where Roberto was chatting with her and asked him to leave for a moment. "Alwanianon, Mireio has told me that she wants to become your new mother, and Roberto, your new father. What do you think about adopting them as your new mom and dad? If we do this, then they will look after you until you grow up and get married and start your own family."

"That would be really, really great. I like them a lot and I can help her too, when her new baby comes. They are much nicer to me than my real mom and dad ever were. Is it okay if they become my new mom and dad?"

"It sure is. We will have an official ceremony right now to make it official so that no one can ever separate you three. How's that?" She was very excited, to say the least. A few minutes later, with everyone who could be spared from their duties gathered in the galley area, I began the ceremony. "Alwanianon, do you hereby accept Mireio and Roberto Milienne to be your new mother and father, until death separates your bodies?" She giggled and said she would.

"Mireio, do you vow to accept Alwanianon as your own daughter, to raise her as if she were your own child?" She certainly did. "Roberto, do you vow to accept Alwanianon as your own daughter, to raise her as if she were your own child?" He did as well. "Then, I now pronounce before all these witnesses that from this day forward, Alwanianon is now the legal daughter of Mireio and Roberto Milienne. Let no one break this bond between parents and child."

Everyone clapped and the three hugged each other. I let them all celebrate for a time, before taking Alwanianon aside for her therapy session. Because I did not know the language of the Spice Islands, I had Natale sit with me handling the translations as needed. I discovered that Mireio had done a good job teaching her the basics of our language, which made the process much easier.

She began rolling through that fateful day like a well-oiled top! "I am out in the fields helping mom pick some tea leaves. I see this black creature flying our way. I yell to mom and dad. We all start running for our house. I stumble and fall. I watch the big bug swoop down on me. I scream. I am so scared. I pee my pants. I try to get away; it's weird. I am up here a long ways from my body and the bug. Like I forgot my body somehow. I watch it as it starts biting into my right arm, where my elbow used to be. I can feel it, kind of tingles, but doesn't hurt. I think maybe this is not a bad bug, maybe it is playing with me. I move closer to it thinking to pet it, as I did with our stray cat that mom let me keep. But I can't move my arm anymore. I see my arm is unhooked from my body. He's holding it in one of his many hands. I get really scared now and move back from him."

"I hear mom and dad screaming, running towards us. Dad is waving a machete and mom is waving a big stick. Now the bug is biting my other arm. I tried to say please can I have my arm back? I need it, mister bug. He doesn't answer me, but his eyes look at mine, and it somehow makes me black out. Yet, I hear mom and dad attacking it. I hear them scream horribly. Then all is silent for a long time. I am getting hotter and hotter now. I cannot wake up even when I try. I still see things. I am in the meeting hut all by myself. No one is looking after me. I am still afraid. I am so hot! I get tired and float up into the sky a ways. Then, I see this big, big boat coming to our beach. I see many villagers running down there, so I go along with them too. I see you all coming onto our beach in the two smaller boats. I follow you."

"Now I feel Tonia wiping my body clean. It feels good. I am going back close to my head now. She is saying nice things to me. Sleep now little one; you need to rest. She is so nice, so I did; I went to sleep. I wake up, see my arms, and scream. I want my arms back so I can learn to play music, but no one listens to me then. That's all. I am sorry that I wet my pants, though."

"Very well done, Alwanianon," I praised her and had her go through it all once more. This time she yawned heavily all the way through it. Then she started laughing. "Always before I was inside my head. I didn't know I could be out here. I love it out here and am going to stay out here, that is, if it is permitted. It is so much more fun being out here. I can see more things. Please is it permitted to be out here all the time?"

"Excellent, Alwanianon. Well done indeed. Yes, you can be out here all the time. Most of the rest of us are out here too." So much for her therapy! I wished that all cases were so easily done! Thankfully, her trauma was so very light. Her bubbling enthusiasm for life was only heightened. I could see now why Mireio had been so taken with this young girl. She dashed off to tell her mom what had happened.

Natale just grinned at me. She also knew that this had been the easiest case on record to handle! Now we had to start in on the others. Most of these were in their early twenties. Seven had been married, but their husbands had been killed while trying to protect them from the bug. For once, we did not have a disaster on our hands. With all nine, they had lost only a single limb or portion thereof. Some a leg, others, an arm. None of these would need extensive assistance with life or retraining on how to do the simple chores of living. Finally, we got a break with this aspect.

For the record, during the course of the sessions, five of these women contacted an earlier episode with the mantis creatures, often between fifty to a hundred years before. Similar to the Wanakan people, over a long period, they had watched the bugs slowly devour parts of their bodies, until they at last welcomed their deaths. All recovered nicely, though it took the better part of a month to handle all of them.

August 1, we anchored off the largest of the Spice Islands. There waiting for us was the Horn of Plenty, another of our caravels from Velona. We spent two days transferring our cargo to their ship and vice versa. It was one sweaty, hot mess, here in this incredible heat! We entrusted Michelle's copy of the map to their captain, who was given strict orders to get this to Jenna without fail! The nine women were the last to be moved onto the other ship. Once more, we all promised to visit them when we returned from our lengthy voyage.

Our supplies replenished, on August 4, we set sail for the next island on our map, which contained a star. Presumably, here was yet another base or nest of the mantis creatures. The Big Killers were on the move once more.

Chapter 9 Isle of Right

Alexa giggled, "Come on, let's go see if anything is different today." The eighteen year old bronzed skinned young woman had pale blue eyes; her blonde hair reached to her upper thighs, a fact of which she was very proud. Alexa was a very independent young woman, free spirited some said, a rule breaker others suggested. For a number of years now, she was the driving force behind her foursome, who had earned the name Rule Breakers.

Her companions in arms, also eighteen, included Chara, the Quiet, Dione, the Beauty, and Enyo, the Foolhardy. Alexa's nickname was the Deep Thinker. Chara had a soft voice, which gave others the impression that she was just shy. She was anything but shy; in fact, many of their escapades had been her idea, such as climbing up to the Forbidden Walkway. Like Alexa, she had blonde hair, paler than Alexa's and thinner, with somewhat deeper blue eyes. Dione had the good looks, or so everyone kept saying. Her long blonde hair was nearly a light brown just touching her thighs; her lips were full as were her perfectly formed breasts. She was unquestionably the prettiest of the foursome. Enyo had thin lips and small breasts, which she continually prayed would somehow fill out, at least to those of Dione. Her eyes had a shade of green mixed in with the blue, enchanting some said, devilish, others thought. Her pale brown hair reached only to the small of her back, this, too, she prayed would continue to grow.

Chara said quietly, "But Alexa, it has only been a day since we last peeked. What could possibly have changed in the world in one day?"

Challenged, Alexa suggested, "Well, for one, we might see if the men have returned. Wouldn't that be exciting?"

"Yes, it would," Dione spoke up. "Alexa, we all know that the men have gone off and left us. What else can explain their absence? There hasn't been a man in the House of Right for at least ten years. You know as well as we that Adelphe and Gaia are now ten and they are the youngest and last children born here in the House of Right. Ten years, Alexa. Why should today be any different?"

"Perhaps we will see a large fire. Maybe we will see a boat bringing strangers. Maybe we will see a deer. Dione, just think of all the thousands of possibilities that we may see!" Alexa replied in a pleading tone.

'She's quite right, you know," Enyo spoke up. "Just think of all the Forbidden Sights that we four have already seen! The Town of Men, the deer, and all the other animals out there in the world. Don't forget the storm and the lightning strike that smashed the tree down the hill a ways. Look, no one is watching or around. Let's do it! Go ahead Alexa. I'll keep watch. Remember if I whistle, freeze. If I start making a cooing sound of the pigeons, hide somehow."

The four were standing at the far corner of the House of Right. The complex was five hundred strides long. Enyo had measured it a number of times, proving to Alexa that it was square in shape. The outer walls were thick limestone, another fact that Enyo had proven two years ago when the four had sneaked a small about of vinegar from the kitchen and poured it on a section of the wall. It had fizzed. From their secret observation post, they also knew that the walls were three strides thick. Again, Enyo had cleverly come up with a way to measure it indirectly. It had taken all four of them to do it, however. While she had sat in their post looking, Alexa stood at one spot in the courtyard and Dione was directed to another spot. Between these two spots, Chara paced out the dimension.

Going around the massive outer walls, which stood seven strides tall, again as measured indirectly by Enyo, was the Forbidden Walkway, barely one stride wide and six strides above the ground. No guardrails protected against an accidental slip, and the fall could be very deadly, which is why Alexa concluded it was forbidden to be up there. Of course, there was only one normal way up there, through that section of the Main House of Mother Primus, Zona, who was the eldest of the women here at sixty-five. Near Zona's room, there was a door with a strange circular knob that must somehow open the heavy oaken door, though no one knew how it operated. There was no need to know because it led only to the walkway, which was forbidden — a set of logic that Alexa thought was absurd, but then Alexa thought many things here in the House of Right were absurd. They had discovered that the door did indeed lead only to the Forbidden Walkway last year when they followed the walkway around to that side, went down the stairs, and found the other side of the same door with a similar knob protruding from it on this side.

How then did this foursome get up to the walkway? Ah, clever Alexa found the gnarly oak tree here in the northwestern corner of the House of Right. It had numerous large limbs set only about a foot apart. While it took each young woman nearly a quarter of an hour to climb carefully up the distance, they found that they could easily step from one branch directly onto the walkway. Oh, that had been a glorious day for the Rule Breakers, some four years ago now. For the first time, they could see the Town of Men, the beautiful sea, as blue as their eyes, Dione had claimed, and many other things that they ought never have seen, if they followed all the rules set down by the Book and enforced by Mother Primus.

"Let's do it," Alexa said and began her very careful climb from tree branch to branch. When she was finally on the walkway, she ducked back so that the tree would hide her, calling down for Chara to come up. An hour after they started, all four women were high above the ground on the walkway. Now they peered over the side, looking north.

Far off in the distance, the white marble pillars of the Town of Men shone in the sunlight, just as they had every time these women had seen them. Today was no different; no smoke clouds could be seen. No smoke, Alexa had said, meant no men. "Still deserted," she said absentmindedly. They looked far out to sea and saw no boats. Of course, they had never actually seen a boat, but Mother Secundus had and often described them to the women here in the House of Right.

"I wish a man would come," sighed Chara, "I would really like to have a child of my own. You know there haven't been any new children for ten years. Ah well, we'll just have to be patient, as Mother Primus says. She keeps saying that the men will return when it is the Right Time. Really, I have been ready for lots of years; you all have too."

Enyo teased her, "Ah, Chara, you just want to have a Holy Man in your bed, we know, we know." Chara, the Quiet, blushed; yes, she wanted a man in her bed, holy or not!

Alexa suggested, "Shall we sneak around to the other side? Maybe the deer is back." Carefully, the four women pressed their backs to the wall and stepped sideways along the walkway. None of them trusted themselves just to walk normally. One misstep meant a disastrous fall! A half hour later, the four peered out over the grassy hillside to the west. "Oh look, there's a mother with her fawn!" For a half hour, the four women watched the delicate life of a mother with her recent newborn. At last, they inched their way back to their secret tree. An hour later, all four were down safely.

"I'm going to draw that!" declared Dione. All four knew that such things as drawings, depicting anything, was another forbidden action. Dione didn't care; she loved to draw, although it usually took her considerable time to get things just right. Years ago, when these four women had banded together, each supported the innermost desires of the other. With Dione, it was drawing things. Alexa had found an unused cellar deep in the basement of the Manor House. Here the dust on the floor was very thick, ideal for drawing. Enyo had found a number of different sized sticks, destined for the cooking fires. She had stolen them and had spent a week using a kitchen knife that she "borrowed" each day to sharpen their points. Dione loved her drawing sticks. Enyo took pride in the fact that she had helped Dione achieve that for which she longed. Besides, they all marveled at just how good her drawings eventually became!

"Okay, let's slip down there. Now is probably a good time. Enyo and I will steal a pitcher of mead. Chara, you are on guard duty. Everyone remember the signs?" They all did. They had a clever series of whistles and birdcalls that were used on more than one occasion to alert the others to trouble coming their way.

Enyo and Alexa walked to the kitchen. There, Kleio, their fifty-five year old cook was busily preparing their evening meal, although it was only just past noon. It took the woman over half the day to make the evening meal for the hundred plus women who were here in the House of Right. The kitchen was huge. In one corner was the firewood pile. Alexa noticed it, "Kleio, you are running out of firewood!"

"Tell me something I didn't already know, Alexa, and I'll kiss you!" the feisty cook replied. "It's never happened before, never! The Holy Men had better be returning soon!"

Alexa tested the women, "Well, when we run out, perhaps then Mother Primus will unlock the Holy Gate, and we will all get to go outside to gather more."

Kleio laughed heartily. She was a rotund woman with brown hair that only reached her middle back. She had an accident a number of years ago, catching her hair on fire. That had been a scary sight indeed. "That will be the day! Aye, Mother Primus leading you all out to get firewood! Now that is funny, Alexa, really funny! Say, how about you two filling the fireplace for me, and I'll let you have some mead."

That was precisely what Alexa was waiting to hear. She had the cook figured out years ago. Just get her talking and laughing, and she would offer up some trade, which was usually very worthwhile. It took the two over a half hour to get the ten wood pieces carried from the very small pile that remained over to the fireplace and properly inserted. They worked together inserting them just right. If they had a job to do, Alexa insisted that they do it to perfection, something Enyo also insisted upon. Always do the job right was her motto and then you don't have to do it over, which so many of the other women here fell victim to.

Once Kleio Okayed the wood stack, Alexa headed for the pantry and the mead. This was always the tricky part, filling up the pitcher. Enyo once more assisted her and between the two of them got the pitcher filled. Alexa also noted that the huge barrel was very light; she had almost knocked it over. "Kleio, did you know that we are almost out of mead?"

"Aye, that I know too, Alexa. Please don't go blabbing that all over. Lord knows what we will do when the barrel runs dry!"

"But you can make more can't you? You are the cook?" Alexa asked, knowing how awful things would get around here if there were no mead to be had at all, not even for special occasions.

"I've never made it, dear, but a man once told me how it is done. Again, Mother Primus would have to send us all out into the wilderness in search of the beehives. Lord knows where the men keep them! No honey, better enjoy this last bit of mead. We may not have any more for a long time, not until the men return."

"But do you know when the men are to return?" asked Enyo.

"My dear, if I knew that why I'd be Mother Primus! Now get going and don't let the others see you with that mead!"

"You carry. I'll keep a look out," Enyo said to Alexa. The pitcher, like so many pottery utensils here, had a handle. Alexa held the handle in her mouth tightly between her teeth and followed Enyo through the deserted halls down into the basement. Soon, they entered the room where Dione was making her drawing in the dust. Chara had managed to filch a lantern, and Dione was busily drawing when the two arrived with the pitcher. Each woman took turns holding it for the other to drink.

Finally, Dione was finished with her drawing. "There, what do you think?" The three stared down at the rendering of the mother with her fawn.

"Oh, that's so beautiful, so lifelike!" exclaimed Enyo.

"Magnificent as always," added Alexa. "You do incredible drawings. I know that I cannot do them. You are really good, Dione!"

"So beautiful that I have tears," said the soft-spoken Chara.

"Well, I guess I have to erase it now. If Mother Primus finds this, we all will be in big trouble!" Dione said sadly. This marked the two hundredth drawing she had made, only to erase it once done and viewed by her three companions. Hastily, she wiped away the drawing with her feet. "Want me to take the pitcher back for you?"

"No, I had better do it. Kleio gave it to me, not you. She might get suspicious," Alexa replied. Just then, the chapel bell clanged twice. That meant it was time for all women to gather in the sewing room. It was communal sewing time. "Damn, I hate this time of day! Everyday it's the same old thing: sew more of these awful sacks they call dresses. Just once, I'd like to put a bit of color in mine, you know, something to make mine a little different from yours. Come on; we better not be late." She picked up the pitcher in her teeth once more and the four scampered up the stairs. Alexa dropped off the empty pitcher and raced to the sewing room.

She was nearly the last woman to enter. As usual, she walked over to her spot and sat down between Iola and Natasa. Long ago, Mother Primus had to separate the foursome during communal sewing. They talked so much that no sewing was done, so she split them up. Now at least they sewed when they were supposed to be sewing. "Today, ladies, let's see if we can get these new dresses finished. Many of yours are wearing out!" She distinctly looked at Alexa, whose dresses often appeared with rips and tears in them, all of which were unexplained. In fact, all the Rule Breakers seemed to wear out their dresses four times faster than any other women. Mother Primus merely chalked that up to their youthfulness.

Alexa hated sewing with a passion, perhaps because she would spend an entire month making a single sack dress. All the women wore the same kind of dress; the only variation was its overall size. A few of the women, such as the cook, were fatter than others, some were taller. All the dresses looked the same, were sewn the same way, all were off-white linen. Today, Alexa felt more rebellious than normal. Perhaps it was the mead she had just had. "Mother Primus, how much more linen do we have?" She was hoping to know how many more dresses she would have to make.

Mother Primus misunderstood her. "I'm so terribly sorry to have to tell you all this, but now is as good a time as any. What you have is the last of it! We are totally out of cloth until the men return with more. I urge you all to be extra careful with this last dress. Who knows how long it will be before we have more cloth. Also, I have decided to ask you all to look through your clothing on wash day. Any that no longer fit you, please take them to Mother Secundus. She is going to hand them out to those who need them later on, once we've run out of cloth."

This unexpected announcement brought murmurs among all the women, who asked many questions about how this could have happened. Many volunteered to donate as many older dresses as possible to Mother Secundus, Leda. Many now approached their sewing with renewed vigor, for this would be the last time they would have to sew! Excited about this prospect, Alexa asked, "Mother Primus, when we have all finished these dresses, what are we to do during the communal sewing hours?"

"We could have a communal prayer session each day instead," she suggested. All the women moaned. "Just teasing you all," she chuckled. "I've decided that this time period will be free time until we obtain more cloth. Will anyone be too disappointed with that?"

"Yes, I will be," called out the lone voices of Rhea and Sofia. Everyone knew that these two women loved to sew and made the best dresses here. They even had made a pair of dresses for the two Mothers! Alexa joined the rest of the women booing the two, who smiled and took the tease good naturedly. Inwardly, Alexa felt sorry for these two, for no longer would they be able to do what their hearts loved to do. She knew what that felt like, hence her sympathy.

Again further embolden by this unexpected admission, Alexa piped up, "Mother Primus, we were helping Kleio get the fireplace ready a while ago. We noticed that she is almost out of wood too. Whatever are we going to do when the woodpile is gone? How will she be able to cook our meals?"

"Dear me, does nothing escape your eyes, Alexa?" It was meant more as a compliment, really, not a put down. "Yes, Kleio has said that we will be out of firewood by early next week."

"Mother Primus, we would all volunteer to go out into the woods south of here and bring back a stick each time, if that would help." Oops, Alexa realized that she had said too much.

"I know that you all would like to violate the Holy Rule and go outside these protective walls. I know that you all mean well, but the dangers to us out there are so severe, I must find some other way. I will think about it, Alexa. I have thought about it for weeks now." She thought better of asking Alexa how she knew about the forest south of this House of Right. Twice, she had seen the Rule Breakers walking the walls, but did not have the heart to admonish them just yet. She had monumental bigger problems to solve than some rules being broken.

In fact, a terribly vital problem had been troubling her for a month now. Their vast pantry of food supplies was dangerously low. Never in the long history of the House of Right had the food stock been so small, barely two weeks remained. What would she do then? How could the hundred plus women be fed? She had been eating less and less each meal now since she found out, doing everything she could think of to conserve food for the others, especially the young girls. Yet, doom was rapidly coming and still the men did not return. Surely, they must know by now how critical things had become during their long absence.

Alexa now had many things to occupy her mind, not the least was the freedom she would have when this last dress was finished. She worked hard and had it finally done when the chapel bell struck five times. Mother Primus Okayed her dress and she carried it carefully to her room before heading to the kitchen where all the women gathered for their supper. She took her place beside her three dear friends.

Before each woman was a metal bowl, which had a large flange, almost like a handle, save it was flat and only three inches long, along with a large wooden spoon, and a linen napkin. Each week, ten women took their turn at setting the table for everyone else. After the meal was done, another ten would take their turn at doing all the dishes. Alexa hated both jobs and was glad that she only had to do this about once every two months.

Mother Primus said the evening prayers, and then one by one, the women formed into a long line before the giant kettle, which sat above the embers in the fireplace, holding their plate in their teeth. Alexa stepped up, and one of the two servers slowly and carefully filled her plate using a long handled, metal dipper. She walked it back to her place and carefully set it down. She waited for her friends to join her before starting to eat.

"Have you noticed that we have been eating the same thing for supper for the last twenty days?" Alexa complained.

"Twenty-two to be precise," put in Enyo; such things did not escape her keen observation.

"You'd think that there would be some variety," Chara added.

"Oh no!" Alexa suddenly realized what was going on. She whispered her theory to her friends, not wanting to upset the other women nearby. "Maybe we are also running out of food!"

"We ought to find out!" declared Enyo, determined to find out why they had been served the same thing every night for nearly a month now. Breakfasts, why, those were help yourself to whatever was available, such as cheese, milk from the goats, and bread. However, there seemed to be less and less milk each day too, she observed.

Once the meal was done, most women took an evening stroll around the huge grounds. Tonight, the Rule Breakers met in a quiet corner of the big yard. "After they finish with the dishes and before it is lights out time, let's take a peek into the pantry, shall we?" proposed Enyo.

"What's going to happen if we are running out and do run out of food?" asked Chara, very concerned.

"Maybe then Mother Primus will have to let us all go outside and see what we can find. Perhaps the men left behind some food in their town?" Alexa suggested.

"She has the only key to the gates," Dione said. "I saw them once when I was in her room helping her when she was sick."

An hour later, the four snuck into the pantry, normally off limits except for the cook. The panty room was huge; shelves lined three walls. However, only a small amount remained anywhere in the room! All four gasped! They beat a hasty retreat to their room. The four shared a single bedroom, two to a bed, a bed on each side of the room, five strides wide and ten long, as measured by Enyo. A mirror and four boxes lined the back wall. There was no door, just an opening. There were no doors anywhere else for that matter, except the one that led to the Forbidden Walkway.

While there was still a bit of light left, the four women helped each other slip out of their dresses. Now came the grooming hour, just before bedtime. Each brushed out the other's long hair. Finally, as darkness came, they crawled into the beds. Alexa and Enyo shared a bed, as did Chara and Dione. Alexa rolled over and her body touched Enyo's, she whispered, "We are in big trouble aren't we?"

Enyo replied, "Yes, let's sleep on it. Perhaps tomorrow we can come up with some ideas that might help."

The next morning, each helped the other slip into their sack dresses and then the four headed to the water well in the center of the courtyard. This was their morning to be the water-drawers. Their men had made this clever device for them ages ago. The four women each stood behind a wooden spoke and began walking forward, their motion in the small circle that they paced, turned a gear that raised and lowered a large bucket into the well. Twenty times, they raised and lowered the bucket as the other women filled various pitchers for the day. On washday, this would have to be done lots more times.

At last, they got their morning drink and were the last into the kitchen, searching out breakfast. It seemed to the four that even breakfast had gotten smaller. A year ago, lunch had ceased altogether. Now they knew why. Soon they feared even breakfast would no longer exist!

Everyone had finished and was in the process of heading out to enjoy the free time when Mother Secundus came in crying. "Alexa, will you and your group please come with me. Something dreadful has happened to Mother Primus!" They followed her to the Holy House. The House of Right's leaders slept in a separate, vastly smaller building than their big dorm style mansion. Once inside, lying in a pool of blood at the bottom of the steps leading up to her room laid Mother Primus.

Alexa felt her neck, but felt no pulse. "Has she passed away and gone for a new body?"

"I'm afraid that she has, Alexa. It is so awful; the men have not yet returned, and none of us is with child. I have no idea how she will manage, but she has left us with some very big problems, Alexa. I have been watching you and your band of Rule Breakers for a long time. You four are very keen observers and often have avaunt guard ideas. I'm afraid that we need those ideas at this time. First, we must see that she is taken to the holding room, where she must await the return of the men for her proper burial. Will you four help me with this please?"

Alexa and Enyo went with Leda to find the carrying slab. The men had created this clever device a very long time ago. Essentially, it was a board with four wheels on it. The three pushed it back to where the body of Zona lay. Chara and Dione had carried a water bucket and several cloths here and were waiting on the rest to return. It took the combined efforts of all five women to roll the body onto the slab. Then the same three began to push the slab to the holding room at the far end of the complex, where a small single building stood apart from everything else. Already, the room held the remains of a dozen women who had died while the men were gone. With a great effort, the three managed to get Zona off the slab and onto the pile of others.

The three stood there for a moment, crying, while Leda said a prayer for Zona. "I'm so sorry Zona that you cannot have a fitting and proper burial. I promise you that when the men do return, you will be given your rightful burial." The three scooted the board back to its proper location and went to help the other two clean up the blood on the stone floor.

By now every woman in the House of Right was standing in the courtyard waiting words from Leda, Mother Secundus. Tears in her eyes, Leda said solemnly, "Mother Primus has left her body. She took a bad fall down the stairs and broke her head open on the stones. Once more I caution all of you, please be extra careful on the stairs. It only takes one misstep. Until the men return, I will be your leader, as is my position as second. Go now and say your silent prayers for Zona; pray that she can find a new baby body very soon."

As the collection of women began to disperse, Leda asked Alexa and her trio to follow her into her office on the first floor of the Holy House. They sat around her table and Leda began, "Alexa, Enyo, Chara, Dione, I am appointing you as my assistants now. Will you accept this added responsibility?" They agreed.

"Thank you. As you have probably guessed, we are facing some very critical problems here in the House of Right, all stemming from the failure of our men to return in a reasonable period of time. As you know or have guessed, we are nearly out of everything, from cloth to firewood to food. We have long ago run out of fodder for the goats, which is why their milk has so dried up; they are now skin and bones. Zona was reluctant to give them their freedom so that they might find grass upon which to live. She believed that we might have to eat them. I disagreed with her. Now that I am in charge, I want to let all the goats out of the main gate." The four cheered her decision!

She continued, "I will need your help in finding out how to open the gates, however. I've never seen it done before. Zona never told me how to do it. I must caution you four! Out there is a horrible world! All manner of bad things can befall us when we go beyond the gates. Often I have overheard the men talking of such things. It is frightful to hear of so many dangerous things! Yet, I have chosen you four, because often I have seen you doing what the rest of us would call exceedingly dangerous. I've seen you may times walking the Forbidden Walkway!" The four gasped.

Alexa said, "I thought that we were being very secretive about it!"

"I am not Mother Secundus for no reason, Alexa dear. Yet, your secrets are safe with me. I did not share that with Zona, because she had far bigger things to worry about. You four, more so than the rest of us, are willing to try things that might be dangerous. I've decided to ask your help, but if you believe it is too dangerous or that I ask too much of you four, do not hesitate to tell me so. In no way am I ordering you to do anything you believe is far too dangerous."

All four women became very excited about what she was suggesting. It could only mean one thing: finally, they might be able actually to visit the outside world! "What should we do first?" asked Alexa.

"First, we must open the gates, and then you four must see that the goats find their way to the grass fields to the west of the walls." She watched the excitement crescendo in the four women's eyes. "Once that has been done, next, we are nearly out of firewood. I would ask you to see if you can easily find some out there. Please do not do anything dangerous and do not go too far away. You might get lost, and we would have no way of finding you! Promise me that you will not stray beyond sight of our House of Right!"

The four did so. "Okay, then I will go get the keys and meet you by the gates."

Standing beside the gates, Alexa was bubbling with excitement, so too were her friends. Finally, they would set foot beyond their walls! "Perhaps we can see the mother with her faun close up," suggested Dione. All tingled with excitement.

Leda came carrying the keys in her mouth. She handed them to Chara and then asked, "Any ideas how this is done?"

Enyo suggested, "Look there is a hole there about the right side for one of these keys, but which one? Ah, I bet it is the larger one. Let me try to stick the key in there. Hold still Chara while I get the key from you." She took the key in her mouth and after some trouble finally got the key all the way into the hole.

"Now what? The gates did not open," said Leda slightly worried. She tried bumping her side into the gates, but nothing happened.

"Well, something more must be done with the key," declared Enyo. "The only thing left is a rotation motion. Let me try to turn it." She took it in her teeth once more. There were two directions of rotation, she tried each and found one direction easy to move, so she continued turning the key in that direction. She had to readjust her hold several times before they heard a loud clicking sound. Leda leaned on the gates and they began to move! "Yes!" declared Enyo.

With the gates open, the five began rounding up the twenty nearly starved goats, ushering them out the gates. They did not need much encouragement, however. Now the four worked for a half hour trying to convince the goats to follow them. At last, they just walked to the western end, and there before them was the huge grasslands that they had seen from the walkway. All four went into the grass, laid down, and rolled around it, fully experiencing grass for the first time. They looked up to see that the goats had finally followed them and were eating as fast as they could chew.

After a time, Alexa suggested, "Now we should go look for firewood. Probably we should start on the south side. Come on."

"Oh, it is hard to walk on this rocky ground," exclaimed Chara, nearly losing her footing twice. At last, the four stood looking to the south. "Look at all the trees! So many!"

"Well, let's see if we can find some dead branches to bring back with us," Alexa suggested. They walked around the trees and saw much dead wood lying about. Helping each other, all four manages to cradle a piece between their head and shoulder, but found walking back difficult indeed. Great care had to be exercised to keep from stumbling and falling or accidentally dropping the wood piece. Proudly, the four walked in through the gates with the first new firewood the place had seen in a very long time.

At dinner when everyone was gathered together, Leda explained the true situation the House of Right was actually facing. Unlike her predecessor, Leda felt that the women ought to know fully what was happening, at least until the men returned. "Today the cook had gotten four new pieces of firewood, thanks to the Rule Breakers." Everyone laughed.

"From now on, we are going to have no choice but to break many of the long standing rules, unless you all just want to sit there and starve to death."

Several women yelled out, "Can we be allowed to draw things now, please?"

"Yes, from now on, anyone who wished to draw something is allowed to do so, at least until the men return," Leda added.

"When will that be?" called out Delia, a woman in her thirties, and mother of Adelphe.

"Only God knows that, I'm afraid to say, Delia. We all know that none has been seen since you gave birth to your daughter, ten years ago."

"Some say that the men have abandoned us because we were bad and unholy," called out Hestia.

"Not true. We have always been good and holy and more importantly, Right. Never in our long history has there been any serious breakage of the main Righteous Rules, never. Climbing up to the Forbidden Walkway is not a serious rule break," she added for the benefit of the four Rule Breakers. "Only dangerous to yourselves should you fall. No, I believe that the men left on one of their journeys by sea and something bad happened to them, but beyond that speculation, I cannot say. We must ask them when and if they ever return."

"Tomorrow, I am asking each one of you who feels up to the task to go out the gates with the Rule Breakers and help find and bring back firewood, so that our cook may continue fixing our meals. I will not force anyone to do what they feel they do not want to do. It should be each person's individual decision. Yes, the world outside our house is exceedingly dangerous to us; I've heard the men say that a hundred times. We must use extreme caution at all times." For a half hour, she outlined her orders for their safety.

The next morning after an even more meager breakfast, the Rule Breakers led a group of seventy-five other women outside the gates and to the south side of the walls. By suppertime, the wood bin was now half filled with branches. Admittedly, they were not uniformly cut as the men had previously prepared, but it was burnable wood, nonetheless.

Leda took the Rule Breakers aside for a conference that night. "Next, we are very low on food. I have gathered up four carrying sacks, one for each of you. Tomorrow, I would like you to see if you can find anything that we can eat. Just be very, very careful out there in the dangerous world, please!"

The next day, the four women, sacks over their necks, walked out of the gates and stood looking at the world before them. "Where are we going to find food?" asked Chara.

"I have an idea," suggested Alexa. "Let's walk down the road to the men's town. Perhaps we can find some men still there who can help us. If not, perhaps they left some food behind that is still good." Since none had any better idea, the four began walking.

"This is so utterly cool!" exclaimed Dione. "We are out walking in the world for the first time!" Yes, the four were elated, but still very cautious. It took them several hours of slow walking to reach the edge of the men's town. Here they stood looking and listening for several minutes. Nothing but silence greeted their ears, except for the distant crash of waves upon the beach.

"I count fifty houses," Enyo stated flatly. The four walked up to the first house. It had a wooden door with one of those funny round objects sticking out of the wood. They pushed on the door, but it did not open. Undaunted, Enyo studied this round object. At last, she concluded that somehow it must contain the key for entry. She sat down and rotated it first one way and then another. Presto, the door suddenly gave way.

She got up and the four called out, "Anyone home?" No answer. "I guess we go in, but be very careful inside. Who knows what dangerous things might be in here," Alexa stated. They found a bedroom, a living room, a dining room, and a kitchen. Ah, in the kitchen they found the pantry. Unfortunately, it was nearly empty except for some very moldy cheese and a large pot of ground grain. This they could use. It took all four of them working together to get the pot safely into one of the carrying sacks. Cheerful that they at least had something to bring back, they moved on to the next home.

By late afternoon, they had all four sacks very full and could barely carry them. Slowly, but elated, they walked back up the long road to their house. That night at supper, they were cheered! Several other women volunteered to do their laundry so they could continue tomorrow. All four gladly accepted that offer. During the next week, more women decided to help them, and after that, all the houses were searched and any edible food retrieved. Additionally, they also found some cloth and surprisingly many colored threads! These prized items the women took back, and now Leda allowed them to put some color into their white linen dresses.

"Well, Rule Breakers, you have added several more months to our pantry, before we are out of food. We need meat somehow. The dried fish is now gone. No one knows how to make more, except that the fish live in the ocean out there. Perhaps tomorrow you can work out how to catch us some fish. Then we must all put our heads together to figure out how to prepare them." The four gladly accepted their new assignment.

Alexa thought now was a good time to ask about breaking another rule. "Leda, we have checked on the sandy beach. It is quite shallow mostly. Could we all not go bathing there? Many of the women have asked me if they could. May we see if it is safe tomorrow and if so, why doesn't everyone come for a bath? It is probably going to be just fabulous!" Leda gave them permission as long as they were very careful. None knew anything about the sea.

The next day, the foursome helped each other take off their dresses, and all four waded into the cool, clear waters of the white sandy beach. Soon they were excited beyond their wildest imagination! "This is the best thing I have ever done and felt!" exclaimed Alexa. The four spent half the day in the refreshing waters!

Just as they were about to get out and return with the fabulous news about the beach, Enyo called out terrified, "A boat! Here comes a boat! The men return! What will happen to us if they find us out here?"

Alexa looked and calmed her friends down; all three were panicking. "Look, those are very strange colored sails. It does not look like the boat of our men. Maybe it is someone else who can help us? Maybe they will show us how to catch fish and prepare them?"

"That is a lot of maybe's Alexa. I'm scared. What if they are bad men?" said a very worried Dione.

"Well, if they are bad men, then they will get us whether we are here on the beach or whether we run back to the House of Right. I don't see that it makes much difference. If they are going to make us go get a new baby body, it might as well be sooner than later, as far as I am concerned. I hate to get out of the water, but I guess we ought to get our dresses on. Give me some help will you?"

The four walked out of the water. They found their towels in their sacks and dried off somewhat and then helped each other wiggle into their dresses. Finally, they stood on the beach watching as two smaller boats were born from the bigger boat. "How can a boat have babies?" asked Chara.

"Perhaps, the big boat had the littler boats inside it," Enyo suggested. The four waited.

It was August 15 when we finally spied our destination, the smaller island with the star upon it. Following our usual protocol, we circled the island first. We found only one reasonable beach, and it was very promising; there was a village there. No signs of other habitations did we see. More perplexing, we didn't see any smoke clouds curling into the sky as we had hoped. Sailing back to the beach and village, we decided that perhaps the entire island was empty. Suggestions flew that the mantis creature or creatures had devoured everyone on the island already. Of course, that would mean they may have then left this island for other locations where people lived. I hated the thought of that occurrence!

We lowered the longboats. As we all climbed down into them, the lookout called out, "People on the beach. I see four women! Can't tell much else from this distance."

"Okay gang. First contact protocols are in effect. Natale, you are with me as usual. Here we go gang!" We were all excited once more. Still we were hot and exceedingly sweaty and stinky. I longed for a swim on that beach! I promised Renzo that we would do just that tonight! We both stunk.

As we hit the beach and climbed out, I saw the four women clearly now. No arms. "Oh no, not again!" I said to Natale. She cursed.

She and I walked up to the four. We said hello, but the four began chatting away. I almost understood them. Natale caught on even quicker than I did. "Hey, they are speaking some new dialect of Megalos." She asked them to slow down and speak very slowly so that she could understand them.

"Are you from another House of Right?" asked Alexa, now that the armless woman doing the talking finally understood her.

"I'm sorry. I don't know what that is. I am called Natale. I lost my arms to in a fight with some bad men. This is our leader, Bethany."

"She is weird, really weird. Bethany is a man? But she looks like a woman, except for the arms," Alexa said becoming very confused.

Now Natale was confused. "No, Bethany is like me, like us, a woman. She has breasts just like you and I do."

"No, women have no arms. Only men have arms," Alexa stated flatly. Of course, only men had arms. No woman had ever had arms! This totally confused Natale.

"Perhaps here on this island, your world, women have no arms, but in the rest of the huge world out there, all women are born with arms, just like men."

"Oh, she might be right," Enyo said. "We only know what is here in the House of Right. Ask them if they can help us, Alexa."

Alexa said, "Our women are in trouble. Our men have not returned, and we are running out of food and nearly everything. Can you please help us? Perhaps you have seen our men out there on the sea somewhere?"

"Food, now that is something that we have a lot of," Natale said with gusto. "You live in these houses here?"

"Oh no! We have been forced to break the rules. These are the men's houses. We live up there at the House of Right. We have come down looking for food. If you will come with us, we can take you there. Our leader, Leda, the Mother Secundus, can explain everything," Alexa decided that she didn't know what else to do or say, but Leda surely would.

Chara said softly, "Did the big boat have these baby boats or were the baby boats inside the big boat?"

Natale smiled, "Inside. We carry them with us because the big boat goes too deep in the water and cannot get to the beach here. Sure, lead us to Leda. I will tell the others to start unloading the food. How many women are there in the House of Right?"

Enyo answered, "One hundred twenty now."

Natale said, "Gosh, I better tell them to bring lots of food!" All four women smiled, unable to believe their good luck! My group followed the four up the road. I left the Santi crew to begin to unload enough food, at least for tonight.

Chara saw Mireio and asked, "Are you from another House of Right in your world?"

Natale translated quickly. Mireio answered, "No, I had a bad fight with some bad men."

"Oh, these two have half arms?" she asked.

Michelle smiled and said, "A big heavy box fell on my arms and crushed them, this is all that's left. Alwanianon here — a big dangerous bug ate her arms."

Chara looked petrified, until she added, "So we here killed the bad bug." Chara now looked relieved.

Soon we saw the walled fortress complex, and then we saw the hundred plus armless women all dressed in the same type of sack dresses, gathered in the large courtyard, staring at our approach. The next hours can be summed up simply by "culture shock!"

We quickly discovered that all these women had never seen nor heard of a woman who had arms. They were utterly convinced that women were born without them, while men had them; that was the way the world worked! These women had never been outside this walled complex, until the last few days, when necessity drove them out. Their concept and knowledge of the wider world was so limited so as to be negligible.

Yet, we did have some things in common that helped. Several of us could speak their language well enough to be understood. We had two women with whom they could easily relate, Natale and Mireio. We brought food that they desperately needed.

We found Leda, their leader, surprising receptive to new ideas, especially when the Santi arrived carrying boxes of food. The cook led them to the kitchen, and our cooks began preparing a feast for these women. Angel noted the smell of death and found the Holding Room. Leda, when I then asked her about that, begged us to bury them honorably. They had not the means by which to do so and had simply been piling them up as far from their living quarters as possible. When asked where the cemetery was located, she had no idea. I let the Santi decide on a proper location. Leda thanked me many times for burying their loved ones.

That's how I first heard the statement from Leda, "Zona has left to get a new baby body now, but her worn out one needs to have a proper burial."

I began questioning her about their religious beliefs and found to my utter amazement that they all knew that they were spiritual beings, moving from body to body. In fact, every one of these women was outside their heads! They had no idea that a being could shrink themselves so small so as to consider themselves to be inside a head. Once we heard this, we began to look at these women in a different light. As the afternoon progressed, our people began mingling with theirs.

Dione migrated to Michelle the very instant she saw Michelle beginning to make a sketch of their House of Right. "Your drawing is permanent?" she asked.

"Sure, I make a rough sketch here and then take my time with the painting until it is perfect. It takes me ever so long to make them just right."

"I draw too, though it used to be against the rules until recently. We saw a mother with her faun. Let me show you what I saw. I will get my drawing sticks!" A short while later, Dione sat on the ground beside Michelle, remaking her deer scene. By the time that she was done, nearly an hour later, another thirty women had gathered around them admiring the beautiful scene that Dione had drawn. These women told Michelle that they greatly desired to draw as Dione had, but had not been brave enough to violate the rules to do so. Inspired by the beautiful rendition, Michelle took out another canvass and had Dione re-draw it using her charcoal sticks. Near suppertime, Michelle called me over to look at the finished drawing. It was fabulous!

"Now everyone can see the beauty of the mother and faun!" declared an exuberant Dione. I realized that we were dealing with some very able beings here, unlike any that we had come across before. Things only became more impressive during that afternoon.

Enyo carefully listened to our conversations between us. She quickly discovered that Cedric knew a whole lot about how things worked. "Excuse me, sir, may I ask you a question?"

"Sure. I am called Cedric. What's your name?"

"I am Enyo. Come with me. I want to show you something and ask how it works. Here, this is the gate. There is the key. When Mother Primus left her body to get a new baby body, none of us knew how the gate worked. We only knew that Zona had the key. Leda brought me the key and asked me to figure out how it worked. I am always figuring out how things work around here. I stuck it in the hole as you can see. Nothing happened. There is only one other motion that can be made, rotating it to the right or left. I tried one way and it wouldn't move. Then, I tried the other way, and it turned around several times. Then the gates would open. Please, Cedric, tell me how this mechanism works. How does rotating this key cause the gates to open?"

"It's easier if I show you. Let me take it apart and show you."

"Oh no. I don't want it to be broken," she said very worried that the gates would be somehow damaged.

"I won't break it. I will simply take it apart and put it back together again. This way you can see how it works. It is called a lock, and it is a very, very simple lock. Nothing fancy. It will only take a minute to show you." He unfastened the mechanism. "See here is the key."

Enyo said, "Oh, I see, when it rotates, it moves that bar there, which moves that bigger one back. The big one keeps the gates closed, because it slides in there. I see. Ah ha. That must be how the round things work on all the doors in the men's town down there. We could not get inside until I rotated the round objects."

"Excellent conclusion, Enyo. Exactly right. Works the same way. Those are called doorknobs, by the way." She repeated the words several times, committing them to memory. She watched him reassemble the lock.

"I see how it is done. Can I try to take it apart? Aand you can make sure that I don't break it."

"Sure, go ahead." Cedric replied rather amused and interested that she should be so fascinated with mechanical things and how they worked. It was right up the Planner's alley, so to speak. She had a most difficult time handling the screwdriver tool, however, but finally managed it with her teeth, until it was loosened, then her feet did the rest. Cedric found that she was remarkably agile with her feet. She was very happy to find that after she had put it back into place it worked as well as before! Now three others gathered around asking about the doorknobs.

Enyo then asked a completely different question. "When you first came, we saw the big boat give birth to the two smaller boats, at least that is what Chara called it. I saw these ropes and wheels hooked to it. One rope goes off to the side, then the rest of the rope goes over the wheel and down to the little boat and then back up to the wheel and then down to the little boat. Big pull on slant rope makes little pull on little boat. Does not that make the little boat seem to weigh only half as much?"

"Wow, Enyo! You are right again! Perfect. Yes, that way we can lift something that is heavy very easily. You are a very observant, sharp young woman indeed!" She beamed. For the rest of the afternoon, she and three others followed Cedric everywhere he went, plying him with questions as they thought of them.

Alexa heard Linda mentioning "culture shock," and moved over to her. "What is this culture shock? Is it like this: when we, the Rule Breakers, discovered that we could go bathing in the waters of the beach and what great fun that was, we came back to tell the others. They did not believe that a woman could go into the waters. It was against the rules even to be outside the House of Right. Only after we took them into the waters did they see for themselves that bathing in the beach waters is just fabulous indeed."

"Yes, that is very similar. Our world, actually, Alexa, the rest of the world out there beyond the sea, is very different from your little house here. We see you and you see us so very differently."

"Oh I see. Is it true that women out there are born with arms and hands?"

"Yes, absolutely. I've seen hundreds of thousands of women; all had arms. The only ones who do not, like Natale and Mireio, have experienced something quite bad, which cut off their arms — you know, like chopping them off with a sword or knife," Linda explained.

"Oh, that must have been terribly painful for them. But why is it then that we here are born without arms? It cannot be that there are two kinds of women in the world. That would not make sense. How is it that we women here in the House of Right are born without arms? No, if what you say is true, then we are born with baby arms. That means they must have been cut off, like Natale's, but I've talked to the mothers here, and they were given their babies to nurse the day after they gave birth, and the girls had no arms then. Hum, that must mean that the baby's arms were cut off while the men were preparing them for their mothers the next day. That would explain it, but why, Linda, would our men want to cut off our arms?"

"Excellent conclusions, Alexa! I'm impressed with your reasoning skills. You are almost certainly right; your men used that one day to remove the girl baby's arms, before they gave the baby to its mother."

"But that could only mean then that our men deliberately wanted all of we women to only believe that women were born with no arms. Oh, I see. If I knew that they were cutting off my baby's arms, just because she was a girl, I would do something to stop them. Oh, I'd be rebelling against them. Ah, they would not be able to control me anymore. Ah, as long as I believe that women are born with no arms, then I will accept my life without arms as normal, which it must not be! Our men must have been bad men then; there is no other explanation, is there?" Alexa asked.

"Alexa, I am very surprised that you so easily grasp how things go. It is a very impressive gift for seeing the truth of a matter that you have. Such is one of the skills that I have, just like you, to see the truth of a thing very quickly. I'll tell you a little more that may allow you to understand why your men were doing what they were doing to you." Linda began to tell her about the mantis creatures and what they had been doing to other peoples elsewhere on Tarra.

"You see, we are trying to find out if there are any more of these bad bug creatures around and if so, kill them, before they hurt anyone else," Linda explained.

"I see. I know nothing of these bugs. None of us here does. Yet, that would mean that either our men were forced to do this thing by the bad bugs or they, in their stupidity, believed what these bad bugs were telling them to do. Either way, our men were bad men."

"You are right again."

"I will ask around and see if any of the older women have seen these black bugs and let you know. I love talking with you, Linda. You are much like me. We see things so easily, but I always get us into trouble by breaking the rules, when I am just looking for the truth."

"Well, that has now changed forever, Alexa. Never again will you have arbitrary rules you have to obey. Let your own observation of how things are control your life! That's what I always do."

"That is freedom, is it not?"

"Yes, why?"

"Well, that is what we have had lacking all this time here in the House of Right, which is now not very right, is it?" Linda chuckled, while Alexa went off to try to find out information for Linda.

Another bunch of women followed Rosina around asking about our meager clothing. When they found out that we all wore other clothing when it was not so hot, they just had to see them. At once the women asked her where to get the cloth, how it is sewn and so on. Although none of this was Rosina's specialty, she did her best to answer the women.

At last, the cooks had dinner ready. Again, shock set in. We discovered that these women had always had what could be generously called a stew, but it was really just everything thrown into one pot and cooked to into a uniform mush. Now they had their special plates filled with several different, colorful foods, including meat, which had been sorely lacking of late. The comments we received about the food were a bit overwhelming; the women loved it! Only when our cooks promised to teach Kleio how to prepare these various foods did the poor cook stop crying.

The next surprise came when Mireio and Roberto, now accompanied by their daughter, Alwanianon, played a round of after dinner music for everyone. Suddenly, we had thirty women just begging to learn how to make music! Even more surprising, an hour later, Mireio declared that most of those who wanted to learn music had perfect pitch. Once they heard how the song went, they reproduced it exactly right! She and Roberto were flabbergasted!

Once the music and conversation over the music ended, Alexa came up to Linda, bumping her to get her attention. "I have found something that might help you. While none has ever seen this bug that you talk about, some of the older women recall that many, many years ago, the men who took the babies after the mother gave birth, took them up the hill behind our house. Maybe there is something unknown up there?"

Finally, while everyone was chatting after the music was done, two dozen women began asking us about our beautiful earrings, and how they were made, and so on. They asked us if they could learn how to make such fine earrings.

We all said good night, promising to bring them a good breakfast the next morning. On our way back, we all hit the beach for an early nighttime swim! We needed this bath!

On the ship, we compared notes. It was clear that we had just stumbled into an entire collection of very able beings; all were probably artists in some way. The only conclusion possible was that the mantis creatures were entrapping the artists and great thinkers of their part of the world into these female bodies with no arms, while convincing them utterly that women were born this way, and giving them no outside contact with the rest of the world. A perfect trap indeed — one that kept these "trouble makers" out of the way. I began to see the methods being used by the mantis creatures much more clearly. Every one of us insisted upon bringing these women back to Velona with us, to train them, and to regain their artistry for the world.

When we arrived with breakfast for them the next morning, Alexa was waiting for us at the gate. "Excuse me, Bethany. You must come with me. I must show you something very important about what you were asking about the bugs!" While the others continued carrying the breakfast supplies on into their kitchen, I followed her over to a corner of the courtyard. There Dione was standing guard over something she had sketched on the wall, using the charcoal stick Michelle had given her yesterday.

"Is this the bugs that you spoke about yesterday?" asked Dione, a note of fear in her voice.

On the wall was a perfect representation of a mantis standing over a tiny baby body and in the act of eating one of its arms! "Yes, Dione! This is it exactly. How were you able to draw it?"

"Mother Secundus, Leda, she came to Alexa last night crying. She's had this nightmare very often all her life. She said that I had to draw what she was seeing. Now today, many others have seen this, and they too have such nightmares. Me too. We all thought it was normal to have them, but we never spoke openly of them; we didn't think it was real. After what you said to Alexa yesterday, we know them to be real. We are all very scared and upset. You must see Leda, please."

We three went to join the others in the large kitchen. Since there was now a long line, I went to Leda's table where she had already begun eating. "This is a fabulous breakfast! On behalf of all of us, thank you very much!" Leda said. I saw dark pockets under her eyes, and they were still reddish and puffy. I knew that she had not slept well, very likely crying.

"I saw the drawing that Dione made. You are precisely correct. To the best of my knowledge that is what has been going on in many other places and now here too, it seems."

"A tear formed and trickled down her cheek. "Alexa has told us much. We believe truth is important for us. Now we all know. She has discovered that most all us have similar nightmares, though not as bad as mine have been. No one was willing ever to mention them because we all thought they could not be real. Then it is so; we have all been unwilling, unknowing victims of some horrible plot. Worse, while we all thought having no arms were normal; we are now terrified, because all the other women in the world out there are not like us. I am their Mother Secundus, but now even that is a lie — well what I was supposed to be counseling was a lie. They still look to me as their leader, but I do not know what to say."

She went on, "Now I understand Mother Primus Zona better. I believe that she intentionally fell down the steps so that she could leave and get a new baby body. Is that what we should all do, fall down the steps so that we can end this nightmare, and go find new baby bodies?"

"Heavens no, Leda! First, my mother and I have perfected a therapy that totally erases the entire trauma a person may have experienced. I promise you that I will work my therapy on every one of your women. Second, I would like all of you to come and live with my mother and me at our large complex. There all the women, who have been so harmed like you, are staying. All your needs will be met; you shall not want for a lack of anything. Of course, we will ask you to help, as you are able. Third, we Santi possess great knowledge and skill, and you have my word that we will teach every woman here, as much as she is willing to learn, in the areas that she desires to learn, such as art for Dione. In short, Leda, we Santi offer you hope for a bright, happy, and worthwhile future. If you need proof, just look at Natale, Mireio, or even Michelle."

"You would do this for us? We are total strangers."

"Would you not help an injured person who came to your gates?" She smiled and understood.

"Perhaps it would be wise if you told everyone here this right now. Many are very distraught and have been considering falling down the steps," Leda confessed.

I stood up and told everyone what I had just offered Leda, adding more words to make it even clearer. The women began yelling and cheering, offering their thanks to whichever one of us was closest to themselves. We brought a ray of hope into their lives. "Before we can begin any of this, I and my companions must find where the bugs used to live and make sure that they are totally gone and can never come back and do this to anyone else. This should only take us a day or two at the most. Meanwhile, you might work with Captain Henry here to figure out what all of your belongings you desire to bring with you."

I finally got to eat my breakfast. Linda and Henry sat down beside me to discuss a few things. Linda said, "We have not bedding for this many women. They cannot just sleep on the cargo hold deck. Realize that they have been living a very cloistered life. All this is going to be totally unfamiliar and new to them. I would like to maintain as much continuity as possible during the long voyage. Alexa has said that they are organized into units of four women who help each other with basic needs. I suggest we keep them so organized. Henry believes that we should take their simple beds onto the boat, maintaining their groups of four. He wants to keep things as close to what they are used to here." I gave them my okay.

Next, we packed up our few supplies and headed off to try to find the mantis creature's home. I left the Santi and several others behind to guard them and work out the arrangements for travel. I found out later what happened from Mireio.

Dione and Chara came up to Mireio looking rather shy. Dione said, "It is so good that you are going to have a baby!" Mireio smiled and she continued, "We also very, very much want to have a baby, but now we no longer know how that may be. Our men were supposed to return and bed us, but that has not happened in over ten years now. Do your men bed you often? How do we get men to bed us so that we may also bring forth new life? I have tried to make myself as pretty as I can, Chara too, but now we no longer know how it is to be done."

Suddenly, Mireio found herself having to wear my shoes! "The rest of the world believes that a man and a woman should first care very much for each other, love we call it. When they both are ready to settle down, they get married. Only then do they bed, and once married, they only bed with each other. Bedding with someone who is not your marriage partner is considered very bad and is rarely done, except by bad people sometimes. Roberto and I are married. It is his and my baby growing here." She nodded towards her growing belly.

"When the baby is born, it will be both Roberto and my responsibility to raise the baby together. This way, the baby has both a mother and a father looking after its needs, playing with it, loving it, and caring for it."

"You mean the fathers are always around after the baby is born and help with its raising?" Chara whispered. "Oh my. That was never done here! None of us even knows who our father is!"

"Yes, you have been cheated out of half of your parents."

"But how do we find this love, a man?" Dione complained. "Now that we know we are the freaks and not a normal woman, who will want us like this? Compared to those like Bethany, we are so helpless, who would want to marry us?"

"Back in Velona, where we live, there are many good men. I met Roberto there. He loves me because of me, not because of how my body looks. We share many interests in life; we are both musicians; I love to sing and he, to play. We understand each other very well. My advice is look for a man you both admire and respect. If he is the right one for you, love will blossom. But yes, it will take some time. You all will need to meet many people and many will meet you. You both are very pretty and that helps attract men's attention too. But remember, looking pretty is very transitory. Look how age has changed Leda. Look for one you admire and respect; he will be doing the same thing with you as well, if he is a wise man, for this does not grow old. Roberto and I love making music and that will never grow old, so neither will our love for each other. Does this make any sense to you?"

Both women looked a bit confused, Chara asked, "So the men where you live won't look at us as some kind of freak?"

"Oh there will always be those that stare at you. People like us are very rare in our world, so it gets their attention. Some will gush sympathy and pity at you — always happens. Oh you poor little thing — crap like that. Just ignore that. I always get stares, but then there are many others who really would like to get to know you. Those are the ones who will look at you, not your bodies."

"We don't like thinking of ourselves as freaks! Until now, we never ever had such a notion!" declared Dione.

"So don't start thinking that way now! Forget such nonsense! You are you. I always just be me, so the heck with the rest of it. Be yourselves and everything will work out just fine, believe me it will."

Both smiled, "Okay we will! We must go tell the others. They are worried about now being freaks. So we will not be freaks; we will just be ourselves. Thanks, Mireio." When Mireio told me of this later on, I said that she handled it well.

It was a long, hot hike up the hillside. Fortunately, the road had many switchbacks, making the grade easier to walk. By noon, we were near the top of this large hill. Ahead was a wooden building, the road led straight to it. Benet pointed out that no one had been on this road up here in many, many years. We were leaving very telltale tracks! We found that encouraging.

Inside the building, we found an operating table and many sharp knives, needles, and even threads. Long dried blood covered the sides of the table and the floor. Evidently, the latest work had been done by the men here, not the creatures. That would make sense, because for fifteen years after Alabaster and I had gotten rid of them, the men had to carry on the tradition of removing the female baby's arms up here. We found nothing else of interest in the cabin. Even outside, we found no trace of the removed limbs. Now came the hard part, finding where the mantis had lived, probably where the men had taken the arms as an offering.

"Fan out and search," I suggested. Just then, huffing and puffing up the road came Alexa and Enyo.

"Are we too late?" Alexa asked. "We wanted to see too. Have you found anything yet?"

I laughed, no wonder these were the Rule Breakers! "No, nothing key. Come, I'll show you what is inside." I took them inside. Both went to the table, looked at it, and cried.

"It is really true, Alexa. See the dried blood that our many arms have made," Enyo pointed out.

"Yes, I see. I wonder where all our arms have gone too? They are not inside here," Alexa added bravely.

"We are looking for them now. Come on." I led them back outside this gruesome building.

"Over here, Bethany," Benet called out. "Oh, hi Alexa, Enyo." Everyone scampered to where Benet and Michelle were standing. A white marble slab, an offering altar large enough to hold an adult lying down, was littered with the desiccated arms from a large number of babies.

"Two of those are probably yours, Enyo, and two are mine," Alexa commented. It was a ghastly sight because of what it meant. "Our men brought us up here after our bodies were born, removed our arms back there, and left them here for the bug to eat, only the bug was not here."

"Yes, in my last lifetime, I helped kill all the bugs that were plaguing Tarra, Alexa. I wish that we had known about your island here, we would have attempted to free everyone and stop these misguided men. We also didn't know that the bugs laid eggs, which might later hatch and begin to cause new harm to others. That is the main reason for our arrival here. We found a map of all the bug's hideouts, and we have been systematically visiting them, destroying newly hatched bugs and any remaining eggs. Gang, the hideout must be somewhere close to here. Keep on searching." The two women said little more and continued to examine the pile of bones.

After a thorough search, Benet found no cave entrance that we could enter from here. Enyo now began looking around as well. She said, "Look at these rocks here; they are different from the rest of the stones, more reddish. I wonder where they came from?"

"Hey, good observation, that must be it," Benet pointed to the rocky peak of this hill, which we would need ropes to climb, if then. "I bet it has a roof top entrance, where it could fly into its den. Bethany, take a look please?"

Alexa whispered to Linda, "What's he mean? Can she climb that steep slope?"

"No, Bethany can move out of her body and go up there and take a look. If there is an opening, she will carry all of us inside." Alexa looked at me, as did Enyo.

I opened my eyes and said, "Excellent, Enyo and Benet, you are right, there is a big opening up there. Does everyone have their lanterns ready? I'll lift you all in." I took the two Protectors inside first, and they got their lanterns going to make sure that we did not bump into anything that might be dangerous. One by one, I lifted the others gently inside. "Now it's your turn. Just relax. I won't drop either of you." I picked up Alexa and floated her up and over and down inside with the others. I noticed that she was holding her breath. Then, I did the same with Enyo. Finally, I was standing outside by myself, and I lifted my own body up, over, and down.

"Wow that was great!" exclaimed both Alexa and Enyo together. Alexa then asked, "Can all your people do this?"

"No, mostly my mom and I have learned how. Several others are getting really close to being able to do it. Let's see what they have found."

"Nest, Bethany. Four eggs are intact," Benet called out.

I decided to let the two women stomp and break two of the eggs themselves, a small blow for their people. They really enjoyed destroying these last remnants of the bugs, which had harmed so many of them. Benet eliminated the other two.

"Over here, look what I found under these reeds," Linda called out. We went to see, and there, neatly stacked, were another large number of similar golden ingots!

"Alexa, Enyo, this is gold and is what most everyone in the rest of the world uses as a means of exchange," I pointed out.

"Oh, I get it," Alexa picked up on the idea immediately. "If we want to get some food supplies, we give the trader some gold bars, and he gives us the supplies."

"Yes, only the amount of gold here will pay for anything your whole group of women could possibly want or need for the rest of your lives. There is a fortune in gold here, not just a little bit, a huge amount. You and your people will never have to worry about being out of food ever again!"

Both women smiled. Enyo asked, "But how do we get it out of here and how heavy is one of those bars?" I had her sit down and I gently placed one ingot on her feet so she could lift it. "Wow, this is really heavy! Alexa, you lift it." Alexa sat down beside her and Enyo repositioned the ingot onto her friend's feet, with a similar result.

"I'll just lift them out like I lifted you all inside. Let's see what else might be here," I replied.

"Hey, over here, I've got another writing desk but none of their books. Anyone got any ideas? There ought to be some here somewhere, because the others had some," Natale asked.

While the others went looking, I explained to Alexa and Enyo that Natale loved learning new languages and already spoke more than the rest of us. We had found what must be the writings of the bugs and she wanted to see if she could learn their language to read what they had written.

A half hour later, Cedric found and opened a secret compartment. Natale added six more books to her growing collection of mantis writings. Finding nothing else of value, I began lifting everyone outside. Then, I spent another hour lifting out three hundred and five ten-pound gold ingots, one by one. Cedric was already working on how we were going to transport over a ton and a half of gold down to the caravel! Enyo was at his side, asking questions and offering ideas.

She said, "When we have something too heavy to carry, we put it onto the wooden slab, which has rollers instead of feet. Then, we can push it along. Maybe we could use the marble slab with the baby bones and put all the gold on it. All we need is to make wheels."

"Good thinking, Enyo. We don't have any wheels though, but we can make do. How about putting logs that roll under it?"

"Oh, I see. We push it a ways and then take the logs that come out after it has moved and put them back in the front," Enyo replied.

"Enyo, you are an absolute genius at this stuff! Perfect. Gang, scour around, find us about ten logs. Bethany, can you move that slab or is it too heavy?" I lifted it up and floated it around, teasing him. Everyone laughed. "It's all downhill, so we shouldn't have too hard a time moving it."

"Yes, but," Enyo added, "if it is downhill, what will keep it from rolling away from us really fast?"

"Hum, how about another log acting as a brake? Stick it under the front the wrong way to, which ought to provide enough friction to stop it if it gets to rolling too fast for us to manage."

A half hour later, they had enough logs made, and I laid the slab onto the logs, with Cedric operating the brake log. Next, everyone piled the gold onto the slab, spreading it out evenly. Then, with others holding spare logs and the rest of us ready to collect up the logs that rolled out the back, we began our slow walk back down the hill side. Several times, Cedric had to stop it. Either it began going a little too fast or we couldn't get the new logs under the front in time. It was nearly dark when we finally returned to the House of Right.

We ate supper slightly late; most of the others had finished. Then, we all headed down to the beach for an early evening bath to wash off the sweat and dirt from our day's exertions. That night, Henry outlined his plan for transporting our new guests and I Okayed it. I then contacted mom to brief her.

Hi mom. Guess what?

I know you have another two hundred wounded women for me to handle.

Not that many! Only one hundred twenty. But these are very special women! I related what we had discovered about these women. She was very impressed. In fact, Allan had already begun work on yet another dormitory housing project, expecting me to find more women to bring home with me. I told mom to thank him for me and to design it with four women to a room, since that was the way that they were organized. She promised me that they would be ready for our new additions.

The next day, the crew began to start the lengthy moving. All their beds had to be taken out to the caravel and positioned properly and secured so that they would not move in a storm. Each woman's few possessions also had to accompany their move to the ship, along with their chamber pots, food tins, and wooden spoons. All this would take at least a week to accomplish. Hence, I decided to begin therapy sessions while we waited.

I began with Leda, their leader, whose nightmare continued to bother her. This time, I had a break on locating the trauma incidents. Obviously, they had occurred right after birth. I began by sending Leda back to her birth, which she easily found. "It's all black and warm. I feel like I am being squashed from all sides." She was off and running. Once her body had been born, cold male hands picked her up, wrapped her in a blanket, and carried her up the hill. There, she was laid on the slab.

"I am crying for food and am freezing cold, when I see this

enormous black creature moving over me. I am terrified. I am screaming my little head off. It leans over me and bites into my shoulder. I can't move, but then it stops hurting. I watch as it very neatly cuts around my arm, and its claws remove the bone from my shoulder socket. It spits something up on my shoulder that somehow heals it and stops the bleeding. My stomach is in such a tight knot that it hurts. Now it does it to my other arm. I have no arms any more. I am wrapped in the blanket, and the man carries me back. I am laid down beside my mom, but I can't eat for a long time. My stomach is one big knot. Then I fall asleep. When I wake up, I am nursing. Now I feel better. That's all. Bethany, my stomach really, really hurts!"

"Thank you Leda, you are doing well. Now let's go through it again." I had her go through it six more times, but it did not change at all. Following Jenna's procedure, I asked for an earlier time she had a similar trauma. Immediately, she began running an almost identical incident, her birth the lifetime just before this one! Before I actually finished Leda, she had run through five complete, nearly identical birth incidents. If she had lived, say an average of sixty years each life, she had been trapped here at this place for over the last three hundred years, maybe more!

Laughing heartily, she realized that this whole thing had been precipitated because she had run for her town's mayor position! She had won and had been killed and entrapped by the bugs.

Her incredible recovery and resurgence of life did not go unnoticed by all the other women. Rather the opposite! Now they all wanted to get sessions at once. I continued my methodical treatments with the Rule Breakers, taking Alexa first. Two days later, she too was laughing her head off, totally rejuvenated. She had been trapped here for six lifetimes as well. She had been a powerful Megalos Senator, promoting peace, justice, and truth among her people. Like Leda, she had been killed by a bug and entrapped here.

Enyo had been an engineer who had actually designed and built many of the ancient aqueducts, which still provided water from the mountains to the lower elevation cities of Megalos. She too had been killed by a bug and entrapped here for seven lifetimes.

Now the pattern slowly became clear. By the time we were ready to sail, I had finished the Rule Breakers. All their stories were incredibly similar. Even more interesting, many wanted to learn how to do this therapy. Hence, I began conducting training lessons in the morning. Each afternoon and evening, we ran the sessions. Since all these traumas were so nearly identical, it was easy for me to monitor many sessions simultaneously, while running my own. By the time that we reached Velona, four weeks later, all were fully recovered and twenty were now quite competent with the technique.

We were now in possession of one hundred and twenty incredibly able people, the artists, engineers, and great thinkers of ancient Megalos! Even more impressive, all were outside their heads, had full knowledge of their own spiritual natures, and were greatly desirous of learning all that we could teach them! September 24, we sailed into Velona.

During the voyage, Dione asked me, "Bethany, do all the women wear such large, beautiful earrings? Do your men find them attractive? We are all wondering if those might help us find the right man so we can marry and have a family."

I explained how we came to have them and told her that we had hundreds more of them. "After you are settled in and if you then decide you want some as big as these, let us know. We can fix you up."

Poor Renzo, he and the rest of the Circle spent most of their time either helping with the nearly constant cooking or washing dishes! The caravel was not set up to handle so many passengers; that is an understatement. We were all very cramped in the cargo hold! We had no space to play ball nor did we have any time to spare either.

Natale was not idle either; she had to teach our new guests our Sea Prince dialect. Since so few of us actually spoke the Megalos dialect well enough to handle their more ancient form of the language, they would have to pick up ours. The sooner the better. Hence, when they were not in a therapy session or giving one, Natale worked on their language skills.

Meanwhile, Linda quietly asked each woman what her favorite color was and took down her measurements. After compiling the lengthy list, she had Rosita relay it to Paulette. When the women arrived, the first thing that they would be given would be a new dress in their favorite color. No more of these bland, off-white linen sacks!

What a sight we made as we sailed into Velona. On the main deck, the outer rows of women were sitting down. Behind them, the next bunch was on their knees, while those in the middle were standing. All were tightly together so the crew could still move around to carry out their vital duties in docking. To say that they were impressed with the sight of such a large city would be an understatement. This was beyond anything they could imagine. The sights, sounds, and colorfully clothed people made a lasting impression on them. Never having seen a carriage, much less a carriage ride, this was also quite a hit.

Yes, Elona Po welcomed them to her city. They were very surprised to see that mom had no hands and was yet the Santi leader, and this gave them tremendous hope. True, they were stared at and watched by many eyes, as we told them they would be. However, with their therapies completed, it didn't matter, for they had recovered fully their own self-respect. However, the many whistles of admiration did cause several of them to blush. Dione commented to her friends, "I think some of them like us already, and we haven't yet met them!"

As we entered the estate, the first stop was at their new living quarters, where each room held a plaque with the four names of the group who would stay here. Allan had constructed very comfortable beds and on each lay their new dresses. As it turned out, maintaining their organizational pattern worked perfectly, allowing them to continue their familiar methods of helping each other. I led the Rule Breakers to their new room. "Mom has had her seamstresses make each of you a new dress. Can you figure out which one is for which of you?" I teased as they carried their small sacks of personal possessions, such as their hairbrushes, inside their new room.

"Blue! Mine is the blue one!" declared Dione. "Oh this is so pretty!"

"Mine has got to be the green one," said Enyo, "like the grass under the mother with her faun."

"Mine's the yellow one," Alexa pronounced.

"I get the red one," Chara said quietly, all smiles.

I helped them quickly change. "There, now you all look super. Come on; now I want you to walk with us up to the Manor House where I live as do mom and many of the other women who will be helping you learn so many new things." One by one, all these new arrivals walked the short distance to the brownstone manor house. Of course, it was entirely dwarfed by the twin palaces of the Laird Arts Foundation.

There waiting to greet us all were all of our friends, including Teyacapan and Teiuc, who gave a hearty welcome to Alexa, Enyo, Chara, and Dione. The four were amazed at how well Teiuc could move around on her own, claiming her situation was far worse than theirs was.

While the rest of us began unpacking our gear, which Henry had brought up while we were assisting the new arrivals with their new clothes, mom began the lengthy introductions and took them on a guided tour of the estate, the art foundation, and the heated public bath. Poor mom was besieged with many, many questions from Enyo. She saw at once, what I had meant by how incredible these women were.

That evening, Bard Tal introduced them to the music of many lands. Impressed and thrilled, he found himself and his group members surrounded by more than half of the new arrivals, all wanting to know about music, singing, and the incredible dancing done by so many other women who were just like themselves. He had made an indelible impression on them, just as he had planned. His estimates were that at least twenty of these women might be musically inclined and wanted to attract them to his large troupe!

Later that night, I found out that Lenkova and Andre, with a number of others too, were due to arrive in Velona within a week. Renzo and I finally could set our wedding date. Thus, we allowed them two days to get accustomed to our estate. Our date was to be October 4, 649. Also, Rosina and Cedric would marry with us, a dual wedding. However, Benet and Michelle came and begged us four to allow them to marry along with us. Okay, now it would be a trio wedding.

No sooner had we four agreed to have Benet and Michelle join us, when in walked Emil and Tonia. How had I missed all this! They were madly in love with each other and begged us to allow them to be married along with the rest of us. Laughing, I swore that I knew nothing about love any more. We agreed, now it would be a quartet of marriages.

No sooner had I agreed and began laughing, when in walked Linda Sarah with my youngest brother, Damien. "Hi Damien. Congratulations on making Protector! Mom's just told me about it. Good going. I know you had to work awfully hard at it."

He gave me a big hug and kiss, lifting me off my feet and twirling me around. "Yes, I finally did it! Sis, Linda and I want to ask you for a really big favor."

"Sure, little brother, what is it?"

"Ah, we want to get married along with you too."

"What? Linda? Damien? But how? I..."

"We've been in love for years, Bethany, only we kept it pretty secret, because he was having such a hard time learning all the needed spells. Now that he's made it, we can finally marry. He wouldn't hear of it until he made Protector. He made me promise to keep it a secret all this time! I guess I did a pretty good job of it," my very best friend said.

I gave them both a long hug. "Okay, now it is a quintet of marriages! Does mom know?"

Damien grinned sheepishly, "Yes, she has known all along. You know that it is impossible to keep anything secret from mom! But we thought we'd ask to join you four last, to make sure that the rest would get your okay to share the day. By the way, what day are we getting married anyway?"

"October 4. Golly, now we all have to get so many presents for everyone and so little time. I suppose that we all should get together tomorrow and try to figure this all out, make our plans and all," I answered. Then I thought of a serious problem, and asked, "Say, Damien, where are you going to be stationed? Linda is going to be spending a lot of time with me at sea, you know."

He looked at the floor and shuffled his feet, his arm still around Linda's waist. "Er, I've been assigned to a caravel by mom."

"Great, you probably will like it, I sure do. What's your ship's name?"

"The Sleepy Hollow," he whispered.

"Oh you rascal you! Why didn't you tell me?" I began chasing him around the room, tickling his sides. He always was very ticklish like

Renzo.

He finally blurted out, "Mom wanted to surprise you. Stop! Now Linda knows how awful ticklish I am!"

"No problem, love," exclaimed Linda, who took over from me and began tickling him herself, until he turned on her and gave her a loving embrace. That stopped the tickle match.

Chapter 10 Five Weddings, an Interlude

The next day, we all went shopping. I won't bore you with all the presents, but I can't help but tell you what I got for Renzo. I found a super high quality short sword, made by the best sword smith in all the Highlands. Also, a new game had now become very popular around Velona; it was called Kings and Queens. In your world, it is similar to chess. Since we would likely be playing it at sea, I got him a beautiful set, which was designed to be played on a moving boat.

I was not prepared for the present that he gave me or that mom gave me. They had worked together on them, behind my back even. I had no clue until I came back from shopping and gave Renzo his presents from me. "Let me get your mom, and she and I will give you our presents." I had no idea what was going on, my curiosity rose, especially when mom came back with him, a twinkle in her eyes. Dad was with her too. What were these three up to anyway?

"Dear, your father and I have a wedding present for you and Renzo. Renzo added his wedding present to you to ours. Will you follow us please?" I dutifully followed them.

"Why are we going outside?" I asked. "Did you get me a horse?"

Suddenly I saw a new construction. A small brownstone home had been built here behind the manor house, only a short walk separated this new building from the manor house and the bathhouse, which lay just to the right of the brownstone. "This is your new home. We decided that you ought to have some privacy when you desire it. We hope you like it."

I loved it! The home was small and prefect for our needs, as we walked through it. "This way to the special room, Bethany," Renzo added. Behind the living room was a large square room. On the opposite wall was the line. It was our very own Torque Ball room! Now I could play any time I desired! I was thrilled to say the least. "Only don't get so good at it that I don't stand a chance," he teased me. I hugged all three. This was really an unexpected surprise.

The next interesting event was the public concert and the public dance held on Friday and Saturday nights. I helped all of our new guests get dressed up for the concert, making sure their hair was nicely brushed. Well a lot of us actually helped them. Then, we led them to the huge performance theater, where they met many of the others who were living here on the estate. Further, about a thousand public showed up from Velona. At last, the new arrivals had an opportunity to meet new people, especially men their own ages.

Of course, Bard Tal's show had greatly improved, only I've run out of superlatives with which to describe it. The Greenway dances, the stomps, now featured twenty-five women who had no problem keeping their arms from moving, since they didn't have any. I got a surprise when two dozen of the Isle of Loving women, were introduced as the Line of the Old Way ensemble. There was Gesa, Emiri, and Amiria leading the group in a set of evocative songs and dances from their island, with Tal's band performing the percussion-heavy, accompanying music! When the concert finally finished, Tal and his ever-growing group received a standing ovation, and they had to do six encores.

Our new guests were thrilled beyond words with the performance and the lengthy conversations held among the attendees afterwards. Many had friendly chats with very eligible bachelors.

Shortly after that, Dione came up to me and asked me, "Bethany, a man has asked me to go to the dance tomorrow with him. I said yes, but I do not know what exactly this is. Have I done wrong?"

"Say, that is wonderful." I then carefully explained it. "You will easily catch on. Trust me, you will see. He knows that he will have to come here and ride to the dance hall with you in one of our carriages. Besides, we all will be going, and we'll look after you for sure! Many of these men you met here tonight are fellow artists. Like you, they are trying to meet many people, hoping to find just the right person for them."

Andre and Lenkova arrived the next day, bringing Donata and Sarah Amber, Linda, and my sisters, with them. We spent much of the day showing the twin's parents all around Velona and the estate. Neither could believe the sheer size of Velona nor the incredible beauty of Elona's church in which our ceremonies would be held. However, the estate was beyond anything they ever imagined! "This is utterly unbelievable!" Lenkova kept saying as we moved from one spot to another.

We toured the Laird Foundation. At first, the sight of so many superb works of art on display they found breathtaking. Neither had ever seen so much quality art in one location before. Then, they met many of the artists themselves, both male and female. That so many women were able to produce such art, considering their circumstances, left them speechless. If that was not enough, we then sat in on some of the many rehearsals that were going on during the afternoon. Bard Tal was working up their routines, again, providing numerous outlets for creative performances by so many women.

Just before supper, they presented us four with our wedding presents from them. They gave each of us a horse. Not just any horse, these were four of the finest horses in the land, very well trained and very spirited. At last, we all sat down at the huge table for dinner. An extension had been added so that everyone, including our newcomers, could dine together. Mom finally admitted to us that she had finally exceeded the capacity of our enormous dining hall. Allan teased her, "Ah, we shall just have to add on another extension, Jenna. There is tons of space out front!" Everyone roared.

Personally, I enjoyed seeing all these women whom we had rescued all dining here together, faces beaming with happiness, chatting gaily among themselves. It was so rewarding that I felt light as a feather. Mom brought up a new problem though. With so many very able women now in need of Guardian style training, either she had to recall every existing Guardian back to her estate to train all these or we would have to break with our long-standing tradition of taking on only one apprentice at a time. Everyone voted for multiple trainees, however.

Once supper was done, the mad rush to help everyone get ready for the big public dance began. Even Lenkova was pressed into service helping; those with arms, assisting those without. She was particularly impressed with those from Wanakan, Teiuc and Teyacapan, along with Cazamel, Xilonen, and Iacotl. That they would even consider going to a public dance and then actually attempt to imitate the dance moves as best they could totally consumed all her thoughts and attention. She watched in awe as Teiuc met Shorty, who took her arm and helped her into the coach. Shorty never left her side the whole night. In fact, Lenkova quickly saw that the two were quite in love with each other. He had finally found someone who was his size and more importantly was as interested in painting as he was! "I don't believe it!" Lenkova said to me on more than one occasion that night.

The next morning, Lenkova had an idea, which she and Andre pursued, with our help. That afternoon, she proudly led four small ponies into the complex. They had scoured the city for these specific ones, very well trained, very gentle, and with an easygoing temper. I brought the four women outside to meet her. Of course, Teyacapan accompanied her friend. "Teiuc, Cazamel, Xilonen, and Iacotl, I want you to meet the most famous fighter and guardian of women's rights in the entire Zargarb sector of the Sea Princes. This is the legendary Lenkova Pazzio le Gouer. Lenkova: these are our friends from Wanakan: Teiuc, Cazamel, Xilonen, and Iacotl."

After the hugs were done, Lenkova said, "You four have impressed me beyond words! I watched how you handled the dance last night. You are an inspiration for all women everywhere. I wanted to do a little something for you. I have gotten a pony, a small horse, for each of you. Andre and I have modified the tack to fit your special needs. These are very gentle animals and after I am done training you how to ride, from now on, you can ride anywhere you want. You will have an even greater freedom of movement. You can take them back to your land when you return and will be able to go more places far easier." The four women were quite impressed with the ponies, especially when they found that they could very easily mount them and were not that high off the ground.

One by one, we helped each one into their saddle, show them what to do, and we led them around the grounds, allowing them to get used to the motion.

An hour later, Teiuc was yelling at Teyacapan, "Look at me! I am moving around now effortlessly! This is so great and so easy to do! You must get one to so you can come with us!"

Shortly after this, Shorty came by to chat with Teiuc; he had not known about the ponies. When he saw her riding proudly around the yard, he exclaimed, "Oh Teiuc! I didn't know you could ride a pony! This is fabulous. Now I can take you to my special place, the one I showed you in my painting where the waterfall and yellow buttercups grow!" Teiuc was incredibly happy, for now she could actually visit the place that Shorty had been telling her about so frequently. She had a vast new vista of mobility.

At last our wedding day came. The Rose Cathedral was packed with well-wishers who came to watch we five couples get married. Nervous? Yes, we five, Tonia, Rosina, Linda, Michelle, and me, were wearing our new white dresses, but were continually fidgeting with nearly everything.

"Mom, I'm so excited and just a bit nervous, well a whole lot nervous," Tonia said to her mother, Elona Po, who was about to marry us all.

"Dear, I am too! I just can't believe that my little girl is all grown up! Why it seems like only yesterday that I was holding you in my arms. Time flies so fast these days! Oh, I'm supposed to be telling you how this will go. Oh, Tonia, your brothers are back. Adrien and Gascon just got back in time. They will be with your father and me." Her older brothers were nineteen and seventeen and had just gotten back from a trip to the northernmost Santi fortress along the border with Barcella.

Also, Paul and Jovanna Barcella Wilkins had come to the wedding as well, bringing their entire Circle with them. She was the ruler of the Barcella sector, which had turned the corner on it dire plight during its lengthy occupation by the Holy Paladins. They had just gotten here today and would meet with us all later today.

I won't bore you with the details of our ceremony. However, I do want to tell you about what Bard Tal did. Before the ceremony began, he had his many vocalists sing a number of sacred songs, which echoed within the enormous church, like angels on high. I was impressed with the sound!

After the ceremony, we went to the public dance hall, which used to be our old estate before we expanded into our current, much larger one. While all the old buildings had been torn down and replace with this huge dance hall and an arts building, still the place held fond memories for so many of us. Here, we partied. I lost count of the hugs, kisses, and well wishes we received. Jovanna, as expected, just loved our earrings. Naturally, when she returned home, she, Leslie Ann, and Aura now sported their own set. We were starting a new rage in fashion, just teasing.

Me, I just waited out the hours. Soon, Renzo and I were finally alone in our new house, just behind the giant manor house. "I cannot believe that you and I are really alone now," I said, holding him tightly.

"Me either. Come on, let's," he didn't finish his sentence; he couldn't; my lips sealed his mouth. I felt fabulous the next morning. We both slept in, way past the normal rise and shine time.

Someone knocked on our door. I went to see who; it was Linda. "Jenna needs you at the morning meeting at once. Something is up with Vito and Bonilla. Hurry up." Hastily I roused Renzo, and we dressed quickly, heading to mom's meeting room. All the other Guardians were already there.

"Sorry to bother you, Bethany, but we just had some alarming news. In both Vito and Bonilla the Holy Paladins have just set sail for Megalos! No, they have not abandoned the sectors. Rather they left the local Holy Paladin recruits in charge now. From the haste of their departure, something is happening way down south. Paulette is checking on what's happening in West Reach as we speak." Those were the three areas still under the control of the Church of Jehosanity, Megalos.

"Why would the Holy Paladins desert these sectors?" I asked. All these years we had been trying to get them out of there and now, they left of their own accord? Why, I wondered. No one had any explanation. In fact, everything had been quite for well over a year now. Later Paulette reported that the soldiers were still in West Reach, however.

Jenna decided to ask the Santi in our two fortresses close to the two cities to investigate and see what the true situation was. Did we need to send in forces? Were we finally about to regain control over these sectors? Since nothing more could be done until we had more facts, we left to get some breakfast.

While the days passed waiting for further news, we five new couples definitely began enjoying married life. However, Renzo and I began giving the four new pony riders lessons, and of course, we found a smaller horse that Teyacapan could easily handle as well. Even Shorty and Matlali, that is Iacotl's fiancé, came along with us. Each day, we took them for longer rides around the area. Finally, when we were sure that the four could handle a longer ride, we accompanied them to Shorty's favorite place, about fifteen miles north of Velona, an isolated area of virgin woods and meadows. Here a small stream cascaded over a twenty-foot rock wall, making a beautiful waterfall. We ate a picnic lunch lying among the field of yellow buttercups. Yes, we allowed Shorty and Teiuc some private time together here.

The four women sat tall and very proud in the saddle, when, near suppertime, we entered the gates of the estate. For the first time, they felt like ordinary people again, out for a ride in the countryside. While on their ponies, they were just another rider. They did not stop talking about this little trip for days.

A week had passed. The only real news from Vito and Bonilla was status quo. Those in power remained in power, although the enforcement was now weaker, since the local Holy Paladins were nowhere near as competent fighters as those from Megalos. The only clue our forces gathered was a rumor that some battle was eminent somewhere around or on Megalos.

On October 15, 649, we once more set sail for the southern areas. Jenna's orders were to investigate the situation down there. We needed more information. This trip we took along double the food supplies, because mom was tired of having to make rush refills on our supplies. As usual, we were all on deck watching Velona slip slowly behind us. Michelle was at the helm, compliments of Henry, who took this opportunity to both study our map we had gotten from the mantis creatures and to spend time with Natale.

Michelle had actually issued all the orders to the crew to set sail, a tremendous honor, especially since she was the first woman ever to pilot a ship of any large size out from the docks. It did not go unnoticed by those on the docks either!

Once we were at sea, Henry wanted to hold a conference, so the bosun relieved Michelle, and she joined us, all crowded into the captain's cabin. "Okay, I thought that we might take a slight detour as we head south and seek out these unknown islands here. We've had rumors that they existed, but no firm confirmation. They are on the mantis map, however."

We chatted for a while and agreed. Then, Michelle spoke up. "If we are going to these islands here," she pointed with her arm, "I have some distant memories of them. Good harbors as I recall. However, could I ask you all to do me a small favor on the way?"

"Sure, what is it?" I asked.

"Well, I've got some memories of a small island near this group. I would like to see if that island does exist. If so, I'd like to put ashore there and see if anything else exists there. It is possible that I left something there when I as there as Antonio Zar."

"Sounds cool, why not?" I replied. No one had any objections, so Henry plotted the course using his new navigational methods. With luck, we could sail right to the island group without having to search for it — well that is if this map of the mantis creatures was correct in its spatial dimensions.

Life quickly settled back into normal for us. Renzo and I played ball in the cargo hold at least once a day. Since we now shared my cabin, we could stay up at night and play the new Kings and Queens game that I bought him. We both found it an interesting challenge, often staying up a little too late perhaps. However, hardly anyone noticed, since all five newly married couples were trying to spend as much private time together as they could. Even the not-newly married couples wanted to do the same thing. It was a nice, relaxing easy sailing week to get to these new islands.

Of course, when we reached them, all went on deck to see these new islands. Several had strange as yet unknown animals on them. The Loremaster made notes, but we decided not to land here. The largest of this group of six islands Henry named Midway, because it was somewhat midway down the coast of the Southlands. Well, not really halfway, barely a quarter, but Quarterway or Partway didn't make a good sounding name, we agreed. Now it was Michelle's turn to find her island.

For two days we zig-zagged in a small fan or arc south and east of Midway. She was about ready to give it up when the crow's nest look out called out "Land ho!" There ahead of us was a small island no more than two miles across. As we drew near, we saw that it was little more than a tall rock protruding from the sea, no trees and not much flat land. All of us were wondering what could possibly be here. Michelle, on the other hand, became very excited about the find.

"We need to anchor there — off that rocky thumb. Lower the longboats and wait for low tide. Then we will see if it's still there or not. God, I hope so!" What was there she would not answer. I suspected that she feared it would turn out to be nothing and wanted to avoid the embarrassment of it. Besides, she was actually using memories from a distant past life to guide her, and so many things change in hundreds of years.

We lowered the longboats after dropping anchor. We were at least a hundred miles off the main shipping lanes that paralleled the coastline of the Southlands to the east of here. Michelle also had us bring along a number of lanterns just in case we needed light. By now, we were intensely curious about what she expected to find; still she gave us no hints. We waited for an hour, Henry's wild guess on the low tide was somewhere between an hour to three hours. It was nearing suppertime and some began grumbling that they were hungry. Yet, we waited patiently, though exceedingly bored.

Michelle continued to stare at the rocky thumb all this time. Then, she noticed that the water level was definitely getting lower. The waves were now breaking far lower on the rocks. Suddenly, she called out, "There, see it, there, a cave entrance is opening up! I was right. Come on; make for that entrance." We all began slowly padding the two longboats toward the slowly widening opening.

By the time that we got there, most definitely the opening was large enough for one longboat to enter at a time. Michelle's boat, with us on board, went into the opening first. Quickly, we had to light the lanterns so that we could keep from banging into the rocky sides of the tunnel. Ten minutes later, we entered a large underground grotto and beached the boats on the shore. Stalagmites and stalactites were everywhere, reflecting in our lantern lights. It was certainly a beautiful cavern.

Michelle said, "So far, so good. Let's see which way?" She looked at her memories for a time and then led us off towards one side. Here the roof came down to meet the rising floor. Benet noted that we were now on dry land. Evidently, when the tidewaters came back inside, the water level didn't quite flood the entire grotto. "There! There it is! Just as I left it! Wow!" We looked where she was pointing. An ancient sea chest with rusted iron bands lay tucked tightly into the highest point in the grotto.

Emil and Benet crawled up to see if they could retrieve the sea chest. It slid down the slight incline easily. "Golly, Michelle, this is heavy. What's inside?" Benet called out.

"Not sure exactly, maybe nothing anymore, but it's locked, and I don't have the key. Besides, we best head out of here. We don't want to be caught when the tide starts back inside. I don't think we can oar against it to get out and would have to camp out here until the next low tide tomorrow evening."

We made haste after that sobering thought! Already, the tide was slowly rising, but we made it outside. A half hour later, the crew began raising the longboats back onto the deck. The men lugged the heavy chest down into the cargo hold, where we could open it at our leisure and with sufficient lanterns. However, we decided to eat our supper first, since the cook had it waiting for us.

I put off doing the dishes so that I could watch Cedric open the chest. He had to oil the lock and work with it for some time. The chest was still solid, but hundreds of years old, an historical relic, he claimed, and he wanted to preserve the chest if possible. Ten minutes later, the lock made a telltale click and opened. "Do you want to open the lid, Michelle?"

"Thanks. Again, there might not be anything left in here; it's been so long ago that I put it there," she said hesitatingly. Using her arms, she lifted the lid, which made a creaking sound, even though Cedric had oiled the hinges on its back. Our semi-circle of bodies looked over her shoulders at the chest. "Oh my," Michelle said.

"Good god!" Henry exclaimed. Gold, jewelry, gemstones shone back at us, along with various leather pouches. "You've got a fortune there, dear lady!"

One by one, we all began to take the items out and arrayed them on the dining table. "This was my wife's, Melinda's, tiara, before she died," Michelle commented, remembering the golden tiara with five shining gemstones on its front. All told, one thousand three hundred and forty-two gold coins lay stacked on the table, all ancient coinage, worth more as relics than their weight in gold. Seven gem encrusted broaches, sixteen rings of various sizes and stones, and three necklaces were carefully placed on the table.

"What's in the ten leather pouches?" asked Natale.

"I'm afraid I will need you to open them," Michelle replied, waving her arms, as if we needed a reason why. Carefully, Benet opened one and pulled out an ancient scroll.

"I cannot read it." He suggested, "Natale?"

She looked at it for a time, sounding out the words. "Oh, this is Old Megalos. Oh, this is a very neat document, Michelle!" She read it to us.

> I, Emperor Titolos, do hereby grant Antonio Zar royal permission to open up trading routes between Megalos and the Sea Princes.

"It has his signature on it and an imperial seal. Oh, the date is 432! Wow, this is really fantastic, Michelle!" Natale exclaimed, and we all agreed!

Another pouch contained the Official Land Grant Registry of the section of the Sea Princes known as Zargarb to Antonio Zar and the Church of Tur. It was dated 425. It also specified the boundaries of that sector, which were still the boundaries today.

Another two pouches contained a real mystery. One held the most unusual shoe that any of us had ever seen. It was well worn; one look at the soles told us that. However, the wearer had impossibly small feet! Either that or they had perhaps lost over half of their foot, the entire front part. Mostly the shoe would fit a heel on one of us. The other pouch contained a scroll with writing on it. This was terrifically interesting to Natale, who did not recognize any of the symbols. None of us did. All the symbols were most strange; we'd never seen anything like it.

Michelle explained, "I remember that I once found these washed up on the shore somewhere along the bottom of the Southlands. I believe that they came from some shipwreck and had washed ashore. No one could read this then, and no one back then had any idea where these had originated. Even the material of the shoe is unique to the known world. So I kept them safe, though I never knew anything more about them. I still haven't seen anything like this, have any of you?" None of us had either. This was indeed a complete mystery.

The last pouch contained several dozen more rings, completely anticlimactic, we thought. "What should we do with these?" asked Michelle.

"I know, how about putting some into the museum we have going up at Mont Blanc, in the limestone caves?" Benet suggested. "We have all the original inventions of Helios there; we can add these. I know that Ariana Zar would just love to see this original land grant document. I bet it is the only remaining land grant document in existence today, to say nothing of the Emperor's grant. Dear, now there can be absolutely no doubt about your past life, Mr. Antonio Zar!" Everyone chuckled and she blushed.

"Pretty neat, Michelle, this is the first time that we have had concrete proof that a lifetime that was examined in our therapy sessions has in fact been real and not just imagined! Jenna will love to hear about this!" She smiled and asked Rosina to let Jenna know. I, unfortunately, had to do the dishes, while the others looked over all the treasure. Ah well, at least I didn't have to swab the decks!

Chapter 11 The Decision

It was summer of 650. Royal Princess Sho Lin Wu looked in her mirror to check on her appearance. This she never trusted to her many servants, not ever. As the third in line to the throne of her father, a throne that she had coveted since she was five years old, her appearance meant everything. She had to be perfect. She checked the black shadow around her upper eyelids, yes, perfect. She perused her lips. Ah the cherry red lipstick was just right, accentuating her thick lips, which gave her part of her seductive look. The reddish blush on her cheeks, perfect. The gold interlocking rings of her seven earrings on each ear tingled as she moved her head. Of varying sizes, the longest touched her shoulders, and as the wind blew or she moved her head, the soft chiming sounds announced her graceful, elegant, royal presence.

Carefully, she examined each of her ten cherry red, painted nails, six inches long, her desired length for them. Sho Lin had worked long and hard to get them just perfectly right as they now were, sharpened to a point. No scratches or chips did she see. Satisfied with her nails, she turned her attention to her long brown hair. Her servant girl had just finished brushing it out. Sho Lin turned her head this way and that, surveying just how her long tresses fell, adjusting one here and there with her long, capable talons. Sho Lin had been blessed with good quality hair; hers now exceeded that of her two sisters, her rivals for the coveted throne. Hers was down to her knees, which she always displayed prominently by parting it in the middle and draping it over her shoulder and across her full bosom and down into her lap. When she needed to be very seductive, she would pull it all over one shoulder and down her front side, leaving the silhouette of one breast visible beneath her clothes.

Next, she checked on the eight rings on her fingers, making sure her servants had put the correct rings on for today's meeting. All were right, so she adjusted her necklace to be sure it was hanging properly, making a slight adjustment. Now she began to examine her clothing.

Sho Lin wore only the lightest, finest silks in all the land of Tashien. Each garment was especially made for her under the tightest of specifications. Her clothing must at all times be perfect, utterly seductive, and utterly feminine. Indeed, many of her garments had been original inventions of her loyal seamstresses. Their latest invention had revolutionized her appearance enormously, raising her stature higher than that of her two sisters. As yet, it did not have a name other than the shrinker, though the name corset was beginning to be used to describe it to others. Sho Lin did not want to reveal its truest purpose: to help her display properly her fourteen inch waistline. Yes, it took several of her servants nearly a half hour to get her into it and the strings tightened fully each day. Yet, the visual impact of her tiny waist more than compensated for its severe restriction of motion and breathing.

Over this magnificent form shape, today Sho Lin wore her pale blue silk dress, which fit her extremely tightly all the way down to her tiny toes, displaying perfectly her many seductive curves. Now she examined her lower body to make sure all looked just right. The narrow waistline added to the appearance of her plumb buttocks, while the tightly fitting dress highlighted her long, well-shaped legs. Her servants wore similar dresses, but these had walking slits in them, while hers, of course, did not. However, these servants had been thoroughly taught to take only the tiniest of steps. It would be a major social affront to appear walking with larger strides than their Princess did.

At last, Sho Lin examined her feet and shoes. Of these, she was the proudest! Her feet were unequivocally the tiniest of any of her sisters! This alone gave her a decided advantage for the throne!

Everyone knew that the Empress of Tashien always had the tiniest feet of any woman in all of Tashien. Both her sisters had worked long and hard to achieve what they called a size 4. However, at age five, Sho Lin realized that, as third in line, she had to outdo both her rivals. Hence, she endured the pain and forced her servants to bind her feet far tighter than normal, and now as she reached her twenty-first birthday, it had paid off perfectly; her feet were at least a size smaller! Her toes bent permanently above her foot nearly touched the beginning of her ankle, making her feet the smallest of any woman that she knew, a size 3!

Of course, Sho Lin never walked anywhere! Royal Princes never walked, such would be the height of disgrace! Well, at least in public she never walked. Alone in her quarters, she was assisted by her servants on short walks for the necessities of life. Even as a child, she was always carried on her royal divan, which steadily grew in size as she did. Her Royal Divan was a soft couch, covered in exquisite silks as well. This one was a shade darker blue to accentuate her beautiful, elegant form as she lay upon it. Finally satisfied that her appearance was perfect, she waved her hands, and the Royal Porters stepped quickly to her divan, lifted it up, and carried her into her Throne Room, where she would deign to accept audiences from her subjects, as she chose.

Her Throne Room was as elegant as the Princess. Bolts of various pale-colored silks hung from the ceilings, waving in the gentle breezes, which blew in through the many opening in the walls. While made of stone, because of the heat of summers, large openings were left in the highly polished walls. Indeed, her walls glistened in the morning and evening sunlight. Ten stone workers had lost their heads because the walls were not as perfect as she had ordered!

She ruled over the southeastern Provincial Capital of Tal Lon. Her father had given two far more desirable provinces to her older sisters, while Sho Lin had been stuck here in the far south, where the temperatures soared in the summers. Yet, even this she endured, knowing that one day, she would succeed in gaining the throne of all Tashien, surpassing both her sisters. Then, Sho Lin would have her long sought revenge on them, banning them to the frozen north and here in Tal Lon!

Her seneschal Wan Tou and her advisor Yan Dahou entered. "You may speak, Yan Dahou. What progress has been made?"

"Your Highness, all is now ready. Ten thousand soldiers are fully armed, fully trained, and await only your command," the thirty year old advisor explained.

Years ago, she and Yan had held lengthy discussions about what requirements had to be met before she was guaranteed the throne. She would need an army of loyal soldiers, but not just any army, for her sisters also commanded such forces. Hers would have to be battle hardened; her sisters were not. In a power push move, her soldiers must not fail. Her sister's provinces, ripe in the breadbasket of Tashien, were flush with gold. Thus, Yan had counseled her to do what she could to acquire much more gold. Finally, it had been more than two centuries now since any Province had acquired additional lands; the last acquisition had been the far northern realms where coldness prevailed. The Empire of Tashien now encompassed the entire known world, at least all that could be reached. The entire continent east of the towering Kathas Mountains was now the might Empire of Tashien. No one could climb these impassable mountains, though five had tried and perished, attempting to follow Sho Lin's orders to climb them. Beyond them was nothing but the Desert of Despair, a desert wholly devoid of water.

Yet, several centuries ago, historians here in the southern province of Tal Lon had made mention of a sailor named Yang Tse, who had sailed beyond the desert and found new lands, peopled by strangely colored people who were bronzed skinned, quite unlike the normal yellowish skins of those in the known world of Tashien. The historians also said that this Yang Tse never returned from his second voyage to this new land.

The Princess Sho Lin was a pupil of history, determined not to make the mistakes of her ancestors. The throne meant everything to her. It must be hers when her father past away. Hence, she left no stone unturned seeking to find every conceivable advantage that she might bring to bear on her ultimate quest. Those in her court fully supported her, because if she succeeded in becoming the Empress of Tashien, they would become the most powerful men in Tashien as well. Hence, all of those in positions of power in her court had a highly vested interest in helping her succeed to the throne.

Indeed, last year, they had sent spies to get closer to this land, which they discovered was called by the awful sounding name of Megalos. Unwilling to reveal their presence, for none knew how powerful these people might well be, her spies had captured a small fishing boat. After questioning the man, an action that took considerable time owing to the barbaric language that the man spoke, the spies, wearing his clothing, took his boat in for a closer look at this new land. By all reports, it was not only wealthy, something that Sho Lin admired, for her coffers could use more gold, but also it was very weakly defended, ripe for their picking.

In earnest, Sho Lin ordered the military buildup. Now her army was a thousand larger than her rivals were, but she must make them battle hardened. What better way than to put them to use? She dare not attack either of her sister's provinces, not until her father, Ho Lan Wu, died. Then, most certainly, the three sisters would vie for the throne. Ho Lan showed no signs of dying anytime soon, unfortunately. Yet, this gave her time to build up her forces.

"Excellent, Yan. At last, we are ready. Send in the huan, and I will bless them as they lead forth my army to victory." He bowed and backed out of the room. A huan is equivalent to our general, the man who commands the entire army. "Wan, send for the wine — the best wine for our huan. They shall be in my presence shortly." She gave a flick of her long nails, and Wan also backed out.

Shortly, Wan returned with seven serving women, carrying a golden tray with a number of golden goblets, along with a glass bottle of wine. "You may place them before me," Sho Lin ordered, as one might order a recalcitrant dog. Carefully, she poured a measured amount of wine into each goblet, making sure no drop spilled. Again, she was a perfectionist in all matters. Satisfied the wine was properly prepared, she again flicked her long nails, and the serving women backed out of the room. Just in time too, because Yan was walking toward the room with the five huan who would lead the assault upon this wealthy but barbaric land.

"You may enter," Sho Lin commanded when they reached the portal of the doorway. Everything had its proper place; court etiquette meant everything in the royal empire. Such was observed at every level of government. Some may say theirs was a refined society.

"Ah my loyal, able huan! Come, you may kiss my hand." She held out her right hand, making sure that her nails looked their best. Each huan walked to her throne and knelt down; she felt the warm touch of the virile man's lips upon her hands. "Come, share wine with me. We toast your eminent victory over these barbarians." She gracefully handed each man, including Yan, a golden goblet, taking the last one herself.

"To victory!" everyone said in unison. Then, they chatted informally for a time, she stressing just how important it was to have her soldiers battle hardened. The huan agreed fully, knowing that one year soon they would be moving against her sister's armies. If they won, these huan would become the huan of the entire Empire of Tashien!

"Your Highness, I have but one question?"

"You may speak," Sho Lin replied, using the precise etiquette.

"During our attacks, we expect to be taking many prisoners. What does Your Highness wish us to do with these men?"

Ah, she noted that he was also following the precise script the Royal Court demanded. So refined, so handsome, this huan. "They are all barbarians. Of what use is a barbarian? I can find none. Just behead them. The civilized world has no need of barbarians."

All five of the huan smiled; this was to their liking. None desired to be tied down with prisoners, especially barbarians. Finally, as protocol demanded, Sho Lin said, "Approach me now that I can bestow the Royal Kill upon thy hand that thee may carry my presence into battle and become victorious in the name of Sho Lin Wu, Princess of Tashien."

One by one the huan approached her. She had to do this action absolutely perfectly! She took each man's hand in hers, making sure that her nails touched his wrists, which was sure to get the man's attention. Next, she leaned over, allowing part of her long hair to brush the man, and then placed her lips in the center of his hand, making sure that she pressed hard enough to leave a visible trace of her red lips upon each hand. This she double-checked as the man got up from his knees. As she desired, each man had a perfect representation of her lips upon his hand, which she took as an omen that their assault upon the barbarians would be entirely successful.

"Go now and return with victory upon your shoulders! Do not forget to send for me when it is safe. I wish to see our conquered lands." They bowed low to their Princess and backed out of her presence with great respect. Having the visible presence of the lips of their Princess upon their hands was held in the highest regards. They had received a very high honor indeed! All five strutted out of the palace to their awaiting army with their heads led high. Their aides all discretely looked to see if their Princess's mark had been bestowed upon their huan. Elation spread through the ranks of the entire army. They had been personally blessed by their Princess on this assault. Now they knew with utter certainty that they could not fail!

As soon as the men left, Sho Lin flicked her long talons and her personal servant appeared, bringing her mirror and her lipstick. Quickly, Sho Lin touched up her red lips once more, before dealing with others who had requested an audience with her today. It was her obligation to appear perfect and elegant at all times; such were the duties of a Royal

Princess.

Unfortunately, she found her mind drifting for much of the day. The presence of such virile young men kept bringing up visions of pleasure. Although she told herself there was time enough for that this evening, still she could not get the most pleasing sight of the huan out of her mind.

Chapter 12 Chaos in Megalos

It was late summer of 650 in Megalos, hot as usual. Still the Church of Jehosanity had not yet elected its new Pope. Pope Anaxagoras had been quite old when he was elected and had died late last year, though many said that he did little during the last few years of his life. The Conclave of Cardinals was bitterly divided on his successor, with the entire church anxiously awaiting news of the new most holy man on Tarra.

During this time, the Supreme Prelate Thondakas, leader of the security wing of the church, the Mano del Dio, ran the daily operations, until the new Pope was chosen. While he could accomplish much in the way of security, his hands were pretty much tied until one man was chosen. He knew better than to take a policy decision to the Cardinals for their approval. A group could never agree on anything, witness the Senate, which now ran the country!

However, at this time, he stared at the latest dispatch from his associates in the easternmost city of Lathlox, a coastal town of some hundred thousand. They were being invaded? How could this be? The Santi del Dio had become utterly placid way up north in the Sea Princes, dying out with so many women leading it. Never in its five hundred year history had the island of Megalos ever been invaded. The dispatch made no sense to him whatsoever! He sent for his dispatch riders.

"I want all five of you to take ample supplies along with you. Ride hard to Lathlox or as near to it as you can safely come. Find out who is invading and what the situation actually is. As soon as you have any information, one rides back here at once. As more information becomes available, another comes back. Do not fail me. We must know what the devil is going on here."

"Do you suspect that the Santi are behind this?" asked one young man. These days it was fashionable to attribute all manner of ills to their archenemy, the Santi del Dio.

Thondakas shrugged, "It is not like them. I would have expected a direct, open assault, long announced in advance from them. Yet, it makes no sense. Megalos has never been invaded. Go now and let me know as fast as possible!" The five bowed to their leader and left. A half hour later, Thondakas heard the clapping of horse hooves on the cobblestones as they left, heading for the eastern coast of the large island. He estimated two day's hard riding there and then back. He would be stuck in mystery for at least five more days.

Late that same night, the Church's Senate representative, Dax, arrived to see Thondakas on very urgent business. He'd ridden all evening to get here from the capital city high in the mountains, Galantas, some twenty-five miles from Constanza City and the Church. "Thondakas! We've been invaded!" he burst out.

"Come, not so loud, here, in my chambers. What news?" he led the anxious, worried man into his private room, where the thick stone walls muffled any sounds. He poured the Senator a glass of fine red wine. "Sit. Tell me all that you know."

"Three days ago, a fleet of anywhere between twenty-five to fifty strange ships landed near the port city of Lathlox. The count varies upon the person reporting the figures. These ships are not as large as ours are, but no one has ever seen anything like these before. By all reports, they just suddenly appeared off our eastern coast! Even stranger men got off them. They have a yellowish skin. Their eyes are just as strange, slanted some say, as if they are piercing into your very soul. I say how can eyes be slanted? Anyway, they are armed with unusual looking bows and curved swords. They wear unfamiliar leather armor."

"By all reports, they have begun attacking the legion that is stationed in Lathlox. How strong their numbers are is anyone's guess. Some wildly claim that there are thousands, while others put the numbers well over a hundred. The Senate is in a furor. Today, they issued an order dispatching five of their legions from nearby cities to Lathlox. I thought you should know this."

"Thanks, now we have some idea. Here, we only heard a rumor of an invasion. I sent five dispatch riders to find out the details. I don't expect to hear back from them for five days," Thondakas replied.

"The Senate wants to know if they can count on the Church fielding our Holy Paladins to the defense. I told them that I would have to ask the Church, but I don't see how we cannot send them. If we didn't, we would lose the respect of our people," Dax said very worriedly, rubbing his sweaty brow.

"They still have not elected a new Pope, but until then, I have control over our forces. I will issue a full battlefield alert. Within a week, our entire army will be mobilized, some thirty legions strong. However, they are scattered widely around the central regions. Do we have any idea of the enemy's plans? Perhaps this is only a raiding party, and they will leave after sacking the Lathlox," Thondakas wanted to sound hopeful. It was just too awful to think that the entire country was going to be under attack. Never in its history had the actual island ever been attacked.

"Tell the Senate that the Church will fully mobilize all its forces to come to the defense of our homeland. We just won't say where they will be deployed at this time. Will that do?"

"Yes, Supreme Prelate. I will relay this to the Senate. I must ride back yet tonight. They want to meet earlier than normal tomorrow."

"I'll send three dispatch riders back with you. Use them to relay word to us. It's too much to ask of you to keep making these long rides after spending all day in the Senate meetings." Dax smiled, thankful for this consideration. He bowed and left.

Thondakas walked solemnly to the large chamber in which the Cardinals had been cloistered now for several months, arguing, debating among themselves over who would be the next Pope. When he knocked and was allowed inside, the fifty Cardinals ceased their discussions; each knew that their Supreme Prelate would not interrupt them unless it was some emergency.

"Cardinals, I have some very alarming news. The Senate has received word that Lathlox has been invaded by some army, whose country of origin, strength, and intentions are as yet unknown. Apparently, these soldiers are an unknown people, yellow in skin tones. I have sent dispatch riders to ascertain the truth of the matter for us. Senator Dax has just briefed me on the Senate's actions. They are deploying five of their nearby legions to Lathlox. It appears that we are facing some new and as yet unknown enemy, definitely not the Santi del Dio. I will order a full mobilization of our Holy Paladins here on Megalos. It would be prudent if you elected our new Pope soon. I will return when I have more facts to report." He turned to leave, but many called out with questions, which he could not answer.

Five days of utter confusion of messages, rumors, and soothsaying inundated Galantas as well as the Church. Most of this Thondakas ignored. He waited and reserved judgment until his own dispatch riders began reporting to him. These, and only these, he could trust, for they were Mano del Dio trained.

At last, a much harried dispatch rider returned on the fifth night. "Supreme Prelate, it is worse than we thought! Already the legion defending the city is gone. The enemy put all their heads on their spears, arrayed in lines outside the city as a warning to the five legions that have moved into position on the city's perimeter. At least half of the city folk are fleeing, most on foot. Fifty thousand refugees are making their way along every possible road and path from Lathlox. The best estimate we have on the initial study is that the enemy landed with ten legions. However, their strange vessels have all left! In fact, they left the very day that they finished unloading the soldiers. It is a safe assumption that they have gone to fetch more soldiers. Within fifty miles of Lathlox, it is utter chaos, very difficult to get through."

"Damn, five legions cannot hold off ten for very long! I want you to go to Galantas and tell Dax all that you have told me and then return to the others. You have done exceedingly well. Jehosa blesses your untiring efforts my son." He made the sign of the cross over the man's head, who took this as a very high blessing indeed, coming from the Supreme Prelate himself. He left with renewed enthusiasm for his tasks.

Once more, Thondakas interrupted the Cardinals, relaying the accurate news. Shocked, the Cardinals renewed their efforts to come to a decision. At last, the gravity of the situation swayed many of these holy men. A consensus was reached; they opted to elect a younger man to lead them during this crisis, forty-two year old Agropolis, who had at one time been a soldier, a Centurion, himself, before becoming a priest and then a Cardinal. He wisely chose the papal name of Pope Yazi II, hoping to inspire, instill the wisdom, and power of the original Pope who had founded the Church. In hindsight, this was a very significant choice of a papal name!

Two days later, after his coronation, Thondakas thoroughly indoctrinated the new Pope in all the many details of the Church's operations including the secret vault, which contained journals meant for the Pope's eyes only. Not even Thondakas had seen these. Indeed, the news that filtered back for the last few days had been somewhat better. The five legions were holding their own on the higher ground outside the port city. Perhaps this would all be over soon now.

However, the good news was short lived. Two weeks later, the same strange boats had returned, again unloading another ten legions! This time, his dispatch riders, sitting high in the mountains above the port were able to make an accurate assessment of the numbers unloading. Further, many ships were now plying the waters around the eastern portion of the island.

Later, their reports said that the ships did indeed arrive from somewhere far to the east, and thus from some unknown land! Days later, the combined forces broke through the defensive ring around Lathlox and were now pushing on up the coastal road along the southern shores of the island. Worse still, all the ships left for the east just as soon as they had unloaded the soldiers!

"What should we do?" Pope Yazi II asked Thondakas at their meeting.

"Your Holiness, I am neither a soldier nor a general. Security is my specialty, not wars. Our Holy Paladins are now fully ready to be deployed and are awaiting your orders. However, perhaps we should discuss options. I am a good listener, Your Holiness," Thondakas needed to understand his new boss, and this was an excellent way to get into his mind set.

"Yes, perhaps. I was a soldier once, just a foot soldier, mind you. As I see it, the ships intend to bring even more of their army to our shores. It must be an invasion, a full-fledged one at that. I cannot imagine any general just dumping ten legions onto an enemy's shores and then leaving them there without transportation. No, I suspect more will be coming."

"Where to defend, that is the question. One plan would be to muster all our forces into one combined group and attempt to overwhelm the enemy and drive them into the sea. I believe that the Senators are considering that plan. However, with these boats, what is to prevent them from launching many other invasions way behind our forces, cutting them off? I fear that if we place all our men in one location, say near Lathlox, then this leaves the other cities without any protection. Any smart enemy commander would then just invade those cities, looting them and cutting off the main defending army."

"Ah, so then we leave each city well defended with a much smaller number of legions. Now we are protecting against many other potential, but unseen invasions. Yet, then we do not have enough forces to stop the enemy army from advancing. This will make it easier for the invaders to slowly and methodically take each city, reducing our soldiers piecemeal."

Thondakas saw no way out and asked, "Then are we doomed?"

"No, the decision may well be taken out of our hands by the Senate. If they request that we send all the Holy Paladins to the front lines, while they send their remaining legions to defend the other cities, I have no choice but to comply. Any other move on the Church's part would appear treasonous to the Senate and to our people."

"We could send word to recall all the Holy Paladins stationed in the Sea Princes, Your Holiness. That would give us some backup here. If we send out all our Holy Paladins, I will be unable to defend our Church here!"

"I think it prudent to do so now, at once. As I understand the Sea Prince situation, in Vito and Bonilla, there is no real need for them to be there at this time. All is calm and the Santi are indeed dying off with all the foolish women leading them. They have taken no actions against us now for almost a decade."

"Aye, that they have not." Thondakas did not mention that this was in part to the priests ceasing to utilize the highly effective metal encasements that the Mano had developed. Ah well, they were working very well here in Megalos!

"Yet leave the twenty legions that are in West Reach there, just in case they are needed in the Sea Princes later on. I don't totally wish to eliminate our mighty army from there just yet. Surely twenty legions will not make the difference in this invasion."

"I will send the orders by fastest courier tonight, Your Holiness."

"One more thing, Supreme Prelate. How many members of the Mano del Dio are stationed here in Constanza City? And how many ocean-going ships are now under our orders or will obey a direct Papal order?"

"Your Holiness, we have but five legions of Mano del Dio here within the city, providing security. Another five are on duty scattered all over Tarra. As to the ships, I will have to consult the records. Your predecessor began slowly building or buying ships and crews. The idea, as I understood it, was that the Church needed its own fleet to send out supplies to our men in the field and to send out relief supplies to those in need. My rough guess, and this is only a wild guess until I consult the records, is thirty ships, somewhere in that range."

"Excellent. Please get me the precise number. I will issue a Papal order to their captains. I believe that it may well be prudent to see if we can double that number, quietly mind you, on the side. Will you see to it for me please?"

"Yes, Your Holiness." Thondakas left to write the needed recall dispatches and to find the precise tally. How he would acquire more ships, he didn't know or why the Pope would ask for them. This he began to ponder; surely, the Pope had something in mind, though he was evidently not yet willing to share with him.

By early October, the situation had become alarmingly grim on Megalos. Fully a hundred enemy legions had landed on their shores, a mighty army indeed. The entire eastern quarter of the island was under the total control of the invaders. No one knew anything about what was now happening within the conquered land. The Senate had ordered the entire Holy Paladin forces to hold the southern line, while they moved all available legions under their control to defend the northern line. Further, at this time, all available legions in the Southlands had been ordered to return to Megalos and organize on the western portion of the island, opposite Sud. It would be at least another month before these widely scattered legions could be combat ready in one location.

The thirty or so legions of Holy Paladins from the Sea Princes were not due to arrive until December at the earliest, perhaps January. However, Pope Yazi II worried that they might arrive too late to defend Constanza City from these invaders from the Far East, as they had become known. Pope Yazi II met daily with the Cardinals and the Supreme Prelate. Today, he began with a dire warning.

"I've asked you all here to discuss the gravest of matters. I have prepared a map of Megalos, with the latest information about the war on it. The enemy lines are here; our forces are deployed here and here. I point out that the enemy is but a mere thirty miles from us here in this building. If our forces are flanked here, they can make a straight shot into Galantas. From there, as you know it is a mere twenty-five mile downhill ride into our Church. On the other hand, if they break through here on the coastal road, the can be here within days as well."

"Our Holy Paladins in the Sea Princes will not be able to get here in time to defend our walls. The Mano del Dio, while powerful, is greatly outnumbered. Alone, they cannot hope to defend our partially completed walls from these attackers. In short, we must be prepared for the distinct possibility that the battle will come to our very doorsteps here in this very building, a battle that we cannot hope to win as we now stand."

"Are we going to be overrun? The Church sacked? Our gold stolen? Our Church vandalized? Our incredible art works destroyed?" asked a terrified Cardinal Thalos. Many others had the same ideas, though had not spoken of them.

"Cardinals, I must be totally honest with you. Unless there is some divine Holy Miracle, I do foresee this happening, perhaps as early as November, but surely by December." Pope Yazi II was a shrewd man, coldly calculating, which was why he had not been elected sooner. Too many disliked his demeanor. Thondakas watched him like a hawk; this was the side of the man that keenly interested him. The Pope had just said doom was inevitably coming to the Church here. He knew that, unlike his weak predecessor, Pope Yazi II must already have worked out a solution, though he had not yet been so informed.

As if sensing Thondakas's ire and displeasure, Pope Yazi II added. "Only today, has Divine Guidance come unto me. I have been praying for enlightenment for weeks now. Only this morning have my prayers been answered. I heard a voice reply unto my mind, 'Go forth Yazi; take thy flock to thy brethren, thy long forsaken kin.' That is the answer for which we have been seeking."

"But what does that mean, Your Holiness?" asked several confused Cardinals. "What forsaken kin?"

He paused for dramatic effect and then answered, "Our cousins on Acropolis, with whom we have had only minor dealings with over the last few centuries. Far to the south lies their mighty island kingdom. I propose that we begin evacuating our precious Holy Items onto the many ships, which are anchored off our city here, even as we speak. Our Holy Supreme Prelate has added a few more to our fleet. We should take with us everything of value, go forth into the Wilderness, and convert more to our cause. Once we have added to our numbers, we can then return to Megalos and retake our homeland. It will be the holy Church of Jehosanity, which shall free our people from the invading army from the Far East! Imagine the power our Church would then have? Beyond imagination."

"But does anyone know where Acropolis is located?" asked another concerned Cardinal, still reluctant to leave this Holy Church.

"Yes, I do and so do several of our captains."

"Then, I say let's do it at once! I for one do not want our many Holy Relics, to say nothing of our fabulous art works, to be despoiled or destroyed by these wild barbarians from the Far East. How soon do we begin?" asked another Cardinal.

Those were the magic words that the Pope had been waiting to hear. He smiled, "With your permission, we begin today. Let's make this an orderly move. Make sure that nothing is left behind. Let the invading barbarians find nothing but the stone shell here!" Everyone cheered, and nearly every Cardinal was greatly relieved. They now knew beyond any doubt that they had elected just the right man to lead their Church in this time of ultimate crisis!

Fully two weeks of constant work was required to load the forty ships with the gold, art works, Holy Relics, and other valuables of the Church. Vestments and clothing were carefully stowed for the ocean journey. Thondakas and his top twenty men were to accompany the Pope and the Cardinals on the Royal Yacht. Everyone one was extremely busy organizing their massive exodus. Adding to the confusion, many of their priests who had fled the invading armies in the occupied portions of the island at last had made their way to Constanza City. Immediately, they were also put to work loading the many ships. One positive aspect was that the ocean going ships of Megalos were twice the size of the invaders. Hence, the invaders gave their ships free reign to sail where they pleased.

However, at the Pope's orders, they would not actually depart Constanza City until it was about to be invaded. Because of their isolated, well-protected dock, they could afford to wait to the very last minute before evacuating, as long as it was merely men who had to get on board. Hence the loading in advance was an extremely crucial action to take.

On November 15, the coastal defensive line was breached, and the enemy raced toward Constanza City, due to arrive with twenty-four hours. At last, Pope Yazi II gave the order to evacuate to the boats.

Now Supreme Prelate Thondakas had a new problem with which to deal. Below in the maze of underground passages, years ago, he had a special prison built in which to house all the metal encased recalcitrant women. The plan had been for the Sea Prince sectors to ship the women who refused to work toward obtaining Good Marks, that is, the ones who refused to obey the Church, down to Megalos in secret. Thondakas and his Mano del Dio would then keep them hidden permanently in this secret, soundproof prison. This way, the hated Santi del Dio would not find out about them and would not then have a pretense with which to launch an attack against the Occupied Sectors.

It had been a good plan. However, because of the damnable pirates, none of the women ever arrived. All had been lost as sea, presumably. Those women had never been heard of or seen ever again, and it had been nearly a decade since they were lost. However, here on Mcgalos, many women still fought against or spoke out against the Church. It was inevitable that eventually the Church would have to silence these outspoken critics. Quietly, for years now, the Mano del Dio abducted these recalcitrant women, encased them, and imprisoned them here in their secret prison. Not even the pope knew about this prison. The befuddled old man would not have understood. Besides, he could swear honestly and truthfully that he had no part and no knowledge of any such actions, something that the Santi del Dio Evil Witches would surely check.

For years now, this had worked to perfection. All the women who protested against the Church had vanished, never to be heard from again. No dead bodies ever appeared, no ransom notes, just vanished in the night. The skills of the Mano del Dio were exceedingly good.

What then was this problem facing Thondakas on the eve of their mass evacuation from Constanza City? Over the years, encased in the metal devices, with rings permanently forcing their mouths open, many had died. However, some two hundred still clung to life in their damp, dark underground prison. Speaking to his wall as he packed his last sack, he said, "Well, I cannot bring them with us. That would ruin everything. We are all leaving, so there will be no one to care for their petty needs. I will leave them plenty of water and let them starve to death. Even if the complex here is overrun, they are not likely to be discovered. Even if they are, the invaders will probably just kill them outright or continue to let them starve to death. Besides, I like the idea of letting them starve slowly to death. They can better contemplate how they have so utterly wronged the Church. Problem solved." He grabbed his sack, took a final look around, and headed to the underground passages, which led to the secret entrance by the dock and the Royal Yacht.

On his way, he met the last five of his men. "Your Holiness," one reported. "By your orders, we have searched the entire complex. Nothing is left that has any value."

"Well done. Come, let us go," Thondakas said, and turned his back upon the secret entrance to his special, private prison. They walked out into the daylight and climbed onboard the Royal Yacht. The captain drew up the gangplank after they boarded. Slowly the large ship slipped away from the dock and joined with the large flotilla of ships. Soon, their sails were set and they headed eastward. They had no choice but to sail past those areas of their island under the control of the invading army. The Shallow Firth at the western edge was only a few feet deep, not enough to support these large ships.

A week later, some fifty miles beyond Sud, Southlands, they passed by a small fishing boat with a young girl lying in it, apparently unconscious. This they ignored and sailed onwards. Ten days later, now off the southern coast of the Southlands, they began their sweeping arc-turn to the south. As they were making their maneuver, they spotted a Santi del Dio caravel, flying its distinctive sails with the red crosses. For a moment, the captain of the Royal Yacht became concerned that they might come under attack from their enemy. However, with over forty ships in the armada, the Santi ship did not approach them and the flotilla slipped off to the south unmolested.

Chapter 13 Discoveries

The morning of November 27, our caravel was nearing Megalos. Several times now, we had met other caravels, which were making cargo runs in this area and swapped news. We learned that the Pope had died late last year. Now the relative peace in the Occupied Sectors began to make sense, their Church was currently leaderless, until a new Pope was elected. However, more importantly, we learned that indeed Megalos had been invaded by some unknown army that had sailed in from the Far East, wherever that may be located.

The last ship with whose captain we met had more information. Rumors were now running wildly all across the Southlands. This invading army was slowly taking over the entire island, well at least the eastern third. Many said that the capital city of Galantas was about to fall to these invaders. Worse, the horrors of war also circulated. The enemy was ruthless; all killed or captured soldiers whether Centurion or Holy Paladin were beheaded, their heads stuck upright upon a spear at the outskirts of whatever town or city had just been taken. Yes, it was simply a fear factor used to control the local captured populations. Still it was a gruesome act.

No one knew much of anything about these invaders, however. Our ships stayed away from the island. Yet, reports told of a flotilla of ships anchored off Constanza City. Our best guess was that the Church would make an evacuation attempt, rather than submit to being conquered. I know that we certainly would make just such an effort.

On this morning, Henry had the caravel moving slowly. I wanted to discuss the developing situation with everyone, before I made a decision on our next move. "Little to nothing is known about this new enemy," I was saying to everyone in the galley, while the thoughtful cook poured our tea. "While Megalos is about as far from us as you can get, I still think that we should at least see if we can get some facts."

Renzo added, "We should know something about their fighting style, their weapons, and their tactics. Who knows, perhaps this will be a reverse direction barbarian invasion — I mean before the Galts of the Northern Steppes charged down through all the Sea Princes and then the long way down here to just north of Sud before they were stopped. These invaders might just decide to head on up north towards us. Really, there is virtually nothing to stop them from doing so. Prudence would suggest that we learn all that we can."

Benet added, "I'd sure like to know where they came from; these rumors of the Far East are intriguing."

"No kidding, Benet," Natale added. "We might be dealing with a new civilization and new languages to learn!"

"To say nothing about new customs and commerce," Linda concatenated on to Natale's idea.

"But what about the mantis creatures?" Emil interrupted. "We still have two more sites to check on; there could be women in dire need at those locations as well. Can we afford the delay?"

"I know, this is a tough call, that's why we're having this meeting," I refereed. "With the other two sites, it is unknown what may or may not be there. Here, it is another matter. We know something critical is happening. How about a compromise? Let's take a quick sail around Megalos and see if we can glean any information using our far seeing eye. Once we have learned something more about these invaders, we can finish our main mission and check these last two sites." Everyone agreed with my compromise and Henry left to issue the sailing orders.

Around noon, Henry called us all onto the main deck. "Flotilla ahead! I count forty-one ships."

"That one is the Royal Yacht," I told the others. I remembered it from my last lifetime when I had snuck by it to get into the Church's secret underground tunnels to steal the assassins journal of Pope Yazi I. All the boats were riding low in the water: conclusion, heavily laden, probably with their valuables.

"Hey, that is an interesting course they are following, why go south from here?" asked Benet.

"If memory serves me and the bug's map is correct, they may be making for our next destination, the island of Acropolis," Henry called out to us.

"Well, isn't that an interesting development!" Emil said. "Our worst enemy is heading right where we were supposed to be. Had we already been on that island, we might have had ourselves a conflict with their assassins. Luck must be on our side."

"Orders?" called out Henry.

"Stand to and let them pass," I replied, continually watching the many ships, as they made their graceful turn to the south. We could see the crew members moving about adjusting the many lines and sails. A half hour later, we tightened the mail sails lines and resumed our eastwardly journey, heading for Sud and then Megalos.

For nearly a week, we saw no other large ships, only the small fishing boats of those who lived along the coastline of southern Southlands. We rode out two squalls as well, but no blows. Since it was typhoon season here in these southern waters, Michelle and Benet did daily weather scans at least two hundred miles to our southwest. If a typhoon came our way, we would need time to get out of its way. I had no intention of sailing into some small port along the coast and riding it out. Too much chance for major damage to the ship and right now, we really needed the Sleepy Hollow.

"Ship ahoy!" the lookout called from the crow's nest. "Looks like it is in some kind of trouble, captain!" Okay, that got our attention. At sea, a ship in trouble demanded instant assistance, regardless of its nationality. This was the golden rule all mariners followed, for one day it might just be themselves adrift in the ocean with a broken mast. We all dashed onto the deck, leaning over the rail trying to get a glimpse. Henry issued orders and the ship began slowing down.

I marveled at the command and judgment that Henry needed to bring our big ship alongside another small fishing boat that was adrift, floating helplessly on the waters. Unlike a horse, this big ship could not stop quickly. A wrong call and we would fly past the disabled craft. Still, it seemed like slow motion, as we gradually lessened the distance between us and this little boat.

A one man fishing boat from Megalos, I determined from her lines and single mast. I saw no sails, however. Perhaps it had been caught in a sudden squall. As we drew closer, our much higher elevation allowed us to see down inside her. "There's a person lying in the bottom of the boat," Renzo called out, but we had all seen her. It was a young woman, bronzed skin suggesting she was from Megalos. She was not moving, even though we began calling out to her.

Because of the wild difference in height, I watched as the bosun, safety rope attached to his waist and a mooring line in his hand, crawl over the side on the main rigging lines. He bent low as we closed the final few feet. He latched onto the craft and secured it to the mooring line. Quickly, other crew members tightened the line, pulling the little fishing boat snugly up to our side. Next, the bosun dropped a rope ladder and descended into the boat. "She's alive, got a pulse," he called out.

Other crew members lowered a life cradle. This was essentially a rope contraption in which items could be placed, such as her body. Once tied to the main ropes, it could then be raised using our pulley system, whose boom extended way over the side of our main deck. Five minutes later, the crew swung the cradle over onto the deck and lowered her. Immediately, Tonia went to work.

"Say, I can put my new skills to work, Bethany," Tonia said. I knew that she meant that she was now pervading her patient's body looking for what might be wrong with her. A few minutes later, Tonia opened her eyes. "She is severely dehydrated and half starved. Let's get her below and get some liquids in her immediately. Otherwise, she is healthy." The strong hands of Benet, Emil, and Renzo carried her down to the galley area.

For an hour, Tonia worked with her, putting water on her parched and cracked lips. The woman began sucking on the cloth and finally was able to open her mouth enough for Tonia to get a little more volume into her mouth. It was rough going because the inside of her mouth was also very dehydrated as well. At last, with enough liquids in her, the woman regained consciousness, opening her eyes, staring around in fear. Tonia held out a mug of cooled soup and she took it and drank it down rapidly. "Not so fast, easy does it," Tonia said, but she did not appear to understand her. Natale repeated it in the Megalos tongue.

Startled, the woman looked up at Natale and gasped, seeing her shoulders and absence of arms. Natale said, "You are safe now. We've rescued you. You are on board a Santi del Dio caravel. Relax and drink. You very nearly perished at sea. You've had a very close call." At the mention of Santi, the woman jerked and tried to set up, suddenly becoming frantic, attempting to say something.

"Easy, easy. You can talk once your body has recovered a bit," Natale urged, with Tonia's approval. The woman still refused to relax and made writing motions. "Oh, you want to write something?" She nodded.

I brought her a paper and quill. The woman wrote, "Help. My sister was taken. Mano del Dio. I went to find Santi. Help us. Please."

"Sure, we will help," I replied. "First, we need you to rest up and drink plenty of soup and get your voice back. Then you can tell us what has happened." This seemed to satisfy the woman. We made a makeshift bed and laid her on it here by the galley so that Tonia could continue to see to her needs.

"Well, looks like luck is still with us," Renzo commented to me as we watched the crew raise the small boat up onto our main deck. "We were just in time. Another few days and she would have died."

Henry said, "On to Megalos?" I nodded affirmatively. Now we had even more reason to get there.

The next day, she had recovered enough to tell us her story. All of us gathered around her bed in the galley to listen. Of course, only Natale and I could speak descent Megalos dialect, so she translated for the others.

"I am Medeia Phoros. It's my sister, Natasa — she's been abducted by the Mano del Dio men!"

"Please, Medeia, start at the beginning, and tell us everything," I said.

"Our father was a sea captain. He died when I was young. Mom and Natasa are painters. But the Church has outlawed all of mom's beautiful paintings! When she protested against this, one night she didn't come home from her studio. Her body washed up on the shore a few months later. Since then, Natasa has been looking out for me, because I am only thirteen; she's twenty. Natasa kept on painting very beautiful things and sold them discretely to others. Then on my birthday, last August 31, we were out celebrating, when the Mano del Dio came into the restaurant and abducted her!"

"She whispered to me to go find the Santi del Dio somehow, and they might rescue her. But I didn't know how to do that. So I followed them to see where they were taking her. I followed them up the streets of Athos to their city, Constanza. I watched them take her inside the big church there. I snuck inside, thinking I might be able to rescue her. When the guards went into their little guard house to light their pipes, I snuck through the gates and went inside. I heard her struggling noises and followed that. The church is so big inside! I nearly got lost, but I found the room in which they were holding her. I hid behind one of the tall marble columns and waited. I heard awful noises though."

"It was late at night. She had not made any noises for hours, and I was afraid that they had already killed her, as they did mom. Just as I was about to give up hope, the door opened, and the men looked around to see if anyone was around or looking. Then, they led my sister out. She was wrapped up in a metal case, as if she didn't have any more arms, but afterwards I figured they must be locked inside the metal thing. Also she had this big metal ring in her mouth, forcing her mouth open. She looked terrified. I've never seen her so scared, not even when they found mom on the beach."

"I had to rescue her! I followed them a ways and they went down some steps into some underground tunnels. I had no light, and I was forced to go back. I couldn't see! Maybe I should have kept trying anyway." She stopped to wipe her tears.

"For weeks, I watched the entrance to see if they would be bringing her out and taking her someplace else. I only saw more women being taking inside late at night. They never came out either. After a month, I decided to do what she told me, find the Santi, only I didn't know what that was. I kept asking around, nearly got beaten by one man who said the Santi were Lucifer's Spawns, whatever that is."

"Finally, an old seaman told me about the Santi and that they were way up north and that I could only get there by sea, following the coastline to the Sea Princes. So I stole a fisherman's boat in Athos and tried to sail to the Sea Princes. I got all the way around Megalos, but I was starving and very thirsty. I didn't know how far this Sea Princes is, so I stopped and stole some food and water in Sud. I almost was caught, but I escaped and began sailing, though I don't know how to sail, really. A storm came and broke my sail off. I couldn't see land anymore either. So I lay down to rest and think. Soon I had no food and then no water. I figured that I would just die out here and one day my body would wash up on the coastline like mom's had. I had failed to rescue my sister."

"Then, I wake up, and I've found the Santi! Please, you must help me rescue Natasa, please."

"We are heading to Megalos right now," I replied. "However, we saw all the Church people sailing in some forty ships, leaving Megalos. Did you know that your island is being invaded by some foreign army?"

"No, do you suppose that they are taking Natasa away with them? Now I am too late!" She began crying again.

"Well, perhaps they did and then again, perhaps not, Medeia. I cannot imagine that they would be taking all their prisoners away with them," I answered. "But we will see. We are a few days from Megalos, so you rest up and get your strength back. We want you to come with us when we go look for Natasa."

She smiled bravely. Then, we introduced all of our party. Naturally, Natale, Mireio, Michelle, and her daughter, Alwanianon, had to explain what had happened to them. I thought it best at least to let Medeia know the consequences of those metal encasements. Lord knows what we would find, if anything, but I wanted her prepared for the worst now while she had time to get over the shock.

A few days later, we were nearing Megalos and Sud, at the extreme southwestern shores. The sight was incredible. Hundreds of people, carrying sacks and bags were crossing the Narrow Firth; the lucky ones were being ferried across, though most were wading across the three-foot deep waters. Refugees were swarming down the hillsides of what had once been the estate of the artist and inventor Niccolo Helios. Many small boats were also making their way towards Sud, loaded with passengers and often in danger of capsizing, so overloaded were these fishing boats. Even though the Church of Jehosanity and these Megalos Centurion soldiers were our major enemies, we felt saddened at the plight of these people, for our quarrel was not with them.

We didn't catch sight of the invading army or fighting until noon the next day, when we were about halfway around the island. Henry slowed our progress so that we all could get a good firsthand look. He loaned us his smaller far seeing eye, and Renzo hooked up our large one. Everyone had a turn looking, but I allowed the Protectors to look as long as they desired.

Indeed, the enemy did have a uniformly yellowish to brownish hue to their skin, not the bronzed skin of those from Megalos, but lighter in color. Most of their hair seemed to be black. Their eyes did appear as though they were looking through elongated slits. They wore strange body armor, greyish in color, probably a mixture of some kind of cloth and hardened leather. Their weapons consisted of a very short bow, about three-quarters the length of the standard short bow found in our world. These were thus lighter and easier to fire and manipulate when in combat.

Their swords caught the attention of our Protectors. The blades were slightly curved, with only a slight hand guard. From the fancy maneuvers of the wielders, they concluded that these weapons were very well balanced. However, their fighting style was unique. While they did use their swords to dispatch their opponents, the use of the sword came last. Using various martial arts kicks, spins, and twists, they would seek an opening. Only when that opening appeared, did their swords strike, often a deadly blow. As if following orders, once they had felled an opponent, they paused to cleanly sever the head, dropping the head on the ground before moving on ahead to face the next opponent.

Renzo concluded, "These invaders are excellent fighters, definitely superior to the Centurions we have seen of late and vastly better than the Holy Paladins. Bethany, we should take these men seriously!"

An hour later, we had passed all the fighting. Now our eyes caught the aftermath in the already conquered towns and cities that we could see, along both the coastline and a little ways up into the hills. Along the roads, we spotted enemy troop supply wagons carrying food toward the front lines, while others were piled high with glittering objects, golden objects we presumed. The local populations seemed vastly smaller. I had been around this area several times now, always one saw bustling crowds of people in the streets, but no longer. Only a few togas were seen darting here and there on the streets. Some marble pillars had been pulled or knocked down, but most of the buildings seemed unharmed from this distance. How does one seriously harm a marble building?

As we rounded the eastern corner where the large port city of Lathlox stood, we spied the large enemy fleet of boats. These were strange ships indeed, unlike any that we had ever seen before. About half the size of the outdated Megalos ships, ours was at least four times larger than theirs were. Further, their construction seemed very flimsy. As we watched, we could see cargo, probably the spoils of war, being loaded onto a dozen of these ships.

However, as soon as we were spotted, the alarm went up. Soldiers dashed to form a battle line, the ships closest to us attempted to maneuver closer to the docks. They had seen our two flame throwers that we had on deck, plus our four ballistae. Yes, I had ordered them assembled and manned, just in case we were attacked. Now I could see the futility of their ships making such an attempt. Our Sleepy Hollow could easily ram into theirs, destroying it. The naval advantage was all ours.

We slowly continued our wide arcing around this extreme eastern edge of the island. Many eyes on land watched our every move. We had most certainly been observed. What I found so striking was the almost total lack of small fishing boats out plying the waters! None, to be exact, whereas normally I would have expected to see hundreds of these little boats. An hour later, the last view of Lathlox disappeared from the horizon, and we headed on up the northern coast bound for Athos, which was about midway between Lathlox and Sud.

At noon the next day, we again saw the supply and looting wagons going in opposite directions and not too long after that, we began seeing the enemy fighters on the move along the coastal paved roadway. Late afternoon, we finally arrived off Athos. Several of its wooden buildings near the docks were smoldering, sending dark plumes into the clear blue sky. Apparently, the fighting here was over, and we caught sight of the soldiers going from building to building, often carrying out sacks, presumably of plunder. Smoke clouds were also clearly visible from the capital city of Galantas, some twenty-five miles up into the mountains from Athos.

We slipped around the port and docks. A large rocky outcropping separated Athos from the concealed docks of the Church of Jehosanity and their huge walled city. On foot, these would be nearly impassable, which made this location an ideal one. The place was eerily deserted, as we expected. With all of us on sharp lookout for the enemy soldiers, the crew and Henry sounded our ship into the dock, where the Royal Yacht normally was moored. Five minutes later, the ship bumped into the dock, deck hands leaped onto the dock and fastened the mooring lines. Now it was time to go exploring, in search of Medeia's sister and any others.

The area was obviously under the enemy's control. Docking here was exceedingly dangerous. I had discounted the idea of anchoring at sea and sending in the longboats, the landing party could easily be picked off if the landing boats were compromised. At least with the ship docked here, no worry of that. However, we now needed to leave the ship heavily defended. Also, Natale was a little upset with me because I insisted she stay behind on the caravel. I explained, "If the invaders attack the ship, Natale, I desperately need your skills here, holding them off until we can get back!" At last, she realized the wisdom of that and took her place beside her husband, Henry on the forward deck beside one of the huge ballistae.

We grabbed many lanterns and got them going. "I know my way around this maze of tunnels somewhat. Renzo and I take point. Emil, Benet, you are behind us. Tonia, you and Medeia bring up the rear. Rosina, you and Sammy maintain a constant Mind Link. Let us know if the ship comes under attack. Okay, let's go exploring."

We walked into the cool tunnels. I had memories of the last time I was inside these tunnels. I had my dying Ket Bethany body then. My body was so paralyzed that I had had to slither along the floor, which was polished very smoothly. It was utterly silent, only the soft sounds of our leather shoes broke the stillness. "It's a maze!" whispered Renzo as we passed the tenth side passage.

"What are we looking for?" whispered Benet.

"A prison room. When I saw the assassin's memories of this place, I did not see anything like that in here. Probably, it is new construction so I'm looking for such signs and heading for the steps that lead up. We'll post guards there so we cannot be taken by surprise while we are hunting or whatever."

"Okay, that's my alley," Cedric replied. "Now that I know what I'm to look for, I'll keep my eyes peeled."

Before long, we reached the steps heading up into the vast church complex. We did hear strange voices. Obviously, the invaders were about. I posed Emil and Damien here, with Rosina in mental contact with them as well. I had no intention of being taken by surprise.

Now it was back into the maze of tunnels. After a while, we found the burial crypts where the previous Popes had been interred. It took us two long hours to find the new construction. We all had to use our keen powers of observing the obvious finally to find this spot. Here, there was a new wall, I say new wall because the stone was fresher than the surrounding walls, which now sported some fungus growth here and there. Now Cedric went to work, bringing all of his Planner technology to bear.

It took him nearly ten minutes to finally figure out how this disguised entrance worked. He found a stone in the floor, which when pressed, caused the wall to slide off to one side. "Very clever design. Someone wanted this room to be totally secret!" I speculated what that might mean as we shone our lanterns inside and then entered.

All manner of torture devices lined the walls, some under construction. "That's like what she was wearing," declared Medeia, as we came upon a stash of over two dozen of these devices, all shiny and new.

"Hey, they are back here," called out Benet, who had gone ahead of us. Around the corner, we came upon a large room, which had a set of metal bars enclosing it, keeping its prisoners inside. "Oh my god!" he added.

We rounded the bend and gasped. Hundreds of women were piled into this relatively small space. They had no room to move around. There was neither food nor water with them. Urine and feces covered them, as there was nowhere for them to even perform the call of nature. I spoke quickly, "We are Santi del Dio. We have come to rescue you. Please do not make a sound. There are enemy troops nearby. Get this gate open now," I ordered Cedric, who was already picking the lock.

Medeia called out, "Natasa! Natasa! Where are you? I've brought the Santi like you said." She was in a near panic, trying to find her sister among this large mass of women lying on the floor behind the gates. As the women began clumsily rising, the lock clicked; Cedric was keen with locks. One woman moved closer to the gate, "Natasa! Natasa!" exclaimed Medeia. "That's Natasa! Right there," she pointed out her sister.

We have company. It was Emil, via Rosina. *Large group are coming down the steps. We are backing up. I hope that we don't get lost in here! I think we were spotted. Little help here.*

"Okay, the rear guards are under attack. Benet, Renzo, you are with me. Cedric, you are in charge here. Get these women out of here and back to the boat as fast as possible. "Come on; we need to hold them off until Cedric gets them all out of here." I began racing back toward the entrance.

Emil and Damien worked together. The width of the tunnel they used to their advantage. The enemy soldiers attempted to circle kick them, to knock them around, and bust through their line. They needed every scrap of their Protector training to avoid these flying kicks. Their strategy: slowly fall back. They had no chance to strike back, however, because all their concentration was focused upon this strange combat form. They had been forced back some fifty feet when we came running up behind them. At once, Renzo threw up a wall of flames separating the two sides. A cry of pain told us that one of them had decided this must just be an illusion. He found out the hard way that it was not. Emil and Damien were out of breath, so I had Benet throw up yet another wall of flames.

"Okay, let's move the flames slowly back up the tunnel and force them back into the church," I ordered. In a matter of just a couple minutes we had pushed them all the way back up the stairs and out into the massive room, with its high arches and vast open spaces held up by enormous marble pillars.

We moved out into the open of the room, forming a circle, with myself at the point. The Protectors kept their wall of flames roughly V-shaped out in front of us. Now we watched and waited, observing our opponents, who were also observing us. More and more of their soldiers came running into the room, including one who may have been their leader. At least, he issued their orders. Three men made a running dash, intending to fly through the flames and knock us off our feet. I grabbed each man and gave him a toss, throwing him high over the heads of the mass of soldiers. In response, four began to shoot arrows at us. I stood my ground and simply snatched them, mid-flight. Renzo did likewise with two others. I slowly let them fall to the ground, staring directly at this supposed leader, who stared back at us.

Unlike the Centurions and the Holy Paladins, I had the foresight to order us into our chain mail with our black tunics and red fleur-de-lis crosses on them. Very probably, the arrows would not have penetrated our mail, but I was taking no chances with these men; perhaps they used poisoned arrows.

Next, the leader spoke another command. Instantly, a hundred men raced to form a line, readying their short bows. I saw his idea.

Where we could catch one arrow, we could not catch hundreds. "Good move on his part," Renzo whispered to me.

"Ice wall now, Renzo!" He and I threw up a wall of ice just beyond the flames, which Emil and Damien continued to hold in place. The huge volley of arrow thudded harmlessly into our ice wall, shattering it. Bits of ice fell to the floor, covering it with chunks of all sizes. Several men picked up some pieces to see if they were real or perhaps what they were. Now we had a standoff, which was precisely what I wanted here. I had no quarrel with these men; they had not harmed us in anyway. I could not condone what they were doing to Megalos, but I was not about to start a war with them over Megalos!

We have company back here! Sammy sent to me. *A number of them are scaling the steep rocks overhead. They just seem to be looking right now.*

Okay, hold them off. Has the women gotten there yet?

No.

Alright, we are holding them off here just fine. Keep me posted.

"Let's slowly back up into the tunnel now. Perhaps they will not attempt to enter again. Some are nearing the boat, and the women haven't yet begun to get there," I ordered. Slowly, in a non-threatening manner, we began to back up to the stairs. "Renzo, keep the flames covering the entrance. I'll lead your body along down here."

He smiled, "See how useful I've become now that I can keep my spells going from a distance from my body?" I gave him a little pinch, and we began descending the steps.

I received a strange image from Sammy. There was Natale standing in front of the caravel. Sammy said that one of the men slipped and was falling to his death on the rocks nearby; she stopped him and was holding him there. As I watched, she ever so slowly lowered him down. He was falling head first toward the rocks. Henry and the bosun were scrambling to get to his position. As he neared them, the men took away his sword and prepared to catch him. As I watched, Natale slowly let the man slump into the waiting arms of the two men. Several others pointed their longbows at the man. They helped him to his feet and motioned for him to stay put. The look on his face was one of utter shock. Now Natale began looking upwards once more at the others, who now paused in their descent. Evidently, they were content to watch from where they were at on the rocky ridge overlooking this small dock.

At last, we caught up with the end of the long line of women. It was grim. Linda was up front leading the way, along with Medeia, who was helping Natasa. All the others were back here at the end of the line, dragging several women who were in very bad shape. "Six are dead back there," Tonia said grimly. We are having a devil of a time, Bethany. Almost a quarter of them can't walk on their own, and the others, just barely. Please lend us a hand if you can." At once, I began to see what I could do to help. I concentrated and began lifting woman after woman. Finally, Tonia said that I had them all.

"Push on them please," I whispered to her, not daring to break my intense concentration. I had something like seventy women suspended just above the tunnel floor. The rest began to push. As I hoped, the group floated along nicely. After an eternity, I saw the light at the end of the tunnel!

A few minutes later, I saw the crew of the caravel and the many Santi assisting those women who could at least walk onto the ship. A half hour later, those who were unconscious had finally been carried onto the ship. Renzo extinguished his flames and returned to his body, confident that even if these soldiers tried to follow them, they would easily get lost in the maze of tunnels.

I looked up to see nearly a hundred of these fighters watching us from the top of the rocks. Some were perched halfway down. They made no threatening moves, though Angel and Mary Beth continued to have their longbows notched with an arrow. There was no time to attempt to get the women below deck, not with this army so nearby. We were pressing our luck. Henry barked sailing orders; the mooring lines were dropped, and we slipped ever so slowly out of the private dock of the Church of Jehosanity.

We stopped about a mile off shore and dropped the anchor. Before we could do anything for these women, they had to be bathed and cleaned up. Either that or risk a massive outbreak of disease, if they were not already sick. Hastily, it was all hands on deck, bringing all available water buckets, towels, and rags to bear. We began with those who were in the best physical shape, washing them off as best we could, then drying them off, and wrapping them in a blanket. These were carefully taken down into the cargo hold and allowed to sit down propped up against the hull.

While Tonia began her careful examination of each woman's state of physical health, Mireio, Roberto, and several others began to spoon feed a nourishing mixture that the cook had concocted, just as soon as Sammy had relayed that we had found them. My compliments to the cook, for he did a marvelous job with this batch, tailor made to what these women needed, nourishment-wise.

I had to smile; even Michelle and Alwanianon were hard at work washing off a pair of women as best they could manage. Everyone was working together as one team. We had to, so many were gravely ill. If we delayed, more might die, which I wanted to avoid if possible.

All the rest of the afternoon and far into the night we worked, until the last woman was finally clean and safely below deck. Now came the tough part, Tonia had already separated them into healing categories, seventy were quite ill, running a fever. She believed their illness stemmed from the unsanitary conditions in which they were forced to live.

Cedric examined each woman's encasements. As he feared, each had permanently disabled locks on them. "Bethany, there is no way that we can transport all these women in this condition all the way back to Velona. Some are just not going to make it. We must do what we can to get these hideous devices off of them. I know that if we take it slowly, there will be time for us to handle the surgeries. There are a lot of us who can do it on board now. May I have your permission to at least see what I can do to undo the mouth rings, so that they can at least eat properly?"

I have visions of having to perform hundreds of surgeries here on the ship! However, the alternative, another six weeks of living like this, suggested that we might well lose half of these women. We simply could not administer the medicinal herbs and nourishing food this way. Reluctantly resolving to face countless surgeries, I agreed, "Yes, start with the rings first. Wait until we are in safer waters before you try the arms. Surgery on a moving ship will be incredibly challenging, none of us have ever tried that before."

It was the middle of the night when we finally got to bed. I posted a heavy guard, however. Dawn came altogether way too soon for all of us. As I stumbled to the galley, there was Medeia sitting with her back against the hull, her sister's head resting on her lap. She'd fallen asleep like this.

Cedric joined us, a smile on his face. "Why are you so cheerful?" I asked sleepily.

"I've been awake all night pondering this problem. I believe I have devised a clever way to get these off without hurting the women. I will experiment as soon as I eat."

"Well, take Natasa first, please, or Medeia will be pestering you no end, if I know her," I replied.

Michelle wandered in next. Rubbing the sleep from her eyes, she said, "Bethany, yesterday when I had nothing really to do, I went out looking at the weather, figuring that we would set sail for home soon. But we had better not sail just yet! There is an enormous typhoon out there in the southern ocean. I cannot tell yet where it is heading, but it is a big one. Benet and I will go have a look see after we eat."

"Damn. Thanks for the head's up. I'll let Henry know. Looks like we don't sail for several reasons." I left to let Henry, who was on deck, know the unfortunate weather news.

The day was picture perfect, as so many days were down here. The weather was only warm, not the searing heat of summer. Not a cloud was in the sky, but somewhere to the southeast of us, a typhoon was raging. There was no sign of the invader's; none of their boats could be seen. It was also spooky, because normally this close in to the shore, at least fifty fishing boats ought to be plying the waters.

I went below to watch Cedric's experiment, hoping against all hope he would be successful, at least with these damnable rings, which were preventing proper care of these very ill women. He had stoked the cooks fires and was about to begin on the contraption around Natasa's head. "This should not hurt, but maybe it will feel warm. Wiggle if it gets too hot for you to stand. Now we are going to lay you back slightly. The idea is to get the metal to melt and flow out of the lock. Here we go, keep your toes crossed." Medeia grinned and watched with her fingers crossed.

While Emil and Renzo held her at a forty-five degree backwards slant, Cedric began pressing the rod to the lock, while holding his universal key in his other hand. "It's working," called out Renzo, who saw a drop of shiny metal drip onto the deck.

"Hang in there Natasa, one more minute," Cedric encouraged her. Then, he quickly inserted the key and turned it. The mechanism gave way and clicked open in the back. Carefully, Cedric removed the head harness, removing the ring from her mouth. "Viola! Success!"

"Thank you! Thank you!" Natasa said and began crying, as the men helped her up.

"Okay, to the table with you," Tonia ordered. "Now we must get the herbs in you and get you well fed! If you need to go to the bathroom, nod your head." She led the woman with Medeia at her side to the galley table.

Cedric beamed at me. "Well done, Mr. Planner," I said. "Very well done indeed!"

One by one, each woman had the awful device removed from their mouths, while one by one, Tonia administered her healing herbs and oversaw what the woman would be fed, though usually feeding them herself. She wanted to make doubly sure that each got precisely what she had sensed that body most critically needed, in terms of nourishment. Her recently acquired skill was now being put to great use.

By noon, all two hundred thirteen women had the mouth rings removed, but seventy were still delirious with their fevers and unconscious. Now I had to address the women, but worse, only Natale and I spoke a reasonable Megalos dialect. She and Mireio stood beside me. "We are all Santi del Dio. We found Medeia adrift at sea near death and rescued her. She told us of her sister's plight and we decided to rescue all of you. However, half of Megalos had been taken over by some invading army from the Far East, wherever that may be. No one knows for sure from where this army has come, just that they have wiped out half of your island. The entire Church of Jehosanity has packed up and fled the island and left you all to die where you lay."

"We know all about these horrid torture devices that you are wearing. Long have they been used on the women of the Sea Princes — on any who would not go along with the Church of Jehosanity's mistreatment of women. We Santi have been extremely vigilant in locating these imprisoned women and then rescuing them, so you are not alone. Both Mireio and Natale here were encased just as you are now when we found them."

I noticed the terrified looks from many women as they looked at the two beside me. "Over the years, we have cracked open perhaps half a thousand of these encasements like these that you are wearing. However, I have really bad news for many of you. Uniformly we have found that women who have been encased for a number of years will have had their arms atrophy into something that resembles a corpse — in short, their arms have died. Their arm bones became so brittle that the slightest touch caused them to crumble into tiny pieces. Yes, this has happened to my two companions here." I listened to the wails and cries from so many women.

"Yet, I say this to all of you, you are among the greatest Healers on Tarra. Every one of these women we have saved, performing the surgeries, which saved their lives. However, that alone is not enough, not nearly enough! Who can stand the horrors of facing a life without arms? The trauma is more than enough to make one end one's life! Ah, but we are great healers. We have perfected a therapy technique, which will totally erase the entire horrible trauma that you have endured, giving you a new feeling of life!"

"Still, even that is not enough. We also have the Laird Foundation for the Arts in Velona. This entire foundation is made up of hundreds of women, such as these two are. In fact, both Natale and Mireio are members of the Laird Foundation. Even Michelle here, who lost her lower arms due to an unfortunate accident with some heavy crates in a warehouse, is a member. She will be showing you her paintings. Yes, we offer some fabulous, nearly incredible rehabilitation training which may help you once more to create the art, which you used to do. I know, it sounds unbelievable at this time. However, during the day, I will have these ladies give you all a little show of just what they are able to do in life."

"Further, the Laird Foundation and all of our Santi training and services will cost you nothing! The foundation exists to help women, such as you, who are in great need. We Santi also pledge to help you in any way we can. All that we ask of you is to do what you are able to do and to help us and others as you are able."

"Now as to the removal of these arm bindings, here how it must go. Those who have been encased less than a year, we will attempt to remove yours first. Expect your arms to be incredibly weak and sore, probably for many weeks. We will work on a massage therapy to help you regain their use."

"Those who have been imprisoned longer must wait a little longer. Why? Because it is likely that the very instant it is removed, you will need emergency surgery or face a painful death as the bone particles flood throughout your entire body. Worse, we are at sea and have a limited number of us who can perform this surgery. Worse still, our weather people, Michelle and Benet, are predicting a typhoon is coming our way. So I ask all of you, please be patient; we will do everything possible to make sure that you not only survive, but also can regain your ability to create. Yes, life is still possible. Mireio got married while armless, ditto with Natale, ditto with Michelle. Ditto with hundreds of other artists and women back in Velona. Please, please be patient with us and do not lose all hope. I promise you that I will perform your therapies as soon as humanly possible."

"Oh, finally, bear in mind that only myself and Natale speak your language fluently. Some of the others speak a few words. So don't fret if they have to have things repeated, keep at it until we understand you, okay?" Many nodded.

"Okay then, I want those of you who have been encased like this for less than a year to please stand up and go over to where Cedric is standing." Forty-three women managed to get to their feet and began to form a line. The hopeful look on their faces was moving, and yet the looks of horror on the others filled me with a great sadness. I knew what they faced: the emotional trauma that was staring them in the face. I felt a great sympathy for these women. Yes, many broke down and began crying. Natale and Mireio went to these, offering sympathy and kind, upbeat words.

Now the real work began. While three men held a woman horizontally, Cedric began working his miracle unlocking. The cook kept the fire going and kept each of the three rods that Cedric used red-hot, handing them as needed to Cedric. It took nearly ten minutes per lock to melt the shiny metal so that the key would turn. Next, the encasement had to be very carefully undone because their arms were very stiff and sore and easily broken if we were not exceptionally cautious.

"Oh my shoulders and elbows hurt so bad that I can hardly move them," Natasa exclaimed as she was freed. "But at least I have mine. How can I ever thank you all?"

Natale said, "As soon as you are able, lend a hand with all your fellow women who are going to need tons of care for quite some time." Natasa and Medeia both promised they would. Now Tonia took over, showing Medeia how to perform the massages. I knew that this would be an action that all of us would be doing later on. There were just too many women who desperately needed physical therapy, and we had no hot bath here at sea to help as mom did at her estate.

By lunchtime, the forty-three had been freed. However, several found their arms were in very poor shape, requiring months of rehabilitation to regain their mobility and flexibility, to say nothing of their strength. While we ate, Benet and Michelle reported that they had now plotted the path the typhoon was taking. In a little over a week, it would smash directly into Megalos! Just what these folks needed — an invasion followed by a typhoon!

Hence, Henry made the decision to set sail, and we put off any further removal operations, because the ship's rolling motion made surgery a very risky thing to attempt. I believe the women understood. Meanwhile, Natale began spending her time working on teaching all the conscious women the basics of our Sea Prince dialect. This kept their minds off their horrid situation and onto the future.

Chapter 14 West Meets East

A day later, we neared the port city of Lathlox, where the large enemy fleet was stationed. As we rounded island and came into view of the edges of the city, we found seven of their ships out in the water, attempting to block our passage. "No wait, I see white flags," called out Henry. "I think they are asking for a parley. Orders?"

"Heave to and let's see what they want, if we can somehow understand their language. Someone fetch my wife please," Henry said, following up with orders to drop the sails before we ran one of these flimsy boats down.

"A parley?" exclaimed Natale, very excitedly. This was a linguists dream! A completely new language spoken by a completely new people!

By lunchtime, I could tell that we were going to be delayed several days, even though the typhoon was pressing down upon us. Hence, I asked all the Guardians to join and see if they could somehow delay its arrival a bit. Meanwhile, Natale, Henry, and I worked with the new arrival from the Far East.

He was tall and perhaps thirty, with black hair and eyes. I could tell now that they were not slit or slanted as the reports had suggested; they had an unusual eyelid fold. His hair was short, his clothes, immaculately pressed silks, of various shades of brown, with a pale blue waist sash. He sported an unusual moustache, which was very long on its ends plus a tiny bit of long beards on either side of his chin, like a pair of ponytails. He carried no weapons and seemed exceedingly polite, though obviously very intelligent. His language was foreign, as ours was to him. Still he continued to smile and was quite eager that we learn to communicate, though at this time I knew not why.

We spent the rest of the afternoon and evening relaxing on the deck, working out words. As Natale, Henry, and I figured some out, I carefully wrote their phonetic sounds on paper along with our word for it. After a short while, he figured out what I was doing and borrowed some paper from me to do the same with our words. As darkness fell, we finally understood his language well enough for an important meeting. The ruler of Tan Lon Province, Royal Princess Sho Lin Wu, was here in Lathlox and very much wanted to meet with us. We agreed to meet with her the next morning. Additionally, we shared with him that a typhoon was barreling this way and would hit within a week and that we were doing our best to stall its arrival a few days. He seemed much impressed with this information, as well as very concerned.

His name was Yan Dahou, the advisor to the Royal Princess. We learned some surprising information. There was an eastern lobe of our continent, which lay east of the Desert of Desolation, also separated by an impassable mountain range. Now I could understand why our two civilizations had remained unknown to the other. Apparently, the Princess Sho Lin's province occupied the southern portion of their land, which was collectively known as Tashien. From what I gathered, the country was huge, stretching from here in the south all the way to the frozen northern lands. Her father, Emperor Ho Lan Wu, controlled the breadbasket central region, while her two older sisters controlled other regions.

He also explained just how formal this meeting would be, that his people were highly refined, well educated, and abided by a strict, formal protocol, which held one's respect and honor at the highest levels. We were not entirely sure what all this meant, however. Natale decided that we should dress in our finest clothes and look as presentable as possible. She had a hunch that this coming meeting would be very important and that first impressions would go a long way for us with these people.

We spent the evening hours massaging arms and helping care for so many passengers. Tonia was being run ragged taking care of so many sick patients. At least five were doing better by nightfall; their fevers had broken, and they had awaken and eaten some. She specifically ask me not to crack open any encasements until those that were sick had recovered, "I can't handle delicate surgery with so many ill patients, please," she begged me. I agreed with her.

The next day, we women decided to wear our finest dresses to this critical meeting with the Royal Princess, while I had the men wearing their chain mail with tunics. If there was any kind of trouble, the men would be in a good position to protect us, I hoped. Finally satisfied with our appearance, we joined the others in our longboat and headed to the shore and the big meeting. Henry, Natale, Linda, Benet, Emil, Renzo, Rosina, Tonia, Cedric, Damien, Michelle, and I formed the meeting party, while Angel and Mary Beth would stand guard over our longboat during our meeting with the Princess.

We arrived and tied up the longboat, our two Santi sergeants immediately took up their defensive positions. Yan Dahou came forward to meet us, along with an armed escort. The meeting was to be in the Sun Temple. A dozen beautiful white marble columns supported a marble roof. All the sides were open. However, Sho Lin added her own temporary touch: numerous bolts of pale blue silk cloths were hanging down and waving gently in the morning breeze. Sho Lin was waiting for us on her blue silken divan, having spent several hours this morning making sure that her appearance and the temple were perfect for this meeting.

While our conversations were a bit jerky, with Natale and Yan doing their best to get new words figured out, I will present our meeting without those interruptions. Natale and I were at the front of our group as we walked up the steps of the temple. Yan notified Sho Lin that we were present, and she signaled for us to approach her. I believe that both she and we were surprised with each other!

The first thing that I noticed was her long black hair that was perfectly draped over her left shoulder, down across her breast and out onto the side of her dress. It reached to her knees, as she lay slanted across her divan. Her waist was so tiny and the tight fitting dress followed her every curve down to her feet that I wondered how she could walk in such a tight fitting dress. Then, I noticed her extremely tiny booties, and I thought at first that she had lost the entire front half of her feet in some kind of accident. As my gaze went back up to her upper half, I noticed her incredibly long nails, painted a magnificent red color. At last, my eyes latched onto her face. She wore some kind of face paint, but I had no words with which to describe this as yet. Her lips matched the color of her nails, and her cheeks were permanently flushed, some kind of powder I surmised. A black color highlighted her eyelids.

Of course, her eyes were examining each of us at the same time. She stared long at our earrings especially those on Natale and Michelle. She noted the chain mail armor the men wore and their tunics. At last, she motioned with her fingers, and six similarly clad servants appeared. While their dresses matched Sho Lin's, theirs had a pair of long walking slits. However, each took only the tiniest of steps as they carried a large, ornamental teapot, steam rising, along with quaint flowered porcelain cups, which had no handles. They were also smaller than our mugs. I knew that I would have to assist Natale with her cup, besides which she was wearing her fancy shoes with tie strings.

Next, several men brought a number of soft pillows before Sho Lin, who gave a flick of her long nails, signaling they were acceptable. They arranged them in a wide semi-circle before her, placing each one with great care. Sho Lin then motioned with her hands that we were to sit before her. Per Yan's instructions, each of us bowed to her before we actually sat down.

"Please accept some of our finest oolong tea," Sho Lin spoke. Carefully, following a well-learned protocol, she poured each of us a cup, although she hesitated when she came to Natale. I indicated she should sit it before Natale, which she did, and before Michelle. Sho Lin then picked up her cup, indicating that we should join her now. I held one to my lips and one to Natale's. Oh, was this ever good tea! She seemed very pleased that we all really liked the tea. It was a good start. It seemed so out of place — the invading army conquering Megalos, well half of it at least and here was the refined, elegant woman who was in charge of the war.

Sho Lin began the real conversation. "We came to this island expecting it to be filled with nothing but barbarians. However, my huan then discovered you and your people. Are you from this island? Unless my eyes deceive me, you are anything but barbarians."

"No, we are not from this island; we are far from home, here on a rescue mission. Our homeland lies far to the north, approximately as far north as Yan has said that your father lives in your land," I replied.

"Ah, now the events make so much more sense! I am enlightened and gratified to find that there are other refined and civilized people on Tarra. My huan has told me many tales of your meeting the other day at Athos or near there at some holy site. Is it true that you yourself picked up and threw the soldiers out of their front line attack? Is it true that many of you can catch arrows as they fly at you? Is it true that you can create real flaming sheets and walls of ice to stop arrows? Was my huan correct in deciding that you were not going to harm his men, but only wishing to keep them back for a time? I have many more questions, but perhaps I should just ask them all and let you answer. Is it true that the beautiful woman next to you, who has now visible arms, actually caught one of my soldiers who slipped and was falling to his death? Is it true as my huan has suggested that you were at this place to remove those women who wore metal things which made their arms useless and invisible and with metal rings in their mouths? Why would someone do that to women anyway?" She flicked her long nails, which I interpreted as time for me to reply.

"Yes, to all these. We are called Santi del Dio, Knights of God. Long years have we here studied and trained to learn how to do these things and many more. Yes, we are all immortal spiritual beings inhabiting these fleshly bodies. Spiritual beings can be quite powerful. I can indeed lift even these marble pillars supporting this roof here, when the need is great. Natale did stop the man who was falling; she held him a few feet from the rocks, while the others gently rotated him so that he would land on his feet, and she lowered him to the ground. All of us here can easily create sheets of fire and ice, though we normally only use these and lightning bolts in defensive actions. We are not out to kill others, just to prevent them from harming us and those we are protecting."

"So yes, we did not want to harm your soldiers. I ordered my fighters here simply to keep yours from harming us and entering the tunnel for a time. The men who made that holy place, which is called a church, the Church of Jehosanity to be precise, are our enemies, because of what they are doing to women. They are treating all women as less than a cur dog. Those who do not obey them used to have their hands cut off, such as my mother, have their tongues cut out, or were blinded. We Santi eventually forced them to stop doing that. Instead, they invented those metal encasements that your men saw."

"Women would be imprisoned in them for the rest of their lives, living worse than a dog. Worse, we have found that when imprisoned this way for several years, their arms atrophy, becoming dead arms and have to be removed to save the life of the woman. The Santi have now rescued many hundreds of so mistreated women in the lands these men control far to the north. Natale is but one of hundreds of such women to lose her arms in this manner."

"However, Sho Lin, the Santi are great healers. We have great skill healing the sick and injured. We also now have learned how to heal the scars such traumas leave in one's mind as well. These women that have been so badly mistreated have usually been the artists, musicians, and dancers — those who create beauty in this world. Through our teachings and training, most all these artists are now able to paint, sing and dance, and to continue to create their beautiful things for this world. Michelle, here, lost her lower arms due to an accident; a heavy crate crushed them. Yet, after our physical, mental, and spiritual healing, she is once more a very good painter of seascapes. Back on our ship, we have another woman who lost her arms with these metal devices, yet she has been healed fully and has resumed making music."

"A week ago, we learned that these evil men were imprisoning Megalos women, artists for the most part, as they were doing to women up north where our land is located. Since we saw those evil men sailing away, we came to rescue them. All are onboard our ship at the moment just beginning the long healing process. I believe that answers them all, unless I forgot one. May I ask you if you have had an accident with your feet? We can't help noticing they are so small."

She smiled, "Oh no. They are perfect! I have bound them tightly since I was a baby. Having such small feet is held in the most-highest regard, the very highest respect, in our land. Indeed, the Empress is expected to have the tiniest feet in all Tashien! Unfortunately, I have two older sisters who are first in line for the throne when our father dies. It has been my lifelong goal to become the Empress of all Tashien. To achieve my goal, I must be better in all ways than my sisters are. My feet are now fully an inch smaller than theirs are. My waist is many inches smaller, thanks to my dressmaker's invention. My hair is a foot longer, and I wear my beautiful nails fully two inches longer than theirs. When the time comes, all will see that I, more than they, embody the vision of Empress."

"But how do you walk like this?" I asked, somewhat aghast at their customs.

She giggled, "I do not walk. For a Princess or Empress to walk in public is the highest disgrace imaginable! It is much worse than even shaving her head or cutting off her nails! Never in a thousand years has a Princess or Empress ever been forced to walk in public. Yet, my servants assist me when I must walk, but only in private, for private matters.

Then too, they must never take bigger steps than I take, you noticed them, I saw, when they brought in the tea. Yes, they have worked long and hard to match my tiny steps. They are very honorable servants indeed, highly prized, highly respected, highly honored women."

She then asked, "Tell me of your huge ship. Do you have many? Are they sea worthy? Our ships are mere trifles compared to yours, which are more than twice the size of these barbarian ships around here."

"Yes, they are called caravels. A twelve year old boy invented them several years ago. They are very fast and can carry a heavy load. They are most trustworthy in a storm. I once rode out a typhoon in one, suffering no damage to the ship. Speaking of which, we are also keenly aware of the weather. Do you know that a large typhoon is approaching this island? It was supposed to hit here in four more days, but we have been holding it somewhat at bay so that we may still have time to sail around it before it hits here."

She had a very startled look on her face, so I knew that they were not aware of the storm. She looked worried for the first time, and spoke rapidly to Yan. "No, thank you for the warning. We have typhoons, which sometimes strike our shores near this time of the year. Please continue to delay the storm as long as you can. We will evacuate this island before it strikes." I agreed that we would do our best.

"A small matter, but your earrings. They are so beautiful, so expensive. I would love to have a pair. I will pay you gold for what they are worth."

"Sho Lin, I will give you a pair like Natale's as a token of friendship between our peoples."

"I am indeed honored." She bowed to me slightly, though her waist undergarment prevented her from any major movement. "It is as I suggested to Yan. I would like our people to become allies, close friends. You are refined, elegant, and honorable. We have much in common and perhaps our peoples would find much that we could trade with each other. However, we do not have such ships as yours to make the long journey to your land. I would like to invite you to come and visit me at my palace. I would learn from you as you learn from me."

"That would be absolutely perfect for us. Our people make their living trading with all the other countries on Tarra, excepting yours, which we did not know existed until now. We have hundreds of these large ships sailing the oceans in our part of Tarra. Many would love to open up trade with your land. I can tell you right now that we would like to import a whole lot of this exquisite tea! Oh and cloth from which your dress is made. We can't get enough of silk cloth. Oh, what about music? Do your people make music, songs, and dances? In our lands, these are wonderful, and we all love to dance."

She smiled, "Yes, our tea is most refined. I'm pleased that you like it. Our musicians are very sophisticated; soft and refined is our music. Unfortunately, I did not bring my musicians along with me. One day soon, you must visit my palace and hear for yourselves. Our dance tells ancient tales and legends. The dancers study for years perfecting their precise moves. Ordinary people do not dance. How is it that everyone in your land knows such dances?"

"Oh, our dances are mainly for fun and enjoyment, not the telling of legends. Men and women enjoy dancing with each other; it's romantic and fun, a social thing." I could see that she could not understand this; she would just have to see one of our dances sometime.

Next, we discussed how we would be able to find her city and palace. She suggested that perhaps we could swap ambassadors who could learn each other's language, customs, and such. With so many Megalos women on board, I really couldn't spare anyone just now. Sho Lin understood. I promised that when we came back that we could exchange ambassadors then. I suggested that she start looking for us around March at the earliest, allowing us six weeks home and back and sometime to reload supplies.

"Yes, I understand that you have so many injured to heal right now. However, what if I sent along just my ambassadors? They could work on learning your language and suggest things to bring for trading when you return. They could tell you about our country and customs. When you return, perhaps we would find it much easier to communicate with each other. I would like to count upon you as my dear friends from this Sea Princes land." She was persistent. Sho Lin most definitely wanted us as her allies. I decided that even if this was some political treachery and she ultimately wanted to invade our land, with their puny naval fleet, they would not be a serious threat at all. I relented.

"Thank you, Bethany. I will send Ming Lau, one of my personal assistants, and Jin Han, my Court Historian. She is knowledgeable about the royal courts and our customs, and he knows our history and our material needs." She signaled again with her long nails to Yan Dahou. He bowed respectfully and backed off. A short while later, he returned with the two who would be her ambassadors.

Ming Lau was also around twenty, dressed similar to Sho Lin. Her long black hair reached to the tops of her legs. Her nails were at least three inches long. Ming had an oval face and was quite pretty. She bowed and said, "I am most honored to be your ambassador." I noticed that her feet, too, were small, yet she still walked. Well, time enough to worry about this feet thing later.

Jin was a small man, even Ming was taller; he barely stood five feet, if that. His black hair was somewhat long, but his moustache and beard were similar to Yan's, like small ponytails dangling from either side of his mouth. He wore yellow, silk robes. Bowing low, he said, "Most honored to go with you on behalf of Princess Sho Lin Wu. We will get our things and be ready to leave as soon as you desire." He appeared to be about thirty years old.

"We should get sailing, Sho Lin; we must get around the incoming typhoon," I said, intending to wrap up this historic meeting. Time was precious to us just now.

"I understand. It has been a high honor to meet you, Bethany, and all of you Santi del Dio. I will prepare for your visit in the spring. In our land, spring is a very beautiful time of the year. The fresh scents of the blossoming flowers are a wonder to behold. May I ask how long it will be before the typhoon reaches this island?"

Michelle replied, "Three to four days at the outside."

"You might seek shelter for your men in the tunnels underneath the holy place where you found us," I suggested. She thanked me generously. Bowing, we all backed off the temple floor to the steps. Back at the longboat, we waited for the two ambassadors to arrive. They came walking rapidly about ten minutes later, though she still took only very tiny steps, but had to take them very rapidly indeed. What an unusual way of walking we thought. Jin carried both of their sacks. I began to wonder if they had planned this all beforehand; perhaps Sho Lin had. Still, we now could learn much about our new friends.

Sammy vacated his cabin so that our two new guests could have one of the luxury cabins. However, it was not permitted for an unmarried maiden to share a sleeping room with a man. We should have guessed, so Sammy and Jin shared Sammy's room while Cathy and her husband, Jason, moved into a lower deck cabin, allowing Ming Lau to have her own private room. That handled, we raised anchor and set the sails, heading due south.

After the two watched the sight of the island drifting off into the distance, Natale and I gave them a tour of the ship. They were stunned when they saw the horrible plight of the many women in the cargo hold however. Ming even cried quietly to herself at the sight. Jin merely said, "I am glad that we were able to put a stop to such barbaric practices."

I turned my dictionary-writing task over to Linda. She and Natale were constantly with our two guests, while I went back to work with our rescued women. After lunch, I addressed them all, "As you know a large typhoon is bearing down on us. We have been holding it at bay or slowing it down for the last few days. Now we are going to try to get around the worst of it. Expect a rather bumpy ride for the next week or so. However, Tonia and I have decided that we will start removing more of your encasement devices. Because surgery is likely to be needed, we will stop the caravel for the short time she needs. Then, if surgery is needed, I will begin therapy on that woman right after that, while we continue to sail. This way, there won't be any wasted time. We all want you out of these horrid things just as soon as possible."

One woman asked, "How long does the surgery last? It does not hurt?"

"If your situations are the same as all the other women that we've rescued, the surgery will take less than an hour, and all that you will feel are pin pricks, nothing more. As far as the therapy goes, I usually do it in a private room. Just now, that is more difficult, but can be done. However, if the person is willing to have her therapy done right here, then all the rest of you can witness how it is done and see the results. It might give you much more hope."

The same woman said, "If so, then I would be most willing to have the others hear mine. Honestly, Bethany, we have so little hope now, and so many of us just wish that we were dead rather than to have to live so horribly crippled."

"That is what anyone of us would fully expect to hear from each of you, even from us if we were in your situation. I would think you crazy if you thought this was a wonderful way to live." She smiled bravely at that.

"I guess the question is does anyone of you want to be first?"

The same woman spoke up, though most were silent, unwilling to be first and to have to face the likely outcome of looking like Natale or Mireio. "I am Adonia. I was a painter, but probably never again. I will go first unless someone else wishes to be first. I knew my life was over when I was put into this thing. I have come to terms with being a hopeless invalid for what time yet remains to me."

"Adonia, you are a brave woman. Cedric, get her ready, and when you and Tonia are all set, let me know, and I'll get us halted." For a few minutes, there was a flurry of action, and then we waited until the iron pokers were red hot. When they were finally ready and our dining table converted into an operating table, I relayed word to Henry.

He suggested that he just keep slowing down until the ride was sufficiently calm for Tonia to proceed. In the end we were able to continue forward at a few miles per hour while she did her work. After twenty minutes of applying heat allowing the metal to drip out of the main lock, Cedric was at last able to open the back. A slight tap and the hinge pin on the front slid out of the hinge, and the men carefully removed the device, without moving her arms. It was good that they had not tried to move her arms. As with all the others, two dried up desiccated arms became visible. Many of the other women who were watching gasped, and several fainted from the shock and realization that was what their arms must now look like. Adonia, like a stoic trooper, said nothing.

Carefully, the men laid her on her stomach on the operating table. Forty minutes later, Tonia was done. "There, that didn't hurt much did it?"

"No, I didn't feel much of anything," she said and looked at her shoulders where the neat stitches of Tonia were now visible. Next, Tonia spread her healing salve on them and wrapped them. "There you go, Adonia, all done."

"May I see them, what's left of my arms?" she asked.

Tonia pointed to them. Adonia stared at what had been her arms in disbelief. After a time, with tears streaming down her cheeks, she said, "Well, that explains why I could no longer feel them for a long time now."

We helped her to a sitting position against the hull, as the ship resumed making full speed southwards. "Okay, Adonia, let's begin," I said, sitting down in front of her. I explained what I wanted her to do, "Close your eyes. Go back to the time when you were first abducted by the Mano del Dio." We were off and running. By supper break, she had pretty well viewed most of it. She felt a whole lot better after she spotted the fact that she had decided that, if she continued to paint what she wanted she to, then she would eventually be abducted. "I just went into agreement with everyone else: that I'd get wiped out if I continued. Certainly did." However, she was not entirely cheerful or laughing over it, just relieved.

At dinner, the caravel began really rocking and rolling. The seas had become much rougher than normal, due to the nearby typhoon. Feeding everyone became more difficult. While Linda, Rosina, and Renzo did the dishes, Tonia inspected the still ill women; two more fevers broke, however. I took Adonia back into her therapy session. Once more, we had a large audience listening to us.

This next time through the recent trauma produced nothing new, so I asked her if there might be an earlier time she had experienced some similar trauma event. In fact, there was! Something like three hundred years ago she was a young girl who had accompanied her father who was a stone works engineer. There had been an accident and a huge stone block fell on her. She'd tried to get out of the way but fell and the stone landed on her outstretched arms. She started laughing wildly, "Right there as I saw the stone coming down and couldn't get out of the way, and I just knew that my life was over! Damn if I wasn't right! I went into a coma. They are cutting off my arms, but blood poisoning and an infection takes over and I never did come out of that coma!" She laughed some more and then sat upright, startled, "Wait, this can't be real can it? It would mean that I have lived before!"

I launched into my usual explanation about spiritual beings and she resumed laughing, telling everyone, "Hey, I've lived before! I am a soul, I don't have one, I is it!" Her laughter was contagious; smiles spread over many other faces.

By the next morning, the swells were the largest I had seen in a long time. The rains had begun as well. Still, we continued to head south by west, hitting the surges head on. Below, Linda and the others had their hands full with the women, helping them hit the chamber pots, which was difficult because standing was becoming a real problem. The cook was unable to fix breakfast, so it was left overs and cold biscuits for everyone. Yes, they spent much of their time after that trying to keep the women from panicking. No, the ship was not about to sink under them.

On deck, Natale was lashed to her usual place with Henry, while Michelle and I were tied to the back railing. Afternoon, we were relieved for a while by other crew members so that we could eat and warm up a bit. An hour later, during a slight lull, we headed back to our positions, expecting the worst. It didn't come, by evening, we sailed out from the last of the outer reaches of the squalls into relatively calm seas; we had passed beyond the typhoon's reach.

After warming up, drying off, and eating something warm, we hit the sack. The next morning, with calmer weather, they un-cased another woman, Delia, who had also been a painter. Soon thereafter, I began her therapy. The others reached a decision, however, while I was occupied. Since the sailing was now rather smooth, Tania wanted to continue with more women. Linda and several others were now sufficiently trained in how to run the therapy sessions, and they wanted to help as well. By evening, six more had been freed and had begun to erase their traumas.

On the average, Tonia managed seven surgeries each day. In twenty-four days, the last woman was freed from her metal cage. Of course, the therapies were greatly backlogged. Tonia deserved a medal. Every one of those who were ill recovered. We lost not a single patient! Now she too could sit down and work a therapy session to help us. It took us nearly two months to finally reach Velona, docking there on January 20. To our credit, the last woman finished her therapy as we neared the docks! We had done a herculean task, delivering the two hundred thirteen women to mom in top condition, ready to be taught new ways of doing the basics of life and to relearn how to create their works of art. Yes, every one of these women had been involved in either some aspects of the arts or politics as a leader.

Linda and Rosina also attempted to identify the people who had done this to these women. As their skill with the Megalos language improved, they began questioning each woman about what had happened to them. Specifically, they only interviewed them after the woman's therapy was finished, since neither wanted to add to the woman's emotional upset until the trauma was gone. Always the abduction and imprisonment was done by one of four men, with their leader overlooking the action. A name dropped here and there by accident, spread out among the two hundred thirteen women, gave us the names of the guilty, which included the head of the Mano del Dio, a man named Thondakas. Via Mind Links, Rosina now had a face to go with each name.

The problem was how to arrest these men, assuming that they could be located. Undoubtedly, they were at sea somewhere and out of our reach. Even if we could approach these men, they were incredibly dangerous, trained, and skilled assassins. I joked with them one night saying, "Well, Natale holds them still, Linda makes their bodies surrender, and I just pick them up." We laughed, but really, any other way was fraught with danger, especially with their propensity for using poisons.

Perhaps more exciting was the birth of Mireio and Roberto's first child, a lovely baby girl, whom they named Adrienne. Alwanianon, now eleven, was an immense help to Mireio, who faced another major learning curve, caring for her newborn. The three were inseparable — Alwanianon constantly hovering over her little sister, helping Mireio with everything. It was hard to tell who was the happiest about little Adrienne, Alwanianon, Mireio, or Roberto!

What of our ambassadors during these two months? At first, they listened and learned our language, but did have trouble with many of our customs. They observed and asked many questions about the therapy, our religious beliefs, and of course about the ship and our homeland. For example, we just brewed a pot of tea and helped ourselves with whoever made it often pouring it for others. Ming explained that in Tashien, the taking of tea was a very important occasion, requiring that every detail be perfect, to honor the recipients.

One morning, Ming gave us a demonstration. The great care that she took with each step of the simple process was a wonder to behold, down to the act of pouring the cup and its precise placement before its receiver. One had the sense that the tea was somehow more delicious this way. I must admit I've never tasted a better cup of tea than Ming served, though it was the very same tea that we drank daily.

I asked about her small feet. "The size of a woman's foot is very important in our society," she carefully explained. "The Empress of Tashien always must have the tiniest feet of any woman; that is the way it has always been for centuries. Peasant women who work the rice fields normally have their feet unaltered, unless they have been at a higher status, have been disgraced utterly, and is now only a rice field worker. My mother was a chef for the previous Princess of Tan Lon Province. Her feet were six inches long, but she wanted me to have a higher status than mere cook. As a young girl, she kept my feet in tight bandages so that they did not grow so big. Mine are now five inches, like those of a young girl. Thus, I have honored my mother and have a much higher station in life now. Here, I will show you, for it is permitted for a maiden to show her feet to another woman, just not a man until we are married."

She took off her stockings and revealed her feet. Yes, they looked just like any other feet, only the size was not proportional to her body. Ming explained, "My Princess Sho Lin, has to have the smallest feet if she is to become the Empress. Hers do not look like mine. Her toes, they are folded up here against her ankle. Mine did hurt some while I was growing up, but hers must have hurt terribly so. Yet, if she becomes Empress of all Tashien, then it will have paid off enormously."

"Is being a servant of the Princess what you wanted to do with your life? I mean are your people free to choose what they do in life as we are?" I asked.

"Most important is to honor our parents and ancestors. Honor is everything among our people; without honor, all is disgrace. I enjoy being the personal assistant to my Princess. We all honor her as she, us. When she becomes the Empress of Tashien, she has promised me that I will be allowed to marry any man that I choose. I will then be free to marry Lon Zu, a gardener, which will raise his status enormously. Our children will then have more opportunities to rise even higher. Yan will become the advisor for all Tashien, the second most powerful man in the empire. Only the Emperor wields more power. All of Sho Lin's huans will become huans of the entire empire's armies, the highest honor that can be bestowed upon those who fight."

"Everyone around Sho Lin will gain enormously in honor and status when she becomes the Empress of Tashien. We are all very loyal to her, for through her we stand to gain much honor for our families. Those in the Emperor's court now will become retired, when Sho Lin gains the throne. For all their many years of service to the empire, they will be held in the greatest respect as well."

Something was still bothering me. I asked, "I understand that she is the third in line to the throne, that her two older sisters have claims before her. How is it that she will succeed over her sisters?"

"His wife joined her ancestors several years ago. He is old and in failing health, it is said. When he too joins his ancestors, then the, how do you say, Great Council, will meet. There, the three who claim the throne will be judged on many things: who has the smallest feet, who has the longest nails, who is the most properly attired, who has the longest hair, who has the best rituals, who has the most gold, who has the most knowledgeable staff, whose staff handles all the courtly rituals the best, who can provide the best commerce. The Great Council judges them by many categories. Yet, sometimes they cannot make a decision. In all these centuries, this has happened a dozen times. Jin can give you the details. Then, the contender's armies decide for the council, and the winner takes the throne. Sho Lin has invaded the barbarian lands so that her army can gain much valuable experience, should they be needed in order to decide who gets the throne. You see, it is in everyone's best interests to make very certain that no disgraces befall our Princess, that she is perfect in all ways. We all work very hard to see that this happens. If disgrace befalls her, not only will she be dishonored, but we will be disgraced too, and all of us will lose our opportunity to gain the highest of honor and respect in our land."

"One other thing, does Sho Lin have a boyfriend? I mean when she becomes the Empress, who will become the Emperor?"

"She will choose her mate at that time, giving them and their family the highest honor possible. When it is time, she will choose, though I do not know who that will be, male or female."

"What? She could choose to marry another woman?" I asked quite startled by her offhand mention of Sho Lin's mating.

"Yes, it has happened ten times during all these many centuries. Jinn can give you the details. To have royal heirs, they would use the Royal Consorts, which in this case would be strong, virile males. Sho Lin has not said a word to us of her desires for a Royal Mate, not yet anyway. I believe that she has too many other details to perfect just now. She has told me that with the throne of all Tashien at stake, personal pleasure is a very minor thing."

I could tell that there were vast cultural differences between our two lands. I hoped that the culture shock would not be too great when Ming and Jin began to see what our country was like. That finally happened on January 20, beginning when we pulled into the huge port of Velona. Twenty caravels were either docked or docking as we were or just leaving. It was a typical winter's day, a bit on the chilly side.

At the dock, Elona greeted the new arrivals, speaking a few words in their language, which pleased the women. Of course, mom and her crew were there, along with Bard Tal and members of his music group. They played some welcoming music for these Megalos artists. Since our rescued women had scant clothing and this was wintertime, though the temperature was still in the forties, once each woman was helped into a coach, a warm blanket was wrapped around them.

Like a well-oiled machine, mom and her group got all the women into the newest dormitory and dressed in new, warmer clothing. The Explorers Circle was there too, lending our hands. Once that was done, we led them all over to the mansion and the twin palaces. As we were walking the short distance, Adonia, now the self-appointed spokeswoman for these Megalos artists asked mom, "On behalf of all of us, I want to thank you and everyone else for rescuing us, healing us, and for the incredible therapy, which has so rejuvenated each one of us. However, Commander Weston, will you please be honest with us? Is it possible for any of us to be anything but a hopeless cripple for the rest of our lives, so utterly dependent on everyone else for nearly everything in life? I mean we all feel so completely helpless as we are."

Mom stopped and spoke loudly so that all could hear. "There is no doubt that your lives have been drastically and horribly altered. No one will say that your lives will be easy. Gone forever are many simple actions that normal people take for granted, even the simple scratching of one's nose. Yet, here on our estate, if you are willing and apply yourselves, we can teach you new ways of doing most everything. Once you regain some semblance of self-reliance, then we can help you learn new ways of producing the creative art that I'm told so many of you were doing."

"As we enter my estate mansion building, I want you to observe for yourselves. Notice no door anywhere on this entire estate has a doorknob. All are hinged to swing in either direction, merely push with your feet. After I show you where you will be eating and where the hot public bathhouse is located and such, I will take you over to the Laird Foundation, the twin palaces there. As we tour, notice the art works on display first, then meet the artists who have created them. Yes, some of the artists in residence are normal, but the vast majority is like yourselves. After you have seen with your own eyes the finished products and have met those who made them, then make your judgments. Come. Let's see the expanded dining hall. We gather here, all of us, for our meals. Mealtime around here is a time to share with others."

Sometime later, as we all filed into the massive art gallery, where the artists put their works on display in hopes that someone would purchase them, the women gasped at the magnificent paintings and ceramics. Michelle had to point out her works to Adonia, "Here, these seascapes are mine, only now there are only six left. I guess some more have sold while I was off on this last trip."

"You did these, Michelle? They are really good!" Adonia praise her sincerely. Many others gathered around the two to admire Michelle's paintings. Yes, with well over a hundred works on display, these artists from Megalos were truly impressed with the quality and variety of finished works.

Next, Jenna took them upstairs to the painting studio, the finest on Tarra, so all the new arrivals declared. The vast open spaces with plenty of natural light from the hundreds of windows were superb. This turned out not to be a quick trip through the studio! With Natale and me translating away, our new arrivals just had to chat with the artists, particularly other women who were like themselves. They just could not believe what they were seeing. Uniformly, each of the artists explained using nearly the same words, "We just have had to learn new ways to do what we used to do with our hands. It does take a whole lot more patience than it used to and tons more time to get one done right. Yet, it can be done, usually. You just have to keep trying until you succeed."

During a late lunch, at which many of the others began showing the new arrivals new ways to eat, Bard Tal and some of his ensemble provided both music and dance. Many were keenly interested in these aspects, because they had been either a musician or a dancer. Afterwards, he was besieged with questions and inquiries. I knew that he intended to usurp as many of these new arrivals as he could. His was an ever-growing music and dance troupe.

After the meal, I had an unexpected surprise. Enyo came running up to me. "Bethany, you just got to come and see what I have been creating!" She was very excited to say the least. Her constant companions, Alexa, Dione, and Chara were only steps behind her. To my surprise, Allan and several other Planners and engineers, whom I did not recognize, came as well, bringing up the rear.

Allan added, "Bethany, bring your entire Circle, even the two new ambassadors. You have got to see what Enyo has been designing for us."

"Okay, Enyo, let's go," I grinned at her and gave her a hug.

"These are my new engineer friends, who are helping me get this built just right," she explained.

"Hey, it works, it really does work!" put in Alexa, proud of what her comrade had designed.

"Yes, it is all her design," Allan added. "Her ideas are rather revolutionary to say the least!" We walked over to the previous new addition built to house Alexa and her group. I noticed some new constructions, narrow, long holes in the ground, and a big wooden cylinder that stood ten feet above the ground.

"The demonstration model is in here," Enyo led the way into the communal latrine building. "Da ta! I call it a Waste Remover. See you sit on it, as we women do, or you can stand up. You go to the bathroom in it, and then press this lever down and hold it for a minute. Water from the tank goes through the pipes and into this ceramic stool, flushing the waste down some large pipes into a big, tile-lined, underground latrine. No stink even."

"Incredible!" I exclaimed, very surprised.

"And this one over here is for us women. You sit and push the lever with your foot and hold it down. Water from the tank comes up and sprays your bottom area. We shall be the cleanest women on Tarra now!"

"You thought of all this yourself?" I asked incredulously.

"Yes, but it was spurred on by our situation, you see. It is so hard for us to keep clean. I knew there had to be an easier way. Once we get twelve of each working here and if they work as well as these two, then Allan is going to assist me in making a Waste Remover system for each building on the estate. Already, several Velona engineers want me to design some for other buildings in the city and are offering me quite a lot of money to do it."

I gave her a big hug. "Very well done indeed, Enyo!"

She continued, "I have many other ideas to try. In the spring,

Allan will help me with making an aqueduct system to bring fresh water into the estate so we don't have to use the wells."

Ming and Jin, who had also tagged along, were also impressed with her new system. Ming asked, via me, "One day, we would like you to come to Sho Lin's palace and build one of these systems for us!"

"We have a large number of aqueduct systems on Megalos to bring water to all the towns and cities," Adonia said to Enyo. "They work really well until they break down, then no one seems to know how to fix them."

"Yes, Adonia, I know. I was one of the men who built them over five hundred years ago. I found that out when I was getting my therapy from Bethany here," Enyo replied, as if everyone knew all about their past lives. Adonia was speechless, staring at Enyo.

"Excuse us, but I am supposed to take our two ambassadors to meet formally with mom now. I'll drop by and chat later, Enyo. Keep up the stellar inventions!" She beamed and we headed back to the mansion.

On our way, Adonia asked, "She, Enyo, she is, was, one of the ancients? One of the builders of Megalos?"

"Yes, we rescued her and a whole bunch of others who had a great deal to do with the original building of Megalos. There's not time now to explain it all fully. Just ask Alexa or Enyo about it sometime or I can explain later when things calm down a bit. You ought to go join your companions and start learning some new things."

In the meeting room, with all of her Circle present and mine, Jenna explained to Ming and Jin, "I'm sorry that we couldn't meet at once with you two honored guests from Tashien right away. However, it was very important to see that the new arrivals got properly orientated right away. They have to start learning how to care for themselves somewhat, because we just don't have enough people with arms around here to do everything for them. I hope you understand and are not affronted by this delay."

Neither was. In fact, they were just as eager to see everything as the Megalos women were. I won't bore you with the details of the meeting. We all decided that they would be given a grand tour of Velona during the week. After that, they would suggest items that we could take back with us with which to open up trades. Plans were then made to sail on February 7, 650, back to the Far East. Mom planned to send along two other caravels with us, one of which would remain there for a time. In addition, mom decided to send along several linguists and a full Circle as well, who would act as ambassadors and to learn all that they could about this new land.

Later that night, Renzo and I had our first chance to play Torque Ball in our private room. After he won, we then had a fine romp in our bed. How we both missed having private time to ourselves!

For several days, our ambassadors were driven all over Velona, from the docks, to the magnificent Rose Cathedral, to the abundant shops and open-air markets. They found the diversity of people very interesting as well as the free and openness of everyone. While they claimed that we were a very free people, we could benefit from some refinements, some formal hierarchy, that we lacked the refined discipline of culture.

Come Friday night, they, as well as our newest rescued women, attended Bard Tal's grand performance in the Arts Center. His show now lasted over two hours with a fifteen-minute intermission, when tea and sweets were served. The very wide variety of musical styles and dance groups made a long lasting impression on all, especially the Megalos women, who had never seen such dancing. However, as expected the real showstoppers was the Expressionistic Dance Suite performed by Zita and her group and the Greenway Stomp. Both had to perform an encore, so enthusiastic was the crowd. Our ambassadors were very taken by Zita's performance. Hers was the closest to their formal dance form.

The next night was the usual Public Dance at the old estate. As usual, the mansion was utter chaos, as everyone helped everyone else get dressed and ready for the fun night of socializing. Even Ming was pressed into service helping many women change into their elegant formal dresses. This kind of an event was foreign to our ambassadors. Ming explained in her country young maidens were not allowed to so interact with men.

At the dance, I was not about to have her just stand and watch, so I began dancing with her. I had to take unusually small steps, however, so as not to force her to disgrace herself by taking too large a step. Later on, many other women danced with her, and she ended up thoroughly enjoying herself. Jin, on the other hand, found himself with partners too numerous to mention. It seemed every woman in the building wanted a chance to dance with the ambassador.

However, the whole evening was a total shock to the women from Megalos. They stared in disbelief as Shorty and Teiuc danced nearly every dance. At least half of the women there were normal, in that they were from Velona and had arms. Yet, the new arrivals could see clearly that the absence of arms made little difference to the many men. In fact, they were frequently invited to dance by all sorts of men, even though the men could barely understand the few words of Sea Prince that the women spoke. They quickly discovered that words were not needed, for it was the music and dancing that mattered. One might say that they were swept off their feet by the whole affair, especially when they learned this happened every Friday and Saturday night! That men doted over them during the frequent refreshment breaks, helping them with everything, also impressed them as well.

Adonia commented to me on the way back, "The men did not look upon us as some kind of freak! We could only understand a little of what they said, yet words did not seem to matter."

"No. Still, around here, some will look at you that way. Always some will. Yet at the dances, most men are very understanding and really are out to meet women, you know, looking for that special someone, as are all the women looking for the right man. It is the socializing event in our land. Works out well, I think."

Adonia replied, "We have nothing like this on Megalos. This is great, I think. And the other women's silk dresses — they are so tight, form-fitting, so unusual — and the men cannot keep their hands off of them!" She was referring to the Laird Foundation women, of course, with their special party dresses. "I thought that having long hair was always a bother when painting and all, but they have their hair so long and they fling it out so — well, I thought that was very romantic indeed."

"As soon as the seamstresses get your measurements, they will be making party dresses for each of you as well. It'll probably take them a while to make so many, but soon, Adonia, you can dress up as fancy as you like as well." She smiled appreciatively.

"At least half of the women in the same situation as you have already found wonderful husbands. Some have families now as well. About half of them moved off the estate to live with their husbands, though they still commute daily to the foundation to do their art and such. The other half moved their husbands here to the estate. In some ways, it is helpful to be surrounded by many others who can help, but you forgo some of your privacy. There's always so much activity going on around here."

"Can I ask you something else?" she changed her mood to a serious mien.

"Sure, ask away."

"It's about Enyo and Alexa, those people. Were they really raised to believe that women were born without arms? That is so utterly unbelievable. Who would do such a thing? They would have to cut off the baby's arms to do that."

"Yes, it is true. They lived in a walled complex on an isolated island that no one knew existed. When a mother gave birth to a baby girl, it was taken away after it was born and its arms removed before being given to its mother to nurse. All they ever saw were women without arms." I now had to explain about the mantis creatures and our several rescue missions.

"Now I understand little Teiuc. She had direct contact with these creatures. Golly, that must have been horrible! She is so brave! Did you see her out there imitating the dancers with that short fellow?"

"Shorty, that's his nickname. Yes, those two are madly in love with each other. I did her therapy, and she is certainly a trooper."

"Is it true that she can ride a horse, that she has a horse? I just can't believe that one."

"Yes, a pony to be more precise. She and her three other companions who are like her frequently go for rides. Since she still has some arms left, she has an easier time riding than those like you. However, Julianna and Rachele, who are now in Zargarb, are just like you, and they have become excellent riders. They took me on a ride when I last visited them. They even mount and dismount without any assistance. It sure surprised me when I saw them doing that. The more I'm around you women, the more amazed I become with what you can accomplish, once you set your minds to it. However, I won't fool you. Without having erased their traumas, they would probably be languishing in some home for the sick, doing nothing." She laughed.

"Another thing, Adonia, based upon Alexa and Enyo's people, we've discovered that it works best if you are grouped in foursomes. It seems to be an ideal organization for mutual assistance. I think mom will be going to try to arrange your group that way soon."

She looked at the ground for a moment, took a deep breath, and looked me squarely in my eyes. "Bethany, we in Megalos have had a totally wrong viewpoint of you Santi del Dio people. You are not heathen barbarians, but God's Angels! Thank you for helping us, for saving us."

"You are most welcome. Pay us back by making fine art and helping round here as you are able," I gave the standard reply. As an afterthought, I added, "I know that your lives are going to be much tougher and so darn, well inconvenient isn't the right word. Yet, you are filled with life, and we will do all that we can to help you achieve your goals."

"I know, it's a damnable way to have to live like this, but I've never felt so utterly alive in my life. I'm going to learn all that I can. You realize, don't you, that all of us would have died in that prison if you had not showed up when you did?"

"I know. I sometimes wonder how many other women have suffered and died, while we didn't even know that they were in trouble or where they might be being held. I won't rest until we get that Church to stop doing this to women. That I swear to you."

"I do appreciate it. I know the others do too." I gave her a long hug.

Two days before we were to sail for the Far East, Bard Tal asked all the women staying at the estate and the Laird Foundation to come to a short, but very special concert in the Grand Music Hall. He only would say that this was to be a very, very special song being debuted. I knew whose song they were going to play, but I was under oath to say nothing about it.

Bard Tal took center stage and looked out at the huge crowd. He spoke slowly and clearly. "Ladies and gentlemen, girls and boys, it is with the greatest pleasure that I am allowed to introduce to all of you this first musical composition written by the eleven year old Alwanianon Milienne. Her song is both revolutionary in nature and in sound. It is a tribute to and written for all the Megalos women that she's helped on the recent, long voyage back here. She hopes that all of you from Megalos will enjoy it. I give you Alwanianon Milienne making her debut on bass drum on her first song!"

Without waiting for any kind of applause, Alwanianon began by thumping a single, low, loud, slow, but solid beat on the big bass drum. Thump! Thump! Thump! Thump! Then Tal came in on one of his largest stringed instruments, whose notes were very low. He played a single note, paused a drum beat, then repeated that note and played a couple of rising notes, followed by a long string of descending single notes, then holding the very last one several beats. This he repeated three times. Between the steady, driving thumping and his pattern, one got a feeling of anger being somehow expressed.

Then Tal's wife, Lia Ines, and Mireio, Alwanianon's mother, came in with vocals perfectly blended, joined by Roberto on his guitar's higher strings, playing a fast melody line.

> Sitting in the shadows
> Staring in the face of life.
> Watching the winds blow
> Rain down upon my face.
> Damn your hate!
> Damn your lies!

After holding lies for an entire beat, then came utter silence for a beat. When once more, Alwanianon's regular thumping began, joined after four beats by Tal's bass theme, the other three began again.

> Cannot touch my face,
> Cannot hold my babe.
> Cannot wipe my tears,
> Cannot hold my love.
> Damn your hate!
> Damn your lies!

After holding lies for an entire beat, then came utter silence for a beat. When once more, Alwanianon's regular thumping began, joined after four beats by Tal's bass theme, the other three began again.

> After quite a number of similar verses came a resolution.
> I'll be damn if I'll live your lies!
> You are never beating me!
> I will thrive and I will grow!

I will create and I will survive!

Damn all your hate!

Damn all your lies!

After holding lies for an entire beat, then came utter silence for a beat. When once more, Alwanianon's regular thumping began, joined after four beats by Tal's bass theme, Roberto and Tal and Alwanianon took off! Faster and faster they went, louder and louder, with Roberto driving a hard, fast melody on the highest strings, echoing many notes repeatedly. The two women joined in singing, "I will survive!" over and over until at last they were nearly drowned out with the volume from the other three. When one thought that they could not possibly go any faster or louder and without any warning, they all ceased playing at once, leaving a huge vacuum of silence!

We sat there mesmerized, stunned for many seconds. Then people began wildly clapping, others stomped their feet; even yelling and whistling filled the entire room. Alwanianon's new rocking sound was a smashing success! I spotted tears in many of the women's eyes. The young musician had captured the essence of their situation.

Me, I cried too. Here was this young Spice Islands girl, who had lost her arms below the elbows to the mantis creature, whose parents had died trying to save her, and who had been forsaken and left to die by her people when we arrived and rescued her, creating such highly emotional, incredibly moving music that captured much of what so many women here on the estate felt. Yes, I cried too.

The noise just didn't die down! At last, Bard Tal got up and stood before the audience, raising his hands. Finally, the crowd became quite enough for him to speak. "I take it that you would like to hear it once more?" The roars of "yes" were louder than the music. He smiled and looked at Alwanianon, who grinned back at him. He took his place by the large stringed instrument. Once more, the incredible thumping filled the room.

Before we finally sailed, they had to repeat the song six more times. The last time was for the benefit of nearly all the other musicians in Velona, who had heard about it and demanded to hear it firsthand. All this from an eleven year old child — incredible.

Chapter 15 The Pure Society

Pope Yazi II, still recovering from a bout of sea sickness, sat up on his bed. The Cardinal watching over him smiled, "Ah, feeling better today, Your Holiness?"

"Yes, a bit better. How's the typhoon?"

"Gone, Your Holiness. We had a very narrow escape indeed. Jehosa was on our side. Only lost one ship. Smooth sailing now. Think you can eat something light now?" The Pope nodded and the Cardinal went to fetch some cheese, biscuits, and mead.

While the Pope ate slowly, the Cardinal went on, "I'm told that we ought to make landfall later today. If you are feeling better, you might come on deck and watch the sights. I'll come let you know when it's time."

That afternoon, Pope Yazi II leaned against the mast, holding on to the ropes. He did not trust his legs and refused to be anywhere near the edge of the yacht. Acropolis lay on the horizon. Even at this distance, it looked much like Megalos, save greener. The island was three hundred miles long and a hundred wide. A range of low mountains ran down its center.

Even from this distance, he could see the telltale signs of large towns and cities scattered about this northern side. No one knew anything about the people who dwelled here, save that they originally came from Megalos some five hundred years ago, settling here around the same time that Megalos was settled. Behind the Royal Yacht, Yazi II saw the other thirty-nine ships, their bows breaking the waves. It was a reassuring sight; he had at least rescued his men, the wealth of the Church, and all of its Holy Relics, including the contents of his private vault.

Soon they were close enough to see the people on land. Many small fishing boats plied the waters not too far from shore. Towns and villages dotted this northern coastline. The captain was looking for a large city, however, and they continued paralleling the coastline. About midway along, they spotted what had to be a city of substantial size. Indeed, the architecture was very similar to that of Megalos, only the stonework was black basalt not marble.

Great open sided temples or buildings with large black pillars supporting the typical stone roofs dotted the hillside on which the city lay, sprawling into the distance. Unfortunately, there was no dock! The captain looked in vain for docking facilities and found none! "This is most unusual, Your Holiness. There is no place for us to dock."

"Perhaps, we should sail around the island and see where their major shipping ports lie," Yazi II suggested. Two days passed by and they were right back where they had started. Seven large port cities had been passed, but not one had any docks. Further, no ships larger than small fishing boats had been seen anywhere around the island. "Could it be that Acropolis has no shipping, no trade with other lands?" the Pope asked in disbelief.

"It sure looks that way," his captain replied. "We are running low on fresh water. Perhaps we should lower a longboat and go visit them here." A half hour later, the captain and six crew members began rowing the short distance to shore.

While the others watched from the main deck of the yacht, a dozen soldiers wearing bits of bronze armor, very similar in nature to that worn by Megalos Centurions, came rushing to the shore where the longboat was intending to beach. As the captain drew near, he could make out the symbols on the soldier's tunics, a large, black praying mantis. One of the soldiers spoke; the language was very similar to that spoken on Megalos. "Halt. You are not allowed to land anywhere on this island. If you set one foot on our soil, you will be arrested and thrown into prison for the rest of your life, however long that may be."

"Greetings, we are from Megalos. We are your cousins," the captain pleaded. The soldier merely repeated his warning.

"We are nearly out of fresh water and are seeking sanctuary here for a time," the captain tried.

"There is no sanctuary here for anyone who was not born on this island. However, we will not allow you to die of thirst at sea. Bring your water barrels hither and we will see that they are filled and reloaded onto your small boat. Just do not set foot on our shores. Under no circumstances are any visitors every allowed on Acropolis."

"Why is that? I could understand such a restriction if we brought the plague with us or if you had an outbreak of the plague," the captain queried.

"No plague. We are the Pure Bloods, the Master Race on Tarra. Every man, woman, and child on Acropolis is dedicated to maintaining the purity of our bloodline. For hundreds of years, no one has been allowed onto this island. Although a ship beached here in a storm once, its crew were summarily executed, and the ship chopped up for firewood."

"I see. Say, what is the meaning of the praying mantis on your tunics?"

"Ah, that is the emblem of our god, the Black God, who looks after us and guarantees the total purity of our bloodline. Now go and fetch those water barrels."

"But there are forty ships in our flotilla," the captain tried to protest, hoping that they would be allowed on shore to fill that many water barrels, at least ten from each ship.

"Tie them into a mass and float them in. We will see that they are filled. In a few days, we will bring them back here and load them onto your longboats. Go now, I have wasted too much time talking to inferiors already!" He turned and walked back up the beach a ways, clearly indicating the meeting was finished. The captain had no choice but to return to the yacht, where he relayed the entire conversation to the Pope and Thondakas.

The men discussed the situation for quite some time. In the end, they had no choice but to do as the soldier had asked. They needed fresh water in any case, no matter what else they might do. A day later, a giant mass of floating, empty water barrels was rowed close to the shore. A number of soldiers waded out to fish them onto the shore. A number of wagons arrived and their crews loaded them onto the wagons, ten barrels per wagon and left.

Over the next few days, the wagons returned; their crews loaded them onto the longboats and picked up more empties. Three days later, the last of the many water barrels had been filled and returned to the flotilla. Throughout the day and night time hours, a squad of soldiers was always watching the shoreline.

Thondakas was all for landing a group of his men and teaching these men a lesson. However, Yazi II vetoed it. "We are in a very precarious position here, with all of our treasures aboard, fleeing from an invading army. We cannot risk losing even one more man, let alone our security forces. I fear that we will need all of you when we return. No, we must accept this minor setback. It must be the Will of Jehosa that we seek another route to safety. Let us sail back towards Sud. I have a feeling that the typhoon may have changed the entire situation on Megalos. It has been a very long time since our land was directly hit by a typhoon. This one was definitely headed to our homeland. Perhaps, Jehosa sent the typhoon to rescue our people."

While Thondakas did not like this point of view, he had to accept it. He retired to his cabin once more, while the Pope explained his orders to the captain. The message was received a short while later by all the other captains. Once more, the flotilla began to sail, this time retracing their route.

Back on Megalos, the Head Nun at the large Nunnery in Galantas, Sister Zosime, a matronly, plump woman, surveyed the damage. Trees were down everywhere; several temple structures had collapsed. Rock slides and mud slides blocked all roads out of the capital city. The only good news was that the invaders had left before the typhoon had struck. A rider had come into the city this morning crying out the news that the invading army was leaving the island. Already one thousand had left on their flimsy ships. The many legions of the enemy were all marching towards Lathlox. However, the city now had only half its usual population, for the rest had died or fled before the invaders had arrived to sack the once proud city.

Many of her nuns had complained bitterly about having been left behind when the Pope had also fled. Sister Zosime had said, "Weep not, sister, Jehosa knows of this and has a purpose here for us. We will know it in time." Well, the time had come, as far as Zosime was concerned. People were in dire need.

"Break out the supplies, blankets, food, and the water reserves," Sister Zosime ordered. "I want signs put up outside, offering free food, water, and shelter. Also, let's setup an infirmary for the sick and injured. We'll use our commons room for that. Sisters, now is the time that Jehosa is calling for us. We have much work ahead of us, if our people in Galantas are to survive. Let's get busy!"

By nightfall, the word had spread; one could get much needed food and water at the Nunnery. By the next day, hundreds of men, women, and children filled the makeshift infirmary. Some had the usual diseases, but others were wounded by the invaders and had been very fortunate not to have been beheaded.

A week later, the Nunnery had become the focal point of life in Galantas; so many had come, that there was no more room anywhere in the Nunnery! Sister Zosime took on more and more responsibility. Now she began issuing orders to those who were here who were not injured to begin clearing the mud and rocks, so that water wagons could once more travel to the reservoirs. Soon, the first of the water wagons began returning with fresh water. Not long after, fresh fish came up from Athos.

After a month, the people of Galantas began calling Sister Zosime, Saint Zosime! The sick had miraculously recovered. Many of the wounded had healed or were on the mend. So many had been saved from starvation or thirst that she had long ago lost count of them. This one woman had stepped in and literally saved the entire city from ruin. Through her relief efforts, the Church of Jehosanity rose to new heights in Galantas among the poorer people, so much so, that when Pope Yazi II finally returned to Constanza City, he was besieged with requests to declare Zosime a holy Saint.

Thus, on January 31, 650, the Church of Jehosanity declared its first saint, Saint Zosime. All over Megalos, the day was celebrated with many feasts. Thereafter, January 31 was declared Saint Zosime Day. Each year thereafter, most families celebrated with a feast in her honor. She was the first living person to gain sainthood.

True, all over the island, the other Nunneries, after hearing what was happening in Galantas, opened their doors as well, aiding the hungry, thirsty, and injured. Yet, these others were simply following the lead set by Sister Zosime. Thus, the upset with the sudden departure of the Pope was offset by the kindness and generosity of the Nunneries.

Meanwhile, Pope Yazi II took his flotilla to the old secret trireme construction bay, known as Port Bay. Here in the still waters of the bay were facilities for his men and their ships. On February 1, he sent his yacht with the Mano del Dio members off to reconnoiter Megalos and ascertain the current status there.

On February 28, the Royal Yacht was sailing back to Port Bay with the great news that the invaders had fled Megalos just after the typhoon had struck. Now, they could return home and work on rebuilding the damage suffered by the many churches during the invasion and the typhoon. The ship had just rounded the southern tip of the Southlands, heading north some three hundred miles from Port Bay.

Chapter 16 An Unexpected Capture

On February 5, 650, the Sleepy Hollow set sail for the Far East and the land called Tashien. The Long Nose and the Peanut caravels accompanied us, loaded with an entire newly formed Circle that called themselves the Traveling Circle and the trading goods that Jin had suggested his people would want. Our two ambassadors were currently on the Long Nose with the Circle, teaching them how to better speak their language. This gave all the Explorers Circle some quiet, relaxation time. Things had been rather hectic for the last few months.

Mireio, with Alwanianon's constant help, was now handling her new baby much better. She'd also gotten some tips from the many other mothers at the Laird Foundation, who were like her. Her sense of helplessness had once more become a thing of the past.

Renzo and I spent a good deal of time playing Torque Ball in the cargo hold, working up a sweat. Usually, after the game, we ended up in bed. Can I plead that we were still newlyweds?

On February 25, we rounded the bottom of the Southlands, changing course from south to east. That's when the lookout called out to Captain Henry. We all rushed on deck to see the Royal Yacht of the Megalos Church heading our way. Emil had the far seeing eye trained on the ship for some time as they approached our three vessels.

Suddenly he said, "Rosina, come take a look. Isn't that the man who was responsible for imprisoning all those women?"

She looked and replied, "That's him. I also see the other four. Bethany, we have to arrest those five men for what they did to those Megalos artists!"

"I don't see any of the priests there on deck, just those Mano fellows," I noted.

"I wish we could just reach out and pluck those guilty men up and bring them all captured over here and send them to Isla Roca!" declared Linda. "Bethany, we've got to stop them from harming more women."

Acting spontaneously, I did just that, floated over their ship and spotted the five that Rosina had identified as the ones who had encased the women and left them to die of dehydration and starvation when they fled the island. Rosina quickly linked to me, sending me once more the images she had retrieved from the women's minds. *Have Natale hold these men still when I pick them up,* I sent to Rosina. I felt the tug of Natale's mind joining us and several others as well.

One by one, I put a line down to each of the guilty men and then energized the beam. Up went the five bodies flying high into the air. I felt Natale's impact upon the bodies right away; she held their bodies rigid. I slowly moved them over to our ship and sat them down on our deck. Instantly, the Protectors began disarming them, and searching them for concealed weapons, especially poison. Several vials of an unknown liquid were tossed overboard. Emil took no chances!

One by one, the five men were tied up, while Natale continued to hold their bodies absolutely still. Over on the Royal Yacht, men were running about, yelling, and grabbing weapons. As our ship closed the distance to theirs, Emil yelled out as loudly as he could, "These men are under arrest for murder and attempted murder. They murdered a number of women in their secret underground prison beneath your church in Constanza City. They imprisoned over two hundred other women and left them there to die when you evacuated the city. They will be taken to Velona and tried for their crimes. You are free to continue your voyage."

One yelled back, "You cannot do this. We demand you release them at once."

"You cannot get away with murder and torture of helpless women any longer. If you continue to torture women by locking them into those metal encasements, you too will be arrested. Murder of innocents is a crime against humanity and is not tolerated by the rest of the world, even if you somehow find murder of women justified." Emil was getting rather angry with these assassins.

However, further conversation became impossible, as the two ships sailed past each other. Both were going rather swiftly but in opposite directions. A minute later, the Royal Yacht was far in the distance behind us. They made no move to attempt to circle back around and chase after us. It would have been foolish anyway, since our caravels could sail much faster than their yacht.

With the five men secured, Natale released her hold on the men. I spoke, "Thondakas, you are under arrest for crimes against the women artists of Megalos. Many that you ordered to be encased in those horrid devices died in your secret prison cell there in the underground tunnels beneath your church. Two hundred thirteen survived, although you left them there to die when you fled the island as the invaders approached your city. Three quarters lost their arms to your sick perversions. You and these four who have been positively identified by the survivors will be taken to Isla Roca and imprisoned there until you come to your senses."

He stared at me, violently angry at having been abducted himself. However, he began to realize that he had just been lifted, as if by magic, and transported over to our ship. Worse, he was totally tied up, his weapons thrown overboard. His vials of poison, likewise. He attempted to spit into my face, but I saw it coming, caught it mid-flight, and threw it back into his own face. Thondakas was shocked to find that he had somehow managed to spit in his own face!

"Serves them bitches right," he snarled. "They continued to paint blasphemy!"

"That does not give you the right to murder them, to abduct them, to encase their arms, put rings in their mouths to force them always open, and to leave them that way until their arms died or even their bodies died! If I still had some of your devices with me, I would put you five in them and see how you liked it! Those women have survived and are now recovering. One day they will paint again, even though you took their arms, you have not taken their spirit and will to paint beauty, you fiend!"

As the reality of his situation finally sunk into the man, I saw his anger turn into fear and then terror. He was trapped, caught like the animal he had become. His past deeds had finally caught up to him. Thondakas would at last have to answer for his numerous crimes committed under the guise of "holy deeds" for the Church of Jehosanity.

Linda added, "You will be taken to Isla Roca and presented with a list of your crimes. Then, you will be taught the truth of the situation. If you come to your senses, then you will be allowed an opportunity to make amends for your many crimes, although personally, I cannot envision how you could make amends to so many women whose lives you have ruined! Yet, if you somehow manage to do this to the satisfaction of all the women, then you will be released from Isla Roca a free man. Take these foul excuses for men below and make sure that they are securely tied."

Once they were below, Linda let out a whoop! "Bethany, we did it! We got the five guilty men out of circulation! I cannot believe this!" Everyone shared her wild enthusiasm.

"One slight problem, Linda," I pointed out, "we are sailing the wrong way. Are we taking them to the Far East with us?"

"Absolutely not!" declared Captain Henry. "Keep a sharp lookout for another caravel heading towards home. We'll transfer them to that ship."

"Now you are talking!" Linda declared. "Besides, I will hate to have to feed these beasts!"

Sure enough, two days later, just such a caravel appeared, coming our way. She was heavily laden, riding very low in the water. We hailed the ship and came along side. The Water Witch was carrying a load of timbers back to Velona for the shipwrights. They agreed to transport our prisoners, especially when they learned who they were! Again, to avoid any possibility of escape, I used my powers to lift them one by one from our ship over to the Water Witch.

Even better, their captain was able to put the five men in chains, alleviating the necessity of having someone watch them day and night as we did, otherwise they might find ways to untie each other. With chains, the key was needed. We all felt this was the perfect solution. Back home, many, many people cheered our action. Two hundred thirteen were especially pleased by the news, as you might expect.

However, three weeks later, we learned that during the night, Thondakas had used his chains to strangle the other four and then committed suicide himself, strangling himself with his chains. In the end, while they had been prevented from committing further harm, they were now free to acquire new baby bodies and perpetuate their perversions in their next lifetimes! While this aspect concerned mom and me greatly, almost no one else worried about it. The perpetrators were dead and that was enough for them. I kept wondering what I would be facing, say another twenty or so years down the road. Perhaps they would not continue their crimes, but the odds, I thought, were against such hopeful thinking. The reasons that they were doing them had not been viewed or erased.

March 7 we arrived off Megalos, giving it a wide berth, continuing sailing eastward. Now our two ambassadors were transferred over to the Sleepy Hollow, so Jin could provide sailing directions to his city. Once more, Henry and the men began taking careful measurements, averaging them, and plotting our course on the main map. Interesting or curiously the mantis maps did not show anything further east than Megalos. Either they did not know about this other civilization and landmass or they were not operating there.

I had a horrible thought, what if some other aliens were in operation over there, aliens that we knew nothing about? I quickly squashed such speculations. After all, with the elimination of both the Grey Creatures and the mantis creatures, nothing would have prevented such aliens from taking over control of our portion of the world.

As the days slipped by, I had Ming Lau teach me how to perform the tea making procedure properly. By the time that we arrived, Ming said that I was actually nearly perfect with it. I did notice that somehow my tea actually did taste significantly better than it normally was. Even though so many steps of the ritual seemed utterly pointless to me, doing them all in the proper way and in sequence yielded a superb cup of tea, no question of that. She was also very pleased that I had actually learned it.

By March 15, we began to sail near the coastline of Tashien. Now we could see scattered smaller port towns with their many fishing boats plying the coastal waters near land. Often these were made from bamboo poles lashed together. We passed great stands of bamboo growing in the wild, shooting up as tall as smaller trees did in our land. Other sections of the countryside were covered in irrigated fields of rice and similar grains. Jin explained that at the start of the season, the fields would be flooded and the rice shoots planted. Then, the water level was gradually lowered. Indeed, we soon passed by one such field, where we could actually see the labor-intensive planting of this year's crop.

Finally, on March 21, 650, the great southern city of Shansee appeared on the horizon. The sheer size of the city took us all by surprise! Velona sector boasted nearly a half million people now, but Shansee was home at least to double that number! Since the weather this far south was often very hot in the summertime, most of the dwellings were made from thin woods and even the all-purpose bamboo, with very large windows that had pull down blinds made from split bamboo. Dingy yellow was the predominate color of the city.

Chapter 17 When in Shansee. . .

Their docks were large with some twenty of their larger ships currently there, loading or unloading. Unlike our ships, theirs, Jin explained, could travel a long way up the great Yonshu River all the way to the Emperor's city of Zau in the central province of Wontun. As our caravels began to head into the three empty berths that Jin said were reserved for Royal Guests, the people around the dock area stopped what they were doing and began to stare at us. They had never seen such ships before; ours were nearly four times the size of theirs and vastly sturdier. While theirs had a single mast, ours had three, with great billowing sails with our trademark red crosses prominently displayed upon them. We certainly gave them something to watch and talk about for days!

Henry sounded us all the way in, unsure if the water's depth would support our deep keels. It did, with five feet to spare at low tide. Once the mooring lines were secured, Jin walked down the gangplank and explained to us their equivalent Harbor Master and guards. He requesting a runner be sent to the Royal Palace, notifying Princess Sho Lin of our arrival. With the arrangements made, Jin returned on board.

"I have sent word to Sho Lin. When you wish to unload the trade goods, those men will help you transport them to an empty warehouse where you can put them on display for all to see. Many people will greatly desire to view them. Perhaps Sho Lin will come to look as well. We should now get the things that we wish to take with us to the Royal Palace and place them on the dock. As with your estate, the Royal Palace of Sho Lin is several miles inland.

Henry turned command of the Sleepy Hollow over to Bosun Thad. The ship's Guardians and the Santi would remain here providing protection of the ships. Interestingly enough, we had long ago run out of available Guardians to put on caravel guard duty. Both of our sister ships merely had Santi fighter protections. It took the Explorers Circle over a half hour to get our things together and onto the dock. In contrast, the Traveler Circle had theirs ready to go in half that time and was standing on the docks awaiting us! Their Circle had only eight members.

Finally, with our gear ready, the strangest of transportation devices began appearing! A man pulled a funny two-wheeled cart in which two people or baggage was carried. The man then lifted up the front two poles and pulled the cart through the streets! A bamboo roof kept the direct sunlight off the passengers. Jin explained that these men made their living transporting others around the city for a copper a ride. These were called shushus and the carts, riks. We all gave our shushus a silver, for which they effused great gratitude!

The streets were all cobblestones, but they were densely packed with people going about their daily business. Many shops lined the sides of the streets, though some vendors walked about selling water or tea from large copper kettles. The odors of food cooking were everywhere. While we stared at the strange sights, the people here stared right back at us, for we were also the strange sight!

It was hard to tell the distance traveled but our best guess was that we traveled about five miles inland before the city decor suddenly changed. Now the densely packed houses and streets gave way to magnificent formal gardens, complete with small streams flowing through them. The cobblestone street began to wander through these gardens and all sight of the bustling city was left behind. One now got a sense of immense tranquility, a peace of mind. Occasionally, we spotted a person walking slowly through the garden, and sometimes a young couple stood holding hands. The gardens seemed to go on forever! At last the Royal Palace of Sho Lin appeared, embedded within this garden.

All the many buildings were single story and of wood and bamboo construction. Many decks and porches connected the quaint structures, often going over small streams or ponds filled with lily flowers. Surrounding these buildings and among them were numerous varieties of flowering trees, all budding out with so many shades of color I could not count them. The combined flagrance of so many was heady. Many of the buildings had silk banners draped over one or more of the large windows, and these waved gently in the slight breeze. We swore that the palace had grown out of the gardens so well did it blend in to the garden.

This was a picture perfect palace indeed. However, we did see a number of guards patrolling the perimeter of the grounds, dressed in their unusual cloth and leather armor. Each carried a sword and held a long spear in their hand, which had a pale blue banner fluttering from its tip, the chosen color of Sho Lin. Jin explained that there were some fifty buildings in the palace. The one with the smoke curling up among the trees was the kitchen building, where all the food was prepared. Occasionally we spotted a servant, likewise dressed in a pale blue silk dress just like Ming's, walking with short paces to and from various buildings.

The shushus pulled up before the main entrance, where four soldiers stood erect, guarding the main entrance to the complex. Jin said that we should pile our bags on the porch, which had a little bamboo roof to protect it from the rain. Servants would carry them to the guest quarters while we met with Sho Lin. After piling up our many sacks onto the porch, we were finally ready to enter. Ming had already gone inside to let Sho Lin know that we had arrived. Jin waited patiently for us and we then followed him just inside the door, which was also made of thin bamboo draped with the familiar sky blue silk banner of Sho Lin.

Inside, we found numerous wicker chairs and a table. Here guests would wait to be presented to the Princess. Two more guards stood at the entrance of her court room. Jin explained, "Please remember how we have taught you to be presented. There will be many others present along with the Princess. These nobles, sages, merchants, and scholars will all be observing you. As I said, some will resent outsiders being allowed into the Royal Palace. It will be these that will be quietly looking for you to disgrace Sho Lin. They want some excuse to insist that you be thrown out." Ah, courtly intrigue — it seems such is present in every palace. I hoped that we would not give them any such reasons.

An unusual musical stringed instrument played several quaint notes, the signal for Jin to present us formally to the Princess. We entered a very large room. At the opposite end sat the blue divan with Sho Lin lying in a perfect pose, just as we had seen her do before in Lathlox, Megalos. However, seated on mats upon the wooden floor in a U-shape going all down either side were numerous men of various ages with a few women present as well. A quick guess suggested we had an audience of at least fifty people. As Ming and Jin had drilled us, we waited for Sho Lin's flick of fingers before we bowed to her and stepped forward to greet her with Natale and me leading the way.

As we drew close to her divan, we bowed once more, watching her fingers with their long nails for another signal. She waited just long enough for her audience to observe that we both respected and honored her before giving us her final sign that we may speak. "We bring greetings from Velona, Sea Princes. It is good to be before you again, Princess Sho Lin Wu. We have brought presents for you, and our ships have brought a sampling of trading goods that Court Historian Jin Han has suggested would be of interest to your merchants, nobles, and sages. They are being unloaded and setup for their review in the designated warehouse. With us are the promised Velona ambassadors. I hope they will meet with your approval. Ming Lau and Jin Han have taught us much. Thank you for allowing them to visit our land."

"It is good to see our new friends from the very distant land of Velona," Sho Lin replied. "I see that you have learned our language much better than when we first met." She smiled, "Ming and Jin have taught you well. Although we have met formally, my esteemed colleagues assembled here to meet you have not. Would you please formally introduce your members to them?" Per Jin's coaching, we knew what was now required of us.

I bowed to her and turned to the left first, always the left first, since those would be the most important of those gathered here. First, I bowed to them and then said, "I am the leader of our group. We are all members of the Santi del Dio, the Knights of God. I am called Bethany Rose Wilkins Pazzio le'Goeur, and this is my husband, Renzo." He bowed to the group as well. We turned and I bowed to those on the right and repeated the introduction and Renzo bowed again. "This is Natale and Henry Freeze, our ship's captain."

"This is Linda Sarah Rose Wilkins and her husband Damien, who is my brother." After their bows and the repeat for the right side, I said, "This is Michelle and Benet Donegal." Continuing, "This is Rosina and Cedric Pazzio le'Goeur Dietz. This is Tonia and Emil Po Woodgrove. This is Mireio and Roberto Milienne and their daughters Alwanianon and Adrienne."

"I am very pleased for you to meet our ambassadors from Velona. This is Muriel and Hendrick Gaston. This is Helena and Tomasio Pelia. This is Virginia and Samuel Backwater. This is Ellie and Albert Muskgrove. This is Flavie and Renoir Deegs, both are painters. We hope that they will please you and honor us."

So far so good, I thought, well no major blunders that I could see. I did notice many eyes staring at Natale, Mireio, Flavie, and even Michelle. Many eyes focused on our long earrings. Jin had confirmed that gold and gems were their means of exchange here, but that emeralds were far more valuable than jade. Now for the next step.

I bowed again to Sho Lin. "If you will allow me, I would like to present you with a small present on behalf of the Santi and Velona." I waited for her hand signal. She smiled, knowing what was to come and gave me the go-ahead sign. I retrieved the mahogany box that a Santi had found to hold the earrings. I opened the box and presented it for her to see. Yes, here was an identical set of these very expensive, very long earrings that we wore. She broke into a big grin and held the box so that first those on the left and then those on the right could see.

She gave me a slight bow. Her corset prevented a deep bow of course, but such was not needed here. "I am very pleased with such an expensive, elegant gift. Thank you very much, Bethany. I am honored to receive them." I smiled back.

"I now must see that the noon meal is properly prepared. I would be pleased if you would join me for lunch in an hour. Many here have questions for you. I will leave you to answer them. An hour then?"

I bowed, saying, "Most honored are we to share your lunch." She then signaled her staff, which came and carried her on her divan out of the room using a rear door. However, I was uncertain what would come next or its protocol.

Yan Dahou, her advisor, spoke first, after bowing to me, "Your present is a queenly gift indeed. You do our Princess a very high honor and the rest of us here as well. Thank you. At this time, many here would like to ask you questions. There is no ritual format for these questions, save please be truthful and honorable in your replies." I had not thought about others having someone who could detect whether a person was telling a falsehood or not, as we had with Jolina's special skills. "If you do not understand something, please let me know. Who wishes to ask the first question of our honored guests?"

"How long will you be staying with us?"

I replied, "Our ambassadors are prepared to stay as long as you desire their company, though perhaps they might like to return home after a year. As for us, we have made no plans. While we have other business to deal with, we can stay as long as the Princess might wish us to or you too for that matter."

"Why do they have no arms?"

And so the questions came. What samples had we brought? How much could our ships carry? How fast could they sail? How sea worthy were the caravels? Why did we all have such long earrings? Do women run our country or do men? Did our people have a written language? Did we have many books and scrolls? How could an armless woman paint? What was our music like? Did we have formal dance, which told of our history? Did we have a history? How old was our civilization? What exactly were the Knights of God?

Finally, one man asked what I had expected all along. "We have heard from the huans, who were attacking the large holy site near the port of Athos, that you did many strange and mysterious things. Is it true that you can conjure fire and ice? Is it true that you can lift men and throw them without using your body? Is it true that the woman with no arms can hold a man still that is falling? Is it true that you were rescuing many imprisoned women that these barbarians were torturing?"

I answered for us. "Yes, to all of those. Yan, is a small demonstration here in the Princess's meeting room permissible and not a disgrace, since the Princess is not here?"

"Yes, it would perhaps be wise to show a small demonstration. You see, many here find these things rather hard to believe. Yao Liu always says, 'A sight is worth a thousand characters.'"

"Renzo, a small bit of flames out here in the empty space please?" I asked. He smiled and put up a small square of flames. To my shock, one man dressed all in white stood up and approached the flames. "Sir, please be careful; the flames are real. You can be harmed!"

He said a word that I did not understand, faced the flames, pulled back his white sleeve, and immersed his arm through the flames! Many others, who were watching, grunted and nodded. The flames did not harm his arm in the slightest! Then he pulled his hand back and spoke, "Real flames." Everyone then nodded and muttered excitedly amongst themselves.

"Emil, a small bit of ice please?" I said, figuring that ice would cause no real harm here. He placed a small wall of ice between himself and those on the left side. Once more, the same man in white approached it, said another word that I did not understand, and thrust his hand through the wall, shattering it into pieces. Several of the bits he picked up and handed to several men, who felt them and watched the pieces melt in their hands. More affirmative grunts came from the assemblage.

Since this man in white seemed to be the deciding factor, I said, "Sir, with your permission, I will pick your body up." He grinned at me and nodded. I nodded back, honoring him. I then floated over him, lifted him three feet off the ground, and sat him back down gently. He immediately bowed respectively to me and I, to him. This time, the grunts were rather loud, and the whispers, intense.

"Natale, your turn." She stepped closer to me. "Sir, I wish you to rush towards Natale, as if you meant to harm her. She will hold you still, if that is acceptable to you." Again, the man in white bowed to me and then even more so to Natale, who returned his bow. He said a sharp word and came running at her, attempting to do a flying kick. To everyone's amazement, the man froze in mid-air, motionless. Slowly, Natale lowered him to the ground and gradually relaxed her grip on him. She did not want him to follow on through and punch her out! He stopped his movement and again bowed even lower to Natale, who smiled and bowed back.

"Please, worthy gentleman, realize that we only use these abilities and skills in defense when someone is out to harm us. We do not go around burning down people's houses and stuff like that. Natale held the soldier who had slipped and was about to hit the ground with his head. We do not like to see people die, and she rescued him the only way that she could. At that holy place, we only wanted to rescue the imprisoned, tortured women. We had no quarrel with the huans and their soldiers, so we used our skills to keep them back, while we got the women safely to our boat. I picked up the men because they were about to dash into the flames and get badly burned."

The man in white answered me, "Bethany of the Santi, you have done us all here a very great honor by showing us that you speak the truth. I am called San See Tou, the Princess's Protectorate, sworn to protect her with my life. We could learn much from each other. We will speak more later." He again bowed to me, and I, to him.

A distant gong sounded. Yan said, "That is the signal that the Princess Sho Lin has your lunch awaiting you. This session is now over. We must not delay the Princess with our talk. If you will follow me, I will take you to her table. If you have more questions for Sho Lin's guests or the new ambassadors, please get word to me, and I will arrange a personal meeting. Thank you for coming today." He bowed to the left group and then to the right group. Not knowing the expected actions we should take, we too bowed to each side as we left to follow Yan.

As we walked the short way to the Royal Dining Room, Yan whispered to me, "That went better than I had hoped. Several doubted you and wished for you to be expelled from the palace. Now they will think twice before saying such again."

We entered the Royal Dining Room, but it was not what we expected at all. It was really a sheltered porch! Long tables lined the porch, which had a bamboo roof so that rain could not fall on the diners. Sho Lin sat at one end of the table. This was the first time we had actually seen her not lying on her divan. She motioned for Natale and me to sit close to her. The others sat on down along the long table. We all had a front row seat looking out onto the Royal Gardens, with its bubbling tiny streams and small ponds filled with water flowers that floated on its surface. All around, flowering trees were in full bloom. It was gorgeous beyond description!

Her servants brought in trays of food, sitting them at various precise locations along the length of the table. Sho Lin herself poured my tea and handed the pot to Ming, who then proceeded to go on down the line, filling the other's cups. These cups were exquisitely made, very fine china, though a bit too small for my liking, being a tea guzzler. Next, a plate with two wooden sticks was placed before each of us. Sho Lin then identified what each of the dishes was, going down the line from herself to the end of the table. Before her was her favorite, chicken with broccoli and pea pods, though I cannot say the name that she called it.

We all watched in complete fascination as she deftly used the two wooden sticks to fill her plate and then picked up a small bite to eat! None of us was prepared to eat using a pair of sticks! After much laughter by Sho Lin and her servants, we all got much-needed lessons before we starved to death. Many of us had an awful time managing the sticks! Actually, Natale and Mireio had the easiest time of it, perfecting a method they called shoveling it into their mouths. I could see that formal eating was going to take us an enormous amount of practice!

After the hour-long lunch was over and we had emptied the teapots three times, Sho Lin said, "Now my servants will take you to our Guest Houses. But I must ask you, do you women wish separate quarters from the men or should we put husbands and wives together? I do not know the customs of your land."

"Families should be in the same room, if that is honorable here," I replied.

She nodded that it was. "I have province business to handle this afternoon. Someone will come and get you when it is time for dinner. I will not be able to attend diner tonight. I must host another visitor from the north. However, please feel free to take a walk in the Royal Gardens; they are most beautiful at this time of year. Bethany, if you and Natale will honor me with your presence this evening after dark, I would like to speak with you privately." I nodded and she added, "Ming will come for you when it is time."

With that, we all got up and followed Ming, who lead us off the porch and over to a set of identical wooden buildings, each with connecting porches. Over each door was a symbol, and quickly we memorized the symbol over the door of the cabin in which we were now staying. All of our many sacks were neatly arranged along the porches, so we had no trouble finding our things.

Renzo and I explored our small room. It had a very nice bed with silk sheets and a heavier silky type of blanket. Three more were neatly folded on the dresser. Two wicker chairs and a table were also present. Out the spacious back window with bamboo blinds that could be lowered for privacy, we had a grand view of the gardens, which seemed to go on forever. After unpacking, Renzo and I took a lover's walk through the gardens. We decided that should we take such a walk here every day, in a month we might be able to see everything!

That evening, the temperature was perfect! Combine that with the heady fragrances of so many flowering trees, bushes, and plants, I felt really alive and alert. Ming came for Natale and me just after dark. "My Princess will see you now. This is a very great honor that she does for you. Never has she done this for any guests. Follow me please." I had no idea what she was talking about, unless having a private meeting was this important a thing around here.

We were led to the Royal Dining Room. There sitting on the steps waiting for us was Sho Lin herself, still wearing her beautiful pale blue silky dress. Ming bowed to her Princess and then backed away and went inside, leaving us three alone. I noticed that there was not another person around anywhere.

"I heard what you did for the skeptics at the meeting today. Very wise decision. Thank you, Bethany."

"Well, I sensed that many did not believe your huan and couldn't think of any other way. At least they know that we spoke truthfully."

"Tell me, what do you think of the Royal Gardens?" Sho Lin asked.

"Princess, I have never seen anything so remotely beautiful! All of us are impressed beyond words at its beauty. Renzo and I took a walk today and decided if we took a walk every day for a month, we still would not have seen everything."

Sho Lin smiled, "Yes, my gardens are the nicest gardens of any palace in Tashien. Every night about this time, I, too, walk among them. It gives me great peace of mind, removing all the stress of the day from my mind, and then I can sleep most restfully. Tonight, would you two like to accompany me on my walk in the gardens?"

"But I thought that it was a disgrace for you to walk in public?"

"Oh it very definitely is about the worst disgrace imaginable! But here at night, there is no one else around. My guards guarantee such, so it is not public at all. It is permissible for other women to accompany me, just not men. Besides, I do need such assistance, for I walk only with difficulty. Yet, such walks are needed for my spiritual growth. Much of our spirit is captured in these gardens. Will you accompany me?"

"Sure, we would be honored. What do we need to do to help you?"

"Let me put my arms around you to steady myself. I do walk very slowly of course." She rose and we did as well. I was on her left and she slid her hand under my hair and over my shoulder. Then she did the same with Natale.

"This way. I wish to show you my favorite spot in the gardens." Her steps were indeed quite small. I could see that she was walking mostly on her heels, with very little foot left with which to keep her balance. "I can walk on my own, but it is so inelegant, so ugly, and wobbly that I prefer company like this. I am so glad that you do not mind walking with me like this."

"If you go slow, then you can see more of the garden," I volunteered.

She grinned, "Wise observation. Haste makes waste or so the philosopher Yao Liu always says. In this, I believe he is correct." We walked on in silence for a time, observing the dim woods around us, illuminated by the yellow moonlight.

"Here, this bush here. See how the gardener has found the spirit of the tree and brought forth its essence in its shape?" Sho Lin pointed out the very careful trimming that made the bush look so keen, so vibrant, and so alive, as if it did have a spiritual being within it.

"Ah here is my spot, of all the spots in the garden. Help me to sit please?" We helped her sit down, which was made somewhat difficult because of her very tightly fitting dress, which had no leg slits, and the tight corset she was wearing. "When my mother went to join her ancestors, I began forming this spot in her honor. The little pond is like how I saw her in life, gracefully touching all with her presence, yet never overpowering. For many years, I have come here at night and worked with it until I feel that I have captured her essence in this little pond." I could tell that our Loremasters were in heaven if they were not already there! Indeed, we were seeing a side of the Princess that we had not known existed. In her own way, she was an artist too, only working with things that were alive as well, forming a unified whole.

We three chatted for a long time, before we helped her up to return. On the slow way back, she asked, "I would like to honor you and the other women and in so doing, if you agree, you would be also honoring me and helping dissuade those men who are upset with your presence and very different customs."

"What did you have in mind?"

"I would like to present you with a set of clothes nearly alike to my servants. They can show you how to properly dress and assist you until you have learned it. They will be made of the very finest silks, mind you. Yet, they will also be the style of the trainers. That is, they will be like mine, with no walking slits. New servants wear them so that they can learn how to walk perfectly so that they can be seen in my Royal Court. As Ming has explained to you, women are expected to take no steps larger than mine, when in public. I know that this is much to ask of you and will take an awful lot of getting used to walking this way. Yet, if you do, it will show me great honor and that will put some of the men at ease. You would only need to wear these dresses during official public meetings. At all other times, you are free to wear what you desire."

Natale replied, "I'd love to so honor you, Sho Lin, but do you realize the sacrifice that I would be making if I wore such dresses? I use my feet where you use your arms and hands. In such a dress, I would be nearly helpless and others would have to look after my many personal needs."

"I do understand, Natale. I have watched how you, Mireio, and even little Alwanianon manage. I just cannot believe that you can do what you manage to do. You have such powerful spirits within your bodies. I do know that I am asking a very great deal of you, especially, Natale. Yet, if you did so, it would really help bind our two cultures more solidly together. I will be honest with you two. In my position, I have really very, very few friends. Oh yes, lots of servants and others, but not real friends, due to my position as Princess. Nearly all will at some point withhold from me because I am their Princess. Not so with you two. Always you have spoken you will, your heart, to me, and not because I am your Princess. This I greatly admire, respect, and appreciate. If I did not consider you to be such close friends, I would not be making this offer that I have made."

"If you, Natale, or the others would prefer not to so dress, then I do truly understand and will not be dishonored or think less of you. I know that I am asking an awful lot of you, in particular. Worse, still, without your arms to help you keep your balance, it may be very difficult for you to keep from falling. Even if you do agree to try it, if you find that it is too difficult, too risky, then please, please no longer make the attempt. I can have Ming give you dresses with walking slits in them."

"In that case, Sho Lin, I will give it a try. It may be that I can master it, but then again, I might not. As long as I know that you will not be upset with me if I cannot wear them, then I should at least try it. Besides, your and your servant's dresses are so sexy, that it is driving my husband quite mad over them," Natale replied. We all chuckled.

"Thank you both. Tomorrow morning, send the men out for breakfast and I will send my servants around to assist you. Should we try to clothe all the women in your party or just your Explorers Circle?"

"Better start with just us. If we can manage, then perhaps the ambassadors will want to try it too," I suggested. We helped her up the steps of the porch.

"This way," she said. "I will let you escort me to my personal bath. I always bathe before going to bed."

A little while later, we two returned to our bungalows, that was their proper name, the men had found out. Everyone was sitting on the porches watching the beautiful evening. Mireio, with Alwanianon's assistance, was nursing Adrienne, when we came up. "How did it go?" she asked what everyone wanted to know.

"We helped her go for a walk in the gardens," I began relating what had happened, carefully explaining the misconception that we were under. "This was not considered walking in public," I said. Then, I told them what she had asked us to try, wearing outfits similar to hers.

The women giggled and Mireio commented, "Ah, here we go going native once more. Seriously, Bethany, I had better not. I have Adrienne to nurse so frequently. I'm sure Sho Lin will understand." We agreed.

The next morning, after Renzo teased me and took off for breakfast, Ming appeared carrying a complete outfit for me. After I undressed, she helped me into the corset thing, tightening it up quite tight, I thought. I could scarcely breathe in it. It was so restrictive of bending motions! However, it pushed my breasts, which were now the size of my mom's already and showing no signs of ending their growth spurt, up even larger. We both giggled over them. Then, she helped me slither into the incredibly soft, silky, curve-fitting dress. I had to admit that it felt incredible to the sense of touch. However, the bottom was so tight that I could just put one foot in front of the other.

When she had me all fixed up, I tried to walk by putting one foot in front of the other. I nearly fell over! "No, silly, you cannot walk that way! You will lose your balance surely. Like this, see, shuffle them forward." Now I could see why these women all shuffled along; they would fall over if they tried to put one foot in front of the other. She and I, soon joined by the others, shuffled our way to breakfast. Natale and the others had to wear dresses with walking slits; it was just too hard for those without arms to keep their balance.

Sho Lin was very pleased with our appearance, and to be honest, Renzo just could not keep his hands off me; his arm was constantly around me. Many of the other husbands had similar reactions. However, I found that with the tight waist, I could only eat a fraction of what I normally did.

After breakfast, we were asked to join her Royal Court for a brief meeting. For Sho Lin, this was the perfect opportunity to show them that we were indeed giving her a tremendous honor by not only mimicking her style of dress, but also by not taking any larger steps than she might have taken. I, however, found the meeting rather boring.

Renzo and I, along with most of the others, spent much of the afternoon strolling, slowly through the gardens. Each evening thereafter, Natale and I were invited to join Sho Lin in her evening walk about the gardens. Only now we did so, dressed as she was dressed, a fact not lost on her many servants. It soon became readily apparent that we were truly honoring their Princess, which made the discomfort worthwhile. However, we soon discovered that changing into and out of this costume was far more trouble and hassle than it was worth, as long as we were not really expected to do anything. Hence, we quickly stopped even bothering to change out of the new outfits.

During our many evening walks, Sho Lin chatted about many things. I quickly discovered an interesting aspect. When one does not have close personal friends with which to share one's deepest thoughts and feelings, one becomes rather starved for such communication. Sho Lin was a perfect example of this. We were now her closest friends, and she told us many of her very private thoughts, feelings, and emotions. No, we did not share much of this with the others, respecting her privacy.

For example, she and her Protectorate, San See Tou, were in love with each other. However, dishonor and disgrace would befall both should they even appear to be touching each other, much less speaking of things other than official business. Yet, they managed to carry on a relationship by very subtle means. A raised eyebrow, a blink of the eye, a touch to his moustache, a touch of her hair, a twist of her long nails, these carried their secret love messages in a manner that no one else would notice. Had San See been a Prince or perhaps even a noble by birth, then they might at least share words over a public dinner.

Yet, when she became Empress, she could then choose any man or woman to marry or mate. Only this way could they ever hope to consummate their love, their deep feelings for each other.

This raised a fascinating point, according to Linda, and I was instructed to ask Sho Lin about this while on one of our walks, "When you become Empress and you marry, making the man the new Emperor, who actually rules Tashien? You or he?"

"I do, silly. Always, the woman leads, whether it is the government, the business, or the family. However, it is unseemly for a woman to, how do you say this, get her hands dirty. The woman allows the man the illusion that he is the one in charge. That first day when you met all those merchants, nobles, sages, and philosophers, they were merely gathering the data, the information, to take back to their wives. The few women you saw there are without husbands at this time and have to suffer the disgrace of being so open in the public eye and among other men. It is a bad step down for them, you see."

"Every so often, calamity strikes, as it has my father, when my mother, the Empress, died unexpectedly. Now he must suffer on alone, making decisions that she would have made or marry another woman who would then be elevated to Empress, but then her children would become our rivals as new Princesses and Princes. My father did not wish to put his daughters through that and so has honored our mother by not remarrying all these years. Now he is quite old, though he says he feels young, but I know differently."

"Every first day of summer, I go north to visit him; it is the anniversary of his marriage. It helps him if I am with him that day. He can see the fruits of his love. If you are still here when summer comes, I would be honored if you would accompany me to visit my father, the Emperor."

"If we are here, I wouldn't miss it, Sho Lin. Thank you for inviting us."

Linda's comment was, "So this is a matriarchal society. I would never have guessed it, though perhaps I should have from all the gardens. This really helps, knowing that the women behind the scenes are the ones calling the shots. Very interesting indeed."

Unfortunately, we did not get the opportunity to visit the Emperor. On April 3, 650, a messenger came to Sho Lin with the sad news that Emperor Ho Lan Wu had just gone to meet with his ancestors! Sho Lin summoned us to a private meeting. With tears in her eyes and wearing none of her makeup, she told us the news. "Tomorrow we must journey to Zau and attend my father's funeral. I would be most honored if you, Bethany, and your group, would come up north with me. I could use the support just now. I promise to show you the Imperial Palace, if there is time and such a private meeting can be arranged."

"We would be dishonored if we were not allowed to come with you, Sho Lin. This is a time for friendship. What must we bring?"

"Thank you so much. Ming will bring you the details. We must leave later tonight to get there in time. I have much to do now." We left and a short while later, Ming came by to see us.

Ming said, "I will bring more of these clothes. It will be very important for you to be dressed like us; the funeral is a very public affair. We will have all the other necessities, so you do not need to bring anything. We will go by boat up the Yonshu River and will be there in about two weeks for the funeral. Until the funeral, our tradition is for women to wear a black orchid in their hair, as a sign of the highest honor to the dead person. I will have them for you when we board the boat. Please follow Yan when he comes for you right after supper."

Many lanterns illuminated the long path from the palace to the river. Everyone knew the meaning of this lighted path at night. I saw many people lining the sides of the road, heads bowed, sending a sign of honor to their Princess in her hour of morning. We traveled along the road in the flimsy man-pulled carts and an hour later arrived at the Royal Dock. I was expecting to see some kind of large ship, but instead found a pair of covered barges, really. Ming was there awaiting us and she had Natale and I, along with our other women join her on her barge, while the men went with Yan onto the second barge. Sho Lin was sitting as usual on her divan, with a black orchid in her hair. Quickly, Ming fastened one in each of our hair as well.

"I have made this trip many times, only now I do not wish to be seen by the many well-wishers. Yet, I know you wish to see. I have had Ming make a small divider to separate the front half from this part. You may sit up front and she will raise the blinds so that you may watch. It is worth seeing, though just now, I am too sad to watch." We thanked her and moved to where Ming had already arranged for us to see outside. I was very glad that she had!

The moonlit river was beautiful, very wide, and very calm here. Along the banks were teams of horses, hooked up to the front of the barge. When Yan gave the all set signal, Sho Lin made her sign, and Ming relayed it to the men on the horses. Now I saw how they would travel upstream! The horses pulled the barges along at a fairly good pace. The horses, I estimated and later compared notes with the men, moved along at about five miles an hour. However, they did not stop, but continued all night and all day. Periodically, fresh teams were hitched, and the lathered horses led away. Over a thousand miles was covered in just eight days.

It was a fabulous eight days of sights and a horrible eight days of cramped legs, yearning for a stretch, especially since we were all so confined by our clothing. We passed by many river villages, with small fishing boats out plying the waters. We learned that many larger reed boats were actually the home of whole extended families — river rats was the colloquial name given to these people. Slowly the terrain changed and rolling hills appeared, dotted with farmsteads. Occasionally, we spotted a larger city not too far from the river or on its edge. Without paper on which to jot down all their names, they quickly became a long fog of names, however.

Clothing also changed the farther north we went. Here the climate was not so hot and people dressed in sturdier clothing with brown cottons predominating. As we passed by, many recognized the Royal Barge of Sho Lin and waved or bowed to the craft as we moved on by them. During the daytime, Sho Lin explained what would be occurring at the funeral, preparing us ahead of time, so that we would not accidentally bring disgrace to anyone.

"Many in Tashien now know of you and all eyes will be on you and your party while we are in public, though they will be discrete with their stares. It would not be honorable to do otherwise at a time such as this. By wearing our clothing as you are, this will do much to enhance your acceptance by many, many people outside my province. This, I am very, very sad to say, will become increasingly important in the days to come."

"Oh yes, I remember, you said when your father has gone to meet his ancestors, then the Grand Council must elect one of you three sisters to become the new Empress," I replied.

"Yes, precisely. This will be my hour to shine as the evening star above my older sisters; I have had to live in their shadows all these years. For so many years now, I have been doing my absolute best for my people and myself to ensure that everything is just perfect, no blemish of dishonor. I have every confidence that the Grand Council will pick me."

"However, Bethany, since I have now gotten you involved in my attempt to gain the throne of Tashien, I must be frank and honest with you. Should some calamity befall me and I am not chosen, but cast out in disgrace, you and your people will be in grave jeopardy! If one of my sisters gains the throne, then she will pick one of her children or relatives to become the new Prince or Princess of Tan Lon Province. All that I have done, all the agreements I've made, all the new commerce that we are working together to establish, even your presence in our land shall be reviewed by the new ruler. The worst that I expect would be for them to banish you from Tashien, although Yan has told me that there have been times when they were murdered instead of being told to leave at once. This should not happen, but since I have now gotten you, my dearest friends, involved in all this, I owe it to you to allow you to be fully prepared, if I am disgraced."

"Thank you. But what will happen to you if you are disgraced, Sho Lin? Where will they take you? What will you do?" I asked, very concerned for her well-being.

"That would be up to my sister who took the throne. If history can be a lesson to us, either she would have me banished to the far north, where it is eternally cold, there to live out my days as a pauper in disgrace, or she would have me slain. Knowing my sisters as I do, I would probably be killed, for even in the frozen north country I would be a threat to them, what with the smallest feet and all. Ever they would fret that somehow I might be able to make a comeback into power."

"Sho Lin, if such a disgrace should befall you, would you please consider coming with us, bring San See Tou and your staff with you as well. The Santi would give you full protection and help you create a new and fulfilling life among our people, where you would be able to live with great honor and respect."

"You would take a disgraced person and give them sanctuary?" she asked in disbelief.

"Absolutely and without any hesitation. Even if such a calamity should befall you, in our eyes, and all the eyes of our people, such a calamity is never, ever viewed as a disgrace! We consider it more of a slight bump in the long road of life. We move on and continue to live and prosper. Please let us take you and all who might want to stay with you along with us. That would greatly honor me." I played the honor card; no way was I going to allow her to be killed or sent to the frozen north, wherever that may be!

Ah, the honor card convinced her. "You mean if I and others who are disgraced here should go with you to Velona that would give you much honor?"

"Yes, we are always rescuing other people who are in need. You and your people would be in dire need. Thus, great honor." She bought it completely and so agreed to do so. It did give her much to think about and to discuss among her staff.

Slowly the Yonshu River began to narrow until finally the outskirts of a very large city could be seen just ahead of us. Ming announced, "Zau, Wontun Province. When we arrive at the Imperial Dock, please fall in line behind Yan. He will be giving you guidance. We just barely made it here in time. Her sisters purposely made the funeral so soon in hopes that Sho Lin would suffer the disgrace of missing her father's funeral. It should be taking place in Central Park, about a half mile from here. We will probably have to walk it. I hope that you are up to it. I must see to my Princess now."

"Boy what kind of sisters does she have?" barked Linda. None of us had an answer just yet. Instead, we stared at the huge city, which was at least twice the size of Shansee. As we drew near the docks, already they were nearly full of many other barges and small boats. There was barely enough room for us to dock. Our men lifted us off the barge, and we fell into a line behind Yan. A dozen of her guards took up a flanking arrangement on either side, while her carriers, four very strong men, lifted her divan with her on it off the boat. Guards lifted her six servants off as well. Ming walked just before the divan along with two guards who led the way. I noticed that already a large crowd had gathered to catch a glimpse of us, Sho Lin in particular, though many eyes were upon us as well.

Now we began the very slow walk into the city and to this Central Park. The first thing I noticed was the buildings. Unlike those in the south, these were more like ours, made of timber and stone. All the streets were cobblestones, right up to the doorsteps of the many buildings. The buildings were all packed in tightly against each other, with narrow, dark alleys separating the many rows. Larger side streets periodically appeared, though not at regular intervals.

Some buildings, especially those made of the brown stone, were two stories tall. Nearly all of them had a pagoda style roof, quaint and rather pretty, I thought. What I found interesting was that these pagodas were each painted a slightly different color, contrasting sharply with the nearly uniform browns of the stone and wood buildings below them. Every so often, the buildings gave way to market places nearly a block long. Here, countless open-air shops thrived, although today all were closed down. Many people stood at the sides of the road, watching our slow procession, while others were walking much faster than us, heading in the same direction, to the funeral, I presumed.

Finally, as my feet were tiring from the constant tiny shuffling steps, we spied what must be the park ahead. Great throngs of people were flooding into the massive gardens. Now our lead guard continually called out, "Make way for Princess Sho Lin Wu!" Instantly, those in front of us would back out of the way and bow towards her. Thus, in spite of the enormous gathering, we were not in fact slowed down, but we were already going excruciatingly slowly in these tight dresses. I felt sorry for the poor men who had to carry the divan all this distance.

It took us over a half hour more to get to the main location. Ahead, we saw an enormous stack of wood, ready to be lit. High atop lay the nicely dressed body of Ho Lan Wu, his arms crossed over his chest, as if he was at peace with the universe. Each piece of wood in the funeral pyre was very carefully placed, perfectly arranged. The care someone had exercised was plainly evident.

I noticed that we were positioned up wind from where the flames and smoke would eventually drift, that would be fortunate, but then I realized even this had been carefully arranged. We were near the pyre's end by his feet. They placed Sho Lin's divan down close to the bottom wood. Now I saw to our left two other divans, her sisters. Ah, they were arranged in order of their ages. Furthest from us, some hundred feet, sat Tao Lin, the thirty year older sister. As we arrived, she bowed respectfully to Sho Lin, though I detected a great flow of either hatred or spite coming from Tao Lin, as though just seeing Sho Lin here was a disgrace to her. Between the two some fifty feet from us, lay Mi Lin, who was twenty-five. Tao Lin wore a pale red, tight fitting silken dress, much like Sho Lin's, while Mi Lin wore a similar dress of lavender.

I studied Tao Lin for a minute; she had a crooked nose, but glints of light suggested that she wore much rather gaudy jewelry, perhaps to compensate for her nose. I wondered if she had fallen and broken it as a child. I caught Tao Lin also studying us!

I turned my gaze upon Mi Lin; she was prettier than either of her two sisters, but a little later, I heard her speak. She had a squeaky, mousey sounding voice, not at all regal. Further, she was intensely shy. I suspected that she often did what her older sister asked of her. No doubt about it, Mi Lin was simply a follower, not a leader. Tao Lin had the bearing and manner of a leader about her.

Then, the advisor to Tao Lin walked over to Sho Lin. After a respectful bow and acceptance that he could speak to her, he said, "Tao Lin sends her welcome and says that she is glad that you could make her father's funeral. She asks why you are disgracing her with the presence of these foreigners?" I detected a note of cold covert hostility in his voice and wondered how Sho Lin would respond.

She bowed slightly. "We too are glad that we could make this all too soon funeral of my father. These are my friends from a distant land and have chosen to honor greatly both my father and me with their presence at his funeral. As you can see clearly, they wear trainer dresses, far more than our tradition demands. They do me the highest honor possible at this time of my great grief. Tell Tao Lin that I hope she has others with her that are offering her the greatest possible honor at this time of grief."

He bowed and returned to his Princess. I saw him bend over and repeat her words. A bit of ire flashed from Tao Lin's eyes, but it was gone in a second. Now it was time for the funeral. A trio of holy men walked as slowly as we women had, though I am not sure from where they had come. Each was chanting the same prayer, though I could not grasp their words. Incense flowed from a swinging chanter before them and they carried a large metal container. Coming behind the three were another three holy men carrying burning torches. A pair of each stopped before each of the three divans.

They spoke quietly to the three women. Then, many unseen musicians began to play haunting music. We had thus far heard little of their music. Soon many voices took up the song. I noticed that many of those in the crowd were now signing along. Louder and louder came the singing as thousands of voices continued to join them. As this was happening, I saw Ming and another woman rise and move to either side of Sho Lin. I glanced quickly over to the other two sisters, who also had a pair of servants beside them, helping them to stand up.

The holy man handed Sho Lin the metal container and she poured a token amount of the liquid upon the wood before her, before she handed it back to the holy man. Next, the holy man emptied the rest of the container at strategic locations nearby. With the haunting melody sung by tens of thousands of voices hanging in the air, the other man with the torch handed it to Sho Lin, bowing and backing away from her. Sho Lin looked over at her two sisters. Tao Lin moved first and the other two sisters quickly followed her lead, touching the torch to various spots within their arm's reach. Flames began to burn rapidly now. The holy man bowed and took the torch from Sho Lin and she again lay down on her divan, at which point Yan signaled all of us to begin to back up, after bowing to the deceased, which we did.

For a couple of minutes, we continued to back away, though we were now far enough back from the raging flames to be well out of harm's way. I wondered why we were so far way. The huge crowd continued to sing as the flames consumed the late emperor's body. By now, it was dark, but what happened next shocked us all. We had never seen anything like it. Suddenly, a great explosion was heard above the singing. Yan pointed to the sky and we saw a burning streak heading very high overhead. Without warning, it exploded into a huge ever-expanding sphere of red, sparkling flames, and then died out.

Boom. Boom. Boom. More and more explosions, then blue spheres, green spheres, and even yellow ones, overlapped the sky high overhead. Yan yelled out "Fireworks." This had our full attention like nothing had before! Yan called out, "The last one will be a red dragon that will lead Ho Lan Wu to join his ancestors, at least symbolically."

This was the most spectacular display any of us had ever seen. We had nothing whatsoever like this in our part of the world; this was totally new and extraordinary! By some magic these people had captured fires and could send them flying high into the sky, even cause them somehow to explode. This immediately demanded our full attention, and this we just had to learn all about, somehow! For nearly an hour, we were treated with this incredible aerial display of unparalleled proportions, from our viewpoint at least. Yan gave us a split second warning when the finale began. Yes, the last one exploded and began to form a monstrously huge red flying creature that they called a dragon. It was utterly unbelievable!

After it faded out, I noticed that the music and singing had ended. Most of the huge fire had gone out; only dying red embers remained of the pyre. Behind us, people were bowing to Sho Lin and retreating. I presumed that the event was now over. It was. Yan said urgently, "You are to stay right here at this spot. Do not move for any reason. I will be back shortly." He went up to Sho Lin, bowed, and received her finger signal. He leaned over while she whispered something to him. He bowed and backed away and left heading toward where the other sisters had been. Ming, thankfully, stepped back to our side.

"Yan is going to check on whether Sho Lin will be allowed to spend the night somewhere within the Imperial Palace. Yan will report. Sho Lin is very worried that her sisters will attempt to cause trouble of some kind. We must attend one more very important ceremony tonight, before we can retire to the palace or elsewhere. It is our custom upon the execution of the funeral for those who are vying for the throne to appear at the Holy Temple of Airs, there to announce to the Holy Airs that she is seeking the throne. Everything must go perfectly with this! Though unseen by us, the Grand Council will be watching our every move, looking, and grading us! Sho Lin is most worried about this, because this will be the first time for her sisters to make an attempt to disgrace her somehow."

Yan returned and whispered to Sho Lin. She gave the signal and her divan bearers once more picked her up. Ming hastened to her assigned position, and Yan fell back with us. "Trouble at the Imperial Palace — her sisters claim that there is no more room there for her to spend the night. This cannot be true, unless the sisters have somehow managed to find five hundred guests with which to fill it. We will return to the barge and head home once this final ceremony is completed."

Yan continued, "Now I am beginning to be very worried for Sho Lin. Has Ming told you where we are headed?"

"Yes, to the Temple of Airs, where she must somehow declare that she is a candidate for the throne," I replied as we shuffled along, hoping this would not be another lengthy walk!

"It is not far," he was reading our minds! "However, at the temple, her bearers must carry her perfectly up the many stone steps to the top, where she makes her simple declaration of intent. Then, they must carry her back down. I do not trust her sisters. I feel it in my bones that they will try in some way to disgrace her before the unseen Grand Council."

"We'll keep a sharp lookout, Yan," I volunteered. He seemed pleased that we cared so much for his Princess. I just concentrated on shuffling and not falling down.

Finally, we saw the temple ahead. Twenty stone steps led up to and open air temple with a typical pagoda roof. It was very well lighted with numerous gaily-decorated lanterns. A small crowd of people gathered, but was kept far back from the actual temple grounds. One Holy Man stood at the top, evidently there to witness the sister's declarations.

Then I saw the other two divans also at the top, one on either side. Evidently, they were waiting on Sho Lin to make her appearance. We all walked up to the steps, where we halted. This was as far as we were permitted to go. I thought it interesting that the other two sisters had their crew at two adjacent sides, which forced Sho Lin to go up the middle between them. Yet, what possible trap could they have created for Sho Lin?

I wanted to hear what was being said, so I moved out of my body, and floated along just over the head of Sho Lin. Gracefully, her bearers carried her perfectly arrayed body on the divan up the steps. At the top, she smiled at the Holy Man and said clearly and distinctly, "I am Sho Lin Wu, third daughter of Ho Lan Wu. I am most honored to be a candidate for the position of Empress of Tashien." That was all, plain and simple. The man bowed before her, and she signaled her bearers to take her back down. At the same time, her sisters did likewise. Perhaps it was to be a showing of the care with which the bearers carried them down the steps?

About half way down, the stone beneath the lead bearer's foot gave way, and the man fell down. Instantly, Sho Lin's divan nearly fell over. I latched on to it at once and lifted it, carrying the vast majority of its weight. I sent to Yan, *Someone has sabotaged this stone step. Come at once.*

Sho Lin looked utterly petrified, so I sent to the bearers and her, *Relax. I am carrying most of the weight. Continue going down as if nothing has happened.* Unfortunately, the rear bearer also stepped on the broken stone and fell, just as Yan and Cedric were rushing to help the first man, whose leg was broken by the fall. *Just keep going, this will give them something to ponder,* I sent. Everyone looked on in complete and utter disbelief! Here was the obviously heavy divan with Sho Lin on it being carried gracefully down the steps with no one holding onto one entire side of it. Magic, perhaps.

Cedric pointed out the telltale marks of a tampering. Someone had intentionally chiseled away at the underlying stone so that the slightest pressure on the outer portion would cause it to break loose! Yan called out, "Sabotage here!" Immediately, six men came rushing to the step, while Cedric and Yan carried the man with the broken leg down; the other man, who had fallen onto him breaking his fall, walked down behind them, his head held down in disgrace.

One official man declared, "Yes, it is sabotage! Council members, you may see for yourselves if desired. There has been a deliberate attempt to disgrace Princess Sho Lin and her bearers here. I declare officially that no such disgrace has occurred here." The other men agreed and came down to Sho Lin, who had regained her composure, signaling that they were allowed to speak.

"Princess, please forgive this horrible attempt to disgrace you and your staff! Officially, there has been no disgrace to either you or your bearers. I do hope that the one recovers swiftly. We will conduct an official investigation into the deliberate tampering of the steps here. Please accept the forgiveness of all the Temple of Airs staff! We are most sorry at this awful event."

"Thank you. I accept your findings. Please find out who has attempted to disgrace me and see that they are dishonored for their crime. We will return to my palace tonight. Again, thank you." She bowed and he returned her bow and backed away from her.

"Sho Lin, I cannot carry your divan and walk myself in this dress. It takes all my attention to keep from falling," I whispered to her and Yan. "Is there someone else who can take the injured bearer's position? If not, would it be a dishonor if one of my men helped carry your divan?"

"You, you did that? I nearly fell out of the divan! Had I fallen, I would have been disgraced anyway! You have saved me! Thank you dearly! Yes, I have a spare bearer with us. We must talk once we are safely on my barge. Come. Let's get out of here fast."

I smiled, "Hey not too fast in these dresses!"

She chuckled, "In a manner of speaking, I meant." Quickly, we fell back into our marching order, except that Renzo and Cedric carried the injured bearer. The rest of us tried very hard to not stumble or fall down on the long shuffling walk back to the barge. I was never so glad to get lifted into the barge as I was this night — oh, just to sit down finally!

Once we were safely moving downstream, Tonia wanted to go over to the men's barge to set the bearer's leg. However, since women were not allowed to be on the men's barge, Cedric did it for her. About a half hour later, the barges stopped and several of her men went ashore, returning in a few minutes carrying sacks of hot food and most importantly lots of hot tea!

Safely hidden behind drawn blinds, Sho Lin could finally relax. "I hope you like the food. I signaled my men what to get just before we stopped."

"But how? You didn't say anything that I heard," I asked. She grinned.

"One of the very useful features of such long nails is that they can be used to make many different signs to my staff. Now then, Bethany, I do not know what to say or how to thank you for what you did for me back there. You totally saved me from a complete disgrace and being sent to the frozen wastes or killed! How can I ever repay you for such great kindness and honor?"

"This is what friends are for, Sho Lin. Friends help each other when needed. You needed all that I could do on such short notice. I have to admit though, had I not moved out of my body and been standing over you so that I could hear your short speech there, I would not have been able to react in time to save you from a disastrous fall. You could have been seriously hurt with a fall on those stones! We were very lucky tonight, very lucky. I am starving, may I eat?"

She laughed, "Eat, eat. You do not need my permission to eat when the blinds are closed. I am so nervous right now that I cannot eat. I keep seeing myself falling hard onto the stones!"

Ming added, "I thought for sure that it was all over in that instant when he fell. I heard his leg crack when he fell too. He is in much pain, but he does not show it. Who would have done that to you, Sho Lin?"

Between mouthfuls, I replied, "My bet is on Tao Lin. Mi Lin is too shy. She is a follower, not a leader. Can I have some tea please, Ming? This one is hot, hot, hot!"

"Sweet too, but yes, very hot." Ming handed me a teacup.

"I guess I will try a bite," Sho Lin sighed; she too was now feeling quite hungry. I watched her incredibly deft usage of the wooden sticks and marveled at her skill. I was mostly shoveling the food into my mouth. Eating calmed her down further. "I decided that with this attempt on me, we should return home as soon as possible, limiting the chances for another attempt to disgrace me or my staff. However, I doubt that the investigation will uncover the guilty party. If it was Tao Lin, she will have gone to extreme measures to see that it would not be traced back to her."

Over tea, we continued our discussion. She said, "I am so sorry that I have brought you into this mess. If I had known that my father was going to join his ancestors so soon, I would never have insisted that you stay around the palace this long. From now until the new Empress is chosen, we are all in dire peril. I will see that the guards are doubled around the palace, Bethany. I could not live with myself if any harm should come to you or your members!"

"Thanks, Sho Lin, dressed like this, we are pretty helpless ourselves. Yet, I can see the great wisdom you showed in asking us to wear them. Repeatedly, I saw eyes watching our every move. That we are deliberately honoring you by dressing this way I am very sure has not gone unnoticed by the Grand Council members, unless they are blind. Personally, I'm glad that we could help by such a simple thing as wearing these really tight, restrictive dresses." The rest of my group totally echoed my sentiments.

"Say, Sho Lin, there is one way you could thank us. What were those incredible flames in the sky? We have nothing like that in our part of the world, only the conjured flaming sheets that a few of us can create. What are the called? How are they made? Can we purchase some to take back with us? The sky show was the most fabulous thing that we have ever seen!"

Both Ming and Sho Lin giggled. Sho Lin replied, "Fireworks, we call of them fireworks. I know not how they are made, though. We have such displays many times each year, to celebrate many things. There are six very large factories in Shansee, which make them. I will send all of you with Yan to visit with them when we get home. I am sure that they will gladly make as many fireworks for you as you desire. It will be my thank you present, Bethany! Please let me do this tiny thing for you."

"Thanks! Wait until the men hear about this!"

"I'm telling them right now," teased Rosina, who was already making the telepathic connections. All of us were totally enthralled by the fireworks display!

"But how is she doing that?" asked Sho Lin. "Oh, how did I hear you in my mind back at the temple?" She finally realized that I had actually somehow spoken to her right then when the nearly disastrous fall had occurred.

"Sho Lin, some of we Santi have a very special skill. We can communicate across any distance with what we call telepathy. Rosina is telling the others as I spoke to you and your bearers back then. It is a very effective way for one spiritual being to communicate to another. May I show you?"

"Please do!" Sho Lin replied.

"Me too," added Ming.

I reached out and touched their minds and made a Mind Link between us three. *See how's this? You only need to think your thought and we all will hear it. Try it, think something.*

This is the most incredible thing! It is so, so sensual, so intimate! Sho Lin thought.

Yes, so utterly intimate, so delicate like frost on the spider's web in the fall, Ming sent.

Well said, Ming. Exactly like that, so delicate.

But can you read my private thoughts? I sensed a bit of concern from Sho Lin.

While a telepath could well do that, we would consider the doing of that to be a horrible, horrible disgrace! None of us would ever do that — read the innermost private thoughts of a person, not even our spouses.

Sho Lin flushed very red, but I did not inquire why, though in hindsight, perhaps I should have. I broke the connection, and we three chatted about this until I nearly fell asleep.

Chapter 18 Sneak Attack

April 23, we arrived back at Shansee and familiar ground once more. While Sho Lin handled matters of her province, Yan escorted us into the city, riding once more the man-powered carts. Yes, dressed as we women were, our men had to lift us in and out of the carts, but they seemed more than eager to do so. For half a day, we shuffled around the six fireworks factories. I let Renzo and Cedric work out how these marvelous devices were made, while we women spent our time picking out fireworks to take back home with us. Len Shu, one of the kindest managers, spent quite a lot of his time helping us pick out fireworks to create a perfect aerial show. Again, we faced their attitude of "if it is worth doing, then it must be done perfectly." In the end, we chose sufficient fireworks to put on four displays. I hoped that this would not seem too greedy to Sho Lin.

Next, we placed an order for ten more show's worth of fireworks, but these would be paid in full with gold from the next Santi trading caravel. Our order would not be ready until the fall, so there would be plenty of time for the caravel to arrive. Around noon, we had finally finished the orders, all the looking, and window shopping, when Len Shu bowed to me, saying, "Please, will you accept lunch with me? It would give me great honor to host you all for a simple lunch." Hungry, I agreed.

We all shuffled after Len to a nearby restaurant. This was the first time that we had eaten out in a local dining facility. Len was around fifty years old with a typical oval face and neat moustache with the two pigtails on either side of his mouth. "This is one of the finer dining establishments on this side of Shansee," he explained as we entered the Dau Doh. As we entered, a waitress bowed to Len and then to me and then the rest of our party. She was dressed in a light green dress rather similar to ours, though hers had a walking slit.

The plush red carpeting beneath our feet felt soft and elegant. I noticed that she adjusted her shuffling steps to match ours, going no faster than we could manage. We were seated at a long table covered with a silk tablecloth, which had various flowers in its design. Many candles provided the illumination and gave off scents of springtime flowers. While we waited to be served and sipping carefully prepared tea, Len said, "I wish to thank you all for so greatly honoring our beloved Princess Sho Lin Wu. While we have occasionally had foreign visitors here, none has ever so greatly honored her as you have. Long have we merchants been waiting for you to visit our shops. I hope that you will be able to come to our business district more often now. I'm sure that Yan will permit it." Yan smiled, nodding that he would. "However, for such great ladies as yourselves, I would insist that you avoid the far west end. All towns have a, shall we say, seedier section."

After an exquisite meal, we thanked our host, who was very pleased that we also enjoyed the meal with him. He added with a twinkle in his eye, "When you hold your fireworks display, you will find a small token of our thanks for immense honor you have done for our Princess." Now my curiosity was aroused. Only much later was it satisfied when we eagerly rummaged through the many crates of fireworks. There was one very large unit that we had not ordered. It was labeled Red Dragon!

Back at the palace, a great deal of the usual pressure was lifted from Sho Lin. Gone was the everyday worry about being perfect because of some vague future event. Yet, the reality that the judging was now going on added new concerns and worries; some suggested that a monitor was actually present in her daily court meetings, disguised somehow. Sho Lin was even more vigilant to dress immaculately perfectly and to follow diligently and vigorously every protocol. With her time so occupied, we were allowed much more free time to visit the fabulous shops and markets within the city proper.

However, as before, Natale and I accompanied her each evening for her slow stroll through the formal gardens. One night she explained their construction. "You have seen all the many architectural constructions blended into the gardens?" We said that we had. "Well, that is one of the primary objectives, to blend such constructions into the pure, essence and beauty of nature, such that it appears as if the structure itself is a natural part of nature. This takes a very great deal of knowledge and wisdom to create. I believe here in these gardens, our many gardeners and artists have achieved a most perfect result."

"Yes, they have indeed. Now that you point it out, I can most definitely see it. We were wondering why all these little constructions were here. Some we assumed would be to protect someone from the rain, should they be out on these grounds."

This night, we wandered far into the garden, because Sho Lin felt like walking more than she normally did, though for her, any walking was not only awkward, but somewhat painful, given the condition of her feet, being so out of proportion to her five foot seven inch frame. Hers were five inches in length, but three inches of that was her heel. Her toes had been bound and forced back so that now her toes touched her ankle. By having kept them bound so tightly as a child and into her teen years, she had restricted their overall growth so that her feet might be the size of those of a six or seven year old child. With her heel occupying most of the five-inch walking surface, she had nearly nothing with which to maintain her balance easily. Yet, if this action she had endured with her feet helped her achieve her goal of becoming the Empress of all Tashien, she would be well repaid for her sacrifice. This was her viewpoint, which she carefully explained to us once more this evening.

"Yet, just between you and me, there are times that I wish I had not done this. Sometimes I would just like to be free to come out and walk in the gardens by myself. Yet, always, this I cannot do alone as I am now."

"Say, I've been meaning to ask you, Sho Lin, if you do become the Empress, will you then be able to take a sea trip and visit our land for a short while? We would love to share our world with you one day," I asked.

"Oh yes, the Empress is free to do what she will, unlike a Princess. While I am here, always there is the day that I am facing now, the time of the Choosing. Think of the horrid disgrace that would befall me if I was in your land when my father died. Why, I would miss his funeral and lose the opportunity to declare my desire to become Empress! Yet as Empress, I would be free to visit your land, and I would dearly love to come one day, if you permit it."

"Permit it? I insist on it, Sho Lin, when you become Empress, that is." She smiled and bowed slightly to me. "How long does it usually take the Council to choose the new Empress?"

"It is only May Day; one must be patient, Bethany," she replied. "This is a very important decision that they must make, and I am sure that they wish to weight everything so that we have the best possible Empress chosen. According to the historians, sometimes it has been nearly a half a year before a council has made their choice known. However, I do not think they will be so long this time. I have so many perfects that my sisters do not. Yet, perhaps I have overlooked something that I should not have, who can say. It is done now at least — the long years of striving to be perfect every day. At least now I can relax from all that. What is done is done. We have walked a very long way tonight. I thank you for this. Perhaps we ought to be starting back now."

Tonight, dark clouds occasionally blocked out the moon, which was near first quarter. Rain was on its way here, but not eminent. Slowly we began walking back toward the palace, which was at least a half mile from us. When we were about halfway back, we heard distinct cries and shouts of alarm. "That's the sound of a sword battle!" I exclaimed! "Something is terribly wrong at the palace!" Damn, dressed as we were, we could only shuffle along very slowly.

"Bethany, if we are attacked, you can barely move! We have no weapons with us," Natale whispered urgently.

"What can be happening at my palace? Never have there been sword battles at nighttime! Bethany, I am very worried! Could my palace be under attack? If so, I cannot be seen walking around the gardens by those that fight! I am doomed to disgrace or worse."

"Let's keep walking and see what comes of it. Your guards are there and so are all of our people. If we see anyone, I will pick you up and somehow carry you, Sho Lin! Come on." We continued our snail's walk back to her palace. The sounds grew louder by the minute, and it sounded like a wholesale battle was occurring. We neared a clearing from which we could at last see the distant palace.

Dozens of men dressed entirely in black from head to foot were swarming over the grounds, the porch, the roof, even filling out of the back doors and windows of the palace. Many of her guards lie on the ground just beyond the porch, dead or wounded, which, we could not tell. From their positions, we determined that these guards, knowing that Sho Lin was out in the gardens, had tried to set up a defensive line to prevent them from entering the gardens. Off to our right, we saw our people fighting away. Renzo and Emil had formed up a battle line, while our women were standing behind them using defensive spells as they could; too much fire was a bit dangerous here. Yet, lightning bolts would work, and now I saw they had switched tactics and were blasting bolts at some of these men in black.

Instinctively, I picked up Sho Lin. She put her arms around my neck and held on tightly. "Ninja! These are very wicked, evil assassins, the very best of fighters, who far exceed the skill of my poor guards! I was not expecting that my sister would resort to having me assassinated! I am afraid that not only have I signed my own death warrant, but also I have doomed you to a horrible death here at my palace. Oh, god, what have I done?" She wailed.

"Dressed like this, I can barely walk! Natale, if my body begins to fall over, hold me still please!"

"Absolutely. If any come after us, I'll get them too," she said determination in her voice.

Now we were finally spotted by the ninja. At least a dozen began scrambling towards us! Over two dozen were swarming all over Renzo and my group. From the corner of my eye, I saw that only our Protectors stood any chance at all with these highly skilled assassins! Emil, Damien, and Renzo had now formed a defensive line, protecting all the others, with Henry, Benet, and Cedric desperately trying to hold either flank. Inside their small protective circle stood Rosina, Linda, Tonia, and Michelle.

Rosina, move out of your body and lightning bolt any of these here that Natale holds still please! I frantically sent her. She looked our way and responded at once.

The first ninja was rushing us now, curved sword held behind him, ready for his deadly strike. Natale stopped him mid-stride, like a frozen statue! Boom! Came the peal of thunder as Rosina struck the target; the man went flying through the air. One down, far too many to go!

Just then, San See Tou came racing into the battle, knocking three ninja over as he moved to a position just before us. One against two dozen plus, bad odds.

I had a choice to make. I can only do one thing at a time. Either I could lift us three up safely out of the assassin's reach or I could begin to pick up and pitch the assassins. There were too many of them coming at us at one time. Decision made. I couldn't leave San See to fight them alone. I floated up above us, grabbed a hold of a ninja who was rushing towards us and threw his body into a tree. I hear the crack of bones; he did not get up.

I called out, "Natale, keep your eyes open, hold any that are shooting at us, if none, hold one so Rosina can get a bolt to him."

Boom! Boom! Boom! Came the echoing thunder, such as had never been heard before in this city — so deadly close, so frequent in occurrence. San See took on those that got to close to us, while I continued picking up their bodies and throwing them into any available hard surface. Several in the rear of the swarm now thought better of rushing us and began to throw spinning disks at us. Thank god for Natale, as soon as she saw one coming flying at us, she acted, holding it still; then by letting it go, the disk fell harmlessly to the ground.

San See took out another one, but one dashed around him. Natale froze him mid-stride. Boom! Rosina blasted him. Still we were in danger of being overrun as they continued to race towards us. San See was now backed into a corner, three ninja after him, giving him no maneuvering room. I picked up the one behind him and gave that one a pitch. Natale froze yet another one and boom came Rosina's reply.

From the corner of my vision, I could now see the other Santi and the Traveler Circle racing to our rescue, if only we could hold on for a bit longer. While San See eliminated another one, he took several sword cuts in the process; he was tiring rapidly. Five ninjas farthest from us began to shoot arrows, hoping to get the Protectors or us. Again, Natale was challenged, but stopped all but two, but one hit San See in his right leg while the other zipped towards me. I had barely enough time to grab the shaft before it would strike Sho Lin; its tip just barely touched her dress. Boom, Rosina handled one of the archers, who pivoted to shoot back at her. However, too many of their own men were in the way.

During their momentary lapse of attention, San See managed to hobble back closer to us. "Can you get it out?" he asked. I bent down, putting Sho Lin close enough to grasp the shaft.

"Pull on it hard, Sho Lin," I ordered. She gave it a pull, while I braced us from falling. I nearly fell over backwards when it came out. Only Natale's quick action to hold me still prevented me from falling. During this brief time, three more closed to battle San See.

I pitched one into a tree, while two lightning bolts knocked the other two over and nearly knocked us over as well. Natale had to hold both San See and me from falling. Boom! Boom! Boom! Now the lightning bolts came much more frequently; the Traveler's were aiding Rosina.

I spied ten over on our right, who were fighting my group. Then suddenly and without warning, they fled the area, running back around the left side of the palace. Four did not make it, because lightning bolts sent their bodies flying wildly through the air! Three eventually did escape, however.

Just as suddenly as the attack had begun, it ended. San See collapsed onto the ground, bleeding from numerous wounds. "Natale, see if you can keep him from bleeding, I have to get Sho Lin to the porch." I lifted us both up, moved our bodies over to the porch, and sat us down gently onto the soft ground right in front of the porch. As soon as my feet touched down, I gently lowered Sho Lin to the porch. I flew my body back, yelling, "Back soon!" I rushed to join the others, though Sho Lin was mostly in shock now.

"Damage report!" I barked out. Tonia was already working on Renzo; Linda had gone to aid Damien; Ronina was helping Emil. They were wounded, but I hoped not too badly. Our Santi fighters, Angel and Mary Beth, were already going from fallen assassin to assassin, stabbing them in the heart to make double sure they would not rise again. Muriel and Helena rushed to begin aiding the fallen guards, while Virginia raced to assist Natale, and Ellie ran inside the palace. The other Traveler men raced around the complex looking for other ninjas and to see who else was injured that was not out back. For a time, it was chaos, which I attempted to organize rapidly.

"Let's get the wounded moved into the throne room. There is a lot of light and open space there." Several of Sho Lin's servants came out on the porch, visibly shaken up. Some had large bruises. They had been roughly handled and physically thrown out of the way of the swarming ninjas in their search for the Princess. I let them carry their Princess to her divan, which was still in the throne room. At least Sho Lin would have a front row seat. The Traveler men reappeared, saying they found bodies scattered all over the place. I told them to place the dead back here on the porch and get the wounded into the throne room.

Next, I spied Natale over by Henry, applying pressure to stem the blood flow from a wound in his arm, while Muriel was putting a temporary bandage on him. Since there was nothing else I could really do out here, I went inside to get the throne room ready for healing operations. "So many wounded," exclaimed Sho Lin, who was starting to recover from the shock. "What should we do?"

"We need tons of boiling water, many blankets, and all the bandages you can find. Here, I'll start making places for the wounded to lie," I replied taking a stack that Ming had brought in, noticing that she was bleeding from a bad fist smash to her face. "You go get more, old ones; these will be covered in blood soon." Like a mother hen, I kept the seven servants busy. The cook and her helpers came running in, so I set them to work on the boiling water project. One by one, others brought the wounded inside. I could barely keep up with making the temporary resting places. A half hour later, with many pots of boiling water steaming up the place, forty-three were resting on the makeshift beds.

I followed Tonia around like a mother hen as she quickly prioritized our wounded Circle members. Renzo had taken two sword cuts, one to his left arm and one to his right leg. I was grateful that he only needed stitches. Emil had one bad cut and several smaller ones. Damien had two nasty wounds to show for his fight. Henry, Cedric, and Benet each had one nasty sword wound. Thank heavens none of our people were critically wounded!

Tonia with the assistance of her pressure applier, Natale, began working on the many others, while we worked on our fellows. I began to sew up Renzo, who complained, "Ouch, dear. Say, that was a good move throwing them into the trees. These men were the best fighters I've ever heard of, better than I am, as you can see. Sorry that I couldn't get to you in time, I tried."

"Hey, you had to protect the others, buster. I think you did a great job of it, now hold still, will you? None of our women was hurt and none of you is critically wounded. I think that you all did very well indeed." It took me a half hour to get him all fixed up.

After I put the final touch on his bandages, he said, "I think I will just sleep a while." He was utterly exhausted and drained. I moved on to check on the others. Henry put up a forced smile; he was hurting. By morning all of them would be hurting, of that I knew firsthand.

I joined the others who had moved on to the many wounded of Sho Lin's personnel. Tonia and Natale were working to save the life of Jin Han, the historian, who had taken a bad belly wound. It looked horrible, Tonia, with the able assistance of Natale, who could precisely apply holding forces, had half of his guts out and was carefully sewing them back together. Muriel was working on Yan's right arm, trying to save it; it had been sliced clear to the bone. I cleaned off my needles and knives in a pot of boiling water and knelt down beside San See, whose wounds were many. Removing the temporary bandages, he began bleeding heavily again. I set to work quickly.

While we were working, several of Sho Lin's huan came into the room; none said a word, just surveyed the situation, looked for permission of Sho Lin, and went to her side. Soon, they left, and I forgot about them, concentrating on saving the life of Sho Lin's lover. It must have been near dawn when we finally finished the last one. My back was aching from all the bending over. I stood up and stretched. All of us were one bloody mess. These dresses were now history. There was Sho Lin, still sitting on her divan, nearly asleep, but staring at San See, who was now unconscious.

She said softly, "Will he live? Thank you, thank all of you! I have hot food waiting. Will you sleep here or in your rooms? What should we do here while you sleep? My huan have sent a hundred soldiers to guard us. I believe that we are safe enough for the present."

"Food!" we all chorused. At once, Ming, whose face had been doctored but was now swelling up, came at once with a tray for me. Her helpers brought in many other trays. I sat down and told her, "San See is unconscious, but I believe that he will recover." Then, I ate quickly. A bit later, I added, "I think it will be wise for us to sleep right here. Some may need our attention at once."

Angel, who had been helping as she could, spoke up, "Commander, the official count as of this moment: thirty-one dead ninja, three escaped. Twenty-five dead guards and staff, mostly the grounds keepers, I am told. They were the first that the ninja encountered when they raided this palace. I've pulled in half of the Santi from the caravels; they are on duty outside. You can sleep in peace, sir."

"Thanks Angel. I need sleep now." I forgot everything else and lay down beside Renzo and was asleep at once. It was late afternoon when Tonia roused me.

"I could use a breather, Bethany. I've checked everyone's bandages. Could you spell Muriel and me for a few hours?" She had not yet slept! I got up and helped her to get comfortable. She and Muriel fell into a deep sleep almost at once.

I looked over the bodies; many were now stirring. Dried blood was everywhere, but they all lived, including Jin, who was still unconscious. Sho Lin still sat on her divan, but I'd never seen her look so disheveled. "I've been giving instructions and orders all night while you slept," she whispered.

"How many of your staff is up and able? I'd like to start cleaning up everyone who is awake and then cleaning your room here. Sorry about the mess, but we needed the space."

"I've got a dozen volunteers; my staff is now sleeping. Just tell them what you want done, please." She signaled and twelve women came in carrying buckets, mops, and rags. Other had towels and soap. I decided to be methodical, starting with our group who were in the best shape.

"Okay Renzo, bath time," I nudged him awake.

"Oh, I hurt all over!" he complained. I began washing him off. Once he was cleaned up as much as possible, Sho Lin had a food station ready. I helped him hobble over to the far side and let him eat.

"Normally, back home, we have an infirmary building where all the wounded could stay. That way it is easy to watch over the wounded while they recover, at least until they are on the mend," I explained to Sho Lin.

"How about the banquet hall? It is seldom used. Ming, will you show Bethany where it is at?" She and I shuffled off to see this room, which I had not yet seen. It held a very long table, but was large. This would work. I sent Ming back to tell everyone to come here when they had eaten. I set to work rearranging the room. Soon, six men arrived carrying small beds. Sho Lin had thought ahead and put her staff to work. Together, we began arranging them side by side along one wall. Not long after, Renzo came wandering in, and I pointed him to the first bed and put him to sleep again.

An hour later, all but two men had been cleaned up as much as possible, fed, and put to bed in the banquet hall. The two who had been most critical were still unconscious. One was Yan; the other was a guard who nearly lost his arm. These two were carried in by the men; both had been cleaned up. San See was at least up and drinking liquids, pretty amazing for one with so many wounds, I thought. I returned to the throne room. Only we women were present; her servants had already begun to clean the floors, and the blood-soaked blankets had been taken away already.

Sho Lin said, "If you will all come with me, it is time that we all had a bath. We will use my private tub. Everything there has been already arranged for us." To our total surprise, she stood up and offered me her arm, which I took at once, and Natale rushed over to her other side. Since this was now no longer public, she could walk us personally to the bath. We dutifully followed her, forced as usual to match her short strides still wearing our blood-covered dresses. It was not too far, however.

Her private bath was large enough to hold all of us. In the center was a large wooden tub, just barely fitting all of us in it at one time. We saw that clean clothes, towels, and wash rags were already laid out for us — in a perfectly arranged sequence no less. "If you will assist me," Sho Lin said to me. I carefully undid her dress and under garments, and then I did the same for Natale. Surprising me, Sho Lin undid mine!

Now we could all see her incredibly tiny feet. Yes, we stared at them and she smiled, for here in this land, her feet were the ultimate in feminine beauty. I was glad I didn't live here for this single reason. Even more surprising, Sho Lin insisted on washing off both Natale and me! We in turn washed her as well. She whispered to me, "I owe you more than I can ever repay you, Bethany." I knew that she meant it and believed it. During the bath, Sho Lin asked, "Are there bad men in your country? Here, we have bandits in the outlands and evil ninjas who may be anywhere."

"Yes, we have them too. However, Sho Lin, I will say this: there are far more good people than bad. Only a very small number of persons have evil in their minds." She took heart in that even in our land there were evil men around. To her, this whole affair had been quite shocking and terrifying.

One thing, don't let a bunch of women into a relaxing bath, all on their own. We did not reappear for nearly two hours! With our hair nicely brushed and in clean clothing, our small troop shuffled once more to the throne room. We found it was now spotless. We helped Sho Lin to her divan and then went to inspect all the patients.

A few days later things were mostly back to normal, even a few of the men had been released from the makeshift infirmary. At last after supper, I said, "Well, Sho Lin, we've finally got everything under control again. How about going for a walk in the gardens now?"

She looked terrified, "Perhaps I shall never walk there again. Such bad memories."

"Oh come on, we've got plenty of guards around. I am sure that they will not strike again. You haven't been out of the palace in days. Fresh air will do you good." I knew that I needed to get her out into the garden again or she might not ever face it.

Slowly, Natale, Sho Lin, and I shuffled out into the gardens once more. I was right; soon she began to relax. "You know, there will be repercussions from this attempt on my life. My huan identified the bodies and searched them. When a ninja takes on an assignment, he must carry something given to him from the person making the assignment. They found tokens that could only have come from my sister, Tao Lin. It was she who hired these assassins to kill us. In this universe, for every action, there is an opposite reaction, so it is observed. So be it."

"What do you mean?" I asked, not quite sure what she meant by this.

"If the wind blows in your face, you feel it and your hair blows out behind your head. If you push on my hand, either I push back or I move my hand back. If you drop a stone into the pond here, a small tower of water rises up and then falls back down, ripples float across the pond hitting the sides before rippling back to the center once more. Each action that we take will meet with an opposite reaction. My sister has taken a very bad action. That she has hired the ninja to assassinate me is now widely known in Tashien. Every day, word spreads to even more people."

"Had the ninja been successful in killing me, she would never have been discovered as the one who ordered the assassination. She would then undoubtedly become the new Empress. However, because of you and your people that effort has failed completely. Now she must face the reaction back on to her. Tao Lin's disgrace is now just as monumental as the honor that she stood to gain if she had succeeded, but now it has gone beyond my power to control."

"What do you mean? What will happen to Tao Lin?" asked Natale.

"Had she merely personally tried to disgrace me, nothing, unless I chose to retaliate in kind, which I have never done. However, she chose to have me assassinated — a Princess and a contender for the throne. What happens to her is the reaction against what she attempted here. If she is very lucky, she will only lose her head. I am utterly powerless to stop the inevitable reaction back flow. Only the Emperor or Empress could save her now, but there is neither at the moment."

"But who would do this thing to her?" I asked.

"The lowest peasant who works the rice paddies, the bread maker, the tinsmith, the merchants — any of our people who are not evil men, if given any chance, would strike her down. However, it is far worse than that, I am afraid. My huans, having seen the assassination attempt, consider it now a matter of personal honor to bring the reaction to Tao Lin. My entire army is probably already approaching her as we speak. Only the Emperor or Empress has the power to override a huan's sense of honor and make them cease in their attempt to bring the proper reaction back to Tao Lin."

"But won't that just bring about another blood bath? Won't Tao Lin's army fight back against yours when they get close to Tao Lin?" I asked, afraid of yet another bloody war.

"My huans have taken several of the dead ninja with them. They will throw them at the feet of her huans, to show them the disgrace she has created. Her huans then will turn on her as well. My sister, Tao Lin, is doomed beyond words. If she is very lucky, one will cleanly slice off her head. If she is unlucky, well, I don't even want to think about that possibility."

I thought about how to respond. She and her people were mimicking the physical universe, in that for every action there is an equal, but opposite reaction. However, we are spiritual beings and are not subject to the physical universe and its laws. We can show mercy and compassion, for example. I decided to explain what we Santi had done with our method for the rehabilitation of those who have brought harm to others. Case in point was the Holy Paladin General who had cut off the hands of Ariana Zar and then had given himself up to the Santi, seeking a cure for his recurrent nightmares of what he had done. He had come to his senses, repented his actions, and was now working hard on making amends to his victims, by serving as a priest to those in need all over Velona. By the time that we returned to the porch, I believe that Sho Lin finally understood, though there was nothing that she could do about it at this time. By her sister's own action, it was taken out of Sho Lin's power to make any difference in the outcome.

She did say, "If I should become Empress, I will make an attempt to try your method with the criminals. Perhaps it will work here too, though it is much faster to dole out the reaction."

I agreed with her, "Yes, it certainly is easier and faster to strike back. It takes a really big spiritual being to not retaliate but to work towards the rehabilitation of another." She smiled and we entered the palace.

San See was finally able to get up and move about on his own power. He bowed to Sho Lin, and said, "I go now to my quarters to recover, Princess. I am yours if you need me."

"Go now, Honorable Protectorate. You have shown me the highest of honor, bravery, and courage. It shall never be forgotten." He hobbled out and returned to his own quarters.

On May 11, a messenger arrived from her huan. Tao Lin was dead. Her own head huan got to her before Sho Lin's huan could find her. He had slit her throat in one clean cut. Sho Lin's men found her dead on her divan. Half of Sho Lin's army was now staying in Zau, watching over the Imperial Palace, while the rest would be here to protect her tomorrow. A somber Sho Lin told us the sad news. "Her own huan — she even disgraced and dishonored her own army leader. By now, even he is dead, probably by his own hand. He would not be able to live with the disgrace she cast upon him."

"Will there be a funeral for her like that which was held for your father?" Natale asked.

"No, her body will be cremated and her ashes spread upon a pig sty, befitting the utter disgrace that she brought upon herself by her actions. She must have been awfully desperate to have taken such a gamble," Sho Lin said sadly.

The next morning, the fanciest coach that we had yet seen in this land pulled up outside her palace. At once, her entire staff suddenly became instantly formal. As we gathered with many others into the Royal Court room, we saw an elderly man waiting for us. Immaculately dressed, his grey hair was long and his twin ponytail moustaches the longest I'd seen. His fingernails were also quite long, perhaps approaching five inches. He was dressed in the finest yellow silks. His back was slightly bowed from old age, and he walked very slowly into the room, pausing to bow to Sho Lin, who gave him permission to enter. Ming whispered to us that he was a representative from the Grand Council, their spokesman.

"Princess Sho Lin Wu, I have come to give you the decision of the Grand Council. I have already been to the palaces of the other two contenders to the Imperial Throne. It is the final decision of the council that you, Sho Lin Wu, are to be our new Empress. On behalf of the council, please accept our congratulations. You embody all that can be asked of any Empress of Tashien. The throne is yours. May you guide us well in the many days to come." He bowed low to his new Empress. She returned his bow as well.

Then, to everyone's surprise, including Sho Lin's, he turned to me and bowed, I returned his. He spoke, "Commander Bethany Rose Wilkins Pazzio le'Goeur, over these many centuries of our long history, we have had foreigners visit our lands. Never has a foreigner ever so greatly honored one of our Princesses or Empresses. I see that even yet you do so honor her. You have earned the complete respect and honor of the entire Grand Council. Be it known that you and your people will always be most welcome in Tashien." He again bowed and I returned his. Without saying another word, he slowly backed out of the room, pausing at the entrance to bow to Sho Lin. Then, he was gone.

The room was utterly silent; you could hear a pin drop. Now that the official notice had come, everyone was speechless, stunned. Sho Lin spoke first, her voice but a squeak, "Someone pinch me; tell me this isn't real!"

Ming found her voice, "Oh Sho Lin! You did it! You are now the Empress of all Tashien! Let me be the first to bow to our new Empress!" She immediately did so. Now the room exploded with congratulations and great joy, so much so, that all formality was completely lost!

I went up to her and said, "In our land when something this wonderful happens, we give her a big hug. Permit me?" Sho Lin smiled and opened her arms and we hugged tightly. Natale wanted a hug too, and Sho Lin held her tightly as well.

At last, recovering her composure, Sho Lin said, "Go forth and spread the word; tonight we shall have a great feast to honor the occasion. The plans that we must make are quite lengthy. Ming, as my first formal proclamation, I hereby declare that you may marry the man of your choosing. Please, you must go now, find him, and rejoice together with him. You have brought him great honor!" Ming squealed with joy and happiness, so much so that she forgot to bow before rushing out! Sho Lin merely smiled as she watched her faithful servant's joy.

For the rest of the day, Sho Lin entertained numerous callers who wished to express their best wishes for her stunning achievement. The confusions and commotions finally ended as we all sat down for the banquet. Sho Lin said that tonight all over the city, her people would also be feasting in her honor. It seemed the entire province was rejoicing in the tremendous honor that she had brought all of them.

After the meal, Sho Lin asked to have a private meeting with me. We still sat around the now empty table. She carefully prepared the tea for us, only she placed three cups on the table. She had a mischievous look in her eyes, I noticed. Presently, San See Tou appeared at the doorway, bowing to her. "San See, please come and sit here by me." He bowed again and took the indicated seat across from me. I sat on her left, he, her right.

"This is a very private meeting. The customs and traditions of Tashien have been firmly established now for many centuries. At this time, the Empress must choose her mate, who would become the Emperor of Tashien. She should choose for love as well as for honor and many other reasons. This is very awkward for me to say," she flushed, becoming rather embarrassed. She took a sip of her tea. Politely, he and I followed suit.

"In my case, the choice comes down to love. All other aspects are in perfect harmony; none would disagree with these other aspects. For me, the deciding factor must be love. Unfortunately, I am deeply in love with two people. My heart belongs to both of you." San See flushed; this was his proudest moment in his life. However, I began to wonder what she meant by this.

"History has shown that the Empress may choose another woman as her mate; she would then be the Emperor in name. Bethany, I am deeply in love with you. The absolute greatest honor and reward that I can possibly give to you, one that my heart yearns to give you, is to have you as my mate. Yet, I know that you are already married to a wonderful man. Ours would be one of loving pleasure only. San See, I am madly in love with you also, as you have known all these many years. We have worked so hard to keep it a secret. Now at long last I can choose you to be my mate, and for the first time we can at last share a kiss!"

"I have thought long and hard about this, often not falling asleep until near morning. What I am proposing is very simple. When Bethany is in Tashien, she and I would share my bed in loving pleasure befitting our love. I know that you will be leaving soon, and it may be years before you can return. Yes, I still greatly desire to be taken to your land and see this Velona with my own eyes one day. I realize that our time together is very short, Bethany, but the love that I have for you, I shall treasure forever. I will also mate with you, San See, and you shall be Emperor of Tashien as well, yielding the post only during those few days when Bethany is here with me. Worry not, no jealousy, ours can only be a love borne of pleasure. We would not detract from your marriage, Bethany, nor would it lessen our marriage, San See."

"So I must ask you, San See, will you be willing to accept this compromise and allow Bethany to share my bed during the few days that she is here?"

"Sho Lin, I would do anything for you. The compromise is a very worthy one and very practical as well. I would be most honored to have Bethany sleep in your bed with you, to share your love."

"Bethany," Sho Lin continued, "I know that it is not the custom in your land for two women to bed or two men either. I have asked Linda discretely about this many days ago. Yet so strong is my love for you that, though so utterly embarrassed as I am to speak of this openly now, I must, if only to be completely honest with myself and with you. If you feel that you cannot do this, please, it does me no dishonor to so say. I can understand if you do not. Many people love another who does not share that love for themselves. Wonderful is the couple who do love each other, as Ming and her gardener, as San See and myself, as you and Renzo."

"Even if you do not share my love, consider allowing me to share mine with you. I am not like you or any of the rest of your women. I can barely walk and have none of the skills that you women possess that I know of — I only know how to be a good ruler and how to give much personal pleasure. I am highly skilled in the giving of pleasure to my mate. Compared to anyone of you, this is so insignificant a thing that I can do, but it is all that I have to offer you for all that you have done for me and San See. I would dearly like to share the two things that I can offer to you, pleasure of the body and the undying allegiance and support of a vast country."

"If you need other reasons, perhaps to help explain it so that others from your land can understand it better, if we mate, then great honor and power lies in your hands, a power that can unite our two countries for all time. My people will see our union in just such a light. Further, if your land is ever threatened with attack, all of Tashien and its armies will be at your side, just let us know."

"My last plea uses your own words to me, while on our walks at night. Love is composed of both great admiration and a great respect for the other person. I do feel this for you, Bethany, as deeply as I feel it for San See! You need not answer me tonight. Go now and discuss this with your loving husband, Renzo, and whomever you wish. However, please pledge them to secrecy about this. It would disgrace me to have this become widely known among my people. This is a very private matter and decision we make."

My face was hot, very probably red. I didn't know what to say to her. She had given me a way out, at least for tonight. "Yes, thank you for the great honor, Sho Lin. You are right. I must discuss this with Renzo. Am I right in thinking that tonight you and San See can take a walk in the garden by yourselves?"

She and he both grinned from ear to ear. "Yes, that and very much more!" she replied. I bowed to them both and headed for our bungalow. I needed Renzo now!

"She wants to what?" exclaimed Renzo, his eyes nearly popping out of his head. I'd just explained what Sho Lin had asked me. "Marry you? I thought she wanted to marry her Protectorate, San See."

"She does. I could see it in their eyes tonight. Both are in love with each other, and now at last, they have a way to fulfill their love. However, she apparently also is in love with me, equally, if I believe her. Of course, I am not in love with her. I respect her, but I love you, not her." He smiled and gave me a hug.

Renzo thought for a bit and replied, "Well, if we try to take her point of view for a minute, she certainly had seen a great deal to respect and admire in you, my love. You are one hot woman indeed, to say nothing of what you have done for her, saving her life and from the intended disgraceful fall at the funeral. If I were her, I certainly would consider that I owed you a tremendous thank you and I can see how she could also believe that she now loves you as well. Tons of admiration and respect is really going to translate into deep feelings for you, Bethany. Honestly, Linda and I were both discussing this point."

"What point?" I was slightly missing his point.

"We have both done and given her things she considers of immense, nearly monumental value. Enter the exchange factor. She must find something to give back that she considers worthy of what she has received. We all work on that same basis, don't we? We both know what happens to someone who is always given things that they consider valuable, but are never permitted to give back something they consider valuable in return."

"Yes, they eventually go criminal on us; they lose their respect for themselves. Damn, am I ever in one fine pickle!"

"My dear, I believe that is the understatement of the year!" He laughed. I poked him.

"That's not funny! I am truly in the pickle barrel! I need some help, buster." I playfully tickled him again.

"Okay, okay, let's bring our Judger in on this one, dear. This is way out of my league." I agreed, and Renzo went to fetch Linda to our bungalow. Now I had to explain it all once more, from the beginning, leaving out no details, even though I found them somewhat embarrassing.

Linda commented, "Well, Bethany, you are in the pickle barrel this time, but I told Renzo weeks ago that you were very likely to get us into some kind of mess over this. Okay, let's look at all the facts, shall we?" I agreed. She went on, "Regardless of whether or not she is in love with you, by offering you the position as her mate, she is giving you a position of power in her land. Along with that comes the fact that the Santi would now have a very powerful, huge ally, enormous trading benefits, and armies to help defend us, should the need ever arise. She, of course, in return has the Guardians on which she can all for help at some future time, when she is in need. It works both ways. She knows perfectly well that soon we must sail off on our other missions and that our lives lay elsewhere than in her Imperial Palace. As her mate, this would cement the ties between our two countries and the Santi and her."

"Are you saying that she is just using me?" I asked, somewhat confused. I noted that it is lots easier to be objective, when you are not the topic of the mess.

"Oh no definitely not using you. I am sure that she is wholly sincere. However, she is a shrewd leader, so she must know that such a union benefits her and her country as much as it does ours."

"I see what you mean, but. . ." I knew there had to be a "but," but I couldn't think straight at the moment.

"Now let's look at it from her subject's point of view for a minute. Their newly chosen Empress goes and marries a foreigner, and a woman at that. Don't you think that more than a few are going to be very upset with such a move? Making a foreigner the equivalent of their Emperor? Certainly, some people could interpret this as a great dishonor, a disgrace to the very people she is ruling. While it might not go so far as to become a civil war, it certainly is going to cause a big fracture in many people's loyalty to the Empress. While Sho Lin undoubtedly means well by this proposal, I fear that if implemented, serious damage and unrest would likely follow."

"Yes, I can see how it would. I knew that there was something really wrong with this, I just couldn't vocalize it. I just can't allow her to marry or mate or whatever. I would be bringing serious damage to her reign if I did."

"True. However, Bethany, as Renzo has wisely pointed out, there is also the exchange factor to be considered here as well. We, and you in particular, have given her monumentally valuable aid as well as honor. Now, she is desperately trying to find something equally valuable from her point of view that she can give back to you and to us. You just said that she knows the stark reality of her situation: she can barely walk, has no real life skills such as a trade. She doesn't sew, cook, or anything. All she can do really is sit on her couch and look pretty. Her only real contribution to her society is being a very good ruler and making sure that her closest supporters are well paid for their loyalty and assistance. I'm being very hard-nosed and blunt about her, mind you. I'm not attacking her or her values or her country's notions, just the stark reality of her situation."

"We've seen that she does a very good job as a ruler and until now, that has been her primary, if only, means for exchange with others, who must do nearly everything for her. However, you mentioned that she revealed one other thing that she is trained to be able to do: give pleasure to others. As a Princess, we all know that she was literally in a straightjacket with this. A man was not even allowed to touch her even.

Now as Empress, she at once enters a new position where she can begin to use the giving of pleasure as a means of exchange, but very probably only with her mates. We've seen no indication of wide spread promiscuity anywhere in this land, although we have only seen a tiny fraction of Tashien. I'll grant these people the benefit of the doubt on this point, no promiscuity, until we actually find something to contradict it."

"So what we are really facing here, Bethany, as I see it in my official position as Judger, is how to help Sho Lin get her exchange between her and us back into balance. I think that allowing her to mate with you is out. There are too many bad or potentially damaging side effects of going through with that."

"Whew! I agree with you," I said emphatically. "So what can we do?"

"Find an alternative. We could ask instead for rulership of a province — that would be balancing. Yet, we both know that is unacceptable to us really, but it would balance the scales. Let's put our heads together and see what else we can devise." Linda suggested optimistically.

We began throwing out ideas, but they were all totally wild and not remotely workable or acceptable to us. Finally, Renzo had a good idea. "You know what we Santi really need here in Tashien is some small bit of land where we can build better docking facilities and a fortress, in case of troubles. I know that is likely too small and won't measure up on the scales, as far as she is concerned, but really, isn't that all that we Santi could possibly want at this time? That, and a mutual defense treaty or pact that says we will come to their aid and they will come to ours, if and when it is ever needed."

"Renzo, I could kiss you!" Linda replied enthusiastically. "But I'd better not or I'll find myself flying out into the garden!" She teased me and I grinned good-naturedly at her jest.

She continued, "Seriously, you have it exactly. We need proper facilities from which to conduct trading and a mutual defense pact. However, that isn't going to be enough for Sho Lin to balance the scales as she sees them. Moreover, it doesn't address the fact that she believes that she is in love with you, Bethany. I have another idea. What about Bethany becoming her Royal Consort? Look, we all know that it is only pleasure that can be exchanged between like couples. Such cannot harm your true relationship with Renzo. I wonder what the ramifications of the Royal Consort actually are in this country?"

My face was hot again. Renzo added, "She's right, Bethany. It is only pleasure that can be exchanged and not even the kind of pleasure that we swap!" He winked and raised his eyebrows.

Linda gave him a playful slap for me. "Men, always in your pants are we?" Now Renzo's face crimsoned, served him right. This was serious for me.

"The question is how do we find out what we need to know without breaking Sho Lin's request for confidence? We cannot go asking Jin or Yan or even Ming about this," Linda said, twisting her hair between her fingers, as she often did when she could not think of any reasonable answer at once. We sat in silence for a time. To me, it seemed everything hinged on just what the ramifications of the Royal Consort actually were.

At last, I said, "I should go and ask her." Both looked very relieved. "I know that they were going out for a walk in the gardens, perhaps I can find them there yet. I would like to have this thing resolved before I go to bed. You both stay here until I return, please." They agreed and I left, shuffling off to the gardens.

Considering the size of this enormous formal garden, finding them would be most difficult, especially at the snail's pace that I walked. I expanded my mind and located Sho Lin, being very careful not to intrude into her mind. I walked directly toward them. As I drew close to the pair, I began making a bit of noise so that they would not be startled or caught in anything embarrassing.

When I saw them, I paused and bowed to her, watching her long nails for the sign to approach her; she was quick to give it. "Please excuse me, Sho Lin, San See. I have been trying to work out what you asked me earlier. I have found that I need to know something about your culture that none of us know. It is important. May I ask it of you?"

"Ask anything, Bethany!" she replied, very keenly interested in what I might be asking.

"The position of Royal Consort: what does that entail and what are the obligations and ramifications of that position?"

"It is a position in which much pleasure is exchanged between either of the rulers. Oh, I see where you are heading with this question, Bethany!" Damn, she was a very observant leader. "Yes, the exchange of pleasure plus if the sexes are right and a child is needed, that is done too. We have had several Emperors and Empresses who used the services of the Royal Consort to create royal heirs for the throne. It is perfectly honorable to so do. The Royal Consort commands very high respect among our people because of what they do for the rulers. Often the consort is given a small parcel of land and has a well-cared for home built on it. Sometimes they even have their own small court to rule."

"Bethany, both San See and I could tell from your reactions that you did not share the love that I feel for you. You must forgive me for being so bold and for putting you in such discomfort, for giving you this, this problem to face. Yes, perhaps the best choice would be the Royal Consort."

"Thanks for understanding, Sho Lin. Yes, we discussed it and all of us are horribly worried about the potential for a political backlash against you for mating with a foreigner and making her their Emperor, having a foreigner rule over them. I just cannot live with myself if I caused you anything remotely like this!"

"You are very wise, Bethany. Yes, I was aware that I would face a great deal of unrest over such a decision. Yes, I would have to force it upon many to accept my ruling as Empress."

"Then, we agree, Sho Lin. I cannot become your official mate. That should be San See's role, and his alone! But Sho Lin, I also know that you are trying very hard to find some way to give back to me and the Santi for all that we have done for you."

A tear formed and trickled down her right cheek. "Yes, yes, I am. I must. I will suffer great dishonor if I cannot find some way to really thank you all. It is the most important thing that I must do and do quickly, before I go to the Imperial Palace and begin to rule."

"Sho Lin, we have found the solution. What we Santi really need is some shore land where we can build docks large enough to handle our large ships. We can barely dock at yours. Also, we always build a stone fortress and walls around our docks to guarantee our security at all times, in case of trouble, such as we had with the ninjas. To us Santi, this is an extremely valuable thing to acquire in any land that we desire to have a continuing relationship with: a permanent, small location to call home and to be able to guarantee the safety there of our people. It would seem to me then that if you made me your Royal Consort, then everyone wins. Would that be enough to satisfy you, Sho Lin? It certainly would more than satisfy all of us."

From the huge grin on her face, I could tell just how much she was relieved to hear this. "Oh yes, yes. Yes it does. No one would raise even an eyebrow over the giving of land, the building of a fortress and docks, if it were for the Royal Consort. Such is nearly always provided for him or her. You would not mind being my consort? I would treasure the giving of great pleasure to the ones that I dearly love, even though I know that you do not feel the same about me. Are you willing to allow me to express my love for you without any need on your part to do so to me? I must know this, Bethany. I would feel awful if you were going to hate every minute that we might spend together."

"Yes, I am willing to allow you to express your love to me, Sho Lin. I would not hate it or you nor think less of you because of it. Yet, I do not think of you as I do Renzo. Expect me to be a little apprehensive about it. However, I will be content if you are not going to be offended if I do not reciprocate towards you."

"That is most acceptable to me. In your country, do they not hand shake to seal a bargain or deal?" I said that we did. "Then, let us shake hands on this, Bethany." I grinned, for she was reaching out to my world.

We shook and then I gave her a hug as well.

"We hug those that we really like or love a lot too," I explained. "So what must I do or how does this Royal Consort thing become known?"

"When we go to the Imperial Palace, I will make the first two public proclamations, one for San See and one for you. Once that is done, then it is official. We can work out the best location for your base, and we can find time for pleasure as well. I also know that your people are probably anxious to get on with your other missions, but can you stay for another month or two before you leave? That would give us ample time to make all the arrangements. If not, I can move things along faster somehow."

"No, that will be fine with us, especially now that it gives us some great purpose for staying longer: the location, design, and construction of docks and a fortress. My people will be very excited about this. Thank you, Sho Lin, for giving us this great honor. It means the world to us!" She beamed and I knew that finally she began to feel that she had given us something that we considered of great value, as we had given to her.

There was a bounce in my step as I shuffled back to the bungalow, so much so, that I forgot that I was still wearing this restrictive dress and fell flat on my face. Ah well, undaunted, I continued on my way. Renzo and Linda were most pleased with the results. I told them all that had passed between us. Linda was very interested to hear that Sho Lin had wanted to shake hands to seal the bargain. This, she thought, was a very significant change in her attitude.

We had no more than finished our discussion when the sounds of many fireworks resounded in our ears. We all rushed outside and watched. The city of Shansee was celebrating their Princess's becoming the Empress of all Tashien! For over an hour, the skies were filled with enormous bursting globes of colored flames and sparkles.

Partway through the display, Sho Lin and San See came shuffling up to our porch. Seeing our shock, she said, "I am the Empress now. I have much more freedoms. I can be seen walking a little. My people are celebrating tonight, as much for themselves as for me. We all have received the greatest of honors. This they are celebrating."

We watched in silence at the awesome display. Finally, as it died down, we saw a huge firecracker, a lone one, hurling high into the sky, higher than all the others. It burst into sky blue flickering flames and formed into the shape of Sho Lin!

"How the devil did they make that one?" exclaimed Cedric. It was unbelievable indeed.

We said good night to everyone. Renzo and I went inside. He said, "Now I am going to show you how pleasure is done properly, Bethany."

"Oh no you don't! I'm going to show you how it is done properly,"

I taunted back. I lost. He carried me physically to our bed. Okay, I let him.

A week later, Sho Lin left for the Imperial Palace in Zau, Wontun Province. Half of the Explorers stayed behind, working out the details for the right location for our newest Santi fortress and docks, suitable for a fair number of ships. Besides Renzo, Benet and Michelle, and Damien and Linda accompanied me along with Sho Lin's rather large group. Cedric had ordered Benet and Michelle to take copious notes and make significant paintings of this new city and the Imperial Palace, which they promised to do.

It took us two weeks to get there. Her huan had spent the past many weeks getting all the arrangements made. Her father had pretty much let things go after his wife had died; hence, much cleaning had to be done. The Imperial Palace was a huge, walled, brown stone complex, with many buildings within its walls. Every aspect of the main building spoke of great elegance, of great forethought of design, an even of great opulence, as far as I was concerned. The Imperial Bedroom was enormous in size; the bed could sleep ten people! Draped bolts of sky blue silks adorned many of the rooms, the colors of Sho Lin. There was even a Royal Garden next to the main building in which we all walked with Sho Lin and San See every evening.

Renzo and I were given the Royal Consort's room, which was about half the size of Sho Lin's bedroom. Still, the bed was five times the size of the beds to which he and I were accustomed, plush, soft, and luxurious indeed. Upon our arrival, I was given two young servant women to look after my courtly needs. They insisted on bathing me and pampering me in every conceivable manner.

During these past few months, we women had been letting our nails grow longer, due in part to Sho Lin's influence. Now my personal helpers insisted on painting them cherry red and even painting my face similar to the way the Sho Lin and many other women we had met did. Further, I was given a complete new wardrobe of clothing, all made of the finest silk, sky blue, naturally. However, the dresses still did not have any walking slits in them, so I was still shuffling my way around the place. In some ways, I really did enjoy all this pampering I was receiving, especially because these young women really loved to dote on my appearance.

Two days after we arrived and with the domestic situation now under control, the time came for Sho Lin's first official Court. With Renzo holding my arm, I shuffled into the enormous throne room, while San See held onto Sho Lin as she walked in from another door. We two couples shuffled at the same speed towards each other, grinning all the way to the thrones.

The Empress's throne was covered in plush sky blue velvet, and even the two steps up to her throne were so covered, making it more comfortable for her to manage. I noticed a big change, gone was the divan. Now she sat upright on the ornate throne, her very tiny feet were clearly most visible to any who approached the throne. Her thin waist was also highlighted. She carefully arranged her long tresses so that they came down equally on both sides of her. The throne for the Emperor was identical but was now empty. San See currently sat upon the floor beneath her.

A smaller throne sat just to the left of Sho Lin; here was where the Royal Consort would sit. Per protocol, I stood beside the throne with Renzo holding my waist. Sho Lin looked at us, took a deep breath, and gave the signal. At once, the doormen opened the main ornately painted main public access doors, and many well-dressed men and women appeared, bowing first to Sho Lin and then entering and arcing out around the sides of the room. Once all had gathered and the doors shut, Sho Lin spoke.

"Welcome everyone. It is with the greatest of honor and pride that I have been chosen by the Grand Council to be your next Empress. I promise to always do my very best to guide and serve you. Please feel free to bring anything to me that you desire."

"As is our custom, my first Royal Decree is that San See shall become my husband. Arise, San See, Protectorate no longer, arise, and be seated beside me as my husband and Emperor." He stood and bowed to the gathered people, faced Sho Lin, bowed to her, and walked up the steps, taking his seat at her side. "At this time, I also choose Bethany Rose Wilkins Pazzio le'Goeur as my Royal Consort. Come, my dearest Bethany, who has given so much to me already, and take your proper place at my side. Along with my presence in our bed, please accept a small parcel of land on which to build your official residence."

This was Renzo's signal to assist me in climbing the step to my seat beside her, but at a lower elevation. He then returned to our previous position and sat down on the carefully positioned mat just to my left. "Be it known then throughout Tashien, San See is my husband and your Emperor. Bethany is my loving consort. Honor them both as you honor me. I have spoken this decree." The assembled group began clapping, a sign that it was accepted.

Next, an hour of official decrees and appointments, even some re-appointments, followed. Sho Lin kept on many of those who had held similar positions in her father's court. However, I did recognize quite a few faces from Shansee, who had been promoted. Among them was Ming's husband, who became a Royal Gardner. Yan was appointed the Royal Advisor, and Jin, the Royal Historian.

Finally, with this round of appointments finished, Sho Lin dismissed them, charging them with creating and bringing an agenda to her for the afternoon session. Thankfully, this was the first and last time I had to sit on the throne.

That evening, after dinner, Yan took Renzo and the others on a grand tour of the complex. However, to see it all would take several days. Perhaps Sho Lin had planned this all along. It gave time for her and me to have private time together in her luxurious bedroom. I am not about to go into the details of those evenings. However, I will say this. This was my third female body since arriving on Tarra. I thought I had the role of being a woman down pat. I was utterly and completely wrong.

Two weeks later, it was time for us to return to Shansee. Sho Lin showed me that my room would be maintained just as it was, with several sets of clothes ready for me anytime that I returned to visit here. "When the time is convenient and proper for you, I greatly desire to come to your Velona for a visit. The time should be of your choosing. I will eagerly await that day." We hugged each other and said our farewells.

Another ten days later, we arrived back in Shansee. During our absence, the others had not been idle. Cedric had found the perfect location for our new base of operations here in Tan Lon Province. Part of his criteria had been to not displace other establishments, if possible, and yet still be near the main docks where the cargo would be stored. Our location was just south of where our caravels were currently docked. Already, he had the construction underway.

After each group brought the other up to date and after I took a bit of ribbing about being the Royal Consort, we decided on our departure date. Water, food supplies, and our cargo of precious fireworks, to say nothing of all our other acquisitions, had to be loaded. One ship would remain for the use of the Traveler Circle. The other would carry most of the goods that we had gotten, less the fireworks, of course. Finally, on July 15 and during the heat of the summer, we all boarded the Sleepy Hollow. We watched the great city slowly recede as Henry directed the caravel back out to sea, followed by our sister ship. Our plan was simple, escort each other to the Spice Islands, then each ship would go its own way.

The first thing that we women did was to get below and change our clothes! We stowed all of our local clothing carefully, knowing that one day we would be returning here. It felt so great to be wearing our good old comfortable clothes once more! The big decision that we women had to make concerned our nails, which by now were overly long. Mine were cherry red, but long. Should we cut them to their usual lengths or keep them long for a while yet? Ah, the luxury of having the time for such decisions. What a contrast this trip had been from our previous ones. All of us decided to keep them long for a while yet.

Chapter 19 Of Acropolis and Babies

The weather turned hot as we said farewell to the Peanut, who turned to the north as the two caravels reached the extreme southwestern corner of the Southlands, here on July 31, 650. Our comfortable life aboard ship had returned to normal once more. All of us sweated profusely by day and wore only very short pants. The voyage was a relaxing change from all of that continuous honor considerations running so rampant within Tashien.

Two known locations remained on the mantis map for us to visit; one was an unknown island far to the south of us called Acropolis. The other was deep within the Southlands, perhaps eight hundred miles from the western side, rather centrally located within the width of the landmass or some four hundred north of the southern side. Access to this unknown site would be far, far more difficult for us. Hence, we decided to check out this last remaining island.

On August 15 in the middle of a nearly unbearable heat wave, we made landfall. We spent a week circumnavigating the island, examining it carefully with our far seeing eyes. Many cities were spotted and the construction was similar to that found on Megalos. We spotted numerous soldiers and they too were armored in the same way as the Megalos Centurions. We could only conclude that these people here were in some way related to those on Megalos.

We saw no large ships, no docks for outside trade. Only small, one man fishing boats dotted the seas near the sandy shores. At last, we decided to put in at the largest town on the coast, which was in the middle of the northern side. Sweating like mad, the crew lowered the longboats, and we began to make our way slowly to the shore, Natale and I were at the front of the lead boat, ready to make first contact. Natale felt confident that these people probably spoke some dialect of Megalos.

As we got to within a hundred feet of shore, over two dozen soldiers came trotting down to the beach, where we had intended to land. One called out, "Go back. No foreigners are ever allowed to set foot on this island. If you set one foot on our land, you will be arrested and thrown into prison until you die. Go back. You are not welcome here."

"Well, the language is nearly the same as that spoken on Megalos," Natale declared. "How should I respond?"

I spoke up, "We are the Santi del Dio. We come in peace. Is there someone in authority with whom we can plead our case to be allowed just to visit?"

"We just threw off the Pope and his flotilla. We don't care who you are. No foreigner has ever been allowed onto these shores in our four hundred year history! We must keep our bloodline pure from all your imperfections. We are the master race, chosen to one day lead all of Tarra. Now be off with you. Or land if you want a fight. I guarantee you that you will be swiftly executed."

"There is no use trying to reason with an angry man," I said. "Head back to the caravel. Do you all notice the markings on their tunics? I swear that is a representation of a black mantis creature. Let's use our far seeing eyes a bit more! I don't like this reception. What are they trying to hide from us?"

An hour later, our longboats were once more secured, and the far seeing eyes were both in constant use. "Fairly primitive people," Linda commented as she studied the common people in the streets of the town going about their activities. "Nothing unusual. Women have both arms though I rather expected to see some without them. Many soldiers and more seem to be coming down to the beach area, probably because we aren't leaving. I don't see any way that they could raid us out here, nothing larger than a one man dingy."

"Well, they've certainly got a disproportionate number of soldiers per person, at least here in this town. I count one soldier for every two others at least," Renzo added while peering through the other one.

Linda gave Rosina a turn to study the people, and added, "We've pretty much seen how many large towns they have during last week. I can hazard a rough guess that the island has a population of no more than a hundred thousand, somewhere in that range. None of these is what we would call a substantial city. Now what, Bethany?"

"Let's go have another look at Henry's map. I want to see if we can possibly locate where the mantis cave might be. The map has thus far been accurate in the position of the symbols representing their bases. Come on." We headed down to the Captain Henry's cabin, where he had the unusual map spread out on the navigation table. Based on the dimensions of the island, we estimated that it lay some twenty-five miles further east and near the center of the width of the island. After Henry relayed his sailing orders, the caravel weighed anchor. With only one mainsail up, we slowly moved westward, trying to estimate the distance needed to put us just north of the mantis complex, if one was indeed here.

Bingo, at the precise location indicated on the map rose the highest mountain peak on the island. This seemed logical to us, since the other complexes were similarly located on the other islands. The far seeing eyes showed us that several smaller villages and one town lay between us and the peak. The others now looked to me for our next step.

"Well," I began, "we best not trespass. While we could no doubt defeat some of their soldiers, I suspect that they would just funnel every one down to this spot. We cannot take out thousands of them. We are not at war with these people; we only need to see if there are mantises about or if there are eggs."

"Hey, don't forget about tortured women," Natale added. I smiled; I hadn't.

"They explicitly forbad us to put our bodies on their shores, but they said nothing about us floating over their island and having a good look around," I suggested. "Five of us are going to go have a look-see. Renzo, Rosina, Benet, Michelle, you are going with me. Here's the plan." I outlined my idea and everyone thought it an excellent one.

We five sat down, leaning our backs against the poop cabin walls, and backed out of our heads. Rosina was in charge of maintaining the Mind Link. I gave her time to bring everyone into the massive link. This way, everyone on board would see what we were seeing. If we failed to spot something, they could let us know instantly. Once we were set, I led the way, floating some hundred feet above the water, heading towards the shore.

Ten minutes later, we rose higher and higher up the mountainside, looking for any cave opening or some way inside, where we expected to find a cavern complex. Sometime later, we found it at the very peak. Here was a giant caldera, and in its base, a dark opening led deep inside. It was a wide opening, large enough for the giant creatures. We headed inside.

A hundred feet nearly vertically downward, the tunnel opened up into a large cavern. The lighting was very dim; only a small amount of sunlight came down the tunnel. I conjured some blue light to increase our sight. Now we began to search carefully.

The place was a mess. Linda suggested that it appeared as though someone left in a great hurry. Thick dust lay upon everything. At last, Benet found the nest. All five of us studied it carefully. We counted two dozen eggs. However, every one of them had dried out and cracked open, rotten. None of these had ever hatched nor would they ever. We all breathed a spiritual sigh of relief!

Although we found nothing at all that interested us, no gold, no maps, no writings, we spent an hour looking anyway. Finally, I ordered us all back to the ship and our bodies. "Well, so far so good," I said. Linda agreed wholeheartedly.

"Now, let's go to Phase Two of the plan," I suggested. Once more, we backed out of our heads, with Rosina in a Mind Link with everyone else. This would take considerable time. Phase Two consisted of floating over the entire island in a systematic manner looking for any armless women or any kind of place that might house them, such as the House of Right that we had come across months ago.

Talk about a boring two weeks! Systematically we scoured the entire island from one end to the other, but found no sign of any armless women. Yes, nearly all the soldier's tunics bore the mantis symbol, evidently torturing women was not happening on this island. Natale and Mireio were very much relieved when we turned up nothing, but they didn't have to do this incredibly boring sweep!

Finally, on September 7, we set sail, heading northward, satisfied that this island, though weird, was not a threat and did not have any mantis creatures living on it, nor were the inhabitants practicing mutilation of their women. We did celebrate this finding, however, drinking a toast of mead together. Now we had to figure out how to check out this last place where the maps suggested a mantis creature or creatures had lived, somewhere in the remote central Southlands.

We had essentially two choices to get to this weird place, deep inside the unknown Southlands. Neither was appealing, because both were overland routes. The shorter route was to put into one of the southern ports and bushwhack due north several hundred miles, scaling one mountain range. The longer route required traveling more than twice as far from a western coastal port, following perhaps rivers through dense jungles. No mountains blocked this route. The southern port towns were all controlled by Megalos and would not be particularly friendly to us. The western coast towns were all free and open ports, though with these towns lawlessness and anarchy rained. These were rough and tumble towns on the fringes of society and civilization. Our choices were not good ones at all.

When we reached the southwestern edge of the Southlands and finally had to make a decision, a completely unexpected decision occurred. Tonia, in making her periodic health checkups on everyone aboard the caravel, gave me news I was not expecting. "Bethany, do you know that you are pregnant?"

"What? How can you tell so soon? I haven't missed my . . ." my voice trailed off. Yes, I had forgotten that Tonia now had the skill to effectively sense what was going on internally within a body.

"Yes, most definitely, probably within the last few weeks I'd say."

"Wow. I'd better go tell Renzo about this! Thanks!"

"Me, a father? Already? Oh boy. That's great, Bethany! I wonder if it will be a boy or a girl?" Renzo was elated. "Are you feeling okay? Guess we'd better lay off the Torque Ball for a while. Need to sit down?"

"Renzo! I'm not sick, just going to have a baby! Silly. I'm fine, don't even know it yet. I'll let you know when we need to take it easy. I wonder what we should do about names?"

While he and I began proposing names, Tonia returned. "Say Bethany, you will never believe the rest of this."

"What now?" I said, wondering what other exciting news our Healer had for me.

"Linda is one month along now. Rosina is too. Natale and I are also pregnant, and so is Michelle! Can you believe this? All of us are going to become moms at around the same time. Pretty darn impressive I think. We can all share the new experience together, with Mireio lending us a hand with the ropes, so to speak, since she's had her first now. Everyone's so excited about this!"

"I guess I should have seen this one coming, what with all of us being newlyweds. Well, I guess this changes everything. We're not going to go tromping through jungles and have our babies out there in the wild! I'll let mom know this exciting bit of good news; she's going to be a grandmother again. I think that we need some different orders now." Tonia left to spend some time with Emil. They were just as excited as Renzo and I were.

Mom agreed, though we both felt that this last location just had to be checked out, now was not the time to do it. However, I really didn't want to just come home and sit around for another eight months or so and then however long after that to nurse. It would be long enough just with the nursing time. She and I compromised; we could spend a few more months filling in the empty spaces on the ocean west of us.

"Henry, here's our new plan," I explained, with everyone standing around squished into his cabin looking at the large map of the ocean. "Plot out a zigzag course through the middle of the ocean between here and Grun, the name of the landmass further north from Wanakan. Our objective is to spend a few months seeing if there are any other unknown islands out here in the vastness of the ocean. It would be convenient for sailors if there were a few out there. We should try to be home by March next year or so."

For six weeks, we sailed west by north across the ocean. We did discover Benet's Isle, a very weird island. Yes, it had fresh water, but it had very strange, unknown animals living on it. Located about halfway across the ocean and roughly in the center, the Loremaster's loved this unusual island. The rest of us enjoyed its vacation style beaches. This was the only island we found during the entire time.

However, once November came, we discovered that this was the beginning of the stormy season in the northern half of the ocean. Not only were the seas rough, but the frequency and severity of storms and blows increased three-fold, especially the farther north one sailed. Thus, we arrived home in Velona on January 1, 651, several months early.

We five were now about four months pregnant and showing it. Mom had a nice welcoming surprise. She had had Allan build a whole row of brownstone homes similar to Renzo and mine, abutting ours in a little line. Linda and Damien took the one next to ours; Natale and Henry, the next; Rosina and Cedric were beside them with Tonia and Emil in the next one; Mireio and Roberto, with their growing family, had the last one. Everyone was extremely surprised and very pleased to say the least.

On January 4, we held the first fireworks display for Velona, launching them from the middle of our estate with a huge crowd of people from Velona just outside our walls watching them. Yes, this became the single topic of conversation for a month. We had to launch a second display on February 1 just to satisfy the incessant demands for more. Already, a caravel was en route from Tashien with a whole cargo hold full of fireworks, so this summer we promised more of these incredible displays.

Allan and Cedric dismantled several of them to find out how they were made and how they worked. For months, both men, joined by Enyo, worked together to see if they could not reproduce the active ingredients. By December, they had succeeded, although they had nearly blown themselves up in the process.

During the time that we were gone, Enyo's new inventions for bathrooms, now called toilets and washers, her original names were too long, had proved successful and every building on the estate had at least one bathroom with a dozen of each type in them. By our arrival, Enyo and her crew were halfway along with aqueduct construction, which when done would bring in an endless supply of running water to the estate. In September, a ribbon cutting ceremony was held as Enyo, sitting on the ground, twisted the main control level that opened the gates. Everyone cheered as water from far up north came flowing down into our estate, filling up the many wooden water towers, as we began to call her inventions that held a very large volume of water each.

On the music front, Bard Tal brought us up to date on what the many musicians had done. It was revolutionary in both scope and nature. Some of the musically talented women from Megalos, Black God Isle, and the Isle of Right joined to develop a completely new concept in music! Led by Chara of the Isle of Right and using the notation techniques developed by Roberto, they created polyphony, music in four to six parts, each part of which was not the same as the others and when played together formed musical chords! The result was the most incredible music anyone had ever heard anywhere.

The women involved were the following: from the Isle of Right, Chara, their group leader, Gaia, Ioanna, and Rhea; from the Black God Isle, Amiria, Gesa, Emiri, Emere, Roas, and Tama; from Megalos, Cymone, Hermi, Iolanta, Sophia, and Korinna.

While they all worked together, there were essentially two very different kinds of music being created or composed. Amiria and her subgroup were creating vocal motets for four voices mostly which had a rather holy sound to them, more or less sacred type of musical sounds. Within a few years, every church in Velona had their choirs singing these as hymns before their services began. Chara and her subgroup created both vocal and instrumental polyphonic popular type of songs. Cymone and her subgroup created larger instrumental works, which were often variations on popular dance tunes. Fifty years from now, the names of the prolific composers, Chara, Cymone, and Amiria will become legendary, known throughout our portion of Tarra!

A couple weeks after we got back, Allan took us all down to the Velona shipwrights to see something very new. "Pietro Alvarez is at it again," Allan explained. He had invented the revolutionary caravel when he was just a boy of twelve. Now he was thirty-seven and one of the wealthiest men in Velona. "We keep on wanting to carry more and more cargo per shipment, so he's designed another new type of ship. He calls it a carrack. Wait til you see the sheer size of this one!"

At the dry docks, dozens of new ships were under construction. We could not miss the new one! It dwarfed the caravels, standing twice as tall and nearly double everything else and with several decks of cabins for the passengers and crew. "We can transport a whole regiment with their horses in this one!" exclaimed Allan, who was quite excited about the long-range possibilities of this new style ship. Me, I liked the cabin space as well. "Pietro claims it will be about as fast as the caravel, perhaps slower when fully loaded. The possibilities are staggering."

"Yes, but what is this other ship?" I asked seeing another unusual looking ship next to the carrack.

"Ah, Pietro has this thing for speed. He is trying to build the fastest yacht on the seas. If it works as predicted, it will carry only half of what a caravel does, but go half again as fast, making this sleek ship the fastest sailing ship on Tarra! It's his personal ship. With the talent he has and the money he has made off of his caravel design, he can afford to splurge," Allan explained.

The first carrack would not be ready for its maiden test run until a year from this spring. Duly impressed, we began to wonder if our next explorations might just be in one of these newest carracks. I began to hope so, because we would have vastly more space and comforts!

When spring came, Allan took us on a trip to Southway, Greenway. Specifically, he wanted us to see what else had been invented. Some years back, Leann Finn, the longbow maker who had become fabulously wealthy with her unique bows, had moved her entire factory from West Reach to Southway because of the invading Holy Paladins. I learned that she had finally remarried a local armorer. Like Renzo and I, Leann and Walter loved to challenge each other.

Allan explained that Walter had now invented a new kind of protective armor that made chain mail obsolete. "Look, we saw how we lost the combat edge when the Holy Paladins themselves began to wear chain mail instead of their leather armor and bits and pieces of metal protections. Walter has perfected an armor, which even Leann's bows cannot penetrate except at close range! A sword strike does nothing, bounces off and not even a bruise is left!"

"This I've got to see!" cried Renzo. Emil and Damien echoed him. Naturally, this was of keen interest to the Protectors.

"That's why we are making this trip!" Allan replied.

Leann looked much older than I last remembered her. Golly, how the years pass. Walter was in his fifties, and I could tell at once that they had the same kind of special relation that I shared with Renzo. First, Leann took us on a tour of her factory, proudly declaring that they were making fifty bows per week.

Then, Walter reappeared wearing his new armor! He looked like a shiny, silver tin man! From inside his closed helmet, he said, "I call it plate mail. Here, take a sword and strike my chest with it." Cautiously, Renzo did just that. Bang, we heard the sound of steel upon steel. It did nothing at all to Walter, who took off his metal helmet and laughed.

It took a good deal of work to put it on and take it off. Renzo tried it on and found it was very heavy indeed. "Now here is the acid test," Walter explained. "We know that Leann's longbows are far more powerful than the normal short bow. I have one of the breastplates propped up out there on the test firing range. Take one of her bows and these razor steel tipped arrows and see if you can penetrate the breastplate."

"See these marks on the ground — they indicate long range, medium range, and short range. I suspect you can't hit it from long range, so try it from medium range," Walter suggested.

Emil took a shot and hit the plate. We all went to see what it did. Had the target been wearing chain mail, the sharp shaft would have penetrated the chain mail. We could not even find the dent made by the arrow that Emil shot! Impressive. Next, we moved back to close range and fired again. Only at close range did her shaft finally penetrate the steel armor breastplate.

"A man or woman wearing this armor is going to be immune to all projectiles, unless it is one of Leann's longbows and then only at close range. It will drastically reduce combat injuries as well," Walter explained.

"Yes, but it is heavy and awkward to move about in," Renzo commented.

"True, but on the battlefield, you will be nearly invincible, you can walk where you will," he replied.

Allan added, "We've ordered a fair number of these suits of armor. One whole attack regiment is going to be outfitted with plate mail. If they work out, we have plans to make such armor for all the attack regiments. We are going to get our combat edge back once more."

Indeed, new inventions continued appearing throughout our lands at an unparalleled rate. The Director of Printing and Writing at the Laird Foundation was swamped with requests for publishing printed material, from books to musical manuscripts. Another of the Megalos women whom we rescued had put her engineering talents to work on this problem and invented a new, faster printing press. Now some fifty editions were coming off their presses each week, truly impressive.

In fact, so much development was going on now in Velona and all of our other locations that I found it a challenging task to keep up with it all. I certainly didn't know how mom did it!

However, in June of 651, we received some bad news from Zargarb. Lenkova Pazzio le'Goeur has passed away. The twins, Renzo and Rosina took the news hard; she was their mother, and they had been very close indeed. The most famous freedom fighter in Zargarb had died at sixty-two. As soon as we heard the news, the Explorers Circle took the Sleepy Holly and headed at top speed for Zargarb, setting a new record for this run, arriving in seven days. Of course, the caravel was nearly empty.

Sad was the overall mood in the entire city. The sense of loss was great. She was given a funeral fit for a queen, and rightly so, for this woman had devoted her life to achieve freedom for her people. Her husband, Andre, took the loss particularly hard, he had been utterly devoted to her ever since they had met so many years ago. The twins did what they could to comfort him, and the prospect of grandchildren kept him from a complete emotional breakdown. He asked us to let him know where we finally would settle down and he would put in for a transfer there to be with his grandchildren. I promised him that I would make sure he got the transfer.

As we returned to the caravel to sail back to Velona, I noticed that a presence was in our cabin. I expanded my awareness, extended a communication line to it, and found a very bashful Lenkova! *Hi, I, ah, hope you don't mind me being here. I know that you and Rosina are going to have babies, and I, ah, kind of wanted to have one of you to be my next mother, if that is all right with you. I'm not at all sure how to do this, though.*

Great! We were wondering what happened to you. Let me get them into this link. Your twins miss you very much!

Quickly, I linked Renzo and Rosina into our Mind Link. It was fabulous watching their grief so altered by simple communication with their mother. Both twins were delighted that Lenkova wanted one of them to be her parent.

But mom, what if I have a boy? Rosina asked, worriedly.

Well, maybe Bethany will have a girl, she replied.

Yes, but what if she too had a boy? Rosina responded.

You wouldn't do that to me, would you? Lenkova feigned being annoyed.

But we don't have any choice, mom. Rosina continued to be worried about it.

Look, it's fifty-fifty chance and there are two of you, so one of you ought to have a baby girl. God, I hope so anyway! Lenkova replied. *Bethany, what do I do now?*

Simple, relax and just hang around us until it is time. Won't be that long now, probably six weeks or so, I sent. *Rosina will probably be chatting with you all the time now!* Indeed, she did just that, one benefit of being a Communicator.

On the trip back, we all began to finalize our picks for baby names. I insisted that we agree on both a boy's name and girl's name. Renzo insisted that whichever one didn't get used this time, we would use that one on the first opportunity that we could. I teased him, "Renzo, what if your great boy's name doesn't get used this time and we keep on having girl after girl?"

"Oh, that's a simple one, Bethany dear," he teased me back. "I'll just have to turn you in for a newer and better model!" We both roared with laughter.

"Yes, so I just have to keep on having babies until I get a boy is that is?"

"Yes, indeed!"

"Well, buster, if we keep on having boys, then I get to keep on having babies until I get a girl, how's that?" Again, we laughed long and hard.

Beginning the last week of May, the babies began coming over the next four weeks. Natale had hers first, and she and Henry named their little boy, Charles Angel. Michelle came next, giving birth to a girl, who she and Benet named Aimee Elizabeth, somewhat after me. I had mine next, twins! The boy we named Benjamin Andre; the girl we named Lena Jenna. Yes, I helped make sure that Lenkova now had her new body, and she liked the name as well, Lena. Now I was glad that my breasts had grown so large; I had two mouths to feed.

Later, Linda had her boy, whom she and Damien named Zachary Allen. Rosina came next with a little boy, whom she and Cedric named Felix Andre. Finally, Tonia had hers, a girl, whom Emil and she named Elaina Elizabeth. All mothers and babies were perfectly healthy.

Yes, for the first few weeks, it was general chaos around the place. Mireio was a very big help to Natale, who had to face dealing with a baby now. Her friend shared all the tips and techniques she had learned from others like them. Me, I just relaxed and enjoyed being a mother for a time, though dealing with two was quite challenging indeed.

Realistically, we could not resume our mission until the babies were at least a year old. Hence, we spent our idle time planning this next mission, crossing the jungles of the Southlands. Once we traveled ten miles inland, we would be in totally unknown and unexplored lands. It was daunting, since we had something like four hundred such miles to travel. We would take our young children with us and bring along several nannies to care for them while we were off exploring. None of us wanted to leave them behind, but we dare not take them with us into the dangerous jungles.

Finally, on June 1, 652, we at last set sail to continue our voyages of exploration. All of us were more than ready to continue; we had enough pure idle time.

Chapter 20 Off into the Unknown

The Sleepy Hollow again slipped slowly out of the very busy harbor of Velona. She had had a complete overhaul, barnacles removed from her hull, and more cabins added in the stern of the cargo hold. She was loaded with supplies and babies. Our two nannies were Lisa and Molly Sterns, a pair of sisters who just loved children. Both were sixteen and had cared for their younger siblings. Neither was married as yet.

We also brought with us several pack mules. The plan was for our pack animals to carry our provisions as we hiked into the interior of the continent. Provisions for a large party were prohibitive. Living off the land would have to be part of our experience, so no way could we carry enough food for the long journey. Even if our estimates of four hundred miles was accurate, that meant eight hundred all total for the round trip. If we adopted a very optimistic rate of twenty miles a day traveled, this meant at least forty days of provisions per person!

Since the land was completely unknown, we could not count on replenishing our supplies at any point along the journey. Hence, we decided that Henry and Natale would stay with the caravel this time. While we certainly could use our language translator, by all accounts, the trek would be exceedingly difficult for her to make. To add to our provisions as we went, we needed expert archers, and Jenna insisted other Santi accompany us for protection as well.

The party to make the journey now consisted of myself, Renzo, Linda, Damien, Rosina, Cedric, Tonia, Emil, and Benet. Even Michelle was asked to stay behind with Natale and Henry, but she didn't mind because she could use the time to paint. We also took along the two caravel archers, Angel Hattfield and Mary Beth Blackstone. Additionally, John Waterberry and Jason Marks, two Santi seasoned fighters, came along as well. Thirteen in number, we brought along four mules to carry the provisions. Based upon the descriptions we gathered from those in Velona who had been to this general area, we women also followed their advice and left our long earrings on the ship. Bushwhacking through dense jungle with these long earrings would be a problem.

On July 1, we anchored in the small port harbor of Dingray's Bay, where the proposed river that we would follow reached the sea. However, after careful consultation with the local men, we became convinced that this route was not doable. The jungle was extremely dense here; we might make five miles a day if we were lucky. The river was full of flesh eating fish; one misstep and your entire foot would be eaten to the bone! Several men had witnessed just such an unfortunate accident. The alternative route, coming up from the south, while shorter was vastly more dangerous, not because of the mountains which we at first thought was the problem, but rather the many gem mines of Megalos located in this area. These were vigorously defended against all outsiders. Kill first, ask questions later was the philosophy followed by the men in this region.

After much consultation with the local men who were very familiar with the area, at least familiar with the first fifty miles inland, the consensus was our best chance was to travel back north to Lulu and hike through the well-known timber regions until we reached the dry savannahs. There, we could head diagonally down. However, here we faced a six hundred mile journey one way, with constant danger from vipers and large carnivores, to say nothing of any native tribes. This, we decided, was the best approach to follow.

On July 7, we checked in at Lulu, the exotic timbers port. After consultations there, they agreed that if we followed the logging trails some fifty miles through the dense forest, and then we would strike the savannah and have a clear shot southeastward, though no one knew what lay along that six hundred mile path. The mantis creatures sure made this location a tough one to get to, of that we were convinced.

Now we changed tactics once more. We sold the mules and bought seventeen horses, four to serve as packhorses. These were overworked horses and not in great shape, but we calculated that with our care, we could nurse them back to full health. On July 9, we packed everything we could get onto the four horses and our personal items in our own saddlebags. It was a tearful farewell to our young children. I hated going off like this and leaving them behind, but this was no journey for a year old to be taking.

Cool and dark was our two-day ride through the heavily cut teakwood timberland. The tall iron wood trees obscured much of the sunlight this far down at the ground level. There was no chance of becoming lost, for the logging trails were very well worn paths. During the quick two days it took to reach the highlands of the savannah, we saw no other living person — animals, yes, people, no. However, we did hear the distant sounds of chopping; workers were far off the trail felling valuable timber for boat construction back in Velona primarily.

A century ago, I had traveled some of this vast savannah as the leader of the Lightning Circle. Now past memories began returning to my mind. It was hot and dry. That meant it was also dusty too. Scattered trees offered the only shade from the baking sun, yet the trees also held vipers, and we generally stayed away from them. Sometimes we came to a dense patch of grasses so tall that they rubbed up against our knees. Other times, we rode across parched earth.

What kept everyone's interest up were the strange wild animals that we passed by. Herds of all kinds, giraffes, elephants, deer of many unknown types, cow like creatures, hyenas, even lions and cheetahs. Mostly we steered clear of these larger animals. Angel and Mary Beth, excellent markswomen with their longbows, continually added fresh meat to our diet as we traveled. In our favor was the speed of travel across the savannah. With the long daylight hours of summer, we spent ten hours each day in the saddle averaging nearly forty miles.

Our biggest problem was, of course, finding water holes. Here, Benet, our Loremaster, shone! While we Guardians all could easily find our way across country, even though he was unfamiliar with this land, he developed an uncanny knack for finding watering holes. He tried to explain it — something about the track patterns left by the wandering herds, which also needed water.

Our typical day consisted of rising with the sun. Carefully inspecting our bodies and all our gear on the ground for scorpions and snakes, which often snuggled with us for warmth, we would then rise and shine. After making a breakfast, we women would clean up and pack everything, while the men saddled the horses and packed them securely. Then, we would mount up and ride at a good clip while it was still cool. During the heat of the early afternoon, we would stop for a light lunch, resting the horses and generally allowing them some grazing time. We'd ride on until there was about an hour of sunlight left, while looking for a watering hole or a good place to camp for the night. Once found, we hastily got a fire going, and while we cooked, the men unsaddled the horses, rubbed them down, and tethered them for the night. Because of the many predators out here, we kept a guard watch on our camp all night long, each taking a two-hour turn. It was not hard to keep a fire going all night long, for there was much dried deadwood all around.

There were occasional black-skinned native villages along the. These we carefully avoided whenever possible. On this trip, we were not interested in making contact with these people. While I suspected that they would be friendly towards us, we did not want to delay our trip. It was far too long a journey anyway to be wasting days learning new tribal languages and visiting with them. However, during the first three weeks of travel, we did meet five men who were out walking by themselves. They were friendly, but neither could understand the language of the other, so the encounters were short.

For eighteen days, this pattern continued unabated, one day turning into the next. Always we tended to head east by southeast. Finding a needle in a haystack you might think was our trip, but it was not as difficult as that. If the map of the mantis creatures was correct, there should only be one tall mountain out here somewhere, isolated and thus very prominent, easy to spot when we neared it.

On the nineteenth day, we saw our first glimpse of our objective. Rising blackish above the horizon was definitely a lone mountain of some kind. However, on the twentieth day, a new problem arose. The land began to change and become vast grasslands. Even from our vantage point, as we looked into the distance, we could see that the native villages here were much closer together. We were heading into a more populated area and could no longer bypass all the inhabitants. By nightfall, we had no choice but to enter a village of some thousand people.

Linda suggested that this might be a good time to stop, make some friends, and find out any information on the mountain, which lay ahead of us. We entered the village and caused quite a stir among the people; many had never seen people whose skin was white before. Often the children would come and touch our skin to see if we were real. Yet, everyone was smiling, a good sign I thought. Now we could have used Natale's skills. Awkwardly, we all fumbled around trying to pick up their words, and they, ours. It was frustrating, and our respect for Natale's skill rose enormously!

Just when we were about to forget the whole idea, one man began talking to us using a crude dialect of Megalos! His name was Jintu. Eagerly, we began chatting with him! He used to work in a diamond mine far to the east of here, but had escaped one night. We learned that the miners used slave labor to do their digging. Jintu was very glad to hear that we also considered Megalos to be our enemy. Here, everyone considered the bronzed skinned men to be Evil Ones. Since our skin was not bronze, we were accepted. Naturally, they wished to hold a feast in honor of our appearance, to welcome us here to their village called, Utu.

At my suggestion, we had brought along with us a few small items to trade or give away, mostly small knives, and such. After presenting the village leader and Jintu with a knife, both treated us as if we were family. Now information flowed swiftly and honestly between us. We did not like what we found out, however.

Our destination was called Hudu, or Black Evil. The lower mountain sides were home to a very warlike tribe called the Hudu Tikki. Further to the west where the jungles began, tribes of head hunters lived, who collected the skulls of their victims and somehow shrunk them into small heads. But the Hudu Tikki were not head hunters. After hearing this, we were very glad that we had not tried to get here on our original course!

These natives painted their bodies with grey ash and often raided out here on the grasslands, taking captives back with them. Mostly the captives were women, none of which was ever seen again. While Jintu and these villagers carried very long, slender spears, the Hudu Tikki used blowguns with poisoned darts. If a dart hit you, your body became paralyzed, and you were captured or killed, or so Jintu and the village leader explained to us. Very bad men, they continually repeated.

We asked about strange creatures, if they had seen anything strange or unusual around the mountain or close to it. None had, just the normal wildlife. I thought this was encouraging at least. An hour later, Jintu described strange flying birds, very black and very large that had been seen flying about the mountain. We discovered that we had not asked our question properly! These people distinguished between land animals and flying birds. We'd used the wrong expression when we asked the original question! Now we began to worry and asked them to describe these flying birds. However, no one had ever seen them close up, only flying at a far distance. Not much help, they could just be giant scavengers, of which we had encountered many on our trip thus far.

Apprehensive, that would describe all of our feelings that night as we tried to get some sleep in a hut provided to us by the leader. Were there actually mantis creatures living on that mountain or not? How dangerous were these inhabitants? Could we possibly get around them to search the mountain? We had far too many unanswered questions, and all of us were rather worried that night. Rightly so.

The next day, we got a good look at Hudu. It lay about a day's ride from us to the south. A rounded black boil on the brownish and grasslands of the savannah, Hudu was out of place, a dome structure rising several thousand feet above where we stood. Yet, it was a gradual rise from these plains, not a steep, rugged climb to the top, where we expected to have to get to find the entrance. The black surface rock was covered densely in places with clusters of relatively dense low trees. Other places the grasses of the savannah were slowly encroaching upon the black roots of Hudu. We counted at least five valleys on this side that led upwards and there were numerous smaller plateaus on its sides. We estimated its base to be at least twenty miles wide; perhaps a crow's view might show us that Hudu was nearly circular and twenty miles in diameter. At least, that was our guess at this point. While this was a lot of area to have to search, based on the other mantis caverns, in all likelihood we only needed to search the top of the peak.

Getting there would not be a problem, just another day's ride. Rather, handling the tribe that lived on the sides of this peak would be a serious one. Did they number a few hundred, a few thousand, or more? How good of a fighter were their warriors? Was there any truth to the reports of their use of blowguns with poisoned darts? Yes, the Hudu Tikki was undoubtedly going to be a major problem for us.

Now it was decision time. Which route would we attempt to follow to the top? Where would we leave our horses and supplies? Or should we attempt to ride all the way to the top? Emil cautioned us, "If we take the horses and get attacked, we risk losing our transportation. If we go on foot, we will take longer there and back and limit the amount of food we can take and limit what we can bring back, if anything."

"What about taking four packhorses and going on foot?" suggested Renzo. We liked his compromise. Of course, now what do we do with the horses and tack? These villagers had never seen a horse, and I didn't want to leave them in their care.

"May I make a suggestion?" put in Angel, hesitatingly. She was not used to working this closely with a Circle of Guardians.

"Sure, anytime, Angel," Emil encouraged.

"We could ride them a ways yet, until we found a secluded spot with plenty of grass and water. Mary Beth and I could then stay with them and guard them while you all went the last way on foot. I would not trust one of our mounts to these villagers, and we don't dare leave them tethered. There are too many beasts of prey walking these lands," Angel volunteered.

This was the best idea yet and was adopted. We thanked our village hosts as best we could and rode out in the middle of the morning, heading to the most promising area of Hudu, where there seemed to be a fairly easy route to the peak itself. Gradually, the ground began to rise, though the grasslands still predominated. Now low trees began to dot the otherwise open landscape. Around noon, we came to a secluded glen cradled beneath a steep rocky cliff. A small stream trickled down the rock forming a small pool at its base before forming a very narrow creek trailing out into the grasslands. Here was the ideal camping spot. Carefully, Benet searched the ground around the pond.

"All clear, no large cat footprints, only a few cloven hooves, probably some of the strange deer-like animals. This is a good place to leave the horses. Let's make our base camp here," Benet decided. An hour later, camp was fully setup, and those of us who were continuing had packed a sack to carry on the four packhorses that we'd take with us.

Now I had to issue the standing orders for Angel and Mary Beth. "Okay you two, this is an exceedingly dangerous mission we are embarking upon. You are our rear guards. If we lose the horses, our return trip is going to be one very long mess. The horses are your prime duty. However, how long we will be gone is unknown, and it may be several days. Under no circumstances are you two ever to leave here to try to come and find us, is that clear? If we do not return in say fifteen days, you can assume that we have been killed and are then free to make your way back to the caravel. At night, whenever possible, either Rosina or I will contact you and keep you updated on our progress. If you suddenly stop hearing from us for a lengthy time, use your own discretion to decide whether to pack up and return or wait a little longer. However, always use extreme caution. These Hudu Tikki are likely very evil men, and those flying birds might just be the mantis creatures. If either of those appear near here, hightail it out of here as fast as you can. Under no circumstances attempt to fight them. Questions?"

"But, Bethany, we are Santi; we cannot leave without you," pleaded Angel. "We've never gone off and left anyone yet!"

"Use your discretion, Angel. If we no longer communicate with you, we are likely already dead or worse. It is critical that headquarters then knows about this place! If there are mantis creatures here that we cannot handle, all Tarra is doomed! I've fought the adults a century ago and only succeeded in surprising them, not harming them. These foes, as adults, are unbelievably formidable opponents! We may not have anything that can harm them. So if we are lost, I am depending upon you two to get word of this back to headquarters, along with how to get here."

"Yes, Commander," Angel replied with a sigh. Mary Beth just looked at the ground.

With lunch under our belts, we began hiking up the chosen gully. We four women led the packhorses, bringing up the rear. Benet and Emil took point, with Renzo and Cedric behind them. Jason and John trudged behind them. Ten of us headed into the unknown, determined and resolute, but very apprehensive.

Shortly, Benet called a halt. "Look at this. What do you make of it?" We gathered around a small rock cairn, which stood about two feet tall. On its rocks were painted in grey several long streaks. Speculation suggested these could be crude mantis representations. However, from the villager's descriptions of the painted faces of the Hudu Tikki, these were more like tribal markings. We concluded that this was a marker indicating that we were now entering their land or country. Benet continued up this gully.

The heavy grasses began to give way to the rockier, black soil. Small trees became more numerous. I say trees, because they looked like twenty-foot tall trees, but none of us had ever seen such trees before. While a normal tree has a single trunk that grows thicker at its base, the base of these trees forked into at least ten independent root-like tentacles that clawed their way into the black ground.

We were steadily going upwards, though the gradient was gradual. Occasional large boulders had to be avoided, and the frequent stony patches were both slippery and noisy when the four horses stepped on them. None of us liked the noise, which might announce our presence here. In the back of our minds was the idea to slip quietly up to the peak, inspect it, and then quietly leave, all without contacting these Hudu Tikki.

Near dusk, we estimated that we were at least halfway to the top. During the last hour of our climb, we kept a lookout for a safe place to make camp. As the sun dropped over the side of the mountain, we found an ideal place. Cradled against twenty foot tall cliffs, a box canyon offered us a good site, where we only had to guard against one entry point. Here we set up camp, though we lit no fire, figuring that would be a dead giveaway of our position. While we made a light, cold meal, Rosina contacted Angel and relayed to her the little news that we had. In turn, Angel reported that everything was quiet there as well. The two women had seen nothing all day.

We posted two guards that night, who were relieved every two hours. During Renzo and my watch in the wee hours of the morning, I felt the skin on the back of my neck prickling. *I have an eerie feeling that we are somehow being watched!* He slowly began moving toward the perimeter of our camp, sword at the ready. However, neither of us actually saw or heard anything. When we roused Linda and Damien to relieve us, we let them know about our uneasiness as well.

I was never gladder to see the sun rising over the eastern rim of the gully than this morning. We were still safe; all was completely quiet, except for the birds chattering away in the trees. After eating a cold breakfast, we assembled our gear, tying it securely to the packhorses. Benet and Emil again took point, but requested that we stay put until they reconnoitered the short distance back into the gully we had been climbing. They found nothing amiss. As we began to walk back out of our secluded campsite, I carefully studied the ground for footprints that Benet might have missed. I found none. I took a deep breath and felt better about everything.

Shortly before noon, the gully leveled off onto a plateau. Here the trees grew thick and dense, obscuring our vision drastically. We all paused here for a time, knowing that this patch might easily hide trouble ahead. The men all took out their swords. Renzo handed me one of his spares as well. Tonia had her staff, Rosina, her dagger. Linda drew her short sword as well. Satisfied that we were armed and ready, Benet and Emil began picking a route through the dense trees. Our estimates suggested that we were three-quarters of the way to the top. Surely if we could get through the next few hours, we would reach our destination!

The going was slow, twisting and turning, as if the very trees were attempting to block our passage! Again, I had an eerie feeling as if we were being watched. I looked left and right and even behind us, but saw nothing. Creepy. For what seemed an eternity, we hiked onwards. Suddenly, I realized what was bothering me. The bird sounds had vanished; only our heavy breathing and dull footsteps broke the silence. Just as I was about to sound the alarm to the others, I heard a low, short, puffing sound from my left. I turned to look and felt a slight sting on my left shoulder. I turned my head and saw a little dart, no bigger than an inch sticking out of my shoulder. Instinctively, I pulled it out. As I did, I saw a black skinned man with ash grey lines on his face and chest. His hands held a long tube, and he silently slipped back into the cover of the trees, out of sight.

I tried to yell, but my voice didn't work. My body was numb; my sword clanked on the ground. I couldn't move! A greyish mass moved over me. Though I fought against it, the mass swamped me, and I lost consciousness, doped off into a comatose sleep. That's the way I would describe it later, a comatose-like sleep. The last thing I remembered was the world slowly lowering. My body was falling to the ground.

Chapter 21 The Choices of Angel Hattfield

"Mary Beth, they didn't contact us last night!" Angel exclaimed as she got up from her restless night's sleep. "This is the fourth day now that we have not heard from either Bethany or Rosina! Something is horribly wrong, I know it; I just know it!"

"I feel it too, Angel, but what can we do? She gave us the strictest of orders. Remember she said and I quote, 'This is an exceedingly dangerous mission; you are our rear guards. The horses are your prime duty. How long we will be gone is unknown, it may be several days. Under no circumstances are you two ever to leave here to try to come and find us, is that clear? If we do not return in say fifteen days, you can assume that we have been killed and are then free to make your way back to the caravel. At night, whenever possible, either Rosina or I will contact you and keep you updated on our progress. If you suddenly stop hearing from us for a lengthy time, use your own discretion to decide whether to pack up and return or wait a little longer. However, always use extreme caution. Use your discretion, Angel. If we no longer communicate with you, we are likely already dead or worse. It is critical that headquarters then knows about this place! So if we are lost, I am depending upon you two to get word of this, along with how to get here, back to headquarters.' That's what she said." Mary Beth had a knack of remembering precisely what was said, orders-wise.

Angel fussed with her short hair, fluffing it out from her night's sleep. "Okay, I think that not hearing from them for over four days now constitutes a lengthy time. Now I am to use my own discretion, right, Mary Beth?"

"Well, I suppose that not hearing from them this long is a lengthy time. Granted that, then you are allowed to use your discretion, Angel. What are we going to do?" Mary Beth asked, quite worried about their predicament. Her fears had steadily been growing, ever since the first night that they failed to contact them. True, the first night, Rosina had spoken with them via their minds and nothing was amiss. After that, four nights had now come and gone without word. This would be the fifth day now. Something was horribly wrong.

"As I see it, Bethany is the most powerful Santi of all time, even more so than our Supreme Commander Jenna Rose Weston. If she were awake or even if her body were dead, I know that she would Mind Link, as they call it, to us and let us know what to do. Look, we both have seen her talk to spiritual beings that have just had their bodies die. If she were able, she would have contacted us long before now," Angel reasoned.

"Yes, but where does that leave us, Angel?"

"I can only conclude one thing, Mary Beth. She and the rest, well at least Rosina, must somehow be unconscious. Maybe they took a bad fall; maybe they were attacked and were seriously injured. Maybe many things, but both Bethany and Rosina must somehow be unconscious. That can be the only reason why they are not contacting us, Mary Beth," Angel declared, still fussing with her short hair, which she often did as she tried to work out a serious problem.

"Well, that does seem reasonable, so what are we to do?"

"I get to use my discretion, that's what. If they are unconscious, then I can't just leave them. Lord knows, I might be able to save their lives or something. Yet, we have the rest of Bethany's orders to consider as well." She paced wildly around in little circles, forming a way to satisfy all of Bethany's orders to them.

"I've got it. Mary Beth, you take your horse and most all our provisions here — all the water too. I want you to ride back to the native village. Wait there two days. If you have not heard from any of us by then, you are to retrace our route back to the caravel. You can hunt as well as I, so you won't starve. I charge you with getting word of this back to headquarters as we were so ordered."

"Okay, I can do that, but what about you? Aren't you coming with me?"

"No, they must be unconscious. I don't know why, but four days unconsciousness sounds terribly bad to me. I have to go find them and see if there is anything that I can do to help. If I find them dead, I'll rejoin you at top speed. If I am attacked or anything like that, I'll do the same. Yet, if I'm not, it shouldn't be too hard to follow their trail; ten of them and four horses leave a clear path. I will take the gamble that the horses here will be fine until I return for them. We have seen no predators these last five days, so I'm willing to take that gamble. I'll travel light and use all the tracking and stealth skills I possess. I believe this is covered under the clause that I am to use my discretion."

"Angel, do be extra careful. I do love you, you know. I would hate to lose you too. We've been on so many adventures together. Yet, I think you're making the right decision. I'll do as you say, wait for two days before making my way back. I'm a better long-range marksman than you, but you are better at stealth and tracking; you always were. Go rescue them, Angel!"

Angel smiled, "One last thing, just in case I don't come back myself. I think that Jason really likes you. I've seen him watching you constantly when he thinks we're not looking."

Mary Beth flushed, "Really, but then he is likely to have been hurt too. Just our luck, Angel, when we finally find some fellow who is interested in us, they go and get themselves killed." Both women smiled; they had very rotten luck finding husbands.

They hugged each other and then began to pack up everything that Mary Beth would need. A half hour later, they hugged once more, and Mary Beth mounted up and began riding cautiously back down the hillside toward the distant savannah village. Tears filled her eyes.

Angel made sure that the horses were all set for an extended stay on their own. She packed up every arrow she had, three quivers worth, packed up a small amount of dried food and a water skin. At last, she checked on her short sword and picked up her longbow. Taking one last look around to make sure she'd forgotten nothing, she turned and headed to the gully without looking back.

As she suspected, their trail was impossible to miss. Steadily and silently, she began to follow the route taken by the Guardians five days before. Haste made her passage more rapidly that we had. By nightfall, she reached the plateau where the dense trees began. Our trail led straight into this dark mass. Angel couldn't follow the trail at night, not when the trees obscured all traces of the moonlight. Hence, she found a sturdy tree and climbed up, hiding in the foliage. There, she ate lightly and rested, waiting for morning's light. She half hoped that she would receive word from me or Rosina that night, but she did not. At dawn, she steeled herself.

She had found our first campsite from where the nighttime message had been sent to her from Rosina. The next night, no word. Thus, whatever happened to her people had happened just ahead, likely within the dense woods. It was a perfect place for an ambush. After eating a bit more, she climbed back down and listened to the sounds of the many birds, greeting the new day. Satisfied, she began to follow our clear trail wandering among the trees.

Around noon, she spied where the ambush had happened. Signs of fallen bodies littered the ground. She picked up a tiny one-inch long dart. Ambushed, she declared to herself, taken by total surprise. She bent over and began studying the ground. Hundreds of barefoot prints covered the immediate area. Angle noted that our leather boot prints completely ended here. No trace of them could she see beyond this spot. However, the barefoot prints leaving this location were deep, far deeper than those around where the bodies had fallen. Angel reasoned that everyone was now unconscious and had been carried away from here, horses too.

Satisfied with her observations, she notched an arrow and began to follow the unmistakable trail as it led deeper into this dense forest on the plateau. Three hours later, going very slowly with her eyes ever alert, she saw a black man with grey ash markings watching the path just ahead of her. He also saw her and raised his blowgun to his lips. She was far faster. Twang! Her steel-tipped arrow, driven by the powerful bow, flew completely through the man's head. He fell out of the tree onto the ground, dying instantly. She quickly notched another and crouched down, watching for others to appear. After the initial flutter of birds, the forest became normal once more. No more men appeared. She waited a long time before moving again. At last, she moved to the dead man and pulled him into the brush to hide his body, but her arrow was deeply imbedded in the tree and could not be removed easily. She left it there as a warning sign to others. Angel was getting mad. Do not get an expert archer angry!

She noted that this lookout was about ten feet from the main path. Thus, since the path was now very wide and unmistakable, she moved twice that distance off the path before pushing on ahead. She calculated that she would likely be able to see other lookouts before they saw her. The wisdom of her decision soon became apparent. Three more lookouts died from her arrows, all arrows passing cleanly through the victim's head. She continued to push on hoping that she was getting close to where our unconscious bodies had been taken.

Just as night was falling, she halted and hid among the trees. Ahead the forest opened up into a village, a rather large village at that. Hundreds of men and women and children, all with black skins and those strange ash grey line marks on their faces and chests moved around the village. Angel decided to observe for a while, hoping to discover where we might be located.

The houses were crudely built structures of thin wood with leafy roofs. Most all were very similar in nature and size. Slowly, she studied each building that she could see. Occasionally, someone would enter or leave the building she was observing, their residences she concluded.

Just as night fell, she spied an unusual looking building. It was hard to see all of it; other buildings partially concealed it. This one had unusual walls, more like vertical poles evenly spaced about six inches apart. Angel focused her full attention on this one. A few minutes later, she saw a naked woman, who did not have the grey markings on her body, yet did had something shiny about her neck, carrying a bowl or something like that from one spot over to another. Her eyes drilled onto that woman, straining to see in the failing light and at this extreme distance. Then she was rewarded; she spied the woman lifting up a white arm! Try as she might, she could see nothing more. However, out here, this could only mean one thing.

Angle did not sleep a wink that night! Her conclusion was obvious. We were all being held prisoner in that pen or building. All night long, she tried to envision ways to rescue us, but no viable idea came to her. She spent the last few hours crying to herself before the dawn came. She was this close to helping us and yet could do nothing. She was one against hundreds.

As the dawn broke, Angel heard two of the loudest, most awful shrieks that she had ever heard! It sounded like some of us, however, and they came from the pen where she had seen the white arm the night before. Hastily, she laid out her three quivers for fast action. If nothing else, thirty of these beasts would be felled before she ran out of arrows and had to go hand to hand with her sword. She waited, but thought she heard moaning or crying sounds. However, now there was a whole lot of movement within the pen. Other women with something shiny around their necks were scuttling about, carrying what looked like bowls. Just where they were going, she could not see; buildings obscured her vision.

Angel waited, but saw nothing harmful. Then, she spotted many villagers coming out of their huts. Strange, they all lined up in two parallel lines, one on either side of the village. Evidently some kind of ceremony was about to take place. She still had a clear line of sight to the pen. The villagers began chanting and stomping their feet, raising small black dust clouds around their feet. The ground was parched. Overhead, something momentarily blocked out the sun!

She looked up, as did all the villagers. Angel nearly vomited! It was one of these horrible mantis creatures that Bethany had often told them about and just like the ones she had seen killed by Bethany before on the islands and at the Wanakan temple. Only this one was much larger than those she had seen dead! It was at least thirty feet long!

Slowly, it descended to the ground, raising a black cloud as it landed right between the lines of the natives. Once the dust settled, it slowly moved toward the pen! Oh my god, it's going to eat them, thought Angel to herself. She rechecked her arrows and prepared to fire every one at this truly demonic beast.

Then she saw Bethany being pushed out of the pen. She could see some kind of struggle going on between me and the creature. It twisted around, and now she could see that the mantis had me held tightly in its front top arms if that is the right term for them. Its mouth was drooling saliva on me, that much she could see. Just as it opened its massive jaws to begin to dine on me, Angel acted, doing the only thing that she could. For her, this was a medium range shot. Her aim was, as always with this Santi, at its head. Never did Angel ever aim elsewhere. She always took the head shot, her trademark. One arrow, one kill was her motto that she had lived by all her life. Besides, from our attack on the mantis down in the Spice Islands, arrows through its soft middle section did little harm to the mantis.

Twang! Her arrow flew, backed by the full draw of her very powerful longbow. The steel-tipped armor-penetrating shaft flew straight to its mark. It pierced the bony exoskeleton around its head and came partway out of its right eye cluster. Instantly, a horrid shriek deafened everyone. Angel saw Bethany's body fall to the ground. Twang! Five seconds after the first shaft found its mark, Angel's second arrived as well, only at a slightly different angle, passing only half way through the creature's head. Damn, the mantis is well armored around its head, thought Angel. Never had she not seen her shaft exit a man's head, unless he wore a helm, then it might come halfway out, as they did here with the mantis. Five seconds later, she was ready to fire a third arrow, muttering to herself, "Die foul beast from Hell!"

Chapter 22 Captured

I was encased in a grey foggy mass, surreal, everything was dislocated, disjointed, and my thinking was nearly non-existent. I tried to move, but which way? Up was down was right was left. The more I tried to move, the more swirling the grey fog became and the more confused I was. Fight it, Bethany, fight it, I kept thinking to myself. We've been captured; you have to get out of this fog! Yet the more I tried to move, the more confused I became, the more disoriented I was.

How long I was fighting, I do not know. How do you tell the passage of time when all you can see is a swirling, disorientating grey fog? Rise above it, I kept telling myself. Yet, which way is up? No matter how I tried to move, the fog only suppressed me further. Finally, I decided that I was indeed in a drugged stupor!

At last, I could reason. I stopped fighting it and tried to relax. The only thing to do was to wait it out; eventually the drug's effects would wear off. I panicked. What if I'm given more of the drug? Sometime later, I managed to begin to relax once more. I could do nothing about that eventuality. Why would they want to keep me permanently drugged? That made no sense either. None of this made any sense, for that matter.

Wait, just relax, and wait it out, Bethany, I kept telling myself. If you can't figure out which way is up to move out of the mass, then just wait until it wears off. I took a deep spiritual breath and calmed down. I stopped resisting the effects of the drug. While the grey fog was still encasing me, at least I felt better about it.

I had the strangest sensation of something touching my lips. Do I still have lips? I wonder where they are at now? Yes, it most definitely is my lips that I am feeling. Oh, something cold is on them. No, it's liquid. I can feel it trickling down my chin. Yes, I do still have a chin somewhere around this grey fog! Say, I seem to be drinking it. I can feel my insides now. Oh, am I ever thirsty! Whoever is doing this, yes, yes, give me more, more!

Slowly feeling came back into my body; the grey fog slowly subsided and evaporated. I opened my eyes. I saw several black women with these gold colored metal bands encircling their necks all the way up to their chin; these seemed to be very tight, and they could not move their heads. I heard the sounds of Tonia and Rosina; they were waking up too. I decided to get up and pushed up with my arms.

Nothing happened. I tried again, still nothing. I tried to bend my head to look at what was going on. I couldn't bend my head either! Shocked and with a horrible feeling in my stomach, I lurched my body upwards. I could see that we were in some kind of pen with many other women. There were Tonia, Rosina, and Linda. We all had these gold colored metal bands around our necks, which were so tight that we couldn't move our heads at all.

Good god! "Linda, what happened to your arms!" my disembodied voice shrieked. She was sitting up, but had no arms left. She looked at me and shrieked as well. I tried to raise my arms to feel these metal bands around my neck, but nothing happened. I twisted a bit and finally saw my own shoulders. I too had no arms. Terrified, we looked at each other and shrieked at the top of our lungs!

Tonia yelled, "Bethany, Linda help! Calm down. Help. Help. Help!"

Her voice pierced me, and I regained control of my mind. I looked around. Both Rosina and Tonia were still unharmed as far as I could see. Several other black women with the same metal bands around their necks came to us offering a drink from a bowl. We accepted and I drank and drank. Thirst quenched, I looked around. Five other women here also had no arms. Two more had no arms and half of their legs were missing. One poor woman was nothing but a head and torso!

"Bethany, we have got to get out of here before we are eaten up like her," Tonia exclaimed. We four got up. Tonia came over to help me, while Rosina helped Linda to her feet. The other women kept waving their hands trying to tell us not to try to walk out of the pen. The gate was locked, but Tonia kept trying to push it open, to somehow break it down, but to no avail.

"Damn, damn, damn," I said. "Where are the men? Anyone see them?" No one did. Now I was getting mad, really, really mad. I moved outside the body, latched onto the locked door of this pen, and ripped the entire door off! "Damn!" I said once more. There was only room for one person at a time to leave, so I went first, followed by Tonia.

We four had just gotten outside, when we spied the entire village lined up in two neat rows on either side of the street before this pen, if street it could be so called. The sun was momentarily blocked out but something flying overhead. Twisting my body so I could look up, I saw a huge mantis creature coming in for a landing. With this damnable neck thing on, I could barely move around. To see, I had to turn my whole body, slowing my reactions horribly. Now the mantis landed before us.

I yelled, "Good god! It's huge! Get back inside all of you. You are no match for this beast!" My three companions backed up into the relative safety of the pen.

I moved up and over the mantis, figuring to grab a hold of it and bash it around some. Just as I latched onto it, the mantis creature picked up my body in its top front appendages, leaning its ugly head over my head, its mandibles dripping juices on my face. It was going to eat a bit more of me — that was certain. If I were going to pick it up and bash it around, then I would also very likely be killing my own body. I made the conscious decision to do just that; this creature had to be destroyed before it got the chance to eat my friends and many other women. My life to stop this demonic creature — it was well worth the trade.

Just as I was about to begin, from nowhere an arrow pierced its skull and came partway out of its left eye cluster! The horrid cry that it made nearly pierced my eardrums. My body fell to the ground, released from its devouring grip! Thud! A second arrow slammed into its skull coming out close to the first one. I delayed no longer.

Mad, angry, violent hatred — yes I felt all these running through me at the time. I grabbed its huge hind legs, picked it up, and began thrashing it into the ground, much like thrashers do wheat when they are harvesting it.

The creature struggled violently to free itself from my grip, but I held on so tightly that I crushed its bony skeleton surrounding its legs. Over and over and over, I smashed its head into the ground, into the nearby huts, even into the line of shocked Hudu Tikki. Ah, the Tikki, they had captured us, and now my rage turned onto them. Using this mantis body much as a club, I began smashing it into their bodies. Suddenly, they began running in all directions trying to escape this incredible act of God that was striking them down. I did not stop. I began picking them off one by one, wham, smash, thud!

I had not noticed it before, but now I had help! Flames, three sets of flames appeared over the buildings and over the fleeing men. My three friends were in on the action too. Wham. Bam. Thud. I continued pounding the mantis into everything imaginable around the village.

After some time, I heard a far off voice saying, "Bethany, you can stop now. It's quite dead. Please stop. We need help!" It was the disembodied voice of Tonia. No, I was disembodied! I let go of the mantis and looked at it. It had been beaten into an unrecognizable pulp! I gave it a spiritual spit and floated back to my body, which the others were holding upright.

"Damn," I said, hearing the sound of my own voice at last. "Well, at least this time I did not go insane, that's something. Where are the men? Are you all right? Where did that arrow come from? Good god, what had happened to Linda and me?"

Someone came running towards us. Tonia called out, "Angel, is that you?"

Angel, carrying her nearly empty quivers, ran up to us. She stopped short and gasped, "Good god! What happened to Bethany and Linda? They've no arms! I should have come sooner! I am so sorry that I have failed you, Bethany."

"Angel, it is good to see you. We've only just now woken up. None of us knows what has been going on or even what day it is."

"This is the fifth day that we haven't heard from you. I sent Mary Beth back home and came looking for you. I should have come sooner! Woe is me, I've failed you both!"

"Hold on, Angel, you have not failed us. We were completely drugged the whole time. Golly five days? Wow. If you had come, you couldn't have done anything. Instead, Angel, I owe you my life, such as it has now become. If you had not shot it when you did, I would be just as dead as the mantis. I was just about to thrash us both into the ground, which would have wiped out what remains of this body. So Angel, I owe you my life." Right now, I had to think of her emotions and conclusions first or lose her, and I needed her mind free and clear. Mine sure wasn't!

"Linda, concentrate your thoughts only on the situation. Don't think about yourself right now, please. Me too. I've got to focus or we are lost."

"I'm trying, Bethany, I'm trying. God what has happened to us?" Linda wailed, but fought for her self-control.

"God, this neck thing — I cannot even turn my head. Can one of you get this thing off of me, please," I ordered. Three examined the rings carefully.

Angel replied, "I don't see how it comes off, Bethany. It looks like it was somehow forged around your neck. Damn!"

I sighed, "Well, okay. The men, does anyone know where the men are at?" No one did.

"Okay, spread out; let's search the village. They must be here somewhere," I declared. We began searching the smoldering remains of the village. Angel also began collecting what arrows survived. In the end, she refilled two of her quivers, thankfully.

After an hour of searching, we found no sign of the men. They simply weren't here! I had an awful sensation in my stomach over this revelation. Linda came up to me, "Bethany, the other women, who were like us — they are also gone. Not here, only the one poor woman who had no appendages left. She's got a knife in her heart. The others have fled somehow. We are the only ones here. Now what? We have to find the men!"

"Okay, I have to do this. Someone please help me to sit down and watch over me. I will try to find them." Tonia and Rosina quickly came and helped me sit down, made all the more difficult because I couldn't move my neck. I tried to relax, but that was most difficult, especially pushing everything out of my mind. Under the circumstances, this was a minor miracle in and of itself!

At last, I was out and expanding my awareness, searching for my loving Renzo. Having no idea at all where he might be, I had to go in expanding circles, centered on our position. An hour elapsed before I found them, all six of them!

Renzo! Are you alive? Where are you? Are you men hurt?

I immediately picked up stark, utter terror from Renzo! *We don't know. We think we are underground. We are chained up in a viper pit. Hundreds of them are swarming at our feet and over us. Benet has been keeping them calm, but he keeps falling asleep. Help us, please, please, please!*

Hang in there. We are coming. Back soon. I broke the connection. I only had the vaguest idea of the direction.

"They are alive, chained in a viper pit, hundreds of them crawling over them; they don't know where they are. I think it is that way," I tried to point only there were no arms with which to point. I sort of used my foot.

"Commander, if I may, allow me to see what I can discover," Angel broke in.

"Sure, go ahead, like this, we can hardly see the ground!"

We watched as she began walking in wide circles around the perimeter of the village. After a short while, she yelled, "Over here. This way." We moved to her as fast as we could go, but Linda and I were experiencing a great awkwardness, having a very hard time coping with our bodies.

"I noticed the heavy imprints back at the place where you were captured. They carried you from there, making these very deep footprints. Come on. Let's follow these; they must be carrying the men this way." It was in the general direction I had discovered, so we followed her.

Soon, we could tell that we were continuing to climb up the mountain, and the plateau was now behind us. Tonia now had her arm around me to steady me, while Rosina did the same for Linda. Still, we four found it tough going. If only we could get rid of these awful neck bindings!

Higher and higher, we climbed, tougher and tougher going for the two of us. We needed constant assistance to keep from falling. At last, as the sun was setting, we came out onto a clearing and the plateau at the top of Hudu.

"Damn, it is so dark that I can't see the trail any longer," Angel cried out in dismay.

"Okay, calm down. What is the last direction the steps were heading?"

She pointed. "Okay, hold that point. Let's form a line and continue to move in that direction. Since Linda and I are going to have the most troubles, let us be the first markers. You help me move on out in the right direction a ways. Then I'll stand still, and Linda, you get on out further from me; together, we will mark the direction for the others. A sort of human chain. Those men carrying our men are going to go in a straight line up here since there is nothing in the way."

A minute later, I was in position. Somewhat later, Linda was out in front of me. Now Tonia sighted along us and moved out ahead of Linda. Angel went last, surveying what lay in front of us.

"Hey, there is some kind of temple thing here. I wish we had light." Very carefully, I walked up to her position. Now I was experiencing what so many other women that we had rescued had to experience every day. Hastily, I drowned that thought out of my mind. I had to rescue Renzo!

"Blue lights everyone," I ordered. With four blue lights hovering just in front of us, we could see the small temple like construction with a stone slab which I had a feeling was used for torture. Search as we might, we couldn't find them. At last, feeling awfully frustrated with an awful depression beginning to creep into her mind, Linda sat down on the slab, dejected, tears beginning to trickle down her cheeks.

The very instant that she put her full weight on the slab some enormously powerful lights turned on, fully illuminating the top of Hudu! We all jumped very shocked, pivoting this way and that, trying to see what had happened. The tight neck rings forced us to twist our bodies to see in any other direction than straight ahead. We heard a low-pitched humming as well, coming from somewhere underground! The lights were located in four concealed positions making a square with the temple here at its center.

"What the heck is happening?" Linda called out, frightened far more than she normally would have been — both she and I were just beginning to come to grips with just how vulnerable we both had become! A pole poked its way up from the ground until it stood twenty-five feet above the plateau. Distant memories of a similar pole that was used by the Grey Creatures came into my mind. Their pole energized, and any free spiritual beings were sucked into the pole. Next, their memories were scrambled, and then the Grey Creatures gave the confused beings orders to go get a new baby body, and report to the pole when it later died. Obviously, the mantis creatures had similar technology.

"I've found them!" yelled Angel. "There is a hole in the ground over here. I can see Renzo barely." We rushed over to where she was standing. Indeed, a low row of stones marked the rim of a six-foot square hole in the ground. We moved our blue lights over and sent them down inside.

None of us was prepared for what we saw there — well, I was, sort of, anyway. Our six men were chained to the walls of this six-foot square chamber, some eight feet below us. Slithering all over the floor was a giant mass of poisonous snakes, hundreds of them. Our fellows were motionless, even though several vipers had managed to slither up their bodies and were wrapped around their heads, trying to get out of the pit. None of them made the slightest attempt to say anything; they were petrified beyond description. I smelled a strong odor of urine coming from the pit.

We stared at the scene for a minute, before Angel whispered, "How are we going to get them out of there?"

Compared to our situation, theirs was horrid. One slight muscle twitch at the wrong moment and the vipers would strike. They would be dead long before we could ever get to them. "Damn, if only my neck wasn't in such a vice! I can barely see. Okay, I will bring the snakes up and free them one by one. You all stand way back, and Tonia, use your pole to convince any that threaten me to go away."

I moved slightly out of my head and then began. I carefully picked up the first viper which was wrapped around Renzo's head and pulled it on up and out, laying it carefully on the ground some distance from my body. When I let go, it slithered rapidly off towards the light. At this slow rate, it would take me all night!

Then, I had an idea. "Angel, drive one of your arrows into the end of Tonia's pole. I think that it will then be just about eight feet tall. I'll stick it down there and see if the snakes can climb up the pole themselves."

"Hey, now that is using your head," Linda commented.

"About all we got left," I joked grimly. A few minutes later, Tonia brought me her pole. I latched onto it and lowered it slowly down. The feathers of the arrow just reached above the top of the hole. Almost at once, the snakes got the idea. They began fighting each other to climb up the pole! "It's working. Damn, I had better get out of the way!" Indeed two vipers appeared and began slithering close by my feet. Making only the tiniest of motions, I backed away, joining the others who were watching.

Just then, we heard two noises. One came from the pole, which energized, casting a pale bluish glow over the area. The second sounded like a door sliding behind us. We whirled and saw that a section of the ground was in fact a sliding doorway! The head of another giant mantis creature appeared. It stared straight at us!

You dare interfere with our operation! Die now! we five heard in our minds. It came from the mantis that continued to climb out of its hole in the ground. Before we could think properly, it picked up some of our memories! Damn, this creature was both intelligent and powerful, I thought. *Baby killers! Wife murders! Race murders!* This last pronouncement was intended for me, because it was Alabaster and me who were the ones responsible for the near elimination of both the Grey Creatures and the giant mantises so many years ago.

With these cursed neck rings, the four of us were at a horrible disadvantage; our mobility was drastically reduced. Linda and I were almost completely sitting ducks! "Watch out for the energy blasts from its eye clusters!" I yelled, while looking for a way to grab hold of it as I had done before. Too late, Linda took a blast full force; she just couldn't maneuver at all. I saw her body fly backwards and land on the ground.

Tonia and Rosina began to move about as best they could, made horribly difficult by the confining neck rings. Me, I tried my best to keep from falling down and to get out of its direct line of sight, looking for an opening to attack it. The only thing we had going in our favor was that this energy blast was chemically created somewhere within its eye clusters. Time was needed to recharge between blasts.

I moved around to my right. Just as I was at a reasonable spot to avoid its gaze, Tonia took a blast in her head and went spinning to the ground, hitting it hard. She, too, did not get up. Rosina launched a wall of flames right on its head, temporarily startling it, and causing it a slight burn. Angel shot an arrow and once again pierced its hard shell head with the shaft making it only part way out the other side. It shrieked wildly, blasting Rosina with a blast. Like the others, constrained as we were, she could not duck and roll out of the way. She was stunned and fell to the ground as well.

I took this opportunity to reach out and grab its hind legs. The second it felt my beam latching onto its legs, the mantis twisted and turned towards me, but I was not in my body and it could not see me. To it, it must have seemed like magic — my solid grasp on its giant legs. Distracted as it was, Angel fired a second shaft into its head. As it swung around towards her, I pulled the creature up into the air so that it could not blast Angel. Now it began flapping its wings in a vain attempt to break my hold on its legs.

Die Bug! I placed that concept into its alien mind and swung it hard onto the ground. It tried to break its collision with the stone ground by flailing its small front appendages. Wham! Its head hit hard. Now I knew I might have it bested. I began swinging it up and down, smashing it relentlessly onto the ground. Any relief I might have felt was gone in an instant. I saw more of the bugs crawling up out of the hole in the ground!

Angel also saw them. She ducked behind the stone slab and began firing arrows at their heads as fast as she could, an arrow every six seconds or so. Many found their marks. I just kept on smashing this large mantis repeatedly, praying that the others would not get to us before I finished this one off. Then an amazing thing happened. As the mantis died, its spiritual being floated out of the crushed body and was instantly caught in its own electronic pole trap!

Wild energy flows arced around the pole as the mantis fought to get free of its entrapment. It did the wrong action; it resisted the pull of the pole's energy, which from experience I knew was the precisely incorrect thing to do. All one had to do was relax and not resist at all the pole's attraction and you were free of it. The being smashed into the pole, which now energized even further, scrambling the memories of the creature.

"Bethany! Help! I'm out of arrows!" screamed Angel, drawing her sword now and cowering behind the small shelter of the stone slab. She intended to wait until a mantis showed its ugly head by her and then chop at it. However, she didn't duck in time. One of those just climbing out sent a blast her way, knocking her over, sprawling onto the ground.

I now put my attention on these new arrivals. Ah, they were much smaller mantises! Angel had severely wounded three of them, the forth was now trying to assist the others by somehow pulling the barbed shafts out of their heads. While they were distracted, I latched onto the stone slab. Angel didn't need it any longer. I gave it a gigantic toss at the pile of mantis children. Only the unwounded one was able to get out of the way. The slab squashed the other three.

Unfortunately, for my body, it was the only one still standing. The fourth one instantly blasted it. I felt my body fly backwards and hit the ground, while my arms vainly tried to break its fall. Of course, there were no arms there to respond. Yet, the body was still alive, and I kept my attention on this fourth one. It now thought that it had eliminated the slab thrower and was now trying to lift the slab off its three siblings. I could see it straining to lift it. I latched onto the slab and jerked it high into the sky.

The poor mantis looked up completely astonished, unable to grasp what had happened to this very heavy block of stone. Gravity did the rest. Boom! The ground shook as the slab hit, crushing the entire lower body of the mantis child. The top half wiggled to get free, while writhing in intense pain. I had a choice. I could lift the block and risk it doing further damage to us with its energy beams or let it slowly die.

Evil creature or not, mutilator of women and me or not, I could not see it continue suffering like this. I floated over to Angel's dropped sword and took hold of it. One swift movement and its pain ended. I watched as all four mantis babies were also sucked into their own pole trap! Their memories flashed by as a complete jumble. Then, the energy of the pole stopped. A great stillness enveloped me.

Since nothing at all moved, I floated over to each of my dear friends and sensed their bodies. All four were alive and breathing. They were just knocked out or stunned, I couldn't tell which. I am not so good diagnosing things when exterior to my body like this. Relieved, I then floated over to the opening from which they had come and looked inside to see if more might be issuing forth at any moment. A dim light came from inside, but I could see nothing. I decided that I had better not go in there alone like this, without a body and with everyone else unavailable.

I took up a guard position at the head of the ramp they had climbed and waited for more to come out. After a time, with nothing happening, I made contact with Renzo.

Are you all okay now? Snakes gone? We've been attacked by five mantises up here. They are all squashed now. I'm standing guard over their hole. The others are all knocked out, my body too.

A very faint reply came to me. *Yes, as far as I can tell they are gone, but I can't see well enough to tell for sure. If there is even one left, we are doomed. I am so weak I can hardly stand up, but if I move, a snake might strike.*

Make your blue light, Renzo.

I'm so shaky I can't concentrate. Haven't slept in days. None of us have. Bethany, I'm so terrified! He was beginning to panic utterly! I had to do something fast.

I floated over the hole, created another blue light, and floated down inside bringing it with me. I saw their awful predicament. All six were chained to the walls with their arms held out horizontally with heavy clamps on their wrists, which were fastened to chains coming from the walls. Likewise, their legs were also chained to the wall, spread slightly apart. They had been forced to stand this way for days without making the slightest motion or the vipers would have struck. All their pants were soaked in urine and feces. Poor Benet had worked overtime trying to keep the snakes calm, but now he had collapsed into a deep, unconscious sleep.

No snakes remained. I triple checked and then checked again, looking in every conceivable spot where a snake might be hiding, up a pant cuff, behind a leg, any place. I found none. All had been very, very grateful to have at last had a way out of this trap, for the vipers too had been entrapped here as well.

None, Renzo. No snakes. You can relax now, maybe get some sleep. I'll keep watch over all of us until the others wake up. I watched as he did just that, collapsed into a deep sleep, his body slumping against the chains. Slowly, the others did as well. I floated up and back over to the mantis hole. Still no more had come out. That was a relief.

Only now, I noticed movement just outside the bright lights. Slowly a large number of the black skinned men with the ash grey stripes on their faces and chests began cautiously approaching, spears and blowguns in hand. Damn, would this nightmare ever end? I grabbed Angel's short sword and began attacking them before they could shoot or stab our five bodies lying on the ground all over the place. Three died before the rest fled terrified into the night.

Then as suddenly as the lights had come on, they went off! Instantly, complete darkness filled the Hudu peak. I heard the pole sliding back down underground. Fortunately, the heavy stone slab was sitting on the door entrance to the underground hole and the mechanism could not close it. Eventually, I heard an awful noise from deep inside the hole. Shortly an acrid burning smoke drifted up and out into the night sky.

I waited in the total darkness, very worried that more mantises would appear or that the natives might regroup and attack. The one thing I knew that I dare not think about was what had happened to my body and Linda's! I could tell that I had an enormous amount of fear, terror, and grief sitting right there, to say nothing of the utter hopelessness I would feel, just like the other women I had salvaged. If I allowed myself even to touch on this, I would lose control over everything. All the others were now utterly dependent upon me to watch over them. If only someone would wake up!

Then my body did wake up. I tried to get it to stand up. With this metal neck collar, the challenge was made ten times worse, which was already quite horrible to manage. I began to have an even higher respect for Natale, Mireio, and all the others! At last, I gave it up and just lifted my own body upright, floated it over to the slab, gently sat it down on the stone, picked up the sword once more, and placed it in my own hand. Oops. I forgot, the body had no hands. I just held it there where a hand should have been. Damn, damn, damn, I thought to myself.

Finally, Angel stirred and rose. Quickly she rushed over to me, stumbling over all sorts of unseen obstacles. "Are you alright?"

"Yes, I got my body smashed too, but I was outside it at the time. I took care of the rest of the creatures, and have verified the snakes are gone. The men are chained horribly down there. They are finally sleeping, though I suspect they are in poor shape indeed. I have no idea how we are going to free them, much less get these horrid rings off of our necks."

"Thank you, Commander. You saved us all once again."

"No, Angel, once more, you helped save us all. You had three of the four that were coming out mortally wounded. If I had to face four more, we all would be goners by now. Thank you Angel!"

We chatted a bit more, when she remembered Mary Beth. "Can you locate her and let her know that we need some real help here?" Angel asked.

She stood watch now and I reached out and made contact with a very worried Mary Beth. She was now in the last friendly native village. *I'm so glad that you are alive!*

Angel saved us all from the mantises. However, alive is about all. We are in big trouble here. Linda and I have lost our arms. The men are chained in an underground chamber. At least, I got the several hundred vipers out of there before they could be bitten. We have these horrible rings around our necks and cannot even turn our heads. Only Angel and I are now awake, guarding the others from any more mantis creatures that may be here and from the Tikki who have made one appearance already here at the top of Hudu. So alive is about the best I can say!

I'm on my way to you. I will follow Angel's path. Should I try to bring the horses too?

I fear that you might get yourself captured by these nasty Tikki men, Mary Beth. However, our need is great. I know — when you get back to the horses and have them ready to lead on up the trail, wait until I join you. I will ride guard for you and protect you while you join us. How soon do you think you would be ready to follow Angel's trail?

I'll be there by dawn. I'll not fail you all. Help is coming.

Okay, I'll float down to you at dawn then. Thanks Mary Beth, we really need you!

I relayed our plan to Angel. "If she rides hard, she ought to be up here by early afternoon. It isn't all that far, if you can just ride swiftly," Angel sounded quite hopeful. "Besides, she'll bring me more arrows. Then, we can provide better protection all around. She is the better shot."

"You were superb, Angel! Without you, we would have all perished most horribly. God, I am so tired now and hungry and thirsty!" I desperately wanted to add, and now I cannot even feed myself, but knew that I dare not entertain that thought! I had to stay alert and help get Mary Beth and the horses up here or we may still be doomed!

"Forgive me, Commander," Angel said. Quickly, she retrieved her water skin and held it up so I could drink. God, this neck ring thing made drinking unbelievably difficult! Next, she rummaged in her small sack for something to eat. In the near dark, it was a challenge. At last, she placed some dried fish in my mouth. It tasted delicious right about now. She and I sat there munching away for some time.

"Whatever happens, don't let me fall asleep, Angel. I have to be awake at dawn so I can help Mary Beth get here."

"I won't Commander. Here, have some more."

A while later, Linda stirred, followed by both Tonia and Rosina. I made another blue light so that Angel could see to help them up and bring them over to the slab. In a little while, we were all eating and drinking up the last of Angel's water. I explained what I had to do next so that Mary Beth could bring up the horses and much needed food and water. All promised to help keep me awake.

Chapter 23 Aftermath

Finally, dawn arrived. "Okay, I'm off. Linda, you are in charge of everything now, particularly watch over my body here while I am gone. Angel, you have security; keep a sharp eye out for the Tikki, who might try returning in the daylight. The rest of you, see what can be done to rescue the men. Good luck." I floated up and off down the side of Hudu, heading towards our horses and campsite. I had to give Linda a large load of responsibility. I knew that if she had nothing to do, the stark reality of our new condition would hit her like an emotional sledgehammer. I was doing my best to keep mine suppressed for the time being. I had too, everything depended upon it.

Sure enough, there was Mary Beth waiting for me. Her horse was well lathered. I knew that she had pushed him hard to get here so fast. She had all the horses tied into one line and then tied to her saddle. Thus, she had her arms free to fire her longbow if needed, though that would be difficult from horseback. I made the Mind Link.

Thanks, Mary Beth. We are in dire need up there. Come on; I'll guide you. Let's make haste. Leave the blasting of any Tikki to me. You just concentrate on getting these horses up the mountain.

You got it, Commander! She kicked her horse into action. I stayed well out in front of her.

Part way up the gully, I spotted a Tikki with a blowgun hiding in a tree. I grabbed him and threw him clear over the mountain, that's how angry I had become. Okay, slight overkill on my part. Sometime later, we rode through the burned-out village. A few had returned, but seeing us come charging into the village, they instantly fled for their lives. It is good that they did. I was in no mood to be kind just now. By the time we got to the top of Hudu, I had wildly pitched a dozen blowgun shooters an awfully long ways away!

Around eleven, Mary Beth and our string of horses came galloping onto the open top of Hudu. I slid into my very tired, exhausted body. "Report?" I heard my body say. Unfortunately, I did not hear the replies. I fell into a very deep sleep, a horrible sleep. Nightmares wracked my body. I kept seeing mantis creatures eating what remained of my body — feeling their saliva dripping onto my face. I tried to wipe it off with my hands, but no hands were there. What an awful nightmare.

I woke up. It was near dark. I tried to get up using my arms. Nothing happened. I looked at my arms, but they were not there. I shrieked loudly and all the others came running over to me. I looked sheepishly back at them.

Earlier this morning, Linda had watched me slip out of my body and head off to find Mary Beth and help her get to us. Taking charge she said, "Well, at least we can see now. God, the bugs are all over the place! How many did Bethany kill?"

"One giant one and four middle sized ones," Angel called out.

"How are we fixed for defending ourselves? How's our food and water supply? Any ideas on how to get to the men?" Linda asked, trying to focus on leading our group and not on herself.

"I've ten arrows left and my short sword, and I've lent my dagger to Rosina. My waterskin is empty, but there is a small bit of dried fish left," Angel quickly answered.

"We're screwed!" exclaimed Rosina dejectedly. "No water, no food, no weapons, no rope, no way to get to the men, and no way to unlock them even if we got to them. I cannot even move properly with this neck thing. Linda, we're really in the pickle barrel this time!"

"Well, it could be worse I suppose. Let's see what we can do that will be useful here. Angel, you and Tonia go check on the men. If they are still sleeping, let them sleep. See if there is any way you can get Tonia down to them. At least she could then check on their health and examine their bindings. Perhaps an idea will come, but you stay on top, in case the Tikki should return. Rosina, look around and see if there isn't something we could collect some water in. We could make a wall of ice and let it melt to make a little water, if only we had something in which to put it. I'll watch over Bethany and keep watch for the Tikki."

Rosina wandered around the hilltop, but found nothing with which to collect water. She joined the other two and helped Angel lower Tonia into the hole. The men were all sleeping. Tonia quickly went from man to man, using her skills to pervade their bodies and detect their state of health. When she got to Damien, Linda's husband, she gasped, putting her hand over her mouth to keep from waking the others. Tears came anyway, and she raised her arms over her head so that the other two could pull her back up. After a great struggle, Tonia managed to get out of the pit trap.

"What's wrong?" Rosina asked immediately. Even Angel looked very worried; the tears were obvious to both women. Something was wrong.

"It's Damien. He's dead. His heart gave out during the night. I have to tell Linda. Oh god, how do I tell her? She's lost her arms and now her husband!"

"I'll do it," Rosina volunteered. "Angel, you stay here with Tonia." Rosina walked slowly over to Linda, who waited for the report on the men.

"How are they holding up?"

Rosina sat down beside Linda and put her arms around her. "Five are sleeping, but in bad shape. One has died. It's Damien, Linda. His heart gave out. Their ordeal was too much for his body to handle. I'm so sorry for you." She felt Linda's body react in response to her mind registering the awful news.

"Oh god! No! Not Damien!" Linda wailed. She buried her head on Rosina's shoulders and cried for a time. Linda saw a huge wall of black grief moving in upon her mind. Lost, everything she valued in the universe was lost! She sat upright like a bolt. "Get control of yourself, Linda. I'm in charge. I must stay focused. I can grieve for Damien later." She took a deep breath, but it had a catch in it. The grief was still near at hand. "Thank you, Rosina. I must stay focused. Help me stay focused!" She sniffled to clear her nose. "Can you wipe my face a little, please?"

"Thanks, now has Tonia been able to see any way to unlock their bindings?" Linda sniffled once more, regaining her composure. She had to stay focused on the here and now — she just had to, she kept telling herself.

"No. She says they look like simple locks, but we need a key or a lock pick."

"Damn, damn, damn this whole mess!" Linda cursed. She looked about, "Damn! Tikki! Form a line around me immediately!"

Around four dozen of the black skinned men with the ash grey stripes on their faces and chests had appeared at the edge of the hilltop. They had quietly moved there from the trees, their eyes surveying the carnage of their Holy Gods. Revenge filled their minds. Shouting and yelling, they charged toward the four women. Four walls of flames suddenly appeared on them, searing their exposed flesh. Ten also dropped to the ground in less than a minute; an arrow had gone completely through their heads. For a moment, they dropped back out of the way of the flames.

"Move the flames closer to them; make them backup some more," Linda ordered. For a couple of minutes, it was a standoff. However, another bunch of men appeared, re-enforcing their numbers. As the women watched, the new arrivals flanked to either side of the four flaming walls, preparing to rush them once more. Angel, out of arrows, now moved out in front of the four, her short sword at the ready. She took her usual defensive combat stance, her feet spread slightly apart, ready to battle these monsters to the death. Steel anger seethed through her powerful muscles. She was ready to face them; no other thought than to protect the four behind her was in her consciousness. Rosina, with her dagger, took a flanking position.

The two groups yelled and then began to charge the women from two directions. "Fires now!" yelled Linda. Four more walls of flames appeared, two on each side. However, only two were not sufficient to stop all these men, hellbent upon revenge for the slaying of their gods!

Two dozen of the men managed to dart around the flames, running towards the nearly defenseless women, waving their spears wildly.

Several threw their spears at them; however, the women dodged them. Three reached Angel and began to find a way to attack her, poking at her dancing body. Her short sword was way out of reach compared to their long, thin spears. She danced and dodged, looking for an opening.

Just when Linda thought that this would be the end of them, she heard the sound of galloping hooves. A rider with a very long sword came galloping up over the hilltop behind the Tikki lines. The man let go of the reins of five other horses that he was leading and came charging into the melee, taking the Tikki by complete surprise.

Man and horse began attacking them. His sword was so long that it took two hands to wield it. He swung it this way and that, while his horse kicked with its hind legs and pawed into bodies with its front legs. The two acted as if they were one being. Angel took advantage of the confusion to strike deathblows to those closest to her.

Linda began using her skills to control other's bodies and make them do her bidding. Now she had half of the left flank attacking the other half. Rosina ducked and stabbed one who was trying to get his spear into Linda. Tonia kept throwing up walls of fire to block others from getting too close on the right flank. Men fell right and left. Suddenly, their morale broke utterly. Individually, they turned around and ran as fast as they could off Hudu's summit, racing for the cover of the trees. In seconds, the battle was over.

Linda stood staring at the scene. Angel was gasping for breath; she had felled five Tikki. At this point, they turned to look at the stranger wearing brown leather, who was calming down his prancing horse. "Thank you sir for the timely rescue," Linda spoke first. "I'm Linda and temporarily in charge of this Santi del Dio party."

The tall young man, who she judged to be about eighteen and slightly older than her, dismounted. His outfit was unique, she noted. From the back seams of his arms and legs, leather streamers dangled. He wore a beret hat with an eagle's feather flopping to one side over his short black hair. He was a handsome young lad, but he had the saddest blue eyes she'd seen.

"Guardian Chaucer de'Grange, ma'am, at your service," he bowed to her.

"My horse!" exclaimed Angel. She rushed over the field of bodies to retrieve her horse and the other four. "Hey, these are your packhorses," she added.

"Yes, I was following you, miss. I picked her up where you had left her and found the other four on my way up here. I was just in time it seems. Are you all right?"

Linda shook her head, "All right? God that is a relative term! No, we are not all right! Bethany and I here have just lost our arms to these vile bugs. We have these horrid metal neck chokers that prevent us from doing much. My husband is dead down in the snake pit, where our other five men are still chained to the walls, probably dying. We have lost our food; we have no water; our leader, Bethany, is out of her body here, trying to protect Mary Beth, who is trying to bring up all our horses and supplies. And we've just been attacked again by these abominable Tikki who don't know when to stop attacking us. Are we all right? Well, thanks to you we are not yet dead, so I guess so."

He roared with laughter and gave her a big hug, which, without arms, she couldn't prevent him. "My dear Linda. I meant are any of you wounded? I can see that you are in a fine pickle here. I rather expected far worse when I headed here a couple days ago. At least you are all alive. God," he just noticed the dead mantis creatures. "You killed them? How on Tarra did you manage that?"

Angel, leading the five horses up to us, said, "Well, I put two arrows into the head of this big one. and Bethany then picked it up and bashed it to death, as we did to the other big one down in the village. I was knocked out and didn't see how Bethany killed the other four, though."

"Gang, we have water again!" Angel declared, removing her other water skin from her saddle. She also got out her drinking cup and poured a cup full for Linda.

"Allow me," said Chaucer, taking the cup from her. He gently helped Linda drink the whole cup.

"Oh that tasted good. Thank you, Chaucer," Linda said gratefully. She took an instant liking to this man.

Tonia, who had not said anything yet, finally spoke up after taking a long drink from the water skin. "Chaucer de'Grange, Lilly de'Grange." He pivoted to face her. "You are both dead, been dead for two years."

"I recognize you. Aren't you the daughter of Elona Po?" he replied.

"Yes, Tonia Po Woodgrove now. My husband is chained in the viper pit over there, in bad shape, I'm afraid. But you are both dead!"

"I'm sorry, Tonia, but I am not dead yet. However, my wife is, Lilly. She was captured by these very creatures." Suddenly, Linda saw the origin of the grief in the man's eyes. She spied a tear forming, as he struggled to gain control. "I had to kill her. I had to kill my own wife!" He broke down completely, sitting down beside Linda and my lifeless body on the stone slab, crying.

"Tell me about it," Linda said, her voice full of compassion.

"We were assigned to the Santi Fortress at New Barq. Three years ago, merchants traveling up from the Southlands and Sud began reporting strange lights at night from out here on Hudu. She and I were finally sent to investigate. The Tikki never allowed us to get close enough to see really what was going on. Then, when I was out hunting — our provisions were running low — one of the larger bugs swooped down upon our campsite. I saw it abduct her, carrying it away in its claws as it flew. I rode like the wind after them."

"It took me several days to sneak up to the now burned out village back there. I spied on them and saw her being held captive in a wooden pen. Her arms were gone, just like yours! I wanted to rescue her and the dozens of others being held prisoner there too. However, there were over a hundred men with deadly blowguns constantly guarding them. Try as I might, there was no way I could get to her, though I tried several times. I saw the creature come to the pen several times, watched helplessly as it ate other women's legs too. Gruesome. Then, I saw it take what was left of two women, a head and torso only, and fly away up there to the peak with them. I presume that they would finish dining on what was left up here. To my utter horror, I watched the creature come after my wife. It was about to devour her legs too! She saw me hiding in the trees. I knew what she wanted me to do. That was the hardest thing I have ever had to do. Yet, I could not allow the creature to dine on Lilly. I pulled down a lightning bolt onto the metal choker around her neck. I killed her. The creature dropped her body. They do not dine on dead bodies; thank the gods for that. I watched in grief as the Tikki dumped her body into a hole."

"Ever since then, for two years now, I have been scouting this area, looking for a way to get revenge and kill these creatures. It looks like you have done it for me. I saw the lights last night and came as fast as I could. I saw Angel here coming after you and followed her, but she had a good head start on me. I found where she had left her horse, brought it along with me, and then found these other ones along the way."

"So, Elona Po's daughter Tonia, I am not dead, though I suspect the Guardians have long written us off as dead. We've had no contact for over three years now. I am not fit to be a Guardian any longer. I am a wife killer. How can I possibly face the world this way? I am as good as dead already. Enough of dead me. Let's see what we can do about this mess you are in." He gently pushed Linda's long hair aside and over her chest so that he could see the backside of the rings.

"Hey, these were forged onto your necks," he announced.

"Can you get it off?" begged Linda.

"I think so. Let me know if I am hurting you." He took his dagger point and began wedging it into the tiny crack where the two ends of a ring met at the back. Twisting and bending, he made a slight opening. Then he used his fingers and pulled hard. Ever so slowly, the metal began bending out straight once more. At last, the first ring came free, releasing the taut tension that was holding Linda's neck in a vice grip.

"Ah, that is so much better!" Linda exclaimed, finally able to move her head a little. Ten minutes later, Chaucer had all the rings removed from her. He had Tonia rub and massage her neck while he went to work on Rosina's neck. An hour later, all the women had been freed from the restraining neck rings, even mine, though I knew it not at the time.

During this time, Angel had piled all the dead Tikki bodies off to one side and gathered up their spears to use as weapons. She salvaged only a single arrow, much to her dismay. Her spare food sack, she carefully divided into portions so that each of them could have a little to eat, reserving the two larger portions for Linda and Bethany. She took the smallest portion.

With the rings removed, the group munched a welcome meal as the sun reached its zenith. Just then, the sounds of many running horses brought cheers from the group. Soon, the form of Mary Beth came riding up the top of the hill, a herd of horses behind her. I returned to my body and opened my eyes. "Report?" I said, and then promptly collapsed into a deep, nightmare-filled sleep.

"Hi everyone! I would not have made it without Bethany's help. She killed a bunch of Tikki who were guarding the path. Oh god! What happened to Bethany and Linda? Oh my god!" she shrieked as she dismounted, handed the reins to Angel and rushed to Linda and my now sleeping body. She threw her arms around Linda and hugged her tightly. "We have all failed you so badly!"

"No, you haven't, rather the opposite, you are saving us. We are out of food and water. The men are still chained in the viper pit and in terrible shape. You have come just in time in our hour of desperate need! The damn bugs got Bethany and me."

"Oh, who are you?" Mary Beth suddenly saw the newcomer. After a round of introductions and explanations, Linda again forced herself to focus on the present, at least until I awoke.

"Damien's dead. Tonia found out this morning. Come on, everybody. We must find a way to free them now," she ordered. The group went over to the pit and looked down on the chained men. Renzo was now awake, looking pitifully up at us.

His voice was terribly weak, "Please help us."

"I've an idea. Angel, bring my horse over here and tie my rope to the saddle. I'm going down there," Chaucer requested. While Angel held his horse, Chaucer slid down the rope inside the pit. "Hi there, Renzo is it? I'm Guardian Chaucer. Let's see if I can figure out how to get you out of this mess. Ah, my kingdom for a lock pick!"

"Cedric. . .pick. . .boot," Renzo whispered, his voice barely audible.

Tonia pointed out which man was Cedric. Chaucer then began removing Cedric's boots. In the right one, he found the lock pick. "Good man," he said to Cedric, who merely moaned a little. A few minutes later, after removing the leg locks, he removed the right hand lock of Renzo, whose body collapsed upon him. He struggled to get the other lock removed, and then carried the limp body to the rope. He fastened a special body hitch around Renzo's torso and gave Angel the signal.

Angel then walked the horse a short ways, pulling Renzo up to the top, where Tonia, Rosina, and Mary Beth managed to pull him out. "He stinks badly," Mary Beth commented. Indeed, for six days, they had no choice but to go to the bathroom in their pants as they stood chained to the walls. They carefully dragged him over to Linda by the slab and Tonia began to help him drink water.

By late afternoon, Chaucer had all the men freed and out of the pit. Damien's body they carefully covered with a saddle blanket. Linda didn't know what to do about his body just yet. All five men were in poor shape, weak from dehydration and lack of food for six days now. For the rest of the day, Angel hovered over John; Mary Beth, over Jason; Tonia, over Emil; Rosina, over Cedric; Linda and Chaucer, over Renzo and Benet.

After getting a good deal of water in them, Tonia mixed up a nourishing broth, and they got a good amount of that into the men's stomachs. Next, all the men were stripped and their highly soiled clothing put back into the pit. A large number of ice walls were formed inside the pit, followed by a few sets of flames. Soon, there was hot water for washing. Tonia scampered down the rope and did her best to get them somewhat clean.

After she brought them up, they wasted a bit more of their water on a good rinse and then laid them all out over the rocks to dry in the afternoon sun. Next, Chaucer and Angel decided to go back down to the burned out village to get more water from their well and to see if they could find their possessions that they had with them when they were ambushed.

Late that afternoon, the two returned with all available water skins filled and much of their possessions, stuffed into many sacks. "How are the patients doing?" asked Chaucer, as he and Mary Beth began handing out the sacks. He noticed that the men were now wearing their underpants, a good sign he thought.

"They are starting to recover, but are sleeping now," Tonia replied. "We'll probably need to feed them a watery supper as well. I don't want them on solids until we get their overall water levels higher. They are very dehydrated. I'm so glad that you found their stuff. At least they have their weapons now."

I woke up. It was near dark. I tried to get up using my arms. Nothing happened. I looked at my arms, but they were not there. I shrieked loudly and all the others came running over to me. I looked sheepishly back at them.

"Bethany! Are you okay?" asked Tonia, her voice full of concern and anxiety.

Embarrassed, I said, "I had these horrible nightmares, losing my arms and all, and then I woke up and tried to get up and discovered that I don't have any arms anymore. I spooked, that's all. Sorry to scare you all. Oh, is my neck ever better! Oh, you got those damnable rings off me! Thanks. I'm starving. Report, please? Oh, who are you?" I noticed a strange young man looking at me as well.

"Damien's dead," Linda blurted out, tears forming again. "Tonia said his heart failed. We've got the others out, and they're beginning to recover, but they're in terrible shape, but alive." She sniffled, and Tonia once more wiped her cheeks.

Rosina said, "We just about have dinner ready. Why don't we eat and tell Bethany everything while she eats? Everyone is starving."

We did just that, only I paused to look at my sleeping husband. Renzo looked so gaunt, so pale; I became rather worried about them. While Rosina fed me, I watched as this new stranger insisted on feeding Linda. "He's Chaucer de'Grange," Tonia explained.

"No, he and his wife were reported dead a couple years ago now, if I remember mom correctly," I replied.

"I'm alive, but not really. I had to kill my own wife, so I am not really alive anymore," he sorrowfully explained.

Tonia retold his story and then related all that had happened here while I was asleep. Chaucer then asked, "Linda, how come all those Tikki on the left flank began attacking each other? I can't figure that one out."

"My doing. I took control over a bunch of their bodies and made them attack their companions. Nature did the rest," Linda calmly explained.

"What? That is not possible!" declared Chaucer. "No one can do that — well expect perhaps the Judger Jovanna Barcella."

Linda didn't feel like talking much; her massive grief was barely at bay. She simply took over his body and made it dance a jig! We all laughed. He had a red face, but said, "Oh! Please accept my humble apology, Linda!"

She managed a smile in spite of everything. "Another thing that I don't understand, Bethany, they said that you were off with Mary Beth, and she said that you eliminated a bunch of Tikki who were blocking the path. How is this possible?"

"You've heard about the new skills that mom has?" I replied.

"You mean the ability to move things without a body?"

"Yes, I can move around at will and move things like her. I left the body here and rode protection over Mary Beth to get her safely here. Yes, I can tell that you also want to know how we managed to kill the bugs.

Simple. I picked the big ones up by their hind feet and then smashed them into the ground as if I was harvesting wheat. Sometimes I hit them with stones. This slab that I am sitting on here — I threw it on top of the three little ones that Angel had shot with arrows. The other one — I lifted the stone way up into the sky and just let it fall. Chaucer, you are among the Expert Bug Killers of Tarra," I jested.

"Yes," added Linda, "only this time it cost us dearly, Bethany and me — my husband too. Dangerous business, this bug killing." She looked at me, and I knew that we both were in dire need of a large amount of trauma erasing sessions! Even Chaucer needed one too, I noted, for he had given up on life already. *Keep it at bay like you are doing, Linda. You are holding up beyond my wildest expectations,* I sent her. She managed a brave smile.

"Well, it's getting dark out. This is an awful place to camp. I'm awake now, so I'll take the first watch. The Tikki have attacked us now several times, so who is ever on guard duty, stay sharp. You all get some sleep. It gets chilly out here, and we don't have much to keep us warm. Probably the smartest thing to do is to have everyone snuggle into a big pile to conserve heat." I suggested.

Without any more coaxing, everyone snuggled in beside their husbands, and Angel lay beside John, Mary Beth lay between Renzo and Jason. I watched Chaucer help Linda to lay down, and he snuggled up to her to help keep her warm. Using my teeth, I pulled blankets over the sleeping forms as the chilly night wore on.

Pacing around the vicinity of my sleeping companions, I debated on whether to contact mom and fill her in on what had happened. I would have to tell her that my brother had been killed and Linda and I were maimed. I found this hard to do, unless I had the full picture of what it was that we had accomplished, that my brother had not died for nothing. While I was pacing, the decision was taken out of my hands, so to speak, as I didn't have them anymore.

Paulette here. I have Jenna with me.

Dear, is everything all right? I have had these awful premonitions that something is terribly wrong.

Oh mom! I was just about to contact you. Your hunch was right. We have succeeded with the mission, and it is far, far, far worse a situation than anyone ever dreamed possible. I guess the bad new first. Are you sitting down?

The worst news is that Damien's heart gave out, and he's passed away under the most horrid conditions imaginable. The other bad news is that Linda and I lost both of our arms to the mantis creatures, but we are all right otherwise. I waited for the shock to sink in before saying more. A while later she wanted to know more.

We were drugged in a surprise ambush. We awoke five days

later missing our arms. None of us actually saw the creatures doing this; we were all unconscious from the drugs. We women were locked up in a pen awaiting further mantis feedings. We found out later on that the men were taken to the top of Hudu and put into an underground chamber, chained hand and foot to the wall, with several hundred viper snakes writhing on the floor, climbing all over their bodies trying unsuccessfully to get to the hole in the ceiling to escape. They were like this for six days before we could rescue them. Every one of them held out somehow, but we have not had them talk about it yet. They are in bad shape and just now recovering. Damien's heart gave out after we got the snakes out.

I'm getting ahead of it all. We awoke and found ourselves in the pen and another mantis was coming to eat the rest of me. I ripped open the pen so we could escape, but the mantis grabbed my body. Angel, who had followed us in hopes of rescuing us, shot two arrows into its head, causing it to drop me. I picked it up by its tail and smashed it to death. The others burned down the Tikki village and drove our captors off. Then we went to find the men and rescue them. However, mom the mantis situation was far worse than we dreamed possible.

There were two nearly adult mantis creatures here. I killed them both with Angel's assistance. Then, there were four younger ones, like the ones we have fought before. She and I got those too. However, mom, the adults already have Hudu back in operation. When a body is placed up here, somehow lights are activated, illuminating the place. The pole thing rose up out of the ground, and began to trap any spiritual being that came in contact with it, scrambling their memories and all that. Mom, this place is in full operation! The mantis creatures were caught in their own pole trap after I killed their bodies!

We were nearly lost here, been attacked by the Tikki several times up here on the top of Hudu. However, there is a piece of good news. Chaucer de'Grange is not dead, only his wife. He came to our rescue. Without his aid, we would be in even more trouble than we are now.

We have not yet gone inside to see if there are more mantis creatures. I want to get the men able to walk on their own before doing anything further. Mom, Linda and I are in the middle of a huge trauma, and I am doing my best to keep it at bay, not even thinking about it. Linda's even worse, because of Damien. If we lose it now, everyone is doomed here. So far, she and I are managing it, coping — I just hope long enough until the others recover.

I would have contacted you sooner, but it has been a continuing crisis here. Right now, they are all totally exhausted and asleep. I'm awake on guard duty. I slept all day while they were active.

Mom sent, *Thanks for telling me everything. I won't ask for any more details. We both need you coping with the situation. Time enough for the trauma later on. If Rosina can send Paulette a daily report now, that would help us. I will see if there is any possible thing that we can do from here. The only request I have of you is to have them find some way to destroy this abomination of a place. I want it out of operation!*

You and me both. I don't have any more arms to donate. I tried to jest about it a little. *Seriously, mom, if we had not taken the time for me to learn how to move objects as you do, we would all have been dead several times over. These creatures are more than a match for us otherwise. I'll get this place destroyed somehow, mom.*

She sent me her love, and we broke the connection. I thought that she took the horrible news about her son and us rather stoically. However, Beth Ann was there at the estate, and I knew that she could give mom a therapy session if she was too upset over the loss of her son and our mutilations. Ah, good old mom, she had given me a new order: destroy this place. I was going to do that anyway, but now it was a direct order. She was helping me keep my mind off the trauma, to keep it at bay a little longer. I smiled; I really loved my mom!

"You were supposed to wake me," Rosina said as dawn came, warming us up. She was rubbing the sleep from her eyes. For an instant, my stomach nearly heaved as I realized that I would never be able to rub my eyes with my hands like her ever again. I quickly blocked the thought from my mind! I had to or all the trauma would come flooding in over me.

"I wasn't sleepy, Rosina, and you all were. I need some help going to the bathroom, and I am thirsty and hungry. Can you lend me some help?"

A half hour later, everyone was up and at it; breakfast was prepared, a cold one yet again. On the top of Hudu here, there was no firewood of any kind. The five men were scarcely able to sit up, and their arms were so weak and sore that the others had to feed them. Renzo bawled like a baby when he saw me and then Linda. Then, they all cried even harder when they learned that Damien had not made it.

After everyone had eaten, I took the time to tell the five what we knew had happened, especially with the bugs and the pole trap thing. I wanted them to know right now just how terribly serious this installation actually was, that our sacrifices were not in vain.

Their story was very short. They had awaken at some point and found themselves in the pit with the vipers. Only Benet's cool head and love of animals allowed them to survive. For days, he had kept the snakes calm. Then, we rescued them. I knew that there was an awful lot of trauma locked up in them as well.

"Don't you worry now, John Waterberry. I'm looking after you now," declared Angel.

"You neither, Jason. I'm on you," Mary Beth added. "I honestly don't know how any one of you could have possibly survived being in that pit with that many poisonous snakes, chained to the walls, and for six days! I know I would have been dead the first minute." She rattled on, which amazingly was just what Jason needed at this point. In fact, they all needed the encouragement for their feat.

After the others helped them go to the bathroom — their legs still couldn't carry their weight — we had them lie down and rest some more. "We are under new orders now. We must see that this place is destroyed. While you are recovering, see if you can come up with some ideas how this might be done. We will wait until you are recovered before we attempt to go inside," I gave them something to occupy their minds in place of the trauma.

Chaucer asked, "Commander Bethany, we should bury Damien. Can we do this while you are sleeping? Is there anything you want done special? I understand that he was your brother and Linda's husband."

"No, that would be good of you to do it for us. I checked and Damien is long gone from here. I don't know where, but he's probably off grabbing a new baby body back home. If he was still around, I would have Mind Linked him to Linda and me so we could say goodbye. I think he was just too terrified to stick around here. I cannot blame him; I don't like snakes at all, now even less. Wake me if anything comes up. Linda, you are in charge during the day, while I sleep."

While the activities during the day were at a lull, Chaucer sat down beside Linda. "Can I ask you some questions, Commander Linda?"

"Sure, but just Linda, please."

"Forgive my ignorance, but I've never met Bethany. How do I ask this? Is she the one who used to be Ket Bethany, our leader before Jenna Rose Weston?"

"Yes, that's her."

"Oh my! *The* Ket Bethany. Oh my. That makes her about the most powerful Guardian since Alabaster Benjamin Crowley! Oh, so that means she or he, well she, was teamed with him to destroy the Grey Creatures and the mantis creatures in the Red Desert. I always thought that was a lot of exaggeration, until these last couple of years."

After a pause, he asked, "Are you a Circle or just a band sent here on this mission?"

"We are part of the Explorers Circle. We have our own caravel, the Sleepy Hollow." She began relating the lengthy story of our many adventures. Chaucer was keenly interested in the mantis creatures and had her relate those incidents in detail. He was positively stunned to learn of all the many hundreds of women that we had rescued.

"Now I am beginning to understand," he said. "I would sooner cut off my own arm as ever harm a hair on a woman's head. I just never could understand why those priests of Megalos would do such things to the women of the Sea Princes. Now they have even done it to their own women! I couldn't understand why, but I'm beginning to see why. People, beings, we live lifetime after lifetime — well, that's what I believe, though I can't personally remember any that I may have had. If one had the misfortune to have an bad encounter, such as you and Bethany, have had, with one of these mantis creatures, I can see where in another lifetime, you might be inclined to act out what was done to you, that is, harm a woman. My theory now is that those who have done these despicable things to women have had it done to them in an earlier lifetime."

"Chaucer, you show a remarkable ability to grasp precisely what we believe has occurred. I think that's rather remarkable. Good show," Linda praised him. He now had her interest up. Chaucer was not just another Protector only interested in fighting. "This is precisely what Jenna and Bethany have concluded!"

They continued to chat and the day passed very rapidly for both of them. He ended their conversation by asking, "How does one get to become a member of the Explorers Circle? I think that I would like to do this very much. I am no longer fit to live among normal townsfolk. I've had to kill my own wife. I cannot face other people anymore." Linda didn't know how to respond to this and said that she would inquire.

I didn't wake until roused for supper. The five men's strength was returning more rapidly now, I noticed. They were able to feed themselves. Linda brought me up to date. It seems that around noon, the pole thing activated again, rising up from the ground. Everyone perceived a spiritual being that was sucked up tightly to the pole. When the being was completely confused, he was sent on his way, and the pole deactivated and went back underground once more. Renzo commented, "Bethany, this place is fully operational, even without the mantis creatures here!"

"I'm glad that you were all able to see it. This is why we must destroy it. Think of all the lives destroyed by this contraption. Can you imagine trying to live with all your memories totally scrambled? I hope this is the last one, because I am rapidly running out of arms to donate," I added a playful jest. They smiled, even though the situation here was awful. It was good to see the men more alive and alert, because I needed them now more than ever.

After the cold dinner, Renzo and I sat together, his arm around my waist, under my hair as usual. He whispered, "I'm so sorry about your brother, but I want you to know that I still love you dearly. Nothing has changed between us, except I think that we've got a wee bit of traumas to handle." He squeezed me, and I knew he was playing with me.

"Yes, dear, just a wee bit. Seriously, don't let anyone think about that or even start down that road. Somehow, we have to hold it together as a group until we get back to the caravel."

"I figured that's why you are insisting Linda be in charge while you are sleeping. You are the best!" We hugged — well, he hugged me, and we embraced passionately. He stayed up with me for half of the night. I awakened Angel and Mary Beth to spell me. This time, I wanted to be awake in the morning. Thankfully, no attacks came this night.

The next morning, once more we ate a cold breakfast. How I missed a hot cup of tea! Today, the men were up and about. Though their arms and legs were still very sore, they were moving on their own steam. "Time to see what lies below. Chaucer, Mary Beth, John, Jason, you are to stand guard and come if we need help. Angel, bring your bow with us, but I hope that we don't need it. Let's go see what lies below. I caution all of you, please be doubly extra careful. We are into alien technology of which we know nothing. Besides, there could be more mantis creatures down there."

The men got their swords and lanterns, just in case. We looked down the entrance ramp into a large underground complex. Its lights were still on, but nothing was moving. Emil took point. Renzo, Linda, Angel, and I brought up the rear. I wanted her and me to have help going down the ramp. Without arms to help maintain our balance, it was a challenge. I could see that this was going to take us an awful lot of getting used to before we'd feel any confidence at all again.

Inside, we saw a bank of strange dials, gages, and levers lining the wall opposite the ramp. Overhead was the same kind of lights that had been in the underground tunnels of the Moon People who had lived underground for centuries in the Red Desert. I pointed these out, reminding them of their history lessons about the Moon People. I began to see connections with the past — how things were beginning to become understood, where once it had all been a complete mystery.

This first chamber, we concluded, was some kind of control center. At the far left end, the sides narrowed into a tunnel that led downward. The floor sloped gently downward, conveniently for us. It also curved around and opened up into another huge cavern located below the one that we first entered. Here was some kind of workshop. We observed but did not touch. On either end of this chamber tunnels sloped downward once more, deeper into the mountain. We took the one on the right.

The next chamber yielded a cache of their metallic books, two dozen of them! "Natale will love this find!" Linda commented. A number of what must be writing devices were scattered on a desk. Evidently, the adult we surprised was working on something at the time it came out to check on what had activated their devices.

"Wow! Look at this gang!" I called out, trying to point with my hands, giving up in disgust and nodding my head toward the wall. "It's another map. This time it looks like it has the whole world. It has those navigation lines on it like the other one. This could be our find of the century!" Everyone gathered around me examining the map on the wall.

"I can't tell," Linda complained, "does anyone see any more of those star things? Are there any more we haven't seen yet?" She was worried, so was I for that matter. In this light, we could not tell for sure.

This room had one curving, sloping downward tunnel so down we went. "Oh my goodness," exclaimed Angel as she walked into the room with us. Against one wall was stacked a huge pile of gold ingots, similar to those we had found at other sites. There were hundreds of them. Beside them was a smaller stack of shiny silver ingots. What caught Angel's attention the most were the shelves with little bins all full of various colored precious gemstones. Here was a fortune in gems! This smaller room had no exits, just the perpetual lights similar to those of the Moon People.

We backtracked to the other exit in the workshop. Down again we walked. The next room that appeared contained supplies of various types. Neatly stacked were dozens of the Perpetual Lights. One pressed a switch and the device produced a beam of light. We found metal bands, bits of lumber, hammers, saws, even nails; though we had no idea what use these mantis creatures might have for this stuff. Six coils of rope were fastened to the stone wall as well.

Next, we followed the single exit around and down further. Benet commented, "Bethany, the temperature is getting warmer the deeper we go."

"Isn't that backwards, Benet? I thought it got cooler down to a point, where it then stayed constant, like in all the caves in the Langdoc region," I asked.

"Precisely," he replied, but offered no explanation, just the observation.

The next chamber was full of dried grasses, dried flowers, packed nearly to the ceiling. "Ah, their pantry," Benet suggested. "They are after all related to the praying mantis we have on Tarra. Perhaps they eat grasses?"

Finally, we went on down again. As we rounded the bend, the temperature definitely rose significantly. Then we saw the sight we had dreaded. Nests! In one nest, six-inch baby mantis creatures were crawling around, evidently playing. However, the second they sensed our presence, they began crawling out of their nest heading straight for us. Food! "Don't let them touch you! They will start eating you!" I screamed out. I was frightened mostly because now I had no arms with which to defend myself, having forgotten that I only needed to slide out of my body and go into smashing mode. I spotted that this was a reaction coming from the massive trauma I had suffered. I noticed Linda had similar reactions.

"Not a problem," Renzo declared. The men began skewering them with their swords. The battle of a dozen hatchlings versus five men lasted a minute. When this small, they were not a serious threat, unless they started amputating and eating your fingers and toes, that is.

We saw two more nests filled with eggs. Then we saw something horrible! Lying in a third nest lay a black skinned woman, head and torso only, for the rest of her had been eaten long ago. She began talking pleadingly to us, but we understood her not. Finally, Rosina made mental contact with her to try to see the concepts the woman was thinking. "Oh my god! I think the bugs have put something in her womb!" Rosina exclaimed quite shocked.

Tonia sat down beside her, placed her hands on the naked woman, closed her eyes, and began perceiving the woman's internal state of health. Tonia made a motion with her hand as if she were putting something into the woman's body and the woman nodded her head yes. Now Rosina began to get a clearer picture. The woman kept rolling her head over to the previous nest. "She's saying something about another woman in this other nest."

Renzo began poking around in the nest. As he removed the surface grasses, the rib cage bones appeared and skull! "Oh, I get what she is saying. The bugs put something in her that will hatch inside her body and eat her internal organs. She saw it happen to the woman you just found, Renzo. She wants you to stab her with your sword. She doesn't want to get eaten by the bugs that hatch."

Tonia said, "My god, too late. Look!" We stared at her abdomen and saw little bumping movements. The bugs were hatching even as we spoke. The woman looked terrified, but couldn't even move. Renzo hesitated no longer and did it mercifully. Next, he opened up her belly and out came a dozen of these bugs, only an inch long. These we immediately dispatched. Now we knew what they did with the women! How utterly gruesome indeed. I wondered how many women had died like this until now? Linda and I looked at each other. Simultaneously we realized just how close we had come to being just like this woman here. It was unnerving to say the very least.

We searched this whole hatchery thoroughly but found nothing else, thank heavens for that! During the search, Benet came upon a strange thing. He found a crack in the floor near the point where the wall met the stone floor. A dull reddish glow came from the crack along with intense heat, which accounted for the warm temperatures needed here in the hatchery. My conclusion was that this crack in the floor had appeared some time ago, and the heat had caused some eggs to hatch, probably the two small adults that we killed. These, in turn, had begun raising children of their own, probably on their fourth set!

"Gang, had we not come here, soon there would be so many adults that all Tarra would have been doomed to be under their control once more!" This was a terribly sobering thought, which gave added meaning to all our sufferings, losses, and sacrifices.

We stood there stunned, thinking about just what might have been for a couple minutes. Benet, then, spoke up. "I have a way we can destroy this place."

"How?" I asked, baffled. I'd seen nothing at all that would be useful to me, anyway, if I had to destroy it.

"We somehow enlarge this crack here, and the hot rock down below comes up and fills this whole place with more solid rock. I just don't quite know how we make it bigger, though." The men liked his plan, however, and decided it would work.

"Okay, then, first, we need to salvage what we can from here. Second, how the heck are we going to get all this stuff back to the boat on horseback?" I asked.

"You are not, Bethany," Cedric replied. "Besides, how are you and Linda going to ride your horses back, for that matter? Granted, Julianna and Rachelle are able to, but they have had some years to work out how to get along as they are." I nearly broke down and began bawling — Linda too. We both fought back the terrible inrush of horrible emotions that threatened to crush us as we stood there.

Cedric continued, "Don't worry, you two, I have it all figured out. I will build you a large wagon. We can put all the stuff in it and both of you as well. Maybe you can even work out how to drive the team somehow."

Renzo saw the state that Linda and I were in — a hair from being overwhelmed utterly by our trauma and loss. He quickly stepped in, "Okay, then Cedric, let's all get to it. Some of us will help you build the wagon, while the rest of us will start moving the stuff we want to salvage up and out of here. Come on everyone; let's get busy. The sooner we get it done, the sooner we can get back to our children and the caravel!"

Thank you Renzo! I could have hugged him for a week! Everyone began to do something, which gave Linda and me time to recover and regain control. She and I brought up the very rear now. She whispered to me, "Bethany, I don't know if I can hold up much longer. I almost lost it all back there! I'm so terrified of the future now."

"Me too, Linda. I just barely kept from bawling like a baby. We have to keep on going, Linda. We just have to, until we get back to the caravel. Think of little Zachary; he's lost his father. He just can't also lose his mother!"

"Yes, but thinking about him reminds me that I can never pick him up and hug and hold him. I just can't do this anymore!"

"Yes you can, Linda. You and I have to — we just have to. We've depended on each other since we could walk. Let's keep on doing it. Lean on me." She did and felt a bit better. We wandered topside and told the others standing guard that it was now safe and for them to go down and look.

At last, she and I were alone and could just look around at the vast space of this mountaintop and calm down. We looked at the tops of the very distant trees that just barely poked over Hudu's summit. We gazed off into the far distance on to the vast savannah, and we began to feel better; a bit of tranquility returned to us. Linda commented, "I feel like I'm a volcano about ready to explode."

"Me too. Me too."

Soon the men began carrying up some of the scrap boards. Cedric began building a wagon from scratch. Linda and I felt so useless just now. However, Cedric soon found odd jobs that we could do, such as using our feet to hold a board in position while he nailed. I think he realized just how close he came to setting off both of us. Probably Rosina spoke with him. Anyway, we now were contributing and felt somewhat better.

We spent several days building the wagon. Cedric wanted it extra sturdy. His fear was having a major breakdown out there on the endless savannah. Besides, it had to carry an awful lot of weight. The wagon was the ugliest wagon any of us ever saw, but without a doubt the sturdiest. The wheels took an entire day to get right, and he also made two spare wheels, just in case.

Twice during these days, the Tikki reappeared at the edge of the summit of Hudu. However, both times, after seeing all of us in good health and well-armed, they wanted nothing to do with attacking us again. Yes, I threw up a wall of fire close to them each time, just to remind them that we were serious.

Another whole day was needed to load everything on the wagon. The ingots went first and formed the bed on which everything else was placed. Our two horses and the four packhorses were hitched together forming a team of six, and Damien's was added up front as the lead horse. In the absence of any leather for the harnesses, Cedric improvised using the rope and other various odd bits he found useful. I think that he was in heaven on this project, for the engineer in him shone brilliantly. Rosina was very proud of his achievement. Oh yes, the piles of grasses we used as fodder for the horses during these days. Finally, we were ready to leave, but we were also completely out of water!

Renzo lifted me up onto the wagon, piled high with everything including our rapidly dwindling food supply. Then, he lifted up Linda. We made ourselves somewhat comfortable. Because there were no springs on this wagon, the ride would be bumpy. Since we could not "hold on" at all, Cedric designed a recessed seat such that only our heads were visible. We had many solid objects to keep us from falling out. "Going down, ladies, will be the worst part. If it makes it to the savannah, from there on it should be a sweet ride. I'd say hold your hats ladies, but you aren't wearing any. Here goes." Cedric was driving; Renzo leading his horse for him.

"Hey, wait a minute," I called out. "We forgot about destroying this place!"

"No we haven't, Bethany," Benet called out. "We are going to do it once we are off this mountain and out onto the grasslands. We think it will be safer for you two. If something doesn't go right, we might have to make a run for it. Trust us, Commander." I said I would.

Yes, going down was a nightmare for us. The wagon heaved left and right. Without arms to hold on to anything, we keenly felt our new helplessness, more so now than ever before! It took every ounce of sheer willpower to keep from caving in to the horrible emotional trauma we both keenly felt!

Part way down, with the wagon bouncing and heaving wildly, Renzo leaped onto the back of the wagon. "Cedric forgot to build a brake on it. Don't worry dear; we've worked out another way." We twisted around to see him catching a rope and tying it to the heavy frame of the wagon. Then, several other horses pulled in behind and latched on to the other end and pulled backwards. We slowed down, for which I was eternally grateful!

Twice, huge boulders in the gully stopped us. A horse could easily ride around them, but not the wagon. Time was needed to move them. It was full dark when we finally hit the grasslands! The wagon now leveled off, and we no longer felt like we were constantly falling forward. Renzo rode along side, "We are going to go a little farther until we get to that small stream. We must have water, since we're totally out."

An hour later, the wagon stopped and helping hands lifted us to the ground. It felt wonderful to have our feet on the ground once more. After drinking our fill, we set up camp. While they all worked on making a fire and hot food, Linda and I began to fill the water skins. This we could do using our feet.

For me, that hot cup of tea tasted like ecstasy in a cup! The first hot meal in days brought everyone's spirits higher than they had been for days. We got a very good night's sleep, including those on guard duty, for we were back to only needing two-hour shifts. After breakfast the next day, we looked back at Hudu, miles behind us. Emil said, "Okay, ladies, into the wagon you go. If something goes awry, we might need to put a whole lot of miles between us and Hudu there." In fact, everything was made ready for an instant ride, before the men grouped together. Now I realized what Benet had in mind! This was a spell that I did not know, used primarily by the Protectors, and then only very, very rarely.

"Watch this or feel this," I whispered to Linda.

The men chanted away together in unison for over an hour. Finally, Emil seemed satisfied, and they all mounted up. We were off once more. "But I didn't see or feel anything," Linda commented to me.

"It hasn't happened yet. I think there is a time delay in it. Whoa! Feel it?" The ground beneath the wagon began vibrating! My teeth chattered together, making little noises. I watched Linda's head move slightly up and down. Even the horses seemed spooked, and Benet had to work rapidly to keep them calm. The earth shook for only a minute at most, and then all was silent. In the far distance, we saw flocks of birds rising off the trees that covered Hudu. Then all was quiet once more.

We continued to move along slowly across the grasslands. "That was an earthquake, Bethany. The men actually made the earth shake!" exclaimed Linda. After a pause, she asked, "But how's that going to destroy the nest?"

"I think that Benet's idea was to make the earth shake to open up that crack in the floor much larger and let the hot rock come out. I suppose that we could send someone back there to make sure it is gone, maybe tomorrow?"

Suddenly, we heard a huge noise and the ground shook once more. An incredibly loud boom echoed across the land. Horses reared and spun around, nearly dumping their riders. We all turned to look back at Hudu. A giant red streak rose high up into the sky from the very peak of the mountain. The red stuff slowly fell down onto the ground while more rose up. Soon the entire peak was one mass of red-hot rock. Giant clouds of smoke rose, as trees near the top burst into flames.

Cedric called out, "Commander, I believe that is total destruction of the site, is it not?"

Everyone yelled and cheered! Then, Cedric decided we best put a lot of distance between us and it, since now half the side of Hudu was enveloped in the red glow! I began to wonder if it could reach out this far and fry us! It didn't however. Months later, follow up reports came back saying that Hudu now was fifty percent taller and broader than it had been. No trace of the Tikki was ever seen after that.

That afternoon we rolled through the friendly village. The people there were all standing around watching Hudu and pointing it out to us. We smiled and waved goodbye; well, all but two did. Again, Linda and I shed a tear or two before we regained some semblance of emotional control.

Chapter 24 Across the Savannah

The second full day of our slow ride through the heart of the Southlands, both Linda and I were going stark raving mad. All we could do was sit there, heads looking at the scenery gradually moving by us — all day long, minute after minute, hour after hour. Our will power to keep our traumas at bay was failing rapidly! At the end of the second day, I knew I would not last another day of this. Neither could Linda. We just had to have some therapy fast or become utter basket cases for the rest of the journey, which was likely to be months long!

In fact, the only thing that kept me together that second day was thinking about giving Linda her therapy. However, I realized that I needed it just as much as she and that we probably shared nearly the same incident! If I began running her, I would be seeing my own trauma as well. When she would go unconscious, very likely so would I, since it happened to me exactly at the same time! This scared me stiff, because then there would be no one running the session!

I thought about having Tonia or Rosina run us together, but then they too had been captured at the same time and drugged as well. They had nearly the same situation as we. I dare not ask them for that very reason! Next, I thought about the men. Could I get Renzo, for example, to run Linda and myself? Or perhaps Angel or Mary Beth? No, they had only witnessed a little of it while on the caravel. Besides, they needed to forage for our fresh meat, if we were going to have anything to eat. Renzo — he and the fellows had their own horrors to face, all of which were right here and now. I had been noticing very subtle changes in all the five men's behavior. At the tiniest surprise, they would wildly overreact, fear kicking in something fierce. Renzo wouldn't admit it. I certainly didn't press him or I would have him right there in the middle of it all as well.

Mom, sorry to disturb you so late.

Ah, children again. Hank and I are in bed enjoying ourselves, now that all of our children have flown the coop. And her you come again. She was enjoying teasing me. We both laughed. I had reached out to her for help again.

I brought her fully up to date, although Rosina had been giving Paulette daily reports. *Mom, Linda and I aren't going to make it through another day. We sit in the wagon doing absolutely nothing at all. I know that I simply can't hold this enormous trauma back another day like today. Neither can Linda. I can't ask the men, because they are in a similar mess themselves and are now trying to get us back to the caravel safely. Angel and Mary Beth are out foraging and hunting all day, trying to keep us in food.*

Ah, but you have an idea, don't you Lizzy Ann. She always called me that when I was growing up. Only when I came of age did I change it to Bethany. It was really Elizabeth. Once more I was flabbergasted at her keen insight!

How could you possibly know that? I asked dumbfounded.

I know you well, my dear. Out with it.

The only one here who is not burdened down with recent trauma is this new fellow, Chaucer. Yes, he needs the trauma of his wife being eaten and then his mercy killing of her handled, but he's come to grips with it sort of; it happened two years ago. At least it is not current. Is there any way that you could somehow Mind Link someone with him and have him run Linda and me? If we can somehow get over ours, then she and I can begin to handle all the rest of us. Otherwise, she and I aren't going to make it through tomorrow; we'll be bawling, sobbing, and useless women.

*Lizzy Ann, I'm ashamed of you! Haven't you learned anything from me about giving these therapy sessions? When you are delivering one to someone, you must put your full and I do mean **full** attention on the other person. You can't look at your own situation, because then you aren't helping the other person. You plus the other person is greater than the trauma. Individually, you are not. So kick yourself in your butt with your feet, Elizabeth Ann Rose Wilkins Pazzio le'Goeur. You face Linda's trauma along with her! That's an order! Now get some sleep and tell me how Linda is doing tomorrow night.* My face was burning up as I dropped my connection with mom.

She was absolutely right! I was playing victim here, when I had a job to do. I was doing an "oh woe is me" kind of thing. Yes, mom had most definitely kicked me right where it hurt the most! I felt awfully small, awfully embarrassed, awfully foolish, awfully everything! I was alive and well. I had all my faculties and wits about me. I just had to use them.

At breakfast the next morning, I announced, "Today, once we get rolling, I will begin therapy sessions. First up will be Linda. So ignore any noise we may make. If an emergency arises, consult with me first before jarring Linda. Okay?"

Chaucer asked Rosina what I had meant. She gave him a very lengthy explanation — good for her. I found that Chaucer chose to ride close to the wagon all day so that he could witness the session. I allowed it.

I faced Linda in the wagon as we began to roll slowly along. "Okay, Linda, time to do this. I want you to close your eyes and go back to when this all started." We were off and running. Mom was precisely right. I had to stay constantly alert, constantly observing Linda, constantly listening to what she had to say. Together, she and I were indeed more powerful than the trauma she had experienced.

I suspected it would be slow going, and I was correct. We had been drugged for five days straight. The first pass over this yielded nothing but a grey fog. Then she re-experienced waking up with the shocking discovery that her arms were missing; having those nasty neck rings only made matters worse. She repeated her high volume shriek, as she re-experienced that shocking moment. Then, she continued to go through the rest of it, which was much lighter in nature. On the third pass through, when she got to the discovery portion, her screams subsided, and the rest from then on was nearly gone. On the fourth pass, she finally contacted the images made during the drugged state.

Here, I had to work at keeping my full attention on Linda, because I also wanted desperately to know what exactly had happened to us. I just could not let my desire to know for my own sake interfere. She had images of people walking around; people forcing more liquid into her mouth. She saw the men bending and forming the rings around her neck, pounding them tightly together so that they couldn't be removed. "The man is lifting my neck, trying to see if it moves at all. It does, so he pounds another ring on making it even tighter. He tests it again. Now my neck doesn't move at all. He seems satisfied; he smiles. He and another man carry me back and lay me down in the pen. All is quite. Now the sun is up; the same woman pours liquid in my throat. I am so thirsty. I drink it. It keeps me drugged. I think it is water though."

"Now I see the people. They are all lining up in two rows outside the pen. I'm carried out and laid on the ground. I'm an offering. This huge mantis flies down and lands by me. They are chanting something, looks like a prayer or something. The mantis drools on my right shoulder, then my left shoulder. It seems very numb. I see its mandibles; they are clicking. Now it bends down onto me. I see they are like knives. I can feel them cutting into my shoulder, in the socket, severing my right arm from its socket. Oh, it is being careful to leave a lot of skin and flesh around there. I don't feel anything except the pressure of the cutting. Now it's kind of sewing my shoulder up. It drips something else on my shoulder. It feels very good to me, healing-like. Now it goes to my left shoulder. I feel the pressure as it cuts around the shoulder socket. Now it is dripping the same stuff on that one. It too feels as if it is healing somehow rapidly. I remember thinking I wish I had some of this healing slobber. It works really well. I could use it in surgery or Tonia could. I'm wondering how I can get some of it. I'm thinking if I could ask it for a sample, maybe we could mix up a batch ourselves."

"Oh, it sends to me 'Thank you maiden.' I wonder what it means. Why is it thanking me? Is it going to give me a sample? Then it flies off. I'm carried back inside the pen. More liquid is poured into my mouth. Now it is dark. I'm supposed to sleep now. Now it is day. They are lining up again. Oh, here comes the mantis. Is it going to give me that sample healing slobber today? I can't move though. I see Bethany being carried outside. Maybe it is going to give it to her today for me, since I don't have the arms to take it from the mantis. No, it is cutting off her arms, just like mine. Gee, I always have wanted to be just like Bethany. Now we are alike again. This is good. I wonder if it gave Bethany my sample of its healing potion? Now they bring her back and lay her beside me. They pour more stuff in her mouth. Now it is dark. I am supposed to sleep."

"Now it is day again. One woman in the pen is very sick. People are very confused. They are working with her. Hey, you are supposed to give me my drink. They forgot. They forgot to give Bethany hers too. Oh, they forgot to give us all our drinks. The woman dies and they go off to bury her body. The sun is getting hotter. Oh, I'm beginning to wake up now. My eyes are seeing again. I look up. I try to sit up but my arms don't work; my neck hurts too and won't move. I twist and see that I don't have any arms. I shriek."

Now Linda began yawning heavily. We went through it all once more. As expected, more details appeared. However, it was now lunchtime, so I ended the session. She felt a whole lot better, and we ate a good meal. As the wagon began rolling again, we resumed the session. After going over it three more times, nothing new was discovered, and she was content with it, chuckling a little over the silliness of some parts of it, where she had to be like me and wanted a sample from the mantis. Hence, following mom's protocol, I ask her if there was something earlier like this.

She remembered something from her last life as Sarah, my daughter. We had been traveling home from delivering a number of Sunday services at distant towns, when this flying ship came overhead and began energy blasting us. She was utterly terrified and shrieked. The stark terror was the similar thread. However, after several passes, this one also did not result in laughter and the complete erasure of her trauma. I asked her if there was another one similar and earlier.

"I see something. Might not be real. I see a young girl, maybe all of ten." I had her go through the happening, telling me what happens as she went along.

"I see this pretty girl; she's having a birthday party. Then she is jumping into the river. Oh, I'm choking and drowning, and I can't breathe. I can't make my arms pull me up out of the water. Oh, I don't have any arms anymore. I die, no the body dies, and I float away."

"We went through the incident several more times, Linda began yawning very heavily. "I adore my older sister; she can walk on a tight wire that is high above the ground. I want more than anything in the world to be like her. She is so pretty, so graceful. Everyone loves her, and she walks this tightrope in a pretty costume. Oh, it is a traveling circus.

We are a circus family. After my party, I decide to try to walk the tight wire as she does. I'm not allowed in here though. I'm breaking all the rules. I want to be as her so badly that I'm doing it anyway. I climb up high as she does. I wiggle my body around as she always does. Then I slip and am falling down. My arms hit the wire." Linda screamed as if her arms were being pulled out, startling everyone around us, who turned to stare at her.

"I hit the stack of hay, but my arms are not there! I am screaming. Everyone comes. I pass out. I'm still seeing them. Someone is sewing my arms up — stings like a needle prick. I wake up but I cannot get up. I see I have no arms. I scream and scream. Then I cry for hours. Now I can never be like my sister, not ever! I can't do anything anymore. I can't feed myself. I can't even go pee by myself. I'm totally helpless, totally useless. I can't be like my sister. Ah, so I jumped off the bridge into the pond, knowing that with no arms I can't swim anymore. Well, I got out of that one!"

She continued to yawn as we went through it a few more times. Suddenly, she opened her eyes and started laughing. "I just heard what the physician was saying when he was sewing up my shoulders! He is saying to mom, 'She will be totally useless the rest of her life. She won't be able to do anything at all for herself. If I were her, I would go kill myself, jump off of a bridge or something.' Bethany, I did exactly what he told me to do! I just agreed that I would be totally useless the rest of my life, that I would be utterly helpless, and I did just what he said to do, go jump off of a bridge!" Now she roared with laughter. I smiled and ended the session. She stood up in the wagon and laughed all the harder. She kept saying, "Go jump off of a bridge! I did!" Ha, ha, ha. "What an idiot!" Ha, ha, ha.

Over supper, she finally stopped laughing enough that she could eat. "Bethany, you saved my life just now. I'm certain that just as soon as we got near a river or lake, when you all weren't looking I would have just jumped in! I was following those orders from way back then! I even felt totally useless, as if there was nothing left to live for, totally helpless. Yet, I have seen nearly a thousand women like us who are absolutely the direct opposite! Enyo is probably the best engineer on Tarra! You have saved my life, Bethany! Thank you! I know I will miss Damien, but I am only sixteen and quite young and have our son to raise. I have everything in the world to live for! How can I ever thank you?"

"You do me tomorrow," I replied.

"You bet!" she exclaimed.

A little later, I spied Chaucer, who had heard nearly all of it today, talking to her. Okay, so I eavesdropped on my best friend. "Linda, that was the most powerful thing that I have ever witnessed. I can see it fully, how you were following the words spoken by the physician while you were unconscious. How did you ever remember that?"

"On my own, never. I was unconscious, silly. If I tried to, I'd be unconscious again. It is because of the therapy that Jenna invented and Bethany has mastered. Together, we are able to see what lies under that unconsciousness. I will be doing her tomorrow. Have a listen. I'm sure she won't mind, but I will check with her first."

"Thank you Linda. I would greatly desire listening in; this is such an incredible thing they have discovered. Is it hard to learn how to do, this therapy?"

"No, not really. There are a few do's and don'ts to learn, but it is awfully simple."

"Okay. Oh, one other thing, I would really like to help you. I've heard that you have a young son. You and Damien have given so much to help all of us on Tarra that I would like very much to give something back to you. Please allow me to help you and your son in any way that I can."

"I'm sure I'm going to need a whole lot of help until I figure out totally new and inventive ways to do things. Thanks for the offer."

The next day, Linda and I reversed roles. I was very apprehensive about this, terrified of losing control of myself. I kept telling Linda this, about a hundred times. She began the session just as the wagon began to roll along again.

"I hear this puffing sound, whirl around, feel the dart hit me. I go unconscious. They have hit me with a very fast acting drug. I'm in a greyish mass. I can't seem to move out of it. I try all directions and only get more confused. I wake up. I try to sit up. My arms don't raise me up. I try to bend my neck. It doesn't move. I twist and see I've got no arms."

At this point, I screamed a blood-curdling cry that got everyone's attention as they rode along! Renzo later told me that I have a good voice for screaming — it was a tease, of course.

We went through it a number of times. I lost count. Fear, panic, terror, I don't want to be like this, utter helplessness, total worthlessness — these grew steadily, stronger and stronger, but always even stronger than these was the stark terror of losing control of myself! Yes, I began yawning. I too cracked through the veil of the drug and saw almost exactly the same things that Linda had seen, except I had no thoughts of being like her or of desiring to obtain its drool. By lunchtime when we stopped rolling along, I was finding nothing new in the whole thing at all.

Worse, I was in terror, total fear. I was panicking completely! I felt a complete and utter helplessness. I knew that I was so worthless now that they should not even waste their precious time feeding me. Worse, I had lost all control over my mind and emotions. How they managed to get food into me I do not know! I peed my pants. I pooped them as well with a stinky diarrhea. I vomited up half my lunch all over my now filthy clothes. I was shaking violently and completely out of control of my body. Poor Linda, she definitely had her feet full with me today.

Once they had me mostly cleaned up and some food in me, I found myself back in the wagon, and Linda was asking me to go over it once more. I did, though I don't remember doing it. She asked me, "Is there something like this that is earlier?"

"I see a girl on a farm."

"Good. Now go through it and tell me what you are seeing and feeling and smelling as you go along."

"I see this pretty girl, maybe twelve. She's on a farm somewhere. I'm screaming. I'm falling. My arms are gone. I can't stop falling. I'm peeing and pooping. I've lost all control of everything. I'm dead." I sat there like a dead body.

"Okay. Let's go back to the beginning and go through it again."

"I see me. Oh, I'm this girl. We live on this farm. I don't think there is another farm anywhere near us, very isolated in deep woods somewhere. Dad has these sharp threshing blades stored in the shed. He tells me a hundred times not to play in the shed because it's dangerous. I'm bored and I play in there anyway. I'm fearless. I'm climbing all over the rafters, chasing pigeons. Oh, I slip and fall." Once more, I let out a blood-curdling scream of terror and great pain mingled.

"I land on those sharp blades. They cut my arms off completely! I'm screaming and screaming, totally scared, totally terrified. I cannot even get up. Dad comes running in and finds me. He picks me up and I pass out. He carries me in the house. Ouch, it burns me. And again, it burns. Oh, he is touching a red-hot pan to my one-inch long arms. It stops the blood. Dad is bandaging my shoulders up now. Mom says, 'Why are you bothering, you know that she is going to be utterly helpless the rest of her life. She will be worthless around here. She's just a total liability; it's not even worth feeding her now. Why didn't you just let her die and be done with it?' Dad says he loves me anyway. I am in my bed now sleeping."

"It's morning. I try to get up, but my arms don't work. I look down and see that I don't have any arms anymore! I scream and scream. Mom comes in. I say, 'I don't want to be like this! Please put my arms back on. I promise not to play in the shed ever again.' She says, 'You are going to be like this forever.' I yell mom, 'I don't want to be like this.' She says, 'You are now just a worthless girl, totally helpless. I have to do everything for you. Now get up.' I can't; my arms don't work. Somehow I got up."

"I try to go down the steps to the dining room from my loft. I'm so scared. I have no arms to hold on. I'm panicking. My stomach is a knot. I fall the last way. I cannot control anything anymore. She shovels food into my mouth too fast. I choke, but I have no arms to help myself. I get more and more scared. I can't do anything anymore. I'm worthless, so totally helpless. Mom says go outside and play."

"I can't even open the door to go outside. She scowls at me and says, 'See you are worthless, helpless. You cannot even do that simple thing.' She opens the door for me. I go outside. I stumble and can't keep from falling. I hit my face hard on the ground. I'm getting more and more scared, more and more afraid. I have to find my dad. He loves me still. He is out working in the woods. I go looking for him. I can't find him. Now I'm getting even more terrified and scared. I pee my pants again. Then, I poop them too! I can't even go to the bathroom anymore. I get even more terrified. I don't want to be this way. I cry and cry, and look for dad. I stumble and fall again. I can't keep from falling. I get even more scared. Now I'm shaking all over. I have to find dad. I begin to run, but then I fall again. My arms just don't work. I don't have any anymore, I realize again. I'm so sick at my stomach. I'm so terrified, so scared! I'm lost. Now I think that I'm lost in the woods!"

"I'm so helpless, so worthless, so lost, so scared, and so terrified. I panic and then I hear a wolf howl! I peed my pants again. I have to run! I see the wolf coming for me. Stark terror grips me. I'm so helpless. I try to run and trip — no arms to help me. I poop my pants again. Somehow, I get up and run some more. The wolf is getting close to me. I'm losing control of everything. I can't control anything anymore. I'm so terrified. The wolf is right behind me now. I hear its breath. It is going to eat me, and I can't fight it off. I have no hands anymore. I don't want to be like this. I'm stumbling. Oh, I'm falling over a cliff. I try to catch hold of something, but I have no arms anymore. My stomach is in a knot, terrified, stark fear. I'm spinning out of control. I can't control anything anymore. I have lost control of everything. I hit the ground, everything goes black, and I'm floating above my body. Oh, so that is what I look like now without any arms. I sure don't want to be that way. The wolf is eating on the body. I don't feel it, so I leave."

"Very well done, Bethany," Linda said. "Now let's go over it again."

Part way through it, I began laughing like a hyena. "Oh, I just spotted something. When mom was pregnant with me, she kept saying that she didn't want another girl. Yet, I turned out to be just that, another girl. No wonder she hated me. She never wanted me in the first place! I just had a lousy mother that time! She wanted sons to work the fields and make her more money so she could buy more things. It wasn't me after all! I just went into complete agreement with her because I was not used to doing things without any arms, that's all! Babies have to learn to walk and to talk and to use silverware and to read and to write and to do things. If no one is there to show them how, they are then useless, helpless, and worthless. Duh!" I roared with laughter, what a stupid thing to have happen to me.

Linda ended the session, with a huge smile on her face. Chaucer was stunned at the results and the change in me. Renzo was riding close, evidently watching over me.

"Hey, get that spare horse over here. I'll be damned if I'm going to ride all the way back to the boat in this wagon! Now, Renzo!" I ordered.

"Yes, ma'am," he grinned in jest. He brought the spare horse up. He helped me into the saddle. "Hang on a second. I remember how Julianna did it." He tied the reins into a knot, and I took it in my mouth. We began to move out once more, and I was riding a horse. I had little control, but by golly, I could sure learn how to do this. If Julianna and Rachele could, so could I!

A little while later, I saw that everyone else was watching me. Spontaneously, they all began clapping for me. I grinned with the reins between my teeth. "Can't talk very good this way," I muttered. Renzo laughed. I was alive once more.

At supper, I commented, "Well, at least I will not be bored for a long time. I get to learn how to do everything in life all over a new way." Everyone chuckled at my jest.

While we sat around after supper drinking our hot tea, Chaucer came up to me and said, "Bethany, this therapy thing that you do, it is just so incredible. Can I ask this of you, you did not know about this earlier life with that awful mother?"

"Nope, I had no idea it was even there. I often have seen a sort of greyish mass where this was located. Now that greyish mass is gone."

"It seems to my perhaps too simpleton view, that the terror and fears you were experiencing at lunch today came from this earlier one, not from the current attack just a few days ago with the bugs. Your terrors seemed all out of proportion to my way of thinking." He was trying to be as diplomatic about his questioning as possible. I could tell that he was both on unfamiliar ground and was working something out for himself.

"Well, yes, I rather made a complete fool of myself at lunch today. Embarrassing to say the least. You are right. At lunch, I was so absolutely terrified that I even threw up. Yours is a good observation. My reactions and fears were way, way out of proportion to what happened with the mantis. Actually, the mantis mutilation was nearly painless, very humane in a twisted, sick way. After massive battles, I've seen an awful lot of men and women who have horrific wounds and have to have all sorts of amputations. Now there is excruciating pain, often intolerable. Yet, with the mantis, physically all I felt was a bit of pressure and a prickly sensation at the end of it."

"All this I find extremely interesting indeed. What you and Linda are doing is so vastly more important than what I do as a Protector. I find that I'm like feeding the pigs, while you are running a country, just no comparison in worth or value. Is it possible for others, such as me, to learn how to do this therapy of yours? I know that I'm worthless now as a person, having had to kill my own wife. Yet, if I could put that aside, I would give anything to learn how to do this therapy and then devote my life to doing this to help others, that is, if they don't mind having a wife killer as their therapy giver. The help that I give as a Protector is so completely insignificant when compared to this new therapy."

"Chaucer, in fact, it is very easy to do, so simple that we are all astounded that no one has discovered this before. Yet, it requires something that many people find most difficult to do. When you are running the session, you must put your full attention on the other person with none on yourself. You have to listen carefully to what they are telling you and let them know that you have heard them. At no time can you ever make less of something they say, contradict them, or tell them what something might mean or be. When a person is going through their unconsciousness and pain, they are not very observant and aware, because if they were, then they wouldn't have been unconscious at that time, now would they? They often confuse things, misidentify things, like calling a horse a dog. While you might know that it was a horse that stepped on their leg, those whose pain you are trying to erase, if they call it a dog, you must not contradict or correct them. In time, they will do so themselves, when they fully view what is there. Many people find this hard to do — to just sit there, full attention on their patient, listening carefully, and not advising or correcting or arguing with the patient. If you can do these things, you will be successful, I think."

"I believe I see. If they are really out of it, they may not see things as they are. Yet, one thing puzzles me. This grey mass that you said you could see — how is it that you yourself could not see what was there, getting hurt as a child? How is it that you could then see it when Linda was doing the therapy? This I do not yet understand."

"This is also simple, Chaucer. All by oneself, at that time whatever happened, it was too much for one to see, so they are unconscious. If I had even tried to re-experience it and see what was there, I would have been unconscious again. Since I couldn't experience it then, I'm certainly not going to be able to do it now. Yet, in my therapy session, it wasn't just me looking. Linda was there, another spiritual being. Somehow, two beings are always bigger than the unconscious pictures and so it becomes viewable and can be erased by viewing it. Can you see now why it is so utterly important that the giver of the session must be fully alert, with their attention on their patient, and listening to their every word?"

"Now I see. Ah, but now I can see more. At first, yesterday, I was very confused. Both you and Linda have endured nearly the same traumatic event. All you women did, though only you two were harmed forever by it. Having seen just how awfully powerful your own trauma actually was at lunch yesterday, I asked myself how is it that when you were doing Linda with your own nearly identical trauma sitting right there totally raw, so to speak, how is it that you were not thrown right straight into your own as she described hers to you? Does this make any sense to you?"

I flushed. This man had just seen my own victim folly, for I had this exact thought, how could I handle Linda with my own identical trauma sitting right there too? He noticed my flush. "I made the same mistake — thinking that I dare not do Linda for fear that mine would activate and overwhelm me completely. I had that very thought too. I even begged mom to help us. She kicked me in my spiritual butt, so to speak. Look, if this were the case, that when helping another through their trauma, your own kicked in full blast, no one could ever do the therapy! No, mom reminded me that when I am doing Linda, I must always keep my full attention on her and what she is saying. If I do that, I am obviously not looking at my own traumas, now am I?"

"Brilliant, positively brilliant. I beg you to teach me how to do this!"

"Chaucer, I certainly will. Nearly every one of us here has undergone severe trauma on this trip. Linda and I could use the help. However, it must wait a little while. I had already intended to give you some tomorrow. After I finish you, then I'll teach you how to do it, and, believe me, buster, I'll put you to work!"

"Thank you, thank you. I'm ready to work, though you needn't waste your time on me. I'm just a wife killer, pure and simple. Nothing can ever change that. I did it, end of story."

"We'll see tomorrow. Can you pour me some more tea, please? I haven't yet learned how to do that. Gosh, I haven't really learned how to do much of anything yet!"

The next day, we made room on the wagon for Chaucer to sit and for Tonia. Linda and I would each do one person today. I figured Chaucer would be the tougher case. I was right.

"Let's start at the beginning when you arrived around Hudu," I said, and we were off and running. He began describing things vividly. He commented about how very real his mental pictures actually were. He told how he could really re-feel the tall grasses as he had at that time, several years ago. As they learned the local language from the villages near Hudu, both he and his wife had growing fears of what was going on up on the mountain. They had ventured there, but were ambushed. Lilly took a dart and was drugged unconscious as we had been. Fortunately, Chaucer had been able to get her out of there and she recovered. Sometime later, their provisions were low and he had left her at camp while he went hunting.

"I see hundreds of them coming down the slopes towards where our camp was located. I gallop back as fast as my horse could go, but I am too late, she is gone. I have to rescue her from these evil Tikki. Yet, I could not go charging up the hillside. It takes me two days of very careful hiking to get to the edge of that village without being seen. I use every bit of cunning that I know to avoid their numerous lookouts with their blowguns. I am sitting behind the trees at the edge of the village and I'm studying the village, trying to find where they have Lilly."

"I spot her in the pen along with a lot of other women. She is wearing the same yellow neck collars that your people wore. She wakes and stands up! I nearly vomit and scream; she has no arms anymore! I want to charge in there right then, but I count over a hundred men with spears and blowguns still in the village. I have to wait for an opportunity. I see other women there like her, missing their arms. Then I see two others who also do not have any legs! I try to think of some way that I can rescue her, like starting the village on fire to distract them. Yet, nothing will work. I feel so utterly helpless! I am failing completely as a Protector. Worse, I am failing the one person in the whole world that I dearly loved. Yet, it is folly to rush in there. I'd be killed and she would not be rescued. Patience, patience, somehow they will make a mistake that I can use to rescue her. I watch day and night. Then, the mantis comes. The men line up in two rows and begin chanting. They bring Lilly out and lay her down before the black creature. I wave to Lilly. She sees me. She is pleading with me to kill her. The mantis is about to chew off her legs like the other women there. She pleads and pleads. I can see it in her eyes, the horror. I act. A lightning bolt hits her neck, and she is gone, released from that terror. The mantis is angry, denied his meal. Big confusion. It leaves. They bury her. I sneak away and vomit. I cannot eat for days. I swear on Lilly's memory that I will never leave here until the beast has been killed."

He spent another hour going through the many days that passed after that, all filled with self-recrimination. After a few more passes, nothing more or new developed and we have to stop for lunch. While we were eating, Chaucer commented to me, "See, I am worthless now, just a wife killer, that's all there is to it." I smiled and said nothing.

After we began to roll along with lunch under our belts, I resumed the session. "Now then Chaucer, let's see if there isn't something like this one that happens earlier in time?"

After a lengthy silence, he said, "Well, I have some strange picture here."

"Okay, let's go through it and tell me what is happening as you go along."

"I see this man who is walking home from work. He is sort of staggering along. He goes into this house, kind of a crude house. There is a woman there. Now they are arguing. She says that he is drunk again. He says he is not drunk. They argue. She slaps him. Ouch! My face hurts. Oh, it is me that she is slapping. I hit her back. She falls down. I am so tired. I lay down on the floor beside her. I really am drunk and pass out. I hear noise. Someone is pounding on the door. It opens and in comes several men. I struggle to my feet. They are looking at my wife there on the floor. She is lying in a pool of blood, a knife sticking out from her chest. It is my knife. You have killed your wife! They are saying that to me. I stare at her. I love her. I would never kill her. I try to explain, but there is my wife dead with my knife in her. I was lying in her blood. I am soaked with her blood. They take me away, calling me a wife killer. The whole village spits at me, throws rotten food at me. I let them. I am a wife killer! Then they hang me. I let them do this, because I know that I am a wife killer. I am floating above my body now. Where can I go now? Everyone knows that I am a worthless wife killer. So I float away, far, far away and sit in a forest where no one is living. A long time passes as I sit there, grieving for my wife, who I loved, yet I had killed her. Finally, I think that perhaps everyone has forgotten me now and I sneak back to a town that I have never seen and find a new mother. That's all. I guess I really am a worthless wife killer after all. There is no hope for me. Every wife I have, I end up killing. So I never marry again, not for a long, long time."

For two hours, I listened to him wallowing in self-pity and despair over somehow killing his wife. He was a drunkard and he did it and was utterly convinced of that for four passes through it. However, then he finally started yawning, and I knew I had him! On the next pass, the veil of drunken stupor began to lift. "I'm passed out on the floor beside her. Oh, the door opens quietly. I see my business partner standing there. He has been asking me to sell him my share of the business all week. He wants it really badly, but I know that we are making a lot of money, and I keep refusing to sell it to him. He's standing in the doorway looking at us. He comes over to me. Oh no! He is taking the dagger out of my sheath. What is he doing? Oh no, no, no! He is stabbing my wife! He killed my wife. Oh hell! I didn't kill my wife! He did. Hell, he made it look like I did it. Everyone believed it. Oh, he was the one who brought the sheriff in the next morning! What an idiot I have been all these years!" He began to laugh, the more he said, the more he laughed. "What an idiot fool I was!" He roared with laughter.

He looked at Linda, who was now watching us, since Tonia was long finished, and said, "I am an idiot, Linda. I am not a wife killer after all, just a moronic idiot!" Ha, ha, ho, ho. He laughed and laughed. I ended the session quietly.

Since it was not yet time to stop for supper, I went in search of Natale and then Mind Linked her with Linda and me. *Okay, Natale,*

Linda and I are in dire need of your aid. We must learn how to do everything all over again. First, how do we eat with our feet? I'm getting tired of sitting like a baby with someone stuffing food into me!

Same here, Linda added. *How do you do it?*

I wish I was with you, I can show you easier than I can tell you. Put the fork or spoon between your big toe and the others. Make sure that as you lift the spoon up, that the bottom side of the spoon is going to lie against the underside of your toes and foot. This way you have support for the weight of it, lying against the bottom of your foot. Do you follow me? Oh yes, you both should begin to do stretching exercises at once. You really have to get your hips and legs limbered up to bend all the way up to your mouth, so you don't have to bend over so far. We chatted for a time, Natale just loved to give us tips, like pulling up your blankets with your teeth. *Remember you two, at first, everything is going to seem horribly awkward and unbelievably slow. Just keep on practicing it and soon it does go faster and it won't seem nearly so bad as it does at first.*

Each day, around suppertime when we finished our sessions, we linked with Natale for more tips, advice, and to get our endless questions answered. I now understood fully why the House of Right women had always operated as a foursome. This was enough women actually to accomplish daily tasks more easily. I was now very glad that mom had followed their suggestion and so re-arranged all the other women into units of four.

The next morning, I spend a couple hours going over the procedure with Chaucer, who was now riding along in the wagon with us. Once I was satisfied, I had Renzo and Benet climb onboard. I did Renzo, while Chaucer did Benet. Currently, Linda was in the middle of working with Rosina. "Don't worry, Chaucer, I will be monitoring your session from here. If you think you need help, raise your hand. If I see anything that needs correcting at once, I'll Mind Link to you, so as not to disturb your session. Good luck."

I was amazed at how well Chaucer actually did on his first session. He didn't need any coaching whatsoever. If there ever was a natural at this therapy thing, I was beginning to think it was Chaucer. Meanwhile, I began running Renzo through his horrid nightmare with the pit of vipers. I knew it would be a terrifying experience for him. As we ran through it, his whole body visibly began shaking wildly out of control. This experience had really shaken him up badly!

As I expected, Benet ran far more easily, since he loved animals and had a rapport with them. Mostly, his was one of painful confinement. His didn't fully erase after the tenth time through, and Chaucer picked the exact same time as I would have done to ask Benet for something earlier. As it turned out, he had once been drawn and quartered. He had been a farmer who had been captured in a Galt raid. After tying his arms and legs to four horses, the men from the steppes forced the horses to gallop off, ripping his appendages off his body. After heavy yawning and spotting his silly decision buried under all that pain and fear, his trauma erased fully, and he was still laughing at suppertime.

When we stopped, Chaucer was so elated, so excited by his first successful session that he picked up Linda and twirled her around and around, saying, "I did it! I actually did it! This is the greatest thing in the world!" She enjoyed his attention, I noticed.

Renzo, on the other hand, was having a terrible go of it. For hours, he was totally hung up on the fact that he could do absolutely nothing about it. All his training was for naught! He couldn't do anything to stop the life-threatening danger. It was not the fact that he was in a pit of snakes, which would have freaked me out something horribly. No, it was that he, with all his training, could do nothing to stop disaster! In the middle of the afternoon, I finally determined that we had viewed everything that had happened in his six days of captivity. I asked for an earlier one.

"I see men, not snakes. This cannot be right."

"Well, let's go through it anyway. Tell me what you are seeing as you go along through it, please."

"I see all these Axe men coming at us. We are on a hilltop. Many women are defending the hill and a few strangers that I have not met. Oh god. That's mom! That's Lenkova. She's leading us. The Axemen are all around the hill, charging up at us. We are defending it. So many of them. I am well trained. I hold my position, but I know I cannot stand up against this many of them. There are just too many of them. Lenkova says, 'Now, fire all your arrows.' I did. I hit many, but so many more are coming up. Now I am fighting them. Two, now three, now four. I cannot fight so many. I am hit. I ignore the pain. I kill another one. I am hit again. I fall. Oh, I died. Oh, this is Heartbreak Hill! I am fighting in that famous battle on the hill. Oh, I see us falling back now. So few are left standing by the standing stones there. Oh, I see one of these strangers beginning to pull down lightning bolts like mad. He is killing the Axemen one after the other. It is staggering how many he is slaying. This man wields such power that I have never seen before! Oh no. It is you, Ket Bethany, that is doing this incredible display of raw power!"

"Ket saved us all, well not me. My body died there before the display. I decided that I had to find you and marry you. You are the greatest man in the world. Then, you go away. I am floating around trying to figure out how I can marry you. I realize that Lenkova is the key. She knows you and talks about you all the time. So I hang around her, hoping to find a way to get a body and marry you."

Renzo began laughing his head off. "I waited forever until she got pregnant and took one of the twins. At first, I thought I took the wrong one, the male. How was I ever going to marry you now? My childhood was spent feeling sad and sorry for myself! Rosina would get the chance to marry you, I always thought, not me. Then, I heard that Ket was dead, and I forgot about the whole thing." Now he was roaring, "Then I met you and I just had to marry you! Now I am unbelievably thankful that I was so compelled. There is not a greater woman on Tarra than you! I love you dear! Please don't hold my foolishness against me."

"I won't silly. I believe that we are done for today. Come on; let's walk for a while." He lifted me off the wagon, put his arm around my waist under my long hair, and we walked until they stopped for supper.

A few days later, with the three of us working daily, everyone's traumas were completely handled. Our whole group was now back to battery, fully alive, fully aware, fully capable, well, except that last for Linda and myself.

While we were finishing the others, Renzo began carving wooden mouth pieces, similar to the ones that Julianna and Rachele used when they took us all riding when we were in Zargarb. Thus, when we were all done, he insisted that we try to ride again. "Look, if you relearn nothing else on this trip, let's make it horse riding, shall we? First, work on staying on and controlling the horse. Once you two have that down pat, then we will see about mounting and dismounting. I think that is going to be the more difficult thing, you know, to keep from falling."

"Renzo, that is an understatement! Balance, that's the hardest part. I keep reaching out with my non-existent arms," Linda laughed.

While Renzo always rode close to me, Chaucer did likewise beside Linda. She was also being grilled about the many sessions that she had done, whenever the wooden piece was not in her mouth. Chaucer wanted to know as much about how this therapy was done as he could find out. Several times, I caught a knowing glance or wink from Tonia or Rosina. They, too, were keeping an eye on Linda. We all thought that she was really handling the death of her husband and her mutilation well. That she was at least talking with another man we thought encouraging.

One problem that never went away for Linda and me was going to the bathroom, believe it or not. We both preferred wearing our comfortable leather pants and undies, especially out here in the bush. Yet, for us to be able to manage this ourselves, we would need to wear open dresses and no undies. Chaucer also observed us with our dilemma, especially since he was the one who was now helping Linda, while Renzo helped me.

"Look Linda," Chaucer offered, "life offers all of us a set of choices to make all the time. Both of you are facing up to learning how to be independent once again, having just lost so much. I say, choose your dependencies. None of us can live life independent of all others. Think what that would mean. Every scrap of food you eat you would have to grow yourself, prepare yourself, forage to find it, hunt it yourself. Every utensil you use to prepare and eat your food you would have to make yourself. You would have to mine the ore, smelt it, and forge it. Gladly would I trade a few coppers for my cooking gear. Gladly would I trade a few silvers for my week's food. Gladly would I trade some coins for well-made clothes or a fine, well-trained horse. I do not want to spend a month building a saddle; I would gladly swap something for one already made."

"Until now, both of you have lived some sixteen years choosing what dependencies you would accept and where you desired your independence. Now you find that the old familiar, routine is longer doable or workable. Simply let go of the past and chose a new set of things or actions you wish to be independent with and things or actions you are willing to be dependent with, do you follow me?"

"That is a profound observation, Chaucer," Linda replied. "I do love to wear these leathers, though I don't mind occasionally wearing fancy party dresses and all that. If I follow you, then I should choose to be a little dependent on having someone help me dress and to go to the bathroom when I need to, and be more independent with what I wear?"

"Yes. I think you look fabulous in leathers."

"But I feel so funny having to ask you all to dress me and help me go to the bathroom. Besides, do I then insist on giving you a copper every time I need you to pull my pants down?"

"No, silly. Oh I see, you are really concerned about the exchange factor," Chaucer realized.

Linda looked at him with a double take. These were Judger concepts that he was now bringing up, not the usual things that a Protector would even think about, let alone say. "Well, yes, observant of you. I didn't even mention exchange."

"Of course both of your exchange factors are completely turned head over heels by this. How could it not be so? For example, I don't know what all you both did on your trip to Hudu. Certainly, each of you took care of your own personal needs. Did you help out the group with other actions?"

Linda replied, "Well, yes. She and I are or were the usual dishwashers, since neither of us is much good with cooking. The men set up camp and handled the horses; we women gathered firewood and fixed the meals, though usually Tonia and Rosina did the actual cooking, and Bethany and I did all the cleanup work. Now, she and I just sit around like pumpkins."

"Right, so make some new choices. You both used to ride horses, and now you are both back to doing that. See you've decided to remain independent in that area. Now I bet you can still manage to find ways to help bring in firewood. Perhaps you can still deal with the dishwashing chores, if we all find a proper way to set it up for you. There is certainly no time limit on how long it takes to wash them, now is there?"

"Well, probably there is at breakfast and lunch," Linda added. "You are right. We were both sort of going to wait until we got back to the ship and let Natale start showing us how to do things. Bethany, why don't we try to figure some out ourselves?"

"Okay by me," I replied. "I hate sitting around like a pumpkin anyway. Renzo, I will knowingly and willingly let you help get me dressed and help me go to the bathroom so that I can wear my normal pants. In return, will you accept a kiss and snuggle? At least for now until I can figure something better out?"

Renzo grinned, "Oh yes dear." He teased, "Please, decide you need to go to the bathroom, say every couple of minutes?" I head butted him.

Linda laughed at us, then asked, "I suppose that you would like a kiss and snuggle for helping me with the same things, Chaucer?"

"A snuggle, a hug, that would be more than sufficient, Linda," he replied thoughtfully.

"Okay, accepted," Linda replied, but then got serious. "I knew Damien all my life. We played together. It is so hard realizing that he is actually gone from my life. It has left a hole, you know."

"Oh, I know only too well. My Lilly is also gone from me forever. It is a very deep hole indeed. I know not how I could ever fill it. Others say it takes time, but I shall never forget her and our times together," Chaucer replied.

"Come, walk a while with me, will you, Chaucer? Could you put your arm around my waist? I'd like a comforting shoulder to lean on for a time. We both have a big hole in our lives, don't we? I don't know how we can ever fill them." They took a nice long walk around the nearby savannah.

The next evening when we stopped for the day, Linda and I joined the other women fetching firewood. We each managed to drag a few pieces back by holding them with our chins and neck and shoulders, but at least we got some. After the meal was done, we attempted to do the dishes. Normally we would sit on the ground, chat, and wash. We had two tubs, one for washing, and one for rinsing. While we still sat on the ground, the pile of dirty dishes beside us, this time we sat on our butts and used our feet.

We did more laughing than washing this first night. We were so incredibly awkward at this. Try it sometime yourself; it makes a good laugh. "Oh my belly hurts!" Linda exclaimed when we finally were done and stood up. We had been stretching and bending at the waist for some time.

"Well, if we keep this up, our stomach muscles will certainly be tough ones, no flab on us, Linda dear," I teased.

"I didn't even know I had all those muscles!" she declared.

"Hey, ready for a walk, Linda?" Chaucer appeared beside us. Quickly, this became their ritual. After we got the dishes done, Chaucer and Linda went for a walk.

After three weeks on the trail, we two were starting to get the hang of doing some things, anyway. We had a very, very long road ahead of us though. Our progress was much slower than our initial trip to Hudu, however, and over half the distance remained. This night when Chaucer and Linda returned from their walk, he asked me, "Commander Bethany." He was being formal, so I knew that he wanted to ask something. He went on. "I am very familiar with this area around here. There is a particularly beautiful lake not too far from here. I would dearly love to show it to Linda. Would it be possible for us to take a short detour of about ten miles so that I could show her?"

"Any inherent dangers in taking that detour?" I asked.

"None at all. You may like it too."

At noon the next day, we rounded a rise and entered an oasis-like area out here in the heart of the savannah. The lake was still as can be, flat, utterly flat. It was five miles across, fed by underground springs. Here near the smooth shore grew a multitude of wild flowers, whose fragrance was heady. At the far end of the lake, over a thousand pink birds called flamingos, I believe, milled around in the water. Picturesque — did it little justice!

"What an incredible sight! What an unbelievable place!" I exclaimed as I accidentally dropped my wooden mouthpiece holding my reins.

"Oh Chaucer, you are right!" Linda burst out, dropping her mouthpiece as well. "This is gorgeous. Look at all those birds, so pink! Look at the reflections in the water. Wow!"

We made camp here, forgetting the rest of the day! Since Chaucer said it was safe to go in the water, we all decided that it was time for a swim, a bath, and to do our dirty clothes a favor. After securing the horses and letting them have a good long drink, it was time to strip and get into the cool, clear waters. As Linda and I waded out, we once more realized that we didn't have arms. How were we going to swim and play around as we used to?

With the water now up to our necks, we both were a little edgy about this. However, both Renzo and Chaucer were right there with us, so I took a deep breath and flopped onto my back. Quickly, we discovered that we could somewhat backstroke our way around. Gradually, we became accustomed to dealing with swimming, though I was still a bit apprehensive. So much so, that Renzo began our usual games. We would often tickle each other and splash the other as well. He got me good, which isn't saying much. As I was now, I could hardly do anything to avoid it. But I found that I could return a splash by making one with my foot. Tickling him back was another thing entirely, and I forgot about even trying that.

After a fun filled hour, splashing and playing without a care in the world, it was time for a bath. Officially, we women had to wash out our hair. Both Linda and I didn't even try ourselves, content to let Rosina and Tonia do ours. The men with their relatively shorter hair were done far sooner. When we were finally done, Renzo appeared and dropped a large pile of our dirty laundry beside me. "There you go, Bethany. Have at them. I have something else that's really important to do." He darted off without a word.

Chaucer came next with both his and Linda's pile. "If you will be so kind as to do mine for me Miss Linda?" he said and set the large pile down beside her. One by one, all the other men brought their and their wives piles to their wives to do.

Rosina commented, "Well, isn't this just like a man! No stomach for doing the laundry! Leave it for the women! Huh!" She tossed her wet hair back of her in a mock jest.

"Well, Linda, we ought to be able to do this chore," I suggested. We were naked and could not possible get any wetter.

"Now I know why they are letting us do this," I exclaimed. "Take a whiff! It's all those that they were wearing down in the snake pit. Oh brother!" We all laughed.

Soon all we women were doing the washing and chatting amongst ourselves. For quite some time we wondered about how our children were doing. We were really beginning to miss them, yet we were thankful that we had the good sense not to have brought them along. Then, Linda opened up the topic that the rest of us were staying away from, out of respect for her.

"Say, what do all think of the new guy, Chaucer? He's rather nice, don't you think."

"Hey, he's a really nice catch," Tonia said quickly. "Handsome too."

"I think he is awfully bright and very considerate of you, Linda," Rosina added.

"Really?" Linda asked. "I'm not in much of a position to know."

"Haven't you seen the way he dotes on you, follows you around like a puppy dog?" Tonia said, moving a particularly smelly pair of underpants as far from her nose as possible.

"I am having such a hard time with everything. I haven't really noticed all that well."

"Hey, I think he is smitten with you. He'd make a fine catch. You should make a move. I sure would if I were you," Tonia went on, finally soaking the smelly underpants.

"I don't really know. With Damien — well, we grew up together. We knew all about each other. I hardly know Chaucer. Besides, what man in his right mind would want a woman without arms, now really?" she began to put herself down.

Before I could trounce on her for that one, Tonia came right back, "Honey, love doesn't need or use arms, or legs for that matter. He's the most sensitive, kindest man I have met in a long time, our men here all excluded of course. I mean, back in Velona, there are all kinds of men. I've met so many, being mom's daughter and all that. They come to her with everything, you know. So I have met a great many men. I am telling you from experience, Linda, Chaucer is a rare find. You should make a move and reel that fish in!"

"Now how am I ever going to reel him in if I haven't even got arms to hold the pole? Take that one and chew on it," Linda began to tease her back. "Seriously, ladies, I knew Damien all my life. It is so hard to even think about starting over."

"He is probably feeling the same thing," Tonia answered her. "After all he lost his wife too, most horribly so."

"See, so how can I ever possibly replace her?" Linda countered. "What do you think, Bethany?"

"You can't replace her and you shouldn't even try. Likewise, another man isn't ever going to replace Damien. I remember last lifetime when I lost dear Caitlyn. I was devastated, but then I met Lilly Ann, and we developed our own unique, loving relationship. I never ever compared her to Caitlyn. What do I think? I think take your time and really get to know him. With me, well, you know what clicks with me, the spirit of play. I wouldn't have paid much attention to Renzo except his spirit of play is so close to mine. That was the first thing that attracted me to him. God am I ever going to miss our Torque Ball games now! But I can still play kick ball. Sorry gang, this is just so hard to get used to — you know suddenly realizing yet another thing you aren't going to be able to do anymore, something that you loved to do."

Linda replied, "Sorry Bethany. I know that we are just going to run into these things often now, probably lots at first. I just hope that a couple of years from now I am not bothered about it anymore. Hey, now that's useful! Look, the men put up a clothes line. Well, you won't get me or Bethany hanging up these clothes."

"No, but you can carry them for us," Tonia ordered. "You are not getting off that easily!" We all laughed and began hanging out the clothes to dry. I suggested that we get the men to oil the leathers after they dried out because they will incredibly stiff without oiling. They agreed.

The afternoon passed altogether too quickly. Near sunset,

Chaucer took Linda aside, "I want you to come with me. There is one more thing I want to share with you. We are on the western side of the lake, which is perfect. Come on."

"Where are we going?" she asked, curious about his intentions.

"Ah, right here. We have a clear view of the opposite shoreline. Come, I'll sit here. You can sit in front of me and lean back on me. Together we will watch and wait. I hope they come." He sat down and beckoned Linda to join him. She finally did, and he gently laid her back so her head was resting on his shoulders — his hands propped against the ground, holding them both up.

"So what are we seeing?"

"Watch and wait. Sometimes Nature rewards us with a treasure. If she cooperates, then you will see." After a pause, he added, "I used to come here after I lost Lilly and sit here for days. I had always wanted to share this with someone special, someone who could appreciate it. I think that you will."

Linda twisted her head to look at his face, "See what? What will I appreciate?"

"Hey, here comes the sunset." They watched as the reddened sun sank, casting a special hue over the lake.

"Yes, it is a marvelous sunset, is that it?"

"No, silly. Watch. I think I hear them coming now." Suddenly, we all knew that something was coming. The ground began to vibrate slightly. Then a honking sort of noise echoed across this vast space followed by many answers. Everyone stopped what they were doing and looked across the lake. A large herd of elephants ambled down to the lake to drink and bath before dark. Several babies were being led by their mothers.

Sometimes you see a sight that makes an impression that will never leave you. This was one of them. We stared in awe and wonderment at these huge, yet gentle parents, tending their young, splashing and enjoying the lake as we had earlier in the day. After a frolic and bath, they moved back out across the eastern savannah and the stillness returned.

Linda whispered, "That was really special, Chaucer. I will treasure this until I die. Beautiful, really beautiful!" She leaned her head and gave him a thank you kiss.

He whispered back, "Not anywhere as beautiful as you are, Linda."

"Can we lie here a bit longer? I really like to lie here, up against you. I have missed having someone close."

"I'm here for you, Linda, whenever you need me. I could lie here for days." Only when the night chill settled did they rise and head to bed, snuggling in with all the rest of us to stay warm.

The next day, Chaucer took me aside and said in a very serious tone, "Bethany, heavy rains are about to hit here. This whole section of the savannah is going to get flooded, and it will be one big mud mess. We should try to get at least twenty miles further ahead, where the ridge line rises above this basin."

We took his advice and headed out quickly, skipping breakfast. Our progress was slow, the wagon, heavy. By noon, we could see the ridge line far off in the distance. Unfortunately, the rains began, slowly at first for about an hour. Then a deluge came down, as if the very sky opened up on us. Chaucer said that this often happened around this time of year, at least for the last three years it had.

With five miles to go, the ground was now covered in water. The dry dirt turned into a gooey mud. While the horses had no problem, the wagon's progress became slower and slower, until at last the seven horses couldn't move it anymore. Emil now tried to hitch all the other horses to the wagon too.

"Wait, I have an idea. Someone lead my horse. I will try lifting the wagon up, maybe then the horses can pull it," I suggested. Renzo took my reins, and I knew that he would watch over my body while I was out over the wagon. I gave it a lift and a push. Sure enough the horses, surprised to find their load lightened, began moving once more. A few hours later, we made the ridge line and halted to wait the storm out.

This was probably the most miserable time that we had had to date: cold, soaked to the bone, no shelter to be had. No food all day and now only cold, soaked left overs. The men handled the horses, and we women made an attempt to fix something to eat. At last, we all just wrapped ourselves in a blanket and huddled in a mass under the wagon.

Daylight came. Sunbeams slicing down to the ground through the clouds made a very pretty sight indeed. A while later, warmed on the outside by the fire, which we could finally make, and warmed on the inside by a hot breakfast and tea, we stood looking back out over the way we had come. As far as the eye could see lay water. Not deep, perhaps a quarter of an inch deep at most, but it reflected the sunlight and looked surreal indeed. An hour later, the water was gone.

We spent the morning drying everything out and oiling the leather goods. At noon after getting lunch and ready to ride out again, we looked back. What a surprise! The whole land was a sea of pale green! Everywhere new life was beginning to shoot up! Linda decided to call this the Valley of Mysteries.

A week later, we were once more out on relatively flat, smooth savannah lands. Renzo challenged Linda and me. "Okay, ladies. We have been taking it easy on your riding training. Now let's get working on it."

"What do you mean?" I muttered through my teeth.

"Come on, keep up with me." He broke into a trot.

I refused to be outdone, so I nudged my horse to follow. Undaunted, Linda did the same, while Chaucer followed close beside us. I figured the two had already worked this out in advance, but didn't say anything. My attention was focused on staying in the saddle and keeping up. After we got used to this, he picked up the pace.

Finally, he broke into a full canter and then all out run. Oh god! How I had missed this and hadn't realized it yet! The hot wind rushing past my face, my long hair flying behind me, this was the life! I love riding like the wind!

Over the next days, Renzo continued to press us hard. We found that making sharp turns was challenging. Once over that, then we had an awful time with fast changes of pace, reining in swiftly, or starting up fast or even sharp directional changes. In a couple weeks' time, we discovered that we could keep pace with him no matter what he did. At that point, Renzo yelled, "Pass! You both get a full pass on riding! Woo hoo! Way to go. Now we work on mounting and dismounting."

Damn, just when we finally got it all worked out here was a new challenge! At first, they held our horses still, while we worked our butts off, legs actually, trying to mount by ourselves. That proved exceedingly difficult to get the hang of — until we discovered it was a matter of balance mostly. Dismounting was substantially easier, as long as the horse was perfectly still, that is.

Despite our bumbling attempts, both men kept us at it. After a week, we finally could handle our own horses by ourselves, as long as they were saddled and ready. It felt wonderful when Renzo gave us both the words we longed to hear, "Pass! You both pass mounting and dismounting! Way to go!"

Chaucer said, "Linda, you never cease to amaze me! I know of no other woman in the world besides Bethany here who can do what you have just accomplished!"

Renzo corrected him, "We know of two others, Julianna and Rachele in Zargarb. Yet, other than those two, I agree with Chaucer. Fantastic and you did it in less than a month. Now the last part will have to wait until we get back to the estate."

"Wait a minute, buster! What last part?" I taunted him, unwilling to let go of my victory just yet.

"You have to be able saddle and bridle your own horse, now don't you?" Curses! I'd forgotten about that aspect. "You will likely need some boxes to stand on and that sort of thing which we don't have out here. I'm not sure how you will be able to do it, so we will leave that until later to work out, my love."

"Thanks Renzo, for all this. I just realized something, Linda. What we really need is to be pushed intensively, you know, concentrating on one thing at a time, working our butts off to get it down pat, then move on to another aspect."

"I see what you mean. We make great progress as long as we just work all the time on this one thing. Yet, we are facing having to learn how to do almost everything. I was getting overwhelmed by the sheer magnitude of it all. This way, we do one thing until we have it and then move on. Great idea, Renzo!" Linda complimented him.

Renzo flushed, "Thanks, but that wasn't my idea. It was Chaucer's. He came up with it." We both stared at Chaucer.

"Well, I could see that you both were getting over-whumped by it all. We do this all the time when training new Protectors — I mean, get them to master one thing and then move on to the next. I thought it ought to work with you as well."

"Chaucer, I could kiss you for thinking of that!" Linda said and did just that. She leaned over and gave him a kiss. "Thank you! You've found the recipe for us!"

That night, after we got the dishes done, Renzo and I took a walk around the area. We had been following the lead of Chaucer and Linda. Now, all the couples were doing it too, a little private time to spend with each other. I noticed that Angel and John were also going for long walks together as well as Mary Beth and Jason. However, this night we spied Linda and Chaucer in a loving embrace!

Renzo whispered to me, "He's perfect for her."

I whispered back, "And she's perfect for him. I hope it works out for them."

Finally, October 20, 651, we arrived at the docks of Lulu, and there lay the Sleepy Hollow waiting us along with all our children! Both Linda and I became apprehensive. While we had gotten comfortable being around our group during the journey back, now we had to face so many others. We both felt uneasy and worried about how we would take care of our children.

Chapter 25 Overcoming Embarrassments

We rode straight down to the docks, halting at our ship. Linda and I both felt nervous; we were now very different; at least we felt that we were. Yet, we both managed to dismount well and give the reins to the others. As the leader, I ought to walk onto the ship first, which meant that Linda and I would now be front stage with everyone one staring at us.

They were doing that indeed! Henry, Natale, Mireio, Roberto, Alwanianon, the nannies, the crew, I felt sick at my stomach. Linda, the same. I dreaded the expected outpouring of sympathy, oh you poor thing. Instead, Captain Henry called out, "Bethany, Linda, welcome home! We've missed you. May I be the first to congratulate you two for saving Tarra from a hideous fate! Come here you super-heroes!" He gave us a good strong hug.

Natale moved up and said, "Wow. Look at their tans! Come here, you two. I need a hug too." As we got close, I was wondering how we could hug. She whispered in our ears, "Press your body tight against mine; it works rather well, don't you think?"

"It is so good to see you all again too. Thanks." I said, moving down the line to Mireio.

"You have saved us all. There is no thanks worthy of what you have done," she welcomed me. We did their special hug. It felt good to feel the pressure of her body against mine.

"Hi Bethany, Linda. Welcome back. I will help you both with the babies. I am getting good with it. The nannies say so too," Alwanianon chattered happily, very glad to see us again. "Honestly, Bethany, it has been so utterly boring around here I could scream!" She put her short arms around my waist and hugged me, and I pressed into her.

"Bethany," Roberto said, as I moved down the line, he was holding Adrienne. "There are no words for which to thank you for what you and the others have done for us all. Simply fabulously done!" He gave us a hug as well.

Then came my twins, our twins! They were beginning to crawl. I sat awkwardly down before them and let them crawl on me. I leaned way over and pelted them with kisses. Linda sat beside me kissing little Zachary. I whispered to our three little ones. "Now you three can have a bright future. I got rid of the nasty bugs." Of course, I didn't expect them to understand what I was saying or meaning. I said it from my heart.

To my surprise, Lena looked up and me and smiled. Benjamin did too. Suddenly, I realized that they were spiritual beings and had indeed understood, far more than I realized. After all, Lena had been Lenkova!

I heard Linda whisper to Zachary, "Daddy's not going to come home. Daddy lost his body fighting the nasty bugs. We'll just have to see if we can find us a new daddy. Would that be all right with you?" I swore Zachary nodded, but he was only seventeen months old!

Now the others began filing on board, with similar greetings. Oops. I needed to introduce our newest acquisition. I couldn't stand up, because the twins were all over my legs. "Everyone, this is Chaucer de'Grange. No, he is not dead. Yes, without his timely aid, we would be dead. He's the latest addition to the Explorers Circle and a Protector."

I had surprised everyone with this pronouncement. Emil immediately turned and shook Chaucer's hand. "Hey, great! Welcome aboard!" At this point, everyone began shaking his hand and introducing themselves to him. His smile and mild manner was an instant hit with everyone he'd not met before.

"Ah, Natale, the Translator, right?" Chaucer said as he came to her in the line, giving her a long hug.

"Yes, that's little old me," she teased him.

"We must spend some time together. I know three native dialects of the central Southlands. I would like someone else to also know them."

Did Natale's eyes ever light up! Henry moaned in jest, "Oh no, not three more languages! I can never keep up with this woman!"

A while later, Chaucer finally got to us. We were still sitting on the floor with our babies having fun with us. "Ah so these are the twins. This one must be Lenkova!" He kneeled down and took her tiny hand, "Very pleased and highly honored to meet you again. Old Chaucer de'Grange, returning from the dead. We met in Zargarb when I was on my way to New Barq."

"Linda, you didn't tell me what a fine looking lad Zachary is! Hello, Zachary. I'm Chaucer. I've been looking after your mother for a time. I hope you don't mind my doing so. She's a fine mother. I would be honored to look after you as well. I'm a Protector, and that means I help defend people from bad things. I promise to look out for you and your mother." Zachary crawled over to him and began fiddling with his shoes.

"Sit down and he'll crawl on you," Linda suggested, pleased that Zachary was taking a liking to Chaucer.

"Hey, there are my twins! Daddy's back now!" Renzo came over and sat down with us, putting one arm around me and the other all over the twins, who now began climbing on him. I had tears in my eyes. I looked at Linda; she had tears of joy as well.

"I didn't know how much I missed the little fellow," she said.

"Me too!" I replied.

Natale and Mireio came over to us. Natale said, "Bethany, Linda, if you will come with us, we'd like to show you some special changes that we here have all made for you. However, we have one problem. We didn't know what we should do for Chaucer's quarters. We can put him up in the cargo hold on a hammock or eject one of the Santi from their cabin."

I looked at Linda. Chaucer was about to say anyplace is fine, but Linda cut him off, "I would be very honored and pleased if Chaucer would stay in my cabin with me. Natale, he has been my hands these past two months. That is, if you don't mind, Chaucer."

"I would be very pleased to share a cabin with you and Zachary. Thank you."

"Okay then, the crew wants to start loading soon. We all want to set sail. You cannot believe how bored we have all been! If you will follow me below, I want to show you some changes."

Renzo picked up a twin in each arm, while Chaucer gently picked up Zachary, telling him, "Hey, Zachary, let's go show mommy here your cabin." He goggled. We followed Natale below.

"Watch the steps, Bethany, Linda," she called out.

Damn, we had not yet confronted steps. It was a bit scary going down steps without the ability to grab hold of the rail. "Easy does it and watch your balance," Natale pointed out.

In our cabin, I found that my old chair had been replaced with one that was much taller and had a sloping back. I realized that this would make working at the desk drastically easier. She had swapped shelves. My stuff was now on the bottom shelf, while Renzo's was moved to the top. I could much more easily get to my things with my feet. Linda's cabin was done similarly.

Out in the cargo hold, one large section had been turned into a nursery. Railings prevented the babies from crawling where they were not supposed to be going. All of sides were heavily padded to prevent bumps either from the children's actions or because of a rough ship ride. This we thought was a terrific idea. The nannies came up with it, Natale explained.

In the dining area, Natale showed us two new tall, sloped back chairs, which were for us. Now we would be far more comfortable eating. "Henry had a set of cups and glasses made for you two as well. We used mine for a model. Yours are the yellowish ones, Bethany. Yours are the blue ones, Linda. Oh yes, I am supposed to tell you both that this does not mean that you are getting out of your chores around here. You two are still on dishwashing detail. Henry's orders." We all laughed. This had always been our duties and I guess it would remain so.

"Thanks for all this thoughtfulness, Natale. We really appreciate it," I said. Just then, Mireio came up to us here in the galley.

Natale said, "Okay men, take the little ones to the nursery please. Mireio and I need a very private chat with these two, please." Both men gave us a quick kiss and took the little ones back to their play area. I noticed that Alwanianon was standing guard, making sure that we were not interrupted.

Natale said, "Okay, now really, truthfully, how are you two doing, feeling, and coping? Mireio and I have had a long talk with all those on the ship before you arrived. We stressed how awful and uneasy you two would likely be when you actually had to face us. I could see it in both your eyes as you walked up the gangplank."

"God, Natale, I was nearly petrified, nervous, you name it. I felt that everyone was going to be staring at me and all sorts of things," I replied honestly. "I guess you did a good job, because it hasn't happened. I am feeling much better now. Thank you both sincerely! It is so difficult for us."

"We both know Bethany, Linda. We've been there already and have had to confront it. Yes, it never does really go away. Every time we go into a new place that we have never been, we get a queasy stomach. But you just have to do it — have to face it or your lives will be a hell."

"God, I was so hoping that such feelings, such nervousness would go away with time," I said morosely. Linda added a "me too."

"It hasn't for us. Maybe it is so for those like Enyo, who never knew otherwise, but not with us. However, is does lessen with time. Much depends on your regaining your own self-pride in being able to do the normal things of life. Once you two get over that giant hurdle, it does get much better. We just don't want to give you both false hopes. Now then, your mother has ordered us to form up as a team of four, like those in the House of Right. She has found that their solution is the optimum one, and she has implemented it estate wide now. When we get back, you will see that four either are sharing a room or are quite nearby. The married ones are all close together. So whether you like it or not, we four are now a foursome. Jenna's orders."

"That's really a good idea, Linda and I need it, really we do, if only the guidance and moral support. It has been really awful for us, but I guess you already know that from your own lives," I said.

"Yes we do. Now then, there is one thing Mireio and I want to know. We saw you two riding horses."

"Yes, Renzo gave us a pass on handling the horses. We can keep up with him no matter what he does. It took us a month to get it worked out and to be able to do it, though we still have to learn to saddle them and all that. Natale, we also saw that we did best at adapting when we concentrated fully on one skill alone until we really had it mastered. Now that we are back in civilization, I am getting overwhelmed again by so many different things we have to learn to do again."

Mireio replied, "We know; we've been there. That's one of the things that the Laird Foundation has done for us, work with one major thing at a time. Yet, as you both know, suddenly there are thousands of things to learn how to do and all keep popping up at once. We've put our heads together and have worked out a plan. Of course, it is subject to change, as you two desire. We know that the biggest embarrassment lies at the dinner table, when everyone is gathered around so close. Once you two are totally comfortable with all aspects of feeding yourselves, you will begin to enjoy being around so many of us again and not feel so scared and nervous and all that."

"Also right there at the top are personal things, like brushing your hair. The list goes on. To make this work well, we've swapped cabins. Already yours and Linda's are side by side. Ours are now just across from your doors; Natale's is opposite yours, Bethany. Mine is opposite yours, Linda. We four now operate as a team with Alwanianon pitching in all the time."

Natale butted in with, "Also, your mom wants you to contact her as soon as you are on the ship, before you set sail. Sorry, we rather got too excited. We are so glad that you are back!"

I relaxed and connected with mom. *Hi, we made it back to the ship. Natale says you wanted me to let you know.*

Hi dear. Yes, how did it go? I mean meeting up with the rest of the gang. Bit awkward, embarrassing, or feeling a bit strange about it?

Yes, Linda and I suddenly got nervous about it. We had gotten used to life on the trail, but now, well, we are confronted by so many things we can't yet do. Natale has really helped ease us back. I can't believe they all didn't stare and gawk at us, let alone dump sympathies and all that. We just couldn't take it right now! We feel so funny, so different, so weird now, to say nothing about being so dependent on others for trivial things that are now mountains.

I presumed that would be the case. This is a direct order from your Commander, Bethany. You are to sail to the Vacation Island and spend time with your family. I want you to learn how to become independent once more. When you and Linda feel you are ready to handle the world again, then let me know. You see, as the leader, you cannot have your attention being forced inward by your situation. The only way that can happen is being fully adjusted to your new way of life and getting comfortable with yourself as you now are. All the others are also going to be going through a tough period of adjusting to both of you as well. You can't be an effective team until all of you are totally used to the way things have to be done now, do you follow me?

Yes, thanks mom. You've stated what I felt but couldn't quite put into words. We all need to learn to adjust, adapt, and find our new limitations. Otherwise, everyone will be in confusion whenever a situation arises. Can she do this? Does she need help or can I do that instead which is needed? If we are attacked, this could defeat us. Renzo and I knew exactly what each of us could do and we used it to kill the bug once. Now I know that he and I both don't know what I can and cannot do anymore. It's as if a wall has come between us. We really do need this time together. Thank you mom! I love you.

I love you too, dear. I would like to see the grandchildren one day, so don't take forever. Also, why don't you send that pile of gold back on another caravel? That will get rid of excess weight. Now go issue the orders to Henry. I know they have been utterly bored out of their minds waiting these months. Keep us posted.

"Back in a minute, gang." I started to dash through the cargo hold to tell Henry. I suddenly realized I was losing my balance rapidly and slowed down. Damn, I have to be so darn careful now! I took the steps one at a time. On deck, they were still loading the cargo. "Henry, a word please." He came over quickly, but a little hesitant. I could tell that he felt a bit awkward or funny towards me as well. "Sailing orders, Captain. Mom has ordered us to sail to the Vacation Island and take a vacation in the sun and fun. She said to ship the gold and treasure back on another caravel. Do we have enough food and supplies for a long trip?"

"Yahoo!" Henry exclaimed. He was about to hug me as he normally would have but hesitated. Damn, we all needed adjustment. I leaned into him and he then gave me an enthusiastic hug. He whispered, "Er sorry. It so strange seeing you like this you know."

"I know. Mom is giving us all time to learn and to adjust."

"Wise woman, I've always said. Yes, plenty of food. Say, I hear that you have a present for me?"

"Yes, but you are going to have to wait until I hand out the presents once we are underway and settled in a bit," I teased.

"God, it is so good to see that you haven't lost your feistiness, your playfulness!"

"No, just arms. Now give me a hug!" He did. I then went back down to the cargo hold, where the other three were waiting. I told them the sailing orders and we four cheered and relaxed.

Natale began dictating, "Now the first thing we do is a bath, then proper clothes. I know you said you want pants, but you can just as soon as you prove to us that you can take care of your needs wearing dresses like ours. Those armless sleeves are just going to cause you troubles, getting caught on things."

"Linda! We have a new boss! We've been replaced!" I joked, and we four had a good laugh. "Honestly, thank you." I gave her our special hug.

"Just think of all the help you have given to us. Payback time." Natale grinned.

After all the wagon's cargo was lowered into the hold, excepting the ingots and gems, I had every one gather around. "We have a few souvenirs for some of you. Now I would ordinarily hand these out personally, but if you have to wait until I can manage it, you will undoubtedly become very exasperated with me. Renzo is lending me his hands. First, and probably the most important, Henry, we present to you the first map of the entire world of Tarra, complete with the strange navigation lines. I encourage every one of you to spend some time studying it. In the future, we are going to have an awful lot to go explore! Our world has just doubled in size on us!"

Everyone gawked and stared at the huge map. Indeed, we only knew about at most half of our world. "Next, I have something special for every one of you. We found a cache of the Always On Lanterns. I have one for each of you. Renzo, hand me one please. Here, you merely push this button; see, the light goes on. Push it again; see, it goes off." He had wisely placed it on the floor where I could activate it with my toe.

"Natale, you are going to need lots of hands with this one. We have for you forty of the mantis books for you to decode!" She let out a cheer and many hands helped get them to her study desk in the captain's large cabin.

"Finally, each and every one of you, including the crew and nannies, please come forward and accept these pouches with our sincerest thanks for everything. We all have needs and things we'd like to acquire. This should aid you. Thanks for everything."

"Wait a minute, Bethany!" Mierio said with a look of astonishment on her face. Roberto had just opened up her pouch for her. "This is a fortune."

"Yes, we kind of guessed at the relative values. I think it should be about ten thousand gold coins worth. We all are risking everything on these voyages of discovery. You are entitled to a splurge now and then." I received a huge round of applause.

Slowly things got back to normal. Though it was typhoon season once more, Benet and Michelle took up their usual three times a day frontal search, looking for storms ahead of us. Henry was taking it slowly this trip, primarily so that Linda and I could learn to adjust to the moving ship.

As the days passed, Linda and I had to work hard, a constant battle of frustration, awkwardness, clumsiness with a large dose of "taking foreverness" thrown in for good measure. Mom was so right. If I were to remain the leader of our group, I had to be able to perform. First, we spent hours mastering the simple action of feeding ourselves. Natale didn't pass us until we could eat reasonably gracefully and with no attention on ourselves as we ate, that is, until we were very relaxed with ourselves while eating with the crowd.

Personal grooming turned out to be awful. Brushing out our hair, dressing, and undressing almost did us in completely. Here, we found just how critical it was to be acting as a foursome. Together, three working together could manage it, where one alone was nearly impossible with anything but the loosest fitting dress. Shoes, we discovered were highly problematical. Now that we depended so much on our feet and toes, wearing shoes severely limited our abilities to fend for ourselves. Three choices were available. Going barefoot had the liability of getting our feet very dirty which in turn made everything else a mess, as well as splinters from the ship. Easy slip ons worked the best and were what Natale and Mireio normally wore. These proved to be optimum. However, at dances and for our explorations or even horse riding, sturdier boots or shoes were required. Again, with the four of us working as a team, we could at last get them on and off. However, once on, they severely limited other things that we could do. Natale pointed out that it would always remain a tradeoff.

During this time, Renzo was not idle with our training either. Four times a day, he made Linda and I practice running all around the cargo hold. We had to learn to run, obviously, but more importantly, we needed to learn how to maintain our balance. Just as we finally got the hang of it, Henry would increase the speed of the ship! We were back to square one each time. By the time that we neared Vacation Island, Henry had the ship at maximum speed, pitching and rolling wildly, while Renzo chased us around the cargo hold, cracking us playfully in the butt with a bit of rope if we slowed down. That was a fabulous pass, one that we both truly needed! I realized that I now could easily play our chasing games, which Renzo and I so loved to do in the past!

All this time, I wanted to be able to care for my twins. However, Natale pointed out the salient detail that first I had to be able to care for myself before I could care for others. I hated to admit it, but she was right. Just as we arrived at our destination, we finally began learning how to care for our children.

On January 1, 652, we arrived at the first of the new islands that we had ever discovered. It lay around a hundred miles off the coast of Wanakan. Uninhabited, Vacation Island was twenty miles around. Groves of trees grew inland along with a freshwater spring. The calling card of the island was its fabulous beaches! Crystal clear waters lapped upon pure white sandy beaches. Although it was the dead of winter back home, we were so far south here that the days were warm and balmy.

Each day was broken into three training periods. In the morning, we worked with the children. In the early afternoon, Renzo and the men took turns chasing the four of us all over the island. Later afternoons were spent swimming. The purpose was once again for us to maintain our balance and to be able to run like mad, should we ever need to escape some danger. It was all unspoken among us, but every person in the Explorers Circle realized that if we were out on a mission somewhere and trouble arouse and we had to flee for our lives, we four needed to be able to do so and the others needed to know that we could do so as well. Hesitation or carrying us could mean life or death. The others had to have certainty that they could count on us in a crisis. We did too, for that matter. Plus, everyone had to know precisely what the limits of we four actually were. Otherwise, they might accidentally demand more than we could now do, which potentially could also spell major trouble.

Just after lunch, the men did the dishes, while making us four put on our own boots. They would inspect them when we were done to make sure they were tied securely. Then the chasing would begin. Slowly at first, we were chased all over this island. Gradually, they would increase the pace, but only after we were very confident at the current speed of running and dodging. For all of us, the change of elevations were the most difficult to manage. However, here the ground was very soft and sandy, so our many falls resulted mostly in injured pride.

Yes, there was a reward when we did especially well. Our husbands and Chaucer as well, would catch us and give us a very warm, loving embrace, among other things. Carrots and sticks they used on us four for over a month. It worked.

At last, Renzo said on this sunny, warm afternoon, "Ladies, we are now entering the last phase of this training. You pass when you can catch your husband. It would not be fair to make you grab us, so solidly bumping into us will be the yardstick. The rules of this exercise are simple. There are none. We will do everything possible to evade and elude you. All you have to do is to bump solidly into us. No fair bumping into someone who is not your husband, or Linda, anyone but Chaucer. Gentlemen, make this as tough as you can. Keep in mind that we are running for our lives from a swarm of the bugs or from ten legions of Centurions who are out to kill us all. Ladies, we fellows must have complete certainty that you can keep up if we are running for our lives. So do you."

"Further, we do not expect that you will be able to catch us today. We don't care how many days we do this until you succeed. However, we will continue to do this every day until all four of you have passed. That is, if Bethany catches me today, she still has to continue with this tomorrow, until you three have caught your man. We can never have too much of this practice, not if we are going to continue to explore the unknown. I wish each of you the best of luck. Bethany, you are really going to need it! Oh yes, Bethany, Linda, there will be no cheating on this exercise. That is, you cannot pick yourself up and drop yourself on me or pick me up either, for that matter. Linda, no fair taking control of Chaucer's body and halting or slowing him down. This is a dexterity, balance, running skill that you absolutely must have. We must know that we can depend upon you at all times. Got it?"

"But you men are faster than us," Linda complained.

"Well, then, imagine another bug is on your tail and after your legs this time," Renzo teased and challenged her. He entertained no further objections that we had. The chase was on for real now. Thankfully, we only had to do this for a couple hours before we could go for a swim. Chasing after Renzo, I realized that this was different. Before when they were chasing us, I was in control, determining just when I could manage a twist or turn, a speed up or a slowdown to avoid losing my balance. Now, the roles were reversed. I had to follow him and keep up, no matter what he did. More than once, I lost my balance, falling head first into the sand. After struggling to get back up, to my initial disgust, he had not slowed down! He was sending me the clear message not to fall down. I resolved that whenever I caught him, I was going to somehow tackle him and knock him to the ground!

On the third day, Natale caught Henry, and they stopped to kiss passionately! We three cheered. The next day Mireio caught Roberto. Okay, they had an unfair advantage; they were totally used to all this because they'd been armless for years now. I grit my teeth and resolved to catch Renzo somehow!

Two days later, I actually did it. As we entered a relatively level patch of the beach, I put on the biggest spurt of speed I could muster and literally threw my body into his, knocking him off balance. We both tumbled to the ground with me landing on top of him! "Gotcha buster!" I panted totally out of breath.

We rolled over in the sand, and he gave me the strongest hug and the most passionate kiss imaginable. "God, do I ever love you, Bethany!" he exclaimed. The others came running up, saying, "Okay, break this up!" They were teasing of course. Now it was up to Linda.

Still we three had to continue to chase our fellows. Natale and Mireio had caught theirs a couple times now. I discovered that I also could catch Renzo occasionally as well. For two more days, Linda kept doggedly chasing after Chaucer, who like Renzo, did not make it easy for her. In fact, both our men were Protectors, trained to avoid being "caught," which made it vastly more difficult for Linda and me to catch ours, I now realized.

Two days later, Linda began to use her mind while running. Chaucer was always just too fast for her. His stride was significantly larger than hers was; she was only five-five. She watched him curve around a low hill. Anticipating his path, she ran over the hill and saw him coming racing around below her. This was her chance. She raced down the hill and dove into Chaucer, bowling him over as they both rolled into the sand. Linda struggled to her feet and sat down at his side, both were panting. She said, "Okay, Chaucer, I caught you. Now will you marry me?"

We had come running up to congratulate her and heard her proposal. Instinctively, we stopped short and allowed them some time. "What? What did you say? You mean it? Really? Me?" Chaucer, for once, lost his shy reserve. He exclaimed, "Will I marry you? Yes, yes, yes!" He got up, picked her up, and they spun around and around, ending in a long embrace.

Now we strolled up to them with two different congratulations to give. Linda was flushed as she explained, "I have never in my life had so much fun as I have had these past few weeks, running around like this and all. Besides, Chaucer is so shy that he was never going to get up the nerve to ask me, so I told myself, if I catch him, I'll ask him instead. Darn if that didn't drive me even harder. I guess I really, really want you, Chaucer!"

"Hey, this will be my first ship's wedding!" Captain Henry announced.

"Well, let's do it soon!" Chaucer exclaimed. Then he added, "Before this wonderful woman changes her mind!" She gave him a bump with her hips.

Then we four realized that we had done it. "Hey, we did it; we caught them!" Natale exclaimed. "I didn't think it was going to be possible when Renzo told us about it."

"I would not want to do this on rocky ground," I added. "There are limits. We should also practice this on rougher terrain, but that will be far more dangerous to us. Oh, I see, Renzo, it is a matter of knowing precisely what our limits actually are."

"Yes, my love, that is it entirely. You must know and we, too, must know. I promise never to force you beyond your true limits."

"Thanks, but we have to find them first. Thank you for helping us find some of them."

"Right, Renzo, thanks!" Linda added, with Natale and Mireio echoing her.

That night on deck, I bumped into Renzo, "You're it!" The chase was on; we darted about all over the main deck, upon the poop deck. While he could still tickle me, I resorted to friendly bumping. We had a ball. I now realized that I had my spirit of play back again. When we were done, panting for breath, half the crew was watching and broke out into a round of applause. I realized that they too were very happy to see me back into my old playful form, which they knew.

That night as he and I were snuggled into our bed with the twins wiggling between us, I said, "Do you realize what gift you have given me? I have my spirit of play back once more. I am not afraid anymore of running and playing."

"I know. I was horribly afraid that I had lost that part of you forever, and that is one of the things I love the most about you." We embraced long after that.

The next day, it was Henry's turn to drill us four. He'd decided that, if he were going to put Linda and I through this bit of training, he'd also put Natale and Mireio through it as well. "As your captain, I expect that we will be going on lengthy voyages. You all know how I worry so when Natale and Mireio are on deck. Hence, you must wipe out my constant worries. We are going to ask you to master three skills here. First, I have always feared that one of you might lose your balance, fall overboard, and drown before we can get to you. At sea, this is an ever-present worry that I have always had. Since this is a time of total honesty between us all, I am telling you this, which I haven't said anything about before, not even to you, Natale. I do worry. The first drill is to be thrown overboard, and you must stay afloat for ten minutes, which is a rough guess at how long it might take us to get to you."

"We've discussed this at length but cannot find any gradient to it. We will have men in the water close to you, while you are 'surviving' in case it is too much for you to handle. There just isn't any other real way to do this. Good swimming."

He didn't give us a chance to protest or even think about it. Renzo picked me up and threw me over the side of the boat! Oh god! I was falling, trying to fail my arms as a bit of panic swept over me! Once more, I felt so helpless! Ouch! I hit the water so hard. I began sinking, frantically moving my non-existent arms to pull myself back to the surface. Of course, nothing happened. I did the only thing I could: hold my breath. At last, I stopped going down and began going up again. I started kicking with my legs as fast and hard as I could. Just when I thought my lungs would burst, I broke through the surface, my long hair over my face and sides. I gasped and kicked hard and finally caught my breath.

I knew I couldn't kick like this for long but finally the panic subsided. I flipped onto my back and began floating, rolling my head from side to side to get my hair out of my face and nose. Then I calmed down and realized I could float like this indefinitely. Soon, Renzo lifted my body upwards, and Benet slid me into the longboat. I had made it. As I sat up on the bench, I looked around and saw the other three being lifted onboard as well. We had all made it.

When we got back on deck, Henry, all smiles, said, "Wow. You actually did it on the first try. I am amazed. Maybe I was worrying for nothing."

"No, Henry. I very nearly panicked there. I think I need to do this a few more times. I cannot tell you how frightening that was! I was flailing my arms for the longest time! I need to do this a lot more, please."

"No kidding!" Natale exclaimed. "I haven't had that weird sensation of using my arms for so long now I'd forgotten about it. I did too, Bethany! I panicked and was trying to use arms!"

"I nearly drowned," Linda admitted. "It was so weird, the

strangest darn feeling I have ever had! I was way under the water and frantically trying to use my arms to fight my way up! There is just no way to describe that feeling!"

"Unless you don't have arms," Mireio added. "Me, too."

The safety men dove back into the waters once more and soon it was over the side with we four once more. After five more attempts, I began to feel better about the whole thing. "What about diving? I asked Henry. "Can we try diving overboard? We will go deeper. If I can handle diving way down and coming up without panicking, I will have certainty and confidence in the water again."

"Yes, but don't you need your arms to turn yourself around to head up?" he asked.

"I know, that is what keeps panicking me about this whole thing."

I did a dive from the deck into the water. It felt great while I was falling, but once I hit the water and began going down, that panic once more began to creep in on me. I bent my head and arched my back. It worked. I soon came up to the surface, far slower mind you than I ever did before. Yet, I made it and that handled my panic. I took a few more dives until I was confident with myself. One by one, the others followed my lead.

Later, I said, "Well that wasn't so bad, Henry. Now what do you have in store for us?"

He pointed to the slanted rope ladder that led to the crow's nest. Oops, me and my big mouth! "You want us to climb up to the crow's nest?" Linda exclaimed, clearly terrified of this one.

"And get into it and then come back down. In a tight pinch, I might need one of you up there, because the others are injured. We know it is impossible for you to climb up the ropes and other rigging lines, so that has to be a limitation that cannot be overcome. Yet, we think you ought to be able to scamper up there if need be."

I stepped up onto the railing, wobbling to keep my balance. Then I mostly fell onto the slanted rope ladder. Using my neck over a rope rung for support and balance, I began the climb up. At first, it went easy. Then I saw the problem, exposure. What is simple if done at ground level becomes terrifying if done at say a hundred feet above the ground. Renzo was right behind me, in case I started to fall. A rope was fastened around my waist and a crew member held the other end of it way up there in the nest. If I goofed, I wouldn't get hurt.

Initially speed was not a problem. I had all the time to consider each step. We all did make it, though very slowly. For five days, we kept at it, each time going faster up and down. Then, it was solo time: no one below, no safety rope, and no one in the crow's nest. Here, I would use my skills to catch anyone who slipped or fell, including myself. However, we all made it safely and passed. Henry doubted that we would ever have to do this, but now he knew that he could count on us in an emergency to do just this. He, too, had to know our limitations and on what he could depend.

The final drill we all found exceedingly useful in many other ways. They placed a small board on edge, whose width was about half that of the width of our feet. It was only four inches off the ground, however. The objective was to step up onto it and walk its length, some fifty feet in length. Obviously, this was balance training. In fact, it became so popular that soon everyone began working on it. Alwanianon was the first to insist she have a try. Then, Tonia and Rosina wanted to as well. After Renzo had a try, everyone just had to do this one.

By March, both Linda and I finally felt comfortable and secure. Of course, things would never be quite the same with us, but what mattered was our own personal confidence in knowing what we could do, how to do it, and what we no longer could do and would need assistance with from others.

Linda said to me, while the four of us were brushing each other's hair out before heading off to breakfast, "You know, Bethany, I really do feel like I can face other people now. This sure has been a revelation. If it wasn't for all this, I would probably have just found some hole someplace and crawled in to hide from the world."

"Me too, though I hadn't really vocalized it," I admitted.

"Well, every once in a while, Mireio and I get a bit nervous, scared, anxious, or worried too," Natale added. "It never really disappears wholly for us. Perhaps it has for the House of Right women. I'll have to ask Enyo about it the next time I see her."

"Okay, then I say let's head for home and face everyone and get our next assignment," I replied.

On April 15, 652, the Sleepy Hollow slowly entered the harbor of Velona once more.

Chapter 26 Shore Leave

It felt good to see Velona once more, the bustling docks, the many boats loading and unloading. Only now, we saw several enormous carracks whose size was double the caravels docked beside them. I had a sneaking hunch that one of these would be our next ship. Henry had been making many estimates, working out how we might sail to these other landmasses far to the south. Always, he came up with the problem of carrying along enough food and water. A bigger ship was needed and here were several of them.

As the mooring lines were thrown and caught, I noticed that for once, only a few carriages were waiting for us. No large crowd of well-wishers. However, Paulette had already warned us to expect a huge welcoming party at the estate, not at the docks. The average citizen of Tarra knew nothing the Grey Creatures or the giant mantis creatures. Hence, they would not understand the welcome we would be receiving.

For once, it was nice standing around taking in the hustle and bustle of the huge docks, while the cargo was unloaded and put into the carriages. After an hour, we were on the streets heading for home. When we pulled into the estate and rounded the last curve, stopping before the main estate building, the entire gardens and lawns out front were packed solid with people! I was glad that we followed her advice and came dressed up. Our long earrings were back on, hair nicely done, our clothes clean. Renzo had even fashioned a sack-like affair so that I could carry Lena on my chest, while he carried Ben.

When our crew stepped out onto the cobblestone drive, Bard Tal and his expansive group of musicians and dancers struck up a very loud fanfare! After the short bit of cheery music, this enormous crowd began clapping and stomping their feet upon the ground. Many cheers, whistles, and even a yell swamped our senses. It seemed every Laird Foundation woman, every Santi, everyone we had rescued, was here and cheering us!

A temporary raised platform had been erected. Elona Po stood on it, dressed in her finest priestess robes. Even mom was there, dressed in her fanciest Santi clothes. We were told to go up on the stage, which we did, while the noise continued unabated. After our whole crew was assembled in a giant semicircle, Elona raised her hands and the enormous crowd hushed.

She spoke loudly, "This is the proudest day in the history of Velona. The Explorers Circle here has done for all of Tarra, all people everywhere, the greatest of deeds, they have killed the remaining adult creatures which have plagued Tarra for such a long time, alien creatures, which have destroyed lives, given rise to aberrations too numerous to mention, and enslaved the spiritual beings of our world. Commander Bethany Rose Wilkins Pazzio le'Goeur, please accept on behalf of the Explorers Circle the heartfelt thanks, commendation, and praise of all the Santi del Dio and of all the peoples of Tarra. Thank you for a job most well done, despite huge personal sacrifices of you and your group. You and your Circle have given all of us on Tarra hope for a bright and prosperous future, free of the enslavement of the aliens. Thank you!"

The crowd went wild with applause, Tal added to the cacophony with another fanfare. We all just bowed together. Then, it was mom's turn to address the huge assemblage. I wondered what she would have to say.

She raised her arms and again a hush fell. "Ever in the course of achieving freedom, both physical and spiritual, personal sacrifices are often required to achieve that final prized goal. No more so than in this case. Faced with overwhelming, ultra powerful enemy aliens, the likes of which are almost beyond comprehension, you and your team measured up to what was needed and got the job done. I know very well, as do nearly half of you gathered here today to celebrate and welcome back our heroes, just what those sacrifices mean. I have lost my youngest son, and Bethany and Linda, their arms. Yet, despite all this, they did not give up. Many lesser people would have given up and succumbed to the aliens and their supporters. Yes, the easy way out is to abandon the fleshly body and go pick up a new baby body, starting over fresh, forgetting what has happened. Yet, none of you did that. Though mutilated and with all of your men still in chains unable even to move, you did not give up. You chose to continue the fight to its successful conclusion. You have set a standard of excellence for all Santi del Dio to forever strive to measure up to."

"To commemorate this momentous achievement, the Santi del Dio wish to present each of you with the highest medal of honor that we have, the Sterling Medal of Honor, the first such medals ever to be awarded in our history." Again, the musicians played a fanfare, while the throng yelled, cheered, clapped, and stomped. It was a bit overwhelming, I thought. While the music continued to play, Elona stood before each of us and hung the newly made medals over our heads.

Once the presentation was finished, mom again called for silence. "Now I know that many of you wish to personally meet and thank these heroes. If the nannies will come and take the children to the nursery, our heroes can step down here in front of the stage and accept your thanks. Yes, this is my chance to spend some time with my grandchildren, so keep them occupied a long, long time," she teased and many chuckled.

A bit later, we stood in a long line, watching as so many people that we knew formed into lines to spend a moment with each of us. "I just can't believe this," Linda whispered to me.

"I can't either, but I see mom's hands behind this. Cleverly, we will get to meet everyone and they us, so this rather awkward first meeting with everyone will be done all at one time. Actually, I think that was a shrewd move on her part. We just endure the initial meeting of all whom we know once right now and then it's done."

Elona was the first to come through the line. When she got to her daughter, she said, "Tonia, I am so proud of you I could cry! I am crying. Thank you my child for what you have done for us all."

"Bethany, Linda!" She gave us both a hug. "If there is ever anything that I can remotely do for you two, please let me know. Words cannot express the gratitude I feel for what you have done for the spiritual beings of Tarra!"

One by one everyone that we knew and many that we'd never seen before came past us. Linda and I gave hundreds of body hugs to those whom we were now like. Most often, they had tears in their eyes as they thanked us and offered us any help adjusting that we needed.

Chara from the Isle of Right said, "Don't let this stop you. It sure hasn't stopped us. You can do anything you want to, don't hesitate to ask us." This from a woman who had already composed a hundred new pieces of music!

Enyo, the fantastic architect and engineer from the Isle of Right, said, "Once you get used to it, you won't miss them. I haven't. I just keep on making new things. The world, Bethany and Linda, is full of arms, but there is a big lack of ideas, designs, and plans. That's where we fit in. I'm happy to help you any way I can. Actually, now you can really put my bathroom inventions to good use, like us." I gave her an extra hug.

Adonia of Megalos said, "Bethany, thank you for killing the source of these mutilations of women on Tarra. Perhaps now women can rise to their rightful place beside men."

Isabella, the Chairwoman of the Laird Foundation, said, "Bethany, Linda, I just want you both to know that you are members of the foundation and have the full support of it. Please stop by as soon as possible so that we can work to assist your needs."

Then those from Wanakan came through the line as a group. Teyacapan just cried and hugged us. We had ended up as the priests had intended her to be when we rescued her. However, little Teiuc, the woman with half arms and half legs, whom Teyacapan continually helped said, "I hear you still ride horses. I would like to have you come for a ride with Shorty and me one day. I have something to show you." We promised that we would as soon as we could.

Finally the line was nearly done. Tal and his group were near the very end. Tal gave me a big, long hug. "Well, dad, this is the second time that you have rescued all of Tarra from these aliens. I'm so proud of you that I don't know what to say. I loved you last lifetime, been your son this lifetime, and now here in your next one, you are still looking out after all of us. It is an honor, Bethany, truly an honor. Now, if you and Linda here are interested in a change of careers, like dancing, for example, I have two openings in my dance troupe," he teased us. I gave him a butt bump, and he roared with laughter.

His wife, Lia Ines, whispered to us, "You are one of us now. We all stick together and help each other out. Please, please let us help when you need it. Thank you so much for what you did."

Zita, Tal's incredible dancer, said, "Hey, he's not kidding about the dancers! Seriously, as Lia says, you are one of us now. If you ever want to learn how to dance, I mean really dance as I do, I would treasure teaching you both! It is the most rewarding thing in life, dancing. Well, maybe not as rewarding as mantis slaying, but far less dangerous!" We all chuckled along with her. I had a hunch that I just might take her up on her offer later on.

At the very end of the line came Jenna's Circle, some of our mothers and fathers. Lilly Ann, Linda's mother and the Judger, said, "Incredible job, Linda, Bethany. I don't know how you did it. I'm so sorry about Damien, but then I am so pleased that you were able to let that grief go and move on. Chaucer, you must come spend some time with me, bring Linda and Zach too. I am at a disadvantage here, my late husband, Bethany now, already knows all about you, and I, her mother, do not." She was teasing him, of course.

"Ah, Holy Mother of the Best Woman on All Tarra, I, humble Chaucer, would love to come and spend quality time with you," he replied.

She roared with laughter and gave him a hug. "Linda, you picked another winner here, I can see that! Please, I want to see my grandson, so come by."

Beth Ann, the Healer, said simply, "Bethany, wow, do you ever look good! I see you got your wish, larger breasts." I flushed. She knew that I had always pestered her when I was a young girl asking about how soon they would fill out and how big they might become. "Dear, you do look really good. I was worried you might look all worn out, but you are just as bright as ever. Just please do me one little favor, don't go donating any more body parts to the bugs." We laughed.

"Linda, you look radiant. Ah, this must be the man I've heard about. Chaucer, I'm Beth Ann, Lilly Ann's twin sister. My dear, I do approve of him. You've picked a very fine man indeed."

Linda flushed, "How did you know I picked him?"

"Oh I heard about your having to ask him to marry you through the grapevine. Little escapes your Aunt Beth Ann, not when it concerns men." We all chuckled. "All jesting aside, Chaucer, welcome to the family. We tend to enjoy life and have fun. Hope you don't mind."

"Oh, Bethany, I've been meaning to ask," Beth Ann got serious. "Were those mantis creatures really thirty feet long and did you really kill them when you were like this, I mean, after you lost your arms?"

"Yes, on both accounts."

"I saw the dead bug bodies," Chaucer vouched for me.

She walked away repeating, "Incredible, just incredible!"

Beth Ann was the last person. We looked around and saw that everyone else had left. "Well, gang," I said, "that was unreal. Okay, heroes let's go inside and find our kids and our houses. Chaucer, you are with us."

I spent over a week fully briefing Jenna and her Circle, plus a lot of others, who mom also wanted present, on the entire affair. After that, Henry joined us, bringing his prized map of Tarra, of which Michelle had already made five carbon copies just in case of damage. We discussed the ramifications and what needed to be done next. As I expected, we would be given one of the new carracks for this expedition to the far south.

After the two weeks of briefings and meetings, there was little official business that I needed to handle. Our ship would not be ready until late fall, plus Henry and his crew would need to be trained in the operation of the new ships. At least he had lots to occupy himself with during this time.

Linda and I took a day's ride with Teiuc and Shorty; of course, Teyacapan went with us. She and Shorty went riding nearly every day and had come upon a particularly beautiful pool surrounded by a field of yellow buttercups. This had now become their favorite place, and she wanted to share it with us. For once, I let her do the hugging, since she still had something left with which to hug, and she grinned ear to ear afterwards.

Often after suppers, Renzo and I would go outside and play kick ball with the many children. I had not realized that there were so many of them around. However, he and I also tried to figure out how I could do Torque Ball, which had been our favorite game to play together.

After much experimentation, I suggested, "Honey, as I see it, we have two choices. You can let me cheat and do it not using my body or I have use my feet."

"No fair not using a body," he insisted.

"Okay, then we have two more choices. If we leave it as it is now, I can play very slow Torque Ball." I purposely slowed down my speech on that last. "Or we can lower the white line. In fact, let's put in two lines. Lower the main one so I have a chance with my feet and put in a new upper line with the rule the ball has to be bounced somewhere between the two lines. Then I might be able to play medium speed Torque Ball."

We tried my idea and it did work. I also discovered that our daily workouts did wonders for my agility and balance. If I didn't, I fell flat on the floor. Yes, for the first month, I had an awful lot of bruises. By the time that fall came, I was once more giving him a run for his money, something that he found utterly incredible. He began to treat me more like a goddess, that's how highly he thought of me now.

Still there were many hours of the day with little to do. Yes, we all went on shopping sprees. Natale insisted that Linda and I get fancy silk outfits like hers for the dances, because, after all, we were now like them. Actually, I rather enjoyed having Lilly Ann and Beth Ann helping me dress up in my finery for the Saturday night dances. Renzo just couldn't keep his hands off me, and we always had a very romantic time after we returned home.

Michelle had finished forty paintings by the time that we had returned. They were completely sold out one week after she put them on sale in the gallery. She was shocked at their success.

Me, I was still getting progressively bored. It was only early May and late fall seemed ages away. I spent some time wandering the studios of the Laird Foundation, admiring all the many artists and their works. I was not interested in painting, sculpting, ceramics, or weaving. I used to play music and was a troubadour, but without arms, that was mostly out. I didn't feel like singing.

One afternoon, I found myself sitting in the back of the dance studio, watching Tal and his group rehearse new dances. Zita took a break, while the Greenway Stompers practiced. She spied me sitting in the dark back end and came to sit by me. "Ready to try a bit of dance? You could do the Stomp; it is awfully creative they way they do everything with their feet, keeping the body so rigid." She looked at me carefully and added, "No, I think not. You are far too agile for such subtle movements. You need flash and flair. Come with me."

Curious, I got up and followed her into another room, where many of her associates of the Expressionistic Dance were taking a breather. "Basil, let's show Bethany here the jump and spin move." He grinned and took his place, stretching a bit first. I watched as Zita twirled around in a tiny circle for a few times, then she took an ever-quickening run toward Basil. I saw a white mark on the floor. As she reached it, she leapt as high into the air as possible, while going as far forward as possible, as if leaping upon Basil. His left arm caught her chest on the underside and his right arm firmly held her back as he caught her. They converted the momentum of the rush into a flip; her feet went high overhead with her long hair touching the floor, as Basil continued moving her in this great rotational movement. One by one, her feet finally touched the floor, at which point, Basil, sensing that she had her balance back, lowered his hands. Zita said, "Ta ta! Now you try it

Bethany."

"Well, I don't know. I'm not a dancer." I was quite intimidated. I think it showed. However, Zita wouldn't take no for an answer. She and four others like her came over to me and began pushing me up to the front with their bodies. "Here, you stand here. You run as fast as you can to that white mark and then do a springing leap as high and far as you can go. Basil will catch you and convert your momentum into the spinning circle. When you are upside down, open your legs wide and he'll let you touch the floor. Don't worry, he won't let go until he senses you have your balance."

"Zita, I don't think I can do this."

"I know it is scary when you jump like that. Just have faith that Basil will catch you. Now try it. Run really fast and jump."

I was still hesitant. Jumping like that, what if he missed me? I'd land really hard on the floor and probably get hurt. "Come on, on three. I'll count. One. Two. Three." I took a deep breath, ran as fast as I could, and then jumped. At first, it was exhilarating as I went up, but as I leveled off and started down, it became frightening. I was once again flailing with my non-existent arms. Then, I felt Basil's hand on my chest and then my back. Next thing I knew I was spinning head over heels. I nearly forgot to spread my legs. One foot touched and then the other. All the training I had done to date kicked in, and I had my balance at once.

"Holy cow! That was wild! What a sensation! Wow! Can I do it again?" I said wildly excited. "What a rush that was!"

Basil exclaimed, "My goodness! Bethany, that was terrific. Are you sure you are not a trained dancer? You could have fooled me!"

"Huh?"

Zita explained, "Bethany, you are the first to do it nearly perfectly on your first try. Usually, Basil has to catch them and keep them from falling down. You did it smashingly well! I knew you could do it! You were born to be a dancer!"

Basil suggested, "This time Bethany I will spin you around three times. I will call out the numbers and on the third one, spread out your legs for the landing."

Once more, I took my position. Took a deep breath and waited for Zita's signal. I ran with all my might and jumped. Again, exhilaration flooded into me as I rose. However, that was nothing to the spinning! I hardly wanted to stop when he called out three!"

Now the other dancers were jumping up and down cheering wildly. "She's absolutely incredible, Zita. We just have to get Bethany into our dance group," Basil said passionately.

I asked, "The spinning was terrific! How many times can I go around and around before I have to land?"

I was hooked and I knew it! For the next six months until we had to sail, afternoons I spend learning to be an Expressionistic Dancer. Early fall we gave a performance which ended with Zita on one end of the stage and I on the other. Our catchers were about a third of the way from each end of the stage. We ran to the opposite side and did our flying leaps, which turned into rotating spins, only we spun around and around ten times before we landed. The audience gave a standing ovation and we had to repeat it. Such had never been seen before.

Thus, when asked how I spent my shore leave, I answer, learning to be an Expressionistic Dancer. That was as much fun as playing Modified Torque Ball with Renzo. That and one other little detail. All of we women became pregnant once again. Our due dates once more would lie within a month of each other, sometime in January.

Chapter 27 Around the World

The Pinochet was one of the newest ships, a carrack by name. Before making any final plans, we all toured this new ship to see if it would meet our requirements. Our caravel, the Sleepy Hollow was fast and sleek, being some sixty-five feet long and twenty-five wide. Our total weight when fully loaded was sixty tons. The Pinochet was nearly twice as long, one hundred fifteen feet. Its width was also larger at thirty-three feet, and fully loaded carried one hundred twenty tons, double our current capacity. However, its speed was half that of the Sleepy Hollow and required nearly twenty feet water depth compared to ours at ten feet. The main mast was huge, a hundred feet tall, while ours was but sixty. We had but one crow's nest, the Pinochet had three, one atop each of the three masts. The stern mast was as big as our foremast!

The carrack's design was to carry vastly more cargo per run, though slower in speed. It had both a quarterdeck and a poop deck above that and a forecastle deck as well, double the passenger accommodations. The Pinochet offered us more living space, more room, and vastly more cargo. However, the downside for us was the nearly double depth needed to dock and the halving of our speed.

While we liked the spaciousness of the Pinochet, since we were going to unknown lands, we valued speed for fast getaways and shallower draft for entering harbors unused to such huge ships. Once we had established trading, why then the merchants could use these bigger ships. Alas, we ended up opting to stay with our lovable caravel. However, some modifications were done to give us more living space, at the expense of cargo. Our poop deck was extended to become a quarterdeck, adding four more comfortable cabins, one of which was designed to be a nursery. The crews quarters aft and below were also doubled, giving them more room as well.

Food for such a long voyage was a definite problem. While the salted meats, grains, and flower would keep well, our fresh fruits and vegetables would not. We had already seen what a poor diet deficient in these did to the women we had rescued from the Holy Paladins. None of us wanted our teeth falling out or worse. Moreover, we also had our babies to consider. Thus, we adopted a firm policy that if we did not find fresh fruits and vegetables along the way at various lands, our maximum sailing time would be three months.

With this in mind, we then worked out our provisions list. Left over space would then be filled with sample trading goods. This trip, our samples were less than a third of what we normally had been carrying.

On October 1, 652, the Sleepy Hollow set sail on its next voyage of discovery. Armed with the mantis map of Tarra, Henry's own maps, which we had measured and drawn up, and with a new device for measuring our position, we set sail to see these new lands in the far south. This device was called an astro-degree; it measured the angle from the horizon to a star or sun. From that, we could then determine on which of the horizontal lines on the mantis map we were located. This, coupled with the timing device invented by Niccolo Helios, and now modified by our Planners in Mont Blanc, we could get a rough estimate of which vertical line on the map that we were near. Hence, we could estimate our position, assuming this mantis map was correct.

What did the mantis map show the landmasses of Tarra to be? Our portion of the world was in the northern half, shaped like an enormous dog bone. Tashien occupied the eastern large lobe, our known world, the western lobe, including the Southlands. The huge island of Megalos nearly touched the Southlands, and we had found the isolated Acropolis island lying some two hundred miles southwest of Megalos.

The mantis map showed two other huge landmasses. The landmass far to our west across the ocean, which contained the Axeman descendent people called Grun in the far north and Wanakan in the central portion, was actually a huge landmass shaped like a peanut with Wanakan located in the narrower central part of the peanut. Based on comparisons to the Southlands, this peanut landmass was over a thousand miles across and at least five thousand miles long, lying lengthwise north and south.

Located even further south from Acropolis at least another two hundred miles lay the potato landmass, which was at least eight thousand miles long, going east-west, and some one to two thousand miles north-south. The potato was longer than our dog bone by at least five hundred miles. Speculation suggested that the southern edge of the potato would be as cold as Volksholm was up here in our far north.

Captain Henry had a grandiose plan for us to sail around the world! He suggested an initial route that would take us to whatever lay further south from Wanakan, around the bottom of the peanut, over to the far eastern side of the potato. We would then travel along the entire northern length of the potato before veering due north for home.

The problem was the maximum number of days without obtaining fresh fruit and vegetables. If we did not find a way to replenish our stocks completely around the bottom of the peanut, we would have to return home immediately. If we succeeded, then we could sail further west to get to the top side of the potato land. From there, if we exceeded our number of days, we could head due north to Tashien and resupply there, or if over half way along the potato, we could head due north and resupply in the Southlands. The key then was to restock completely somehow along the southern coast of the peanut.

Since it was once again typhoon season, Michelle and Benet took three turns each day moving out southwest from our location observing the weather. With their guidance, we bypassed all rough weather.

Again, during the idle times, I worked my therapy magic on several. First, I continued working with Natale, who was already very close to being able to move objects around. After a couple of weeks, she was indeed able to move smaller objects around. She was elated with her re-discovered skill.

I worked some with Linda, who already could control other bodies. From there, we improved her skill to also being able to move smaller objects as well as well as moving about at will. I thought it wise to see what I could do for her new husband. Chaucer regained his ability to move about as well. He was most surprised to discover that he could do this and very pleased.

On November 20, we sighted land once more, the southeastern portion of the peanut. Per mom's orders, this was to be an orientation voyage. Thus, first contact was to be with the larger towns and cities, if any existed, not the smaller ones. Henry, Emil, Benet, and Renzo all confirmed that the mantis map was as accurate as our measurements! Landfall was within our error range of position! This was very good news, lending more credence to the potential with the rest of the map.

We spied numerous small fishing boats plying the coastal waters along with many small villages. The season took us all by surprise; it was late spring down here, where as it was early winter back home! We changed our sailing pattern to rest at night, so that we would not accidentally pass by any larger settlements.

"It's an agricultural land here," Benet called out. We were examining the land with our farseeing eyes. I took a look. Sure enough, I could see neat rows of stones marking the edges of cleared fields. Already the crop was pushing up green shoots, though we could not tell what crop from this distance. We spied oxen pulling plows, very similar to that found in the Greenway.

"Oh no, not again. Bethany, come quick! You won't believe this!" Benet had found something as he swept the seeing lens over the landscape.

I looked and saw a sight that I could not believe either. Instead of oxen, this farmer had a team of men pulling the plow, a team of four men. But they had no arms! You can guess our fears and conclusions! The mantis creatures were active down here as well, only going after men now.

Now we kept a continual watch on the passing countryside. Renzo got my attention, "Dear, what do you make of those flashes there. Look, now watch. There, see them?"

"Signals perhaps? I remember seeing the Megalos people using light signals when I was there a century ago," I mused. "Perhaps they have noticed us and are sending word."

"That makes some sense, look way down there? See, another flash back this way. If this is what you think, they have a pretty good system going here," Renzo complimented our unknown people.

Linda added, "Ah, then that means we are going in the right direction."

"How's that?" Chaucer asked, unable to make any connection between the observation and her conclusion.

"The signals are going on down the coast in the direction that we are traveling. If these are indeed warning signals, one would expect them to be heading back to their center of command or authority, which is where we desire to go," Linda spelled out her conclusion.

I let everyone know our worry about possible mantis activities in this new land. While we were now at least a thousand miles further south than Wanakan, such might not be a great distance for these aliens. By nightfall, we still had contacted nothing more than small coastal fishing villages with inland farmsteads. As we four were in my room brushing out our hair, Linda said, "Bethany, I am really worried about us running into more of these mantis creatures. Promise me that if we are attacked again and I also lose my legs, that you will just kill this body so that I might get a new one and start over. I do not want to end up head and torso. I could not live that way. Please promise me that."

Natale, Mireio, and I looked at Linda and then each other. "God, you have a terrifying point. I would not want to live like that either," I had visions of such. We all looked worried, and I went to bring Renzo in on this conversation. I explained the awful thoughts that we just had and he sympathized with our fears.

"As much as I love you Bethany, I would do this for you and for me. As spiritual beings, we have the right to let go of this fleshly body and get another one. I would not force you to stay in this one if that happened. If it happens to either of you, I will do my best to convince your husbands of the same. I so swear this to you four." We four stood and gave him a hug — well we pushed our bodies into his and his arms tried to encompass all of us.

At noon the next day, we rounded a bend of the coastline and spotted a large city up ahead. Here we spotted somewhat larger fishing boats, but none longer than about twenty feet. However, there was a series of docks for their smaller boats. Henry decided to take two longboats in to their docks. Carefully, the crew sounded our way in towards their docks. We anchored about a thousand feet from their shore. The buildings were wooden, and many nearer the docks were two stories tall. The streets that we could see were laid out in a square grid pattern. Many people wearing shirts and pants, not unlike those of the farmers of the Greenway, thronged the streets. We spied a number of open-air markets. Henry suggested this was a city of some fifty thousand, based on his knowledge of seeing various cities from this viewpoint.

A half hour later, we sat in the longboats, while the armed folks rowed us ashore. Linda and I both commented to each other, "Well, here's another thing that we cannot do anymore."

As we drew close to shore, we spied a large number of soldiers taking up positions near the docks where we were to land. I hoped that this first contact would go well.

We docked; the men helped us out, and we lined up in our usual marching order. Natale and I were in front with Renzo and Emil right behind us, wearing their chain mail armor. Linda and Chaucer were right behind them, followed by Henry and Benet, then Tonia and Rosina. Michelle and her sketchbook remained behind, along with Angel and Mary Beth, and their new husbands. They would guard the longboats.

We walked up the long wooden dock toward the large crowd that was quickly gathering. However, the soldiers kept them back, giving us an open area to walk. Now that we were close, I noticed that every soldier was a woman, armed with spears and wearing hardened leather armor. I won't bore you with the initial attempts to speak to these people. Natale as usual did a terrific job. My old role of dictionary maker was taken over by Rosina.

Natale began by talking with the soldier, who looked like she was in command. After they exchanged a few words, the line of soldiers gave way to two women, who were wearing colorful, cotton dresses. Most of the people here had light brown hair and blue eyes; their skin was white. The soldier immediate gave way to these women, so Natale began talking with them. After a few minutes and much gesturing, Natale concluded, "Their language is rather similar to that of the Galts. I believe we are each beginning to understand the other. They want us to follow them to the Royal Palace, there to meet with their queen."

This sounded hopeful and we followed them. The soldiers moved to either side of our line, while some remained watching the longboats. As we walked through the streets, people stopped and stared at us. We stared right back at them and their city. I felt as though I were walking through a Greenway city, like Calgary. Things seemed so similar, yet different. After perhaps a mile, we spied a large wooden building, one story tall, but very well constructed. A green lawn with many shrubs lined the cobblestone walkway up to the huge double doors. This palace was actually very pretty, as if some care had gone into its landscaping.

We were led inside and found that the floors were carpeted; fresh spring flowers lined either side of the hallway, sitting on small, ornate tables. Ahead, a large pair of doors was guarded by two more women soldiers, who opened the doors for us. We entered a large room. Again, the scent of freshly picked flowers hung in the air. Paintings lined one wall, while three huge tapestries covered the other three, except where the enormous windows, now opened, allowed fresh air and light into the room. Against the back wall below the paintings were three sofas. Near the back was the throne, more like a large, well-stuffed, comfortable chair. In a circle in front of the throne were three more sofas, with small coffee tables before each. Likewise, a small one was to one side of the throne. A large number of different sized vases, filled with flowers were expertly positioned to either side of the throne.

A woman in her forties sat on the throne; a small gem encrusted tiara identified her position as queen. She wore a simple yellow cotton dress with her long hair nicely braided down her back. She stared long at Natale, Linda, and me, before motioning us to have a seat. Several soldiers immediately positioned themselves just in front and to the sides of the queen, their spears pointing at Natale, Linda, and me.

Natale spoke, announcing who we were and that I was the leader. Again, I won't bother with the broken conversation, the gesturing, and so forth that went on, before we picked up enough of each other's language to talk well.

"I am Queen Ivanna Jelena. Welcome to our city of Kostya in the land of Konstantin. What brings you criminals to our land? Seeking sanctuary from the law? Why do you arm your men slaves?" This was not exactly what we had expected to hear from the queen!

"Greetings Queen Ivanna Jelena. I am Bethany Rose Wilkins Pazzio le'Goeur, the Commander of the Explorers Circle. We are Santi del Dio and are from Velona of the Sea Princes. We are not criminals, but highly respected leaders of our land. Why do you believe that we are criminals? Do you mean like thieves and murderers?"

"Well, I admit it is a little confusing. You three are armless, yet you are women. Around here, the men suffer that penalty for their crimes. Murder and rape are punished with the removal of their arms. They are then sent out to work as oxen, for they are only worth of that as a person. Yet, your men are armed and you are not? I ask again, why are not your women armed and why do you arm your slave men? I do not understand this."

"These men are not our slaves. They are our husbands. Often in our land, the men are the leaders; however, I am the leader of this group. In our land, men and women are equals. We do not have any slaves of any kind."

"You have strange customs, Bethany of Velona. Your land must be very strange indeed, if you allow men such freedoms. Here in Konstantin we women are the rulers of everything. Men must follow our every order. Never are they allowed a weapon, for they would brutalize women. Here a man cannot own property, but must work for his livelihood. Our men depend upon women for everything. Yet, you three have no arms. How is it that you have the marks of a rapist upon you? Here such is the penalty that men pay for that crime."

"We three had a very bad encounter with animals that cut them off. However, we have slain those animals. If you would feel more comfortable, I can send our men back to the longboats." I knew that the men would be furious with me over this; they are our Protectors. *Renzo, do as I ask, but you can then be here with me, while your body is back there.*

"Well, I admit that they do make me awfully uncomfortable. In turn, I will ask my guards to wait outside. None of your other women are armed, and you three certainly cannot harm us."

Her guards escorted Renzo and the others back out of the palace, though I felt Renzo hovering over my head, on guard duty. Soon, Chaucer also appeared over Linda. Only the queen's two advisors remained, along with us five women. The queen visibly relaxed and offered us some refreshments, "Oh, I'm sorry, how will you manage? Forgive me. I will send for some assistance."

"No that's alright. We use our feet, if that is acceptable conduct here. We don't let others do things for us that we can somehow manage. Yet, if it makes you uncomfortable, we will allow Tonia and Rosina to feed us," I replied.

"Well, it is a bit unusual, but I am all for the rights of women, please if you are able, do what you must. Now I do hope you like this beverage, it is a favorite of mine. These are called cookies and this is yan." I took a sip. It was tea, but with an added flagrance of some flower!

We hit it off very well after this! Tea, just give me tea and all is well in the world! We chatted for hours. Trade, this excited her greatly, especially when she felt the silk of Natale's shiny dress. She greatly desired to see fine china, along with whatever metal cooking equipment we might have. Quickly, we realized that trade in this land would be those things that a female-controlled society would prize! Later, we learned that metal farming equipment was also needed here.

"It's getting late. We all have our babies back on the ship, and we ought to get back there to feed them. We will bring many samples for you tomorrow, but I am afraid that we will need to have our men carry them, no arms." I grinned and she recognized this as a joke and chuckled.

"You are very brave leaders of your people to come into a strange land like this. Tomorrow, we will have a big feast in your honor. I will have my musicians play as well. Do you have music in your country?"

"Yes, I have two musicians with me. They would love to hear you music too and play some of ours for you."

"Splendid! Wonderful. Until tomorrow morning then. My guards will see that you get safely back to your ship. You never know when some wayward man might try something, especially with you three." We thanked her and left. An hour later, we sat around the galley discussing what we learned, while feeding the many mouths. Argh, then Linda and I had to do up all the dirty dishes once again.

Linda commented, "How strange to find a whole country where it is the women who have total control over the lives of men!"

"Well, if men dominate elsewhere, I guess it was bound to happen that women would someplace else. Things are out of whack here too, I mean between the sexes," I replied, nearly dropping a plate.

Natale, who was helping us, suggested, "Maybe there are no mantis creatures down here. The men we saw being oxen must have been rapists."

Mireio, who was keeping us company, added, "Well, one thing's for sure, if they were rapists, they will never be able to rape a woman again. Beats cutting their you know what's off. Still, it's a very cruel punishment, but it is terribly effective though, in a twisted sort of way. If I were a man, I sure wouldn't even think of raping a woman, not with this as a penalty!"

Linda added, "Well, they must have had something really traumatic happen in their history for them to be taking such drastic measures and for them to put males as second class people. Maybe in time we will learn their history and this will become more understandable. There is always a reason behind man's actions, some driving force. Perhaps it is another back flash against the mantis creatures. Maybe in their past the mantis and men harmed women and now they are in control, reversing the roles." It was an interesting speculation from our Judger.

We spent three weeks here. Once the women saw our proposed trade goods and had given them a fair amount as a good will gesture, Queen Ivanna wanted to know if she could provide us with anything. Ah, we got our total resupply of fresh vegetables and fruits!

She felt awkward, very ill at ease, listing out to Henry what she and her advisors would like on the first big shipment from the Sea Princes. He was our man in charge of the trading, and she had little choice. In trade, we would receive grain, cotton, and peanuts. Yes, these people grew these underground nuts, which when roasted were fabulous! We told her to expect an even bigger ship, which would arrive in early March, which we learned was their fall; the trees would be in full colors! Weird indeed!

Michelle made thirty rough sketches of various scenes around the city. Later, she would come back and finish them. Even Queen Ivanna was impressed with the skill Michelle demonstrated. Music, well, Mireio, Roberto, and Alwanianon had a ball learning their music and songs while showing off many of ours. Yes, it was a relaxing, enjoyable three weeks that we spent here in Konstantin.

During our stay, Queen Ivanna's advisor, Katerina, took a fondness to us women. Linda was able to get her talking about their history. Their Dark Age ended a hundred Great Cycles of the Seasons ago, when the Rule of the Black ended. Those were evil times, Katerina explained, when men here in Konstantin did many evil things to women, raping was the least of them. In great ceremonies, men would routinely cut of women's hands and arms, offering them to their Gods. Illia, the Great, ended the Dark Age, when she took arms and raided their temples, killing all the priests. Women joined her by the thousands, and they finally took over complete control of Konstantin. Today, all the women were surviving well.

When a woman had a baby, if it was male, she at once gave it to the male slaves to raise, for a male child was next to worthless, except as slave labor and for breeding when the woman desired it. A female child was exulted. She was nurtured by her mother, given an education, and treated with great respect. When she reached adulthood, she could become a landowner, and thus a farmer, and was given a batch of male slaves to work the land. She could become a merchant, a seamstress, or any number of worthy trades. If she had the mindset and physique, she could become a soldier. In short, all of society's doors were open to her.

In other areas, we learned that this was their largest port city, but that there were even larger cities inland. Ten great grain cities lay inland. Thus, if the trade proved worthy, the other cities would begin to place orders through Ivanna, and her city would prosper greatly from the trade. It was a win-win situation for everyone. We took care to suggest that the trading ships, which came here, have a large number of women Santi on board, who would handle the trading arrangements.

Fully reloaded on our perishables, we set sail once more on December 23. A month later, sailing westward around the southern coast of Konstantin, we headed out to deep sea once more. During the month, it was baby time once again for us women!

Renzo and I had Danielle, Linda and Chaucer had Marion, Rosina and Cedric had Flore, Tonia and Emil had Andre, Michelle and Benet had Roland Sam, Natale and Henry had Gwenevere. Our two Santi sergeants also gave birth. Angel and John had Avery, and Mary Beth and Jason had Amy. Yes, we kept the nannies very busy indeed! Between running after all the two year olds who were getting into everything and the newborns, they more than earned their keep!

Thanks to Michelle and Benet, and of course, the careful navigation and map of Henry's, we came upon the eastern side of the potato, right on target, on the last day of January, 653. The weather was warm, early summer was here. We knew that we hit a civilized portion of the world, for almost at once, we began sighting strange coastal ships!

Their captains were just as curious about us as we were them. As we slowly sailed along near the coast, several came along side. Language time once more. Again, Natale got a workout. We learned that this land was called Annelise and occupied the entire eastern third of the landmass; a tall mountain range called Hagan divided this highly refined, civilized land from the rather barbaric country, which lay beyond the range.

Their boats were called dahabea, about a quarter of the size of our caravel. They had one main mast far to the aft of center, which sported a lateen sail on a long boom attached high atop the mast. A tiny spinnaker hung off the rear and was used for control. The quarterdeck was more like a half deck and their cargo capacity was a fifth of ours.

What surprised us even more was their dress! The ship's captain wore a blue linen suit, with a perfectly tailored jacket with two long tails falling behind and over his rear end. He looked as if he were ready to go to a fancy party, not captaining a sailing ship. Yet, the crew members were just as nicely dressed. They wore white shirts and white pants, tailored to a perfect fit. A blue sash was tied around their waists. The captain wore a blue top hat, like a cylindrical stovepipe, rising at least a foot above his head, with a small brim. The sailors all wore white berets with a blue ribbon dangling from its top.

We learned that there were six great sea trading cities along the coast of Annelise. To the south of our current position lay Barborg. We were not far from Lenvig. On around the northern coast lay Grenen, Bjerg, Viborg, and finally Ringenstad. Their capital city of Hodenhagen lay some three hundred miles inland due west of Lenvig. Paved roadways connected their major towns and cities. Of the coastal cities, the dahabea captains suggested that we try the docks at Viborg, because there the waters of the harbor ran deep enough for us actually to dock. It helped that Viborg was also the largest of the port cities, boasting a population of nearly three hundred thousand people.

By inviting several of the dahabea captains on board for a tour of our ship, Natale got the chance to work on learning their language before we docked. We learned that each of the cities and towns were controlled and run by a mayor, while the King of Annelise ruled from Hodenhagen.

We also learned that if we showed up at the mayor's establishment wearing our crude, uncivilized clothing, we would be ordered to go at once and get properly dressed. Their motto was "Proper clothing brings proper respect." The captain also told us that when we docked, the Harbor Master could direct us to a clothing dealer, who could see that we were dressed properly, for a small fee, of course. "A clean crew is a happy crew," one captain told us. He whispered to Captain Henry, "Your women are horribly dressed! You really ought to do something about it. They look so utterly barbaric, so uncivilized! You will find that we treat our women vastly better! It would be the height of disgrace for my wife to be dressed as yours. In fact, if she were seen like that in public, why I would be fired from my position as captain immediately!"

Interestingly enough, Captain Henry made a trade with one dahabea captain; we took his entire cargo of vegetables and fruits in return for a handful of gemstones. Thus, re-supplied, we could take our time here and sail to Viborg. The captains also promised to relay our arrival to their King and to Viborg's mayor. For once, we would be expected.

Yes, Henry also had to explain where we came from and all about our ship. Natale told them about our land and people. We found these ship captains quite knowledgeable and friendly, if not darn right curious about us and our land. No, they thought that the potato continent was all there was to Tarra, and that if they sailed out of sight of land far enough, they would fall off the earth. Their ships were great coastal vessels but were not equipped for sailing across the ocean. Besides, they didn't know that anything else existed out there.

On March 1, 653, we sailed into the great harbor of Viborg, a huge city built on the bluffs overlooking the ocean. Beautiful white stone buildings rose in rows, each one higher in elevation than the next. Streets were all paved and paralleled the terrain, making a rather chaotic appearance. Clean and neat would be a good way to describe the city, remarkably so! As we slowly drifted up to the docks, sounding all the way, we women used the farseeing eye to look at the local dress, especially the women.

"This is amazing. Look at those wide dresses. They are more like ball gowns," Linda commented. While the city was teeming with people going about their business, everyone was immaculately dressed! Now, however, many people began to head to the docks to get a better view of us, as this huge, foreign ship slowly made landfall. It was obvious from their expressions and gestures, that we were presenting quite a sight. Our ship dwarfed every other one in the dock!

As the mooring lines were being secured, we noticed several men at arms taking up positions, where we would have to walk to get into the city from this long wooden dock. Each wore a fabulous costume, with yellow and reds predominating on their spotless uniforms. Each held an enormous halberd, whose cutting edge was quite sharp and impressive. We thought that for guards, their choice of weapons was considerably poor; a sword would be far more effective. Later we learned that the guards were mostly a ceremonial position, but they did occasionally capture a thief. The crime rate was low here, mostly pickpockets.

The harbor master walked up to our ship. He was dressed in a very elegant blue suit, exquisitely made, a perfect fit, from his white linen shirt, to his blue jacket with the twin tails, to his blue creased pants, to his funny little blue tie, shaped rather like a butterfly. Around his waist was a five-inch blue sash. He wore black leather shoes that showed no trace of street dirt. He had a well-kept moustache, and a tall, blue top hat capped off his appearance. "Permission to board Captain?" he said. By now, Henry understood a bit of their language, though Natale quickly translated for them.

The middle-sized man stepped on board and looked about. "Ah, the cleanliness of your ship is vastly better than your dress. Remarkable. One would think the opposite. Poor dresser equals a poorly kept ship, as we say. Well, have you been informed that to go ashore you will need to be properly dressed? We are a highly civilized nation here. We don't allow riffraff on our land."

"Aye, Sir. I am Captain Henry Freeze."

"Ah, forgive me, harbor master Erik, at your service."

"Yes, we chatted quite a lot with other ship captains, who told us about our dress. They suggested that you would be able to help us obtain proper attire for your land." Natale said, translating.

"Certainly, assuming you have some means to pay for the clothing." After a bit of discussion and after Henry showed Erik a sample from his gem pouch, Erik was all smiles. "Ah, yes. Perfect. Now then, am I correct in assuming that you are very important people from your homeland? If so, you will want to dress accordingly. You see, here in Annelise, the better dressed a person is, the higher their status. We have never had visitors from, well, from wherever you are from, nor seen a ship so huge as yours. Thus, I am I correct in believing that you ought to have a very high status? That ordinary commoner clothing is completely wrong for you?" Henry agreed.

"Ah then, there is only one shop for you, Viborg's finest clothier, H & H Clothiers. Bring your gems. How many will there be going?"

Natale explained that many of us were nursing relatively newborns. Erik congratulated us and said for us to bring them along. Children were highly prized here in Annelise. I decided to bring Angel and Mary Beth along with us, plus their husbands, as the Santi representatives, along with our two nannies, who would also look after the babies. Twenty-one of us lined up to get into four carriages, which Erik arranged for us. Atop the carriage, one of the strikingly costumed guards rode along, to ensure that we did go to the clothier and become properly dressed.

The H & H Clothiers was both huge and plush, the finest clothing store we had ever seen. The proprietors, Hedda and Hans Gustav, warmly welcomed us. We stepped into the small storefront, which was carpeted in plush red. Fresh flowers were neatly arranged at the main storefront window, where also several suits and gowns were on display.

"Let us be the first to welcome you honored strangers to our city of Viborg. We have heard of your arrival," Hans began, "and were so hoping that you would grace our fine establishment. We have made clothes for both our king and queen, over the years. Speaking of which, we've heard that they will be coming here to Viborg to meet with you. I must say that this will be a very high honor indeed. Hedda and I cannot recall when our monarchs have ever left their home to come and meet visitors. You must therefore be very important people. Your clothing must reflect your high status."

"Yes, but most of us are nursing our newborns. Will this be a problem?" Natale asked.

Hedda replied with a large motherly smile, "Oh goodness gracious no! Women often must dress for nursing. This does not mean that you have to wear peasant outfits, no, no, no. Our dresses are easily adapted for just such a need. Now the first thing that we must know is how long you will be staying, roughly, so that we may correctly determine the number of outfits we would recommend that you purchase. For example, if you were only staying a few days, why one outfit would suffice."

"Well, let's say that we are going to be here for a month," I suggested. "What would you recommend, bearing in mind that we ought to be dressed for your highest status? We are very important people in our land." I thought that this sounded rather silly, but when in Viborg, do as they suggest. We needed to make a good impression on these people, if new trading was to be established.

"Ah, excellent, excellent," exclaimed Hans. "This allows us far more freedom in the choices that we can offer you. For the gentlemen, I would recommend purchasing not less than six suits. Hedda?"

"And for you ladies, considering you are nursing, wisdom suggests that you purchase ten. You know how messy babies can be. This way, an accident is not a disaster," Hedda added.

"Now then, if you gentlemen will please follow me, we can get started on your excellent wardrobes." The men followed Hans down a hall and into another room. We women with the many babies in tow followed Hedda down another hall.

"There are so many of you, it would be better if we could put half of you in one fitting room and the others in another. That way it will not be so crowded. By the way, if I may be so bold and up front with you, I cannot help noticing that four of you have no arms and the child, no hands. Is this common in your land or have you all met with some positively dreadful accident. Around Annelise, it is rare to find one person who has lost an arm, much less both of them."

"We were attacked by a vicious animal. Yes, it was quite horrible, but we all have recovered very well. Will this be a problem with our dresses?" I replied for us.

"Oh no, no, particularly because you are all nursing. We will go with the nursing models, which you will find are very conducive to meeting this vital need for your babies and yourselves." We split into two groups. Linda, Tonia, Angel, and I went with Hedda, while the others went with another woman. We were in adjoining rooms, so I relaxed a bit. I was concerned about putting all four of us in the same room without someone with arms, just in case of trouble, though I could not envision anything happening at a clothier.

"Now then, let's see what color best brings out your inner selves. Bethany, I would suggest that you wear yellows and Linda, ah, yes, blue. Angel, oh a hard choice, you have a duality within you, warrior or nurturer, ah, let's go with red, if it does not agree with you, then we shall try brown. Tonia, ah, green, yours is easy; some connection to your mother I believe." Tonia looked surprised; how could this total stranger know about her mother, Elona Po, whose robes were green and purple?

"Now then, if you will each step behind the curtains, one of my assistants will help you undress. We will place all these disgusting rags into a sack that you may take back to your ship. Then, we will begin dressing you properly so that you can walk proudly, with your heads held high, knowing that as you dress, you shall be known."

A young woman helped me remove my favorite leathers. I was stripped naked. I looked again at my swollen breasts, nursing was definitely a pain with the twins, but now with Danielle, I needed help with it. Gosh, they were big now. Hedda stepped in beside me, "We will begin with the proper undergarments. You see here in Annelise, a woman's waist is a thing of beauty. A fat waist denotes a glutton. Now many thrive to be as thin as our queen is. Her waist is but fourteen inches. However, I tell all aspiring women that she did not get that way over night. Rather, I know that she wore her corset from age ten onwards. Let me see, Bethany, you do have a reasonable waist to begin with. No fat on you, that is commendable. Women should not be obese; well neither should men, for that matter, though I have heard rumors in the barbarian lands they prize women who are indeed what we here would consider obese. I admit that I do not understand them, but then I am only a clothier. First, we will begin with the corset."

An assistant began lacing me up. I observed that their corset was in many ways similar to those worn in Tashien, yet different. Here, the waistline was about two inches wide, more like a band. "Exhale deeply," the assistant said. Each time I did so, she tightened it further.

"I can't breathe," I complained.

"Oh you can so, just take shallower breaths and relax. Everyone says so when they get their new ones on for the first time. Once more, exhale." She tightened it and I felt I was somehow imploding! "Now look at your narrow waist," she said. I stood before the full-length mirror and looked at my tiny waistline. My large breasts were pushed up even larger.

Hedda stuck her head in to observe, "Ah, very good, Bethany, we have you down to eighteen inches, very good indeed for someone of such high status."

"But I can hardly breathe," I replied. "I can hardly bend either."

"Well, you aren't supposed to bend. Kneel down instead; it is more fitting and proper. Not even the peasants bend over. So inelegant, so crude. Now on with the stockings and nickers."

The assistant had me sit down while she put on a pair of very thin stockings, the thinnest I had ever seen. They did feel nice. The tops of these were then attacked to fittings on the bottom of the corset. Next, she helped me into a fluffy pair of white nickers. Again, Hedda appeared with her cloth measuring strip, measuring how tall my waist was from the ground. Shortly, her assistant returned with another strange article, which she called the hoops.

I stepped into the thing and she pulled it up to my waist and tied it off. Falling or flaring outward from my waist was this huge set of concentric hoops, the last one a foot from the floor was twelve feet across! "Yes, the diameter varies, denoting one's status as well, my dear," Hedda explained. Yours and Linda's should be the largest; Natale and Tonia's should be slightly smaller in diameter, though still quite wide, since they too are important people. Now then, let's put the slips on, shall we?" Her assistant brought in several slips, which she lowered over my head down to my waist. They covered the hoops in several layers.

She said, "You are so easy to dress, Bethany. I usually have to fight off women's arms, which get in the way. But with you, why, they slip down so easily. There now, we don't see any more of the hoops, only a nice gradual flaring. Hedda stuck her head in and agreed.

Both women then returned carrying a very large dress, made from yards and yards of material. Hedda explained, "For women who are not nursing, we usually go with a two piece version, a bodice top and the over skirt. In your case, we will go with the one piece version so that you can easily get to your breasts to feed your new daughter." The two of them struggled with the voluminous material, sliding it down over my head, carefully keeping my long hair out of it. While Hedda adjusted the huge skirt over the covered hoops, the assistant began buttoning the many buttons going up the back. It fit very tightly against the undergarments, that's for sure. The top was strapless. The dress was securely held up by my tiny waist, and the open scalloped top showed off my shoulders and upper chest. I could see how easily it would be for someone to lower the very top so that Danielle could get to my breasts. Whoever designed these had nursing women in mind.

"There, how does this look to you?" Hedda said. I looked in the mirror and was astounded at how I looked. Most of the dress was a pale yellow. Yet a canary yellow ribbon went around the bottom of the dress about a foot and a half above the dresses hem. The ribbon was in the shape of many half circles, opening downward. A somewhat less brilliant yellow half circle of ribbon went around it about half way down. Great ruffles hung the remaining distance to the floor. The bottom hem just barely touched the floor.

"I look really elegant, only I can't breathe in this," I replied, rather stunned with how good I looked.

"Shallow breaths, my dear, shallow breaths. Now then, I do like the way this one hangs on you. Please turn completely around slowly so that I can see how it hangs. We want it to be just perfect on you. Yes, this will do nicely. Now Bethany, how do you like the color scheme? Is it to your liking? If it is, then we shall continue. If not, why there are more styles from which to choose, however, I do think that this one suits you perfectly. I do say you do look positively stunning! Regal and elegant, befitting one of such high status indeed. If only we had months to get that waistline of yours down several more inches. Ah well, we don't, so we will just have to make do as it is."

"I like it. It's gorgeous. I love the bright yellow."

Hedda grinned, "I thought that you would. Now some of the additional nine dresses will have far more yellow in them."

"One question, besides how do you breathe in this. The hem is so close to the ground; won't this dress get dirty quickly? It is so beautiful. I would hate to have it dirty almost at once."

"Silly woman, we are not yet done," the kindly woman replied. "If you will sit on the divan here, we will continue."

"Gosh, with these hoops, how do I sit?" I asked, now occupying some twelve feet across.

"I'm sorry. I keep forgetting that this is your first experience in dressing properly. You must sit on the very edge of the divan; sit up straight mind you."

"How can I sit any other way than straight," I jested.

"Oh you would be surprised at the awful posture some women have. However, we do our best to guarantee that their posture improves. Slouchiness equals carelessness, we always say. Now we need to measure your feet and ankles so that we can get the right fitting boots. They must fit tightly; we do not want any broken ankles around here." I wondered what she was talking about, but she took off to find them.

A while later she returned with a pair of black boots that would come up to nearly my knees. However, that is not what got my attention. It was the heels! The heels were nearly five inches tall! I would be walking on my toes! She saw my surprise and explained, "We all wear these tall heels. This way the dress will not touch the ground or get dirty, as you feared. It has five inches of clearance. Oh yes, they will fit tightly, and we should help you learn to walk in them as well. You must take very small steps and you will do fine. Just remember: small steps are dainty steps." She and her assistant began tying up the laces, pulling them quite snugly around my ankles and lower calves.

"One caution, when you are rising, be careful not to get the heel caught in any of the undergarments. Now let's see how this all works together." With difficulty, I got up. With all the experience I'd had in Tashien shuffling about, these turned out not to be too difficult to master, except the balance part.

Her assistant brushed out my hair, admiring my long earrings. "My, those are the most fabulous earrings I have ever seen. They must be worth a fortune. Yet, all of you are wearing similar ones. I must say, in this dress, they look even better on you," she complimented me.

Hedda reappeared with a canary yellow hair ribbon and affixed it over my head such that it kept my hair from constantly sliding into my face. "There, now take a look at the complete outfit. I would recommend some jewelry, perhaps a necklace. Yet, I am pleased with the look. Definitely, you denote very high status indeed. No one will doubt that in the slightest. What do you think?"

I couldn't disagree. Next, all four of us got together in the main part of the room, staring and gawking at each other. Yes, we all looked fabulous, as if we were about to attend the fanciest of balls back home and then some! "This way please. We must pick out another nine dresses for you." We all walked along very carefully, getting used to these outfits. We spent an hour choosing the other dresses along with the undergarments and boots. These, Hedda said, would be sent directly to our ship for us. The nannies interrupted us; it was feeding time. Therefore, while we handled our young, the nannies got their chance to be formally attired as well.

I was floored at how beautiful little Alwanianon looked in her new dress. She was now fifteen and blossoming into womanhood. She cut a very stunning look, and her waist was the smallest of any of us. She was shrunk down to a mere sixteen inches around. Alwanianon beamed with happiness; she had never looked so elegant, like a grown up woman. She was a godsend with the nursing. We laid back as best we could; Tonia rolled down my top and placed Danielle in the right spot, but Alwanianon then kept her there and even moved her when needed.

Babies fed and nannies properly clothed as we were, we finally went back to the main room, where the men were waiting us. Their mouths fell open when we pranced out to meet them, showing off our fancy new clothes. Yet, we were just as surprised at their incredibly handsome looks as well. All sported very expensive suits, with creased pant legs, shiny black shoes, white linen shirts with the tiny butterfly neckties, and of course, the elegant jackets with the long tails down the back. Each also sported a tall top hat as well.

After we all admired and complimented each other, I reminded the men that we were going to need lots of assistance when dressed like this. Four of us could walk slowly, but that was about all. Henry paid our bill and Hans begged us to come back for more any time. Outside, the harbor master was waiting for us.

"Excellent, truly an amazing transformation, worthy of your exalted status! Well done, one and all. If you gentlemen will assist your ladies into the coaches along with your children, I will take you to meet the Mayor now. He is most interested in meeting you. I would say that he is extremely anxious to meet you!"

Those with arms found getting into the carriage a bit awkward but doable. We four had a most difficult time of it. As we rode through the streets, we watched the local people keenly. We saw that indeed every woman was similarly dressed in such flared dresses. However, many were only a few feet wide and some almost touched the ground. Occasionally, we saw others dressed nearly as fancy as we were, however. All the men wore nice suits, even the men who were sweeping the streets! Try as we could, we saw no one out and about that was not well dressed! I wondered about the farmers, blacksmiths, and miners. Surely, they would not be dressed like this. Later I learned I was wrong on that too.

Everything about the city was clean and neat. We saw no litter along the sides of the streets. Further, all the streets were cobblestoned right up to the edges of the buildings. Each of the buildings was well maintained, often built of stone, actually brown bricks we later learned. Near the edge of the city was a brick making factory, which we later toured. We also discovered that instead of burning wood or charcoal as we did, they burned a black rock called kool. This Cedric investigated heavily, taking a number of samples back with us. He was excited about this discovery, for we had some similar black rocks in northern Velona and Barcella.

At last, we arrived at the mayor's building; City Hall, it was named. A hundred feet on each side, the square building stood three stories tall. Black ironwork fences lined the entrance of the brown brick building. Flower boxes adorned each of the many windows along its front. One by one, the carriages pulled up before the walkway at the front of the building. Our men assisted us gallantly out of the carriage. Renzo, one arm holding Danielle, his other around my now very tiny waist, helped me keep my balance in this confining, yet somehow exciting outfit. We all waited here on the walkway until everyone was unloaded. Then, I took the lead, walking up to the front door.

Right on cue as if he had been watching for us, the mayor opened the door for us. "Welcome, welcome. I am Mayor Aksel Anders, my wife, Herdis." Both were in their forties. He was immaculately dressed in a suit as fine as our men were wearing. His wife wore a pale green dress, similar in diameter to mine, though her hair was only shoulder length. Her dress was not strapless, however. "If you will follow me into our meeting room, please." He led the way while Herdis held the door for us as we entered, pushing our wide dresses somehow through the doorway.

We walked down a carpeted hallway and into a huge room. Tapestries hung on the walls; flowers were located at strategic locations, out of the way of our wide dresses, fortunately. He had leather-covered mahogany chairs set on one side for the men and very wide, cushioned chairs on the other for us women. Our fellows at once helped each of us to sit down and then took their places opposite us. The mayor sat at the head of the table, while his wife was at the other end.

"Perhaps, Aksel, the babies would be more comfortable in another room where they could sleep?" She led our nannies and the fellows carrying all the babies into a side room and returned.

Mayor Aksel said, "On behalf of all Viborg and Annelise, let us welcome you. This is a momentous day in our history, hosting important visitors from far distant lands. Never has this happened in our long, illustrious history. Yet, before we get to talking, may we offer you some refreshments? I understand that you are new to wearing our clothing and might find them a bit uncomfortable at first. However, tight as they may be, surely you would like a little to eat and drink? We have honey mead, a fine red wine from Demokritos, coffee, and tea. Herdis has also gotten some bread rolls and cheese along with a honey dip. If you wish for something more substantial, let us know." We gladly accepted their offer. I wanted to try their tea, which turned out to be a strong, vibrant black tea, highly fermented, with a robust flavor.

A number of servant women entered carrying the many trays, each of them wore very nice dresses, though their widths were only about six feet and but a mere two inches from the ground. From their motions, they too were wearing corsets beneath these gowns. Each also wore an apron over their dress.

Herdis asked what I knew was on both of their minds, "If it not impolite, may I ask what dreadful calamity happened to you five who have lost so much?"

Once more, I explained about being attacked by vicious wild animals, a partial truth that was readily accepted. She, of course, then became very sympathetic. However, I quickly got the meeting back on course. I explained who we were, where we came from, and Henry drew him a sketch of Tarra, showing where we lived. Time flew by; we talked animatedly until it was suppertime.

"It would please me very much if tomorrow you could bring some of these marvelous items that you have been suggesting we might desire in trade here to my office. I have taken the liberty of arranging for your stay here in the city. Forgive me if I seem presumptuous; it may be that you would prefer to return to your ship. However, I thought that it would be easier for your women to stay here in an inn where others can help them dress. Herdis tells me that it is rather complicated for ones new to the dresses to manage. I have arranged for you to stay in the penthouse suite of the finest inn in Viborg, compliments of the city. Your food, servants, anything that you may need is already taken care of, my compliments. It is but a short walk from here so coaches are not needed. I must say that their dining room serves the best food in Viborg. Yet, if you prefer, I can call for the coaches to take you all back to your great ship."

"Considering these dresses," I answered, "we would be most honored to stay at the inn. We certainly do need someone to help us with these outfits. We have nothing like them back home, and we really don't know how to dress ourselves properly. Thank you for your thoughtfulness and kindness."

A few minutes later, one of his maids began walking us down the crowded streets to the inn. Our heels made a definite clicking sound on the cobblestones, and we had to walk very slowly. I depended upon Renzo, as did the others on their husbands. The inn was less than a mile away, further into the city. It was huge and the most elegant establishment we had yet seen. Our room, the penthouse suite, held enough beds for everyone and then some, more like a giant house than a room.

Each of us had our own servant woman to assist us. Yes, we spent a few minutes getting acquainted and answering their many questions. They then said that they would return later in the evening to help us undress. Yet if we needed anything, we only had to ask and they would be here shortly. Next, we nursed the babies once again and then went down to eat in shifts, so that some were there to watch over the babies.

The night was still early, so several of us went for a short stroll around the city, not going too far from the inn. I most definitely needed Renzo's arm continuously around me, as did the others. Yet, the sights were worth the walk. Many other couples were also out for a stroll and we soon found ourselves chatting with them as well.

Finally, quite tired with my feet hurting and chest aching, we headed back. As promised, each of our servant girls were waiting for us. While the men had no trouble undressing themselves, it was a very different story for us women. It took a bit of time to take off each layer of this costume. Finally, she removed my stockings and nickers. "H & H sent over these elegant night gowns for you to sleep in, Bethany. Shall I slip in on you now?"

"Wait, I still have this tight corset to remove."

She giggled, "Silly, you don't take that off! Only when you bathe.

Each year you will find that your waist well become smaller and smaller, perhaps rivaling our queen's. See mine is now down to sixteen inches, only two more to go and I will match her waist. Now that is something." She slipped the soft nightgown over me and adjusted my hair. I'll be back first thing in the morning. Just be sure to use the chamber pot before I arrive. As you have seen, it is difficult to manage it when fully dressed. It has been my pleasure assisting you." She curtsied and left.

Well, I was mostly free at last. With my bare feet, I could once more do things, but my constricted waist ached and it didn't let me bend. Renzo, on the other hand, found it rather exciting as we went to bed that night.

During the next days, we toured the city and even took a ride in the countryside, examining their farmsteads. Trading went well. The silks were a very hot item, as you might expect, along with wool and the paca fleece. They had no sheep in this country. Tonia overrode Henry; she wanted to import many dresses and suits, complete outfits, claiming that we could make a fortune from them. In the end, she won.

A week after our arrival, the King and Queen arrived in town. The meeting took place in the mayor's large meeting room, but only after small thrones were installed. Wearing the finest of our new outfits, we walked to the mayor's office for this vitally important meeting. They were in their thirties, my best guess. "Allow me to present King Thorsten Ryker and Queen Maren," Mayor Aksel proudly introduced us to their royal majesties, who were sitting on a chair and soft wide divan, which sat on a small platform so that they were somewhat higher than we were. He wore a suit nearly identical to that of Renzo. A small gold crown was the only thing that set him apart. She, on the other hand, had a dress that was wider than mine was; shades of red complimented her flush face. She had long earrings, but less than a quarter as long as ours, and she also wore a small crown on her head, blending nicely with her short brown hair. What attracted our interest was her very tiny waist!

According to the custom outlined ahead of time by the mayor, each of us would be formally presented to the pair. Renzo, arm around me to steady me, and I went first. I did my best to curtsey properly and Renzo bowed. I introduced us and said that I was our leader. They both asked about our arms, and then the others, pair by pair, followed us to meet their rulers. Once we were again seated, they began questioning us at length. We repeated quite a bit of which we had already told to the mayor.

Eventually, the topic became trading goods. We had kept all the samples here at the mayor's home, and the two enjoyed examining them. However, King Aksel asked, "What we most would like to purchase is one of these exciting, huge vessels of yours. Would that be possible? And what payment would be desired? It must be very costly to make such a ship."

"Dear, could you also ask if we might also purchase a set of earrings such as they have?"

He grinned, "Okay, you heard the boss, throw in a pair of those earrings as well."

"Queen Maren, it would be our pleasure to simply give you a pair as a token of friendship between our peoples," I replied, taking them both by complete surprise. They both knew quite well that these might sell for upwards of fifteen thousand gold coins. "As far as the caravel goes, it takes considerable time to build and is rather costly. If we were to do this, we would need to train your crew and captain on how to sail it. I am sure that we can work out a trading arrangement. We do not have such elegant clothing in our part of the world and would very much like to acquire a large number of these fabulous dress outfits and men's suits. Although we don't know if your people are able to sew such a lot of them for us, we don't want to deprive anyone here of a new dress or suit."

"See, Thorsten, I told you that these foreigners would have to be quite civilized to make such an historic journey to Annelise." She gave him a look that announced: I told you so. He smiled at her remark.

"Indeed, I am most impressed with your generosity; it is entirely unexpected. In return, please allow me to have H & H Clothiers send along a dozen new complete outfits for your women and men. It is the very least I can do. However, you must allow this fantastic firm enough time to ready them to your measurements. I do not know how long you had planned to stay here with us, but if you could possibly allow them another three to four weeks, then my present to you will be complete."

"Sure, we are not in any rush. We would love to see more of your land and learn of your customs, history, and music. I nearly forgot to ask you if you have music, song, and dance here. We have brought some of our musicians with us to give you a taste of ours," I replied, finally catching Mireio's hints. I kept forgetting to ask about their music.

"Splendid timing," King Thorsten replied, rather animatedly I thought. "In just over two weeks the Summer Collegium Musicum will be meeting at our palace for two days of music and dance, celebrating another cycle of the sun. We would be most honored if you all could attend. Our musicians would be more than pleased to share their music with your musicians, and we all would love to hear what your music sounds like. I am something of a patron of music, you see. I support this group, which consists of the finest musicians in the land. You would honor me greatly if you could attend our concerts and formal dances."

"But dear, they would need ball gowns and far finer suits," Queen Maren interrupted him.

"I don't understand, Queen Maren, these are the finest dresses and suits that we have ever owned or seen. How can there be ball gowns finer than these we now have?" I replied, becoming even more curious.

"Oh these are just ordinary dresses, plain at that, dear Bethany. Ball gowns are much fancier. At this ball, I am hoping that I will be down to a size thirteen waist. I am nearly there now. Thorsten, we must get their measurements from H & H and have ball gowns and suits prepared for them upon their arrival!"

"One complication, we are all nursing at the moment. Will bringing along our babies pose any problems?"

"None whatsoever. You will find many new mothers attending the ball, wearing nursing ball gowns much as you are wearing now, you know strapless," she replied.

"Yes, we will see that everything is arranged. You may expect clothing befitting your very high status in our land when you arrive," the king replied, already assuming that I would agree to come.

"Thank you for your generosity, King Thorsten. We will be most happy to attend." We discussed other things for an hour and then they needed to leave to return to their court. We promised to bring along the set of earrings when we came. Mayor Aksel promised to take us there personally. Both he and his wife usually attended this gala ball each year.

The time passed swiftly for us. Indeed, the discomfort I grew accustomed to rather rapidly. Besides, I rather liked being waited on hand and foot by Renzo. Except at night when our feet were free, none of we four could do much for ourselves. However, he was thoroughly enjoying waiting on me, and he loved the "native look" that we all presented. The only real problem that we had was navigating doors and going up or down steps. We couldn't maneuver our wide dresses, as could Tonia, Rosina, or Angel. Yet we women could plainly see that we were driving our husbands rather wild over our new look.

Sixteen days later the coaches arrived at the Royal Palace in Hodenhagen. We'd seen much of the countryside, which was not unlike that of the Greenway, rolling green hills, dotted here and there with dense forests. Farmsteads dotted the hillsides, usually near the towns and villages. The cobblestone road went all the way from Viborg to the capital city of Hodenhagen. Even the farmers in the fields were nicely dressed. I would hate to be their wife — think of the laundry that must be done.

The palace was actually a collection of many large buildings, stone once more. Along the southern edge neat rows of brown brick cottages lay, the guesthouses where we would be staying. One building housed the Royal Diner, where everyone gathered to eat their meals. Another housed their throne room, from which they ruled. However, the largest building was a combination theater, music, and dance hall, capable of holding several thousand at one time. As usual, the musicians played from a raised balcony.

We were greeted and taken to our new quarters, which were plush indeed. Each family had their own guesthouse; ours were all in a row next to each other, like block houses. After we entered, looked around, and got Danielle's crib by the bed, two servants knocked and entered. One took Renzo into the back room to assist him changing. He said politely, "This way sir. Allow me to assist you in changing. The king has sent over a very fine suit indeed." Renzo smiled and followed him.

"I am so honored to be allowed to service you, Commander Bethany! I heard that you had no arms, but I did not believe it. Did it hurt so?" She began asking me questions as she undressed me. We chatted away. At last, she said, "I must undo your corset. Queen Maren has a new one for you. She followed Hedda's suggestion that you could have a smaller waist by now. I will assist you. You know that Queen Maren is going to debut her new waist, thirteen inches. I know. I saw them measuring it. It is so incredible. Mine is down to fifteen now. I just don't see how she manages it. Ah, now let us see if Hedda is right. She often is, you know. Hedda is the finest clothier in Viborg, and some of hers rivals the best that can be made here in Hodenhagen even. Now breathe out very deeply."

Ugh. This one was far tighter than the other one, which I had just become used to wearing. If I thought that I couldn't breathe before, now I was sure of it. However, she just kept chatting on and I relaxed. Finally, she tied off the long cords. "There, Hedda was right. You are ready for a better one! You are down to sixteen inches, very close to me!"

"Yes, but I cannot breathe or eat like this!" She giggled.

"Yes, you can, short shallow breaths. Eat often and small amounts. This way, you will not get fat. Now let's get the rest on you." This time the hoops were even wider in diameter, approaching fourteen feet! The dress was very heavy, nearly twice that of the ordinary dress. It was made of heavier materials with real golden threads highlighting the bright yellow bands. I felt like I weighted a ton. At last, she tied up the new boots very tightly, saying, "We must make sure that your ankles are well supported for the dance, you know."

At the dance, we discovered that their music was very slow and stately. After all, I realized, what else could women possibly manage in these outfits? Even so, after one dance, I was gasping for breath, as were all the women. However, they had fans with which to cool their reddish faces off. I didn't. In these heels, too, it was very difficult to look elegant on the dance floor. However, I observed the local women who did just fine. Practice I concluded, this would take practice, just like any other skill.

Fortunately, after a set of dances, we all got to sit down a spell, while they played another set of more formal music. Then, it was back to dancing. They timed everything perfectly, giving us enough time to recover enough to avoid fainting or worse.

The instruments were different sizes of stringed instruments, played by holding the body of the instrument between one's legs and bowing across them with a stick with some kind of hair to make the strings sound. Their name translated to viol in our language, though this was merely a phonetic translation. A nasal sounding wind instrument added color, and several sizes of drums added the percussion. This, of course interested Alwanianon the most, as she was a drummer.

Part way through the dance, our musicians gave an hour-long sampling of our music, which was definitely brighter and cheerier than theirs was. They seemed to like it, though many complained it was impossible to dance to such fast music. Indeed, in these outfits, I couldn't agree more.

During the lengthy intermissions, huge tables of food and drink were available, and we made many new friends during the breaks. Everyone wanted to meet us, plying us with similar questions about our land. When we left for Viborg in two days, we had made Velona most welcome here in this new land.

The king insisted that we keep our ball gowns as well. However, the day that we were leaving, I changed back into my original gown; it was so much lighter compared to this new one. However, my servant refused to change the corset back, much to my unhappiness.

A week later, we arrived back in Viborg. There, we thanked the mayor and his wife and promised that the first shipment would be arriving within six months. Both of them begged us to return later when we could. In fact, we had raised his stature among all the mayors of Annelise enormously; he had hosted the foreigners!

Heels clicking on the cobblestones, we women slowly made our way from the carriage to the beginning of the wooden docks. As always, I needed Renzo's arm around my waist to steady me. I even needed him to assist me going onto the ship. I couldn't see where I was placing my feet! Soon we were in our cabin, hugging our twins, who had missed us this past month.

"Dear, please get me out of this now," I said, as Renzo was taking off his fancy suit.

"But dear, I have no intention of taking it off you. You look magnificent in it." He teased me and then passionately kissed me again.

"Please," I was beginning to get annoyed.

"Okay, but you must promise me that on some special occasions, you will dress up like this again. You are so sexy you know." He began getting me out of this dress, only after I so promised. Finally, I could both breathe again and handle my basic needs. I then made it worth his while; I truly loved this man!

Chapter 28 Narrow Escapes

On April 1, we set sail once more, loaded with fresh vegetables and fruits, ready for further exploration. Renzo, Linda, and I stood on deck watching the green hills of Annelise drift by. He said, "Bethany, you were right once more. By adopting the local customs here, we have made a good trading partner and friends with everyone. I admit that I enjoyed wearing the fancy suits, but you women sure gave up a whole lot to match their dress. I just wanted to thank you women for doing that. I don't think that you all are ever thanked enough for all that you do."

"We appreciate hearing that Renzo," Linda replied. "Wids and Judgers often have to make such calls. Worse, we then have to live with our choices. This time, it worked out in our favor. A little discomfort and we've made lasting friends with a new people. Just remember, other times might not work in our favor so much. That's the difference between our specialties. Yet, we do really appreciate hearing your thanks. Now how about a hug?" We both gave him the Laird Bump, as we now called our unique way of hugging without arms.

"However, Renzo, go get Emil and Chaucer; we need to talk about these other two countries that lie here on the potato. We've learned a good deal from our new friends and I am somewhat concerned," I added.

A short while later, I began, "Guys, I need your input about this next land, Vladimir. From what we've learned, this land may be dangerous. Let's go over what we have heard." I outlined the bits of information that we had picked up from those in Annelise. The land was relatively dry steppes, cradled between the Hagan Range on the east and the Katos Mountains on the west which were tall and blocked most of the rain. The people who lived here were horsemen and nomadic for the most part, though they had four coastal permanent towns. They were brutal and warlike people. With few trees anywhere in Vladimir, they only had the smallest of fishing boats, and those were very few. Hence, their raiding parties. Unable to cross the mountains or travel by sea, they occasionally rode up the coast to attack, pillage, and rape the women of the towns nearest the border.

King Thorsten had the situation fairly well under control in recent years by stationing large numbers of his soldiers with their very long pole arms along the passable seacoast with Vladimir. These riders would not sacrifice their prized horses just for a raid. Of their leaders, little was known except that they got their positions by being the strongest and best horse combat riders. Rumors, unsubstantiated, suggested that these rulers had sorcerers who advised them, powerful men who possessed terrible spells. Just what the spells might be, we could get no definitive statement. We were advised to not make any contact with these evil, vicious men. The largest of the coastal towns was called Tanja. This was the extent of our knowledge.

"I would advise against taking the babies ashore," Emil began. "Actually, it might not be wise to take many of you women ashore here. We could run into a nasty situation."

"I agree, except as leader, it is my responsibility to go. However, we don't know what their language is like, whether we could easily pick it up or whether we need Natale's incredible skills. If you men go alone and cannot pick up their language, there's no telling what kind of a mess may result. Yet, you are right, it doesn't sound like a safe place for either Natale or me to venture."

"Yes, I wish you could leave this one to us," Renzo added, "but I don't see how. We have a hard enough time with these languages even with a dictionary and Natale. Emil, can we men really do this without Natale's help?"

"We are up river with no dingy, Renzo. Sure, we can try it without her, but I won't give a copper for our chances of an easy time of it, if we can do it at all. Language is not something in which I am vaguely skilled. If we take Natale, we have to take Bethany. However, let's not put the other women at risk, not until we know for sure that it is safe and that we are accepted reasonably well. Surely, the five of us can protect the two of them. What do you say, Chaucer? You've been silent on this."

Indeed, he had been standing quietly listening to the discussion. He thrust both hands through his hair, "Doomed either way, as I see it. Alone, we are going to have a very tough time with communicating, if at all. We are warned that they are warlike, so patience is probably not one of their virtues. However, it's all that talk about powerful sorcerers that bothers me the most. Bethany is the most qualified in such matters. We should go well armed."

"Okay, I'll put Linda in charge of defending the caravel. Who knows, they might even make an attempt to take the boat while we are ashore," I added.

April 21, we anchored off Tanja, studying it carefully with the farseeing eyes. The land itself, as much of it as we could see, was sparsely grassed, rolling hills, reminiscent of the Northern Steppes. The town, population perhaps fifty thousand, was a step backwards into time and civilization. The buildings were crude adobe for the most part, which made sense if trees were scarce here. The number of stone buildings one could count on one hand; these were the larger structures. Yet all of them looked like rundown shanties compared to what we were used to back home. The streets looked like they had never been cleaned since they were built.

The people wore leather and horsehair woven clothing. The women's dresses were decorated with gay colored embroidery, while the men's tended to be plain. Hair, all wore theirs long; perhaps haircuts were unknown here. Brown was the dominate color, though the men had no facial hair that we could see from this distance. At the northern edge of town lay a huge corral with hundreds of horses wandering about the pasture area. Adjacent to this was the tack storage building, we surmised, one whole side of it was completely open aired.

The townsfolk watched us as we watched them. Some pointed out our ship to others. Yet, they did not seem alarmed that we were just off their beach. Only when we dropped our sails and anchor did the men begin to pay attention to us. We saw three small one-man dingy style boats drug up onto the brown sandy beach. No one was out fishing, which I though unusual being this close to the sea. However, now a number of men with swords pushed the locals out of the way, taking up a position close to the beach, then they stood still and watched us to see our next move.

We lowered one longboat. Emil, Henry, Renzo, Benet, Chaucer, Cedric, Natale, and I got into the boat. All wore their chain mail and were armed to the teeth, just in case we ran into trouble. Natale and I chose not to wear our chain mail because it made normal things too difficult for us to manage. Slowly the men rowed us to the shore. Once we hit the beach, Renzo lifted me out, while Henry helped Natale, and we formed our first contact line.

Natale and I were in front, side by side, with Emil on her left, Renzo on my right. The others stood back in a diagonal line on either side of us, guarding our flank. Now began the language barrier handling. I spoke some words of welcome, knowing that they would not likely be understood. Natale repeated them in many other languages.

At last, she got a reaction from them. "It's a variant of Galt, I think." She rapidly began working out some basic words. Again, I admired her skill and knowledge. In an hour, she was chatting with them reasonably well.

"I am Commander Bethany, leader of this Explorers Circle of Santi del Dio. We come from a land far north of here called Velona. We come in peace and are looking to open up new trading partners. We have brought a number of samples of goods that other lands often would like in trade for goods from their lands. Is there someone whom we can discuss business with here?" I tried to keep it simple.

Up close like this, I could tell that personal hygiene was also foreign to these people. Not only were their clothes dirty, they were long overdue for a bath. One man out of the fifty stepped forward from behind the line of men. "I am Kopon Miho. This is my wife, Koponess Mascha. Welcome to Vladimir. Will you come to our home and feast with us? We have many questions to ask of you strangers." His tone was that of hidden resentment, however. The couple was in their thirties, I estimated. He was definitely a battle-hardened warrior; several scars adorned his arms. She was f pretty, I thought; at least she smiled a lot at us. She seemed very sympathetic to us women, which was a natural reaction to seeing someone like us. We followed them through the filthy streets, with the fifty fighters closing in behind us, following.

Theirs was one of the few stone homes in the town. The first room we entered was his official meeting room, very large in side, with a number of crude wooden tables pushed together to form a long one. The chairs were made of wicker and actually were rather soft. They had various trophies mounted on the back wall. On the opposite side of the long tables sat two more chairs, which Kopon Miho and his wife took.

Kopon was their word for commander or ruler; we were not sure which. In any event, he was my counterpart here. "How is it that you have a crippled woman as your leader and another one as your spokesperson? Is it customary in your land to remove your women's arms? I can see some benefits in this, they cannot protest our advances," he sneered and chuckled. Behind us, we heard his guards also laugh at our expense.

"She and I were attacked by a vicious wild animal and lost our arms. However, we killed the animals. In our land, we pick the best person for our leaders, whether male or female. I am a well-respected field commander. Natale is an expert at learning new languages."

"Here, the Kopon must be the strongest and best fighter if he hopes to command the loyalty of his men. You would not last one minute here if you were in charge, I am afraid." Again, the guards behind us chuckled.

"Perhaps we should offer them some drink," Koponess Mascha replied, winking and smiling at her husband.

"Ah, yes, forgive my manners. We have very good honey mead in this land." He rang a small bell, and a servant woman came in from another room. He whispered to her and she left to bring the mead. Quickly, she returned with another young woman, whom we learned was their daughter, Valerija. She stared long at us women, as she hesitatingly placed a mug full of mead before us.

"A toast to our new visitors from the far north," Kopon Miho roared. His men behind us had also gotten a mug, we noticed. Renzo and Henry picked up two mugs and held it so we could sip as well. It was very excellent mead, I thought.

Kopon Miho took me by surprise. "It is customary for the Kopon and other leaders to show everyone that they are truly a man by drinking the first mug in one drink, like this." He raised his mug, tilted his head back slightly, and began guzzling it. A few seconds later, he pounded the mug onto the table, empty, and belched. He men snickered and catcalled to him, bringing a smile to his face.

I had no choice but to follow their custom. Renzo held it for me and I drank mine down as fast as he had, perhaps slightly faster. Again, the guards behind us let loose and even louder set of snickers and catcalls, evidently impressed. Miho roared and said, "Well done Commander Bethany. You drink like a Kopon!" Quickly, his shy daughter Valerija refilled my mug. I hoped that we did not have to engage in a drinking contest!

Instead, the talks began in earnest. We learned that these people highly prized their horses. A man's wealth was measured by the size and quality of his herd. Only a few people of Vladimir actually lived in these two permanent towns along the coast. The vast majority were nomadic, moving around the land in search of better pastures for their horses. These men were highly skilled riders, who often held a duka to display their prowess and abilities. A duka was something like a large gathering or get-together, which happens quarterly. The town was playing host to a duka in just nine days. We were welcome to stay and see just how powerful a fighter these men were as well as how superb they were as riders.

He wanted to know if we had horses in our land, if we rode and if we fought from horseback. Miho did not believe me when I said that I rode well, though I could no longer fight. Thus, we began to discuss historic battles for a time. Finally, I turned the conversation onto what they might wish to trade and receive in trade. We talked for several hours, gaining useful information on them, as they did us. Our mead cups were continually being refilled. At last, Mascha and Valerija brought in something more substantial, cheese and unleavened bread. This, I thought, was more like it. We ate as we continued our negotiations and discussions.

Then, I realized that I was getting rather groggy, foggy, and slightly spinney. I noticed that the others were too. In our language, I said, "Renzo, I think that we are being drugged somehow. We need to leave here at once." I tried to get up and stumbled slightly. I said, "We need to return to our ship now. We will bring sample trading goods back with us in the morning."

All of us were up on our feet, only with great effort however. Just then, another door opened and a strangely dressed man wearing robes stepped into the room. I saw that there was a small hole in that door and guessed that he had been listening to us the whole time. "Ah, Andelko, there you are, our guests want to leave us now."

The tall, wiry man had a moustache that was long on either side, and he had a six-inch long beard to match. He stared straight at me and began chanting. One instant we were all standing there trying to keep our balance and move towards the door. The men's hands were on their sword hilts, though they had not yet drawn them. In the next instant, all their visible weapons suddenly appeared in a pile on the floor close to where Andelko stood. Before we could react, he spoke another chant, and I felt myself falling down some dark tunnel, my arms were flailing in all directions, though I had none. All was black.

"They should have been back before now," Angel said very worriedly to Mary Beth. Both were on deck staring at the now darkened form of the village. Full dark had come. The other Santi and the ship's Guardians were also on the deck as well. Tonia and Rosina were below feeding our babies, since we had not yet returned and they were starving. The two came up on deck. Rosina was very pale.

"Linda, while I was feeding the babies, I tried to make contact with Bethany to find out what is delaying them. I couldn't make any clear contact with her. I believe that she and the others have been drugged. Whatever should we do now? Launch a raiding party?" Rosina explained becoming more fearful by the moment for our safety.

"No, we are too few and they are too many. We don't know where they are being kept. If I were they and had captured the visiting shore party, my next move would be to attempt to take their ship. Our first duty is to see that they cannot take this ship. Probably they will try a sneak attack when they think that we are all sleeping. They will try to either swim out here or use the longboat. My odds are on the longboat, which means they will be limited to perhaps twenty at most. Let's get ourselves ready to repel them without damaging the ship or the longboat."

"Mr. Farthington, as ship's Protector, what do you suggest we do?" Linda deferred, as I would have, to a Protector.

"We must see that the longboat is not damaged. Let's take advantage of the fact that these people know nothing about ships, particularly where we sleep. Let's get all those who are to fight up on deck, pretending to sleep on a blanket. Allow them to get onto the deck. In fact, let's leave the rope ladder over the side there where it is highly visible. That should force them to climb up in that one spot. We arrange ourselves accordingly so that we can get to them all just after the last one gets onboard. The real question is do we take them alive or just outright kill them when they attack us?"

Linda replied, "Alive if possible. That way we have them to use to bargain for our people."

The twenty-five Santi protection crew quickly setup their positions on the deck; all wore their protective chain mail. Additionally, the three ships Guardians and Angel and Mary Beth's husbands, also joined them, Jason positioning everyone carefully. Rosina and Tonia were ordered to stay below just in case one got by them and came down into the living area and cargo hold. Jason Farthington wanted someone there to protect the ship's crew members, the babies, and nannies. Linda took up her position leaning back against the poop deck walls, where she had a clear line of sight to the entire main deck. She would use her skills wherever needed. However, Jason forced her to don her heavy chain mail as a safety precaution. Everyone now covered up in blankets, while one crew member climbed up to the crow's nest. He would hoot when he saw the longboat coming our way from shore.

Around midnight, an owl's hoot broke the eerie silence. Swords were drawn and made ready. They waited. Presently, they heard the telltale bump of the longboat in inexperienced hands bump into the side of the boat, that and some whispered curses. Linda imagined how these land dwellers were struggling to climb up the rope ladder. Soon one man's face appeared over the railing. He looked at the sleeping forms on the deck and scampered up as quietly as he could, sword in hand. They did nothing until their last man put his feet on the deck. Now they quickly fanned out, heading for a sleeping form.

"Now," Linda called out. Four blue lights suddenly appeared, lighting up the deck, startling the men. The Santi sprang to their feet and moved to encircle their opponents. The clash of steel upon steel broke the stillness, along with the wild yelling of the invaders. They were excellent fighters, however, yet no match for what they faced here. Protected by the chain mail, the Santi were nearly immune to the strikes of their opponents.

Worse still, Linda moved over an enemy, held his body rigid, while a Santi knocked the man out. In five minutes, the melee was over; twenty men lay unconscious on the floor. Mary Beth had a sword cut on her hand, a minor one at that. While Tonia came up and quickly bandaged her up, the Santi searched the unconscious men and then tied them securely to the main mast and the foremast. Once they were all secured, the crew came up on deck, inspected the knots, and improved them, for the sailors were the knot experts around here.

Linda, satisfied that the invasion has been repelled, ordered the longboat brought up on deck and secured. Jason issued orders for six Santi to stand watch in shifts the rest of the night, and everyone else headed below to get some sleep. Rosina reported that she still had not made contact with Bethany. Linda slept rather poorly that night, fearing for her dear friend.

On shore, Andelko and Miho saw the blue glow coming from the ship. "What devilry is that?" asked Miho.

"They may have sorcerers of their own," replied Andelko. "We should find out before you have your way with them." Miho looked slightly worried and the two men walked back to the stone headquarters.

Bethany, where are you now? It was Rosina's thoughts. She'd reached me somehow.

I'm here. Sleeping now, I think. We were drugged. I'm so foggy right now.

Okay. Where were you when it happened?

We were in the stone building, his meeting room.

All right. Where are you now?

Right here, lying down. Body seems to be sleeping. Oh! I just popped out of that greyish drug mental gooey stuff. Thanks for the assist, Rosina. Let's see where I am. I cast a blue light and looked around. I was lying in a bed. I still had my clothes on; that was a good sign. It was a small room. I noticed that my legs were chained to the bed, however. I reported this to Rosina.

See if you can find Renzo and the others and wake them up as you did me. It worked well. Thanks.

They tried to attack the ship around midnight. We captured all their men, so we can see if they will swap prisoners. Okay. I'll get back to you.

Meanwhile, I let my body sleep; it would need the rest to recover. I floated over the chains on my ankles. They were locked on by two cuffs and chained to the rear bedposts, rather securely. Not much I could do about that just now. A little later, Rosina added me to her Mind Join. She had gotten all of us awakened and alert.

Natale reported that she too was chained to a bed in a small room; her body was also sleeping. The men were all in one larger room chained to the stone walls. Renzo wanted to know if they should wake up their bodies and try to get free. I suggested that they let them sleep so that they would feel more alert in the morning. *Just stay outside the body and ready your spells, dear. I think we can handle things. Looks like we found one of their sorcerers.*

Yes, he hit us with a push spell. We were so groggy from whatever they had in the food that the push knocked us all out. Crude, but effective.

Rosina, have Linda see if she can float over us and locate Natale. If she can, have her stand guard over her. She's in the most danger, I think.

Sometime later, a bit of daylight came through a small window, too small to crawl through, assuming I was free. Just then, the door opened and shy Valerija came in timidly. She carried a mug of water. I tried to sit up, but with my legs chained, I had to struggle mightily. "Here, let me help you sit up." She got me sitting up, thankfully. I noticed that she has some fresh bruises on her face.

"Here, I brought you some water, pure water. It will help to clear your head." I accepted the drink.

"What happened to your face?"

She looked at the floor and then at my body. "I tried to stop them from doing this to you. You don't even have any arms to fight against him. He's going to rape you after he eats. I got slapped around by dad for intervening on your behalf, but he at least allowed me to bring you and Natale a drink. I must go now."

"Thank you for your kindness, Valerija. I will see that your father has bruises at least equal to those on your face." She stared at me long before she ducked out the door. Not long after than Rosina Mind Linked us all together.

Cedric sent, *I believe I can get us out of these chains.*

Linda added, *I'm over Natale.*

Shortly after that, my door opened and in came Kopon Miho himself, wiping the last of his breakfast off his face. "Now I'm going to show you how to be a leader. Around here, you have to be the strongest and fittest to rule. I'll have my way with you and show you who is the boss, and it certainly isn't going to be a woman, let alone one with no arms. You are a joke to us leaders of Vladimir!"

"Miho, I will say this one time only. Release me and my companions immediately!"

"Or you'll do what? Hit me with your tongue? I got your legs chained so you can't kick me. What you will try to bit me? Ha. Your people don't have a clue about choosing a leader." He moved over toward me, dropping his pants as he came.

I picked him up, turned him upside down in the air, threw his head and nose hard into the bedpost at my feet. His arms flailed helplessly around in space. The keys to the locks fell onto the floor. I then smashed his back up hard against the wall holding him there, his head touching the ceiling. His nose began bleeding profusely and a large swelling began to appear on his right cheek.

"That was for your daughter, Valerija, who is better suited to rule than you are. This is for me." I floated his body over to the bedpost and threw his private parts down hard on the vertical bedpost. Even though he was hanging there in space, he curled over in intense pain. I had hit him here it really hurts, physically and symbolically. Then, I forced him back against the wall.

I floated the keys up and into the locks. Shortly, I had unlocked my feet. I lifted my own body up to its feet. "Now, let's go get the others. Out this door, I presume?" He groaned, so I took that as affirmative.

Meanwhile, Natale faced the sorcerer himself. Andelko came into her room, "Well, my pretty woman, I've decided to help myself to your pretty body. As you can see, there is nothing that you can do about it, so don't fight me, perhaps you will like it."

Natale answered him, "If you will unlock me at once and help me free my companions, I will forget what you have just said."

"If not, what then, eh? You are the most helpless, yet pretty, woman that I have ever seen. You are in my complete control now to do with as I please. Surely, you can see that. If not, well, I will just have to show you." His hands began to remove his robe.

"Okay, have it your way," Natale said with a sigh. "Men! Always in their pants." She simply held him still, rigidly still, so still he could not move a muscle. She sensed a growing fear entering his mind, as he tried to counter her action. Natale struggled to sit up, finding it as awkward as I had. At last, she looked at the sorcerer standing motionless before her. She spied a set of keys around his waist, under the robes he was in the process of removing.

This she pointed out to Linda, who then took over. She entered the sorcerer's body and took control of it. Against his will, Andelko found his feet shuffling over to Natale's feet. He held one arm on the other, trying to stop the arm that Linda was forcing down toward the keys. In vain, he tried to overcome the force that was now making his hand unlock the pair of ankle locks. He watched helplessly as they fell to the floor, releasing Natale. She stood up.

However, Linda wasn't finished with him. *This is for your intentions on Natale,* Linda sent and then forced his hand into his crotch, gripped his privates hard, and gave them a yank, doubling the sorcerer over. Then, she made him hobble out the door, while Natale walked behind him, ready to hold him still should he break free.

In the hallway, they saw me floating a howling Miho out of my room's doorway. "Hi there, sleep well, Natale? I see you have our sorcerer being well taken care of right now. Now Miho, where are my friends being held?"

"Right here dear," the voice of Renzo greeted my ears, coming from the other end of the long hallway. "Cedric got them unlocked using his lock picks, which he keeps in his boots. Now where are our things, chain mail, swords, daggers? I see Miho is enjoying his little flight through the air. Go gentle on him, dear. He may get air sick flying around like that." He was teasing of course. "Oh, morning Natale, I see you are giving our sorcerer walking lessons. Golly, I would think as old as he is that he ought to know how to walk better than that." He was rubbing it in on these two.

We moved them out into the main room, the only other doorway in this hall. There were his wife, daughter, and his guards. However, what they saw was not what they had been expecting at all. Miho's face was now getting quite swollen, far more than Valerija's; blood covered his face and shirt, to say nothing of being doubled over, moaning, and floating along above the floor. The puppet-like, awkward, enforced steps of their sorcerer also looked unreal as well, though he too was in pain, but could not double over.

Emil commanded, "Guards, where is our gear? I strongly recommend that you do not resist us or you will end up even worse off than these two." One pointed to a pile in the corner of the meeting room. While our men were getting their things sorted out, I surveyed the scene. The two women looked frightened; the two leaders were incapacitated; the seven guards looked stunned, uncertain what to do.

"Valerija, it seems that your father has to learn some manners." She grinned slightly, but quickly suppressed it, when her mother gave her a stern look. That told me everything I needed to know.

"Valerija, could you possibly get your guests their breakfasts? It seems your father has failed to give us ours, most uncivilized of him, rude, and crude. Perhaps you should have your mother lend you a hand. If not, I will have to teach your mother some manners as well." Valerija grinned once more, but Mascha looked terrified, glancing at her floating husband and then me. "Oh yes, don't put any more of those drugs in or food, or we will not be so forgiving next time."

"Now then, Kopon Miho, I suggest that you and your sorcerer take a seat." I plopped the man into his seat, while Linda walked the sorcerer over to the one Mascha had used. "We will release you now, but if you make one wrong move, we will not be so kind this time. Now order your guards to go outside." I relaxed my grip on the man and Linda did likewise, though Natale watched the sorcerer like a hawk, one slight chant and she would act without mercy this time. Natale was somewhat annoyed, though not angry.

Miho did as I asked, muttering to his men, who filed out of the door that we had entered yesterday. "Now that's better, Miho. One more thing, it seems your men attempted to capture our ship last night while they were sleeping. That was a bad thing to try. We have all twenty men nicely tied up, though we did tend to their wounds. We are wondering what we should do with them? Take them out to sea and drown them? Perhaps just cutting off their heads and bringing the heads to you might be simpler. Or would you prefer that we hand them over to you?"

Valerija began bringing in some food, sitting a plate before me first. "Hope you like it," she said shyly.

"Thank you, Valerija. See Miho, even your daughter knows how to treat visitors properly. You should learn from her. By the way, if you ever lay a hand on her again, I will teach you the meaning of pain! Where we come from, the civilized lands of Tarra, men do not brutalize, beat, rape, or mistreat women. We also treat visiting guests with some dignity, honor, and respect, which, with the exception of Valerija, is entirely lacking here."

"But you don't understand," Kopon Miho finally spoke up, "in Vladimir a leader must show strength or he will be overthrown by ones who will. We had to test you to prove that you are strong or no one in Vladimir would accept that you are a leader of mighty Santi. You must look at it as we see it. You come to us from some distant foreign land that we have never heard of or know about. A woman claims to be the leader of these foreigners. If that is not enough to cast total doubt on your claims, she is a total cripple without any arms. That defies all credulity. None of the other leaders would believe me; they will mock me and overthrow me, saying that I am dumber than a donkey, an armless woman leader! I had no choice but to test you, honestly I had no other choice. I would not have harmed you or your companions, not physically — maybe roughed you up so that others could see that you were inferior and not fit to be called a leader. I had to, can't you see that?"

His wife added pleadingly, "You must believe him. The coming of strangers is very important to us. He wanted to take you to the duka and present you to many others. Yet, he must be able to prove that an armless woman is truly a leader as we have them in Vladimir. Please, you must believe him. He meant you no real harm."

"Drugging us, chaining us up, and threatening an armless woman with rape — that's not harming me?" Natale exclaimed disgustedly. Mascha lowered her head and stared at the table.

"Would you release my men and not kill them?" Miho asked.

"We are not barbarians. Obviously, if we wanted you or them dead, it would have already happened," I replied. "Linda will be bringing them ashore now."

"Thank you, Commander Bethany. You have my word we will not harm you again. If we would have wanted you dead, you would already be so as well."

"Point well taken, Miho. I realized that when I woke up. Now then, perhaps it is best if we just leave your country now. I'll see to it that our merchant ships do not ever land on your shores again." I wanted to test him by proposing a total withdrawal on our part.

"Please, there is no need for that. We would like to see these trading goods you spoke of. You have passed our leadership tests; the others will accept you now. At the duka, you can meet many of the other tribes and leaders. It is a time of celebration. There is much music, dancing, and feasting. Then, there is the big horse race, which every good rider enters in hopes of winning the ankat, the prize I believe is your word for it. My daughter, Valerija, will present the ankat this year. Sorcerer, help me out here!"

Andelko, who had been silent all this time, finally spoke up; he couldn't refuse his Kopon's request. "Commander Bethany, that you have powerful spells yourselves is not in doubt any longer. Yet surely, this also means that you and your people possess keen intelligence and wisdom. As a fellow sorcerer, I urge you to consult your reason in this matter. Our ways must seem primitive to ones of such power, and yet they are the ways that we must follow. You and your people have earned the right to enter the duka and race as one of us. Kopon Miho has offered you this very high honor. Never in our history has an outsider been allowed to compete in the duka. Please do not let emotions rule over intellect and wisdom."

"Do I have your word that no one will try to drug or harm our people in any way as long as we are in Vladimir?" I asked.

"I give you my word as Kopon that no one will ever do so again. If someone does, I will have him drawn and quartered most painfully," he replied, a bit of hope returning in his eyes.

"Okay, then we will stay for the duka. What's this about us entering the duka? Is it just a horse race? No violence, no combat?" I asked.

"It is a grueling, long horse race. There is no combat, but there might be some jousting for positions, but no rider carries any weapon, if that is what you mean. Perhaps you will enter your best riders. I will loan you some of my best horses."

"Best riders?" I became intrigued. I love playing games. What better game than a horse race. Renzo and I were the best riders among us. I looked at him, caught Renzo's silly grin, which said, "Let's do it," and added, "Okay, we accept. We will need two horses, one for my husband here and one for me. When is this race?"

After discussing the race further, Linda and the others arrived, marching the captives to the Kopon's door. I left Linda in charge of the further negotiations and returned with the longboat to the caravel. I was very overdue nursing Danielle.

Linda and Henry, with Natale's translation assistance, arranged for trading various goods. The next day, Renzo and I went to check on the offered horses and to see if I would be able to compete. Their saddle was a mere blanket with a cinch, while their bridle consisted of a rope loop around the horse's nose and nothing went inside its mouth. Thus without using my powers, I couldn't possibly mount by myself. As before, Renzo fashioned me a wooden block for the reins. Petar, the eldest son of Miho, took us on a test ride first, so that I could see if I could manage this horse.

Renzo lifted me up, and I noticed half of the town had turned out to watch me. I hope that I wouldn't disappoint them. After some slow walking, I found the horse very receptive to small shifts in my weight. He was very well trained indeed. We picked up the pace and soon I was back cantering away once more, something I dearly loved to do.

As we walked to cool them down, Petar said, "You are a good rider. I didn't see how you could do it. Yet, our riders are experts at riding without using our hands. We shoot bows and swing swords while we ride. Perhaps I should not be surprised that you can ride."

"How about seeing the race course? I assume that the other riders will already be familiar with the path we are to follow," Renzo asked.

It was well marked as we soon found out. On the race day, officials would be stationed periodically along the route to ensure that all riders rounded the poles marking the turns. Yet, it was a long race, ten miles over smooth grasslands, up hills and down. One tricky patch held many loose stones. Here, one had to be exceedingly careful or horse and rider would take a tumble. One long section involved some fifty sharp weaves, in and out of some fifty poles strung out in a long line. Here I could see much jostling for position. This spot would also be tricky to manage. Another section had ten, low stone walls to jump over. Though not high, they would require good timing on both the rider and horse's part.

Although we were allowed to walk our horses along the route, no one was allowed to try it out ahead of time. This kept the game in the game. As we rode along, Renzo and I discussed strategies. Neither he nor I really considered actually winning the race against the many superior riders; rather we had two objectives: make a good showing and beating each other.

Two days before the big day, other tribes began arriving. Of course, we were the big news event. Correspondingly, we underwent introductions several times a day. It got old explaining our "accidents" to these people, however. Yet, I could see how they would be extremely curious about us four.

The night before the big day, Sorcerer Andelko came up to me and asked, "Commander, Bethany, could I have a private word with you? Perhaps you would like to bring your translator along and your husband too."

He took us to his home, a modest adobe house. The front room was filled with herbs, strange artifacts, and even some scrolls. The place was a mess, and he had to move accumulated bric-a-brac off the chairs so that we could even sit down. A bachelor, I thought to myself.

"I have asked you here to both warn you and to ask for your help. Many of we sorcerers have been trying to bring more civilized ways to our Kopons and thus to our people here in Vladimir. We have been trying for years to do this. However, there is one sorcerer called Goran, who continually defeats all such attempts. He is vastly more powerful than any of the rest of us, and he forces his brutal ways upon us in Vladimir. He is a most dangerous sorcerer. I will point him out when he arrives. Be wary around him; he is both mean and vicious."

"Thanks for the tip," I replied, becoming somewhat curious about this new information.

"Also, if you get the chance to observe him, could you let me know if you think that your spells are more powerful than his? I and many other sorcerers of Vladimir would love to see him banished somehow."

"What do you know about Goran?" Renzo asked.

"His spells are many times more powerful than ours. Why? We do not know. Goran is a strange man; he comes and goes as he pleases. He makes his home in the Caves of Roas, in the far north, where the ground is covered in a white blanket in the winter time." (Note to the reader: the direction these people called north is actually south.) "What is most peculiar is that Goran does not seem to be aging. I know he must be at least thirty years old. And yet he looks like a teenager. Weirder still, my father knew a sorcerer named Goran, though I don't know if this is the same man. Also, my grandfather knew a sorcerer called Goran. I find the coincidences disturbing, though I don't know what they mean, if anything. I urge you to be careful around this man."

Just then, someone came for Andelko; apparently. Miho needed him, and our conversation was cut short. Out in the streets of Tanja, large crowds thronged, swamping the local merchants and eating establishments. The population of Tanja had quadrupled already, with more constantly arriving. A short while later, Kopon Miho sent for us, and once again, we had to meet another Kopon. However, this one was the most powerful and influential of all the many Kopons in Vladimir, one Kopon Pavao, whose Sorcerer was Goran.

Our small group followed the messenger to meet these latest arrivals. Kopon Pavao was in his forties, a somewhat pudgy build. I suspected that he relied more and more on Goran to enforce his ruling over others. Of course, we four women faced another barrage of what had happened to us, along with the normal just where is this Velona and so on.

When I explained that we had been attacked by wild animals, but had killed them, Goran looked at me very closely. I felt his steely eyes drilling into me. Suddenly, I felt something cold, something inhuman, attempting to touch my mind. Instinctively, I relaxed and dropped all thoughts, all images, leaving simply an empty mind. Somehow, this touch was vaguely familiar to me; I'd felt it before, but with all the others drilling me with endless questions, I had no time to ponder it. However, I got the distinct impression that it somehow sensed that I was aware of its probing and was blocking it. It was gone nearly as suddenly as it had come, and I focused on answering the many questions being put to me.

That night, safely aboard our ship, as we four were doing our last nursing for the night, Linda said, "When we were meeting Kopon Pavao and his sorcerer, I had the strangest feeling that someone was probing my mind. Creepy feeling, cold."

That jogged my memory. "Yes, me too. I felt it too. Strange." I relayed what Andelko had told us earlier in the day.

"Well, tomorrow you and Renzo have to concentrate on the race.

I'll keep an eye on this Goran," Linda volunteered.

"Okay, but be extra careful until we know what we are dealing with here," I cautioned.

The day of the race was a bit chilly. Winter was slowly making its way here. The seasons were completely the opposite of what we had in the north, though I was not certain why this was so. We discovered many more had arrived during the night. As contestants, Renzo and I were escorted through the enormous crowd, which came to watch the big duka, the big race. Over a hundred riders were entered, so it was going to be a crowded pack that's for sure. As he and I double-checked our horses and he checked my cinch and fixed my bridle for me, I heard many in the nearby crowd placing bets that I would not be able to mount, that I would fall off the horse at the starting line, and so on. Renzo told me not to listen to them.

He said, "Look dear, this is a race between you and me. I am going to beat you today. If I beat you, then you have to be my slave for a day. If you win, then I get to be your slave for a day."

"Yes, but what does a slave have to do?" I teased him back.

"Whatever you want him or her to do, dear. Let's face it, I'm going to win."

"Think so, hot shot?" We hugged, and he helped me into the saddle and made sure that I had the wooden mouthpiece securely in my teeth. He mounted up, and we rode to the long line of other entrants.

I looked up and down the line; they looked at me. Some smiled, some smirked, and some laughed. None looked friendly, though. Kopon Miho walked out in front of all of us and talked loudly. "Welcome to the duka. I want a fair race. No fighting. May the best horse and rider win. We are honored to have a pair of foreigners race with us today. Never in our history has a visitor from another land had the skill and ability to do so. Let's show them what a real horse and rider can do, shall we?" Many of the riders cheered him on, fully intending to show us just that, to leave us in their dust.

"Remember, fair race. No cheating. We have double the usual number of observers at each station. Let's show our visitors how a real duka is run! Get ready. Here is the count down. Three. Two. One. Go!" A hundred plus riders violently kicked their horses into all out gallops, fighting for position going toward the first turn pole a half mile ahead. Renzo and I did not. We allowed our horses to slowly get up to speed, falling in last, eating the dust of the others as they fought their way towards the front of the pack. This was a ten-mile race, and we wanted our horses still to have a reserve of energy at the finish line. After all, what matters was who crosses that line first, not how long one was out in front of the pack.

Soon we were up to the speed that we wanted to begin the race with — a pace that would not tire our mounts too soon. As we approached the half-mile turn, we were nearly up to the rear of the pack. By now, the hundred plus were strung out in a long line, perfect for us to make our first moves. Renzo eased out to the left, while I eased gently to the right. We both passed our first riders, who were now wildly kicking their horses to greater speeds. The awkward jerkiness of their handling and motions only slowed them down.

We concentrated on becoming one with our horses. Marker after marker rose up in front of us and then fell behind us, as did more and more other riders. I was bent low forward, no tension on the reins at all, controlling my horse with the gentlest of body leaning, flowing with him. The wind blew my long hair wildly out behind my head. Exhilaration swept through me. We rode on.

Soon the treacherous rocky zone appeared. Already several riders had been forced to dismount, out of the race, their horses injured by galloping over this barrier. Instinctively, my horse slowed down, way down, and I let him take this obstacle at his own pace, without any interference from me. He knew best. Renzo did likewise.

Once clear, we nudged them back up to racing speed. We passed a few more riders and then hit the jumps. This would be challenging for me to stay on. I gripped my legs tightly and let him do the jumps. I was jostled. More than once, I nearly lost my grip, which would have meant a hard fall and a lost race. Somehow, I managed to stay on, but Renzo was now substantially ahead of me. I maintained our distance separation, unwilling to try to catch him just yet, not with the weaving hurdles ahead of us.

Weaving in and out from closely set poles required allowing the horse to take an optimum speed so that it could make the moves with the minimal effort. Watching the other horses charging ahead of us, my horse saw what was coming. I felt his intentional slow down and allowed him to take these at his speed. Renzo did not. As a result, he had to swing wide several times in order to make a turn. My horse did not. Coming out of the weaves, I had made up the distance, and we were neck and neck once more.

Now it was a race to the finish line. Twenty more were ahead of us. However, I concentrated only on beating Renzo. As the land rushed by us, I was vaguely aware of other horses also falling behind us. Suddenly, I realized that there were only two other riders ahead of us, but they had been fighting for the lead for so long that their horses were running out of energy, muscles tiring. Renzo now pushed his horse, asking for a burst of speed. I did likewise.

Racing at top speed, the four of us pulled alongside. The other two began using their reins to urge their tired mounts faster, slapping them on their sides and rears. Me, I just leaned more forward, making myself as streamlined as possible. Renzo did the same, and we pulled out in front of them. Still I was not beating Renzo. Only a half mile to go. I could see the finish line ahead. Now at last, I asked my horse for more speed, hoping that by having been so conservative, he still had some in him. I inched ahead of Renzo, who bent even lower and urged his mount on, nearly pulling even with me. Now we both urged our mounts on, just a little more.

As the finish line raced towards us, I pulled slightly out in front and crossed it first. Why? I was somewhat lighter than Renzo. For once, lack of arms and a slighter build made the difference of a horse's head! For the first time in the race, I leaned back tightening the reins to slow him down. Gradually I slowed his pace down to a canter, then a trot, and finally a walk. He was sweating heavily and breathing deeply, but he knew that he had won. I had a very proud horse under me. I think he also liked the way I rode him, but then, maybe that was just me thinking so.

Finally, we turned around to head back, while other riders also came past us now, slowing their racers down as well. I saw no one mistreating their horses, which impressed me. These men knew their horses well. Through my clenched teeth, I yelled, "I win. You are my slave for a day!"

Renzo laughed and offered to take my reins and lead us in to accept the winner's prize. I let him take the reins so that I could relax my clenched jaws! I had been really biting down hard, I realized as I wiggled my jaws. "That was the most fun I have had in a long time, Renzo, thanks for the race. We should do this some more. Perhaps when we get back home we can have another challenge race."

"You are on, my dear. Name the day. I seek revenge," he jested. As we approached the throng of watchers, a loud cheering arose. I rather expected to be booed since two outsiders had just beaten their best riders. Yet, they yelled and cheered us. If I had hands, I would have waved back to them; instead, I smiled and nodded my head toward them.

Kopon Miho waved for us to come over to his position. We rode slowly there. Renzo dismounted and then helped me down. Oh, my legs nearly gave way on me; I had been using them overly hard. Two of his men took the reins from us, as Miho began to talk as loud as he could to the huge crowd.

"It is with great pride that my two stallions have beaten all challengers in this duka. Well done to all the riders. This year, the top two riders are our honored visitors from the north! Commander Bethany, none of us here would have ever believed that you could have finished the race, let alone win, beating our best riders by a substantial distance, with your husband only a head behind you. This has been the most memorable duka that I have ever seen! Congratulations on a magnificent race!" Again, the crowd yelled and cheered for quite a time.

"Once more, congratulations. Commander Bethany, would you like to share any tips on how you managed to win this race?" The crowd obviously desired that I make some kind of speech, so I obliged.

"Be one with your horse. He is smart. Allow him to pick his speed over the obstacles. Next, be not so hasty to take the lead early, for you tire your horse, and he will have nothing left for you are you approach the finish line. Also, lean forward as much as possible to lower the air drag on your body. Finally, I am a lot lighter than many of your riders. No arms help, less weight." Several in the crowd chuckled, and then many began laughing at my tease of myself. Again the crowd yelled and cheered me.

"Great wisdom from Commander Bethany, spoken as if she were one of us indeed! I see my daughter Valerija is coming to make the formal presentation of this year's ankat. Indeed, Valerija, wearing a blue dress, probably brand new, walked proudly up to us. She was carrying a large medal on a blue ribbon.

She stood beside me and said loudly, "On behalf of Kopon Miho and the city of Tanja, it gives me great honor and pride to present the ankat to the victor of this year's duka. As I place the ankat around your neck, Commander Bethany, I am denoting you to be the best rider in all of Vladimir for this solar cycle. I now belong wholly to you." She tried to put it over my head, but she was a bit too small, so I leaned down a bit so she could manage.

She whispered, "I'll get it under your hair after bit. Now we must kiss. I belong only to you now. You must kiss me to show that you accept me. If you don't everyone will be utterly disgraced horribly so. Please you must do this."

She stood back and raised her arms toward me. The crowd now began clapping loudly, and she leaned to me, her lips ready for a kiss. I leaned down slightly, unsure of what was really being required of me. Our lips met and she did give me a passionate kiss. As we separated, she whispered, "Thank you."

"What do we have to do now?"

"I have to have my arm around you, I guess, since you cannot put yours around me. We now get to mingle with everyone who wants to congratulate us."

"I don't quite understand this Valerija, but I guess it can wait until we are alone. I will let you guide me through whatever we must do next."

"See, some of the other riders are coming to meet you. Usually, they would shake your hand, but now I don't know what to do."

The rider who had finished just behind me came up to us, grinning, "Well raced, Commander Bethany!" He reached for my arm out of habit.

"A hug will be better; no hands to shake," I replied with a smile. He leaned and gave me a strong hug.

"Well done. You are a very good rider. None of us thought you would even get past the starting line, let alone ever cross the finish line! Amazing. I am so honored to have raced against you. Your people must be fabulous riders!"

Now we were swamped with well-wishers! With so many stopping to chat, my guard was down. Suddenly, I felt that same cold mind pervading into my mind, looking at some of my memories. Fear tingled down my spine. I blocked it out as fast as I could, catching a glimpse of the long forgotten images I had of the Grey Creatures and the fight that Jes Amir and Alabaster had had with them so very long ago. I blocked it from my mind. As I looked up, I saw Goran staring hard at me from a distance, a cold, distant stare, almost inhuman. However, more well-wishers thronged us and I lost track of Goran.

Now I had to go to the bathroom something fierce. "Valerija, I need to pee; where can I go to do it? Also, I could really use a drink. I have a field of dust in my mouth." Renzo added a "me too" to my request.

"This way, we can use ours." She led us into her home and their personal room, as they called it. "Let me help you. I belong to you now, and this is something I can do for you," she said. I didn't like the sound of this at all, but I needed to pee badly. Once we rejoined Renzo, she quickly got us each a cup of mead. Valerija insisted on holding it instead of Renzo so I could drink.

"Thanks, that is a whole lot better now. Can we talk here?" She nodded. "Okay, I don't understand what you mean by you are mine now."

Valerija flushed red, before she spoke. "Ordinarily a man wins the race. Along with the medal, he receives me as his bride or wife — consort or servant, if he is married or doesn't like me. It's a bit strange this time — I mean because you are a woman too. I am prepared to be your consort and give you pleasure or just be your servant, as you wish. I now belong only to you. It is our custom. This has given my father, my brother, and my mother the greatest of honors — to give me as part of the ankat."

"But what is it that you want for yourself, Valerija? Surely, you have a boyfriend or lover."

"Oh no, I have known for years that, when I am of age, as I am now, and when it is also father's turn to host the duka, that I would be given to the winner. I hoped and prayed that it would not be a brutal or ugly man who won. Today, I am overjoyed that it is you to whom I now belong! I hope that I can please you enough. I am all packed and ready to go, just one large sack."

"Hum, just how old are you Valerija?"

"Fifteen."

"I see. If I don't take you, your family will be humiliated and disgraced?"

"Yes, you don't like me?" a very worried look flooded her young face.

"Oh no, nothing like that. You are a fine young woman. I guess you are coming with us. Grab your sack, please." Just then, Chaucer knocked on the door and yelled for me, sounding very worried. Since she was off getting her sack, I had Renzo open the door; in came Chaucer and a very scared looking Linda.

"Bethany! I'm terrified!" Linda gushed. She was trembling. "I feel so utterly helpless! I'm bouncing around all over the place." Indeed, she was jerking and stepping around as if she had a bee in her pants.

"Come on; sit down and tell me about it," I replied. We all sat down at the Kopon's large table. Valerija quietly came in while we were talking.

"Something touched me, my mind! Cold, inhuman. Bethany, it is just like the Grey Creatures that plagued us early last lifetime! Whatever can this mean?"

"You are not imagining it, Linda. I have been touched twice now. It's Goran. Damn, you are right. I haven't been able to figure it out — too busy with this race thing. It's a Grey Creature, that's the only explanation. Another one of those giants still lives, but way down here. We need a conference of everyone immediately. We are in big trouble."

Chaucer countered, "Bad timing, Bethany. They are getting ready for the big feast. You are going to have to be there. As I understand it, music and dancing will be following the feasting. Nearly everyone is ashore now. Can this wait a bit? Surely Goran will not try anything during the feast."

"Darn, okay. Let's meet right after the feast then. Oh, Valerija is now with us. I sort of won her as the prize."

"Yes, it's a big honor for us. I guess I will be her consort or servant," she timidly added, carrying the sack containing her entire life. "My father bought me this new dress I'm wearing so that I would look pretty for the winner."

Linda still was trembling, so I asked her, "Where were you when it touched you?" She told me and I followed up with, "Where are you now?"

Poof! She brightened up at once. "Oh, I'm right here, not back there. I feel so much better. That thing is scary! We'd better get out to the festivities."

Indeed, we had a place of honor at the table where all the dozen Kopon's were seated along with their wives and families. Valerija sat on my right, Renzo, my left. I let her look after my needs, even feeding me, which proved wise. I caught Miho and Mascha stealing glances at us, making sure that I had accepted their daughter. Indeed, several others did likewise. At last, he seemed convinced and stopped peeking at how we were doing. I noticed that Valerija had also seen his looks. Since she was cheerful now, I decided we were doing fine with this aspect.

After the meal, their musicians struck up tunes, playing drums, instruments that looked like guitars, and some flutes. Many sang along, but many younger folk began dancing on the grass. Valerija insisted that we should also dance, even though I had no idea of how to do their moves. She gaily showed me the moves, step by step. Theirs were simple dances, facing partners, moving close and then backing away. Women twirled around, their arms in the air. I managed as best I could. Again, Miho watched us and seemed satisfied that Valerija would be accepted by me. She certainly enjoyed dancing; well so do I.

Meanwhile, Roberto, Mireio, and Alwanianon were hard at work, capturing the music. Roberto notated as fast as he could, usually the first dozen or so notes; Mireio memorized the tunes, while Alwanianon tried to memorize the dances. This was their heaven, learning the music and dance of another people, taking it back to Velona, and sharing it with all the musicians there.

Right in the middle of the dancing while Valerija and I were twirling around each other, Goran struck! Everyone saw a blinding flash of light, an energy bolt of some kind, streaking from his hands through an opening between all the dancers straight at me. I was momentarily facing him and from the corner of my eyes saw the cold stare and flash. Lost within the music, I had no time to react. In slow motion, I saw the body of Renzo flying through the air at Valerija and me, while at the same time I saw the body of Emil flying toward Goran. I realized that my Protectors had been on duty and not enjoying the dancing. Renzo hit us; Valerija and I fell in slow motion toward the ground. I instinctively reached out with my arms to break my fall, but landed hard, my head hitting the ground hard. All went black. I had been knocked out by the fall.

The energy strike hit the ground right where I had been dancing; turf bits went flying wildly in all directions, covering we three and many others nearby. As Emil contacted Goran's body, the sorcerer gave him a mighty shove and sent Emil flying backwards through the air, heading for a crash on top of many dancers. Natale caught him mid-flight, held his body still, and with the help of Linda, gently lowered him to the ground on his back. (This I was told later on.)

The music died instantly. Chaos ensued, as people ran in all directions for cover. Others ran toward Goran to subdue him, probably so ordered by the Kopons. However, Goran simply pushed them all off him like they were leaves. He turned around and quickly fled the area. One by one, the guards got back to their feet and chased after him, but they were too late. They watched him ride off north on a horse.

I awoke and found myself in our longboat being rowed back to our ship. My head hurt. "Put that cold, wet cloth back on her head, Valerija." It was the soft sound of Renzo, though I could tell that he was rowing from the way his words came in rhythm. I felt the cold next to my head.

"Oh, my head hurts," I said. "Can I sit up?" Valerija helped me up onto the seat beside her, and then put the cloth back to the side of my head.

Emil said, "He got away. We're taking you back to the boat now. Andelko insisted on coming along, something about this being sorcerer's business. No doubt about it, Bethany, we are dealing with one of the Grey Creatures down here."

A little while later, we were all sitting around our galley — tea poured all around. This time I insisted on holding my own mug, while Valerija stared at us four in disbelief — that we could do this ourselves. I let Emil explain to Andelko just what this Goran really was, along with a bit of historical context, including the fact that I had been instrumental in their elimination.

Sipping my tea from my slanted back chair, I asked Andelko, "We know for a fact that Goran is one of these Grey Creatures. Are there others like him? That is the key thing that we must know or find out. How many of these are we up against down here?"

"Only Goran. None of we sorcerers are remotely as powerful as he is. No one had reported anything else as unusual as Emil has described. I think perhaps it is only Goran. His Kopon has been utterly disgraced by this. He swore that he knew nothing about the attempt on your life. However, I suspect that his own people will likely depose him when they return home," Andelko explained.

"Well I owe a big thank you to Renzo and Emil. Very well done, men," I replied. "You stopped the attack and no one was seriously injured. Now that is something. It could have been far worse. Thanks for watching after me." Both men grinned.

"You are most welcome, boss," Renzo teased me.

"What's next? Do we go after him?" asked Emil.

"Yes, we cannot allow a Grey Creature to roam Tarra. They are alien and are trying to manipulate and control all of us. We must go after him. Has Rosina contacted headquarters about this?"

"Already done," Rosina said. "Your mom said to be extra careful. She said you don't have any more arms to donate to the cause. I think she meant that as a joke, though." We chuckled.

"I will go with you," Andelko interjected. "I know where his cave complex is located. He will likely head there. I would if I were him."

"We are all still nursing. Just how far away is this cave?" I asked.

"About a week's hard ride, mostly northward, near the Inner

Range," he replied.

"I'll stay here and nurse Danielle for you, Bethany. I haven't learned to ride this hard. I'd only hold you all up," Linda said, offering to stay behind.

"Okay, I understand Linda. When Renzo knocked us out of the way and I was falling to the ground, I was still trying to break my fall using my arms. Strange feeling, you know. Weird. Anyway, I appreciate the help with Danielle. Valerija, will you stay here too and lend her your arms to help take care of my twins and newborn?" She readily agreed, finding some way to be useful here.

"Tonia, we might be injured, so I must ask that you come with us. Benet, Emil, Renzo, Cedric, Chaucer, you will come with me. We'll leave everyone else here. If we are unsuccessful, I want enough Santi left to protect the ship and get everyone else safely home. Mom can then figure out some other means to destroy this Grey Creature, if we can't get the job done."

Everyone agreed with my pick; it was reasonable. "Now, men, ideas on how we can deal with Goran when we catch up to him?"

None had. I explained, "I know that they can be cut with swords. Jes cut one's legs a couple times. I can avoid their energy blasts normally. This time I was taken by total surprise, because I was out there dancing. Perhaps fire and lightning will also affect the creature. If not, there is the old swing and bash that I can try again. If there is only one of it, then we should try coming at it from many angles. It cannot defend in all directions at the same time. I think we have a good chance if there is only one and it does not have those blasters or any of the flying boats that the original ones had up in the Appian Way." Andelko said that no one had ever heard of or seen a flying ship in the skies.

Linda said, "Maybe they hatch from eggs, but it's more likely that its parents left it behind when they went north for the battle, just like you are doing with your young children. That makes more sense to me, since these Grey Creatures look more like us than an insect."

Six days later, we spied a tall mountain range in the distance. Miho had loaned us a number of horses and had also sent along a dozen of his own men as guards for our campsites and to lead us through their land, though Andelko could have done that as well. The Kopon felt that this was the only honorable thing for him to do, since I was nearly assassinated at his festival. "Only a few more miles," Andelko said softly, as if the Goran could hear us from miles away.

We were riding through grasses, which touched our horse's bellies. Renzo and I rode the very same horses we had used to win the duka, the horse race. I had now grown fond of my stallion. I hoped that he liked me as well. At last, we spied a large cave entrance, cradled at the base of a granite sheer cliff. The opening was huge, large enough for one of their flying ships to enter here, I noted, hoping that we would not run into one of those ships.

After dismounting and setting up a campsite, the men prepared their weapons. Andelko continued to insist on coming with us, so I had him agree to stay at the rear of the group looking after me. Emil and Renzo would take point; Benet and Cedric would follow, while Chaucer, Andelko, and I brought up the rear. I also noted that Rosina was also here, floating above her twin brother. I had helped them both learn to be where they chose and to use their attacking spells. Hence, we had an ace up our sleeves, for Rosina would be an invisible attacker. Tonia remained outside. If we were killed, she would then be able to return. If we were hurt, she could bring a rescue party of the guards to our assistance. She was a Healer, not a Protector.

"The advantage goes to Goran," Emil explained as we began walking toward the gaping hole at the base of the cliff. "This is its home, and it is very familiar with it. We don't know anything about what lies ahead. Thus, gang, keep every sense wide open. Let's do everything we can to avoid being taken by surprise."

As Emil stepped into the hole, an alarm went off, a low humming noise. "So much for surprise," he whispered. A little ways inside, the cave opened up into a massively large room. From the marks on the stone floor, something very large, probably metal, had once been in here. In the dim light, we saw an instrument bank of some kind on one side of the walls. A large number of tools and machines lay on the other side, none of which we recognized. Far across the space, three dark tunnels led deeper into the complex.

Inside this room, we fanned out, so that we would not be close together, making it more difficult for the creature to attack us all at the same time. "I have a very bad feeling about this," Renzo whispered. I agreed with him; we were sneaking into a viper's den, and it could strike at any time, taking us by surprise. Only this was no viper. It was a giant that could easily kill each of us singlehandedly! Worse, everything around us was strange and foreign; we'd seen nothing like it anywhere.

The cold, inhuman voice of Goran spoke, "You killed my parents and left me orphaned here, marooned in this desolate land! Ha, at least our enemies, the mantis, got to you before me. Shame they didn't finish the job, but they never could do anything right. Always up to us to clean up their messes." He had suddenly appeared at the far end of this huge chamber from our spread out group.

"What right have you go to interfere with our lives? It's our lives. We are free beings, not your slaves," I replied. I had two reasons in mind. Since it was talking, perhaps I could get some key information from it. Also, I stalled to give the men a chance to get closer to it. "What gives you the right to scramble our memories, drive us into our heads next lifetimes?"

"You are in prison, fools! We are your jailors, what's left of us anyway. I've been expecting replacements now for thirty years, maybe more. Soon, we'll have you prisoners back into your cells."

"What cells?"

"Those flimsy bodies you insist on having. Of course, our enemies were experimenting with controlled societies of prisoners. Always trying to engineer the perfect prison cell. How do you like your nearly perfect prison cell, eh Bethany? Bit hard to manage?"

My face felt hot! So many things were now making sense; yet in doing so, I was beginning to feel more and more helpless, powerless, less and less able. I found that I could think of nothing to say in reply.

"We, on the other hand, could care less what you do within your body prison cell, as long as you stay there. Yet, now that I have seen the work of our enemies up close, I do have to admire their claw work. As you are now, you are so easily controlled and manipulated — you cannot even feed your cell. Funny, I think. I will recommend to the replacements that we also begin similar experiments. If nothing else, it helps pass the incredibly boring time on this penal colony. I have been so utterly bored, stuck down here for my whole childhood all by myself, surrounded only by the prisoners I guard. Perhaps I should just begin my own experiments while I am waiting to break the monotony. I have grown terribly tired of watching the same old thing, body fighting body, awfully dull."

"What do you think about taking every prison cell's arms off? You really don't need those appendages anyway. It's not as if you have anything terribly important to do, except make more prison cells for the ones that die off. I have often thought that the bosses chose the wrong prison cells, because these take too long to mature. Ants, now there's a better prison cell for you; no slowdowns breeding there. Damn ants get everywhere, so maybe that's why they weren't chosen for your cells."

While he was talking, we sized him up. He was grey in color, with the typical three toes on each foot. Goran was only seven feet tall, far shorter than the adults, if that's what they were when we encountered them in the Appian Way. This meant that Goran was still a juvenile. Yet, he must weight twice that of Renzo, maybe more. He had very solid muscles as well, wearing only a loincloth around his waist. I did not see any blaster weapons in his hands. Perhaps he didn't have any or if he had, he didn't know how to use them or maybe they didn't work any longer.

Since Goran was the first Grey Creature that had ever talked with us humans, ignoring when they appeared disguised as and pretending to be a human, I decided to see if he would tell us more. "Goran, if that's what we are to call you, I just want you to know that we have eliminated all the mantis creatures still alive and destroyed all their nests and unhatched eggs. No more mantis creatures, though, as you have seen in our minds, we paid a dear price for doing so."

"Yes, I saw that. I was curious, you know. Armless women were their grand experiment. I read that in mom's journal. Hence, I had to examine your memories to see for myself."

I inquired, "I notice that you do not have one of the flying boats in here. It used to be docked where I'm standing, right?"

He looked a little surprised that I knew so much. "Well, yes, but they took it with them when they left."

"And they never came back from that battle. You've been stranded here ever since with no way to get off this landmass. From our visits of these southern lands, we've seen that you jailers have had little to do way down here, not like all the intervention in the northern landmasses. Why did they leave the eastern half of the dog bone untouched? Why were they fighting over the western half of the bone?"

Goran looked like he was trying to remember something he had read. "Well because in the eastern half, all the prisoners have been here a long time and are staying very nicely in their cells. Besides, those prisoners belong to our enemies. Those in the western lobe are relative new arrivals to the prison here and have to be forced to stay in their cells."

"How do you know when a prisoner is out of his cell?" I asked.

Goran seemed stumped. At last he muttered, "We just know." I knew that he didn't know! Now I knew that we had a decided advantage over this giant; we were out of our cells, so to speak.

"Have you considered what you are going to do if the jailers never come back here, Goran? It is possible that they have forgotten completely about this prison. What are you going to do if this is so?"

"Oh they will come again one day. I must be patient. Maybe another fifty years, who knows?"

"Have you considered that you might be the only one of the jailers left anywhere on Tarra? That they have abandoned this jail?"

"Oh they will return. I will be waiting. Our bodies are built to last at least five hundred of your solar cycles, unlike those engineered for your prison cells. One day, they will return and I will be ready for them. Now I must get all of you into new cells, though I hate to undo the nice cell work of the mantis. Perhaps I should start in down here with a new policy of arm removal from all cells. I've decided that would make my work as jailor much less complicated, far less to do. I've been thinking about doing just this for some time. I've tried it on a couple cells, but until recently, the cells just lost all their juices. However, I've figured out a way that I can just pull these unneeded appendages off the cells without the cells losing everything. Your male cells will become my first test subjects. If it works well, I will begin systematically on all the many cells in this land. So Bethany, I will spare you any further appendage loss. You will then be able to assist these men here in learning how to get by without using their useless appendages. It will give you something useful to do."

This suddenly gave the men an additional motivation factor! Further, I realized that human life in Vladimir was likely to get horrible, if we did not stop Golan right here. "You realize, Golan, that we have come here to stop you from doing this," I replied.

"You? In your armless prison cell, you are going to stop me? Ha. With what? A kick of your feet appendages? Oh, I am mortally bumped!" He ridiculed me, feigning a slight bruise to his lower leg.

I countered, "You don't give us much choice in the matter."

"Oh enough talk. I need to start removing all the prison cell's arms here in Vladimir. You are delaying my official jailor work." Without any warning, he sent our Protector's equivalent of a push spell at my body. I watched as it flew backwards, off its feet and landing hard onto the stone floor. So much for conversation.

Emil, Renzo, and Chaucer rushed him from three sides, while the others closed in towards him. He used his hands to generate the push spell once more, sending Emil flying backwards twenty feet. He dodged Renzo's sword strike, but Chaucer's sliced into his leg. Howling in anger, Goran wheeled on Chaucer and sent him flying backwards forty feet, knocking him out. Benet threw up a wall of flames on his leg with the sword wound, causing Goran to howl even louder.

Goran whirled around and sent Benet flying backwards fifty feet, knocking him out as well. Andelko raced over to Chaucer, pulling him back out of the central area, near where my body still lay on the floor. Rosina backed up Renzo, who took advantage of Goran's distraction to run his sword into the calf of Goran's other leg. As soon as he pulled his sword out, he ducked and rolled, while his sister threw up a wall of flames between them, hoping to give Renzo time to get clear from any retaliation. It worked, Goran howled and spun around confused by Renzo's movements.

Cedric chose this time for his strike. He ran his sword through the left leg, slightly above Chaucer's cut. However, his sword became stuck and was twisted out of his hands, and Goran pivoted. His large fists hit Cedric in the chest, sending him flying backwards towards us. Several ribs were broken, and Cedric was unconscious as well.

Now it was time for me to strike. Goran was hobbling on two wounded legs. I grabbed a hold of both of them and jerked his legs out from under him, sending him sprawling onto the stone floor. He twisted all around looking for his attacker, but did not see me. He had no awareness of spiritual beings, free of a body!

Emil had recovered and signaled Renzo. The two began to rush him from two sides. Rosina added to the confusion by putting another wall of flames directly onto his head, causing him to howl louder and to flail his arms in an attempt to put them out. Both men thrust their blades into his giant sides, but he rolled on them and both chose to let go of their blades. Unfortunately, Emil was in the path of Goran's roll and became trapped. I watched as Goran raised his fist to smash in Emil's head. Emil held his hand above his head, vainly trying to fend off this deathblow.

I grabbed his fist and pulled him over the other way, shocking Goran, who could not see his attacker. Emil hobbled back to find another sword. Renzo pulled out two daggers, one in each hand and circled Goran, looking for an opening in which to strike a deathblow. Instead, Goran shot one of his push spells directly onto Renzo, sending him flying backwards fifty feet, knocking him out for a while.

Rosina got very mad at that point and put yet another pile of flames on his head. This time his hair burst into flames, and the howling was hideous as he tried to put them out. Emil, using Chaucer's sword, ran as best he could, limping on the leg that had been pinned under the heavy giant. Goran saw him coming and timed his fist thrust to hit Emil as he was thrusting his sword at Goran. Poor Emil took the brunt of that in his chest. I heard ribs cracking again, as he slid back across the floor.

However, I saw my chance. Golan's head was now a very open target. I latched onto his head and gave it a twist as I used to do to help the cooks back at mom's old estate, humanely killing the chickens she was about to cook for our dinner. I heard a sickening crack, and Goran's body went limp. His eyes looked up at where I was at, but saw nothing. Then, I saw the being floating out of the dead body. Now he saw me. He spooked utterly. I sensed a fear that grew into an utter terror, as he suddenly saw me as I am. He flew out of the cavern faster than I have ever seen any being move!

Rosina sent, *I'm off to get Tonia in here.*

I floated over to get my body up from the floor. Oh, my side hurt a bit where it had hit the floor hard. Nothing seemed broken though. Andelko had now dragged everyone into one spot. "It is over, though I do not know how, Commander Bethany. I am afraid these are injured."

"Our Healer is coming; give her a minute. Rosina is here and was conjuring the flames you saw. I was over there tripping him, and I twisted his neck like a chicken."

"You have saved all of us. We had no idea about him! He was ready to pull out all of our arms! If you had not been here, our whole country would have been doomed! Yet, this is so utterly fantastic. No one will believe us, excepting perhaps another sorcerer."

"Well, for the time being, perhaps that is best for them, not to know," I replied.

"Oh dear, only you two left standing?" Tonia came running up to us. "Are they seriously hurt?"

"Broken ribs I am sure, what else, I don't know. If you need any help, I'll do what I can with my feet."

"I'll lend you my arms, if you will tell me what I should do," Andelko added.

"First, I have to sense what is wrong inside their bodies," Tonia explained and set to work, putting her hands first upon Renzo.

A half hour later, all were sitting up. Other than large bruises and several cracked ribs, the men survived the attack in good shape, but all would be sore for several days. We moved everyone back outside, where camp had been set up. Tonia began systematically wrapping strong bandages around their chests to stabilize them and to help prevent accidental injuries to their ribs. There was not much else she could do for them, however.

We fixed a meal, and I had a good helping of tea afterwards, contemplating our next move. "We have to thoroughly search this cave. However, who knows what traps lay in wait for us. We must exercise extreme caution in there. I can tell that the wall is lined with instruments, but their nature and purpose is unknown. If we touch them, we could cause irreparable harm to our bodies. Yet, we must search the whole cavern."

"We need to permanently close off that cavern too," Emil added. "We can't leave it open like this; some unsuspecting person could wander in there and get themselves killed or worse."

"I think top priority should be placed on finding the journals of his parents," I continued. "If Natale can translate them, we may learn a whole lot more. We must be prepared if these evil aliens should ever re-appear here on Tarra. That has me very, very worried, gang!"

"Well, let's get searching," Chaucer suggested, grimacing from the pain of talking a bit too enthusiastically for the current state of his ribs.

"Are you up to it just now? We can always wait a while," I replied, concerned about pressing them when they were hurting.

"He said that he had completed an experiment successfully, dear," Renzo offered. "There may be an unfortunate victim in there somewhere. I hate to delay."

Armed with lanterns — me with numerous sacks tied around my waist — we entered the cave complex once more. Three tunnels led deeper underground from this huge area where the dead body of the Grey Creature adolescent lay. Admittedly, I was going to be useless in the search, so I concentrated on observing carefully so nothing would be overlooked. We also stayed together as a group. Since he had appeared from the central tunnel, we took that one first.

Eight-foot ceilings indicated just how tall the adults had been. A little ways down the tunnel, a room appeared on the left. Here were piled various clothes and weapons commonly found in Vladimir — his disguise room was our conclusion. We uncovered spending money mostly in some coins and a few gems. I had Andelko examine the rest to make sure nothing here had any real value to the people of this land; none had.

The next side room further down the tunnel yielded the prize, from our point of view. Books and related items covered a desk and a set of shelves. Carefully, the seven books were placed into a sack. Renzo found a folded up map of Tarra. Strange markings dotted this one too. Our curiosity had to be squashed for the moment; yes, we all wanted to stop the search and study the map. Instead, we continued picking up anything in the room that seemed related to the creatures. Two sacks were then tied around my waist, and I volunteered to be the packhorse.

Further down the tunnel, the sides gave way as it opened into the last room. Here we found considerable wealth in gold and gems nicely stored in strange metal chests. Each chest took two men to carry them, which gave us some idea of the inherent strength of just one Grey Creature! Because of all the broken ribs, I let Andelko supervise the transporting of these chests outside, using some of the guards that Miho had sent along with us.

"Let's try the left one; I have a feeling about this one," Tonia said as we were trying to decide which one of the two remaining tunnels to try next. This time, the rooms were off to the right side. The first room contained many strange tools and equipment, none of which made any sense to us. At my insistence, no one experimented with them. Ignorance can be deadly, more so in this case, since it was alien technology.

Further along, the next side room opened up into a barracks. However, many of the beds had been pushed back out of the way. One small bed sat in the middle of the room; dried blood covered the sides and floor at one end. Here we concluded that Goran conducted his grizzly experiments. With nothing of interest here, we moved deeper into the tunnel.

Once more it opened up into a large cavern. Several dead bodies lay piled in a heap in the back corner. Some were missing arms, others legs. However, in a bed in the center lay a man whose arms were missing. His clothing was a bloody mess, his shirt had been cut away at the shoulders. Tania went to him at once. "He's alive, barely, unconscious."

We crowded around her to see how he was doing. Tonia inspected the two wounds. "This is the grossest, crudest amputation I have ever heard tell of, positively grim. Both are infected, gangrene has set in already. He's running a fever. I'm afraid that I can do nothing for him, but make him as comfortable as possible, though I doubt he will ever regain consciousness. You all go on and continue the search. I'll stay here and look after him. I don't think he should be moved."

Silently, we retraced our steps back to the huge entrance cavern. I told Andelko about the man, and he headed down to Tonia to see if he recognized the man. We headed into the last tunnel. This one was shorter and contained a kitchen and a pantry area filled with local dried meats and grains in clay pots. Again, there was nothing of value here. I dismissed the fellows and let them go lie down and recover from their ordeal. I wandered back to join Tonia with the dying victim of Goran.

At suppertime, she and I walked back out with the news that the man had passed away. However, I had contacted the being as he drifted up from his body and told him that the one who did this to him had been killed. He was greatly relieved and left at once. After supper, Andelko and several guards went back inside, brought the body and those of the other experimental victims outside, and properly buried them after the custom of Vladimir.

The next day, Cedric constructed two crude drag carts from materials gathered from the cave. The seven heavy chests were put on these to be dragged along until we could find a wagon. As we prepared to leave, the question remained: how to seal this entrance. The men were in too much pain to concentrate on making the earth shake here. Besides, the rock was quite solid. Hence, I decided that I would do it myself.

High above the cliff were quite a number of boulders on the foothills. Like a dog digging for a lost bone, I began lifting and pitching boulders down over the sheer cliff. Afterwards, everyone said it looked rather funny, bounders raining down like dirt pitched out of a hole that an excited dog was digging. Well, it got the job done. No one would accidentally enter this cavern complex and get killed or seriously injured on the alien items we left behind. Yet, if we ever understood anything more about their technology, one day we could return and uncover the entrance.

As we rode slowly back toward Tanja, Renzo observed, "You know, this installation was not yet fully operational. The spiritual being trapping mechanism wasn't there anywhere. Perhaps this was just a southern outpost or look out place." I took heart in his observation.

Chapter 29 Shades of Megalos

On May 21, we once more set sail, leaving Tanja behind. Valerija was with us. I had a long talk with her, explaining basic concepts of our world and of personal freedom. While her people may have the idea that she was now my servant or consort, with us, she was no such thing. "I want you as a friend, a close friend. With all the children around here, we could all use another set of hands. In return, I will see that you get trained and educated as much as you desire. If you find a boyfriend in our lands and want to marry, that will be fine with me. If later on, you wish to return to Vladimir and help your people with all that you have learned, I will support you all the way." Close friends, this she could have. I know that she really didn't want to have to be in the position of giving me pleasure, nor did she think of herself as a servant. This way, she could contribute just what we needed and feel like she really did belong with our group.

For a week now, we had been comparing the Grey Creature map with the mantis map. As far as the landmasses were concerned, both agreed well with each other. The symbols were what interested us the most. All the mantis sites we'd visited were marked with the same symbol on the Grey Creature's map. Thus, we felt some confidence that we had found them all. In contrast, the Grey Creature's center of operations had been in the Appian Way. There was only this other one down here in Vladimir, and its symbol was only partially filled in on the map, lending more credence to our conclusion that it was only under construction.

Partially filled symbols became the key. One such mantis symbol lay several hundred miles north of Kostas in the country called Konstantin, which was now run and controlled by women only. Another lay on top of a mountain in the next country on this landmass towards which we were sailing, Demokritos.

However, two special symbols baffled us. Both were different from each other, both lay in roughly the same vicinity, somewhere in the mountains near the west coast of the landmass containing Grun, Wanakan, and Konstantin. They were approximately due southwest of Wanakan, but on the other side of the landmass, where we had not yet sailed. Each of the two symbols appeared to be related to the main symbols used for the mantis and the Grey Creature's main operational bases. We also saw two other tiny notations, but didn't figure they were as significant as the prominent pair. Only years later would I realize how wrong we were to disregard the hint that the Grey Creatures had an installation at the North Pole and in the middle of the Desert of

Desolation.

Although we discussed the significance of the symbols at length, we could draw no concrete conclusions. We needed to know where these aliens would land when they came. Our best hunch was to explore these two special sites. Offsetting that was the fact that both were very close together, unlike their bases of operation elsewhere.

As June came, the weather turned colder; nights now were in the fifties. Yet the daytime warmed up rapidly to a comfortable seventy-five, mild for the winters we were used to having back home. After we passed by the tall Katos Mountains which divided the two countries, we began to concentrate on what we knew from the traders of Annelise. According to them, there was some trading between the two countries. Demokritos was ruled by the Emperor from his palace in Kefall. However, the land was divided into several smaller kingdoms, each with their own rulers. Quite civilized was the opinion commonly held throughout Annelise, which meant something, coming from these well-dressed people.

Further, we were told that after we docked, we should contact the Harbor Master. He who controlled everything associated with the docks. If he did not give you permission to dock, you had to leave. If he did not give you permission to trade, you could not. Laws were strictly enforced there. Four of the kingdoms had coastlines and therefore port cities. However, the Emperor ruled from a city called Kefall, located in the Kingdom of Thrace. Thus, in keeping with our plans to go to the leaders of a country whenever possible, we plotted our course for Thrace. The largest port city in the Kingdom of Thrace was Patri, our first stop.

However, astonished is putting it mildly when we caught our first glimpse of Demokritos! Here was Megalos all over! The countryside was hilly and rocky in many places. Yet, the towns were brilliant and visible from extreme distances. The normal construction material was white marble! We spied long, tall aqueducts spidering their way across the landscape, bringing fresh water to the towns. White paved roads wound through the hills, like snow paths against the brown earth. It was winter and much of the grasslands had become somewhat dormant, though not entirely brown, as was often the case in Velona.

As we passed some coastal towns and cities, we spied many ocean going ships, which were exact replicas of those found in Megalos! We also spied a few dahabea from Annelise plying the waters as well. Red tiled roofs contrasted with the brilliant white marble of the buildings beneath them, as we watched the ports drift by us. Yes, several times we spotted the characteristic open temples so commonly found in Megalos, great columns of marble supporting a magnificent roof with all sides open to the breezes. However, unlike Megalos, the climate here was much more moderate; the ratio of what we called normal dwellings to the open aired temples was drastically larger than on Megalos. This time, we did not need Natale to suggest that the language spoken here was likely to be a variant of that spoken on Megalos.

Finally, on July 1, 653 we began tacking into the large harbor of Patri. Hundreds of smaller fishing boats plied the waters, and seven ships were docked, loading or unloading. The city stretched from the coastline up into the hills, its white paved roads like shining streaks pointing the way to heaven. At the top of one of the most dominating hills of Patri stood an impressive open aired theater, whose seats of white marble were clearly visible from the ship.

Of course, we were noted as we used our spanker sail and jibs to slowly enter, sounding all the way. Our ship had been constantly watched ever since we passed the first coastal town weeks ago. Probably by now, word of our coming had spread widely within all of Demokritos; we had not sailed fast.

Fortunately, the depth at the docks allowed us five-foot clearance even at low tide, which meant that we could dock in a civilized manner and not have to rely upon the longboats to go back and forth. As the Sleepy Hollow slowly bumped into the docks and the mooring lines pitched to the dockhands, we saw a line of Centurions marching formally into position, blocking our passage off the wooden docks into the city. Shades of Megalos! These soldiers looked like the splitting image of the Centurions of Megalos, right down to their bits of metal armor. However, they wore normal clothing beneath this and exposed no skin. Megalos was always hot, and here it was drastically cooler, which accounted for the slight differences. The men stood at attention.

I decided to use our normal marching order, for nothing appeared threatening at this point. We were obviously in a civilized land. As we were preparing to head ashore, a man dressed in a fine looking grey suit, reminiscent of those worn everywhere in Annelise, walked past the Centurions, who nodded to him. He stopped just in front of the line of soldiers, evidently waiting for us. Renzo and I followed by Natale and Henry walked off first, followed by the rest of our gang.

As we four walked toward the man, I saw the sudden surprise in his eyes as he saw my form. Ah well, I readied my animals story once more, thinking that he'd probably never seen someone who lost their arms before. We four, out in front of the others, approached him, and the initial attempts to figure out language began. For the very first time ever, we had no problem understanding from the first words spoken. He spoke perfect Megalos dialect, as if he had come from Megalos itself!

"Welcome Strangers of the most honored Eight Degree! We had no idea someone of such importance was coming here to Patri. I am Harbor Master Demetrios Dido." He bowed low to me and Natale and offered his hand to Renzo and Henry.

"I am Commander Bethany Rose Wilkins Pazzio le'Goeur, leader of this group of Santi del Dio explorers. This is my husband, Renzo. This is our expert Captain Henry Freeze and his wife and our worthy language translator, Natale. We come from a distant northern land called Velona in search of new countries with which to open up new lines of trading."

"Oh my, forgive me Commander Bethany! I assumed that your husband was the leader. Forgive my faulty assumption, I beg your pardon, most honored Commander. I will address you formally. Normally, there is a docking fee to be levied. By Demokritos law, the harbor master must grant a ship the right to dock and the fee it must pay. Likewise, the harbor master decides whether or not to grant trading privileges as well. However, considering your exalted status, the docking fee is hereby waved. If you will please follow me to — oh dear me! I was going to say follow me to my humble office, but for someone of the Eight Degree, such would be an utter insult! It is my sworn duty to take you to my home and there conduct our business. Would you please permit me to send a quick message to my wife so that she can prepare refreshments as befitting so many of you of such high status?"

"Certainly, please do," I replied, completely baffled about what he was talking! I did note that he also observed closely Linda, Natale, and Mireio. Even Alwanionan, now growing into womanhood, did not escape his quickly darting eyes.

A little later, we began to follow Demetrios through the city streets. His guards fell in behind us. As we walked along, the local people gawked and stared at us; we were after all foreigners here. The men were clean and often wore suits or at least well-fitting shirts and pants. The women commonly wore long dresses, reminiscent of those of Annelise. However, I could see no signs of the tight corsets on these women, nor the wide, flaring underskirt hoops. Instead, their dresses flared out by hidden petticoats, I assumed, much more practical and only a few feet out, not the huge distances of those hoops of Annelise.

The buildings tended to be made of white marble, differing only in the colors of the archway stones over the windows and doorways. The streets were wide and filled with people and many shops. Periodically the street gave way to a huge central plaza, filled with an aqueduct-fed water well in the center and open air markets around the sides. The streets resumed across the square. A half hour passed rapidly as we took in our first impressions of this new city and new country. Thus far, I was impressed, very impressed.

The harbor master was a person of some importance in this city, I noted, as we arrived at his home — mansion would be a far better description, occupying an entire city block! A beautiful ironwork fence outlined his block, just inside was a large green lawn, well it would be far greener in the springtime. His house was not ornate, just large, and well made. His doorway color was red, blood red. Flower boxes lined the entire front wall the mansion; of course, only the dirt was now visible. He saw me eyeing it and said, "Yes, it is spectacular in the spring, my wife's passion. If you will follow me inside?"

The entrance hall was adorned with tapestries depicting ocean scenes. He led us into an adjacent room, which held a very long mahogany table with plush matching chairs, done in red upholstery. The man liked red, I concluded. The many windows made this a well-lighted space, cheerful at that. A woman dressed in a long red dress that poofed out several feet around her was waiting for us. She had long blonde hair, quite curly, an expensive emerald broach about her open neck. What caught my instant attention was her lack of hands!

Likewise, she was staring first at me, then Natale, Linda, and Mireio. "Allow me to introduce my charming, loving wife of twenty years now, Evania of the Sixth Degree. Dear, this is Commander Bethany of the Santi del Dio, leader of these foreign explorers. I am sorry that I do not remember your formal title or the names of all your colleagues. Forgive me; I was taken so by surprise when I discovered that we are hosting several of the Eight Degree here in our humble city!" Both were in their late thirties, I guessed.

Bubbling with enthusiasm, Evania came up to me and threw her arms around me in a welcome hug. "So very honored to meet someone of your highest status. You do our house the highest of honors indeed. Please be seated. Some refreshments?"

Acting on a hunch, I said, "By any chance do you have any tea? I dearly love to try other's teas." I let Renzo seat me, figuring to watch closely how Evania managed, intending to follow a similar protocol.

"Why, certainly Commander Bethany. I will send for my best tea. We have similar tastes. I suspect the others may desire to sample the wine that Demetrios himself makes. It is legendary in here Patri, something of a hobby for him, takes his mind off of his work, you know." Shortly several servants came with trays of hot tea, wine bottles, cheese, and breads.

I noticed that Demetrios assisted Evania with everything, so I gave Renzo a nod, and he followed suit. Over a superb black tea, we began our discussions. "Excellent tea indeed, Evania. We have come from a far distant northern land, and unfortunately, we are not familiar with many of your customs and terms. What is meant by this Eighth Degree and the Sixth Degree? We are not familiar with those words." I hoped that I was not being rude, but before we said a whole lot, I decided that we needed to know this detail. Much of how we explained ourselves to these people might depend upon it and what the terms implied.

"Oh yes dear. I can see that would be a problem, you coming from such a different place, yet so very similar to us. I am amazed that you speak our language so well, you've only got a slightly wrong accent." She began to explain. As she did, I became more and more uncomfortable.

Two men, Demos and Kritos founded their country a thousand solar cycles ago. Later, the kingdom was divided among their seven sons, becoming modern day the seven kingdoms: Phindos, Alia, Thrace, Theos, Thallyus, Arolas, and Penelopus. Ever warlike in the early years, at last the kings met and chose an Emperor to rule over them, thus ending a century of nearly continuous wars. Yet, to keep the Emperor honest and to limit his powers, a countrywide Senate was created. Their purpose was to create the laws that the Emperor and the Kings enforced. Members of the Senate are elected by popular vote from all the people within their districts. Hence, the people themselves have a say in the making of the laws of the land. Thus, the conflicts of the early years ended.

Ever since the two men came to Demokritos, people considered the mountain Aylon Orthos to be a most holy place. In time, a great temple was built there, the Temple of Orthos it is known today. Here the oracles began telling the fortunes of anyone who made the long journey to see these women, who are called orthees, a word meaning Holy Fortune Teller or Oracle of the Divine — we never were quite sure of the translation.

A new problem arose in time. Men would often forsake their wives, leaving them destitute to fend on their own. Sometimes, the wives broke the sacred marriage covenant. Three hundred years ago, this became a major embarrassment, since half of the entire population of Demokritos was unfaithful to their spouses. The Emperor journeyed to Aylon Orthos, seeking the great wisdom of the Holy Orthee. There he was guided by the oracles to create the Holy Eight Degrees of Matrimonial Binding. Apparently, this scheme has been in operation some three hundred years now, and the broken marriages are at an all-time low. In fact, the only broken marriages to be found are among those of No Degree.

When a couple decided to get married, assuming that they were not extremely poor, they would journey to the Temple of Orthos to sanctify their union. The woman would sacrifice an appendage, and the man would thus be bound to her for their lives. Only if they possessed wealth and power, would the orthees allow the woman to become of the Eight Degree, losing both arms at the shoulder. This then ensured her new husband of total fidelity for the duration of their lives, as he would have to assist her with everything in life, providing many servants as well. These were the women who were held in the highest regard by everyone, their sacrifice visible to all. They also wielded great power, but of that in a moment.

The Seventh Degree women sacrificed their arms at the elbows. The Sixth Degree, at their wrists, as our hostess had. The Fifth Degree women gave up one entire arm. The Fourth Degree lost one hand. The Third Degree, three fingers of each hand, leaving only the index finger and thumb. The Second and First Degrees, two and one finger on each hand, respectively. Thus, as the degree of sacrifice rose, so did the power, respect, and honor of the union of the woman and the man who were so pledged. While the scheme sounded utterly barbaric to us, here it had achieved its goal, and couples remained faithful to each other for life. Never in the history of Demokritos had an Eighth Degree couple been unfaithful to each other! The penalties were too great even to consider having an affair outside the marriage. If the man did it, the woman was given everything that the cheating husband had: land, property, money, even his job. Similarly, if the woman was unfaithful, she would be sent out into the world to survive on her own, something which none dared do. (This, we learned, was the "party line," and not an accurate assessment of the Holy Degrees.)

Today, only the very poor, who could not afford to make the trip to Aylon Orthos, had unions of No Degree. Here were found the few unfaithful marriages.

Obviously, women of the Eight Degree were very rare, since only the wealthiest and most powerful men could afford such marriages. Further, these women also held great power behind the scenes of normal political life here in Demokritos. While the Senate made the laws of the land, once passed, the women of the Eighth Degree would meet in secret and approve or disapprove the new law. If they disapproved it, the law was void and cancelled! Further, if the Emperor ordered an action that these women disapproved of, they had the right and obligation to cancel his order! Finally, one of these women of the Eighth Degree would preside over trials of those accused of very serious crimes. They would decide guilt or innocence and levy the penalty, including death. Thus, the women of the Eighth Degree were not only highly honored because of their great sacrifice for Holy Matrimony, but also because of the great power that they also wielded.

An aside, Alwanianon was very pleased to discover that here she was viewed by all and held in a very high regard as a woman of the Seventh Degree. Whereas in her homeland in the Spice Islands, she was being left for dead by her own people, when we rescued her and Mireio and Roberto adopted her. She was quite amused by the whole arrangement.

"Of course, King Andreas Gavril and his wife, Calista, who is of the Seventh Degree, will surely want to meet all of you," Evania continued her lengthy chat. "I'm certain that Emperor Alexandr I will send word for you to visit him at his palace in the imperial city of Kefall. His wife, Empress Agata, is like you, of the Eighth Degree. I'm sure that she will greatly desire to meet others of the Eighth Degree from other lands."

Now it was my turn to share. "My mother is our Supreme Commander and is of only the Sixth Degree. It was she who asked me to command this exploration journey." By explaining it this way, it lent credence to why, from their point of view, four of the highest status would be making the journey. Further, having those of the highest status making the initial contact would give the recipients the greatest of honor. Twisted, I know, but it was an acceptable reality for these people.

I asked about the locations of the places she had mentioned. To my surprise, Demetrios uncovered a wall hanging, which held a large map of Demokritos. He pointed out Thrace and Patri on the map. A road led straight to the imperial city of Kefall. From there the road led to Aylon Orthos and the Temple of Orthos. Incredible, the one place that we needed to visit, which was where our maps indicated another partially constructed mantis nest was located, was indeed this mountain! Coincidence? I doubted it very seriously. This whole society had mantis influence written all over it!

After hearing our story, both our hosts were very impressed, and he gave us his official okay to establish trading agreements. "As long as Natale is with Captain Henry, no one would dare cheat him. She is of the Eighth Degree, after all. However, you might find it easier if you were to acquire more appropriate clothing for both you and your men. I do need to return to work, but Evania would be most honored to take you to the finest clothiers." I asked if gems would be an acceptable means of exchange, and they were; I would have been surprised if they weren't.

While we followed Evania to the clothing shop, she explained that there was very little crime in most of the city. Only in the slums were we likely to find pickpockets on the loose. "You can tell by the quality of their clothing, you see," she chatted away, more than pleased to assist us.

Later, we all exited dressed as well-to-do locals. We women now faced wearing five petticoats in order to puff out our nice dresses appropriately — at least no corsets or enormous hoops. We didn't feel so constrained this time. One interesting aspect of our new dresses was the arms. While the dresses of Tonia and Rosina had sleeves, the dresses of us four were nearly topless; two small straps went over what was left of our shoulders, baring our "degree" for all to see, as was their custom.

On the way back, Evania dropped a bombshell on the "civilized" society. "Oh I nearly forgot. There are some people that you should be alert for and stay away from completely, the Kali Assassins."

"What?" I exclaimed my surprise and worry showing.

"Well, unfortunately so. Normal crime is very low. The only ones you need to fear are the Kali, and you always know them when you see one of them; they always dress in black. Black suits, black dresses — no one else dresses like that."

She explained, "The Kali are above the law because no one can catch them; no one knows where they are located. They just appear and then disappear. A century ago, an Emperor decided to put an end to the Kali, and he ordered his legions to kill anyone dressed in black. After hundreds were slain, the Emperor was himself assassinated. His wife sought revenge, for who would deny that to an Eighth Degree woman? After more Kali were killed, she too was assassinated. It is just a fact that we must live with, I'm afraid. Normally, the Kali do not bother us, with the exceptional thievery raid. I suppose they must eat too. I've heard rumors that they make most of their living by accepting commissions to assassinate people, though I do not know who would want to pay someone to kill another. That eludes me, I'm afraid."

"Just remember, if we should happen to see someone dressed in black, just ignore them and keep on walking. Act like you don't even see them — that's what I tell our maids and servants to do, just keep on walking. Honestly, I don't think you will even see one of them, really. I haven't seen one in months, but then I do not get out as often as I used to these days. You know, our children have grown up and moved out now. Demetrios and I are now on our own, so to speak; the house seems rather empty, and we have been devoting more of our time to our hobbies. I do wish you could see my flowers out in front of the house in the springtime, so impressive, daffodils everywhere. Oh my, such beauty." She chatted on and on, happy to have others to really talk to, instead of her maids and servants.

The countryside was rolling by as we watched from our carriages. A week had passed, and we were on our way to meet with the King of Thrace. The day after our arrival, we had received his official document requesting our visit to his palace. Demetrios arranged for these carriages. Following his suggestion, Natale and Mireio remained behind, guaranteeing that all the trading arrangements were made in good faith. Cedric, Benet, Michelle, Emil, Renzo, Linda, Rosina, Tonia, Angel, and I were making the long journey. Our intent was also to extend the trip to meet with the Emperor and then visit the Temple of Orthos, our true objective.

Riding along in the coach reminded me of a similar journey that mom had made in Meglaos, when I was a baby. She had journeyed there to deliver the ultimatum to the Senate and then to the Pope. The wild combat that had occurred flashed by in my mind. The terrain was so similar, the roads, the buildings, the people. At least here they still worshiped the Sun God and not Yazi's perversion of Jehosanity. I hoped that his religion would just die out of its own.

The King of Thrace made his home in the capital city of Axos. Again, the city looked to us just like any other Megalos city, only in good repair. Here, their engineers maintained everything in top working order. We even passed several road crews making repairs to the white brick roadway.

The king's palace in Axos was quite grand, occupying several city blocks, with many buildings and quite a few soldiers present as well. King Andreas Gavril was in his early forties, a strong man, tall and well-muscled, a leader of soldiers, I thought. His wife was very pretty, and her short arms reminded me at once of Jovanna Barcella. She was of the Seventh Degree, and they had been married nearly thirty years now. She welcomed us and gave each of us a hug with her short arms, much as Jovanna had always done. Again, we were well treated, though pumped for data about the rest of the world that lay beyond their land. Unfortunately for the king, the Emperor's summons for us to visit him came the day after we arrived, and he had to send us on our way far too soon for his liking. I promised that we would stop and spend more time with him and his lovely wife on our return trip from the Emperor.

On up the long winding road we drove. Our carriage drivers knew the way and stopped each night at only the best inns, considering the status of their passengers. In a way, it was rather comforting to know that we would always be given the best treatment and did not have to worry about anything. This was turning out to be more of a vacation than work, thus far anyway.

I was concerned about the Emperor, however. I had known several from Megalos; actually, I had killed two of them personally! The first, Hiro, tried to drug and rape me. The second, Justinian, had tried to kill me and our army with his army, as he conquered the Sea Princes. My luck with Emperors was not encouraging, so I was more than a little worried about yet another one.

The imperial city of Kefall was about halfway to Aylon Orthos. Spread out like shining white gemstones across the rocky, brown hills of Thrace lay the grand city of five hundred thousand people. Thriving, bustling, productive described what we saw. The many temples to the Sun God stood taller than other buildings, their white columns standing like fingers pointing to the sun above. Heavily laden wagons rolled by us coming out of the city and we passed many heading into the city. The brownstone aqueducts came down from further inland, and at the center of the city, they forked into three others, heading off to the northwest, southwest, and alongside our road, heading west. Engineering feats were commonplace here in Demokritos, unlike Megalos, where the engineering technology had become lost over the centuries.

In contrast, here the society was alive and doing well, stark contrast to Megalos, which had passed its zenith, turning into decadence and now into perversion of truths. I hoped that this Emperor would be different from those of Megalos.

The imperial palace was markedly different from that on Megalos, most of whose buildings were open-air affairs due to the excessive heat. Here, most of the buildings were large, enclosed marble buildings. There was the Senate Building, nearly an exact copy of the one in Megalos. This spectacular building was visible for miles, sitting on top of a hill. An enormous coliseum capable of seating thousands was also on a hilltop and was the first thing visible from the distance.

Also clearly visible were the Centurion barracks, where tens of thousands of soldiers were housed and trained. Smoke from armories and blacksmith shops curled into the early morning blue sky above the sprawling city. We passed ten wagons carrying raw white marble stone blocks, one in each wagon. Construction was still ongoing, unlike in Megalos.

Our carriages drove straight to the imperial palace, which occupied ten square city blocks, pulling up before a huge building with bright yellow stonework over the doorway arches and hundreds of tall, ornate windows. Ah, in Megalos, bright yellow was the color worn by the Emperor, the parallels continued to mount. Courtiers stood awaiting our arrival, bowing low to us as we exited the coaches and formed into our line. "This way, please," one man said. He was well dressed, the creases in his pants perfectly done. We followed him inside. The domed roof overhead dwarfed us; one could be thirty feet tall and still have headroom in here. Great tapestries hung from the marble columns, though we did not get a chance to study them.

Trumpets announced our arrival, as the great doors of the throne room were opened as we walked up to them, perfectly orchestrated. Inside, we saw the Emperor and Empress standing before their white marble thrones, throngs of others lined either side of the room, a red carpet led from the door up to the throne. Renzo and I led the way, followed by Linda and Chaucer, while the others fell in behind us. Fortunately, Queen Calista had told us how properly to greet a woman of the Eighth Degree.

Both were in their middle forties, I guessed. He had perfectly cut short brown hair, a goatee neatly trimmed, with piercing black eyes and thick lips. She wore her hair long with a sparkling tiara atop her head. She had deep blue eyes and her hair was brown. Her face still looked like an angel; she was one of the prettiest women we had seen, gorgeous indeed.

As per the protocol that we had been told, I spoke first, announcing my name and Renzo's. The Emperor bowed to me and put his arms around me, touching his head to either side of my cheeks. The Empress moved to me, and we did the same, touching either side of our heads to each other.

"I am Emperor Alexandr I and my beautiful wife, Empress Agata.

Welcome to Demokritos and our palace." I then introduced Linda as my second in command and then the others. Each received a similar welcome from the rulers. As the two returned to their throne seats, servants rushed in with plush chairs for all of us. Once we were seated, the hundreds of others here sat down in unison, perfectly orchestrated.

I spent an hour describing us, our ship, our land, our customs, and even a bit of our history, presenting it in a manner similar to what I had done with the harbor master. I had brought along a bolt of the finest silk that we had purchased in Tashien. Renzo presented it to the Empress and had her feel it with her cheek. As I expected, no woman could resist this cloth! She asked her husband to acquire many more such bolts.

Impressed with the fact that the Supreme Commander of the Santi del Dio was a woman of the Sixth Degree, Empress Agata asked, "Are there more women like us, of the Eighth Degree in your Santi?"

"Well, yes, mom could give you an accurate count, but within our extended organization, I would guess that we now have probably close to one thousand women of the Eight Degree. Forgive me if I don't have an accurate count. Two more are in my party. Natale is our translator; she picks up other new languages rapidly. Mireio is one of our musicians. They are back with our ship arranging trading agreements with the harbor master."

She looked stunned. "You have so many of the Eight Degree! This Santi del Dio must indeed be incredibly wealthy and powerful in your Velona." I heard many whispers from the throng of others who were listening in on the conversation.

Emperor Alexandr asked, "How is it that you speak our language so well? This seems so very strange to me." I had to explain about Megalos and even the strange island of Acropolis. He continued to ply me with detailed questions about these two island's people. So much so, that finally, the Empress asked for a break.

"Dear, I would love to chat with Commander Bethany and Linda. Why don't you speak privately with the others, while I speak privately with these of my degree? I'm sure that they can answer your questions just as well as the Commander."

Thus, the formal meeting was broken up. Linda and I followed Agata to a side room, where there were beautiful, plush sofas on which to sit. The rest of my group followed Alexandr to another side room.

"I am so surprised to find that other foreign lands, which we did not even know existed, also have women like ourselves, the Eight Degree. We share much in common, Bethany, including the wielding of power. But we both know that. Can I ask you two some personal questions, having nothing to do with matters of state?" I smiled. This sounded lots better than trying to answer detailed inquiries about Megalos.

"It's about our degree. Often I still do feel so very helpless at times, even though it has been thirty years now since we wed and I became the Eighth Degree at the Temple of Orthos. You'd think that would pass. Sometimes I still find myself reaching out for something with my arms! Silly of me, but it is strange. Do either of you have these feelings? I know that you are so young and only newly of the Eighth Degree."

"Yes, only last month as I was falling down, I kept trying to break my fall with my arms," I grinned. "It sure is a weird sensation, flailing away with non-existent arms. I don't think we will ever quite get over that."

"Me too," Linda confided in her. "When I had my babies, I felt so helpless. How would I ever be able to nurse them? That was and is quite a challenge, but my husband has been a big help to me with it. We'd be in a fine pickle without our loving husbands. I suppose that you would be so too."

"Oh yes, without Alexandr, I don't know how I would survive. I can do nothing for myself and am very dependent upon him. I well remember, just like yesterday, when we went to the temple. It didn't hurt you know, when I became of the Eighth Degree." I could see that she was totally stuck at that moment in time; she had been so ever since that first day! "I was so useless, you know. Every day since then I feel so useless. I know that is silly of me, to think that way. I am the Empress of all Demokritos. I have sat in judgment in a few trials, and I've even vetoed some Senate legislation that would have done more harm than good. Yet, I still feel so useless."

"You know, Agata, we found nearly all our Eighth Degree women have similar reactions and feelings as you have. Mom and I have worked out a therapy that erases those feelings. I can run it on you right now if you are not hungry and if we are not interrupted while we do it."

"You mean your Eighth Degree women do not feel useless?" her amazement was genuine.

I gave her my usual introductory explanation of what I wanted her to do and then we began, moving her back to the day that she and her husband arrived at the Temple of Orthus. Linda knew immediately what I was up to and why I was running therapy on the Empress whom I had just met. Data. What had happened to her and were there mantis creatures there doing the surgery on all these women? Did we have to face more of these creatures?

"We are fifteen. He knew that he would ascend to the throne next year. For hours, we discuss it and finally here we are, walking up the steps of the Temple of Orthos. The High Orthee asks us if we were willing to make this lifelong bargain and commitment to each other. We say so and she leads me inside the building. I am undressing now. She gives me this wine to sip, telling me to drink all of it. I do and am getting so sleepy. I fall asleep. I wake up and my shoulders have a dull ache in them. I feel so useless. I try to get up, but my arms are not there! For a minute, I am panicking, but then an orthee comes, helps me up, and dresses me, talking soothingly to me all the time. She leads me out to Alexandr. I feel so weird, so useless, so helpless, and so dependent. I start crying. He holds me gently and says he loves me. Then, we go home."

Agata began yawing on the third time through. Now she began seeing what had happened when she was unconscious. "Oh, two women are cutting them. They cut about three inches below my shoulders and peel it back. Blood is coming everywhere. They cut around the shoulder and my arms fall to the ground. They use the extra tissue of my upper arm to seal the hole. I see them sewing it up as if I was a dress. One says, 'She'll be useless the rest of her life.' The other woman agrees, 'Yes, she certainly will be completely useless, but pretty though.' They are right, I have been totally useless my whole life."

Rats, it didn't erase, even after three more times through it. "Do you see something there that is similar to this one and earlier in time, Agata?" I asked. After a bit of coaching, she saw something. Once more we were off and running.

This one had happened around a hundred and fifty years ago. She had married a wealthy Senator, and the two had talked about her becoming an Eighth Degree, which would ensure that he rose to the Presidency of the Senate. She'd agreed to do it. This time, however, after she had drunk the sleeping potion in the wine, it was not two women who performed the surgery!

"I see the two orthee women back away from my body with a strange look on their faces, like they are somewhat scared. Now I see this awful black creature coming toward me. It's huge! It wouldn't fit in our palace here. It has these enormous mandibles. God, it is eating into my arms! No, it is taking them off. This hideous thing is doing the surgery on me! I try to scream, but my body is unconscious. Then, it is done. That awful thing goes away, eating on my arms! The two orthee clean my body up. One says, "Well, this woman will now be completely and utterly useless the rest of her life." The other agrees and says, 'I hope she likes it. I certainly would not want to be so useless like this, but we must do as the mantis says. After all, it has taught us our oracle powers. Yet, she is going to be so useless now. I wonder if it is worth it?' The other says, 'Yes, as long as she believes it is worth it, but you are right. She is now useless. Pity, she is rather pretty.'"

"I didn't want to be useless! I thought I was being helpful, giving our marriage a big boost, so he could become President of the Senate! I had not thought of myself now being useless, yet as soon as I awoke, I felt so completely, utterly useless that I cannot find words to describe it!

Gods, I agreed wholly with those two women. No wonder I have felt this way all this life!" She was now laughing about it.

"Hey, Bethany, it's a miracle! That awful feeling is gone, completely gone. I still can't do much of anything, but I don't feel that way, useless! Incredible. I feel so full of life now! How can I ever thank you enough?"

I ended the session quietly at this point. My conclusion was that the mantis creatures had begun this perversion of the society here, but now that they were gone, the orthees were continuing the centuries old practice. However, Agata was not done, "Bethany, what were those horrible creatures anyway?"

I had no alternative but to tell her the truth. I took it gently for her sake. An hour later she understood fully what had happened and just how this vile action had been unleashed on her society. Linda suggested that this well could lead to a change in their society; the mutilations may end. It was now well past suppertime, though the Emperor did not intrude upon his wife. We three joined them, and he looked relieved. Rosina had contacted Linda while I was running the session, and she had explained to him what was happening in general terms.

However, Agata was so cheerful, so happy and outgoing, that he was truly amazed. We dined with them, of course. His comment told all, "Dear, you have not been this happy since we were married!"

"Alexandr, I have been dead all these years! Now I am so alive I can hardly sit still! And it is all due to this therapy the Bethany has been using on her women of the Eighth Degree. Now I also understand why, but I will speak of this to you in private. Bethany, please, you must stay the night here in our palace with us." We had no choice, but were quite willing to do so.

After eating, Agata asked us to follow her. "Dear, don't you want one of our servants to lead them to their rooms?" asked a surprised Alexandr.

"Oh I can certainly walk, love. I am not totally useless anymore. Come on. I'm putting you up in our very best visitor's rooms!"

A little while later, when we were finally alone, Linda commented, "Now that's a positive thing. Agata is now insisting on doing some things for herself. Not bad. What happened with you all and the Emperor?"

"Grilled, that's what," Emil replied. "Question after question about Megalos. I'm afraid that Alexandr knows an awful lot about the history of Megalos at this point."

Renzo added, "I think that the same people who founded Megalos journeyed on and founded Acropolis, and then Demokritos. He sure pumped us for Megalos information. That they all converted to this new religion certainly raised his ire. I think he is a staunch believer in the Sun God."

We enjoyed the comforts of these magnificent quarters, which had six separate bedrooms that opened up into this huge commons room, where we sat on comfortable sofas and chairs. Here we could want for nothing. Servants checked on us several times, offering food, wine, even towels for the private hot bath. This we all made good use of — the hot bath!

The next morning while dining with our two hosts, Alexandr commented, "I must truly thank you, Commander Bethany, for what you have done for my lovely wife! She is so alive and so happy. What a night we had, not since we were married have we had one like that!" She flushed and gave him a naughty look.

"Seriously, Bethany, I wonder if I might impose upon you further?" said Agata. Curious, I asked what.

"I've sent word of what you have done for me to my circle. There are nine others of the Eighth Degree living here in Kefall. Would it be possible for you to stay a little longer and give my close friends the incredible benefits of your therapy, as you do for all of your own women of the Eighth Degree?"

I looked at Linda, and she, me. In all decency, I could not refuse, not and stay true to my own self. "Sure. Linda, Tonia, and Rosina can also perform the therapy as well. We would be honored to help your friends regain something of their vitality of life."

Five days later, we said farewell to the imperial couple. The nine others had similar results to that of the Empress; all recovered a tremendous vitality of life. All had contacted long ago incidents with the mantis creatures, incidents that had hung up their current situation. All had been educated carefully about the truth of the total situation. These were the power leaders behind the scenes in this society. Linda hoped that they would be an impressive force for change, and so did I.

Further, Agata promised that on our return from the Temple of Orthos, she would have a thank you present ready for us. However, she only grinned and wouldn't tell me what it was, in spite of my asking her repeatedly. At last, we all climbed into out carriages, setting out through the imperial city, heading for the east roadway to the Temple of Orthos on the mountain of Aylon Orthos.

We had not gone too far and were still in the densely populated city when the carriages suddenly stopped. Our drivers yelled to us, "Troubles Sirs." At once, we all piled out. I certainly didn't want to be stuck inside a carriage if a fight broke out!

Fifty men dressed entirely in black from head to toe surrounded our carriages; black masks covered their faces. They made no offensive moves, even though our men drew their swords and took up a defensive stance in front of us women.

They made no threatening moves, just stood motionless. "I am

Commander Bethany of the Santi del Dio. What is the meaning of this? Why have you stopped our carriages? Who is in charge here?"

None made the slightest motion; none replied, dead silence. All around us, the streets had become completely deserted, normal people fled from these assassins in black, the Kali. I didn't like this at all and was considering what would be the best action to take, when suddenly we heard the hoof beats of another horse and carriage coming our way. Incredibly, the Kali moved back and allowed this new carriage to enter their circle. Then, I saw why. The carriage was entirely black as well; even the drawn window shades were black. The driver pulled up before us, stepped down, and opened the black door. He raised his arms much as Renzo does for me. I saw a woman being helped from the carriage.

Dressed similar to ourselves with many petticoats poofing out the bottom of her dress, she wore nothing but black. Her hair too was coal black as were her eyes, penetrating cold black eyes. Her hair draped in ringlets down to her waist. As she stepped forward, I realized that her long tresses covered the fact that she too was of the Eighth Degree! She walked up to me, never taking her eyes off my eyes. Such confront I've found is very rare indeed.

"I am Kallisto, leader of the Kali of Demokritos. You are Commander Bethany Rose Wilkins Pazzio le'Goeur?"

"I am. Pleased to meet you, Kallisto," I replied, more than a little bit curious now. Okay, I was exceedingly curious indeed. What was going on here with the Kali?

She moved close and gave me the accepted greeting between two of the Eighth Degree, touching our bodies together, pressing her head against the side of mine and then the other side. "This is Linda Sarah de Grange, my second in command," I added. She repeated the welcome with Linda. At least she was being polite and very respectful of us.

"I wish to talk with you two. If you will please come with me in my carriage? I give you my word that no harm will come to either of you. Since this may take some time, one of my men will escort the others of your party to one of the best inns in the city, there to await your safe return. We mean none of you the slightest harm. I must discuss some things of importance with you. If you will follow me now, please?" She turned and walked stately back to her carriage. Her doorman gently lifted her inside. Only then did she turn to see if we were following her.

We were. I mentally let the others know to go along with this. Rosina would keep in contact with us. Renzo let the others look after his body, perching himself on the top of Kallisto's carriage. He would not be separated from me!

"Thank you. There is no need to wear blindfolds; the blinds hide everything from view. You must not know the location of where we are going. If you did, I would have to have you slain, for none know the secret location of the Kali. Please sit back and relax; it is but a short ride. I will explain later." We had no choice but to comply, my curiosity rising by the minute, as was Linda's.

From the horses' hooves, I knew that we had entered some kind of tunnel and were underground when the carriage halted. The door opened and the driver lifted each of us out and down, taking the greatest of care of us, as if we were a highly breakable doll. Later, I learned it was his reverence being displayed.

We followed her through a dark tunnel into a brightly illuminated room. The scent of jasmine greeted our senses. This was indeed a woman's room! Everything was perfectly arranged, from the magnificent objects of art, to the flowers, to the divans. "Please make yourselves comfortable. I will sit in my favorite divan here. Iole, please bring us the tea." She signaled a servant woman, whom I noticed had no hands, making her of the Sixth Degree. "I know that you are Commander Bethany, but may I call you simply Bethany?" I nodded. She finished, "I also know that you dearly love tea. I have here some of the finest in all Demokritos. I hope that you enjoy it as much as I do. Also, I do hope that you are not as completely helpless as the women of the Eighth Degree are around here. I certainly am not, and I do not encourage such among our Kali. You will find your feet most useful here."

Iole returned carrying a tray with a teapot and three large mugs, whose handles were very much larger than normal, perfect for feet, I noticed. Kallisto slipped off her slippers and demonstrated by pouring the three cups from the teapot, using her feet.

"We would be grateful if someone could undo the laces on our boots. We are dressed in your country's clothing so that we would be more acceptable to your people here. However, we cannot undo our laces easily," I replied, hoping that Linda and I would not be forced to undo each other's laces.

"Allow me to try," Iole said. She was in her late twenties with straight long black hair that reached her calves, very silky and shiny. She knelt down and using her teeth managed to undo the knots, and then using her arms got my boots off. Soon, she had Linda's removed as well.

"Thank you Iole! This is much better!" I replied. Linda and I leaned back and picked up our cups like the pros we were when it came to feeding ourselves. "Oh, yes, this is a fabulous tea. I would dearly love to take some of this back with us. You have excellent taste in teas, Kallisto. Impressive."

"No, you two are impressive!" Kallisto replied. "You are not helpless, useless women of the Eighth Degree?"

"Not at all. In order to fit into your society here, we are going along with your customs. In our world, we pride ourselves on doing as much as possible for ourselves. Linda and I have relearned how to swim in the ocean again. I have reacquired my skill at riding horses, so much so that I actually won the duka horse race of the Vladimir last month, rather shocking them. Of course, I was not trying to win their race; rather I was trying to beat my husband. We are always trying to best the other, a great, loving game we have. So, yes, we are not helpless women; we may look that way, but looks can be deceiving."

She smiled broadly, as did Iole. "Ah, you also display uncommon wisdom as well. Yes, it is the correct action to take, if you wish to be accepted in normal Demokritos society. Yet, you ride a horse? How is this possible?"

"Legs hold you on. Renzo, my husband, made me a wooden block through which he puts the reins. Then, I bite down on the block, and by moving my head and shifting my body weight, the horse knows what my request is. Simple, once you get the hang of it. Only back home, we have better saddles, ones that I can use to mount all by myself. Those in Vladimir are nearly impossible for me to mount safely."

"It is so exhilarating for me finally to meet others of the Eighth Degree like me, who are neither useless nor helpless. Forgive my excitement over this small matter," she said. I also noticed that she was a very attractive woman, perhaps thirty years old.

"Tell me, what do you know of the Kali?" Ah, now we were getting down to business.

I explained that we were told that they were assassins and from our own observations, everyone, including those in power, was terrified of the Kali. Actually, our data was pretty limited.

She chuckled, "That is good then. Allow me to educate you a bit of our history, so all may become clearer to you." She began a lengthy explanation.

The Kali organization formed right after the Emperor and the Temple of Orthos reached the agreement to begin the creation of the Holy Degrees for married women. The Kali were totally opposed to such mutilation of women, and their goal was somehow to take care of the worst off of these women and to end this awful ritual. However, until now, they had been unable to halt the practice. Indeed, over the years it had only escalated in popularity, being seen by all as the solution to so many unfaithful marriages.

However, that was the surface manifestation. Within some marriages, men still mistreated their wives, even though their wives had given them their ultimate sacrifice! These were those who were assassinated. Twice, the woman of the Eighth Degree strayed wickedly from her promises and vows and had felt the knives of the Kali. "My own husband betrayed me shortly after I gave up my arms for him! I caught him in bed with one of my new servants. Furious, I contacted the Kali, and he paid the ultimate price. I then joined the Kali, determined to learn to do things for myself and not be a helpless, useless woman. I have risen up the ranks and have become the leader of all the Kali in Demokritos."

"I am a close friend with all the other women of the Eighth Degree and many of those of lesser degrees as well. Slowly I have been working with them to get laws changed, but I regret that we have not yet changed this barbaric practice."

Iole brought in a tray of cheese and sweet rolls. I watched as Kallisto nonchalantly picked up a piece and munched on it as she spoke. Linda and I helped ourselves to a sweet roll, while listening to her. "The Kali have eyes and ears everywhere. I know what you have done for Empress Agata and her circle of nine others. Such a positive, powerful step forward has never been seen in Demokritos! I am eternally grateful to both of you for doing that for them."

"I could do it for you as well, if you wish," I interrupted her. I suspected that she, too, would not want to be left out. I wanted to save her the embarrassment of having to beg me for it.

"Would you do this for me? A total stranger? A Kali?" she asked surprised, though both Linda and I read her body language which said to us, "Thank god!"

"Sure, we always insist on doing it for all the women of the Eighth Degree in our land. In fact, we do it for anyone who had suffered trauma, big or little. It is the only decent thing to do. Have we the time to do it now?"

"I am yours!"

I needed no further encouragement. We were off and running a therapy session once more. Three hours later, Kallisto was roaring with laughter, her trauma blown completely. She too had encountered the mantis creature some hundred fifty years ago. Again, I spent an hour educating her about the mantis creatures, while we ate a delicious dinner, of course, topped off with more tea.

She looked at me and said, "Bethany, do you realize the gift that you have given me, a total stranger in a foreign land? I feel so rejuvenated, so full of life that I am ready to explode! Are you not a goddess in disguise?"

"I know. When I lost my arms, I truly needed this same therapy as well. I am just a person as you are, Kallisto. However, I have spent lifetimes learning how to do things, not just things using my body, but things that I, as a spiritual being, can do. Like this, for example." I lifted up the entire table on which the remains of our dinner lay.

"Ah, so that is how you could bash these monstrous beasts to death. Now it becomes understandable, whereas before it did not. Is it difficult to learn how to lift things? I can see this would be a fabulous thing for me to learn to do."

Linda came to my rescue; the good old Judger in her activated again, just in time to save my rumpus. "Back home, we have established what we call the Laird Foundation, one of whose goals is to help women such as we three, I mean those of the Eighth Degree, re-learn to do things and to master as much as they can learn. I know that we cannot ask you and the other women of the Eighth Degree to travel halfway around the world to come to our foundation. What would you say if we created an Extension Office here in Demokritos? Here those of you who wished to learn more could come and study. Many of those in the office are trained to perform additional therapy sessions, so that those others here who wish it can get the help they need."

"This would be fabulous indeed! But the cost would be high, would it not?"

"No cost to you at all. The Laird Foundation is fully funded so that it may concentrate solely on helping others in dire need. However, if a suitable building could be donated and perhaps food and essential supplies, that would be appreciated. All we ask is those who are helped in return help others as then are able."

"Bethany, I accept your offer. If I had arms, I would hug you tightly! Such a godly gift!"

"Hey, we can at least hug your style," I grinned. Once more, we pushed up against the other and touched heads together. "I know, it's not anywhere as good as a hug from your mate, but it is something we can share."

"Thank you on behalf of all the harmed women of Demokritos! I know that I am keeping you from your journey to the temple. I will contact the other women and by the time that you return. We will have arranged for the acquisition of a building. However, please exercise extreme caution at the Temple. Those women will not give up their centuries' long practice. Your lives may be in danger. Know this: the Kali will be there with you, watching. If they attempt to harm you, the Kali will intervene! You have my word on this."

"Thank you. Yes, visiting this temple has been our main objective for this first trip to your country. We knew that the mantis creatures once used this place, and we have to make sure that there are no more of those vile creatures still living there. Opening up new trading partners is our cover story, though we are actually doing just that anyway. I'm glad that we met, and Linda and I are very, very pleased that you are doing so much and not being helpless and useless like the others have been doing, wasting away their lives."

"Meeting you two has changed my life forever. I owe you a great deal. I make you this promise. If ever I can get this horrible practice abolished here, I will make the long journey to this Velona of yours and dedicate the rest of my life to learning all that I can so that I may be of much more use to others."

"I accept your pledge, Kallisto. And thank you for allowing us to be ourselves here and not continue to pretend that we are helpless too." With that, we returned to the carriage. The coachman carefully put our shoes back on our feet and drove us back into the city.

Renzo touched me, *Thanks love. You did super. I saw it all. I really love you! Gotta go tell the others all about it.* I smiled for us.

The next day, we once more rolled along the open countryside heading toward the mountain and the temple. Renzo commented, "You know, we are acting as a catalyst for major change in this country." I was beginning to believe that might just be so, but the most difficult part lay ahead of us with the orthee.

After five days of riding in a carriage, I was going bonkers! Linda and I were driving the others nuts. Scratch my nose. Itch this. Help me rearrange this confounded dress. My butt aches. Everyone was glad to see the mountain ahead of us at long last. Not tall, but rounded was the peak of Aylon Orthos, a strange peak indeed, volcanic in nature. Here the very earth had bubbled to the surface creating the black bulge known as Aylon Orthos. The Temple of Orthos was yet another of the white marble complexes set atop the dome. I began to wonder where these people got all this marble!

Three structures formed the complex. The road led to the first one, which looked somewhat like a dormitory. This place was isolated; the last town that we passed was a day behind us. Only people with a purpose came here, and the road ended at this building. As we exited, a woman wearing a white robe, her hands folded across her belly, walked slowly out to meet us. "Welcome to the Temple of Orthos. Why have you returned Eighth Degrees?" She spoke directly to Linda and me, ignoring the others.

"We have come to talk with someone in charge of the temple and its operations," I replied honestly.

"Oh, you have brought two others who wish to become of the Eighth Degree?" She spied Tonia and Rosina.

"No, they do not so wish. We wish to speak to someone in charge of the temple and its operations," I repeated.

"This way please," the woman finally duplicated my request and led us inside, holding the door until Renzo caught it, because Linda and I were following her. She led us down a hallway past several rooms. The smell of disinfectant that we used in our own infirmary assaulted our nostrils. This had to be the rooms in which the surgery was performed.

"If you will wait here," she said, leaving us in a room with a number of comfortable chairs but little else. Stark white walls stared back at us.

Presently, another older woman entered, also wearing plain white robes. "I am Seer Irena. Welcome women of the Eighth Degree. I do not recall your names, so forgive me."

"We've never met. I am Commander Bethany Rose Wilkins Pazzio le'Goeur." I introduced the rest of our crew. "We are explorers and have sailed here from a far distant land called Velona, way north of here. Already we have opened up many new trading partners in these extreme southern lands. Emperor Alexandr suggested that we should visit your temple."

"Your accent is a bit strange. Your skin is so white. The visions of your coming are then true. I accept that you are from a land as yet unknown to us. We take comfort in seeing that even there you also have the Holy Degrees and are honored that two of your Eighth Degrees should come to visit us here," Seer Irena replied, an indescribable coldness in her voice. "How may we help you?"

I was about to answer, when I felt someone moving into my mind attempting to review my memories, my images. This person was powerful and strong and knew what they were doing! *Here you want to see what I can do, look at this!* I rapidly ran my memories of smashing the adult mantis to bits on the ground. Whoa! Somehow, my effect was more than doubled in strength and vividness.

Seer Irene screamed and fell over backwards. Linda caught her body just before it hit and raised her to her feet. I nodded to Linda, who smiled back. Irene stared at Linda and me, and I watched as her total self-confidence slowly eroded, a great fear replacing it. Another woman rushed in at that moment, Seer Hermia, we soon learned. "Irene, I heard you scream. Is everything all right? Who are these people?"

Seer Irene was unable to speak, more than a little shocked at what she had just witnessed with her mind probe of me. "I am Commander Bethany," I repeated the introductions and from where we had come.

"I am Assistant Seer Hermia. Seer Irene, what have they done to you?" Irene was now visibly trembling.

"She attempted to probe my mind without my permission. I didn't intend to shock her so badly. Somehow my intention was magnified," I replied honestly.

At last, Seer Irene found her voice, now shaky and weak, "It is true, Hermia, our visions are true. The Slayers of the Black God have come for us. Doom is upon us now. Kill us quickly, I beg of you."

"I'm sorry Seer Irene, we did not come here to kill you. We only came seeking information, knowledge, not your deaths."

Both women now looked terrified of us. "Look, if we wanted you dead, we could have done so already. How about giving us a tour of this temple? Tell us about your history. I believe that you didn't always have to follow the Black God."

The two women looked at our men, whose hands were not on

their weapons, rather the opposite. Renzo now had his arm just where I loved it, around my waist. Ditto with Chaucer. The others were holding hands, trying not to look threatening. They were good; they had already picked up my intentions to look as peaceful as possible. Somehow, my intentions were being strengthened here — double what I would have expected. Why?

Seer Irene looked at each of us and then began to speak. "This is where we meet with the married couples to make doubly sure that they are truly pledged to each other for life. If you will follow me." She walked out of the room with Hermia and us right behind her. "Here is where we perform the painless Holy Degree surgeries. Back there is where we live our humble, solitude lives, praying for knowledge and wisdom, seeing the future for those who ask it of us."

Now outside, we passed by a smaller building. "That is our private prayer room, where we mediate and pray together daily. It is but one large room. Do you wish to see the actual temple itself?" she asked. We did. She continued to lead us toward the peak and the open aired marble temple perched at its very top. As we neared, several other white robed women backed away and allowed Irene full access to the temple.

"Here is the Holy Oracle of Orthos."

We saw instead a perfect location for a mantis nest, deep underground. From the heavily weathered marble, the structure had stood here for centuries over this deep hole. Somewhere down there the mantis had stayed. "Okay, gang, I'm going down for a look see. Keep an eye on my body please."

"Hey, you are not going down there without me, my dear," Renzo broke in, "I am your Protector. We go together. Sis, keep your Mind Link on us, just in case of trouble."

"You got it, Renzo," Rosina replied. I was outvoted. I smiled and gave him a kiss.

In a panic, Seer Irene exclaimed, "No, you cannot go down there! It is a bottomless pit; we will not be able to get you out! You will be killed."

"We won't be using our bodies," I tried to explain to the concerned woman, who really did not understand what I was saying. While Emil and Cedric surrounded our two bodies, he and I floated up and then down that dark shaft side by side.

It went vertically down a hundred feet before opening into a large chamber. Renzo and I felt so powerful, so utterly strong, like we were gods somehow. *Look, there is the mantis body, long dead*, Renzo pointed out to me.

God, look at all those body parts! They must have dumped all the amputated pieces down here.

Probably sacrificing them to their god, which is long dead. Do you see any nest or eggs?

Nope, look at the dig marks on the walls, this place was definitely under construction and not operational when the creature died, I pointed out the telltale marks.

Ah ha. Look, it died of natural causes; part of the ceiling collapsed and squashed the bug.

Since there was nothing at all of any interest, we began our ascent. However, we both felt so strong, so powerful, that we shot up like one of Sho Lin's rockets! Stopping miles overhead, we laughed our heads off before descending to our bodies.

"Standing stones," Tonia spoke as soon as we were back with our bodies.

"What?" I asked her, confused completely.

"Over there, while you two were off exploring, I had a look around here. See there, grey standing stones. Someone long ago removed them from their proper positions. Look at the stone here around the hole. See all these indentations. They match the bottom sides of the stones in that pile over there. Someone destroyed the standing stones when they erected this temple."

"How could you know that?" asked Irene.

"Linda, that's why our powers are so greatly magnified. This is one of those ancient power points where the forces of our planet radiate upwards from its core. Another set of ancient standing stones. Who would have ever thought that we would find a holy place like this down here?"

I then said to Irene, "We have lots of these holy sites in our land. They are marked by those grey standing stones. They used to stand upright here marking this holy site of power. That's why I accidentally shocked you so badly back there when we first met. These places of power always seem to double our powers and the effects that we create."

"You have oracle holy sites in your lands?" asked Irene in wonderment that there could be even one other such place as theirs.

"Yes, many such places of earth power. However, I think that you need to see what is actually down in the bottom of this holy site."

"Please, don't throw me into the bottomless pit!" she trembled, assuming I intended to pitch her body down there.

"Of course, not Irene. I will show you, not your body. I joined her mind to mine and, while I was at it, I joined with Hermia as well, much to her surprise. With the two women seeing what I see, down I went once more and showed them the dead mantis. Both women were shocked and speechless — their thoughts a jumble, which I made no attempt to view.

Topside again, I dropped the mental connections and asked, "Seer Irene, is there somewhere that we can go and have a talk? We need to have a long talk."

Pale faces led the way back to the first building. A dozen other women in white robes gathered out of concern for the well-being of their two leaders. These watched in silence as we all went into the original meeting room, where they normally addressed the arriving couples.

"That, that was the ancient Black God, wasn't it?"

"Yes, it is no god at all, merely an alien creature who loves to dine on us humans," I replied. I launched into my usual spiritual being discussion and gave them a brief summary of just what the mantis creatures had done here on Tarra, as much as we knew at least.

When I finished, both women were crying. Irene wailed, "We have sold our souls for nothing." I let her cry out more of her grief and despair.

She then began to relate their history, as told from one Seer to her successor over the past centuries. In the ancient days, pilgrims would journey here to the Temple of Orthos to consult with the Seer. Sometimes, the Seer would catch a glimpse of the future for the pilgrim, other times, although the glimpse was of the future, it was not that of the pilgrim. More often than not, the Seer would not have any revelations. Still, these women all knew intuitively that this was a place of power and they continued, based upon their occasional successes, which brought them great fame.

A hundred fifty years ago, when the Demokritos society was hemorrhaging because of so many unfaithful marriages, the Black God appeared to the Seer. It offered a vision of the solution to the marital difficulties within the country, along with visions of the Seers gaining the ability to foresee correctly and all the time. If the Seer implemented the Black God's proposed solution, then the Seer would be given perfect seeing ability. She could not refuse, for it meant abundant survival and power for all of her women and future Seers. Thus began the Holy Degrees and the fame of the Seer of the Temple of Orthos.

However, some fifty years ago, the Black God no longer appeared to do the surgery. However, the orthee women had learned well the craft and began performing it themselves. As far as their surgical skills went, they lost no patients. However, with each amputation, the women felt worse and worse, knowing how awful the lives of these women would become. Guilt crept into their very souls. The Seer before Irene lost her skills at foreseeing and at last took an overdose of the sleeping, anesthesia potion. Irene ascended to the leader position. Although she did not want to continue the long-standing tradition of the Holy Degrees, couples continued to arrive nearly every day for the operation. Although she tried her best to dissuade them from going through with it, the Holy Degree was now firmly entrenched and could not be easily halted by mere words.

Still, Seer Irene had sporadic visions of the future and hoped that not all was lost. A month ago, she had seen our coming and became afraid that their doom had at last come upon them. Of course, the problem with a vision is that it is then believed. She could take no independent action of her own to perhaps alter the supposed future.

"What shall we do? We cannot continue to do this anymore. Should we give up our Holy Temple and do as my predecessor has done, taking her own life? Should we just leave the country somehow? Though I have seen our doom coming, I have had no visions of what we must do," Irene confided in me, asking for guidance.

"Don't be silly. Just don't perform any more Holy Degree operations. Say you have run out of the necessary supplies and that it will take some time to get more. Stall for time, Seer Irene. You have allies that you do not know you have. We Santi had perfected a therapy, which has erased the entire trauma suffered by a person. Already, I have worked these miracles on nine women of the Eight Degree in Kefall, including the Empress herself. These women have erased the idea that they are useless and utterly helpless. Further, they also know the truth behind the Black God of yours. Even as we speak, the Empress and her friends are working to put an end to the Holy Degrees. Also the Kali are fully behind them as well. I believe that, if you can make a convincing argument that you are out of the needed supplies to stall for time, then the Empress Agata may be able to halt this practice."

"The Kali! Woe are we! We shall all be assassinated in our sleep!" shrieked Irene, terrified of the Kali.

"Not at all, Irene. If you do not perform any more Holy Degree operations, the Kali will not bother you at all. If you continue cutting off appendages, then you are right in fearing the Kali. As it stands now, the Kali are behind you, if you cease operations."

"But will not others learning the truth seek our deaths as retribution?" asked Hermia.

"No, you were just as much a victim and used as everyone else. What man in his right mind would tolerate his wife being mutilated? They are as much to blame as anyone else. It is not blame that anyone is seeking. Blame leads nowhere but to more savagery. The resolution is merely to cease doing it and to work on the rehabilitation of those so harmed. Work on making a better future for everyone in Demokritos; that is a more worthy goal, one worth using your Seer powers to assist."

"Yet, there is another way you can help broadly. As a byproduct of this whole mess, you have perfected a very useful drug that healers Tarra-wide could use, when a person needs an operation. We Santi would love to trade useful things with you for supplies of this anesthetic. See, it's not the end of the world, but a new beginning." I tried to put this in a positive light. I didn't want to see these women commit suicide over their past deeds, but to take some small responsibility for it and begin to make a better future for others.

"We have made arrangements with the Empress to establish a foundation in Patri to help the women here in Demokritos. As part of that operation, several of our Healers will be coming. You here have developed valuable surgical skills, which could be put to good use helping save the lives of wounded people. They would love to help you learn more and get established as the local healers. Not only would you still be Seers, but also you may become healers of renown yourselves. There is much good in your future, if you but walk that path."

A week later, we arrived back in the imperial city of Kefall. The coaches took us directly to the Emperor and Empress, who were very glad that we returned safely. Alexandr was signing an official document as we entered their throne room. Agata was looking over his shoulders, a huge grin on her face. Then, she noticed us. "Welcome back Commander Bethany! You look well. Can you also read our language?"

"A little," I replied. "You look radiant, Empress."

Alexandr finished and poured hot wax onto the document and pressed his royal seal onto the soft wax, making it official. "Isn't she though? Just amazing beyond words!" he exclaimed. "Here see if you can read this."

I read aloud for the others:

Whereas the men and women of Demokritos have now learned to be completely faithful to their wives and husbands, as demonstrated by a century of long lasting marriages, the practice of the Holy Degrees is now no longer needed and will be abolished. We continue to revere those who have given this Holy Sacrifice, but the marital situation has long been resolved. Be it resolved that from this day forward, any new couples wishing to utilize the Holy Degrees in their marriage must have official written permission from both the Emperor and Empress before it can be administered.

Senate Law #1245623

As Validated by Emperor Alexandr I

As Validated by Empress Agata, Eighth Degree

I gave Agata a big bump and head touch. Linda likewise. She beamed. Alexandr stood tall, his arms around his wife. He said, "You'll never guess what Agata has done! She is now drinking her own tea from her cup! Incredible, in all these years, she never could do that. How can I ever thank you for giving me my fantastic wife back to me?"

"You already have," I nodded toward the document.

"My dear friend, Kallisto showed me how and gave me a special mug that makes it easier to do. She's promised to show me how to do many other things," Agata grinned. I looked a bit surprised. I had no idea she knew the leader of the Kali! However, I dared not say anything though.

After a big feast that night, Agata presented Linda and me with a specially made broach. Made from gold and tiny gemstones, the broach was in the shape of the country with two small figures representing the two of them. Emperor Alexandr carefully affixed them around our necks. "A small thank you for what you have done for my wife and so many other women," he proclaimed.

Finally, we said our farewells to the imperial family and walked out to get into our coaches for the return trip to our caravel. When Renzo lifted me into our carriage, I was shocked to see a woman in a white dress sitting waiting for me.

"Kallisto!" I exclaimed in surprise. She grinned sheepishly.

"I have fulfilled my bargains. My second in command will be teaching those who wish to learn new ways of doing things. I wish to live up to my pledge to you, to return with you to learn all that I can before returning to help our people. I hope that this is acceptable to you on such short notice."

I leaned over and we exchanged our body bump hug. Linda climbed in beside us and was just as surprised as I. Needless to say, we had a most interesting trip back to the caravel, anything but boring! Kallisto was, as we all discovered, a kindred spirit and was outside of her head, prime druwid material, Renzo noted.

Chapter 30 Exploration Ends

August 20, 653, we set sail from Patri. Kallisto was fitting in with us very nicely. She had brought a pouch of gems for expenses and a change of clothing. She was delighted to meet the rest of our band, floored with the skills that we women like her demonstrated on a daily basis. In fact, she quickly discovered that she was far less skilled in adapting than we were, something which pleasantly surprised her immensely. She knew now that she had made the right decision to come with us. "I never dreamed that we could do nearly everything!" was her frequent saying.

The first thing we did was find her a set of clothes like those that we normally wore, open at the bottom so we could easily manage our own chamber pot usage. While we had been making it a practice of we four getting together in the morning and evening assisting each other with such mundane things as brushing out our long hair, we immediately made it a five-some. Kallisto really appreciated this time together, as we shared our various tips on how to do things. However, she merely gaped as she watched Renzo and me play a round of Modified Torque Ball. Now that nearly all the trading goods were gone, he made us a small playing area.

"How?" she tried to say when we finished our first game. I lost by one point, swearing revenge tomorrow. "How?" she still could not believe what she had just seen.

"Come on, I'll show you. We've modified the game so I can play again. Use your feet to bat the ball to the wall. It has to hit above the lower line and below the top. After it hits, the other person has to hit it back either on the fly after the first bounce. If they don't, you get the point. The hardest part for me is serving, getting it going. That's often where I lose the most points." We played around a while, and she began to at least bounce the ball around somewhat, which delighted her immensely.

The evening we set sail, we five were in my cabin brushing out our hair. I was working on Kallisto's curling, long black tresses and having a difficult time of it, I admit. Renzo popped his head in, "How's it coming? When do I get to be your slave for a day?"

I laughed, "I'd almost forgotten that, dear." To Kallisto, I explained, "When we were going to race in the duka, we had no thoughts of beating their expert riders. Instead, we wagered against each other, the loser becomes the winner's slave for a day. He lost."

"Oh no, you are in really big trouble now!" Kallisto exclaimed playfully, catching on to our game and teasing. "Too bad I didn't win; boy can I think of some things for my slave to do to me!"

"Oh no, me and my big mouth. Kallisto, if you give Bethany any ideas, I'm going to have to chase you all over this ship and tickle you until you give up utterly!"

"You wouldn't, would you?" Kallisto asked.

"Oh wouldn't I?" Renzo dashed to her side and began relentlessly tickling not only Kallisto but also me! Kallisto really enjoyed the attention.

"Okay, buster, now you've gone and done it." I butted into him and began to tickle him with my feet. Unfortunately for Renzo, his sides are awfully ticklish. Soon the tables were turned as we five began chasing after him until at last he yielded.

"Okay, slave, you come over here and brush out Kallisto's hair, while she tells me some clever things I can have my slave do for me," I ordered.

"Yes, dear," he replied, as he stopped laughing at last. While we all chatted during the lengthy brushing session, Renzo asked Kallisto, "You know that you are one very attractive young woman? Back home, men are going to be all over you wanting dates, to take you to dances, even to the concerts."

She flushed, "I fell for that once. Beauty eventually fades, as bodies get older. Look what my vanity got me?" She shrugged what was left of her shoulders. "No, Renzo, what I truly miss is just what you and Bethany have, a love based on the respect of the other. All of you are so incredibly lucky, fortunate, to have such wonderful men in your lives. Yet, I know as I am, in the outside world, men will only desire me because I used to be very pretty, but not anymore. God, how I miss the hug of a lover! That has been the worst thing about this whole thing, but I am reconciled to missing that forever."

Renzo replied, "Well, Kallisto, I hope that you are not too disappointed, when you discover that isn't always going to be so. I, and I believe I speak for all of us here, advise you to look for a man you can admire and respect and build on that. Accept nothing less than a man who admires and respects you for yourself, not for your body. Bethany and I, we are playful spirits; we'd be lost without a game to play with each other. That's how we met. It was terribly hard on both of us when she lost her arms, because all of our games came to a crashing halt. Yet, we kept inventing new ways and means, and here we are once more back to where we belong, loving opponents. My respect for her is enormous. Kallisto, I will make you a wager. If within six months of landing in our land you do not have yourself a fine boyfriend, then I'll be your slave for a day!" We women laughed; I knew he would very likely win that bet!

At last ready for bed, we all went to get our children ready as well. Valerija not only was doing a great job with our many children and infants, but she had our twins wrapped round her fingers! As she helped us tuck them into their small beds in our cabin, I gave her my bump hug, and Renzo gave her a real one, whispering in her ear, "Thank you Valerija!" She blushed and left us.

"Now what would you have your slave do next, my love?" he teased. We got in to bed and I'll let you ponder this one. I put him to good use.

The next morning over breakfast, we had to make the decision on what to do next. Kallisto was stunned to discover that many of us had telepathic abilities. For fun, Rosina Mind Linked Kallisto to me and mom, so she could be introduced formally. Mom got a kick out of that one.

Come home. I think that you all deserve a long shore leave. Do you realize that you are the very first people to have sailed completely around Tarra? It's never been done before! You have all made history! Besides, I want to play with my grandchildren some.

We laughed and told Henry to head for home. October 21, 653, we sailed into Velona to the largest crowd that had ever gathered on the docks! Yes, we were all stunned by the reception! Music, fanfares, yelling and clapping went on for a half hour. Fireworks were set off even though they were not awfully visible. Whether or not we appreciated it, we had made history, the first circumnavigation of our planet.

When we finally arrived at our estate, both Valerija and Kallisto were absolutely stunned with what they saw, but for vary different reasons. In Vladimir, Valerija had seen nothing by which to compare our civilization, so it was hard to convince her that we were not all gods! Kallisto was in complete disbelief over the number of women like us and what they were accomplishing. From the amazing feats of engineering and inventions of Enyo, to the many and varied arts, down to the simple living arrangements, she thought that she had also arrived in heaven.

I moved her and Valerija in with Renzo and me, partly so they had time to adapt and partly because I needed the help with the twins and Danielle.

I never will forget the expression on Kallisto's face when she watched her first Expressionistic Dance performance by Bard Tal and his group, Zita in particular. I was too out of practice to join them, though within a month, I was back on the dance floor once more. "Oh my god!" Kallisto continued to exclaim, as we met with Zita back stage after the Friday night performance.

"We were a little off tonight," Zita said. "Just wait until Bethany here gets back into the groove. Last time she and I performed, we brought down the house. Imagine us on either side of the stage, running towards each other, then leaping as I did tonight, then spinning around ten times in unison on either side of the stage. It's a knock out! Bethany, no one else has been able to hit ten revolutions like you and I did. So I insist that you start practicing tomorrow!"

I think for a week, Kallisto went from one place to another saying, "Oh my god!" She was truly impressed with all of us and the Laird Foundation for the Arts. After letting her become accustomed to life here for two weeks, mom then arranged for her formal training.

Ah mom! She did it again, bless her. Frank Williams was a thirty year old Judger from Mont Blanc. He was quite shy around women and had never been married. Something of a perfectionist, he devoted himself to his art, settling disputes everywhere over the Greenway areas that we still had influence. He'd been one of the Judgers who assisted Jovanna Barcella regain her country from the Holy Paladins. He was a field veteran, yet, he prided himself on his keen observational skills in picking out thieves in the act. Often when in Calgary, he would spend his evenings wandering the streets, spotting pickpockets in the act and arresting them. Yes, he had a strange idea of fun. Relaxation for him was to stroll and see how early he could spot a crime in the making. Of course, there was none in Mont Blanc, his hometown, or around our estate.

Frank twisted his moustache and pulled his goatee as he listened to Jenna. He'd come at once when she summoned him, expecting to receive some exciting new assignment. "You want me to take on an apprentice?" he asked, scarcely able to conceal his emotional letdown. On his journey here to the estate, he'd decided that perhaps she would be sending him off to Tashien.

"Yes, she is a foreigner. I do hope your Megalos speech is up to par," mom added.

"Yes, though I have not had much use for it. I could be better with it if you sent me to Megalos to spy on the Church there," he suggested without much hope that she would do so.

"One other thing, she is like my daughter, armless," mom threw in that significant detail.

"What?" He had carefully been avoiding all the hundreds of such women who had been taking up residence here over the last few years. "You know that I am not, well, comfortable being around them. Why are you doing this to me? Have I failed the Santi in some way?"

"Oh don't be silly, Frank. You are one of the best Judgers in the Santi; only a few are more skilled than you are. No, this apprentice needs the kind of skill and viewpoint that you have. I believe that she will challenge you. I expect that you will give it your best as you always do. If after three months it doesn't work out, I will replace you with no hard or ill feelings between us. Is that acceptable?"

"Three months! You know how addicted I am to catching pickpockets. How can I not do what I love for three months? Torture, you are torturing me."

"No, take her with you; perhaps she can help you capture more of your pickpockets."

"You mean we can go to Calgary?"

"When you believe she is ready for that, yes. Just remember, you will have to provide her much assistance with things she is unable to do for herself while she is away from here." He realized what mom meant. Living with an armless woman required more than a little assistance.

"Do I have a choice?"

"No. Ah, here she comes now. Her name is Kallisto."

The black haired beauty walked in flushed. Renzo had just chased her around trying to tickle her because she was overly concerned about meeting this stranger who would become her teacher. "Sorry I am late. Renzo was after me. Hello, I am Kallisto," she smiled to Frank.

Frank stood up awkwardly, unsure how to greet her. She sensed his uncertainty and helped him out, "I've no hands to shake, sir, but a hug will do just fine." She leaned toward him, giving him no choice but to give her a hug, a gentle one, fearing to hurt her somehow.

"Frank Williams, this is Kallisto from Demokritos. Kallisto, Frank is one of our best Judgers, highly skilled and a field veteran. Why don't you take him to the quarters we have set aside for him, and you can begin training at once."

"Follow me. I'm so new here, but at least I know my way around this building and Bethany's." Frank dutifully followed her, but shot a glare at mom as he left. His room was on the third floor of the brownstone manor, but most of the women were on the lower floor. Hence, it was very quiet and private up there. Frank tossed his sack onto the bed.

"Well, Kallisto, I don't know anything about you or what you might need or can do. So let's begin at the very beginning and see what you are able to do already. Kindly push the latch on the door shut so that we are not interrupted. I never let my training sessions be interrupted. I won't allow it; the trainee loses too much. I want my trainees to become perfect." Kallisto smiled and used her foot to slide the bar across the door, securing it. No one would interrupt them as long as the bar was closed. Privacy was guaranteed, house rule.

"Have a seat, Kallisto. The first thing to cover is the Seven Aspects of Life." He quickly outlined them to her and had her repeat them, which she did without hesitation. "Okay, well done. Now the second thing is to teach people to simply observe what is there, the obvious and not to put opinions, conclusions, and deductions onto it, simple state what one actually sees." He gave her an example, describing what he saw when he looked at her. He then asked her to observe the obvious about him.

To his amazement, she rattled off a long set of completely correct observations. "Doesn't it get harder than this?" she asked when she finished.

"Okay. Given these observations, what conclusions and deductions can you form from them, mind you, they need to be backup by something plainly observable."

"You won't get mad at me, if I speak the truth?" she asked hesitatingly.

"Absolutely not! I cannot recall ever getting angry with any student. Go on; tell me your conclusions and deductions. Mind you, I may ask you for the backup observations."

"Okay. You are uncomfortable around women like me. You have not had anything to do with armless women. Ah, you are not married; no ring or other marital identifiers; no wife in her right mind would let you go out into the world with your outfit messed up like this, shirt half in an half out, mismatched socks. You are shy. Ah, you do not trust women either. You see things that others do not. You are not athletic and do not enjoy playing sports, such as the ball games that Bethany and Renzo play. What interests you anyway? You are an interesting man. Let me observe a bit here. It must have to do with your keen sense of observation of the actions of others. You clearly wanted to see if I would balk at shutting the door bar, because your eyes never left me. If I had a choice, back home where I come from, I would put you out in the streets observing, yes, observing others. I bet that you can spot a pickpocket a mile away. Your eyes just gave that one away, a slight smile as well. Yes, I'll bet you find that fun, being out in a street watching for the sleight of hand."

Frank's mouth dropped. "Damn, Kallisto, you are good — no make that very, very good. Absolutely amazing! Even few Judgers in the Santi could draw those conclusions on such small observational evidence."

"Well I have to be sharp. These things mean life or death back home. I guess I should be honest with you, Frank. Before I left, I was the leader of the Kali, the now legendary band of assassins in Demokritos. We are greatly feared by everyone in the country. I have to be able to size up a man or woman within minutes of meeting them. I will understand if you do not want to go further with my training, me being an assassin," she said, expecting the axe to fall. Yet, she had to be fully honest here in Velona; too much was at stake for her; this was paradise.

Frank swallowed hard. "Damn, Jenna didn't tell me about this. You've murdered people?"

"Usually I've ordered their murder, though I once did it myself with my foot."

"Kallisto, before we go any further, I must know all about your past, if I am to be able to train you. I do reserve the right to refuse to do so, if I feel you are unworthy."

Kallisto sighed, this was probably the end of it all, but she had to be honest. She spent an hour explaining her life and what exactly the Kali did back in Demokritos. "So I can understand if you deem me unworthy. I am not a good person."

"On the contrary, I've never met one more worthy. Assassin is not the way to view it nor is murderer. We've gone over the Seven Aspects. Good and evil or bad are not workable words to describe actions. What may be viewed as good by some can be viewed as evil by others. Good and evil are just a matter of viewpoint. The Megalos Emperor, who thought he was going great good by bringing his version of civilization to the Sea Princes, was viewed as evil by the men here, whom his Centurions killed, and the women here that his Centurions raped. How then should we ascertain a man's worth, or woman's?" he added quickly, unused to being this close to a woman.

"We Santi base our judgments upon whether an action helps more of the Seven Aspects or whether it does more harm to them. If an action harms more than it helps, it is deemed a harmful action. Our standard response to harmful action is to get the person or persons who are doing these harmful actions to cease and desist, one way or another. Sometimes, we can stop them peacefully; other times, I have had to kill the offender to get him to stop."

"You situation with the Kali meet this criterion precisely. You were doing what was necessary to keep them from committing more harm. These women, who willingly gave so much for their marriage only to have that betrayed, had only the Kali to set things right for them. From our viewpoint, you are not an evil assassin, but a righteous righter of those, who would bring more harm than good. I am truly impressed with you. I had no idea you were this observant, this ethical, this well trained! You are not at all what I thought at first. Will you accept my apology?"

"Yes, but I am not sure why you are apologizing. I often do the same thing when beginning the training of a new recruit. I must know their values," Kallisto replied. "If they are but a thief, they are rejected at once. Can I ask a personal question?"

"Sure, my apprentices should feel free to ask anything of me," he replied, trying to guess what she might desire to know.

"We are about the same age, yet you have never married. I find this most unexpected. Why is it that you have not? There are so many beautiful women around here, and I've only seen a bit of this country."

His face flushed, "To be honest, Kallisto, I haven't found a woman yet who is single and who I can respect."

"You've been wounded in love, haven't you?" Kallisto read between his words.

Frank's face went red, "Well, yes, once, a long time ago. She was more interested in running around with a dashing Protector, a fighter. I am not that interested in fighting. A fight has never solved anyone's problems; it only puts the real problem off for another day."

"So very, very true, Frank. I had not thought of it quite like that before, but that is precisely what it does do, stalls it for another day. Yet, now you do not fully trust women in general, correct?"

"Well, yes. I often see ulterior motives in many women's actions, men too for that matter. I've mostly given up entirely. How about you?"

"I was madly in love with Kadmos, a nobleman who was quite wealthy, which I thought would be an added benefit. I thought that he was mad about me as well. We got married, and he asked me to make the ultimate sacrifice, which would bring him even more power. Gladly I did this horrid thing. Not two weeks after I became like this did I catch him in bed with one of the newly hired servants who was to look after my needs. He said that I served his purposes well and to enjoy my new life. I cannot begin to tell you how I felt that night. I don't think anyone could understand. Yes, I made a pair of very bad choices and have had to live with them ever since. I had him assassinated and then joined the Kali to help other women as best I could."

"Like you, I see ulterior motives in most men's actions, much less in women's however. I have never found a man I could truly trust since then. Well, that is not entirely true. I've grown to trust fully Renzo with my life and the other fellows in the Explorers Circle. Perhaps not all men are bad. But I am scared, Frank. I'm scared of even contemplating giving myself to another man. Like this, I cannot even push him off of me if he forces himself onto me."

Something snapped within Frank. She was sitting on the edge of the bed. He moved beside her and sat down, putting his arms around her. Softly he said, "How you must have loved Kadmos to have given so much for him. I only wish I could have been the one to slit his throat. Kallisto, I will do my very, very best to get you trained so that you have the skills and ability to throw any man who forces himself onto your body far off of you. We have certain Judger spells that I will teach you to cast. Once you have mastered them, at least this tiny fear can be lifted from you. I will work very hard to earn your sacred trust, Kallisto."

She looked at him in a new light; a bit of real hope kindled within her. They resumed her training. When she arrived at his room for their next session the next day, Frank said, "I want to take you on a field trip to Calgary, a large city north of here. We will be gone several weeks. I know that it is heading towards winter and you are probably not used to the cold, but I have plenty of warm clothing for you. However, I, ah, well, we will be traveling alone, just us two, in a carriage, so I, ah, well, I will, ah. . ."

"Have to be looking out for my personal needs, helping me with things?" she finished his thought.

"Yes, I'm afraid that I don't know the very first thing about, well about any woman's needs, let alone someone like yours. But I need to see you in the field; there is nothing like the real world. I can understand if you would prefer not to go alone with me. I'm sure that I can find another woman to accompany us, just let me know."

Renzo and I decided to go with them, not because I didn't trust Frank, but because we wanted to visit old friends in Mont Blanc and see Calgary. "Frank, you requested this trip, so Kallisto is your responsibility. Renzo and I will only help out, if you need assistance. We have our hands full with the twins and Danielle."

"Don't fret so," Kallisto said to Frank. "I'll tell you when and with what I need help." I liked her attitude. Because of the cold weather, we had to wear leather bottoms and warm boots, which meant that Frank was going to get an education fast.

By the time that we reached Calgary, he was doing very well with Kallisto, sensing what she needed without her having to ask. She too saw this and marveled about it. Outside, three inches of snow blanketed the city. We rented a sleigh and enjoyed the ride around town. At last, it was time for business. Frank led her to the seedier portion of town. Together they lurked in the shadows and watched. For five days, Frank and Kallisto wandered the streets of Calgary, while Renzo and I stayed with friends and played in the snow with the twins. It was their first snow experience.

Finally, the sixth morning over breakfast as he helped Kallisto with hers, Frank said, "She's just the most incredible person I've ever had the pleasure of training, Bethany. She is a natural in the field. Not only has she not missed a single trick, she pointed out three that I missed! Incredible woman! As far as Judger skills, she is ready for the ninth year, with a few holes here and there in the earlier years. Except that she has already acquired half of tenth year skills and all the fieldwork. Incredible. I would not have believed it possible!"

"Observing it happening is one thing," Kallisto replied, "and for me being able to do something about it is quite another thing."

"Don't worry. Those are the next things we have to work on, the Judger spells," Frank consoled her. "Well, I'm ready to head back. How about you two?"

"Yes, but how about taking the sleigh to Mont Blanc?" Renzo suggested. "It's much more fun and romantic too." He knew I loved sleigh rides.

With Kallisto, me, and the kids all nicely bundled up, we set off on the day-long sleigh ride to Mont Blanc. Yes, it was fun for all. A few days later, we were back at the estate, and Frank and Kallisto began training once more.

Saturday morning, the day of yet another public dance, I found the two of them taking a break from spell casting. "Say, the usual Saturday night dance is tonight. Everyone's going. How about you two taking a break and joining us?"

"I don't know how to dance," Kallisto answered timidly. "Besides, who would I go with?"

"With me, silly. Would you care to go to the dance with me?" Frank asked. I grinned and held my breath.

"Sure, but I don't know what to wear or how to dance. I'll look awfully silly, Frank."

"Oh, dancing is easy. Look, if little Teiuc can do it, you can."

"What? That woman who's lost nearly all her legs?"

"That's the one. Wait until you see her and Shorty going to it."

"I'm sure that I can find a fancy dress that will fit you, Kallisto," I finally added.

Natale to the rescue, she found one of the fancy silk dresses for Kallisto, the form-fitting kind with no armholes and that fit the curves of our bodies as we are. We all helped get Kallisto fancied up, along with ourselves. She was more than a little pleased with her appearance and utterly surprised to see the entire estate emptied as we all headed for the dance hall, which was packed as usual.

Renzo bet me that Frank would be unable to keep his hands off her. He certainly couldn't keep his off my silky dress, and I didn't want him too for that matter. He was right. Once she discovered how easy it was, they danced every dance the whole evening. She seemed happier than I had ever seen her. My mother, the matchmaker, had done it again. I spied them actually kissing when the lights were down for the last dance. I only got a glimpse, because Renzo was all over me, and I, him, as well.

Then it was back to her training. A week later, Kallisto was going around the estate making various people at random do what she asked, using her command voice, a prime Judger skill. It took her a month to master the arts of illusion, making others see what she wanted them to see, not what they were seeing. However, learning the three power spells took all winter. In the spring of 654, she finally brought down lightning bolts. Once that big hurdle had been surmounted, fire and ice quickly followed. Still Frank persisted in her training.

For this last spell, he needed a third person, and Renzo was elected. "Now I want you to flop yourself on top of her, gently at first. Pretend that you are trying to have your way with her. She has to retain her concentration and push you off, Renzo. Ready, Kallisto? Okay, action." Renzo gently laid down on her on the bed. She at once began to use her arms to try to push him off. I was observing from a corner of the room. Frank also spied this as well.

"Look, Kallisto, you don't have any arms. So forget about using arms. Concentrate on the spell; blank your reactions and emotions from your mind. Concentration is the key. Again, action."

Finally, on the third day, Kallisto got mad and at last succeeded, pitching Renzo halfway across the room. I caught him before he crashed into the wall. "Er thanks dear," he grinned.

"I did it! Oh, I'm sorry, Renzo. I could have hurt you."

"You did great. Now let's work on your control. Places everyone, action." Frank was a relentless driver. Finally, on the fifth day, he had Renzo attempting to be as rough as possible with her, and she effortlessly pushed him aside, without hurting him.

"Pass! Pass! Pass! You did it, Kallisto! Well done indeed!" exclaimed Frank. "It's celebration time!"

We all headed to the panty to find food with which to party a bit. Hers was quite an achievement, one that she could really use in life. Over a bit of wine, Frank explained, "The only things remaining are textbook skills, leaning the best way to adjudicate a conflict. A few more weeks and Kallisto will be a full-fledged Judger. There is nothing now standing in her way! Congratulations! You are the best apprentice I have ever had."

That evening, Frank took Kallisto for a walk around the nearly deserted art gallery. "Kallisto, you now have the skill that I swore to you that I would teach you. You can fend off any unwanted advances now. I, ah, well, I want to ask, er, ah, you see I've fallen, well how do I say this?"

"Yes, you have indeed done what you promised, though at the time I didn't believe it was possible, Frank. What is it that you want to ask me?"

"I, ah, well," he faltered. He took a deep breath and raced through the words, "Kallisto, I have fallen madly in love with you. Would you consider marrying me? These past few months have been the happiest of my entire life. You are the most fabulous woman I've ever met. Even if you say no, because love has to work both ways in a marriage, please know this that you always have my highest admiration and greatest respect. Now you can say no."

"Why would I say no? I swore that I would not marry any man whom I did not admire and respect and that he would reciprocate. All that aside, Frank, I want you so badly I can hardly sleep at night. I dream about being in your arms. Yes, I'll marry you, only please, please hug me tightly. My legs are giving out!" He needed no further encouragement! Mom had done it again.

What of Valerija? At the first dance, a young Santi fellow, who assists the breeding of our horses, asked Valerija to dance. The next day he took her riding. The rest is history. She and I found a loophole, in that if I were to allow her to marry, then she could return home still bringing high honor to her family and country. Scott and Valerija married and he was then stationed at our new embassy in Tanja.

Our caravel needed a complete refit and de-ratting after so long a voyage. While in other caravels, the bilge became the latrines, on ours it did not. However, rats are always a problem. During the time that the barnacles were removed from the hull, the rats were also eliminated as well. By the summer of 654, the Sleepy Hollow was once more ready to set sail. And yes, we women were once more all pregnant. This shore leave had its side effects.

This trip was a delivery one. The Wanakan visitors, now fully trained, were ready to return home, along with a Santi support group to help establish our presence firmly there. Another group, including Valerija and her husband were to be dropped off at Tanja. Finally, Kallisto and Frank, accompanied by another group of Santi were to be taken to Patri. Thus, we made a wide circle, going first to Wanakan, then Patri, and finally to Tanja. For all of us, this voyage was more like a vacation, fun-filled and full of conversation with all our friends. Yes, it was very hard parting with so many wonderful people, knowing that we might not see each other for a long time.

Departing from Tanja in December, we received word from Sho Lin that she was ready to visit Velona. Thus, we sailed north to Shansee, where the Santi Fortress and fortress was nearly half built. This was the official home of the Royal Consort, me. Six months pregnant, I decided that some of Sho Lin's protocols would have to be omitted. Fortunately, Sho Lin provided official maternity clothing, which fit perfectly.

She and her husband, San See, were waiting at the Santi fortress as we arrived. Yes, she was shocked by our appearance, although Helena, the Traveler's Circle Communicator, had fully briefed Sho Lin about what had happened to Linda and me, but still, the reality shocked her. She and I spent several days together, following their strict protocols. I was still her Consort and we enjoyed ourselves for a time, while the others restocked the ship for the voyage home.

Again, we all chatted endlessly during the many weeks it took returning to Velona. We took our time and arrived as spring of 655 began. Of course, I had arranged a big surprise for her. The first night that we were in Jenna's estate, a large fireworks celebration was held in her honor. Even Elona Po and her family and group were present. The last sky shell burst into a likeness of Sho Lin, which pleased her immensely. Yes, Sho Lin was incredibly impressed with our land and our people. At the end of summer, we took her back home, along with our new babies.

Renzo and I had a little boy, Adrien. Linda and Chaucer had Samuel; Rosina and Cedric had Edmond; Tonia and Emil had Blanche; Michelle and Bennet had Constance, and Natale and Henry had Barnabe. As we returned home from Tashien, we began to realize that the caravel life was nearing an end. Our twins were four and running everywhere underfoot. Each of us had three or four young children now, and the ship was a continual mess. Although unspoken, we all felt this might be our last voyage for some time.

None of us expected the news that we received on a cold February morning in 656, a week out of Velona. Paulette made a Mind Link with us all. She was barely able to control her grief to maintain the link. We all knew something horrible had happened. *Bethany, it's your mom. There is no easy way to tell you. We are all grief stricken here. Her body has died. We believe her heart gave out in her sleep. She passed away without pain.*

We were a grief-filled, somber group that arrived at the estate a week later. They had withheld her funeral so that we could be present. However, once she was laid to rest in a beautiful crypt in the Rose Church, I began to search for her. She was waiting for me in the panty.

Hi dear. My body just wore out. I love you dearly still.

I love you too mom. I am really going to miss you! Grief flooded over me.

I hung around for you, dear. I have two things to tell you. First, as you will soon find out, I have appointed you to fill my position as Supreme Commander of the Santi del Dio. This was no surprise. I knew that one day I would resume the leadership position. *Second, I will not be taking a new baby body up here in Velona. Jes, the Guardian of the Anuir, has asked me to come down to him and assist him in his task of freeing spiritual beings. I agreed. We've done a great deal to stabilize Tarra so that he can free us. Now he needs help in doing just that. When I can, I will talk more with you. If you need me, you know where you can find me.*

We talked for a long time, private things between mother and daughter. At last, I had to let her go. I watched as she shot southward to the Red Desert. For a time, I sat there wondering what she would be doing with Jes. Renzo found me and held me tightly for a long time that night, just we two alone in the panty.

The next day, Lilly Ann, mom's Judger, read the last official orders from Jenna Rose Weston, whose body now lay in a private crypt in Elona's church, which bore her name. Jenna's words appointed me as the new leader of the Santi. As she read the short document for us all, I looked around at these dear friends — so old looking, all of them. I knew that they had done so much for us all, but they too were in need of slowing down.

Thus, the Explorers Circle took over as the top group of the Santi, while I kept mom's group on as advisors, lightning their daily work load enormously. Now they could spend loving time with all their many grandchildren. Every one of them greatly appreciated being relieved of this enormous burden of running such a large organization. A month later, I really grew to appreciate all that they had been doing. It was a herculean task indeed.

Thus, the Age of Exploration ended. We had opened up a vast, wide new world for everyone. Now came expansion. The world was at peace for a change. Yet, there is one last story to tell.

The second day of my new job here in February 656, Rosina got an urgent message from Mont Blanc. *Bethany, you must go at once to Mont Blanc! Some young woman has come there asking about the talisman of Lachlan Laird! She says that she was told to do this by King Laird. Her name is Cerys.*

A week later, our carriage arrived at Mont Blanc, and I went at once to the room where she was staying. Darn doors, I needed Renzo to knock and open it for me; he was carrying Adrien for me. Inside was a young woman, twenty-two years old, with golden hair and blue eyes. She was exceedingly thin and gaunt, nearly half starved. The Healers here had put her on bed rest and were ensuring that she got proper nutrition. I was told that she was near death when she arrived last week.

"Hello, I am Bethany, the Santi leader."

She sat up. "I'm Cerys Laird. My aunt told us that I am supposed to come here and ask for the Sacred Talisman that she always wore. I don't know why." She told me the awful tale of a dozen years of hardship before she finally had saved up enough funds for the short trip from Cymry to Calgary. From there, she had walked all the way to Mont Blanc and nearly died from cold and starvation getting here. We talked for some time, and Cerys was very relieved to find out that I had known her aunt and that I knew all about the talisman.

I had them bring it to her room. Renzo handed it to her, while I explained what little I knew of its use. "When Lachlan shared its visions with me, she put it around both our necks. She also said that it is disorienting to the senses. That is very true; I nearly fell down. May I suggest that we again share its visions, that I may better guide you? I owe that much at the very least to King Lachlan."

She helped me lie down beside her and put the talisman around both our necks. "What do we do now?" she asked.

"Relax our minds and wait," I said hopefully.

Soon the room began to swirl and a grey mist occluded our view. Then we saw her back in Brea; a stone fortress rose from where Lachlan's old wooden fortress had been. I realized that this woman would be able to rebuild her country, uniting its scattered people once more.

"What does all this mean?" she asked me.

"It means, Cerys, that the Santi del Dio are going to go back with you to Brea and help you rebuild your country. You will become its new ruler, taking your aunt's place. However, this time, the Santi will be there with you to guarantee your safety and the safety of your country! We owe your aunt so very much! You rest up and regain your strength. When spring comes in a month or so, we will get the recovery of your country going full blast!"

When we returned to the estate, my first official major action was just that, the establishing of a complete Santi Circle for Brea, with two Planners and a large workforce of stonemasons from Mont Blanc. In late spring 656, Brea was finally on its road to recovery.

Me, well, I had no choice but to learn to fill my mother's shoes. Hers, I discovered, were enormous!
The End.

A Favor to Other Readers

How about helping other readers? Many readers rely on reviews to make the decision whether to buy a book. You can help them make their decision by leaving your opinions and viewpoint in a short review of the positive things of this book. Writing the review and expressing your opinion only takes a few minutes, and other readers will appreciate your efforts.

Click this link: Volume 6 Age of Exploration
scroll down to Customer Reviews; click on Write a Review, and enter your review. Thank you.

Author Information

Visit My Amazon.com Author Page
Vic Broquard Author Page

Follow My Blog
Vic Broquard's Blog

Follow Me on Social Media
Facebook
Google+
LinkedIn
YouTube

Other Books by Vic Broquard

Without Warning (fantasy)

The Trident Series: (fantasy)
      Volume 1 The Trident and the Book
      Volume 2 The Trident and the Scepter
      Volume 3 The Trident and the Resurrection

The Adventures of Elizabeth Stanton Series: (science fiction)
      Volume 1 The Evolution of the Path
      Volume 2 The Great Messiah
      Volume 3 Of Kings and Queens and Troubadours
      Volume 4 Chaos in the Aftermath
      Volume 5 Power Plays
      Volume 6 Age of Exploration
      Volume 7 Abducted
      Volume 8 The Emperor and Empress
      Volume 9 A Job Worth Doing
      Volume 10 Degradation
      Volume 11 The Second Crusade
      Volume 12 When Worlds Collide
      Volume 13 Dark Ages

The Lindsey Barron Series: (fantasy)
      Volume 1 The Rod of the Apocalypse
      Volume 2 The Board of Governors
      Volume 3 The Crown of Moses
      Volume 4 Dominus for President
      Volume 5 The National Health Care Program
      Volume 6 States Justice
      Volume 7 Cross and Double-cross

Zoran Chronicles Series: (fantasy)
      Volume 1 A Dragon in Our Town
      Volume 2 Dragons, Power, Courts, and War

Planet of the Orange-red Sun Series: (science fiction)
      Volume 1 When Kingdoms Fall
      Volume 2 Dark Ages
      Volume 3 Age of the Towers
      Volume 4 Difficillis Exitus
      Volume 5 Age of the Lords
      Volume 6 The Renegade Tower

The Return of the Wizards: Twelve Companions – The Making of Wizards (fantasy)

www.ingramcontent.com/pod-product-compliance
Lightning Source LLC
Chambersburg PA
CBHW081127020726
47505CB00010B/2269